THE EMPIRE BLUES

A NOVEL BY

Taylor Branch

SIMON AND SCHUSTER

New York

Copyright © 1981 by Taylor Branch
All rights reserved
including the right of reproduction
in whole or in part in any form
Published by Simon and Schuster
A Division of Gulf & Western Corporation
Simon & Schuster Building
Rockefeller Center
1230 Avenue of the Americas
New York, New York 10020
SIMON AND SCHUSTER and colophon are trademarks of Simon & Schuster

Manufactured in the United States of America

1 2 3 4 5 6 7 8 9 10

Library of Congress Cataloging in Publication Data

Branch, Taylor.
The empire blues.

I. Title.
PS3552.R2914E5   813'.54   80-27295

ISBN 0-671-23096-4

For the Families
Branch and Macy

PRINCIPAL CHARACTERS

HENRY WOODRUFF   Senate aide. Estranged husband of Casey Pendleton. Amateur political theorist.

DAVID HOWELL   Reporter for *Washington* magazine. Best friend to Woodruff.

CHARLOTTE "CASEY" PENDLETON   Lawyer. Estranged wife of Henry Woodruff.

PAUL STERNMAN   Author, well-known reporter for the *Washington Post*.

LESTER HERSHEY   Lesser-known author, reporter for the *New York Times*.

HAVEN PINDER   Public-interest crusader. Lily Snow's protector.

SUSAN "SUDS" HARTMAN   Radical heiress, "the queen of the anti-elitists."

CHARLES "ZIGGY" ROSEN   Political hustler, card dealer, Spiro Agnew expert.

VALERIE MANTELL   Director, National Women's Political Caucus. Best friend to Hartman.

MARNER   Co-owner of *Washington* magazine. Rebellious plutocrat.

DRAKE   Co-owner of *Washington* magazine. West Virginia political evangelist.

LALANE RAYBURN   Wife of missing Air Force pilot. Real estate agent.

RICHARD CLAYFIELD   State Department official. Casey Pendleton's lover.

LILY SNOW   Pinder's neighbor, elderly friend of Pinder and Howell. Daughter of renowned insect specialist.

MIAMI

CARLOS MARANA   Cuban CIA agent, mystery spy, underworld legend.

PATRICK SHEA   Special agent in charge, FBI.

EDUARDO "EL NAVAJO" ROMERO   Haunted proprietor of unusual shooting range.

CARMEN VILAR   Maraña's fiery lover.

MAX PARKER   Cuban/American, multiple informant. Maraña's best friend.

EDWARD NOEL   CIA station chief, Miami.

PEPE LOPEZ   Insurance salesman and assassin.

BOBBY ZILLER   Con artist. Entertainer. Friend to Ziggy Rosen.

DAVE DAMICO   Honest, ambitious FBI agent.

MOONBEAM   Resident at Ziller's. Lover of porpoises.

I

HENRY WOODRUFF started breaking down just before he touched the silver door-handle of Moby, his long white Pontiac. He was astonished by his haphazard scrape with Casey. The tears came out of his eyes one at a time. Each one attracted his attention, pausing and retreating and finally heaving its way out of the tear duct. Woodruff was glad he was crying. "What have you done?" he moaned out loud to himself. "You are over your head now." His breath came in short stabs and went out in long sighs.

Across the Buffalo Bridge over Rock Creek Park, then around the embassies near Sheridan Circle, Woodruff guided the car to the 21st Street apartment of his friend, David Howell. He was thankful for the few tears that still showed on his drawn face—they would shock Howell out of his frivolous disposition. Suddenly, instead of coaxing his tears, Woodruff found himself fighting them. He stopped cold and struggled with himself. This would not do. He wanted a suitable residue of crying for his greeting of Howell, but he would not allow himself to be tumbling loose. He turned and strolled around the block. It was past midnight, and Washington's summer sky was the yellowish gray of a catfish belly. The closest things to visible stars were the red beacons atop the Washington Monument. Woodruff recovered himself, rode the elevator up to Howell's floor, and rang the bell.

The door swung open and Woodruff's eyes met the sight of David Howell, dressed only in boxer shorts the color of cranberry juice and in socks the color of a ripe avocado. Howell was not a modest man. He held a half-eaten banana in a hand that seemed oddly minuscule on his ample frame, looking like a raccoon paw. His other hand rested idly on the side of a pale stomach that sloped gently on all sides, like a turtle's shell. Howell was pudgy, short of fat, and he was nice-looking, short of handsome. Women called him cuddly. His features seemed to have been thrown together in some genetic pawn shop, an unlikely assortment that combined to comical effect. He

7

looked like a plump Jimmy Cagney, with dimples and frizzy hair. A magazine reporter, he was curious and merry about most things, but he was known to resent deeply comments that his hair corked out on the sides.

"You look terrible," said Woodruff after a moment.

David Howell stalled for time by taking another bite of his banana, knowing that distress was about to spill out of Woodruff. He sensed it, and at the same time he could think of no person in the world less likely to come undone than Henry Woodruff, who seemed to have a fixity of vision that surpassed his experience and his station in life. Woodruff was well known for this. His cerebral bent, plus his curious appearance, foreshadowed a rising eccentricity in his later life. He stood just over six feet tall, with dark shaggy hair, a thin scholar's nose, a child's eyes, and a serious mouth. He had a scarecrow's hips and scarcely any rear end at all, so that no dress suit had ever fit him. Until now, no one had ever needed to worry about the firm confidence that held Woodruff's disparate elements together. Howell kept looking at him, almost warily. "What happened?" he asked.

Now Woodruff stalled. He felt pressurized moisture seeping out around the cracks in his eyes, and he saw the look of worry on Howell's face.

"Are you all right?" Howell asked again, knowing better.

"I don't know," said Woodruff. He leaned over into the apartment and looked both ways, as though preparing to cross a street. "Are you engaged this evening?"

"I had nothing to do," said Howell.

"Well, I may need a place to stay for a few years," Woodruff sighed, stepping through the door. "Casey impeached me tonight."

"Thank God it's only your wife. I was afraid they were taking your parking sticker." Howell looked off.

Woodruff didn't laugh, and neither did Howell. Actually, Howell was panicked by the thought of trouble between the Woodruffs. They were starkly incompatible and yet so emotionally dependent somehow. Howell didn't understand either one of them even after five years' solid friendship. He had first run into Casey in November of '69 at the gigantic demonstration against the Vietnam War. Howell was crouched next to the driver of the five hundredth or so bus that he had helped park, when he heard a loud treble crunch and felt his nose grind into the bus driver's changemaker. The tip of Howell's nose wound up between the stacks of dimes and nickels, and for years he would imagine faint grooves from the edge of a dime on one side of his nose. It relieved him to discover that the noise he heard came not from his nose but from the smashed fender of a Ford Pinto. He sprang from the bus and the icy wind helped clear his head. It seemed that the Pinto had dipped its headlight and shoulder to sneak a peek under the bus, or, alternatively, that the bus had simply taken a small bite out of the Pinto. Nearby stood a woman dressed precisely, in earmuffs, several matching scarves, gloves, and a heavy beige overcoat. This winter toppage contrasted sharply with her lower garments—skirt, stockings, and Pappagallo shoes. Howell wondered again how women manage to survive the winter, and then he shouted, "Hey! Move that car! I've got to move all these buses to pick people up before they freeze!"

The woman said nothing. She reached into the car and began pulling out contraptions that looked like giant robot ears but were actually expensive megaphones, marked "D.C. Police." She strapped them around her neck, bandolero style, and marched straight toward Howell, through the yellow glare of the bus's headlights. As she approached, Howell thought frantically about how to bulldoze her into moving her car. His mission was of utmost importance. He eyed the long line of gray buses that stretched back down Independence Avenue. They snorted fumes, waiting to take runny-nosed demonstrators out of the cold. He heard the shrill, amplified voice of an excited orator over the roar of the distant crowd. There was a slight smell in the air of tear gas and fear.

"I'm sorry, but I can't move the car now," said the woman, barely slowing down. "I've *got* to get these megaphones to the marshalls! They're from the command center!"

"Wait a minute!" Howell shouted. He saw her organizer's armband, like his own, and realized that he could not pull rank. "The megaphones aren't that important. Do you want to be responsible if these buses don't get through?"

"I don't know about that, but I was told that *a lot* of people will get hurt if the marshalls don't control the crowds! They're using walkie-talkies."

Howell hadn't noticed the walkie-talkies hanging there among the megaphones. He was momentarily intimidated, and the woman took advantage. "Here," she said, holding out her keys and moving away. "*You* move the car and get the buses moving. I trust you." Howell looked into her eyes, which were as tired and desperate as his own, and figured that she was about to throw the keys on the ground and leave anyway. He also noticed a beguiling softness about her, which irritated him because it made him less willing to challenge her ultimatum. So he took the keys, and the two rushed off like firemen on alarm. The next day, in a quieter world, Howell steered the Pinto into the woman's driveway, proud of how he had obtained her name and address from the police with a show of authoritative emergency. The woman was pleased at the return of the wounded car, and she reminisced with Howell over the previous day's excitement. Her husband, Henry Woodruff, joined them. He struck Howell as friendly and yet slightly aloof, a mixture of porpoise and owl. To Howell, he was the kind of person who attracted requests for advice because he gave it so honestly and freely. Casey attracted confessions.

During the mass demonstration, Woodruff had posted himself inside the Mayor's Tactical Command Post, near the White House, from which he had sent Casey out with the megaphones and walkie-talkies. He and his fellow protest organizers looked ogle-eyed at all the communications equipment and the television monitors and the brass from the military and the White House. The protesters and the brass pretended to cooperate in the interest of an orderly demonstration, but they also spied on each other and cracked jokes and had a good time. Woodruff's role, as usual, was to bolster the confidence of his comrades. "What do you mean it's having no effect?" he would say. "Look at all those buses surrounding the White House to guard it. I'll guarantee you everybody in the White House is thinking about us. It takes twenty of them just to put out those statements about how the president is watching football on television. I think they're sweating just as much as we are." He joked about "Woodruff's First Law," which states simply that people inside organizations are still human. "Never overestimate the bastards because of that smooth organizational facade," he would say. He had many such maxims, some of which contradicted others. In later years, Howell and the Woodruffs came to view the big demonstration as a fitting introduction not only to each other but also to Washington life, where perfect strangers fall immediately into calculations over who is more important, each one claiming that the well-being of great masses depends on his or her stature in the scheme of things.

"Well, I guess you sure didn't overestimate Casey this time," Howell called now from the bedroom, where he was pulling on a pair of blue corduroy pants. He returned, mentally fortified for an ordeal.

"What did Casey say? How did it happen?"

"Well, she didn't really say anything. She just polished the silver while I asked questions until I couldn't take it anymore and I left."

Howell gave his mustache a quick, thoughtful twist. "So you decided to split up?" he asked.

"No," said Woodruff. "I still don't want to split up, but I decided she does. So I left. I still can't believe it. It's so sudden."

"I see," said Howell. "She decided to split up, but she didn't have to tell you and she didn't have to do the leaving. Is that right?"

"Hey, take it easy," Woodruff pleaded. He was struggling to control himself.

"I'm sorry," said Howell.

Woodruff took a deep breath. "I must really seem bad, huh?" he mused. "I've never heard you say that before."

"I take it back," said Howell. "Mere apology is quite useless. I agree with Nader on that."

Howell had a way of speaking in disjointed sentences. A listener would, upon reflection, discern a strained but possible logic to them. Upon further reflection, the listener would decide that the meaning was trivial even if it existed. This amused Howell, who enjoyed being on the edge of the absurd. His amiable manner allowed him to explore gullibility in himself and in others, sometimes even in Woodruff.

Woodruff winced at him. "Boy, what a weird day," he said, pacing in front of the sofa. Howell followed. "We were just talking. I have no idea how this happened. I would have bet you a thousand-to-one that Casey and I would never split up. It scares me that I could have been so out of it, and the next thing I know it scares me that I'm already *enjoying* it so much. I mean I've never really had the chance to go out on my own at all, because we got married so early. Maybe that doesn't make sense. And then I get scared because this whole thing is so personal. I mean I know *marriage* is personal, but I mean the idea of losing your first marriage is so chilling because you can't ever get that back. I keep having this notion that you only have one life and that losing your first marriage is like part of your funeral. I don't care what happens to the second and third and fourth ones, because after the first one what does it matter? I've had a lot of terrible things happen to me and around me, but this is the first time that I might have to say that *I* have failed in a way that I can never make up for. I can't get it back, anyway. I've never felt that kind of permanent failure before."

"Welcome to the human race," said Howell.

"Thank you," said Woodruff. "I just don't understand all this," Woodruff sighed. "It doesn't make sense."

"That's all right," said Howell. "In my opinion, the part that doesn't make any sense is the best part."

"That's ridiculous," said Woodruff. "Look, the only thing I can figure is that this has something to do with the fact that I'm off in my own world so much. You know how I'm always wrapped up in my theories and my high-powered political-type friends. Well, Casey is outside all that. To me, our relationship is purely emotional. I feel like a baby around her a lot of the time. You think that might have something to do with it?"

"Maybe," Howell nodded. He thought Woodruff acted like a child around Casey—and treated her like one, too—but he let it pass. "Uh, Henry, you look like you're gearing up for a long one. Is that right?"

Woodruff had his lungs full of air and his hands clasped behind his back.

"That's all right," Howell said quickly, rising to leave the room. "That's all right. I just wanted to prepare a little bit before you get started."

Woodruff nodded and sat down. "It's that obvious?" he said, mostly to himself. He rubbed his right fist nervously in his left palm.

Howell strolled into the kitchen and returned with a six-pack of Coca-Cola, a bottle of rum, two glasses, and a tray of ice, which he plopped on the coffee table. While Woodruff poured, Howell gathered his recorder and his guitar. He tried to be subtle about it.

It took them nearly three hours to drain the six-pack and the rum. By the end Howell was slumped over his guitar, sloppily fingering the chords for "The Girl From Ipanema," a song he loathed. He had started off muttering intelligent responses to Woodruff's monologue every now and then, but as he got drunker he said only "Yowsuh!" and "Jawohl!" His drinking, dedicated as it was, lagged far behind Woodruff's talking. Woodruff let loose his suppressed academic ambitions. He had intended, years earlier, to leave graduate school only for a short time, lured to Washington by the tail end of the civil rights movement and the war in Vietnam. The excitement stretched into Watergate, and Woodruff realized that he actually hated academia. He likened it to a barnyard full of roosters and hens pecking each other over small bits of gravel, a view similar to Howell's idea of politics. He also realized that no university would hire him as Professor of Moral Philosophy and World History. So Woodruff had more or less given up his plan of becoming a professor. He preferred to work as a Senate aide and do his thinking privately—taking advantage, he said, of his perch in the center of the American empire at a pivotal time in its history.

Howell endured a long exposition on some of the standard Woodruff themes, including new refinements about how the Reformation had motorized the psyche of the Western world, and eventually of the whole world, in a forward-looking anxiety that united the secular habits of the Jewish and Christian peoples. Woodruff calculated that one of the by-products of the motorized psyche is an inexorable drive toward centralization, which the people who wanted to decentralize everything always underestimate. From there, he scoffed at the idea that the revenue-sharing plan would decentralize anything, arguing that it was only making the states and cities even more dependent on Washington. "When those people who are begging Washington and the big companies for money tell Washington to go fuck itself," Woodruff declared, "*then* we'll have some decentralization."

"Hear, hear," toasted Howell.

Woodruff explained that his preoccupation with grand visions was pertinent only because it might help him understand how Casey could drift away from him. He wound slowly around to the subject. He discussed Casey's childhood—her upbringing in an aristocratic Tennessee family that stressed Presbyterianism and manners, along with the command that everything should always be locked. Picturing himself as a rebel against the decadent ways of the Lookout Mountain country clubs, Woodruff told of a few social embarrassments that marred an otherwise wholesome early romance. "We never even ran a red light," he sighed. A large part of the courtship, he admitted, was devoted to a seven-year slide toward initial sexual intercourse —an epic struggle that amazed Howell. He always enjoyed Woodruff's tale of the "disaster at third base." This had occurred when young Woodruff and Casey had finally allowed themselves to run naked outdoors on a beautiful college weekend in Massachusetts. After years of tortuous, inch-by-inch seduction, they finally allowed themselves an entire session of bare genital contact, wrestling their libidos, consciences, and bodies in what Woodruff would later call "a rundown between third and home." The "disaster" arrived promptly the next day in the form of head-to-toe cases of poison ivy, which so mortified Casey that she refused to eat in her college cafeteria for a month.

Woodruff acknowledged taking a beating on certain issues raised by the women's liberation movement, especially doing the laundry. Giving himself high marks for cooking and dishwashing, he examined the possible reasons for his aversion to the laundry. The "wasted time" at the laundromat was high on the list. Woodruff described several "bargains" he had offered Casey —more chores in exchange for laundry exemption—and told how she had repeatedly turned them down even after admitting they were rationally to her advantage. These experiences led Woodruff to the conclusion that Casey's views on the laundry were "irrational" and therefore not a bona fide issue. Howell shook his head sadly through most of the laundry discussion, though it relieved him somewhat to see blindness in Henry Woodruff at last. Woodruff circled round and round through careers and political views and comparative attitudes toward having children. He was just touching upon his complete theory of carnal relations when the rum gave out.

"Well, I'll say one thing Henry," Howell mumbled. "For a guy who's all broken up over all this, you sure do have fun talking about it."

Woodruff looked mystified. "What kind of crack is that?"

"Well, I hear you talking about all these painful things like failure and how tragic your romance has become, but I don't feel much of it from you. You know, if you're so hurt, why don't you show it?"

"That's Dylan, isn't it?" asked Woodruff.

"Yes. I personally feel that he lost a lot when he came out for Joey Gallo and Hurricane Carter, but I 've chalked it up to the postwar cause shortage. He's not himself."

Woodruff stared at Howell, lying there in a stupor of rum and fatigue. "Look, David," he said soberly. "I resent the idea that I ought to display my feelings in order to validate them somehow. That sounds like a shrink talking. But since you brought it up, I will say that I already feel like I've got a telephone pole through my chest. And the only relief I get from that is when I think about Casey. That makes up for it. And to me, all I can call it is love. I believe it will last and I know it's strong. And if it isn't love, I don't know the name for it, and you've got to help me figure out what it is, okay?"

Howell stared at him blankly.

Woodruff shook his head and managed a thin smile. "Will you at least talk to Casey for me? I'll bet you can find out more than I can right now."

Howell zeroed in on the answer that would get him to bed most quickly. "Of course," he said.

"Good," said Woodruff. "Now where are my quarters?"

"You're on them."

"You're kidding!" Woodruff was sitting on Howell's slanted, bare-springed, foam-cushioned couch—a refugee from a Maryland flea market.

"What did you expect?" asked Howell. "You know this is a one-bedroom apartment."

"I suppose I have no alternative." He was removing his clothes when Howell returned with a laundry bag.

"I'm afraid your laundry problems may get even worse than with Casey." He tossed a dirty sheet to Woodruff and turned to leave.

Woodruff called after him. Howell turned slowly to face him, like a zombie. "Thank you."

"Good night."

Woodruff conversed with his insomnia for the better part of two hours. He laughed and cried with it, got angry with it, soothed it, tried to surrender to it, and once he even walked to the kitchen and back just to throw it off the track. Always some thought would burst up through a trap door and go swirling through his mind. Sometimes his thoughts were determined and relentless on their way through his brain, squirreling under barbed wire fences and vaulting over barricades like GIs on the obstacle course. Other times they just floated along like bubbles and popped, only to reappear elsewhere. Woodruff's thoughts generated little short stories, and his short stories generated thoughts. Sometimes he would have thoughts *about* his thoughts, and thoughts about the way he was thinking, and so on in regression. Metathoughts, he thought. Woodruff was scrambling for one when the sensation first struck his penis. Ping! It jolted Woodruff straight up off the couch. "My God," he thought in panic.

Woodruff thought he had a doorbell stuffed up inside him, putting out a throbbing electric tickle. It subsided after a second or two and he collapsed. Sweat broke out on his forehead. He knew his hands were trembling. "All the classic signs," he thought. He realized that the feeling, though terrifying, was not painful. In fact, what he sensed lingering on after the jolt was a delicious tingle on the underside of his penis about an inch from the tip, like a mislocated preorgasmic buzz. Woodruff told himself over and over again that there was nothing to worry about. Primordial forces link marriage and the genitals, he reasoned, and they had launched a concentrated protest attack on his penis. Or maybe it's just a supercharged sexual urge, he hoped. He began to massage himself, but he remained limp. The buzz seemed to have an independent life, sexy but not sexual, and it had scared all his blood to his head anyway.

PIIIINGGG! The attack resumed at exactly the same spot. Woodruff gasped and almost cried out, jumping to his feet in one swift motion. He ran around the room in small circles, dumbstruck and frightened. He was grateful Howell was not there to see him so completely out of control.

When the jolt subsided again after ten or fifteen seconds, Woodruff walked shakily back to the couch. He sat down, cupped his crotch protectively with both hands, and started rocking slowly back and forth. He felt at the mercy of invisible powers. The residual tingle was much stronger this time, like an idling engine. Woodruff felt a slight burning inside. There was also a tiny feathery flutter, as though a microscopic hummingbird were revving up its wings in his urethra. Gradually, the pure sensation took on a size and weight. He realized there was something lodged inside him.

He hurried to the bathroom to urinate, but nothing came out. His body had gone haywire. Woodruff turned on the lavatory tap and listened to the gurgling water. He tried hard to think of something to do next. His head ached from strain, and fatigue made it sound like air was whistling out through a thousand small holes in his skull. Finally, Woodruff grabbed his penis and squeezed it punitively. He felt the buzz move slightly forward. He squeezed several more times. A small amount of white pus emerged.

Woodruff retched into the sink. His mouth filled with spittle as his stomach rose, but there was no vomit, and the heaves came back before he could catch a breath. For the next minute or so, his stomach and his lungs waged war over whether air should come in or vomit should go out and Woodruff suffered greatly from the stalemate. When the attack passed, he lowered both toilet seats and sat down like an old man, sucking in gobs of air. "What a night," he said out loud.

There was nothing else to do. Woodruff stamped his foot in determination and marched directly into Howell's bedroom, where he turned on every light. "David, wake up!" he shouted. "This is an emergency!"

Howell stirred just enough to pull the sheet over his head. He was curled up facing Woodruff, still wearing his socks, which protruded far beyond the rumpled sheet.

Woodruff pulled an upright wooden chair across the room and placed it at the edge of the bed. He sat on it backward, leaned forward, and shouted into Howell's ear. "I'm sorry, David, but I'm in big trouble! I think I've got VD!"

A muffled, sleepy voice barely escaped from under the sheet: "Go away. I'm having rapid eye movements."

"VD!" shrieked Woodruff. "David, pus just came out of me!"

Without a word, Howell threw back the sheet and walked quickly into the bathroom. He was groggy with sleep, miserable with hangover, and disgusted by the mention of pus. After splashing cold water on his face, he returned and sat cross-legged on the bed. "How did it happen?" he asked.

"I can't believe it," Woodruff moaned. "All this in one night. This is a nightmare."

"How did it happen? Come on, Henry. You've got to have an accomplice in this kind of thing."

Woodruff stared at the floor and said, "As you know, I'm not much of a ladies' man. I slept with one woman before Casey and then no one but her for all these years. Until a couple of weeks ago. I spent one night with this woman. One lousy night and I have to pay for it at a time like this."

"It's hard to get away with anything these days," Howell sympathized. "Who is the woman?"

Woodruff looked forlorn and dropped his eyes to the floor. "You may have heard of her, but you don't know her," he said. "Her name is LaLane Rayburn."

Howell's jaw dropped down and outward. "LaLane Rayburn!" he said. "What kind of a name is *that?* It sounds like a slimnastics instructor from Dallas."

"Well, that's not as far off as you might think." Woodruff looked up and saw that Howell was covering his face with both hands, pretending to be lost in thought. Little squeaks of merriment escaped from his hands every few seconds. He sounded like a room full of happy mice.

"Take it easy, damn it," Woodruff warned. "She is a *nice woman.* You *can't* laugh at her. She's twenty years older than we are. She's got four kids. And her husband's an Air Force pilot who's been missing in Vietnam for seven years!"

Howell fell back on the bed.

"That's right! Laugh it up!" yelled Woodruff, waving his arms in dismay.

15

Part of Woodruff wanted to laugh, too, and he found himself on the slippery edge of hysteria, where anger and hilarity merge. "Goddammit, David!" he yelled.

"I'm sure she's nice . . . ," Howell said. He looked at the desperate sight of Henry Woodruff. "It's you!"

"Thank . . . you," said Woodruff, feeling a touch of the bouncy chest himself. "I think she's nice. I don't care if she did give me a . . . social . . . disease." Woodruff sat directly on the floor and got washed overboard into laughter.

The release of it made Woodruff feel better by the minute, even though memories kept piercing through the humor. He suddenly remembered being on top of LaLane Rayburn. The memory came out of nowhere, just the way she had come. He pictured her neck, just beneath her earlobe from a range of about three inches, and it all came back sharply—the close-up of the widening pores and loosening skin of a woman in middle age, the odd smell of perfume on old newspapers, the pleasant surprise that the feminine guitar shape of her ass was so much like that of younger women. She said, "It's all right," and pulled him into her. All the status he derived from the Senate dissolved instantly inside her, as she mothered him and squeezed his back with all her might. She patted him and then she hugged him urgently, and it struck Woodruff that he had never felt so needed, so swallowed up that their biographies vanished and it no longer seemed absurd to have his first affair with an older MIA wife who owned two station wagons and three full sets of encyclopedias. Or at least it was human even if it was absurd. When it was over, she said, "God can't hate you for anything you wait seven years for, I hope," and Woodruff agreed. After all, he had waited seven years for Casey.

Woodruff felt the essence of LaLane Rayburn give his heart a twist, and he also realized that he was laughing at this and a hundred other images. Everything suddenly seemed much bigger and more complicated to him. He laughed harder, enjoyed the tears, felt purged.

Some time passed before they could face each other half soberly. "What is she like?" asked Howell.

"Well," said Woodruff, "she's very smart and she's a fighter. She is the former Miss University of Texas, and she has been an officer of that POW group—the National League of Families. She's been buried in that Air Force life ever since she left school. Straight as an arrow, man. Flying the flag, angling for promotions, wanting to bomb things all the time. And she wears a beehive."

"A beehive?"

"It's a hair-do. It's just what it sounds like. Kind of a turban, only taller and made out of real hair. Anyway, I met her several years ago when the POW and MIA wives came marching through the Senate to lobby against the antiwar amendments. Guys from the Pentagon came with them and drilled them like recruits. They were great PR for the war. So LaLane was with them, and even then she was the smartest of the bunch. She kind of

16

sensed there was something fishy about the logic that we should keep fighting the war to get the prisoners back, when in fact the war was making new prisoners all the time, and she didn't mind expressing her doubts. She finally quit going to the League meetings and they hid her away in one of those Air Force communities out in Virginia. I lost track of her after the prisoner exchange in '73."

Howell wistfully fondled an empty rum bottle.

"Okay," said Woodruff. "She called me a couple of months ago and said she wanted to have lunch, and I found out she was in the middle of some ugly stuff. I always knew that POW world was weird, but I didn't know anything. LaLane confided in me that she wanted to have her husband officially reclassified as KIA instead of MIA, and she said the other MIA wives had a smear campaign going against her. She said it was the money. As long as those guys are MIA, the wives get their full pay. But if the Air Force says they're dead, the wives only get a pension, which is about half as much. Anyway, the other MIA wives are spreading the word that she's given up hope on America and that she's been sleeping around with pinkos in Washington . . ."

"Which she has," said Howell.

"Not *then* she hadn't," said Woodruff. "And the next thing I knew she was telling me she really wanted to know more people like me and my antiwar friends because she thought it would help her with her kids. So I told her I'd be glad to take her to a party but that there would probably be a lot of dope around if that bothered her. Then her eyes *really* lit up. She wouldn't smoke it herself, but she wanted to see people smoke it because her thirteen-year-old son is apparently a big doper. So I took her to a party, and she had a great time. And one thing led to another."

"I see," said Howell. "When did this happen?"

"Two weeks ago—when Casey was out of town."

"Something doesn't sound right," Howell said. "Have you slapped it to Casey since then?"

"Don't be crude, David," Woodruff said. "Only twice, I think. And just barely."

Howell jumped off the bed and began rummaging through the books that were scattered all over his bedroom. "Just a minute, Henry," he said. "You sit there and contemplate your dismal fate for a minute."

Woodruff could think of nothing worse than the prospect of notifying both LaLane and Casey that they were unclean.

"Aha!" Howell shouted, as he unearthed a copy of *Our Bodies, Ourselves*. He began flipping through the pages. "Here it is. 'Syphillis and Gonorrhea.' Just as I feared. 'Symptoms of gonorrhea appear within three to five days after contact.' " He looked up. "That's what it says, Henry. I think the tables are turned."

Woodruff looked stony and pale. "That book is full of shit," he declared.

Howell knew he was on shaky ground with Woodruff, but he was too woozy to care. "Well, I wouldn't go that far," he said. "Some of the ideas in the book may be a little syrupy for you, but the facts are straight. You may be the victim."

Woodruff's only response was that the flanks of his neck turned a bright speckled red. They looked hot enough to cook on. His face stayed pale. Internally, Woodruff was still falling through space. "Goddammit!" he yelled. "She can't *do* that!" Woodruff jumped up from his chair and started circling the room rapidly. "Nooooo!" he moaned, and once or twice he gave a swift kick to the empty air. Woodruff's thoughts were racing by in a blur, but the core of him was still falling so fast that it had no contact with the thoughts.

Howell leaned back warily on the bed. He debated whether to attempt a revival of Woodruff's calm or to push him on through to a healthier state of shock. "Look at it this way, Henry," he said. "At least LaLane may be in the clear."

Woodruff paid him no attention. He was elsewhere. Many of the parts of him were scattered around the bed at home. Somewhere in there was a picture of a naked Casey being as enthusiastic about Mr. X as LaLane had been about him, the result of which was that Woodruff found himself unable to swallow. He summoned up the last bit of his psychic reserves, took a deep breath, and walked calmly over to Howell. "You know," he said, "I don't think I'm jealous."

"I can tell," smiled Howell.

Woodruff made a sour face. "No, really," he said. "Look. I don't know if any of this is real. I'm not sure we've broken up. I'm not sure I've got VD. I don't know. There are so many possibilities. But even if Casey has been sleeping with some guy . . ." Woodruff almost choked himself trying to swallow. "Well, I can't imagine that, but even if she did, I can't really hate the *guy* so much. That's jealousy. What I feel is this huge empty space from Casey. I feel so cut off from everything. So lonely. It's like everything is yanked out from under me. Oh, my God!"

For the first time all evening, Howell knew Woodruff was falling apart, and he couldn't stand to see him suffer so baldly over something—his passion for Casey—that Howell couldn't share or understand. He got up on his knees on the mattress, rubbing his hands together. "Henry!" he shouted, scaring Woodruff. "I know how you can put a stop to all that! There is nothing *wrong* with jealousy if you use it right! So don't be such a stupid *gringo*. If I were you, I'd find out who the guy is who's been sleeping with Casey and I'd go over to his house!"

Woodruff shuddered and buried his face in his hands, while Howell sprang from the bed and stalked around in a frenzy. "And I'd take me a sharp hunting knife, and I'd *slice his balls off!* Like this!" Howell made a series of slashing motions in the air. He tottered drunkenly after the final one but managed to hold an Errol Flynn pose. "And then I'd go back to Casey's at midnight and I'd climb up the trellis with a rose clenched tightly between my teeth!" Howell acted out a stealthy climbing motion. "And I'd kick her bedroom door down!" He kicked the arm of Woodruff's chair.

18

Woodruff didn't move. He was holding his face so tightly that his fingertips were white where they were making dents in his forehead.

"Aaaaaaaggghhh!" Woodruff roared, rising with his arms in the air. He sounded like he was being strangled. "You!" shouted Woodruff, pointing at Howell, eyes bulging. "*En garde!*" He snatched the recorder off the floor and pounded the bed next to Howell with all his might.

The cries built to a crescendo as Woodruff spun, staggered, and finally crashed tiredly onto the bed, which collapsed instantly and loudly. Then there was silence, except for the heavy breathing of the combatants and the thud of a broom on the ceiling of the apartment below.

"That's Madame Delacroix," gasped Howell. "She gives voice lessons, and she hates me for making noise."

"Must be a light sleeper."

"Must be," said Howell. They stared at each other for a long time.

I I

ABOUT FIFTEEN hundred miles south of the District of Columbia public health clinic where Henry Woodruff would present himself for examination later that morning, Carlos Maraña was up and prowling about his sunny Miami condominium. As always he moved cleanly. He smelled of talc and outdoor shaving lotion, and he moved with the graceful confidence of a gymnast—always, whether reaching for a gun or for a bar of soap. On this particular morning, he gave off even more energy than usual. It seemed to rise off his shoulders like heat waves off the desert. Maraña wanted to make sure he survived this historic day in American life, so he began his memory exercises early. Spreading the *Miami Herald* on the breakfast table before him, he flipped quickly through the news section from back to front. Then he closed his eyes and tried to read the paper mentally from front to back, concentrating on the names and headlines. He matched the stories with reporters' names, and the names with stories from the previous day. He was looking for patterns and changes. Maraña had to work on his names and faces, but he had a gift for numbers. He could remember the marking numbers of airplanes he had guarded in Cuba fifteen years earlier, and he could astonish his friends by reciting eight or nine of their previous phone numbers. He believed in memory as his chief guardian in a life of intrigue.

The exercises lasted almost twenty minutes, leaving Maraña with a slight headache. He touched his fingertips lightly to his eyelids and the headache seemed to vanish, as it always did. Refreshed, he jumped up from the table and nearly bounced into the bedroom. The recording device he selected from his chest of drawers was a very special one, obtained from an outfit in Fort Lauderdale that sells to governments and gangsters alike. Its microphone, the size of a pinky finger, clipped to the inside of Maraña's French cuffs, and the wire ran around past his armpit to a tiny hole behind his shirt pocket. There the wire attached to a miniature cassette recorder that would fit comfortably behind a pack of cigarettes. Loaded properly, the recorder could be activated casually while reaching for cigarettes or matches. Although "the Mosquito" had a recording time of only twenty-five minutes, Maraña considered it superior to any simple system on the market. It was certainly better than the "wires" he had worn for various federal agencies.

Maraña slipped a remote control beeper into his coat pocket and stepped back to examine himself in the mirror. His face was round and boyish, devoid of harsh angles, his cheeks cleanly shaven up to the dark sideburns only recently flecked with gray. Universally regarded as handsome, that face looked as innocent as a bright moon, in violent contrast to his eyes. Fluctuating wildly from one moment to the next, they were the key to Maraña's mercurial nature. Without warning, all the mahogany color would go out of them and Maraña would stare through unforgettable black discs that looked ten or twenty feet deep, bottomed with nothing softer than porcelain. The eyes, he often said, came from Africa. Their moods whiplashed across the innocent face in a way that inspired primeval lusts and terrors, which calmed down to an abiding air of mystery. His body was well-matched to the moody vitality of his face—catlike and wiry, it could strike a pose of elegant boredom just before exploding. Maraña dressed himself well. He preferred suits of pale green and blue, set off by expensive white shirts, open at the collar. Like thousands of other former CIA employees among Miami's Cubans, he still wore the telltale Rolex wristwatch. Otherwise, the only jewelry he liked was an unusual necklace of leather and stone. He was never without it. Ten years earlier, Maraña had removed the small, cone-shaped stone from a pouch on the hip of a dead Mulele warrior near Stanleyville, in the old Belgian Congo. Maraña was there, he often said later, "killing Negroes" on an official mission that for him stripped war of all its idealism but somehow left its appeal. He never quite understood how it could take one without the other. Imagining, for his own reasons, that the stone was some sort of war charm, he had worn it on a thin leather thong ever since to remind him of the moments when nobly serene, spear-carrying African warriors kept coming in rows to have their lives harvested by Maraña's M–14. On days like today, with accident and ambush strong possibilities, he touched the stone and took heart from the thought that he was still much, much farther from the smothering puzzle of death than he had been in Africa. He felt alive and masterful.

Maraña drove his rented car through Miami toward Biscayne Bay. The sun shone brightly enough to bleach some of the deepness out of the sky, and he enjoyed it. He knew the city well enough to focus on its colors and shapes. Miami is first a visual city. Light reaches everywhere. Exotic objects seem to jump into the eye from a glaring background of white stucco buildings and splashes of aquamarine. Skinny manicured Norfolk pines look like plucked green eyebrows, and the shocking red blooms on the royal poincianas look like whirling skirts at the spring festival in Mexico. Next to such sights, Miami has little to offer in the way of sound or smell. Deaf-mutes flock to the city, while the blind avoid it. Maraña's quick-witted girlfriend, Carmen, said that a man with his extraordinary eyes belongs in Miami.

Crossing MacArthur Causeway, Maraña hit the south end of Miami Beach and made his way up Collins Avenue, past the long strip of glorious but decaying hotels. On his left stretched out the endless row of lesser boardinghouses and condominiums, porches lined with rocking chairs to accommodate the elderly Jewish retirees who make up most of the permanent population. In the summer off-season, they have almost exclusive control of the sidewalks, walking two-by-two, husband and wife, grandma and aunt, on errands to fill their shopping bags with items to help fill their nonerrand time. Most of the all-purpose merchandise stores feature special complaint lines that are also crowded two-by-two and filled with scattered conversation. Patient complaint clerks are highly prized by the managers.

Maraña parked outside the Concord Cafeteria and pushed his tray through the serving line to the breakfast department, where he grabbed a plate of his favorite Concord French toast, thick as the Miami yellow pages. In the cashier's line, he endured a lengthy argument between one trenchant old lady and the clerk over the price of butter patties, and an ensuing argument between the first arguer and the old man behind her over whether it was proper to take up so much time in the line. Maraña wondered whether the argumentative habits of Concord customers came from age, poverty, idleness, or simply from the aggressive nature of the Jewish people. Like pack rats, he thought. Maraña had little use for Jews in the United States, but he held Israel in great respect—especially its intelligence service, one of whose officers had introduced him to the Concord.

As planned, he was seated at a table for four with two quite elderly strangers when Patrick Shea arrived to fill the remaining seat. Burly and pink-faced, with snowy white hair and a benign face, Shea could have passed for a harassed member of the cathedral's collection committee, which he was. He was also special agent in charge (SAC) of the FBI office in Miami, and it was beneath his station in life to meet personally with informants, even legendary ones.

"What's so important?" he growled as ferociously as he could. Shea did not like snitches, and he liked Cubans even less. Among the Cuban snitches, he liked Maraña the least because of his uppity and unpredictable manners. So he growled at Maraña even more than at other Cubans. It was partly to compensate for the fact that his personality was not imposing.

"I wanted you to see the Concord, Pat," smiled Maraña, with only a trace of a Spanish accent. "I'm tired of Kentucky Fried Chicken anyway. Don't you think it's a nice place?"

"For you, maybe it is," said the old lady next to Maraña. "But for me the taste has gone out of it. Yes, it has."

"What did you go and say that for?" asked the lady's companion. "You don't know these people, and you don't know how to eat in the first place."

Shea and Maraña quickly relocated to another table, dumping the notion that they could use Miami Beach seniles for cover. Maraña made jokes about the FBI's performance in the Watergate case, as Shea grunted and drank coffee, and then turned serious. "It's about the Kennedy assassination, Pat," he said over his last bite of French toast. "Fidel had nothing to do with it. The chief conspirator has been right under your nose all along. It's Zapruder, the guy who took the movies. You guys don't even have the real pictures."

Shea drummed his fingers on the table. "Don't call me Pat," he said, "and cut the bullshit. I've got to get back to the office, so let's have it."

"I'm ready," smiled Maraña, "but your three minutes ran out three minutes ago. Someone has to pay the phone bills."

Shea looked sourly at his coffee. Then it registered. "Oh," he said, "I forgot." He pulled out a plain brown envelope, containing $600 in cash, and slid it across the table. It was Maraña's monthly stipend, one of the highest in the Bureau, for what amounted to a few hours' work. Maraña signed a receipt "for confidential services" and put the envelope in his coat pocket next to the beeper. "Thank you," he said. He pulled out a cigarette and started the recorder.

"I hear that a war is starting," Maraña said quietly. "And there will be many prominent funerals soon. The younger groups have declared war on Uncle Sam's *chivatos*."

"What for?" asked Shea, whose meager command of Spanish did encompass the word for informant, or collaborator.

"They say they are tired of waiting for the Americans to give an okay to fight Castro. So they say the hell with the Americans, we're going to fight on our own. The first thing they're going to do is purge the leaders who collaborate with the government."

"Sounds like a quick way for them to get their asses kicked," laughed Shea, much relieved that the message concerned only more rumblings among the Cubans rather than what he had feared—a threat by Maraña to do his informing to the narcs or the Immigration people unless the Bureau forked over more money.

"Yeah, well, that's what you guys said about Fidel twenty years ago," shrugged Maraña. "I'm just bringing you the news."

"Aw, come on, Carlos," snorted Shea. "If I had a dime for every time the young bucks in Little Havana have started beating their war drums, I'd be as rich as you are. That's a lot of hullaballoo."

Maraña cringed slightly at Shea's reference to Cubans as "bucks," but he gave back nothing more than a pleasantly malevolent smile which Shea did not fathom. "I think the first execution will be tonight," he said quietly. "You'd better send your black suit to the cleaners, because this is one funeral you and Señor Noel will have to attend yourselves. It's Taliente."

Shea blinked at the name. "Yeah, that would be a *good* idea," he said sarcastically. "That's about the quickest way I know to have every decent Cuban in Miami down their throats. Good grief, Carlos, Taliente used to be my *friend*. He is about the best hope you people have left. He can talk to presidents and ambassadors, for Christ's sake."

"But he can't shoot them," said Maraña. "He just goes to meetings and takes money and follows the advice of your friend Señor Noel. That's why they're going to make him a famous ghost."

"Let's leave Noel out of this," snapped Shea. Edward Noel, a snotty Virginian of about forty-eight, headed the CIA's small office in Miami. Once a vast and proud possession in the Agency's bureaucratic collection, the Miami station had shrunk through the years to a minuscule size, supported by only three part-time secretaries. The prestige of the station chief had suffered in proportion to the decline. Noel, the latest one, languished on a "career plateau" from which he already contemplated retirement. Shea found him lazy and secretive and pedantic, even worse than the other ones, and he seldom knew what Noel was up to. Neither did Noel, for that matter. His duties were to collect and encourage anti-Castro sentiment—to "keep the flame lit," as the chief put it—but to forestall any hostile demonstration that might cause embarrassment to the United States. Taliente was Noel's most prominent Cuban contact, and for that reason he was a thorn in Shea's side.

"After Taliente, they're going to hit Mendoza, Nino Diaz, Perestevez, and Prio. All the rich and famous ones. That's the main course. There's more on the dessert list, but that's not final yet.

Shea looked exasperated. "Come on, Carlos. Why don't you tell these people to wait until they're out of school before they shoot their mouths off with these cockeyed schemes. I hate to even put this kind of stuff in my report. It's going to make me look like an idiot. Do you realize how many hundreds of times our reports have had these roosters out plotting to kill Castro and Norman Mailer and every other damn person? Even Adlai Stevenson. You know as well as I do that most of those bucks have hot mouths and cold feet."

"I know you've had a lot of rumors in the past," said Maraña coldly. "But this is the first time *I've* told you anybody was going to get killed like this. And I'm not doing it for the food or the company." Maraña's sudden hostility made the FBI man shiver, thinking for an instant that he saw the eyes of a large insect on the face of a smiling man.

"Wait here a second," said Shea, making a quick escape.

Maraña leaned back in his chair and turned off the recorder. The line was still moving, the French toast selling well, and the arguments running on near the cash register. The Concord's most prominent colors were the silver of the cafeteria railings and the reddish, almost purple, hair of several of the old ladies.

"The Mosquito" started back up just as Shea returned to the table, having collected his thoughts and a large slice of key-lime pie. "Okay, I'm going to take this seriously," he said, as he pulled out a small notebook and placed it next to the pie. "But I wish you'd just told Damico about it like always. This story's too wild for me to get involved at this stage." Shea took a bite, savoring the fluffy meringue. "Now exactly who's the big shot on this one?"

Maraña pretended to sweat over the prospect of squealing on the would-

24

be killers by name. Inwardly, he congratulated himself on hooking the timid SAC. "There are three groups now," he said quietly. "Abdala, Zero, and Cuban Power. That's Arozco, Bosch, and Rivero. Each group is ordered to choose one man for the action team, and I don't know who they are yet. It's the youngest ones, though, the second generation. A lot of them think their fathers were Uncle Tomáses. They like Arafat, and they want to prove it."

Shea was scribbling names. "That's just great," he said. "A coalition of Cubans who want to be like the Arabs. I bet that coalition will last at least an hour or two. I don't know why I have to put up with this stuff. Okay, how are they planning to pull it off? Are they going to run over Taliente with camels? A plane crash, a lost boat in the ocean—something to look like an accident?"

"My understanding is that they will shoot him in the head," Maraña replied with pleasant simplicity.

Shea felt a stab of sickness and heaved a sigh to conceal it. "You think they mean business, huh?" he asked. "You think those follows really understand that Taliente is considered a friend and ally of the United States? If they gun him down, they'll have every agency in this town down their throats and they won't have anybody to run to."

"Maybe that's the idea," said Maraña. "These young guys say they have big *cojones*. They say they're not afraid of Uncle Sam like their fathers. They're not even afraid of the Company. They are declaring their independence."

"That's just great," Shea repeated absently. He leaned back, drummed his fingers, and fell into a silent reverie of self-pity. Despite the robust addresses he delivered to the Miami Rotary Club, Shea was basically an administrator and he knew it. Gunplay and street risks were not his game. He had secured his niche in the early 1960s by harassing Hoffa's Teamsters in Miami, whom Robert Kennedy wanted to nail, without disturbing too much the entangled affairs of the other mobs, whom Kennedy wanted to leave alone. This was no small task—especially at a time when J. Edgar Hoover, for his own cosmetic reasons, denied the very existence of organized crime.

The Bureau rewarded Shea by leaving him here in Miami, where he cultivated the goodwill of the local bankers with his Minimum Window Cash program. Otherwise, Shea spent most of his time trying to protect the Bureau's territory from encroachments by other agencies, particularly the local police and the CIA. In 1967, as a member of the Director's Commission on Physical Standards, he had played a part in an elaborate clandestine move to relax Hoover's rigid weight standards—risking career disaster if Hoover detected his role, but gaining the admiration of hundreds of grateful agents. It was the most daring gamble he had ever taken in the Bureau. Only once had he been exposed to gunfire in the line of duty, and that had been after World War II out in Kansas, when a frightened seventeen-year-old bank robber had fired in his general direction. That robber may have been a teenager, Shea always joked, but the bullet was fully grown.

Now Shea wanted to retire, but his wife, Helen, wanted him to wait a few more years on the chance that their friend Sandy Morgan would gain control of the disability committee, where he might wring out some advantage for the Sheas. Helen Shea had cast the deciding vote on most of her husband's career decisions, and on the whole she had cast them wisely. Both the Sheas were proud that he had risen so far from his lowly rank near the bottom of his class at Dayton. They had two white Chevrolets, one a convertible, and they had owned a procession of ever-larger homes, which they abandoned each time the prosperous Cubans spilled into the neighborhood. The Sheas had one daughter, also Helen, who had of late taken up marijuana and heaven knows what other rebellious habits. Patrick Shea hated to think of it.

"What do you want me to do?" asked Maraña, after waiting as long as he could.

Shea was elsewhere, his face clouded with anger. "The nerve of those young Cubans is what gets me, Carlos," he said tightly. "I saw them landing here fifteen years ago with sick babies and no shoes. Now they've taken over the whole city. I see the young ones riding around in fancy cars with their stereo systems and those clodhopper shoes."

"Platforms," said Maraña.

"Yeah," said Shea. "This country has given them everything they've got, and now they're running around like sawed-off gangsters. I think somebody ought to tan their hides."

"I'd be happy to introduce you to them," Maraña offered.

"Very funny," said Shea. "What I want you to do is to keep as close as you can to these firecrackers without getting yourself hurt. If we can, I'd like to get the ringleaders off the street. Get them on a smuggling charge or a firearms rap—anything. Understand? What I don't need is for you to get yourself shot full of holes like last time, because then things get out of control."

"I didn't volunteer for any holes," Maraña replied, chuckling to himself at Shea's assumption that he could still move Maraña around like a chess piece, sending him off to be loyally maimed or killed.

"Good," said Shea. "Now when do you really expect all this commotion to start? You said tonight. Is that American time or Cuban time?"

"Who can say for sure? They say tonight, but it might mean next Christmas. I'll try to speed it up by killing him myself if you want me to."

Shea shivered again. "I'll bet you'd like that," he muttered. "You just keep us informed, all right? Call Dave at home if you have to."

"Okay," said Maraña, gathering himself to leave.

"And Carlos," added Shea, "Try to keep all this to yourself, will you? There's no need getting everybody all excited here at the rumor stage. If the boys over in the organized crime section find out about this, they'll be in my conference room as quick as you can shake a stick. And the first thing they'll want to know is where I got the information, you know. I want to protect you, so help me out, okay?"

Maraña almost frowned. "Do you want me to warn Taliente?" he asked. "He doesn't like me, but I think he would believe what I say, you know."

"Not now, at the rumor stage," said Shea. "I want to be discreet and gentle so Taliente won't tell his friend Noel, because if he does I'll have the Company gentlemen all over me. They don't like it when I fish in their pond."

"Naturally," smiled Maraña, rising. "Well, I'm off back into the shadows. What else will you be doing to help me?"

Shea paused for effect over his key-lime pie. "Well," he said gravely, "I think we'll just knock a few heads together around town and see what happens." He nodded Maraña a farewell.

The SAC had no intention of knocking any heads together. Those were merely the parting words for which he was widely known, having uttered them often in confidence to news reporters, civic leaders, and his agents. After Maraña's departure, Shea meditated at length over his strategy. To make too big a fuss over this report, he knew, would not only cause its dissemination in Washington to other government agencies, but would also expose the Bureau to ridicule if the information proved to be groundless, as was likely. On the other hand, he could not afford to ignore it—knowing that Maraña would be talking to many other people, including the Bureau's Dave Damico, the brightest, most gung-ho FBI agent in Miami. What was needed, Shea knew, was a memorandum constructed so as to land on the Washington desk of the assistant director for intelligence, and go no further. This would maximize the protection of the Miami office while minimizing the obligations and the embarrassments. Shea wanted to fire his memo high but not wide, which would be difficult because memos in the bureaucracy tend to scatter like goosedown in a wind tunnel.

Back at his office, Shea summoned Damico and the two spent the better part of the afternoon fashioning a report, drawing on twenty-five years' experience with language and emphasis. They informed headquarters of a "potentially dangerous and historic shift in the paramilitary activities of Cuban exile groups, which may take the shape of attacks against Cuban leaders sympathetic to U.S. interests as part of a so-called 'go it alone' movement." They cited some of Maraña's victims, including Taliente, adding that "no U.S. officials have been named in the so-called threats to date." As "perpetrators" of the shift, Shea and Damico pointed to "Castro sympathizers, right-wing terrorists, or hoodlum elements in the guise of political activity," which enabled them to place copies of the report under three separate headings in the Miami files so that it would count three times as a report of potential terrorist activity. Shea wrote that until the director so ordered, he would take no action other than to monitor exile activities as closely as possible. In closing, he told the intelligence chief, whom he knew to be fond of suspicious afterthoughts, that he was detailing a special Cuban informant to keep a watchful eye on the informant who had brought this worrisome news, Maraña.

By that time, Maraña was finished with the United Fund and the bank. His business there had been routine. When the Cubans took over the United Fund in Miami in 1971, a wealthy aristocrat from the old Cuba, Diego

Almagro, assumed the presidency of United Fund and carried on its traditions. His personal influence in the community had been assured ever since the day in 1951 when he walked into the treasury building in Havana and withdrew, on some pretext, the entire Cuban foreign exchange balance of $20 million, which he used to purchase most of Key Biscayne.

After this legendary exploit, Almagro devoted himself to charity in exile while suffering from two major impulses in his character. One was an urge to give away money to any and all mendicants; the other to invest in manifestly fraudulent ventures—a habit that invited speculation about a possible guilt complex from the treasury episode. Diego Almagro also exhibited a lifelong sycophancy toward anyone who professed to have physical courage, and he revered the few like Maraña who possessed some in fact. For a hundred years, the death-defying romantic revolutionary has touched the deepest strains of Cuban patriotism—a tender spot for Almagro after charges that his $20 million withdrawal was treasonous—and consequently he obliged almost anyone who wanted money for a gun or a bomb or a boat in the name of Cuban liberation. Twenty years as a soft touch had depleted his fortune considerably, but, owing to the strange legacies of money and social prominence, he still retained enough respectability to carry on as president of the United Fund. He also served on the boards of several large corporations, including the *Miami Herald*.

Understandably, Almagro steered charitable resources into places of benefit to local Cubans. Through his connections in city hall, he arranged for the United Fund to lend substantial sums to the city of Miami, whose officials would take the money and the United Fund's eminent sponsorship to Washington and flash them, in a manner of speaking, before the eyes of federal officials there, who would, after many phone calls and bureaucratic incantations, augment the United Fund's dollars to two and three times their number under various matching programs for job training and supplemental education and community development. Like magic, the money would multiply and return in sufficient quantities to repay the United Fund and also hire extra people in Miami to help out in the area of bilingual development.

Carlos Maraña, for example, served as a program analyst/bilingual, attached to one of the city's youth projects. Three of his friends and two of his relatives were similarly employed. Every two weeks, he strolled into Diego Almagro's plush office in the Flagler Building for a chat. Almagro always received him grandly in his private conference room and gave strict orders that he not be disturbed. In keeping with the conspiratorial ways he admired, Almagro never used Maraña's name in the office, even when they were alone. It was always "*chico*," very friendly, and Almagro would try his best to be nonchalant as Maraña fed him tidbits of intrigue. To Almagro, these were sweet, vicarious moments. He cherished a plot or a counterplot the way the lovelorn thrive on gossip. He did not really mind playing the tail to Maraña's kite. On the day when Maraña, after his meeting with Shea, hinted at the impending wars, Almagro fairly bubbled with excitement. He even tried to make some comments about the situation among the exiles, though of course he was three twists behind Maraña's thinking. At the end of the audience, Almagro promised his silence earnestly and handed Maraña the six paychecks, drawn on the United States Treasury.

Maraña scrawled illegible endorsements on all six drafts and presented them to an old girlfriend at the bank, along with deposit slips that he had correctly numbered for his friends and relatives from his well-exercised memory. He cashed all of his own check and took $100 in cash from each of the others. Then he dropped the "Mosquito" cassette into his safety deposit box. He kept nearly a trayful of them there. This one, he believed, would never be needed.

Eduardo Romero allowed only a few people to call him by his old CIA nickname, "El Navajo," a bastardized play on his Indian features and the Spanish word for razor. Maraña was one of them. They exchanged the Latin *abrazo* when Maraña arrived at the garage, laughing and shouting. El Navajo wiped the grease off his hands and invited Maraña inside to his private office, filled with oil cans and fan belts and early pinups and photographic momentos from the Bay of Pigs. El Navajo's mind was frozen in the early 1960s, the only time in his life when he had briefly overcome all his oddities. Then he had been accepted and happy, drilling himself for real and imagined secret missions with all the enthusiasm of a high school cheerleader. As a night shift bus boy for the Miami Playboy Club, El Navajo had gone so far as to organize his own after-hours boot camp for his fellow dishwashers—marching them through the kitchen and the dressing room, sending them crawling beneath the tables in the dark—until one young trooper pushed the dish cart through a glass partition.

Back then, everyone said El Navajo was skinny enough to cut a bullet in half with his body. They said he would never be killed and slapped him on the back. He was tall enough—six five—to be a scout, and his eyes were beady enough to see in the dark. El Navajo was by far the most angular person any of the Cuban soldiers had ever seen, and they joked that he could use any part of his body as a sword. His arms, which hung to his knees, looked like propeller blades. His legs seemed to fit within the creases of his khaki trousers. His head seemed elongated, mashed between his ears, with his long nose stretched down the middle of it like the business end of a chisel. From every angle, El Navajo looked dark, bladelike, and he felt grotesque except during those military years, when, according to one of war's flipside realities, the ugliest of the ordinary soldiers were the ones who were charmed and admired.

Maraña always laughed with him, just as in the old days. He put his feet up on the cluttered desk and swapped jokes on America's impotence, resting his dark glasses casually on top of his head. Still, El Navajo knew this was a business trip, since Maraña neither asked for a drink nor offered a snort of cocaine. There had been no postponement.

"Hey, *chico*," said Maraña, flipping through the day's deposit slips. "Uncle

Sambo thanks you for your clandestine services." He handed Romero his slip. They shared a laugh. It had long been a joke among the Cubans that to the Americans "clandestine" meant "nonexistent."

"Thanks," smiled El Navajo. "I like his money, but I'd rather have his liver." El Navajo harbored a grudge toward Uncle Sambo, which he expressed in his normal cutthroat manner. In Africa, with Maraña, El Navajo had lost his grip on himself permanently. One stomach-rattling day in a commando jeep, El Navajo's patrol gunned down a party of straggling rebels and then fanned out in the grass to look for strays. El Navajo found one— or what was left of one—lying face down in a circle of mud, perfectly still except for his bare feet, which were together, heels up, taking methodical baby steps to nowhere, toes swishing back and forth through the mud. The sight mesmerized El Navajo. He had seen much worse carnage and been a thousand times more frightened, but somehow the tiptoeing corpse lodged in his mind and rendered it unstable. Useless for the remainder of the African fighting, El Navajo figured he'd lost his courage to a devil's spell and he so confided to Maraña, who already knew. In the decade since then, the former "action man" stayed out of the action and confined himself to support of whatever game was up. This humiliation and the fact that he felt grotesque again, made El Navajo mean and neurotic. He grew worse with time, filling his conversation with knife wounds and ass-kickings. He said more hateful things about the Russians than Evans and Novak. From a pork-'n-beans radio station, he latched on to the idea that Zionists and the Rockefellers had combined to create the Russian Revolution and every un-Christian abomination since then—a view he shared with fundamentalist rednecks and a few Maoist splinter groups. He detected this conspiracy behind everything from Castro to auto inspection laws. His logic was strained, but he didn't bother with it much anyway in his haste to get on to the knife wounds and the ass-kickings he would like to see. Only around people like Maraña did El Navajo recover some of the old Playboy Club sparkle.

He was washing his grimy hands in the lavatory behind his desk when he saw Maraña pull out the wad of cash he had accumulated that day. Without speaking, Maraña pulled out five hundreds and tossed them on the old Gulf Oil blotter.

El Navajo rubbed a wet hand around his stomach. He faked a hungry moan through his smile. This succeeded, as Maraña idly tossed two more hundreds on the pile.

Negotiations completed, they were soon outside in back of one of the queerest auto garages anywhere. El Navajo's sat an hour west of Miami on the Tamiami Trail, on the edge of the Everglades. The old concrete shed lay about a hundred feet off the highway, surrounded by swamp grass in every direction except rearward, where a strip twenty feet wide and three hundred yards long had been cleared. This bizarre path led back through bogs and over cyprus roots to three target stands, near which alligators often sunned themselves. Here, at El Navajo's makeshift but duly licensed target range, customers could run through a box of cartridges out back while their cars were being tuned inside. And very special customers like Maraña could tinker with their cars while Romero overhauled their guns. One of the best firearms men among the Cubans, El Navajo was a magician with his welder and his etching knives and his homemade barrel molds. It was rumored that he could make a serviceable gun out of an ordinary car muffler, and it was a fact that he could cut and file automatic weapon parts to make them interchangeable. His gun wizardry sustained his last link to the glory days. Maraña himself had suggested that he move the garage out to the Everglades, pointing out the advantages of life in the middle of nowhere. Among them was the location along one of the biggest new smuggling routes in the United States. Cubans and old alligator poachers were making parachute drops and guided boat landings and offshore swaps near the thousand-island maze of tunnellike canals on the coast of the Everglades. The traffic between the swamps and Miami was heavy and dangerous, and many customers found it convenient to pick up doctored guns on the way out and then drop them off upon return. Others just liked to get the personal service from El Navajo out there in the swamps, near the old secret training camps where the United States government simulated battle conditions ranging from Cuban jungles to African plains. Psychologically, El Navajo's isolation was a boon because it kept him removed from the city action and constant reminders that he had lost his nerve. He came to like his hermit life out there, where the sound of gunshots went straight to heaven because there were no buildings or trees or hills to bounce off. The guns made an airy poofing sound, so quiet that grumpy kingfishers sat on the power lines and watched target practice like sportswriters.

A solitary door on the back wall of the garage led to a windowless gun room, strewn with crates and worktables and electric tools and weapons of every description. Almost all the guns out in view still bore their serial numbers and were registered. Romero made it a habit to hang on to guns whose papers would trace them to some outlet or warehouse affiliated with the CIA or the Drug Enforcement Administration, knowing from Maraña that such a heritage would usually cloud an arrest beyond the hope of conviction. There was a walk-in storage closet at one end of the workroom, equipped with a trap door leading down to a subterranean storage area. From there El Navajo retrieved four items, each wrapped in its own oilcloth. He handed them proudly to Maraña, who had waited politely outside. The customer unwrapped each one and looked it over. There were two .38s and two .22s, an underrated pistol for close range work, all fitted with silencers.

In Spanish, Maraña asked which of the guns had been loaded with blanks, as requested, and El Navajo pointed to one of the .38s. Part of the handle had been painted red for identification. Maraña nodded and casually fired the red-handled .38 toward his own foot, which survived despite a healthy kick from the pistol over the spitting sound of compressed air. Maraña smiled with satisfaction. "I am always ready to put my foot where your mouth is, *amigo*," he said.

"Thank you very much," laughed El Navajo. "Now that you trust me with your car and your foot, can you tell me who it is who will be shot?"

"The bad guys, of course," said Maraña. "Only the bad guys. The ones who steal money and build false hope in the people."

"You will need more weapons then," said El Navajo. "There are many people like that. I know thousands of them myself, and I only live here in the swamp with the animals. You will need some fire hoses before you're through." (El Navajo had been a "fire hose man," a machine gunner, in Africa.) He noted the sweat on Maraña's forehead, the tightness in his joints, and a cold reality swept over him. He saw a flash of the tiptoeing corpse and felt a pain in his stomach. Ordinarily El Navajo's sinewy stomach could breeze through a diet of hot peppers and steel wool, but one look at Maraña's drawn face ruined all that. He fought the pain as he lit an unfiltered cigarette with his long delicate fingers. "I hope you kill them all," El Navajo said through his teeth. "The Jews, the traitors, and the *pendejos*. And every one of the communists. Fill the gutters with their blood." He bent his sharp body at the waist and knee to spray the area with a blast from an imaginary machine gun.

"Don't worry, *chico*," said Maraña, one of the few living souls who could recognize El Navajo's snarl as an expression of childish sentiment. "You watch closely tonight. I think there will be a few visitors out here on your doorstep. Don't go anywhere. I may call you."

Navajo jerked his head in a military nod and kicked the ground in frustration. He stood there long after Maraña was speeding down the swamp highway past the bib-jeaned families fishing in the canal. By then his tongue was thickly coated with essence of nicotine which he rolled around inside his mouth to feel the sour sting. He thought fondly of Maraña and the guns, spat twice on the sand, kicked the wet spots with his sharp-soled boots, and uttered a quiet prayer of thanks for small pleasures as he turned back toward the garage.

Carmen Vilar arrived first at the Versailles and was followed to her table by several hundred pairs of eyes reflected in the mirrors. The back dining room, while quite small, was completely surrounded by tall mirrors that gave it the appearance of a cavernous nightclub, and was filled with smoke and plain wooden tables and clusters of people, both seated and standing, in animated Spanish conversation. Waitresses elbowed their way through the pandemonium. One of the most popular hangouts in Little Havana, the Versailles was, paradoxically, so public a place that conspirators of all kinds went there regularly to pretend they had nothing to hide. A great deal of very private plotting went on in front of the mirrors.

Carmen ordered a Cuban coffee and waited, acknowledging the respectful nods that came her way from other tables. Like Maraña, she was something of a public figure in Miami. Her father, the city's vice-mayor, owned a large construction company from whose warehouses explosives had a way of disappearing for use in bombings. It was rumored that Carmen facilitated some of the disappearances. It was also rumored that she had denounced her father for being weak and two-faced, for making countless speeches about his desire to return to a free Cuba when, in fact, he had fallen in love with the Yankee dollar. She was a hard and proud woman. In her past were few women friends, one discarded husband, and very few lovers. Fools made her uncomfortable, and she considered most Cuban men to be fools. She thought Anglo men were even worse—salesmen, trying to make everyone happy, polite and tasteless, like a steady diet of stripped white rice. It was a great mystery among the men in Little Havana how Carmen could despise so many people and still keep her zest for life and her great beauty. Carmen's eyes matched Maraña's. When they were not full of scorn, they were laughing. She had a thin, aristocratic nose, which in Miami is taken as a sign of high Spanish blood, but the remainder of her body seemed to be made of circles—circular cheeks and mouth, tall round breasts, sloping stomach and hips—she looked like a bouquet of bubbles, put together in a way that was inexplicably ferocious. With her jet-black hair and perfect teeth, she approached the classical form that Latin men paint on their mental easels, except that she avoided the jewelry and the scarlet paint for lips and nails. Her lack of makeup, so unusual in Miami, made her seem that much more naked to her admirers, who needed no extra reasons to be excited. Many men racked their brains and flailed themselves unmercifully in search of a way to win a small measure of approval from Carmen Vilar. The idea of winning *all* her approval, especially the saucy but dignified approval that lay quietly between her legs, was enough to drive quite a few men to despair, but none had grown so frenzied as to challenge Maraña. To outsiders, Carmen and Carlos were an obvious match of princess and matador, the ideal romance.

Actually, their romance was more in the nature of an understanding between Maraña, who prided himself on his feel for Nietzsche's passions, and Carmen, who prided herself on her grasp of female superiority, which, among other things, allowed her to be like Maraña without having to play all his silly games. The two of them thought they had an understanding, at least. It had begun four years earlier at the Versailles when Maraña had leaned over a bowl of black beans and told Carmen that he did not love her. He had said he didn't think he loved anything, even himself, though he could not yet be sure, but if he loved anything at all he was sure it was not a woman, even Carmen. To this Carmen had replied cooly that to talk of love was to be like moths buzzing around a light bulb. She said Maraña held no love for her but he did hold her interest, which was more than she could say for any other man. She would help him and watch him as long as he continued to interest her, even though she thought she already knew where he was going. Maraña had shrugged and smiled, and the understanding had been sealed. Almost against their wills, they had grown quite tender about each other in fulfilling their bargain's cold terms.

Maraña was feeling tender, in fact, when he walked up to Carmen's table. She took no notice of him and appeared to be the only person in the restaurant who had not seen him coming, though of course she had. She didn't look up even after he put his hand lightly on hers, which was for Maraña an extraordinary display of affection. It was Carmen's custom to be extremely demure around Maraña in times of danger, especially when under such intense public scrutiny. When he sat down, she acknowledged him only by a quick smiling nod and it thrilled Maraña to feel so much communicated in so classy a way. There was nothing wrong, no emergency, all was well.

"Anything unusual?" he asked.

"Not much," said Carmen, still looking at the crowd around her. "Some of the regular customers seem to have left their women at home tonight, but that's all I see."

"They're out on business," explained Maraña. "A few shipments are moving tonight."

"I hope the women have a little business of their own at home," Carmen said.

Maraña pretended to frown. "You've been in this country too long," he said. "A man works hard all night, eating and smuggling drugs, and then he has to come home and find his woman playing around with another guy. This is too much."

Carmen smiled. Most of the eyes she had felt watching them had returned to the food on the tables. She felt more relaxed as a procession of Maraña's friends began coming by the table to pay their respects, one by one, including two policemen, several relatives, and some informants. Most of them left after trying a wisecrack or two. Carmen did not say a word, but she studied them all intently. Maraña valued her character assessments.

They were nearing the end of a hasty meal when one visitor took a seat without an invitation. Pepe Lopez paid no attention to Carmen, nor did his eyes meet Maraña's. He looked at the table and drummed his fingers nervously, offering the sight of himself as a skinny young insurance salesman. He was a salesman because his father had been one in Havana, and he was skinny because he was still suffering from the effects of his ill-fated cruise in the Taliente navy. All the Cubans in Miami had rallied around Taliente's grand plan, as encouraged by the CIA's Señor Noel, which called for naval raids against Cuba to be supported by the dictator nations of the Caribbean, from Brazil to Nicaragua. That way there would be no embarrassment, no American Bay of Pigs, as the Latins themselves would combine to oppose Fidel. Accordingly, amid clandestine fanfare in Miami, Pepe Lopez had steamed around the Caribbean on a grand ghost vessel to collect men and arms for the first attack. Lopez, trained as a CIA frogman, had taken leave from the insurance company to serve as a squad leader. Things had gone wrong, as usual. The arms were always rusty, and the allies always needed extra money under the table. Then the money ran out, soon followed by charges that it had been stolen by Taliente or by the CIA or by one of the factions on board the ship, where the men began yelling and fighting on deck instead of drilling for the attack, as they had done so grandly at the outset.

The ship chased empty promises at sea for months, as the soldiers deserted or resorted to piracy to keep from starving. Lopez, one of the fire-eaters, remained on board, growing more desperate with the passing failures. He was driven by his desire to transcend the insurance business to a more romantic line of work, and he clung fiercely to an idea that many Cuban men grasped from their national history—that if a man were daring and ready, the most unlikely events might line up in an impossible series to propel him to the head of the revolution. It had been so with the students in '32, and with Sergeant Batista, and with attorney Castro. This tradition inspired Lopez to lead an expedition against Cuba with the ragged survivors of the Taliente navy's long cruise. They could only hope to land and capture a garrison briefly, but it would be a gesture and perhaps a catalyst for things great enough to splash glory over the attackers. So Lopez reasoned.

Just before starvation, and just before the Watergate break-in in Washington, Lopez led a party of black-faced guerrillas ashore at the tiny village of Boca de Sama. By the time they arrived it was night, and things began to go wrong again. The town was roused by a loud argument between one of Lopez's men and a local dog. Ordinary citizens spilled out of their homes in nightclothes. Gunshots were fired in the dark, and the attacking party managed a pell-mell retreat to the ship, sustaining only the kinds of wounds a soldier receives by running into trees or rocks at full speed. In Miami, many families hung their heads over this latest of the many secret humiliations after the Bay of Pigs. The bare facts were bad enough in themselves, and at first no one believed Fidel Castro's claim that the only fatality at Boca de Sama had been a ten-year-old girl who was shot through the throat as she tumbled out of her house to see the excitement.

Gradually, however, witnesses from the Cuban village and from the disgruntled attacking party all seemed to be saying that the killer was a skinny man in a black beret who fired the night's first shot. This could only have been Pepe Lopez, who soon learned that no one would look him in the eye. He became the most conspicuous man in Miami, whispered about from great distances, his every movement noticed, his path leaving a trail that smelled faintly of rancid dishwater—or so it seemed to Lopez. He lapsed into a period of savage neurosis. Sometimes he harangued people in public places with an extravagant defense of the attack, praising himself and blaming everyone else, especially Taliente and the CIA. At other times he would not eat or be seen for months, and it was rumored that he had once knocked himself unconscious by ramming his head repeatedly into the bedroom wall. When the shame finally hardened inside Pepe Lopez, he resolved to kill someone. At first he considered himself as the victim, but after discussing the religious drawbacks of suicide with a militantly anticommunist priest, he promised his wrath to someone else. Since then he had been possessed. His physiognomy had changed. He wore a perpetual smile on his haggard face.

His body odor changed markedly in the direction of a vegetable garden. The effect of constant, feverish sweat—quite rare among the Cubans—on his sallow complexion gave it an oily glaze, like a slab of runny brie. Above all, there was hatred in Lopez's tightly quivering jaw. If it is possible for a man to look as though homicide will relieve his condition, Lopez was a demonstration of the possibility.

"What's she doing here?" he demanded of Maraña, pointing at Carmen and looking at neither of them.

"I think she's having dinner," replied Maraña with cheerful sarcasm.

Lopez did not laugh. "I can't talk with her around," he declared.

Maraña drew a patient breath. "If you'll speak with the discretion you ought to use anyway, there'll be no danger," he said gently. "Besides, Carmen knows more about the life than I do and she can rip into a man worse than a bullet. Don't worry about words around her, my friend. Now. Have you gathered up your companions?"

Lopez shifted uncomfortably in his chair. "I think so," he said. "But there are problems. The other groups have agreed in principle, but they want to know more about the plans."

"I'll bet they do," said Maraña. His voice became quieter and yet more authoritative. "Listen," he said, "Don't you tell them anything or they will be bragging about it in this restaurant within an hour. Don't even tell the two friends of yours anything more than you have to. But I want all three of you at your house at nine o'clock tonight. We are going to take a ride."

"A ride?" asked Lopez.

"A joy ride," nodded Maraña.

Lopez felt the panic of nearby violence, just as he had on commando ships off the coast of Cuba when, after months of delay, the moment finally came. What he felt was a strange, downward-moving shiver, which slid down his spine like the metal combs of an escalator. The shiver caused a rush of nausea as it passed behind the stomach. Still, it was the most agreeable sensation Lopez had felt in more than a year. He swallowed. "I'd like to take a ride," he said, "but I don't know about the other guys. They are afraid you will tell, uh, some of your *gringo* friends, Carlos. After all, you have done it before, you know. They say you are the last person we should trust. They say—and I'm only telling you this because I think you should know—that it doesn't make any sense to fight one *chivato* with another one."

"They don't trust me, eh?" smiled Maraña. "Well, let me tell you something, my friend," he said somberly, lowering his voice again to a whisper. "First of all, they have no choice but to ride with me, because I already know everything you are doing. Second, they will ride with me because I know better than any of you how to tangle the *gringos* in their own lines. Third, they will ride with me even though I tell you I have *already* told the chief of the *gringos* what we are going to do. I told him today, in fact."

36

"You what?" gasped Lopez. "You crazy? Who?"

Maraña smiled again. "The king of the wide shoes," he said. "Efram Zimbalist. Like the ones on television with the hats. I told him today."

Lopez appeared stricken. He sucked in some air and was jumping up to leave in flight when Maraña's grip held his wrist to the table. "I told that to *you*," whispered Maraña, "and not to the others because I thought you might be capable of understanding it. You are a Cuban. It is hard for you to see, as it is for me. But a master often has more secrets than his slaves. Sometimes a master has so many secrets that he *is* the slave. And sometimes it is the *chivato*, the informer—I am not afraid of the word—who is more independent than the purest revolutionary."

Lopez looked puzzled.

No one at the table moved or spoke for a few seconds, and then Carmen pulled a pack of Marlboros from her purse. She lit two cigarettes elegantly as Lopez watched her hands, relieved by the distraction. His glance followed the hand upward to the lips, where Carmen left both cigarettes to fume sulkily, and somehow Lopez was drawn to look her fully in the face. He had not done so with anyone for some time, and he felt clear-headed again, as though he had snapped out of hypnosis. Carmen's smile gave him nothing but encouragement. She handed Lopez one of the Marlboros and leaned back in her chair with pleasure.

Maraña let go of the wrist. "*Chico*," he whispered urgently, almost pleading. "This is an act of *defiance*. Your old boss, the great man of the soft drinks, has corrupted himself with the corrupt authorities, and we are defying them *all*. We will notify them and then go ahead, anyway. *That* is defiance."

Lopez felt a thrill from Maraña's intensity before he understood the meaning. "Carlos," he smiled, "you are too clever for your own good sometimes."

"No one will interrupt our ride tonight," Maraña continued. "And after that, nothing matters. Everything we have told them will just put mud in the waters. You and the other guys can trust me. I give you a money-back guarantee."

Maraña rested his case with a laugh. Leaning back, he snapped his fingers and ordered a Cuban coffee. Lopez was studying him, amazement and indecision mixed in his face, as he puffed diligently on the Marlboro. Soon he was shrouded in a cloud of smoke, which the mirrors reflected far off into the distance in all directions. "I think it may be crazy enough to work, and I don't care anyway," he said finally. "But the other guys are young. They read many books. They will never trust you, I think."

"I know," said Maraña. "That's all right. They shouldn't trust anyone. But if we are betrayed tonight, they can deal with me right then and be done with it. They will be equipped to hurt me."

"You will provide all the equipment?" asked Lopez.

"Of course," said Maraña. "And I will buy the gas, too."

Lopez shook his head. "You are beyond me, Carlos," he said. "I don't see how you can play this game of yours very long before coming to the end of the road."

"My end," said Maraña, with sing-song nonchalance, "will come at the end."

Lopez screwed up his face and then nodded slowly. "I think mine has already come," he sighed. He looked miserably from side to side, until Maraña became convinced that he was on the point of breaking down.

"Excuse me," said Carmen, taking her cue from Maraña's glance. She walked slowly through the Versailles, followed by many eyes.

Maraña leaned forward. "Pepe, nothing you do tonight or any other night will erase what happened in Cuba," he said in a philosophical tone. "So forget about that. Your deeds just lie down behind each other until you have a past. You want to have enough big deep tracks in your past to stand out above most people, but you can't expect them to be all good or bad. Just make a lot of them and then decide for yourself what they are worth."

"You talk like a professor," said Lopez. "I don't understand you."

"I don't either," said Maraña, "but I thought a few words might drag you out of your own crazy thoughts." Suddenly, his eyes went blank and hard, like black holes. "The only thought you should have is to be ready at your house with your friends tonight," he said coldly. "Do you understand that? Is that perfectly clear?"

Nothing was clearer to Lopez, who had lost what little will he had. "It is perfectly clear," he smiled.

"Good," said Maraña. "Now get out of here before Carmen comes back."

Lopez stood straight and went weaving through the crowd, out of the Versailles, sensing neither pride nor humiliation from the surrounding eyes, feeling only conspicuous in a strangely neutral way, making big tracks. He was not sweating.

"What do you think?" Maraña asked Carmen when she returned.

"I think he will do what you tell him, but I don't think he will ever be any good to a woman again" she replied. "You should be careful, lover. If you help him recover by showing him a hard place inside himself, he could become a very dangerous man."

"I think you are too smart to be a woman," said Maraña. "I think you should have a sex-change operation."

"I don't need one," smiled Carmen, proud to see that her forceful intelligence could still ruffle Maraña in a crisis. "I'm just saying that Pepe may not always be the little puddle he is tonight," she shrugged. "Anyway, he's yours. I could never do much with him."

Maraña felt a strong urge to sulk over being treated to Carmen's toughness instead of her motherly support, but he knew better. Carmen would only laugh at him and make more witty comments. Besides, he knew she was right. There could be no weakness until tomorrow. He resented Carmen for being so superior, but he appreciated it as well. "You are an angel," he told her with wounded admiration, and then he patted her wrist twice before yanking her up from the table and dragging her out of the Versailles in a

38

rush. Carmen stoically let herself be towed, allowing Maraña the compensation. A silence fell over the restaurant during their departure, as many patrons felt awed by Maraña's apparent mastery over the fiery Señora Vilar. Some of the onlookers were inspired that very night to attempt similar outbursts of *machismo* toward their own women, and of these, a slight majority came to grief.

Carmen followed Maraña to the home of Max Parker, on 27th Avenue a few blocks south of Eighth Street. Parker, a jolly, rotund redhead, surprised them at the door by acting out a comic pantomime of fear—hiding his eyes, knocking his knees, clutching his balls, biting at his fingernails at once—before sinking to his knees in mock terror, eyes bulging, and breaking out into sobs that turned to laughter when Parker could no longer hold the mood of his joke. Maraña waited patiently, accustomed to Parker's antics.

"Carlos, you are a very daaaaaaangerous man," sputtered Parker, clasping his hands and throwing them over his shoulder like a Victorian lady in distress.

Maraña walked solemnly past Parker on one side, Carmen on the other. "Cut the entertainment, Max," he said sharply.

Parker turned around on his knees and affected even greater fear. "Pleeeease, Carlos, do not be angry with me," he begged. "I cannot help it if I think you are dangerous, because a man from the FBI told me so just this afternoon."

This news jolted Maraña, who kicked himself for getting taken in by Parker once again. "Who told you?" he demanded. "What did he say?"

Parker rose to his feet, delighted with himself, and put his hands behind his back to report. "Well, a certain Señor Damico came to see me this afternoon and asked me for a service," he ventured, somewhat coyly. "He said the Bureau had received reports that you were close to a group conspiring to kill pro-American leaders in the Cuban community, and he asked me to keep an eye on you for the next few weeks. Very secret."

"He asked *you?*" exclaimed the astonished Maraña.

"Of course," replied Parker, puffing himself up. He was indeed in great demand as an informant, mostly because he spoke perfect English and could act like an American—a great relief to American agents who knew only enough Spanish to bluff their way past the personnel committee. He had learned English from his American father, who lived and died an expatriate in Havana, and his Spanish from his Cuban mother, who was one-quarter German and who died an expatriate in the United States—both parents having become estranged from each other, and from young Max, before their only son reached puberty. Max had shuttled back and forth between countries whenever one parent managed to foist him off on the other, and in the process of growing up he became intimately bicultural. He also became schizophrenic—more romantic and happy than his mother, Cuba, and also more authoritarian and efficient than his father, America. The long war between Castro and the United States had further subdivided

Parker's identity, leaving him ever more dependent on his Falstaffian humor and on his loyalty to Carlos Maraña.

"I can't believe it," said Maraña. "This is incredible. How much did he offer you?"

"Only one fifty for the first week," sighed Parker. "He said their *chivato* budget has been tight since Hoover died."

"Well," said Maraña, unable to restrain himself, "did you take it?"

"No," said Parker huffily. "I told him that if you are so daaaaaaangerous, I would need at least two hundred the first week and a lot more if you try to kill me. So he sweated big drops like olives and finally said okay. So I am spying on you at this very moment."

"Good!" shouted Maraña. He clapped his hands once and then began pacing the floor, making a steeple of his fingertips the way he did during his memory exercises. Maraña was steaming. While he walked, Carmen laughed at Parker and greeted him with a warm hug. She had already decided to seduce him if anything ever happened to Maraña, but Parker would have been among the last to suspect it.

Within a minute, Maraña returned with his plans, which he delivered in staccato bursts. Carmen was dispatched to check on the shipment and then to return to Maraña's apartment. She departed after blowing a kiss to both men. After reviewing with Parker the sequence of beeper signals, Maraña was on the point of bursting from the room when Parker stopped him for a toast. This was a daring move on Parker's part, given Maraña's latherous condition, but Max pulled it off on the strength of his charm. "I will not leave without drinking to success and patriotism," he pronounced.

Maraña frowned until he saw Parker emerge from the kitchen with two champagne glasses and a large bottle of Canada Dry ginger ale sitting on a silver tray. The bottle sported red, white, and blue ribbons tied around its neck.

"*Salud*," said Parker, and Maraña responded in kind. Taliente, the target, was an international vice-president of Canada Dry.

Ten minutes later, Maraña drove through Coconut Grove, the tropically bohemian section of Miami, in which blue-jean stores and expensive boutiques attract both the slouchy rich and the voluntary poor. He parked in back of the Coconut Grove Theater, walked around to the entrance, bought a ticket, and disappeared inside—observed in these last acts by Parker, who then drove off in his own car.

Casablanca was playing, as it frequently did at the Coconut Grove. Maraña had seen it at least a dozen times there, and it never failed to move him. He usually went alone, but occasionally with Carmen—at which times he would be in the presence of *Casablanca*, Carmen, and his African stone necklace, the three things that still touched him. He would often deny that Carmen or the necklace carried any permanent meaning for him, but he was openly enamored of the film, whose message, he thought, was that no man is too hard-boiled for an act of love as long as he expects to be jilted for it afterward. Maraña was a sucker for that one, and for little else.

40

He was ten minutes early for the 9:30 showing of the film, leaving him almost two and a half hours until the end. Maraña left immediately by the theater's back door and spent fifteen of those minutes getting to the house of Pepe Lopez. He pulled abruptly into the driveway, stopped the car, and got out, affecting a casual pose as he faced the front door with his arms and chin resting on the roof of the car like a dreamy schoolboy.

Three figures soon emerged and walked slowly toward the car. The one in the blue shirt stayed carefully behind Pepe Lopez because he was afraid Maraña might shoot him as part of a complicated betrayal, or simply out of perversity. The one in the green shirt, the youngest, stayed behind on general principle, without any dark suspicions.

"Get in!" barked Maraña. The three jumped to the task but accomplished it only after some fumbling and bumping around. Entering a car smoothly was well beyond the capacities of the three men, who had worked themselves up in the house with a long series of speculations about what Maraña was up to. All that was forgotten as Maraña slammed the door and jerked the car backward in a fluid motion, then screeched violently up the street. The kinetic force of these actions so riveted the passengers that they might as well have left their minds behind in the mailbox.

"Good evening," Maraña said pleasantly a few blocks down the road, slowing to a Sunday pace. "Would you gentlemen prefer steaks or seafood?"

All the passengers stared slack-jawed at Maraña before Green Shirt had he courage to ask, "You mean we're going to *eat* first?"

"Not necessarily," said Maraña. "I would prefer to look for some ginger ale first, but I want you to know that you are free to eat. You don't have to go with me."

"I'm not hungry," Green Shirt said weakly. "Let's go after the ginger ale."

Blue Shirt's normally foul disposition was subduing his panic. "Let's get on with it, Carlos," he snarled. "Who are you working for, anyway?"

"How are you doing, Pepe?" asked a jovial Maraña, ignoring Blue Shirt. He slapped Lopez on the knee and gave him a fraternity punch on the shoulder. Lopez forced a smile while fixing his eyes on the road ahead. Blue Shirt seethed.

Green Shirt cleared his throat after a mile or so, as Maraña weaved slowly westward through Little Havana, parallel to Eighth Street. "Carlos," he said, "I want you to know that our group has considered this action carefully for a number of months. We believe it is correct, morally and politically, at this time as the best single step of courage we can take to combat both imperialism and totalitarianism. We approve of it as a revolutionary act, but I must tell you that we have our doubts about cooperating with you. Our group knows you and your reputation, and we have agreed to cooperate with you hesitantly. We have agreed only because we sometimes have to accept the assistance of many classes and ideologies to accomplish special goals. I am instructed to warn you that the penalty for betrayal is death."

"That is very nice," said Maraña, thinking that Green Shirt had probably written his speech out on paper and practiced it. "You yourself are very nice. But the rest of us are not so nice." Maraña turned to smile at the lean, bespectacled Green Shirt, who was taking very short breaths. "And as for your threat, don't you realize that death is the penalty for living?"

Green Shirt blinked. "A true revolutionary does not die," he said sincerely, "and he has conquered all the fears that held him down."

"I thought we should have hired a regular old hit man like El Estraño," growled Blue Shirt. "But then again, I guess that's just about what you are yourself, eh Carlos?"

"I don't miss anything I want to hit, if that's what you mean," Maraña replied.

"*Mierda*," said Blue Shirt. He was capable of florid political rhetoric, but nerves reduced him to a blind fear of Maraña, whom he envied greatly.

Suddenly, Pepe Lopez covered his face with both hands and began to titter in the front seat. His shoulders rocked gently, drawing the attention of his companions. Maraña was surprised, but amused. Green Shirt, as usual this evening, was amazed and bug-eyed. Blue Shirt was annoyed because he assumed, characteristically, that Lopez was laughing at his expense.

"What's the matter with you?" Blue Shirt demanded.

Lopez struggled to control himself, but funny squeaks and noises escaped between his lips. He knew he could not disclose the real reason for his laughter. It had just dawned on him that he was enjoying himself for the first time in many years, and despite his best efforts, he could not contain the absurdity of the moment, coming as it did on a mission to kill his own mentor in the company of three odd conspirators.

"Nothing is the matter," Lopez managed to say. "It's just that, well, I think I need to go to the bathroom."

Green Shirt laughed explosively through his nose and was obliged to use his handkerchief. Maraña, though instantly aware that Lopez might be taking a major step toward the rediscovery of his will, smiled. Even Blue Shirt laughed with relief at the open acknowledgment of fear. The humor was therapeutic. By heavily engaging the stomach, lungs, and throat, the act of laughing seemed to dispel tension from the places where it had collected, driving it to more manageable places like the extremities and the bladder.

"I need to go, too," Green Shirt said, causing more laughter. By the time the car approached Taliente's house, everybody felt better.

They were about a mile south of the airport, on 47th Avenue, in the endless maze of stucco bungalows that stretches out from Miami toward the Everglades. The intersecting streets and avenues form a dense grid of tiny blocks, with the houses jammed together side-to-side and back-to-back. Most of the Cubans, meticulous by nature, keep their houses clean and neat as a tailor's thread box, and Taliente was no exception.

A chain-link fence ran along the street side of his corner lot, which embraced less than a tenth of an acre, turning to form a common rear boundary with the house sitting about a hundred feet behind Taliente's. From the interior corner, the fence ran to the street in front of the house, through the tiny space between Taliente's garage and the house next door. His front lawn was about the size of a boxing ring, but the grass on it was lush, well sprinkled and often mowed. In the middle of his front lawn Taliente had placed a small shrine. It was a concrete box, about three feet high, with glass on the side facing the street so that one could see inside an alabaster statue of the Madonna, lighted at night by a small bulb that his wife switched on from inside the house. Taliente's home was quite modest for a man of his position. Like most Cubans in Miami, he devoted much effort to the care of his fence and lawn—the smaller the lot, as a rule, the more lavish the care—as though in defiance of Castro's views on private property.

No one spoke as Maraña piloted the car past the Madonna shrine. He turned left and circled the block at a crawl. By all appearances, the house was quiet. There was a single light burning in the front room on the side of the garage. The neighborhood was unusually still, even for a week night. One shirtless man clipped stray grass around the base of his fence, but his house was twice around the corner from Taliente's. Two couples, engaged in conversation over a fence, were as far away. Taliente's large red Grand Prix sat in the driveway in front of the open garage.

On the fourth swing past the Madonna, Maraña turned left, then left again, and stopped—in front of the house behind Taliente's. Nothing had changed during the reconnaissance, except that the man clipping grass had succumbed to the darkness.

When Maraña turned off the car's engine, the silence gave Green Shirt's eardrums a kick. His heart was pummeling his body from within, and his ear bore the brunt of the echo. He had been holding his breath for some time, he realized. Instinctively, Green Shirt rolled down the window to exhale, startling companions who were nearly as on edge as he. Green Shirt looked sheepishly around. There was a chorus of nervous coughs in the car, going on too long and too loudly, like a congregation fortifying itself for a windy sermon.

"Okay," said Maraña. His voice cracked. "Okay," he said again, this time evenly. "Here is the plan. Taliente will be leaving the house alone on business within the next hour, I assure you. When we hear him open the front door of his house, I will give the signal to crouch low in front of his car. When we hear his footsteps stop beside the car to open the door, two of us will walk straight toward him and fire. We will be less than ten feet away when we start. You two should fire then, too, but do not move to your right or we'll hit you. If there are no problems, we can come back to the car the same way we went. If there are problems, we can run straight back through these two yards. Now, that is simple, which means good. The only way it could be simpler is for there to be only one of us. Okay? Is everybody ready?" Maraña was smiling by the end.

"What happens if he doesn't come out of the house?" asked Blue Shirt.

"I have a plan for that, too, but I will tell you when it happens," said Maraña impatiently. "Now let's go. Nobody moves except by the plan, or unless I tell him to."

Before anyone could protest, Maraña was unlocking the trunk of his car. The others followed. Maraña handed Lopez one of the .22s, tossing the oilcloth back in the trunk. Lopez stared at the gun, grinned, and turned casually back to the grass on the edge of the sidewalk, where he began to relieve himself.

"Don't get the gun wet," whispered Maraña, as the other two stared incredulously at Lopez's back. Lopez was beginning to acquire an aura. Before he was finished, Maraña had distributed the guns, keeping a .22 for himself and giving the red-handled .38 to Blue Shirt. Maraña thought that perhaps he should have given it to Lopez, but, on balance, he was satisfied that Blue Shirt was the one most likely to betray them.

Blue Shirt began flipping the chambers to check his gun. The metallic clicks were deafening, like a host of crickets. Green Shirt winced. The noise got to him, as did the leaden mass of his .38. For weeks he had prepared himself for that moment, knowing that a gun takes on an awesome appearance when unveiled for business. His father had told him he would get used to it, but Green Shirt, unlike Maraña and the others, was of a younger generation than the Bay of Pigs and had not been around guns much. For all his idealogical stridency, and his readings from Spengler and Gorki to José Martí, Green Shirt was undone by the very substance of the gun. It was not so much the temperature. He knew that steel feels cold to the human hand. It was more the weight and the inertness. The gun seemed so much a part of the crowd—so domineering, in fact, that even Maraña's presence receded for a time—and yet it just lay there in his hand, pushing heavily toward the ground, giving off a great negative spirit, but no life of its own. Green Shirt felt the capillaries of his hand pulsing around the handle, making overtures, but the gun did not respond at all.

". . . I said do you want to pee, too?" repeated a vexed Maraña, bringing Green Shirt out of his contemplations. He had thought of relieving himself like Lopez, but the complications of the act, especially in the first moments after holding the gun, overwhelmed him.

"No," said Green Shirt.

"Are you all right?" whispered Maraña supportively, without giving offense.

"Yes,"

Lopez and Green Shirt moved out, soon followed by the other two. Before leaving, Maraña activated the receiver of his beeper. He walked last, hoping that the entry would be smooth and worrying that Lopez might lapse into nightmares about his disgrace at Boca de Sama. Maraña worried about the mundane and the unforeseen, which he knew to be the greatest enemies of stealthy work. Children's birthday parties and visiting relatives had spoiled many commando raids into Cuba, he knew, and he recalled an instance in which he and some black-faced CIA experts had burst dramatically into a Cuban home to encounter the startled members of a sewing class instead of the legendary underground leader. Maraña smiled as he walked, his head filled with queer memories and miscellaneous phone numbers. The group was soon within Taliente's garage, with Maraña himself having made the only mistake. Trying to appear too casual while stepping over the fence, he had snagged his trousers and tottered precariously. Maraña was thankful that Blue Shirt had not turned to witness the embarrassment.

The excruciating wait commenced inside the garage. All four men began it with their bodies pressed tightly against the side walls to minimize the chances of being seen. Then, as time passed and muscles cramped, they shifted restlessly from one position to another, like standing insomniacs. Maraña found himself trying to think of boring lists, such as metallic alloys and the names of the towns between Miami and Key West. He admitted to himself that he was frightened. The fear was a peculiar one, but familiar to him, pointed and sharp. He squirmed right along with the other three, though among them he was the seasoned professional. Anticipation ran through him like cold mountain water through a millrace. Twenty cups of coffee couldn't have made him as jittery as he was, and Maraña consoled himself with the knowledge that it would all vanish when the action began. This fact in itself intrigued him. His fear was a form of stage fright, a feeling he had known since playing the part of Joseph in a fourth grade nativity play in Havana, and it carried over into acts around murder and war. It was nature's gift to violence, he thought, that the actor in murder can still count on the deed itself to rescue him from fears, as if he were an opera star or a sprinter in the Olympics.

Maraña longed for the relief. Experience told him to marshal all his strength to fight impatience and to be thankful that he *knew*, at least, that relief would come. He missed Carmen. He was reminded of moments when, after making love to her for hours on nights that found his insides withdrawn into a tight knot, he would fear that all the release in him had dried up, that he would never feel orgasm again, that the very idea of orgasm was foreign to a new and colder reality. And then, on some touch or word from Carmen, who seemed to know, he would feel the hope of release born inside him from a sensation as far away as the faintest train whistle. And even before the physical pleasure arrived, he would come loose with joy over the return and renewal of this possibility, which seemed at once so intimate to him and so separate from him, earned by will and yet so much a gift from the distance.

Maraña, standing in Taliente's garage, laughed to himself about how he could mingle the release of sex and of murder. He considered himself a macabre man and wondered whether there would come a time when the fears would persist right through a murder. This thought he stifled. There was no quantity he could reach and no circumstance that could change things in his mind beyond what he brought back from Africa. So he settled himself, waited, and missed Carmen again. There was hurry in the back of his mind, because he knew things were getting scary in *Casablanca*. Peter Lorre could not be trusted. Maraña figured he had an hour left.

The relief was as sudden as it was troublesome. Green Shirt, standing on his toes, his bladder stretched, longing to be elsewhere, was pointing his gun toward the floor of the garage when a car door slammed across the street with such noise that Green Shirt pulled the trigger reflexively. It was no light reflex, since a .38 requires quite a tug, and Green Shirt would never know what possessed him to squeeze so hard at such a time. The men heard the grunt of the gun. They were in shock by the time the slug had dug into the concrete, ricocheted off the side of Taliente's wheelbarrow, and exited through the roof of the garage. The neighbors heard nothing but one soft ring of metal striking metal, but inside the garage it sounded like the strike force had been attacked by a regiment.

Blue Shirt started to run out the door. Maraña grabbed him roughly about the collar and shoved him into the other two men, who were frozen. Blue Shirt struggled to free himself from Maraña, and Lopez began struggling to get away from Blue Shirt. Green Shirt started to run out of the garage, but Maraña caught him around the throat with his left arm.

"Let go!" whispered Blue Shirt.

"What happened?" asked Lopez.

"Shut up!" Maraña commanded. He stepped back from the lump of men and pointed his gun at them. "Shut up!" he repeated. He lowered his gun a split second before a gun battle at very close range would have broken out among the assailants. The lump of three had a chance to hear the silence outside, to hear themselves panting, and to realize that they were at that moment more frightened of Maraña than anything else. He was very much alive and very much unafraid, utterly different from what he had been before.

Green Shirt realized that his bladder had let loose, probably in concert with the .38. Blue Shirt discovered that the pungent smell of cordite came from Green Shirt's gun, which prompted him to elbow Green Shirt's chest with a heavy thud. Maraña quieted the flare-up of tempers in time for the men to hear a car engine start, engage, and disappear slowly from the neighborhood.

All the men except Maraña felt exhausted, having burned off their accumulated adrenalin. "What are we going to do now?" asked Lopez.

"We are going to wait a few minutes to make sure everything is all right," said Maraña, "and then we are going in after him."

"How are we going to get in?" asked Lopez.

"We are going to ring the doorbell like gentlemen."

Maraña moved out while the others were still nodding their heads mechanically, before they could think too much about the plan. He darted alone from the garage and slinked alongside Taliente's house toward the front. Then, upon reaching a lighted window, he flattened himself against the stucco, held a finger to his lips, and motioned for the others to follow. When they arrived, he took each man by the arm and treated him successively to the sight of Taliente sitting alone in an armchair not six feet away from the window, watching television.

It was *Ben Hur*, being aired for the first time, and costing Taliente a great

46

deal of torment. When Messala urged Ben Hur to cast his lot with the Roman Empire, citing the poverty and impotence of Ben Hur's fellow Jewish vassals, Taliente felt the weight of the argument. It was the same thing the CIA's Edward Noel was always telling him, more urgently now in the bitter times since the disaster at Boca de Sama. Taliente knew that the words of American authorities would always rattle deeply in his bones, for the instinct to mimic, envy, and respect the Americans was bred into the most rebellious of Cubans, whereas the capacity to ignore them had to be acquired from nothing, without support. But Taliente also hated Noel, especially now that he could see freshly how little majesty he had in comparison with the Roman Messala. Taliente hated Noel for treating him like a child. Noel was younger than his son, and harped constantly on the shortcomings of the Cubans while also complaining of the fools everywhere in the American government, high and low. Noel's chief duty was to explain to Taliente how to look upon the latest insult in some favorable light.

Taliente sighed and shifted in his armchair. He wanted to get out of the whole business and cursed the days when visits to the Cuban White House had first planted the idea of high office in his brain. He shuddered to think how his homage to the Americans had come around to oppose his sacred honor. Taliente, a drug pusher! The movement would die without money, and Noel, after giving another speech on the need for self-sufficiency, had shrugged his shoulders when Taliente had been driven by desperation to ask him what he thought about Taliente's raising money by using his men in the ever-lucrative cocaine trade, for which they were well trained. Noel had said no in a way that meant yes. Taliente cursed himself for getting near the drugs, cursed himself for stooping yet again to ask permission, and cursed Noel for approving so deviously, in a manner Taliente knew was designed to prepare the way for later scoldings.

Taliente felt hemmed in from every direction, including a few that he had only recently discovered, and he discharged his hatreds by inflicting vicarious punishments on all his friends and enemies through the scenes in *Ben Hur*. He found himself enjoying the suffering of Charlton Heston as a slave in the galley ship. He looked forward to the chariot race, and found himself hoping that both the mighty Roman and the vassal would be mutilated under the feet of horses and iron. All this profane violence shocked him, lying as it did under the mild-mannered graciousness for which he was known, and for which he had been chosen leader by the Americans.

As Ben Hur was leaving Rome, having won and then rejected its glories, Taliente heard a knock at the door. His head turned to see who it was. In the same instant, Taliente realized that his head had turned in the wrong direction and also that he had not meant to turn it at all. Trying to ignore this odd loss of bodily control, he turned his eyes back to the television set and found that he had no external vision and saw only a shining wetness of oranges and reds, like a germ's view of the inside of his mouth. Astonished, Taliente was overwhelmed by the odor of something like ether, which took his breath away as he felt himself falling through space, having shrunk to microscopic size. While falling, Taliente sensed a vast coming together at the feet of his enormous other body. The collection of vapors was swirling, tornadolike, with unimaginable force, and then it began to rise. He had only a millisecond's glimpse, though it seemed like a long time and was satisfying, of the notion that the swirling force was a gathering of all feelings possible to a human being, the essence of life itself, including Taliente's own fear of death, which was purer and more piercing than ever before, but still only a ray in the infinite spectrum of forces that passed upward with a wallop through the roof of Taliente's old head.

Pepe Lopez was firing more shots when he saw the body stiffen, rise, and then slump over. Lopez wanted to shriek with both rage and happiness, and he would have emptied the entire .22 into Taliente had not Maraña stopped him. Maraña moved him back from the window and took the gun from his hand, whereupon Lopez began to tremble violently. Maraña ignored him.

"Nobody leaves," Maraña told the other two men in a spitting whisper, checking their urge to flight. "All of us shoot him! Quick! Same gun! Nobody just watches!" Maraña thrust Lopez's .22 into Green Shirt's face. Green Shirt stared at it. He was in shock, feeling older, but his passion was up and he almost jumped to the window after grabbing the gun. Once he saw that there was no gore on or around the body—that all Taliente's wounds, including the mortal one in his skull, were as neat as roses—and once he fired his first shot, Green Shirt was over his last psychological hurdle, and he, too, would have emptied the gun. But Maraña stopped him and passed the gun to Blue Shirt. "Hurry!" he said.

There was only one bullet left in the gun when Maraña took his turn. Blue Shirt, who had nearly disintegrated while watching the two men before him, could wait no longer. He bolted. His legs simply started running toward the garage. Maraña saw him leave and fired the last shot into the television screen as he took off in pursuit, the others close behind.

Blue Shirt did not flee by the same route he had come. With no clear purpose in mind, he ran instead through the narrow passageway next to the garage and jumped the fence into the yard of the neighbor behind Taliente, where he was promptly accosted by a female boxer puppy, just let out for the night. The boxer charged from a range of twenty feet, barking furiously, scaring out of Blue Shirt what few wits remained, warning Maraña and his party in time to avoid the scene by scrambling to the side street.

Blue Shirt could have made it back over the fence if he had not wasted valuable time by wobbling around in two inconclusive circles, feeling sorry for himself. Then, when it dawned on him that it was too late for escape, he pointed the red-handled .38 at the onrushing dog and fired three times before she bit gamely into his wrist and ran halfway up his extended arm. The puppy chomped as deeply as she could and growled just like her mother. She did not know that she smelled murder on the intruder, but she hated whatever smell it was and would have gnawed through the arm if her

48

jaws had been stronger. As it was, Blue Shirt let out a terrified bellow and threw the puppy backward over his shoulder into Taliente's yard. She had hardly hit the ground on the other side before she was trying to snarl her way back over the fence. By then Blue Shirt was gone, still bellowing as he dived headlong over the fence to the side street. A dim voice in his instinct region was telling him to hold on to the gun. Blue Shirt scrambled awkwardly to his feet, like a scared drunk. He made himself quit moaning as he ran toward the car, and it was then that he first felt the tears coming down his face. The sight of Maraña did not make him feel any better, for Maraña was sitting there in the car, engine running, and his eyes glowed with a stare that went beyond scorn and derision into a kind of passing indifference. A bank robber in the frenzy of a getaway might look more fondly on a roll of pennies.

No one spoke for the first few blocks. No one even breathed much. The car was so plump with tension that to have exhaled might have broken a window. Maraña kept driving as he reached around toward the back seat with an empty hand. "The guns," he said, and the men produced them. After depositing all four guns under his seat, Maraña slowed the car and turned to Blue Shirt with a smile. "I should have let you shoot first, Manolo," he said, "so you'd have time to go play with the dog."

All four men laughed and whooped it up in the car, taking this as a signal that they were out of danger. Even Blue Shirt laughed, happy to have a pretext for his tears.

"Dogs are the great nuisance for revolutionaries," laughed Green Shirt, bold enough to add a word of sympathy to Lopez about the dog's interference at Boca de Sama. Lopez didn't mind the reference anymore.

"Thieves and burglars don't like dogs either," said Maraña, as he threw a playful punch back in Blue Shirt's direction. Blue Shirt laughed, undecided for now just now much he hated Maraña.

The loud treble hum of the beeper suddenly interrupted the festivities. Maraña called for quiet. He turned up the volume on his receiver. A repeated short-long signal vibrated through the car, and Maraña relaxed. "It's okay," he said. "There's been a prowler call in the neighborhood. That's all." Parker was on the job, as he always was, monitoring police radios and sending alarms to Maraña on the beeper. Maraña knew he was safe at least until the homicide squad was summoned. The emergency signal, a steady blast of shorts, meant that his name or car or position was being broadcast, in which case it would be time to abandon the car.

The beeper signal implanted in Blue Shirt's mind a suspicion that Maraña's work that evening had official status with one U.S. agency or another, probably the CIA removing an embarrassing puppet leader. He was speculating intensely along this line when Maraña abruptly stopped the car. "Get out!" he said.

"What?" cried Lopez. "What are you doing, Carlos? We are only five blocks from my house."

"You have been out taking a walk," snapped Maraña. "Go separately or however you like. In the next few days, let off your steam by sticking your head in a barrel or something and yelling. That'll help. It's better than talking."

The passengers stepped weakly onto the pavement and Maraña was gone, practicing his memory exercises to see how much the fear had impaired his mind. After parking behind the Coconut Grove Theater, he wrapped the guns in their oilcloths, placed them in a trash can, and stepped through the back entrance to a front-row seat. He talked along with the dialogue through the last fifteen minutes of *Casablanca*, exiting with wet eyes. Max Parker, waiting outside in his car, followed Maraña to the rear of the theater in a passable imitation of surveillance. Two cars then went on a meandering convoy back to Taliente's neighborhood, where some twenty police cars had gathered, lights flashing, along with two ambulances and a fire truck, whose men had already unplugged Taliente's television. From a distance, Parker watched Maraña get out of his car for a brief conversation with a uniformed officer. Parker did the same thing after Maraña left, and he went home to report Taliente's murder to Dave Damico. Then he packed up his radio equipment and went to bed.

Maraña stopped at a pay phone to call Patrick Shea, who groaned and growled his way from sleep to a bad mood. Shea got Maraña off the line as quickly as he could. He endured the standard speech from his sleepy wife, who instructed him not to get himself too exposed over the internecine quarrels among the Cubans. The FBI man never cursed in the presence of Helen, and he did not do so now as he gave in more easily to her argument that he should transfer once more before retirement. For several hours Shea lay awake, trying to remember the exact wording of his cable to Washington.

Maraña retrieved the guns and drove all the way out to El Navajo's garage, where he received a $100 return on the unused one. El Navajo recycled his wares whenever possible. He did not need to tell Maraña that he would dispose of the three fired guns that night by packing each one in the hollow of a concrete block, surrounded by a mixture of aluminum and manganese ores and a fuse of pure magnesium, which, when properly ignited, would burn white for five minutes or so as a thermite bomb, leaving a blob of gray metal. The next day El Navajo would put the three blobs in a carrying bag and take a tourist ride on one of the swamp buggies that go skimming over that part of the Everglades. Some distance out, El Navajo would drop his bag discreetly into the dark water, among the cyprus roots and the salamanders. That night, though, seeing the pressure in Maraña's eyes, El Navajo knew better than to ask for gossip about the operation and satisfied himself with Maraña's brisk assurances that his guns had done good service in a real ass-kicking.

Maraña walked into the condominium shortly after four o'clock in the morning to greet Carmen, who had been drinking coffee and reading *Richard III*, though in fact she needed no such stimulus to identify with all the blood and treachery around her. Without a word, Carmen squeezed him tightly about the ribs, then stepped back to see Maraña's wan face, pale and wasted. She nodded her understanding and pulled from her pocket a medicine bottle filled with white powder. "It says right here to take two tablets four times a day for pain," Carmen smiled, reading the label. "I guess that's what you need." She walked to the kitchen for a baby's feeding spoon that Maraña had salvaged needlessly from his marriage, and on the way back she sucked a level spoonful into each nostril. Maraña took an equally extravagant amount and gave Carmen an Oriental bow of thanks before walking silently out on the balcony, where he leaned on the rail and stared across Biscayne Bay toward the lights of Miami Beach. Carmen followed him there as both of them began to feel the cocaine lifting their spirits up over the bay. The drug first struck the spinal cord, allowing the nerves there to luxuriate in something like a cool mixture of palm oil and tears. Both Carmen and Maraña sighed with the rush, which comes upon the tingling of nerves so central that they take full possession of body and senses.

Carmen stood squarely behind Maraña, put her fingertips on either side of his waist and rocked gently back and forth with her whole weight, pushing the heels of her hands deeply into the small of Maraña's back with each forward motion. Maraña moaned with pleasure. There seemed to be a small cushion of fluids gathered there, a waste bag of venerable biles and other troubled humors, and each rhythmic push from Carmen dispersed some of the fluid into the spinal column, where the pain wafted upward and disappeared into the cocaine rush.

Taking a step forward, Carmen continued to push with her left hand as she reached around with her right one and unzipped Maraña's trousers. The penis and testicles inside showed no physical signs of pride over Maraña's *machismo* accomplishments of the day. On the contrary, they appeared to be in hiding, having crawled as far as possible toward the dark inside of his abdomen. The penis itself was shrunken and wrinkled from so prolonged a withdrawal from affairs, and the whole collection that lay lightly and limply in Carmen's palm was on the verge of being pathetic. Carmen smiled. Partly from the rush and partly from her heart, she felt consumed with tenderness toward Maraña in his condition, the very opposite of erection, and she cupped her hand protectively around the portion of maleness she felt, kneading the wrinkles gently between her slender fingertips. Carmen was so lost in this affection that she did not notice how his penis remained small even when his breath quickened to a labored pace, which should have warned her that Maraña's breath was not from the heat of sexual excitement.

It was from anger, or at least a boundless frustration, and it showed on Maraña's face when he turned around. There was hurt in the muscles around his cheeks, but his eyes were deserts, arid and vacant. "I feel so good and so complete," he said, in a voice that sounded far off. "But none of it is me. I am not here. I don't know what you are touching, but it's not me. Maybe it's the drugs. I think you'd better go away from me. Leave me alone." Carmen took one step backward, and Maraña's eyes flashed with rage. "Go away!" he thundered.

Carmen's emotions tumbled a long way before they regrouped and compressed themselves into anger at Maraña for so destroying her tenderness. "You bastard!" she screamed. "How dare you talk to me that way! I know where you've been and what you are, and I will die before I nurse you and coax you and feel sorry for you! Just because you are a big shot with those pigs out on the street . . ."

"Get out of here!"

"*You* get out of here!" Carmen shrieked. "I am here! I have come halfway to you. If you want to feel like a stone, then you go do it, but you will *not* dismiss me like a stone, too!"

As Maraña lunged violently toward Carmen, her mind went blank and then fixed on the image of herself as a child, closing her eyes in stupid faith on the only roller coaster in Havana. Now, as then, she knew she would be all right somehow and didn't care anyway in her commotion. Instantaneously, the hint of a giggle sprang to her face, and it grew some when she saw that the volcanic man rampaging toward her still carried a limp penis, dangling ludicrously out of his trousers.

Carmen's giggle registered on Maraña's mind before he grabbed her shoulders, and it punctured him. His mind would remember the picture of her face as she not only stood her ground in the path of his anger, which no other person he knew would do, but also managed to smile. It was the essence of Carmen, and Maraña realized that the sight brought him the first human contact since he had entered the long coil of events leading up to the murder. Feeling literally rescued, he swung Carmen roughly toward the edge of the balcony, then less roughly back toward the door, then more playfully back and forth until both of them erupted in laughter.

Maraña stopped, dropped his hands, and stuffed himself carefully back into his trousers. "Excuse me," he said, and then looked at the floor. "You know, sometimes you are all right."

"That's better," said Carmen.

Over the years, they had developed a pattern of lovemaking—one that was not invariable but that came most naturally in times of stress. Carmen lay on her back, Maraña curled on his side next to her. She spread herself by lifting one leg over his, sometimes brushing her toes along his calf for a while. Always, she held his penis quietly in her left hand, feeling its heartbeat, pulling gently, and on this night thinking that an erection has its place, too. And Maraña simply made feathers of his fingertips, rubbing them over her nipples and belly and thighs, and all around the contours of her vagina —seldom entering her, for the spirit they enjoyed was to lightly touch and tickle until neither could stand it anymore. In parts of Cuba, it is said that a man who was amply suckled and loved by his mother will focus most of his foreplay on his lover's vagina, whereas the unsuckled and unloved child will still look hopefully to the breast. Maraña spent most of his time swirling

52

softly around Carmen's nipples. She lay always quiet and breathless, which seemed appropriate for a woman who, like Maraña, lived on the edge of denial, but at the end both she and he would whimper "God, take me" like believers.

The late editions of that morning's *Miami Herald* carried a blazing front page story on the Taliente murder, buttressed with tributes to his patriotism from both Cuban and American civic leaders. One side story featured a large photograph of Taliente addressing a throng of more than 30,000 Cubans in the Miami stadium. There were no photographs of the corpse, however, or of any of the sensational scenes that newspapers elsewhere would have prized highly. This restraint was the result of an agreement among both newspapers and the city fathers to downplay any event that might damage Miami's huge tourist industry, which was already sagging painfully. The parties had also agreed to minimize, for patriotic as well as commercial reasons, publicity about strife and criminality among the city's Cuban political groups. Such reports were ugly and sensitive, having a history of being more or less in the realm of official intrigue.

Both the *Herald* and the *News* opened their ears to allegations that the Castro government had somehow caused Taliente's death, reasoning that Castro had much to gain from the elimination of the anticommunist leader and from the attendant grief and confusion in Miami. Some stories mentioned a plot originating in Mexico. Two investigative reporters spent a week working on Taliente's backyard neighbor, who was known to have visited relatives in Havana not long before, and who was therefore under suspicion of operating as an international hit man. In a three-day series, the reporters chronicled the neighbor's futile attempts to explain what his boxer had been doing in Taliente's yard on the night of the murder. Many speculations were cited on this point, attributed to police investigators, including one theory that the boxer had accompanied the killer for protection and then been abandoned in the haste of the escape. There was soon another story reporting the death of the puppy, poisoned by unknown vigilantes.

"Pops" Shea went to Washington. In the wake of the murder a dispute was growing up between him and the CIA's Noel, each claiming that the other possessed vital intelligence on the political forces behind the murder. Unable to reach a compromise, they referred their contentions to superiors in Washington for resolution. Shea and Noel came to something of a mum stalemate, enabling each of them to blame the other for whatever failures he might be called upon to account for.

In the first few weeks after the murder, Shea accepted Maraña's account of having discovered the commotion at Taliente's house after a full night at the movies. Then it became more difficult to believe him, especially after Dave Damico reported being laughed at by local policemen and by customers at the Versailles. Maraña became known as "the man who shot Taliente all the way from the Coconut Grove Theater." Although there was not a word about him in the media, his fame grew so rapidly by word of mouth that Cubans on any street corner or in any high school could identify "the spy with nine lives." Informants in the drug trade reported that Maraña had killed for a spoonful of coke. It was widely rumored that Maraña had arranged for the U.S. Treasury to pay for the murder weapon and for his vacation after the job, which was partly true, and it was also reported that Maraña was in constant radio contact with CIA headquarters on the night of the murder. On some street corners, people swore that Maraña had been working for Castro, and more than one person heard that Maraña was hired to settle a high level feud between Canada Dry and Coca-Cola. Most vexing to the FBI, it was widely believed that Maraña had offered to take some FBI agents along with him on the job but that the agents had been too scared. "Carlos says," went the standard joke, "that if you want to kill somebody, you should tell the FBI in advance." The perfect political crime, according to the new street wisdom, depended not on avoiding the authorities altogether, but on entangling yourself in their secret lives. Upon entering any public place, Carmen and Maraña began to draw more than attention. Crowds would become silent and part for them. Maraña was thought to have played a role in securing petroleum for Israel just before the Yom Kippur war, and to have arranged crime lord Meyer Lansky's return to Miami.

"You will hear many things," Maraña told Patrick Shea, adding that he was going to shut up because he feared for his life. Max Parker also told the FBI that he feared for his life, working so near Maraña, and he successfully negotiated an informant's raise.

Since his CIA days back in the 1960s, Maraña had never lacked for plots and crimes and clandestine gossip, but after the murder he heard more on a single night than he had previously heard in a year. Conspirators besieged him wherever he went. They seemed to feel a need to confess, to plan, to share their experiences and ask advice, in spite of the fact that Maraña might well use the information against them. Maraña filed it all away in his mind. Sometimes even he was surprised at what people would reveal. He was flattered, but he was wise enough to know that he was in more danger than ever. Survival required that he be more alert, keeping a thousand more details straight in his mind. It was only a matter of time before the American authorities would lean on him heavily. He could feel the wars among the Cubans already at hand, and by the gunfighter's logic, he was the one the hungry men would come after—the king *chivato*, the prize of many ambitions. The game was more complicated, and he knew he had chosen to make it that way.

Carmen knew it, too. On the night of the murder, they lay awake for hours like zombies—lost in peace and fatigue and troubled dreams, but with enough cocaine in their blood to make squirrels of their nerves and spotlights of their eyes. Carmen broke the silence only once: "I know you, Carlos. You have done it now. You have called ten more bulls into the ring with you, and you have done it only to amuse yourself. Isn't that right?"

III

THE REGULAR poker game ceased being regular as soon as Paul Sternman's book made him more famous than Lester Hershey. "How about next Thursday?" Henry Woodruff asked many a time, leaving Sternman and Hershey to glare at each other through the cigar smoke, each weighing fears that the other was about to come splashing onto the front pages. Neither reporter wished to admit having free time on his hands if there was the slightest chance his rival would be working. "Nope, can't make it then," Hershey often said, and Sternman claimed to be equally busy. This charade stopped the poker games altogether until David Howell stooped to a bit of chicanery. He called each reporter and told him that the other had already agreed to play on a certain night, so both could show up feeling safe. Woodruff reprimanded Howell for making such false calls, even in the interest of the poker game, whereupon Howell invented and defended his idea of a "benevolent lie." Woodruff denied the existence of such a thing, and the two friends spent several evenings on a high theoretical plane.

These troubles were not uncommon for Washington in those days, when inhabitants were caught up in abstract questions of justice and in compulsions over work, or at least over the appearance of work. Paul Sternman was no stranger to scheduling conflicts. It was widely known that Sternman and his first wife once did not see each other for two solid months simply because they could not agree on a mutually convenient lunch date on which to discuss their ruptured marriage. Their separation ran on steadily to divorce, as the Sternmans made themselves casualties in the complicated but subtle war over who has time for whom, which normally begins in the capital with the question, "When are you free for lunch?" The noon meal, far from an off-duty respite, is the time of significant business. Over lunch, Sternman confided the marital standoff to his lover, Valerie Mantell, who passed the story along to her friends over other lunches. Hearing of this, Sternman promptly broke off amorous relations with Mantell. "You are mighty huffy," she told Sternman, in a message relayed through the receptionist at Sternman's newspaper after he refused to accept Mantell's phone calls.

Tonight at David Howell's poker table, Mantell stared through her silver-tinted glasses, in the octagonal shape of stop signs, at Sternman's solid face. She planned to take monetary advantage of any tenderness that might be lingering behind his impassive features. Every so often she flashed him a young, awkward smile to keep him off-balance. She was good at that. Mantell was one of the city's foremost enigmas. She had arrived ten years earlier and landed a job with a Texas congressman who opposed the Vietnam War, and she proceeded to astound nearly everyone she met by offering an immediate, candid autobiography, focusing on how she, as a proper young Jewish woman from Houston, had nevertheless managed to fall in love with a Mexican heroin addict, with whom she traveled to Europe shortly before the Kennedy assassination, only to be abandoned by the addict and raped in Austria by a bartender of Nazi descent. She sought psychiatric help back home and ran through a succession of therapists, becoming more and more fascinated by the world of the mind and of the plumbing beneath it. In New York, she soaked up ideas and pain with several doctors and many friends before discovering that Washington offered just as many brands of psychiatry as New York, though more quietly. So she moved and kept up her psychoanalysis as a congressional aide and later as a lobbyist for stringent laws against noxious automobile fumes. Mantell came to tell her psychiatrist that something horribly mysterious about the very term "auto emission" attracted her to the job, and she probed inside herself for reasons why the words had such a powerful effect that they filled her dreams with scenes of an inhuman, mechanical, slippery, sexual, and poisonous nature.

These dreams were among the thousands of interior subjects Mantell discussed with her best friend, Susan "Suds" Hartman. Founders of one of the first female discussion groups in the capital, they had taken up women's issues toward the end of the Vietnam War. For Mantell, it was a providential blend of politics and psychiatry. Her skills and reputation, enhanced somewhat by frequent recitals of the Austrian rape episode, brought Mantell a position as staff director of the National Women's Political Caucus. There she performed brilliantly, but her personal behavior was considered so paradoxical that it became the object of criticism among her colleagues. Mantell, casting off the loose and disheveled and unhappy look of the antiwar days, and forsaking the severely analytical look of the early women's movement, braided her long black hair into pigtails as soon as she moved into her office. In addition, she discarded her jeans and her pseudo-cowboy boots from Houston in favor of a large collection of antique white blouses, which she always wore with a black skirt and the kind of sturdy black footwear Susan Hartman called "grandmother shoes." Mantell's new pigtails combined with her naturally red cheeks, fluffed out by a fondness for ice cream, to give the outer edges of her face the shine of a playful farm girl. This competed with the sharp line that ran down her thin nose and over her small oval mouth to a chin of exquisite shape but lacking enough flesh to seem friendly. David Howell, over lunch arranged by his friend Hartman, had found Mantell so intriguing that he invited her to take part in the Henry Woodruff Non-Chauvinist Poker Game, which, since the surprise separation of the Woodruffs, had been transferred to Howell's apartment.

"Play ball!" shouted Charles "Ziggy" Rosen, who, as usual, could wait no longer. For the duration of the night his right knee would bounce speedily up and down off the ball of his foot, housed in a bright green sneaker. Impatient with the usual haggling over the house rules and stakes, he grabbed a deck and began flipping cards around the table. "First jack deals!" he cried. The jack of hearts soon fell before Rosen himself, as he expected it would because he always expected to be lucky. "It's about *time* I got to deal," he said with mock petulance, as he snatched up the other deck and began to deal with one hand. Simultaneously, he shoved the loose cards from the first deck to David Howell on his right, saying "Your make."

"Thanks," smiled Howell, who was actually glad that Rosen was infecting the table with his haste. The group, left to itself, tended to drift toward gossip and anarchy.

"The game," Rosen announced, "is seven-card stud, high-low." He stopped dealing and raised his right forefinger toward the ceiling. "But," he continued, "anybody who promises to bring Woodruff's Tennessee wife back to him this week is guaranteed the low hand's share of this pot."

"Really, Ziggy," chided Valerie Mantell, slowly shaking her pigtails.

"No personal matters should be mentioned at the poker table," Paul Sternman declared.

"That's all right," said Woodruff. "I appreciate that, Ziggy, but for right now I'd rather not have her back anyway."

Rosen smiled. He cupped his hand before his mouth like a megaphone and announced, "News bulletin! Woodruff spurns wife to gamble."

"All he's saying is that he's got a better chance of winning the low hand than he does of making headway with Casey," Howell shrugged, popping open a beer.

Rosen flashed Howell a puzzled look. "That kind of remark deserves a nine," he said. Then he plunked over the nine of clubs onto Howell's cards. Howell scratched his stomach.

"How did you do that?" Lester Hershey demanded. "Are you cheating already?"

Rosen ignored the question. He resumed his dealing, always tossing the cards willy-nilly, back and forth, two here and one over there, instead of in regular order. Rosen was incapable of behaving by regular conventions. In games of draw poker, the players were nettled by his unorthodox dealing, but always impressed upon counting that Rosen's deals came out correctly.

"How *did* you do that, Ziggy?" drawled Mantell.

"C'mon! C'mon!" shouted Hershey, his nasal voice cutting through the giggles like a honking goose. "Let's play cards. My king bets half a dollar."

An hour later he was still complaining that all the nonsense at the table was hampering his game, when someone knocked at the door.

Howell moved instinctively to answer before he remembered that he was sitting on an advance copy of *Washington* magazine, which contained his own cover story. It was highly critical of some of the very people sitting at the poker table. Howell checked himself, looking nervously sideways at Hershey to see if he had noticed, and motioned to Woodruff, who rose slowly to the task. He ambled heavily toward the door, feeling dread and self-reproach. Woodruff knew that he was in a serious scrape. He had known it from the moment he invited LaLane Rayburn to the poker game. It had been an idiocy, born of embarrassment. Just as a humiliated Woodruff had been saying good-bye to Rayburn, after informing her of his gonorrhea, he began stumbling over his words because he was afraid she would think of him as the kind of young man who routinely infects isolated military wives with venereal disease and then abandons them to their shame. He could not bear to excuse himself so coldly and permanently, though his embarrassment had climbed to such heights that he didn't really want to see Rayburn, either—certainly not socially, in circumstances that might make her think he was so brash as to want sex *again*, in the midst of the venereal tragedy. Woodruff had in fact tentatively concluded never to have sex again, having discovered both with Casey and Rayburn that it could lead to emotions more intensely unpleasant than he had thought possible. On top of that, it interfered with more important matters, such as Woodruff's epic quest to understand the world. On the phone then, caught between conflicting shames, Woodruff groped for something between good-bye and the bed, and all that occurred to him was a poker game. He regretted the invitation before the words were out of his mouth, knowing that neither he nor Rayburn could expect any mercy from the poker players, who seemed to toughen themselves for political competition by stampeding through each other's private lives. Rayburn had accepted, and now they would have to pay.

Woodruff took a deep breath and found two visitors behind the door instead of one. "Hi, Sudsy," he said with a wan smile to Susan Hartman, who, by her unusually polite expression, was already calling for an explanation of the phenomenon beside her.

"Hello, Henry," said the phenomenon, who, dressed in jeans and an old army shirt, could easily have passed for a California mother had it not been for the beehive and her extraordinarily large breasts, which had once sent extra blood through the temples of the judges in the Miss University of Texas pageant. Rayburn strapped them down as much as possible, in keeping with the slimmer fashions, but even so they commanded attention. Woodruff realized that he had not even noticed these breasts when he had been in a position to do so, and hard upon this realization came a further one, that he was noticing them now, in the presence of Susan Hartman, only seconds after thanking shame for parching all the sex out of him.

"Uh, have you two met?" Woodruff weakly asked.

"Sure have," Rayburn replied. "Susan has been telling me that most of the players here first met each other at the poker table."

"That's true," said Woodruff.

"Nothing wrong with that," said Rayburn. "Most of my friends met each other in the commissary."

"Huh," said Woodruff. "I guess that makes sense." He stared blankly, not knowing quite what else to say.

"Hi, baby," Hartman said brightly as she threw her arms around Woodruff. Having decided that Woodruff was in obvious trouble, she tried to rescue him with her customary affection—being among the most demonstrative of the natural hugging women. Woodruff was grateful. "Is the game already going?" Hartman asked.

"Yep," said Woodruff. "They're in there now, betting and arguing."

"Oh shit," said Hartman, also one of the natural cussers. She laughed, gave Woodruff a final hug of encouragement, and ran off to leave him alone with Rayburn. "I'll go straighten them out," she said, bounding away.

Woodruff dropped his arms and looked somberly at Rayburn. "I'm glad you could come," he said.

"I'm not so sure about that," laughed Rayburn, "but I'm happy you asked me, anyway." She paused, running low on aplomb. "Uh, where did your friend get the name 'Suds'?"

Woodruff felt more comfortable with such an ordinary topic. "Well," he laughed, "she got it from her boyfriend, Ziggy Rosen. He's in there at the poker table. Actually, the two of them have been on again and off again as a couple for about five years. Right now they're off. But they still like each other, as you can probably tell." Woodruff stopped to let Rayburn hear the wild and joyous sounds from the poker room, where Rosen was shouting, "Sudsy! My dream *shiksa!*" And Hartman was shouting back, "Ziggy! You hustling old running-dog class-traitor bastard!" And the two of them were slapping palms, bumping hips, and doing a dance quite of their own.

"Sounds like they do like each other," mused Rayburn.

"Yes," said Woodruff. "Anyway, during the war, Susan wrote pamphlets against the Pentagon, and they were very dry, academic-type things. Ziggy came along and tried to get her to broaden her audience by putting in more stuff about napalmed babies and soldiers who said they didn't know why they were there and politicians making asses out of themselves—that sort of stuff. He didn't even want her to take the complicated justifications of the war seriously, because he doesn't think that's how most people make up their minds. So he kept saying, 'Susan, put more suds in this pamphlet and you'll end the war.' He started calling her 'Suds' as a joke, but now everybody does it, even though the name really applies more to Ziggy."

"I see," said Rayburn. "How come they've broken up?"

"Nobody knows," said Henry. "Officially, they say they've obtained a premarital divorce. With those two, you never know. They still have affairs with each other.

"Henry!" Paul Sternman thundered from the other room.

59

"Just a minute!" shouted Woodruff. "Deal me out for this hand, will you?"

Woodruff waved his hand to dismiss the general grumbling from the poker room and turned back to Rayburn. "Speaking of affairs," he said awkwardly, "what did the doctor say?"

Rayburn sighed and looked around to make sure no one was listening. "I thought you'd never ask," she replied, with gentle sarcasm. "He got the results back today and he says I don't have anything. Nothing."

Woodruff stole a few moments by nodding. "That makes things very complicated," he moaned. "Let's see. That means I could have only gotten it from Casey. And I had to get it after the night of the party you and I went to, or you would have gotten it from me. And that means . . ." His voice trailed off to nothing. "Ugh," he shuddered. "This is a revolting business."

Rayburn stuffed both hands into the front pockets of her jeans and stretched for relief, shaking her shoulders. Woodruff thought this cowgirlish move made her look twenty years younger, an idea that made his stomach jump. She looked Woodruff over slowly from the thin nose down past his striped, open-collared shirt and his suit pants to his shoeless feet. Woodruff still liked to slide around on wooden floors in his socks. "The test for women is not as accurate as the test for men," Rayburn advised. "I should tell you that. He gave me a hipful of penicillin, just in case. But there's no way I could have given you anything—I mean anything physical—unless I have been carrying it seven years from my husband. I hope I shouldn't have to tell you that, but I wanted you to hear it straight from me." Rayburn paused and swung her shoulders from side to side, showing the strain. "Now I know you don't like the possibility that you may have gotten it from your wife, and, well, what that means, especially at a time like this. And I really think that before you put yourself through all this, you should at least be sure that this is not all a mistake. As I understand it from my doctor, the male penis is subject to a number of secretions and infections, like urethritis, that might be mistaken for venereal disease. And these things are most likely when a man is really nervous, like with, you know, a new sexual partner. Whew. You know how these doctors talk." Rayburn managed a laugh and twisted again at the shoulders.

"Yes," gulped Woodruff, suffering greatly for Rayburn's transformation, in his eyes, from schoolgirl to clinical nurse, and then, across an age barrier, to mother figure.

"Well, anyway," Rayburn said, "I just wanted you to think about that, because I don't want you to go through all this if it's over nothing. I mean nothing physical. I guess I already said that, didn't I?"

"That's true. I mean, God, it would be awful if this were all over nothing," Woodruff said, and sighed. "But I don't think it is. You know, I didn't go to my doctor about this, because I didn't want everybody there to know. And it's Casey's doctor, too. And anyway, I went to the D.C. Public Health clinic. Boy, that was something. It's in this mammoth old building right in the middle of the ghetto. So I went in there, trying to pretend like I was an investigator or something, and when the receptionist asked me where I worked I kind of leaned over the counter and whispered, 'I work in the Senate.' And then this lady, this jolly, chubby black lady, she turned to a friend of hers in the back room and said, 'Hey, Roberta. This man works in the Senate. How about that.' I almost died. I thought everybody could hear that for miles. I think I went sort of numb. And when I told her I was there to be tested for venereal disease, I thought she smiled. It was barely a smile, and maybe I even imagined it, but I thought it was a smile. Then she gave me this little round tag with number 53 on it, and told me to report upstairs. I went up there, trying to look inconspicuous. Which was pretty hard to do, since I was the only white person in the building and I thought everybody was staring at me. I was worried that it was the racist in me coming out, but then I decided that it was no time to worry about racism with all the other problems I had. You know, a man's got to have his priorities." Woodruff smiled, and Rayburn noticed the color coming back to his cheeks, as though the very act of telling the story, even at his own expense, refreshed him.

"Time to declare," came a loud voice from the poker room. Woodruff caught the words above the poker talk and the clatter of chips on the table. He turned to Rayburn to finish his story quickly, happy about a number of things, including the discovery that she no longer made him think of his mother.

"The reception room upstairs was filled with teenagers," he said. "Most of the girls sat around the perimeter and buried themselves in newspapers and schoolbooks, but the boys stood in a group out in the middle of the room, laughing and having a big time. One of them said, 'Hey, man. That's nothing. I been here *nine* times.' And they all laughed and slapped this guy on the back like he was a hero. They teased a lot of the girls, and finally they got around to teasing me. I figured they would, even though I was pretty well enshrouded in the sports section of the newspaper. This young guy in a net shirt and tennis shoes came over to me and said, 'Hey man. Who you been messing with?' And I tried to ignore him, but he went over to one of the girls sitting near me and said, 'You been messing with this pretty little thing here?' And he tried to sit in the girl's lap, but she slapped his ass real loud and said, 'Get away from me!' And then he came back to me and said, 'That's a pretty sassy piece of tail over there. I bet you been messing with her, ain't you?' By this time, all the guys back in his group were joking with him and making comments about me, so I was on center stage in the whole reception room. In desperation, I tried to think of something that would make this guy leave me alone, so I leaned over to him and whispered, 'I think I got it from my brother.' I thought he'd puke or jump away from me, but at least he'd leave me alone. Boy, was I stupid. This young guy just lit up in a smile and shouted, 'Your brother! Hey, the white man here likes the brown!' They all started laughing and jiving about that, and then I really did want to crawl into a wall socket. Those guys were so uninhibited. They kept saying I liked the brown, as though homosexuality were nothing more than a preference for a flavor or something. I decided I would never be in a position to embarrass them, and I had only made things worse for myself.

61

"Finally, a doctor called out my number and I went back to the treatment room, where they took some blood and made me pull my pants down and took a, uh, a smear on a glass slide. And pretty soon, as I was sitting back out in the reception room, this doctor stuck his head in and yelled, 'Number fifty-three! You got the clap!' And he motioned me on back. I felt like a condemned prisoner, and I was a little resentful because I couldn't remember them making such big announcements about anybody else's diagnosis. But I didn't say anything, because I was trying to get them to *make sure*, you know. So I called this doctor into this little curtained room where I was getting treated, and I tried to explain to him that this was no ordinary situation. I told him it was unprecedented for me, that I had just the night before separated from my wife, and so forth. And in spite of myself, all these big words kept pouring out of me, so that I felt whiter and squarer and more miserable than ever. And finally, after he shot my hip full of penicillin, the doctor agreed to double-check. And he brought over this little gray-haired black lady in a lab coat and said, 'Number fifty-three here is worried about his slide. Could you check it again for him?' And the lady, who was the boss, seemed slightly insulted that I might question her work, but she took me over to this big desk with a microscope on it and pulled out my slide and peered at it for a second and then she turned to me and said, 'Yep. You've got the clap all right. That is a beautiful gonococcus!' She invited me to look at it. She was very excited about the quality of my bacteria and kept saying, 'Beautiful gonococcus!' And I guess the point of all this is that I'm pretty sure that I had it—as sure as I am about anything in this mess." Woodruff rested, both hands wrapped around a glass of apple cider in front of his chest. He had worked himself up to the point of merriment over the story, as though he were telling it about someone else.

Rayburn took her hands out of her jean pockets. She seemed soberly amused. "I see," she said. "And now I guess you and Casey are gonna caucus about the gonococcus."

Woodruff looked stunned. The reference to Casey brought back all the personal misery that the story itself had transcended. "Yes," he managed. "I didn't know you made jokes."

Seeing Woodruff on the verge of hemorrhage, she had to make herself stop laughing. Rayburn wiped a few laughs' tears on the sleeve of her army shirt. "I'm sorry," she said. "I don't know what else to do but laugh. This is all so amazing. But I do want you to know that for me, well . . ." She wiped her eyes on the other sleeve of her shirt. "I realize that I'm almost a grandmother and not suited to you at all, but for me it's already been worth it. Even if I *had* gotten the clap, as they say, it would have been worth it."

"Well, uh," Woodruff stammered.

"And that's saying a lot, believe me," said Rayburn.

"Well, thanks," said Woodruff. "I mean . . ."

"I don't expect it to be worth it to you," said Rayburn. "But for me, you know, I have been all tangled up in my upbringing. For seven years, I was terrified of having an affair with anyone while my husband was gone over there. I knew inside me that he was dead, but still it was more than immoral to me. It was treason, you know, like sleeping with Hanoi. And now I've let loose of all that, and I feel like a person again. A woman, too."

Woodruff stared again, not knowing what to make of her.

"Henry!" shouted Sternman from the poker room. "Come on!"

"I'm coming!" Woodruff shouted, turning in the doorway to put an arm around Rayburn's shoulders. "You amaze me," he told her. "I'm gonna need some of your strength tomorrow because I really am gonna caucus with Casey at lunch. Gonococcus is on the agenda, along with love and marriage."

"You'll do all right," said Rayburn.

"I don't know," said Woodruff. "I'll let you know. Anyway, I want to warn you about these sharks in here. They may say anything. Some of them are not normal, and they might wonder out loud about things. Well, never mind."

As soon as he saw Woodruff round the corner into the poker room with his arm draped about a stunning older woman who looked like Hollywood's idea of a southern grocery store cashier, David Howell knew that his friend would soon be tested to the limits. "Good evening, Mrs. Rayburn," he said, rising to shake her hand with a flourish. "Would like a beer or a drink?"

"Nothing alcoholic, thank you," Rayburn smiled. "But I'd like a Coke if you've got one."

"Coming right up," said Howell, who, seeing that Sternman and Hershey were preoccupied with the newcomer, snatched up the *Washington* magazine from his chair for hiding in the kitchen.

"That is David Howell, my roommate, landlord, and friend," said Woodruff, who proceeded to introduce Rayburn around the table. At the sound of his name, Ziggy Rosen tipped his official Los Angeles Dodgers baseball cap with a cavalier jerk, thus revealing the spot on top of his head where the black hair had worn as thin as the grass on a horse trail. Aside from this bald spot, and the fact that he was only five and a half feet tall, Rosen was a physical duplicate of Fidel Castro—complete with the hooked nose, the charming though beady eyes, and the scruffy, conversation-piece beard. He did dress differently from Castro, of course, tending toward rainbow-colored sneakers, children's caps, and a wide variety of T-shirts. At the poker table he wore a standard Fruit-of-the-Loom that had been dyed bright colors in concentric circles around a black bull's eye on his chest, upon which was inscribed the slogan, "Warning: I Brake for Spiro Agnew." Rosen had taken great pains to absorb each highlight of Agnew's political career, back to the earliest connivances outside Baltimore, and he gloried in the cultural purity of Agnew's every deal, bromide, and transparently grasping maneuver. From childhood, Rosen had delighted in bourgeois excesses—especially those such as television, politicians, and fast food that his poker companions made a practice of looking down upon. He was a most unorthodox man. After being introduced, he unconsciously put his right knee through a spell of unusually fast bobbing. It went up and down like the needle of a sewing machine.

Woodruff introduced on past Paul Sternman, who was polite and smiling, though somehow distant. In his crisp blue dress shirt and his conservative tie, loosened precisely to a kind of parade rest position, Sternman seemed orderly and serious even after a long day's work in the grime of daily journalism. He had indeed been a Republican until cynicism corroded his sense of politics, but this occurred too late to affect his personal habits. His appearance was in marked contrast, not only to Rosen, but also to Hershey, one seat past Susan Hartman. Hershey began every morning dressed almost exactly like Sternman, but, within an hour, the clothes would become limp, seedy, and baggy, Lomanesque, as though burned up by Hershey's driven, haggard will. His features were sandy and sharp, eyes beginning to sink early, and he walked with a determined gait, as though leaning into the wind.

He called for more chips from Woodruff, the banker, and the game resumed after Howell returned with Rayburn's Coke and seated her just behind him to observe. Play went on mechanically, without the usual spirit or laughter, and almost immediately there were signs of malaise. During Susan Hartman's deal, all the players passed without betting until the nod reached a sullen Ziggy Rosen, who bet a dollar without even looking at his cards—so late that Hartman had already begun to deal the next round. Although well within the rules, Rosen's late and cheerless bet chafed the crowd, and David Howell didn't help things by whimsically raising a dollar when the bet came round to him. Despite his feeble attempt to laugh, Howell's bet so annoyed Hershey that he took another raise for a dollar, and Sternman raised yet again, not to be undone. No one had intended to bet, but a foul mood had settled over the table and itself pushed money into the pot. It grew to a size that ordinarily would have caused excitement and inspired jokes, but the irritation remained. LaLane Rayburn looked on wordlessly from behind. On the last card, a dollar bet stalled in front of Susan Hartman pending her decision. She lingered over her options, making faces and rubbing the cards in her hands, whose fingernails she kept well-bitten.

"Take your time, Sudsy," chirped Rosen.

"I will," Hartman said with a lemony smile.

"C'mon, c'mon, play cards," said Hershey.

"That's what I said," Rosen protested.

"Knock it off," said Woodruff, who had scarcely been concentrating on the game.

Hartman pushed her chair back and leaned forward until her eyes fell to the level of the table, whereupon she lifted each of her hole cards by a corner and peeked at them once again, as if to make sure none of them had changed. She took sight on them and eyeballed them, squinting and squirming all the while, like a baseball umpire behind the plate. Periodically, she would bend her lips over each other somehow and send a blast of breath straight up her face to lift her light brown bangs off her forehead, the better to peer around the table with her coy and devilish looks. David Howell had long admired this feat of Hartman's. He contorted his lips into every position he could think of, but still he could not make the breath go straight up unless he cupped his hands in front of his face. This time, he succeeded only in blowing air and saliva up his nose with enough force to make him think he was drowning. Involuntarily, he gasped, banged the table with his left fist, and in desperation blew his nose with a loud wet plop in the palm of his right hand. He made a face of grotesque pain while his startled companions tried to catch the chips he had sent flying off the table.

"Dammit, Suds!" Howell snapped. "Why don't you get your mouth fixed?"

"That's very attractive, David," Sternman said.

Hartman stared back at Howell and did her trick again, making her hair lift off her brow as though it were on hinges. She blew again, seeming lost in thought. The corners of her mouth extended on either side a fraction of an inch beyond what would have been perfect, and in this extra space the lines of her mouth curved quickly down and up—so that she could give hints of smiles and frowns at once. Howell doubted that this extraordinary feature had anything to do with Hartman's bangs trick, but he and Woodruff both believed it was a clue to her character. Hartman always laughed with a hint of pain at the corners of her mouth, and cried with a hint of merriment. Her mouth was the only horizontal line about her, for otherwise she was long—tall and lithe, with high legs and thin, bony shoulders and liquid joints at the elbows and knees. Standing, her shoulders and knees slumped naturally to graceful, athletic poses. She had a clean, boyish face, like a fleet mythological runner, and her pale skin was illuminated by a brightness of unusual depth. Her body had a willowy spring to it that was attractive in a special way, as though she had been fashioned from some third, elfin form onto which the female sex had been laid lightly and easily in an inspired afterthought. Hartman wore her jeans over her cowboy boots and plain silver bracelets over both wrists. She preferred patterned blouses, with Indian or Mexican designs stitched over a white base. Anyone could see, through the gossamer fabric, the prominent, unpointed nipples on Hartman's small breasts, and several of the players also knew that these nipples were of a highly unusual light rosy color, like strawberries.

She was trying to understand what had gone so amiss that even David Howell had not laughed at his nasal misfortune, which was exactly the kind of comeuppance that normally amused him most. Ignoring the sniping requests around the table for her to bet or fold, she bent over and checked the corners of her cards once more, then pursed her lips into a frown as she scanned the surrounding faces. "What the hell," she announced to her hushed companions. "I'd watch flies fuck for a dollar."

All spines stiffened instantly at this remark. In the silence, her two half-dollar chips landed in the pot with a crash.

"Really, Susan," Woodruff said hoarsely, his chin tucked down to his chest as though fighting a burp. "I'm not sure that Mrs. Rayburn here, well . . ."

"Please call me LaLane," Rayburn interrupted with a smile.

Woodruff sat back. His face turned crimson, like a glass being filled with wine. To keep from laughing, Rosen and Hershey cupped their hands over their mouths and pretended to yawn.

"Hey, come off it," Hartman said loudly, shrugging her shoulders and lifting her hands to the ceiling. She wore an uneasy grin, with the corners of her mouth twitching. "Let's take it easy. The way it looks to me, we're either gonna sit here all tight-assed and grumpy because Henry's brought this Confederate woman here who's older and has a beehive and a tight shirt and who none of us knows, or we're gonna be ourselves and kid her a little bit and try to have a good time. I mean isn't that right?"

"Hear, hear!" shouted Ziggy Rosen.

"I agree," said Sternman.

"That's right, sister," added Valerie Mantell.

When the noise passed, LaLane Rayburn leaned forward and said, "Well, we have a heap of flies down in Texas. I never *paid* anything to watch 'em, but I don't mind hearing that somebody else will. Don't mind a bit, as long as my children aren't here."

Everyone was pleasantly relieved at this collegial response, and the balmy new atmosphere helped Woodruff's recovery along. "I should apologize," he said during a lull in the Texas jokes, "for not having asked LaLane if she wants to take a hand in the competition here. We can play with eight people, as long as we agree not to play seven-card games. What do you say?"

"Jump right in," Hershey invited Rayburn. "We only play for fun."

There was some surprise when Rayburn agreed to play, and even more when she promptly grabbed the cards for her honorary deal and absent-mindedly cut the deck in the palm of one hand. She leaned forward, slapped the deck twice on the table, and grinned, ready for business.

The other players exchanged wide-eyed, significant looks. "I think we've run into a buzz saw," Howell mused.

"The game is 'The General's Wife,' " Rayburn announced with relish. "We used to play it a lot during the war. It's regular stud poker, five cards, except that you can turn in any bitchy queen for another card at any time in the game. It costs one dollar for an up card and two dollars for a down card."

Cheers greeted this announcement, and the game resumed at a brisk pace. Cards, chips, wisecracks, and lies rolled in every direction. The players became animated and saucy. Most of them presumed to spend their working hours in search of one form of truth or another in a murky world, and poker was to them a holiday of deception in a world that always cleared up at the end of each hand. Out of conviction or ego, the players showed their cards when a hand was completed, even if they didn't have to. Only Sternman was an exception. You had to call his bet to see his hand, and if no one did, he would bury his victorious hand in the deck forever, ignoring the boos of the curious onlookers. He always kept his ruses private, for his own use, which was strategically wise but politically unpopular.

With play running briskly, there was no sustained conversation until Woodruff threw out some stinging comments on the division of household duties, a topic much on his mind. "David has the manners of an orangutan," he remarked between hands. "The other day, he borrowed my toothpaste, left the top off, took it into the kitchen for some reason, then put a gallon of cider on the tube and squirted a big glob of toothpaste all over the fresh asparagus I had just bought."

"It washed off," said Howell. "It was an accident."

Woodruff ignored him. "You have no idea what I put up with," he complained to the group. "I am oppressed in the kitchen, in the bathroom, in the common areas, and in the laundry. I'd love to drag Howell's ass in front of one of those women's groups and charge him with rank sloth and oppression. They'd know what to do with him."

"You'd better stay away from women's issues, Henry," said Mantell.

"Why?" asked Woodruff. "Don't you think I'm a conceptual sister?"

"No," said Mantell.

"Why not?" asked Woodruff.

"Because I think you're really trying to make fun of those women's issues for your own reasons. The last thing women need is you two guys with your tongue-in-cheek household problems, like your laundry."

"Well, I'll admit that I was in something of a jocular mood," Woodruff retreated.

"I think you got him pegged," said Hartman. "It looks to me like a clear case of guilt transference, probably with some repressed anger in there somewhere." She smiled.

"Yep," Howell agreed. "There might also be a dash of sexual paranoia growing out of the uncertain new living conditions."

Woodruff turned on Howell. "Jesus Christ," he said. "What are *you* jumping in there for? I mean you started all this."

"It's all right, Henry," said Rosen. "You've just got to learn how to treat girls."

Hartman threw a disgusted look at Rosen. "That's it for you, Ziggy," she said. "You're cut off."

Rosen stood up as though to fight. "Huh!" he sniffed, miming a boxer. "*You're* cut off. No more of the big lumber for you."

"Cut it out," said Hershey. Almost forty, he was obsessed with the idea that most people only a few years younger than he spent all their time copulating and taking drugs, and he resented being on the wrong side of the cultural divide. It was widely known that Rosen, despite his diminutive size, possessed a sexual member of proportions that rejuvenated certain myths that most men tried to dispel through science and common sense. Talk of the "big lumber" and other references to Rosen's apparatus put Hershey into acute distress, and the cavalier manner with which Rosen and Hartman seemed to go in and out of conjugal harmony drove him to the edge of madness.

"Cut it out!" Hershey repeated, to no avail. Sex roles and related topics slowed conversational momentum, especially after Rayburn spoke of women's liberation among military children and of her son's pending vasectomy. Hershey became so frustrated that he lobbed a comment about journalism at Sternman. Sternman responded warily. His guard was up, and the two reporters circled each other in a discussion of ethics in big-time journalism.

It was well past midnight when Rayburn said she had to rush home to rescue her babysitter. She was tired anyway, and some stray tufts of hair seemed to be crawling out of the tunnel at the top of her beehive. The other players were pleased to gang up on her to stay for the traditional "last round," when the deal rotated once around the table with increasing frivolity and extravagant betting. The hosts had financed the game fairly well, since Woodruff was down over a hundred dollars and Howell about half that, with Rosen and Mantell the big winners. Positions were relatively the same near the end. Ziggy Rosen stood up for the entire last hand, chattering and shifting his weight nervously back and forth. Woodruff barked out the fall of the cards in an auctioneer's voice, and the revelry was such that players raised without looking at their hands. Hartman drew a round of boos when she folded, clutching her small stack of winnings. Rayburn happily shoved her winnings into the pot on a worthless hand, more or less as a sign of gratitude for the evening, and the other angatonists had a good time insulting and menacing each other over the final showdown. There was general shouting and laughter when Mantell nipped Woodruff and Hershey for the high hand with nothing more than a pair of kings, and there was loud protest when Howell won the low with a "sneaky hand." Playful recriminations went on as Woodruff cashed the outstanding chips and glumly wrote checks to nearly everyone at the table.

Rayburn had just left when a deafening kerplunk at the door hushed the commotion without an echo. Some feared the police, but Howell recognized the distinctive knock from the silver knob of an Austrian cherrywood cane. "It's Madame Delacroix," he whispered, with the resigned sigh of the often-punished. "Now I'm in for it." He called for silence and went to the door.

When angry, Madame Delacroix emitted a fiery mixture of French, German, and Hungarian. Howell understood none of these, nor, of course, the mixture, which was all he ever heard. As usual, Madame Delacroix placed her nose little more than her thin walking stick's width apart from Howell's and proceeded to back him once around the living room and then out the door and down the stairs to have a session with the superintendent, shrieking all the while.

During their absence, Mantell and Woodruff managed an exit and strolled over to the basement bar of a nearby restaurant for a drink. Mantell was buying. As a rattled man and the evening's heavy loser, Woodruff felt his tongue reaching for some dark amber bourbon, but, as Number fifty-three, he forced himself to order soft cider so the penicillin treatment could work on the affliction.

Mantell ordered a Scotch. "I don't see how you do it," she said. "Cider after a poker game like that? I'm impressed." She brushed her pigtails from behind her so that they would not get pinched between the booth and her back.

"Will power," Woodruff said truthfully, but shyly.

Mantell nodded and let her curiosity pass by in the quiet. "That was a pretty crazy poker game," she reflected. "Everybody seemed a little loco."

"Yeah," said Woodruff.

Mantell leaned forward. "Do you mind if I ask how you know LaLane?" she asked. "She's a friend of yours, not Ziggy's, right?"

"Well," said Woodruff. He paused and felt the lobes of his brain bumping against each other in protest of this assignment. "Well," Woodruff repeated, "I don't mind your asking, but actually I'd rather not talk about it if you don't mind."

"Wow," smiled Mantell. "Henry Woodruff. That's the first time I've ever heard you decline an invitation to discuss anything of potential significance."

Woodruff was staring at a small patch of Mantell's throat that seemed to be extraordinarily pale and delicate. "Some things have changed," he said sheepishly. "I guess you know."

"Yes," she said. "I'm sorry."

To Mantell, the newly discomfited Woodruff was more chemically attractive than the old, thinking Woodruff, who had seemed mature far beyond his years. She had always known that there was a mighty spark buried in him somewhere, but until now Woodruff's cares had been spread as thinly as all of humanity, polished and so unconflicted that no bulges or edges of pure Woodruff had shown through. Mantell, by virtue of her long labors in psychology, felt like the midwife to Woodruff's personality.

"I saw Casey today," she said.

Woodruff's eyebrows swelled noticeably, but he reined himself back to an expression of moderate interest. "Oh really?" he asked.

"Yes," she said, mildly annoyed at Woodruff's eyebrows. Woodruff was even more annoyed with Mantell for spoiling a reverie that was drifting lazily about her neck. Casey's name chased it away.

"What did she say?" he asked.

Mantell regretted her experiment with Casey, seeing that it had already taken possession of Woodruff's mind. "Oh, nothing unusual," she replied. "She gave me a summary of the facts, you know—when you separated, what movie you had gone to see, where you are staying, how surprising the separation was, that she doesn't expect it to last. Then she said something good about a pending amendment to the alimony laws in New York and went on. That was all."

"She said she didn't expect it to last, eh?" asked Woodruff, pouncing on the information.

"Yes," said Mantell.

"But she's also interested in the alimony laws," Woodruff said, with a flicker of amusement.

"Well, she's always been interested in alimony," said Mantell.

"I know," said Woodruff. Then he stared off.

"I didn't talk with her very much," said Mantell. "We just passed on the street, and I didn't exactly know what to say . . ."

". . . Because she's far too straight for you," Woodruff interrupted gently. "She's too organized and Waspy and coy for you and Sudsy. Even I know that, right?"

"Well, we are different," said Mantell.

"I know," said Woodruff.

Mantell spent a moment analyzing her impulse to apologize for something without mentioning Casey again, and then she shrugged, which Woodruff mistook for a sign that Mantell was securely indifferent to comparisons with Casey. This he admired.

"I'm sorry if I was too tough on you about the laundry," Mantell ventured, "even though I do think you are wrong to toy with women's issues. I mean you're a pig, but not hopeless."

"Thank you," said Woodruff. "No, I didn't think you were too rough on me. In fact, I wonder sometimes how you stay ahead of all your mean old allies and enemies, you're so nice."

"Nice?" Mantell bristled.

"Excuse me," smiled Woodruff. "I didn't mean to call you nice. You know what I mean."

"No, I don't," said Mantell. "Just what do you mean?"

"You're cruel," said Woodruff.

"You're vague," Mantell countered.

"Well," said Woodruff, "I mean that you don't seem to me to have that old killer instinct that the other leatherneck zealots on both sides have."

"Every movement in history has been attacked as a bunch of zealots," Mantell chided.

"I'm not attacking zealots," said Woodruff. "I'm just saying you don't *feel* like a zealot, that's all."

Mantell stared, figuring her angle of attack, and then abandoned the effort. "You get out of corners too easy," she said.

"I'd better," dodged Woodruff, "if I can get into one just by telling someone she's nice."

"I'll tell you a secret," said Mantell. "The only way I can run NWPC is that I'm not really that attached to the job. I could walk away from it, easy, like I walk away from everything else. So that makes me free enough to do all the outrageous things I have to do to draw attention to our issues. I mean I care, but I don't care with everything I've got, you see."

"What do you care about that way, then?" asked Woodruff.

Mantell smiled. "I won't tell you everything," she said. "But besides Marx, Freud, Laing, and Hannah Arendt . . ."

". . . I thought Freud was a bad guy," Woodruff interrupted.

"He is," said Mantell. "That's why I care about him."

"Oh," said Woodruff.

70

"Besides them," she continued, "I care about love, sex, friends, and babies, and a few other things."

"You can't say stuff like that," said Woodruff.

"I know," said Mantell. "Don't tell anybody I did, okay?"

Woodruff noticed that the white patch in the triangle of her throat was dusted now with color. His eyes lingered over the phenomenon while he longed desperately for a shot of bourbon to go with his risky new idea. "Uh, Valerie," he said finally, looking off to the side. "If you don't mind, I'd like to ask you about something that doesn't have anything to do with historical necessity or income distribution or anything like that. It's personal."

"Uh huh," said Mantell, trying not to be eager.

"It's about sex," said Woodruff. "I thought I might ask you because of your professional interest in these things and because of your, uh . . ."

"Experience," she prodded.

"Not exactly," Woodruff skittishly replied.

"Bullshit," laughed Mantell. "Whatever it is, you want to ask me because you know I've gone to bed with Paul and David and Ziggy—all your friends, every man in the poker game, except for you and Les."

"Well, now that you mention it . . ."

". . . Uh huh."

"Which one is the best lover?"

Mantell instantly looked grim, with a sharp line down her nose. "Come off it," she said. "Don't disappoint me."

"Sorry," said Woodruff. "I do wonder how it's so easy for you, though, because it has not been easy for me."

Mantell took a breath. "That's a long story," she said. "But some of it is that I value friends as deeply as anything I know, and part of me says that you can't really have a friend in somebody until you've been to bed with him. You don't really even *know* somebody until you've gone to bed with him, because so much is stored up there. I'm not freaking you out, am I? It's not that big a thing. I just think you've got to know that part to be friends. Sometimes there are big surprises and sometimes not. But otherwise, well, there's something too polite and blind and distant about friends, you know, like a big masquerade party. That's what I think, but I'm not sure.

"Uh huh," Woodruff nodded, struggling to appear casual and unintimidated.

"But that's not what you wanted to ask me about anyway, is it?"

"Well, no," Woodruff hesitated. He looked furtively around, sighed, and then plunged ahead. "You see I have this theory about sex," he began.

"I might have known," teased Mantell.

"I call it my hydraulic theory of the fundamental sexual difference between men and women," he declared, hunching forward confidentially. "The gist of it is this. Men continuously produce sperm in their testicles, where the sperm and the fluid they swim in are stored. Okay? And when that fluid builds up in there, it puts pressure—physical pressure—on the nerves connected to the pleasure centers inside the penis. As a result, the man feels a tingle or a sex drive or a horniness or whatever you want to call it." Woodruff paused, reminded suddenly of the gonorrhea buzz. He wondered where that might fit in.

"So?" asked a wide-eyed Mantell.

"Well, since this pressure buzz needs humanly to be relieved, the man will feel physically compelled to look for ways to do that—whether by love, masturbation, or socially undesirable acts. Now the significance here, as I see it, is that this compulsion is originally physical and in that sense does not arise from the psychology or the ideology or the political stance of the man. He can be innocently asleep, dreaming of daisies or outer space, but all the while those industrious testicles are cranking out the physical components of the fiendish urge he'll feel when he wakes up. Okay?

"Now, as a corollary, I postulate that the female body is such that women have no corresponding hydraulic pressure anywhere in their anatomy, and that, consequently, the female sex drive is not physical in origin. When you sleep, you don't have any little dairy workers inside you ladling mischief into your crotch, because, as I understand it, you have all your eggs ready to go when you are born. So the female sex drive comes not from plumbing but from, well, wherever it comes from—romance or the right man or patterned response or spontaneous combustion or whatever. In any case, if my male and female postulates are correct, it follows that the male and female sex drives are qualitatively different and that it is naturally difficult to strike a complementary balance between the relentless drives inside men and the more ethereal desires inside women. What do you think?"

Mantell ordered another Scotch to stall for time. "You haven't talked very much about this theory, have you?" she asked.

"Well, no," said Woodruff.

"Not even to Casey?"

"I haven't laid it out quite so bluntly, but I think I've mentioned most of the elements at one time or another."

Mantell's Scotch arrived, and she leaned gratefully over it to stifle the smile that her imagination produced as it pictured Henry and Casey going over elements of the hydraulic theory. "That's not a very romantic theory, Henry," she said. "I mean it's worse than a scientist. Off the record again, I've got to tell you that I've got old battle-axes on my board of directors who think of sex the way most people think of cockroaches, and they *still* have a more romantic view of sex than that. You've reduced it all to the sperm count."

"Well, something can feel romantic even if it originates in the body," Woodruff said defensively. "On where things start and first causes—things like that with people—we are back to the old mind-body problem, like Descartes. And that's tough. Actually, I'd be very satisfied if I could establish that all things arising out of sex are as difficult as the mind-body problem. I'd settle for that."

Mantell nodded. "Henry," she said gently, "it's a little dated, though. I think people have been saying that girls are more 'sensitive' for centuries."

72

Woodruff, lost in new thoughts, was paying no attention. "The old mind-body conundrum," he said. "That's not bad at all. Now in my case, I would say that the sex drive has definitely been physical, although I admit that I think about it a lot. With Casey, on the other hand, I would say it's mental in origin. Things have to be just right in her mind, you know, for the physical things to start happening. Although even then, I must say that I don't know a lot about it, because, well, I guess because it's not so observable. I'm not sure."

Noticing Woodruff's discomfort, Mantell uncrossed her legs and began rolling her hands over one another nervously, as though drying them. She was uneasy. "Let me ask you something else you might not want to talk about," she said. "Have you ever seen a woman physically turned on, to the point that there's no doubt she needs and wants an orgasm?"

Woodruff squirmed, having anticipated that Mantell would attack the hydraulic theory by asserting that men are responsible for their sexual urges, no matter how physical they are. "Well, I've seen an X-rated movie," he smiled.

"In real life?" Mantell persisted.

Woodruff thought of LaLane Rayburn, her smell of hand cream and her strange, fatigued moans of relief. His mind brushed over many years and he sighed. "Not really," he said. "I don't think so, anyway."

Mantell drained her Scotch, hiding her eyes and her surprise from Woodruff. "Believe me, women do have those physical urges," she said, without adding that she was experiencing one herself. As was her custom when fighting against it, she leaned imperceptibly from side to side in her chair to remind herself that she was sitting on not one but two buttocks, divided by what seemed like a column of air running through the very center of her to a place, not far beneath her navel, where tiny nerves were dancing in circles. She smiled at Woodruff, who was thinking.

"Maybe they do," he said skeptically, "but I don't think it happens in the same kind of regular, demanding way."

"Oh, come on," scoffed Mantell, though not as derisively as she might have.

"No, really," said Woodruff.

"Come on, Henry," she repeated. "Even a child knows that women's bodies do the same things as men's—their noses run and they burp and fart —but they are taught to do them in different ways. That's all."

"But sex is different," Woodruff protested.

"No, it isn't," said Mantell.

Again, Woodruff wasn't paying attention. After a long pause, he said, "You know, it is possible that a few times in the last ten years—maybe four or five—I've seen a woman, Casey, obviously, go into what seemed like spells or convulsions during sex, but they were so separate from her normal conduct and personality that I didn't know what to make of them. But I didn't think it was essentially part of her. It was like a ghost passed through her body in a hurry to someplace else."

"Wow," said Mantell. She was astonished that Woodruff's mind could be pawing so awkwardly at the nature of women, so basic and close to him, while that same mind could so convincingly portray states of mind far removed from him. In the abstract, his estimates of human nature usually seemed on the mark, untainted by quirks or distortions from his own life. Mantell wanted to believe that no one so ignorant of women could have much insight into people in general. This was a pet idea of hers, with which she had brain-whipped several male psychiatrists. Nevertheless, facing a man who seemed to reach extremes in both ignorance and perception, Mantell was fascinated and more than playfully attracted.

Woodruff mistook Mantell's exclamation as a show of admiration for his descriptive powers, and he leaned back with satisfaction. "Yes," he said, "those were amazing flashes, but they weren't connected to anything, so I don't believe they came out of any normal sex drive. At least I don't think so."

Woodruff's congratulatory air spoiled Mantell's appreciation. She adjusted her glasses by pushing them farther up her nose. "I see," she said. "You want a woman to lose control of herself and *be* herself at the same time, so you can decide . . ."

". . . Wait a minute," Woodruff interrupted, rather wounded that Mantell had lost her admiration so quickly. "I'm not talking about what I want. I'm talking about what I see."

"Maybe that's the problem," said Mantell, her amusement renewed.

"What do you mean by that?" asked Woodruff.

Mantell studied Woodruff's face, which had suddenly become so wholeheartedly inquisitive that it reminded her of David Howell. She rocked in her chair several times, becoming both tender and careful. "Do you think those convulsions Casey had were orgasms?" she asked softly.

Woodruff blushed. "You don't mess around, do you?"

Mantell shrugged. "Well, at least it's not a question about what you want," she said. "It's about what you think."

"Thanks," Woodruff said, and sighed. "Well, I don't think they were. I'm pretty sure they weren't. But I'm not absolutely sure."

"It's all right," Mantell comforted, rocking.

"Thank you," said Woodruff, grateful that she had treated his confession so respectfully. At the same time, he was irritated by his conversational predicament. "But what does it mean?" he asked, with an edge.

"Well," said Mantell, "it means that right now your expectations of women and your experience with women are temporarily out of line with reality, I guess."

"You mean I'm stupid and crazy," Woodruff said impatiently.

"No," said Mantell. "Not at all. You're all right. You're going to have fun, in fact. I just think you've got some things to resolve."

"*Resolve?*" Woodruff recoiled distastefully. "Resolve? Why is it that every psychologically oriented person I know wants to resolve everything? To me, that's like neutering people and draining all the energy out of them. I mean,

74

to me a person's personality is nothing more than what's not resolved about him, and all the rest is just sort of vegetable matter."

"*Understand*, then," said Mantell.

"That's better," said Woodruff. "I can still understand things, I hope. I'm pretty sure I can. Even women and marriage. It's only been a week since Casey and I split up, and already I've been bombarded by so much new experience that I feel a lot closer to being able to figure things out. A lot closer. I have this instinct that just one small tumbler needs to be clicked over and then everything will fall into place. And even if the hydraulic theory turns out to be way off, I can always modify it." Woodruff smiled at the conclusion of his bombast.

"It's a good thing you usually smile whenever you mention your theories," Mantell said. "Otherwise you'd be awful to be around."

"Thanks for reminding me," said Woodruff.

Mantell nodded blankly. She had stopped rocking as soon as she saw that Woodruff's condition would not admit of either instruction or sexual advance. She called for the check. "Henry," she cooed, "I think someone's going to have to give up on telling you these things about women and just show you. That's all. But right now I don't think you're fair game."

Woodruff's erotic imagination, such as it was, stumbled partway through an undressing of Mantell and then gave up. He was too tangled in thoughts of Casey and the clap. "I'm probably not game fare, either," he said.

"Probably not," said Mantell. "Well, that's all right, too."

After a perfunctory conversation on the marmalade habits of the Senate, where liberals were attempting to break a conservative filibuster of a bill saying that women are as good as men, Mantell and Woodruff parted on the sidewalk with an affectionate hug. He thanked her again for listening to him, and she apologized again for being too rough. Then she walked home wondering what his mother was like, and he walked to Howell's apartment debating whether Valerie Mantell represented an exciting breakthrough in the realm of women or merely an aberration, whose keen and physical interest in sexual matters could be understood without too much damage to the hydraulic theory.

Iv

CASEY TOOK a table under the magnolia tree in the Iron Gate's outdoor courtyard. Woodruff was late. The sun and the jitters conspired to bring Casey two rounds of vodka, and the alcohol made her dreamy. She felt like an emotional astronaut. She went into a reverie on the notion of paths—straight ones and crooked ones, through forests and nirvanas so enchanting that she was drifting through Persia when Woodruff appeared.

He was cursing Congress for gerrymandering the taxi zones, but otherwise she found him merry and self-assured. She had no way of knowing what pains Woodruff had taken to fortify himself for the occasion—telling himself, among other things, that the marital ordeal would enrich his experience "one way or the other"—and so she saw him the way she thought nature had made him, strong and generous with a roving wit.

Woodruff shooed away his taxicab worries and sat down with a flourish. "Good afternoon, counselor," he said, handing her a yellow rose. "I thought this might help take the edge off our drama, here."

Casey stared wordlessly, moved by the rose. Woodruff had scorned such trifles for so long that the rose in itself was a portentous offering.

"I know it's only a cheap sentiment," he grinned, "but I'll stoop to anything."

Casey looked down and up several times, her eyes filled with tears and admiration. There was an element of sad nostalgia in her emotion, but Woodruff touched her deeply when he was being at all formal.

"Well," he said, backing away from her open display, "even though you haven't said anything so far, I consider the hello a success." He offered a toast with his water glass.

"I do, too," she replied, and drank.

"Good," he smiled. "So I guess I can go on with the news." And with that he initiated a series of tales. He told of aspects of life with David Howell, a touching story about a senator who held hands with his wife on his first day in the Senate chamber. He told of a New Mexico senator who had his likeness superimposed on a photograph of Venus and mailed out to every science teacher in the state as educational material, and of a senator who joked in the cloakroom that his bill to export Virginia tobacco to Africa was appropriate because "their lungs are already black." ("Virginia statesmanship has gone downhill since 1824," Woodruff sighed.) He also sketched his new theory that self-doubt had begun to eat away at the entire establishment. It would be a sad state of affairs indeed, he predicted, if the trend in Washington continued toward economists and away from lawyers, for economists cannot be proven crooked and they live, by training, apart from any instinctive sense of values.

Woodruff enjoyed himself immensely and kept a twinkle in his eye while saying all this and more, and he did so without eating a single one of his stuffed grape leaves even though he felt ravenously hungry. He adopted abstinence as a means of controlling his appetites, including the passion for Casey that was now under examination. Casey, for her part, ate all her grape leaves and most of Woodruff's even though she was not hungry. She was actually rather nauseated, but she hoped the food might catch up with the vodka at first. Then the eating took on its own inertia as she listened, and she ordered a slice of baklava, which she cut meticulously into small perfect squares, extracting each one as painstakingly as an archeologist numbers the bricks in an ancient temple. This process annoyed Woodruff, as neatness and finery on her part always did, but the annoyance itself helped him keep clear of the emotional undertow so that he could be expansive and entertaining on a wide variety of subjects. His familiar zest made Casey feel all the more guilty and wounded. She controlled her sadness only by channeling more of her attention into carving the baklava.

When Woodruff paused, largely out of fatigue, and said, "I am sorry. I really don't know what the point of all this is except that I want to avoid our business here. How are you, anyway?" Casey was more than unprepared. Water rushed into her eyes and she said, "Oooh, I don't know. I think I've been horrible."

Woodruff was struggling to remain aloof. "I'll bet," he laughed. "I know you. You've been getting up every morning and doing things every day, much better than I have. I've just been staring at the *Congressional Record* every day and talking to Howell all night."

"I don't mean the chores and the clients," she sighed. "I mean I feel like a horrible person. A completely horrible and awful person."

"Oh, come on," Woodruff pleaded. He felt himself losing ground. "Would it help any if I told you it doesn't matter to me a bit that you've been having an affair?"

Casey didn't say anything. " 'Cause it doesn't," he said. "After all, I encouraged you to have one, if it would help, so it wouldn't be fair, would it?"

Casey felt muted. She knew her eyes would make Woodruff keep talking, and she was glad she couldn't help it.

"I'd just like to know who it is," Woodruff said softly. "I'm curious."

"Richard Clayfield," she whispered.

"Who?"

"Richard Clayfield," she whispered again. Casey drew a breath to begin a biographical description of Clayfield, Woodruff's college classmate, but it caught somewhere in her throat. She clutched, as she always said, and quietly watched a dumbstruck Woodruff close his eyes.

He rocked back and forth several times and tried once again to see. His field of vision seemed to back away from him like a movie screen and then dissolve inward from the edges until all he could see were Casey's new earrings and a thin band of her neck. "Richard Clayfield?" moaned Woodruff, still rocking. "My God, Casey! He's a pasty bureaucrat! He has the moral steadiness of a wind sock!"

Casey could tell that Woodruff's disbelief was giving way to shock. His insults to Clayfield dried her tears. "He's very nice to me, Henry," she said. "I know you disagree with his views."

Casey's defense of Clayfield struck Woodruff squarely in the face. "His *views!*" he gasped. "I'm talking about what he *is*, not what he thinks. Christ, you and I both know how he made his way up in the State Department by currying favor with the hawks during the war. Then, just in time, he made a few remarks about how the war was misguided and mishandled. He told you and me to our faces that he was going to lay low in safe jobs like the United Nations Review Committee until the heat blew over. And now he's back. He's written four or five articles in the last six months in the foreign policy journals, with titles like 'The Dynamics of Detente' and 'Multilateralism: The Policymaker's Temptation.' He's doing a job flutter at this very moment, and it's all according to plan."

"Henry, this is personal, not political," Casey said quietly.

"He'll probably be president," he said without hearing her. He was lost in sarcasm.

"It's personal," she repeated.

"I *know* it's personal," Woodruff whined. "To have a foreign-policy type in bed with your wife—that's *very* personal."

The word "wife" set off tremors within Casey's traditional conscience. Her lip quivered. "I *am* your wife," she said. "And I'm very sorry about this. I don't really think this has very much to do with Richard. It's really about us."

"Of all people," Woodruff whispered, rubbing his face with both hands to cool his burning skin. "You really know how to hurt a guy. I never would have suspected him. How long has this been going on?"

"A few months," said Casey.

Woodruff intensified his rubbing, and Casey grew more miserable as she watched him. She could feel his demanding spirit all over her now—on her neck and her face, behind her, everywhere—as all pretense of refinement and decorum were lost. Woodruff appeared to her as needy now as he had been generous some moments before. Casey escaped to the bathroom and

78

peed with all her might, but Woodruff was still rubbing his face when she returned. The lower half of her body felt his eyes as she walked back to the table.

"Oh boy," he said, feigning a smile. "I don't see how I'm going to be able to talk to anybody about this, and I need to. I mean Clayfield is a philosophical embarrassment." He paused, looking old. "But I guess that's not the point, is it? What is it like to be in bed with him?"

"Oh, please," said Casey, drawing back from his urgency.

"I want to know," Woodruff said.

Casey sensed him hardening slightly, and to her this lessened the pressure. She stared at the tablecloth, and her skin offered confirmation: there was less intensity from Woodruff's eyes. Casey felt her insides rush to pull him back, to please him and to communicate with the part of him that listened and talked and held out wisdom to lean on. She realized that her suppressed memories of sex with Richard felt distant and clinical for the first time, and this brought her a streak of elation. "You would be proud of me," she told Henry with a heartfelt gaze. "I think up things to do all the time, and I surprise him and make him do things he's never done before. And I've even tried to do it backward."

As he heard the words, Woodruff threw his chin back like a fighter taking an uppercut, and only his defensive reserves allowed him to mask this move as a professional gesture—head back, looking at the sky, lost in thought while taking it all in. The birth of this fresh, girlish enthusiasm within her arrived at Woodruff's mind with the force of a totem, and the longing he felt to have been the cause of it came from unknown recesses inside him. Yet he had no doubt that she was devout in her wish that the birth would please him.

"But I'm not very good at it," Casey said demurely.

Henry, his head tilted back, exhaled thoughtfully through his nose. "I see," he said. "Well, that certainly is new, isn't it? I guess it's a breakthrough for you."

"I guess so," said Casey. "It could be a breakthrough for both of us." She studied Henry's face closely to see whether his urgent feelings were evaporating or merely being held at bay. When Woodruff was like this—hanging between strength and surrender—she discovered she could talk to him because he would listen, but she had to be careful. It was then that she could least bear to hurt him.

"Tell me more," he said. "This is all new information to me, you know. I'd like to hear the details."

"Oh, Henry," said Casey.

"No, really," he insisted. "Go ahead. How can you tell it's really so different from sex with someone like, well, take me, for example? What is the sign?" He flexed his left bicep and posed with an impish grin. "Go ahead," he coaxed. "I'm tough as nails. It won't hurt a bit."

"Oh, Henry," laughed Casey, who decided then that he could surmount anything. "Well, for one thing," she said, leaning forward, "even when I'm in the office, my pants get wet whenever I hear his voice on the telephone. It's like I'm sitting on a sponge." This phenomenon, being unexpected, had indeed amazed Casey more than her first period, and she gave Woodruff a shrug of puzzled wonder.

Woodruff wallowed in the sexiness of the pert shrug. It was all he could do not to send a baleful howl up through the magnolia blossoms. "Uh huh," he said instead. "Are you sure this is the same Richard Clayfield who does this? What does he say that causes it, anyway? Does he talk about policy components?"

Casey laughed. "It's not what he says," she quipped. "You know that."

"I guess I do," Henry replied doubtfully. "I guess I do." He looked away from her, out through the restaurant courtyard over shanks of lamb and plates of houmous, past political conversations about the correct position to take and what followed from the analysis. He was proud of himself for absorbing all these revelations without coming unglued.

"Whew," he said, blinking at Casey. "That's enough details for right now, I guess. I'm gonna have to think on this, if you don't mind. What else do you have to confess?"

Woodruff eased down into the sweet pain. When it dawned on him that Casey had stopped talking and was watching him in silent distress, he said, "I'm sorry." Then he looked sideways to keep from choking and said, "I just think this is so sad, that's all. I'd do anything to keep it from happening."

Casey was too numb to say anything, and, as always in such situations, she covered her muteness with a look of rapt innocence. This very expression of hers had been heavily criticized by feminists and razor-psyched observers as an instrument of reactionary southern wiles, but it worked, nonetheless, on Woodruff who, realizing his peril, tried to meet the emergency by disguising his breakdown as an act of moral remorse. "I don't know," he said. "I guess a lot of it is that I've got my own confession to make." And he told her at great length of his evening with LaLane Rayburn, stressing his anguish and the environmental factors in his mind while minimizing his subsequent difficulties. Casey remained numb through all this, too, though her mind was sorting through the implications of the gonorrhea for her new physical liaison with Richard Clayfield. She laughed continuously at Woodruff's descriptions of his own squeamishness, throwing in several admiring, "Oh, Henry's," and this encouraged the narrator to take her through the gonorrhea tale. He was pleasantly surprised that she showed no signs of revulsion. They held hands across the table and remarked on the new kind of intimacy they were discovering, fashioned of brokenness. On the other hand, Woodruff felt depressed by Casey's open welcome for Rayburn. After fishing unsuccessfully for the slightest hint of jealousy on Casey's part toward Rayburn, he lapsed back into his cuckolded stupor. Almost murmuring, he compared Clayfield unfavorably to Rayburn and then fell silent.

"Well, what do we do now?" he asked wearily some moments later.

"I think I need more time," Casey replied after much hesitation. She soon left with her yellow rose. Woodruff felt sorry for himself and he watched her glide down N Street, her stationary torso cutting through the air like a peacock while her behind twitched friskily from side to side. The sound of her heels echoed off the brownstones on either side of the quaint Victorian block, and every so often she stamped her foot down to make an extra loud report, which Henry took to come from anger over the danger to their marriage. He did not think Casey might be reprimanding herself for eating so many grape leaves. Following in her perfume, Woodruff went straight to the Burger Chef and gobbled down some fried cardboard and cheese.

Over the next several months, nine negotiating lunches took place, including one through which Henry Woodruff remained aloof, charming, and analytical—without a single weak spot in his debonair comportment—as a result of careful planning and iron will. Unfortunately, this was the same lunch at which Casey had resolved to discuss the laundry question at all costs, so the conversation was steadfastly comical. Woodruff would offer a refinement on his theory that judges were behaving more and more like politicians, and Casey would respond with an ardent query about the various ways to measure the relative worth of peoples' time, especially that spent in laundromats. She went away from this lunch thankful that there had been no disastrous "scene" for once, but convinced that Woodruff would make a vexatious friend, while Woodruff, despite the attainment of his short-term goal, worked himself into a fury over the idea that Casey's hope was for him to put a cork in his head and pass politely around the garden.

He opened the next lunch with a fiery speech about how passion and romance could not be "shoved under the rug," as they were the objects of the negotiations, and how talk was wonderful and all that, but not if he felt constrained to avoid mentioning his deepest feelings, such as the laserlike erotic beam of poetry in his heart. Casey admired the overheated lyricism, but she drew back in fear from Woodruff's ferocious advance, whereupon his ardor melted into an abject plea, which caused her to cry silently and ask for more time, which in due course made Woodruff sullen. Such alternating bursts were the pattern of the lunches. David Howell, who had to put up with endless descriptions of these affairs, remarked that their emotions skated in rigidly parallel figure eights.

Ironically, one of the few subjects that produced stable conversation was Casey's romance with Richard Clayfield. It was an intimate subject of mutual concern, and pain kept Woodruff's emotions subdued enough so that Casey could both enjoy the words and take hope from them. Woodruff sought to prove himself selfless, and Casey was able to thank him for this without precipitating a crisis. Besides, she had no other willing source of advice on a critical problem, namely, that Clayfield had refused to see her since learning of the tumultuous events in her home. He explained that he was under consideration for an appointment as deputy assistant secretary of state for policy planning, and that it would be most untoward of him to be seen squiring around a recently separated women. He also declined Casey's offer to continue only their furtive romantic interludes at his apartment, from which Casey inferred that the gonorrhea had upset him deeply. It was not only personally offensive to him, as a proper Bostonian, but it was also a security risk for someone in his position. Instead of seeking treatment from his own Washington doctor, she knew, he had arranged to have himself added to a petroleum fact-finding team that visited, among other places, Guadalajara, where Clayfield slipped off to see a doctor.

Woodruff, after one of his nightly revelations, advised Casey to pursue her affair with Clayfield to its natural conclusion, which he presumed would be a bad one. He kept up a soldierly resolve. He cursed Clayfield's cowardly delays along with Casey. Then, when Clayfield finally resumed sexual liaison, he managed to counsel patience. He punished himself by playing coach through her hard times, and he punished Casey by doing so with analytical detachment, being constantly preoccupied with related questions of fact, such as who had given gonorrhea to whom.

This was now a full-fledged mystery. Woodruff cross-examined Casey on her report that neither she nor Clayfield had tested positive for venereal disease, though both had received precautionary treatments. "I'm the only one who seems to have anything," observed a perplexed Woodruff. "So there sure is a hell of a lot of penicillin going around for nothing." He felt stymied by the puzzle, and also by the larger romantic one. The confusion went on for months after the separation through "the first stage of idiocy," as he would later call it. Day and night he told himself obsessively that everything was okay, but every morning he awoke with a fresh scheme for reconciliation or revenge—sometimes for both at once.

During this time, Casey planted more than five hundred autumn bulbs in her tiny front yard. She ruined a dozen pairs of stockings by kicking off her shoes right after work and marching outside with an apron, a trowel, and a sack of bulbs. On weekends, she dug all day, dressed in jeans with a red bandana tied neatly in her hair. She caressed each bulb before placing it in the ground, which seemed cold despite the oppressive heat in the air. After dark, she wrote voluminously in her Album. She wrote poems and songs and what she called silly thoughts that were important only to her. She made and revised lists of Henry's good points against Richard's, which always came out overwhelmingly in Henry's favor except for two items in the Clayfield column—"likes ordinary things" and "the way he touches me."

Mantell spent many late evenings with David Howell, shaking her head with him over the trials of the Woodruffs. Howell teased her about her lack of solidarity with Casey. She said that Henry was more "interesting" a case, because Casey could be so easily wrapped up as a southern belle. Howell, the go-between, would demur. Casey was "too easily" classified, he said, citing quirks and strengths outside the stereotype. Initially, Mantell leaned toward the belief that Henry, while a WASP, was "too Jewish" for Casey, as evidenced by his intellectual and guilt-ridden approach to sex. Howell laughed at such ideas, asking Mantell if she found intellectualized sex to be stimulating. Mantell, inferring from this that Howell was accusing her of being after Woodruff, would push her glasses down on her nose and quip that she only wanted to teach him a thing or two. From there, she usually retreated into more abstruse explanations of Woodruff, having to do with fixations in his fantasy life.

Every month or so during such expositions, Howell would explore her eyes for the sign of assent, which was usually nothing more than a glance returned with a flicker of pleasure, and then wordlessly, they would join hands and walk into the bedroom of her apartment or his. Eyes locked, they would undress silently on opposite sides of the bed and then crawl in with a gingerly caution, like puppies meeting on a strange lawn. They almost never kissed. Howell burrowed playfully under her pigtails, while she dived through his frizz to bite him about the neck and ears. After a mutually ferocious hug, they dissipated their troubles into each other's bodies. Mantell explained her tears by joking that she was too busy to make love enough. During the peace, Howell often murmured his only complaint against life in general—that the magic of it came in bits too small to trust or rest upon. This was one of the few things he ever said seriously. Mantell would say she understood, though she did not like talk of magic, and with that the two of them would whisper and rub each other for several hours toward dawn, saying more than once that they were the best of friends.

Howell had even more professional problems than usual after the publication of his article, "Jealousy in Black and White," on the competitive pettiness that shaped scandal coverage at the *Washington Post* and the *New York Times* and thence for the nation at large. "The papers do not exhibit the kind of competition that makes a good basketball league or an efficient pin factory," Howell had written. "It is more like the competition that moved the Yankee General McClellan to let Yankee General Pope's men get slaughtered rather than risking his own reputation to rescue an expedition for which Pope would get the credit. This is the kind of delicious fight for which the heavyweight journalists will get out their knives." Howell himself got sliced up badly. Lester Hershey of the *Times* "did a woodpecker" on him, yelling that Howell's criticism betrayed causes they shared by undermining his credibility. Hershey would remember this "devious backstabbing" twenty years later in a reminiscence. Paul Sternman was low-key. He summoned Howell to his cubicle at the *Post* and pointed to six interpretive passages in the article, two of which made light of him. They were circled in red. In a soft voice, which could nevertheless pave highways, Sternman declared that Howell was dead wrong on each one and challenged him to defend himself. It was Sternman's war voice, by which he communicated that he and the thunder would hold that ground for thirty years, if necessary. Howell shrugged and backed down, as he had with Hershey. Howell, while bold and irreverent in print, tended to avoid personal conflicts by sitting on his opinions—as he had done literally on the night of the poker game.

Henry Woodruff enjoyed the controversy immensely, perhaps because it was the only one near him that did not put him on the defensive. He congratulated his new roommate for contrasting the journalistic motivations of Sternman and Hershey in a way that would match their attacks on the article itself. Hershey found things immoral and therefore incorrect, Howell had written, whereas Sternman found them incorrect and therefore immoral. Woodruff twitted the reporters on this point. But he reminded Howell that he had broken three of Woodruff's Laws for Behavior in the Capital: (1) Do not criticize friends in public, except by prearrangement; (2) If you must criticize friends, make sure they are not journalists; (3) Avoid "monkeyisms." By monkeyisms, he meant descriptions of human behavior by animal metaphors. Woodruff believed such expressions, to which Howell was drawn, would consistently annoy those in the capital who labored to confer an expanded zone of dignity upon their activities through the language of policy. This included nearly everyone, said Woodruff, even Howell himself.

As the sponsor of such laws, Woodruff was more than chagrined when he paid dearly for a monkeyism of his own, which he could only excuse as the temporary lapse of a mind jarred by marital separation. He had endured much during the first three months of his relocation at Howell's. A lamp fell on his head when he was asleep. Twice he rolled off the narrow couch while dreaming of Spanish knives and roses. Inadvertently, he dyed all his underclothes a light orange by putting them in the wash with one of Howell's new T-shirts, and he met disaster when trying to duplicate Howell's incredible feat of catching a tossed raw egg deftly between the lips.

Such adjustments, on top of his new personal worries, wore Woodruff's stamina so thin that he decided to curtail his Senate duties for the first time in his career. Although he still worked an average of twelve hours a day, he abandoned the grueling work of rewriting the entire tax code for lighter projects that he thought would generate less stress. In one of them he collaborated with a staff member of the Government Operations Committee, who also worked for Woodruff's boss, to interview people who had written "dissent" letters about the Army Reserves and the National Guard. Their testimony, in Oklahoma dust-talk and in Vermont lock-palate, was filled with monkeyisms. One soldier said the members of his unit spent all their time "sunning themselves" on weekends. "We graze, that's what we do," drawled a major in the National Guard. "We get there in our uniforms and divide up into units. One unit feeds everybody. One unit processes everybody. One unit pays everybody. One unit makes announcements to everybody. The bulls play cards and supervise, and anybody left over swats flies." There was talk of weekend generals who like to drive jeeps fast and "zoom around in the planes like flying squirrels."

Woodruff found such testimony so candid that he included about thirty similar quotations in a memorandum for the boss on the auxiliary services. "Since the Reserves and National Guard escaped active duty throughout an entire decade of bloody, continuous war, and were instead precisely the places where well-connected men like myself went to *avoid* war," Woodruff wrote, "the wisdom of their very existence should be brought into doubt. The funds spent directly on these militarily frivolous activities over those ten years—quite apart from the enormous pension obligations incurred against the future—could have more than paid the federal share of all welfare expenditures or retired more than a third of the national debt, depending on one's political point of view." Woodruff wrote no monkeyisms of his own, but he knew, or should have known, that the document as a whole was tainted with that offense.

The memo leaked promptly over to the Armed Services Committee and up to its chairman, who would have paid no attention to such a trifle except for the monkeyisms, which were offensive to him as an honorary colonel in the National Guard. He mentioned his hurt feelings to Woodruff's boss, adding that no senator who could conceive of running for president should allow himself to appear as the addressee on such politically suicidal documents. This touched the boss deeply, and he soon announced his support for the chairman's plan to "strengthen the posture" of the auxiliary services against the potential threat posed by the recent international tensions. Plans at the Government Operations Committee for an exploratory investigation into military territory were canceled in the face of the chairman's prickly mood. Aides there heaped scorn on Woodruff's name. In general, Senate staff members agreed sympathetically with Woodruff to his face, but they sighed among themselves about how he couldn't get things done anymore. Woodruff's telephone lost its reach, as the secretaries of the people he tried to call were instructed to fend him off with lies.

He commiserated over several lunches with LaLane Rayburn, once getting so drunk together on the house wine that neither of them could figure the tip without assistance. Rayburn cradled Woodruff's despair by telling him of her own recent troubles with the military. She had been busy. Two weeks earlier, on the eighth anniversary of her husband's disappearance, she and her family minister in Corpus Christi held a burial ceremony over a plaque in the cemetery grass, reading: "To the memory of Lt. Col. Robert Maxwell Rayburn, U.S.A.F., born April 9, 1928, who died in loyal service to his government." The ceremony itself and almost every word of the inscription sparked a venomous controversy. Rayburn, who preferred to think that her husband died when his plane went down, used his rank of that date in spite of heavy pressure to use colonel, the rank to which he had been promoted while MIA. Some of her former in-laws berated her for giving up hope, others for reminding them of their grief. Not a single military wife attended the ceremony, though three of their old Air Force buddies did, earning her gratitude. There were fights about the words "died" and "government," and about why Rayburn refused to add, "Only the enemy knows," as many felt was imperative. Pentagon officials were nervous about their decision to grant Rayburn KIA status instead of the compromise, "Missing, and Presumed Dead," which carries a slightly different legal and financial status. Everything about the ceremony was unpleasant to everyone except Rayburn herself, who welcomed the finality of a stone.

Part of the officer corps around the Pentagon actually welcomed Rayburn's attempt to "stop moaning" and "forget about the one we didn't win." Some of them also shared her low opinion of the war. Still, she was a radioactive personality in military circles, which extend into unexpected spheres. Shortly after landing a job with the Washington Conference Board, Rayburn's name was recognized by two retired colonels on the board of directors. They had a talk with members of the Conference Board management, some of whom agreed to screen Rayburn's clients lest she be assigned to someone who considered her controversial. The people at the office became nervous around her. "I was in trouble before I even found out what the Conference Board does," sighed Rayburn, who told Woodruff that the peacetime military is the most skittish bureaucracy of all. She also told Woodruff that he looked terrible—pale, lost, unkempt, sexually ambivalent —"just the way my daddy always described the communists." She urged him to take a vacation. He would be useless to the taxpayers for a least a month anyway, she predicted, while the National Guard scrape was receding from the mindscans of his fellow Senate functionaries. The more Rayburn talked about a vacation for Woodruff, the better an idea it seemed to her and the more she believed that he was incapable of deciding things for himself. So she drew him up a list of "odd people" she knew in south Texas, made him a plane reservation, and saw to it that Howell delivered Woodruff to the airport on time.

From the moment the capital's lights faded beneath his plane, Woodruff considered himself disoriented, as though in flight from one reality to another, in a phantasmagoria of sight and sound that complemented his inner migrations over Casey. The huge jet rolled confidently up to the gates of the Houston Intercontinental Airport, the galactic headquarters of rawhide and shiny engines. On the ramps, Woodruff confronted people with the appearance of a different species. In contrast to Washington, where people dress inconspicuously so as not to distract from their mental qualifications, the people there favored bright colors, full pants, full wallets, proud flesh, and chests thrust forward with the assurance of those covering familiar ground —an instant blend of California and Dixie. To Woodruff, it was a blur, which lost its noise but not its wonder as he drove his rented car over the peach-colored ground down the Gulf Coast to Corpus Christi. There, from Rayburn's list, he met a loquacious white-haired old man who ran the yacht club as though he were still in command of his navy frigate, dressing in his whites for two crisp flag ceremonies a day; and he also met a clear-faced priest who followed God's calling to the goal of a mixed parish equally made up of whites and Chicanos, which caused many weak spirits to keep their tithes for the devil; and out in the country there was a regular old couple who said howdy to Woodruff and spoke with a remarkably even dramatic pulse about subjects like Franklin D. Roosevelt, food, bank robberies, ration lines, and beer-drinking teenagers who hold target practice along the Nueces River. Back in town, Woodruff stood over Lieutenant Colonel Rayburn's white marble marker, where he sensed a surpassing frustration from angers robbed of their proper end. Within earshot of the marker, he masturbated that night in a motel room, accompanied by a plaintive country song on the radio.

David Howell's apartment was empty when Woodruff walked in three weeks later. He found only a note, anchored to the table by a jar of peanut butter, which read: "Gone south myself. Ask Ziggy for details. Love. David. P.S. Casey says she loves you like biscuits but wonders 'how much is really there.' National Guard still hates you a lot." All Woodruff could learn from Ziggy Rosen was that Howell had left for Miami in a hurry, on the promise of free lodging there with one of Rosen's rich and exotic friends, and that the departure had something to do with the wrath of Howell's two bosses, Marner and Drake.

Marner, junior coowner of *Washington* magazine, was the aristocrat of an unlikely tandem. At Harvard in the early 1950s, planning to be a banker, he volunteered for a series of experiments with new psychoactive drugs, and while under the influence of one of them, it was revealed to him that he hated his father for many slights and injuries, among them for having sent young Marner to Harvard. It was also revealed that he hated Harvard, he wrote then, "for being the rank apotheosis of the worst aspects of both feudalism and communism, of idle privilege combined with the presumption to speak for the masses, of qualified truth and unfettered hypocrisy, of such flabby arrogance that the few whole men of Harvard are destined to fail in its eyes."

Marner then tried to fail. He dropped out of banking, out of stockbrokering, and out of an oil company, convinced more than ever that his father and his fellow executives were frauds, and cads to boot. He bummed around as an "adventurer" and then for two years as a "sportsman," the avocation most loathed by his New England family, which considered sportsmen nothing more than gamblers. But Marner never cured himself of his favorite pleasure—denouncing his peers and his father's peers—and he created *Washington* magazine to do precisely that. He had the time of his life and achieved a reputation for literary flair, having honed the Harvard ornaments off his prose. He did not consider the job a violation of his philosophy, since the magazine was perpetually on the edge of failure. He never tired of pacing his office, an excited grin on his face, exhorting writers to "hold 'em up to public scorn and ridicule!" Such was his anthem and delight, which he embellished with trenchant witticisms.

His plebeian partner, Drake, was a foot shorter, bald, and more thready and rumpled. Drake's father had attempted to surmount his inherited life in the coal mines by marrying the leading actress in a troupe of Bennington seniors who were doing political penance on a summer tour in West Virginia. She described the elder Drake to her friends in New York as an "authentic Appalachian" at first, but their life together had matured into a romance that overcame all incompatibilities. She provided the dreams and he the concrete purpose. He breathed coal dust all week while she did political dramas for coal children, eluding company-owned sheriffs, and then on weekends they gave speeches together for the union.

Their son, young Drake, remembered tear-filled rallies and funerals and marches and mountain meetings at which his beautiful mother would recite John L. Lewis speeches to mining families, and he remembered being lifted by his father into the arms of Eleanor Roosevelt, who looked to him like a kindly camel. As she cuddled him, the godlike raspy voice of Franklin D. Roosevelt himself praised the Drake parents for helping to uplift the entire human race, and in the great supplication of common hope and emotion little Drake's small chest burst like a swelled grape and he felt a happiness that he would never forget.

Many neighbors were astonished that his idealism never soured, even after the double tragedy thirteen years later, in 1949, when his father died and his mother ran away in disgrace. They said the father died of black lung, but young Drake knew that the immediate cause was humiliation. The father had just confessed that he had secretly hocked their house and meager savings to invest in a millionaire con man's promise to win him a share of the "unclaimed inheritance" of his sixteenth-century "namesake," Sir Francis Drake, which was said to run "way up in the billions." No longer able to hide the fact that he had been swindled, Drake loosed his shame and died. Six months later, the mayor of Huntington, West Virginia, accused Mrs. Drake of "unholy fornication" with his political enemy—the local strip mine president, an Ivy Leaguer and the union's archfoe. Some said her "rich blood had finally won out," and others said she was only trying to convert the mine owner. After begging her son to believe that it was platonic and telling him that he could never understand, she put him in the local university and ran off to New York. She dodged his pleas for a visit and communicated with her son primarily by money order. The younger Drake never felt secure in his knowledge of the past, but that did not diminish his visionary calling to rid the world of con men and corrupt officials. He found plenty of both as a young civil servant in Washington, where his patriotic sermons and soliloquies frightened every partygoer in town except the transient sportsman Marner, who hated all great wealth as ill-gotten, but nevertheless wore a gold watch chain and spoke of huge sums as "small money." The two took an immediate dislike to each other. They shared little except eccentricity and a prophet's nose for rottenness. Still, they joined forces because they were bright enough to know that the capital would scarcely support even one publication that derided all its grandeur and social distinctions.

Many writers served them over the years, but none as well as David Howell, whose monumental good humor bridged the chasm between Marner and Drake more than anyone had ever seen it bridged. Howell thought kindly of people because it was more fun that way, a trait that brought him a heavy load of slackers and leeches. He arrived fresh from two Peace Corps years in Kenya among the Tugen tribe and the meat of his home-grown hares, and while his mind was reeling from the contrasting opulence of lights and alarm clocks and two-income angst and strident demands for more, he landed a job between the two maniacs who plastered their desks against opposite walls of the *Washington* magazine's offices so as to avert a raving war.

Within a month, Howell devised an arrangement that allowed Marner and Drake to extend their partnership another ten years. It was simple: the first nine-tenths of any article would belong exclusively to Marner, the last tenth to Drake. The verbal Marner whooped and railed like a sophisticated hyena, laughing, screaming, calling for more entertainment, more puncture wounds, more clowns and fools and rogues, and Howell's satirical whimsy satisfied him, though he found his tone too lenient. Then Howell would take the draft to Drake, who scanned the recorded antics of vagabonds and pretenders in the sandbox of public affairs, and thought with his pudgy fingertips pressed to his cheeks until the spirit of Roosevelt's communion with the miners bubbled up from his soul and he saw clearly again how the problem called for nothing more than a broadbased transformation of human character. Then Drake would erupt into his famous "rain dance," an evangelical fit in which he analyzed and kneaded and moaned over the situation until by the very intensity of his passion one saw that yes, hallelujah, we can wipe out greed and timidity and cultural blindness and status-mongering among the citizens. Howell, always nonplussed by the performance, would go to his typewriter and translate it into a lightly eloquent expression of what ought to be, which satisfied Drake, though he was nagged slightly by the lack of urgency.

The arrangement went sadly awry after the article on Paul Sternman and Lester Hershey, as Howell should have known it would. His position was hopeless, boxed in among four proud foxes from the touchiest and least criticized of political professions. Even before the article, Marner and Sternman held each other in icy, patrician contempt. Sternman had been known to remark that Marner's flashy wit was an elaborate cover for a shielded life that amounted to failure, and Marner called Sternman "a nouveau tweed, masquerading as a thinker after treating his suckers to a Hawaiian tour of scandal." Drake's relations with Hershey were more roly poly, less cordial on the surface.

Marner demanded even more of a whiplash attack than usual against Sternman, but Howell delivered less—protesting that the reporters were, after all, his poker partners. For this, Marner abused him as a coward and buried darts deep into the brick behind his corkboard target photo of McGeorge Bundy. Drake, for his part, demanded the most sober and heartrending of conclusions—he called the article a chance in a lifetime—for he considered the national press to be the catalyst, if not the instrument, of his political gospel. He sent Howell back for ten post-rain dance versions of the ending, but they were all milky because Howell knew the reporters too well to call for any sort of conversion. It was too embarrassing.

So the article infuriated Howell's bosses. Drake brooded for two months before concluding that it was his duty to call Hershey on the phone and tell him that the article was "too soft," that Hershey had "to work up the guts to face" his own limitations, especially the fact that he was "too obsessed with making it" to put aside his petty selfish concerns for the good of the country. All this came spilling out of Drake rather incoherently, for he had worked himself up quite a bit for the call. After a passing show of good form, Hershey threw himself into a swirling telephone dogfight. The call confirmed his suspicions that he was "the real target" of the scurrilous attack, not Sternman, who was merely "the pretty face behind the image." He accused Drake of spending twenty years at "toiletpaper backbiting" that was "less important than a weather forecast." He had to stand up to deliver the woodpeckering, his body quivering with indignation, and finally he threw his entire telephone set across the newsroom of the *Times* bureau and scared the economic columnist, who was calling on the nation to moderate its expectations. This occurred two days after Woodruff had left for Texas.

All these enmities and many more found their way back to Howell. He was fleeing to Miami, really, although he had enough story leads to justify a long working trip. On the plane, he realized that it was the first time he had been out of the capital more than five days since returning from Africa, four years earlier. Ziggy Rosen had warned him to be prepared for anything from a most unusual host, but Howell looked forward to the diversion.

Shortly before noon on a Monday, a Cuban cab driver ferried Howell down an elegant Miami Beach street on the shore of Biscayne Bay. He found himself standing in the courtyard of what seemed to be a miniature version of the Taj Mahal, Spanish style—a white castle of spires and turrets and keyhole windows, with a terra cotta roof, surrounded by an eight-foot wall. He was in the first courtyard, along with half a dozen parked cars and a huge Indian banyan tree. Its bark was smooth, a few shades darker than a winter beech, and its thick limbs dropped four auxiliary trunks to the ground to support the tree's sculptured spread. Howell gawked at the banyan a few moments and then strolled through a second courtyard into the house. Nothing was locked. The garden in the second courtyard appeared to be neglected, and the huge foyer was strewn with rolled Molas, playing cards, and Panama hats. On the left was an imposing three-story living room, furnished only with a record player, a giant aquarium, and more than forty embroidered pillows scattered on the floor. Twin staircases of blue and white tile circled to hallways on opposite sides of the foyer that led off to other rooms. Howell turned right into the dining room where two men were playing backgammon on a long table.

One of them was a tall blonde with long hair, a surfer type who would have been handsome except that he was hideously gaunt and pale. He looked as though he had just donated twenty pints of blood. He lived in the Virgin Islands, on St. Thomas, but he never saw the outdoors because he played backgammon constantly. His opponent was a short, puckish man in his fifties, with a closely trimmed white beard and hair to match, thinning around his dome. He appeared to be a smaller, Jewish form of Ernest Hemingway, enlivened by a glowing face and a body that bristled with energy, like a cricket. From Rosen's description, this seemed to be the host. He moved in constant parody of something. His eyes rolled like Stan Laurel's, and he rolled his dice grandly, like a drunken piano master, palms down with a flourish, ending in slow motion with the dice sliding out of the cup before an excited face.

"Hell—looo!" he cried, the first syllable half an octave high, singing.

"Hello," Howell coughed politely. He set down his suitcase.

"I was talking to my *dice* here, man," laughed Whitebeard, without looking up from the game. He scooped up two of his men and slapped them twice on the board, then celebrated with two calypso shoulder rolls. "Double fours into the old running prime play," he crooned. "And I've got the cube. Peter, my friend, you are *kaka* and *kaput*."

Peter's face registered nothing. He rolled his dice with exaggerated, practiced gentleness. Howell, less than six feet away, looked around. His discomfort over being thus ignored was more than offset by his curiosity about this alien world.

Whitebeard rattled his dice cup next to his ear, like a bartender, then swooped down into his slow motion roll. The results did not seem to gratify him.

"Are you Bobby Ziller?" Howell ventured.

Whitebeard hung his head and shook it slowly to bemoan the intrusion. "I'm trying to get over it," he sighed. He scrutinized Howell like a jeweler and turned slowly back to Peter. "Cracker," he pronounced. "Straight. Works for a living. Asks a lot of questions. Not too smart." He looked at Howell again, then back at Peter. "Good face, no taste. A lot of worries. Would be generous with money, but doesn't have any. Overall, a *más o menos* guy."

Howell felt more than a little diminished. "I'm David Howell, a friend of Ziggy Rosen's," he said lamely. "He said you had room for me to stay here."

"What for would I quarrel?" shrugged Ziller. An afterthought struck him. "Sincere," he declared. "Small town, probably Maryland. Wants to please. Loves snacks in food or women." He put the back of his hand to his forehead, as though checking for a fever. "Oh, the strain of it," he said.

Howell was impressed. He sensed that blunt nonsense was the order. "Not bad," he said. He furrowed his brow, mimicking the way Ziller had studied him. "Hebe," he drawled, by way of diagnosis. "Hustler." He looked at Ziller, then at Peter. "Quite stoned," he concluded.

"*Olé!*" cried Ziller with pleasure. He held out his palm for Howell to slap, and Howell was slow to do so because he was too pleased with himself for obtaining a response. Besides, he was not accustomed to palm slapping.

"Elementary, but correct," said Ziller, still smiling. I think our new *kibitzer* here is way too calm to be the representative of law enforcement. What do you think, Peter?"

"I guess he deserves a little toot as a reward," said Peter laconically.

Ziller lifted the top of a casserole dish next to the game board, revealing a plain round mirror. Neat lines of white powder lay cleanly on the glass. "Have some lunch," Ziller invited, handing Howell a curled fifty-dollar bill.

This is cocaine, Howell thought. His mind fumbled to remember anyone who had ever discussed the proper etiquette, and his Puritan heritage rose in him against using the fifty. "I think I've got a single," he said reaching for his wallet.

Ziller looked puzzled. "Use the Grant, man," he said. "This is a class operation."

Howell squirmed and blushed. He picked up a book of matches and took the fifty. Then desperation brought him an idea. "After you," he said with a bow, and he gave the fifty back to Ziller.

He gave Howell a cloudy look as he rolled the bill nimbly into a tight tube and tamped it on the table. Then he leaned over and sniffed up two lines with pleasure and affection.

By the time Howell received the fifty again, his mirth broke through his embarrassment. He twirled around on one foot, lost in his wholehearted laugh. "Oh, my God," he chortled in recovery, "I thought you were going to *smoke* it. Whew."

Ziller cringed slightly. "You thought we were going to smoke it," he snickered, fanning his brow for air. "You think I'm decadent or something?"

This made Howell laugh harder. He looked around the huge room and through the picture window over the bay. "That's another question," he said. "I'm sorry to be so green. I mean I have been known to smoke dope and pop a beer or two."

"A stiff," sighed Ziller.

"Look, I said I'm *sorry*," pleaded Howell, taking a bit of offense with his laughter. "I'm from Washington, for God's sake."

"Aha!" said Ziller. "So that's it. Why didn't you say so."

"I thought you'd guess," said Howell.

"It's okay," said Ziller. "We just won't be able to take you anywhere, that's all."

Peter rattled his dice. Howell hurried through his two lines, imitating Ziller, who urged him not to sneeze or otherwise blow anything away. "Make yourself at home," he said. "Go on out by the pool, but don't step on anybody."

Howell nodded his thanks and walked out through the door to the pool, his nose powdered white. When his eyes adjusted to the sun, he perceived the shapes of about a dozen nude people, mostly women, lying in clusters around the pool. Howell's eyes leaped, but he was reporter enough to notice by their plump white asses, which lay before him like a field of overgrown mushrooms, that they were newcomers to the sun.

"Ooooooh! What have we got here?" squealed one frizzy-haired woman, in a Brooklyn accent. "A capitalist."

"Hush, Marvella," scolded a tiny blonde. "You don't know that." The blonde stood up to introduce herself to Howell. He soon joined them around the pool. It was the first time he had ever taken off his clothes just to be more comfortable in a group of strangers, he mused to himself as he dived into the water. He swam underwater the length of the pool, and when he surfaced at the other end his face was not more than eight inches from a gorgeous, familiar face. Howell was dumbstruck. "You're not . . ."

"Yes I am," the face interrupted. "Don't spoil it, okay?"

She was one of the few acclaimed movie stars Howell both lusted after and admired, and her face now looked as big as it did on the screen. Howell filled his nostrils with her scent, which was coconut oil mixed with the sweat of an infant's foot, and he read a warning in her luminous eyes not to act like a fan. "Don't worry," he said. "It's just that I've always wanted to go to your dentist." He ducked back under water, wishing that he could have said something cleverer and more endearing.

The movie star, coming hard upon the other surprises, taught Howell to be prepared for anything, as Rosen had said. He remembered how he had stretched his tolerance on the solitary back-country treks in Kenya, but still it was a strain when he heard one woman tell her admiring friends how she had "overcome the last Western hangup" by having regular intercourse with her son, who was three. Hippie talk of stretching karma and hanging things out was easy. A thin brunette swam over to Howell, introduced herself as Moonbeam, and announced that she had recently been having an affair with a male dolphin down at a research tank.

"That's nice," said Howell. "Say, doesn't anybody work around here?"

Moonbeam looked bored and swam away.

"I'm sorry I called you a capitalist," Marvella apologized. "It's just that I'm doing free associations in my group now, and your button-down shirt made me think of Wall Street."

"I understand," said Howell.

"Here," said Marvella. She held out a tray of Wheat Thins that were covered with a thick orange jelly.

"Thanks," said Howell, popping one into his mouth. It tasted like sawdust and apricot, sprinkled with mothball juice. "Ugh!" Howell grimaced. "What the hell is that?"

"Food for your third eye," said Marvella.

"Oh," said Howell. He savored a few gulps of freshly squeezed orange juice from her pitcher, and watched her move on to administer her sacrament elsewhere.

Half an hour later, sitting on the seawall, Howell experienced the first enjoyable hangover of his life. He felt his inner ear engage. A floor, parallel to the ground, slid into his body somewhere between his ear and his chest, and he felt it wobbling slowly as though on a ball bearing. This he recognized as the dreaded inner sea deck, the platform of nausea, whose vacuum drops and rolling portholes had left him clinging to the toilet bowl more than once with his legs waving gently behind him on the bathroom floor, like seaweed. At those times his sea deck had blocked out his other senses so that he could not see or hear and only wanted desperately to breathe, but now the other senses were keenly alive. He could not imagine colors more vivid or pleasurable than the cobalt blue and the white clouds he was seeing over the bay, and even the sounds were remarkable. They were tactile. He could feel the sounds of lapping waves and pattering feet, and the silence of the bay breeze fell on his sea deck like tickling grains of sand. This, Howell figured, was his third eye, and if so he was glad to feed it. He felt as if he were waking up in a new way.

He turned around and saw Moonbeam not more than five feet behind him, looking entranced and very young. She was shapely, though flat-footed, with faint vein lines on her breasts and longer than average arms. Howell noticed how she was standing, one leg straight and the other relaxed and slightly forward, her legs parted at the crotch. He stared at her there, and the sight of the tiny obscured spot where the furrows parted, the minute W of flesh, flooded him with a sense of girl, as opposed to the woman inside. He felt simultaneously free of desire and buoyantly full of sex, in innocent celebration of her body, and the nerve circuits running upward from his legs and penis made his entire sea deck hum with pleasure. In fact, it felt as if the deck rose a few feet in the air.

"Moonbeam," said Howell. "What is this stuff, anyway?"

Her face seemed to make a long journey before meeting his words. Then she lit with excitement. "Psilocybin," she beamed. "The mushroom. Wooooowww! Isn't it something?"

Howell smiled. There was something too urgent about her voice, too needy and enthusiastic for the hushed awe the drug inspired. Howell sensed that she saw that, too, and wanted to call her words back to strip them of the anxiety. This was clearly part of Moonbeam's personality. "That's all right," he said quietly.

"I know," she nodded. "Thank you."

Howell nodded back at her, feeling a light cymbal's rush over the unspoken communication. "Boy," he said. "There's a lot more to conversation than I thought. Words could get hard to follow, couldn't they?"

Moonbeam smiled. "Not really," she said.

"I know," said Howell. "Thank you."

He got up from the seawall and wandered over to the grass by the pool, where he sat down, plucked a few blades, and marveled over the tiny pulsing cell dots of light he saw moving through the shaft in single file, like microscopic rush hour traffic. He thought he could observe the same phenomenon in the capillaries around the folds of his wrist.

An hour later, Howell stood up among the silent group of toweled humans on pillows in the shady part of the living room. He steadied himself against the air currents of heat coming from the musty bodies, and then he made his way into the dining room where Peter and Ziller were still passing the cube. "Excuse me, Bobby," he said, "but I am in need of a silver whistle. Can you tell me where that department is, please?"

Ziller looked up from the board and sighed. "Medicine cabinet, top of the stairs to the right," he said, waving in the appropriate direction.

Howell looked slowly around. "You would not be kidding me, would you?" he asked. "That's a long way to go."

"Nah," said Ziller. "Not the type."

Howell nodded. A few minutes later he returned with a smile and exchanged a few words with Ziller. Then he walked slowly to the top of the stairs leading down into the cathedral room. "I'm not going to blow this whistle unless I have to," he announced with a smile, holding the whistle up before the stoned assembly. "But I hope you can hear its sound anyway, and will respond like the troopers I already know you to be."

There were some groans and incoherent complaints among the pillows, but most of the troopers stared at the silver whistle with amazement. Howell cleared his throat. "Now, druggies," he continued, "I have consulted with Mister Ziller, and he has authorized me to warn all of you that it is not healthy for you to huddle in here like lepers all day. All your vitamins sink into your intestines. Your spirits turn into shadows. And no matter how far your head travels, you are in danger of turning into sacks of moldy yeast."

"Eeeeewwww!" squinched Marvella.

"Easy, man. You're laying some shit on my aura," said a skinny, homosexual attorney of no fixed legal specialty.

"But there is another way," said Howell. "I have here the keys to a magnificent Ford station wagon, which will soon take me, the whistle, and anyone who wishes to join us on a cruise through the sunshine. Bobby has suggested several points of interest, including the new Orange Bowl Parade float headquarters and Hialeah racetrack. He knows the chief resident flamingo keeper."

After some talk of dangers and what could be handled, there were five takers. They all helped each other into passable bits of abandoned clothing and filed out gingerly to the car. Howell considered the trip a failure for the first ten miles. The images came too fast, and every one of them seemed too stark and garish for the travelers, whose hearts were perched on the roofs of their mouths. Roadside billboards, for example, flashed such stillborn images of life that two of them made Moonbeam cry. Several hellbent motorists put a chill through the entire station wagon.

Howell and the others had adjusted by the time they reached the float headquarters and when they arrived at Hialeah they were in good form. They still took precautions, however, such as walking single file from the car, some holding hands. Howell assumed something of a protective function. He realized that the drug had turned up the volume on all their perceptions, so that an ordinary policeman appeared to be a blaring dose of authoritarian enjoyment as he directed people around, and the scratchy yells of the tip-sheet hawkers made one's chest feel like a gong. Roles became more difficult to accept. Screening mechanisms did not work, and normal defenses were lowered.

After some debate on the merits of the flamingos, they decided not to go inside the grandstand itself. The intensity was too great. Instead they remained on the lush grass outside and watched the horses come and go for the races. After one long race, Marvella became upset by the sight of a mare glistening under a layer of foaming sweat, wheezing, and she objected to the violence of the sport. No detail, from the bright gold shine of the horseshit to the proud stiff backs of the younger grooms, escaped their wonder. The other spectators made up a carnival of loud seersucker and greed. White-haired couples came by looking like pairs of ducks. Howell blew the silver whistle on several occasions. Laughter was rampant.

Not long after they returned, Bobby Ziller appeared in the living room and beckoned to Howell, who was happily exhausted by the trip. No one had ever taken them on such an outing, he was told, and he felt that he had given them something. This helped offset the unpleasant sensation he had of himself as a slow-witted gawker outrun by the darting, unhinged new companions.

"I need a strong back for about thirty minutes to help me deliver some merchandise," said Ziller. "Would you mind?"

"Of course not," said Howell. He followed Ziller out the door.

At a warehouse on the upper end of Miami Beach, Ziller changed briskly into patrolman's shoes, green gabardine trousers, and a white, short-sleeved shirt with orange trim and a monogram reading "D.C.I.C." Then he powdered a little dirt from the floor onto his face and arms, grabbed Howell's *Daily Racing Form* out of the car, and hopped into the driver's seat of a small flatbed truck. He motioned for Howell to open the garage door, and they were soon off.

Afternoon ribbon-cutting ceremonies were underway at a new shopping center, though it was only half finished, and Ziller joined in the hearty applause. Howell watched the row of businessmen and local officials without saying a word. He found himself at a loss as to what he was doing there. The drug had calmed down considerably, but his mind was still billowy and there was a bowl of tingling around his stomach.

"That's my kind of event," Ziller laughed, as the ceremonies concluded. Howell only nodded and followed him into the cab.

Ziller drove through the parking lot to the tall office building in back, which was crawling with construction workers and surrounded by trucks and materials. "Wait here," he said, taking a clipboard and the *Racing Form* off toward the construction trailer.

Howell waited outside the truck. He noticed the neatly lettered sign on its cab, "Dade County Industrial Chemicals, Inc.," and he saw seven large drums in the back, each one bearing a sticker with a very long chemical name printed on it.

Ziller came strolling back out of the trailer, congratulating himself silently on the *Racing Form* idea, which had helped put the foreman at ease. He threw the signed invoice into the cab ahead of him and drove to the designated spot where he and Howell unloaded the drums.

"Would you mind telling me what this is all about?" Howell asked.

"In good time, in good time," said Ziller. "All will be abundantly clear if you have a knack for accounting." He launched into a breakfast fantasy for the next day, listing whitefish, nova, shrimp salad, assorted cold cuts and pastries and cream cheeses, and three kinds of coffee. Howell was too tired to make any headway into the nature of his business.

96

Night came back at the house. Howell selected a circular bedroom upstairs and ventured to the backgammon area. "Bobby, do you mind if I put my stuff in that round blue room up there?" he asked.

"The bedrooms are all for sleeping," Ziller replied. "You can have any one but mine." He spoke coldly and vacantly, which surprised Howell.

"It's all right, then?" he asked again, to make sure.

Ziller shrugged irritably. "Whatever's right," he said.

Howell shrugged himself and trundled up to the round room. He was soon so soundly asleep that he didn't notice Moonbeam when she came in and lay down beside him on her stomach, sleeping with her knees under her, bent in the middle like an inchworm.

Before dawn, Bobby Ziller walked out the front door alone to the car. He sagged just before he got in. His shoulders slumped and his face became paler. Dark circles seeped down under his eyes. He labored to move as if he were an old man and sat still behind the wheel for a minute or two. Then he reached into his shirt pocket and pulled out a small vial, from which he took two toots to perk up. He sighed one last time and wheeled back out of the driveway, then off toward Little Havana to look for Carlos Maraña.

V

ONLY ONCE in his life had Max Parker had been early for anything. As a teenager in Batista's Cuba, he had sneaked into the second-class racetrack near Marianao to confer with a cheap gelding racehorse whose Spanish name translated roughly into "Sloppy Kisses." Young Parker had bought and named the old horse without telling his father, who would neither have understood his love for Sloppy Kisses nor have tolerated the purchase of anything on credit. The old man was a stern expatriate, a starched American in every respect except for his Cuban women and his diet. His rampaging appetite had driven him to do such things as to lock away trays full of freshly baked banana bread in his wall safe, lest they be touched by anyone else, and his resulting girth needed support from a thick leather belt that often raised welts on Max's legs even then, well after puberty. The worst sins were gambling and disrespect. Max found himself in a bind. He couldn't make the next payment on his horse, but he couldn't bear to give him up either, as the previous owner was demanding. So he contrived desperately to bring Sloppy Kisses out of racing retirement to earn his own purchase price, knowing that if his father ever discovered the secret gamble the belt would pop loud and hot. This fear, plus the guilt, was just enough to get him to the stable early.

He caressed Sloppy Kisses, and he sweated and apologized profusely to the horse before plunging the hideous veterinarian's needle into the shoulder. Gamely, he hugged Sloppy Kisses while pumping in half a pint of horse speed before the animal reared up in pain. When Max lost control of the hypodermic, its needle broke off in the horse. Max moaned snatches of a long forgotten catechism in a futile attempt to calm himself, and by the time Sloppy Kisses worked the needle out of his muscles the drug was taking effect. His eyes widened into the crazed stare of anarchists near the Caspian Sea. Even in his stall, he broke into a smelly white foam of a sweat. At race time, Sloppy Kisses jitterbugged up to the starting line, turning in circles, and he took off as though he could run across the entire island of Cuba without blinking.

Parker watched the race through the cracks between his fingers. His beloved horse, leading by two lengths at the head of the stretch, did a complete cartwheel except for the neck, which wedged frontward into the turf. There were legs sprawled at angles that were not meant to be, especially after four other horses tumbled over the corpse of Sloppy Kisses. Parker lay down and beat the ground, surrounded by astonished bettors. He never forgave himself. Even when he met David Howell more than twenty years later, he still felt the pain of killing his horse, which he loved, to avoid the wrath of his father, whom he did not. If Parker was having too much fun, a vision of Sloppy Kisses would sober him up. Some months after the catastrophe, as the elder Parker was whipping him over an unrelated matter, the absurdity of his racing scheme and the labored wheeze of his fat father, whipping with all his might, struck Parker in tandem and made him laugh. He could not stop. His father never again beat him, but soon managed to pack him off to his mother in America.

Parker had never mentioned his horse to anyone, even Carlos Maraña, so Maraña had never heard of Parker's being early for anything—not for a commando raid or a payday or a sale of detective books, which were his hobby. This knowledge was lurking in the back of Maraña's mind as he threw open the door of the condominium, expecting some horseplay from Parker. Instead, his mind screamed with the news that he was about to be shot, though he could not see or hear. It happened too quickly and panic made him see nothing but a curved whiteness, as though there were a pillowcase over his brain.

The first bullet struck Maraña just under the mastoid gland on the back of the neck. The second one pierced the fleshy muscle between his neck and shoulder, and a third one, chasing him on the fall, tore a small hole through the white princess telephone in the foyer. By the time Maraña hit the floor he knew it was a mistake to have expected Parker so unguardedly, that early, and he also knew that the killer possessed an exuberant fresh boldness—of the kind that would inspire him to ride an elevator up twenty floors to shoot someone at a hallway door. The killer was a character in transition, who enjoyed the sheer dare of the play more than the killing itself. Maraña decided it was Pepe Lopez and blacked out.

Carmen Vilar arrived some minutes later, wearing tight jeans and dark glasses, carrying a red rose and a shopping bag full of espresso coffee. She screamed in the open doorway just the way she had imagined many times that she would. The neighbors were still screaming and bumping into each other long after Carmen regained her composure kneeling on the floor next to Maraña. She was shaking her head with a hint of a smile behind her spent tears, thankful for Maraña's strong pulse. "You have escaped once again, *gato*," she said softly, wiping warm blood from his neck.

After a news relay and some reckless driving, Max Parker pushed his way through a phalanx of reporters' elbows outside Maraña's hospital room. He found the victim propped up in the bed, all in black and white. A clean white bandage worked its way up from a fresh black T-shirt to the dark hair on the back of his head. Maraña looked fit and alert, nestled between the crisp hospital sheets, holding Carmen's hand. Her rose was on the bed.

Parker's worry left him as he admired the scene. "You two look wonderful," he smiled. "You should get shot more often, *chico.*"

"Thanks, Max," said Maraña.

Carmen gave Parker a warm gaze and a nod of welcome, which was more than he had hoped for. He walked over to the bed and examined the bandage. "How many hit you?" he asked.

"Two," said Maraña.

"A .22?"

Maraña nodded.

"Right when you opened the door, eh?"

Maraña nodded again.

"Did the guy look like me?"

"Max!" Carmen scolded. "Don't even joke about that!"

"Hey," shrugged Parker. "If I can't joke about it, then I know we're in trouble." He looked back at Maraña and became serious. "Who do you think did it, Carlos?"

"I didn't see him," shrugged Maraña. "Who do you think?"

"Well," said Parker, "I've narrowed it down in my mind to about a hundred guys who want to . . ."

"Good work," sighed Maraña.

"But if I had to guess, I would say it was Pepe."

"Congratulations," said Maraña. "I think you'd be right. Carmen saw Pepe in the parking lot just before she found me. He gave her this rose."

Parker whistled with surprise. "Nice touch," he said. "That's going to get around."

"I know," said Maraña.

"Why do you think he'd do something like this after you helped him out?" Parker asked.

"Who knows?" said Maraña. "Maybe he's fallen in love with Carmen."

Carmen rolled her eyes in disgust. "He is a pig," she said. "Besides, he is a zombie now. He can't feel anything for any woman."

"You keep telling me that," Maraña mused.

"That's because you never listen, my handsome young target," smiled Carmen, patting his hand. "I don't think Pepe can be touched by a woman. That's why to me he is so dangerous."

Parker hitched up his pants resolutely. "What about me, Carmen?" he asked. "You think maybe I could get myself touched by a woman?"

Carmen tossed Parker a coy look, so sexy that it made Maraña's bandage throb. "Of course you can," she smiled. "All you've got to do is give a woman a chance. And don't spend so much time touching yourself. You are your own worst enemy."

This comment snapped Parker out of his mock preening. He stared at Carmen and blushed, speechless. She laughed. It was the first time she had ever seen Parker lose his jolly breath.

Maraña wanted to laugh, but his anger was greater. "That is no way for a woman to behave," he said sharply. "No more of that! Max can touch anybody he wants and it's none of your business."

This made Parker laugh; his discomfort never lasted long. But Maraña kept staring at Carmen. Her remark had offended his prudery, his *machismo*, and his conviction that he had to stand by friends like Parker to survive. Women were not allowed to add to the suspicions or grudges between men unless they wanted to take on all the risks of the rough game themselves, which of course was not quite a real choice, since they would not be allowed to do so. In fights, Maraña had conceded Carmen's right to say anything she wanted in private but not in front of strangers and friends, claiming that this was a better arrangement than the reverse. "Okay?" he said harshly after a pause, as though he had reminded Carmen of all this with his eyes.

"Okay what?" she asked. "What kind of joke is this? Max can make fun of the way you almost got killed today, and you think that's okay, but I say some innocent thing about the way he has fun and you get all upset. You are crazy."

"It's nothing," Parker shrugged. "It's okay."

"It's no way to behave," Maraña persisted. He spoke vacantly, however, and lay back against his pillow. It finally registered on him after these many hours how close he had come to a death of someone else's choosing. His breath burrowed several miles inside him, and he sighed.

"I'm sorry, Max," said Carmen, diplomatically. "I'll help you find a woman."

"Ooooh, God help me," smiled Parker. "Not too tame, not too mean, please. Are you all right, Carlos?"

"Of course," said Maraña unconvincingly. "I was just thinking about what the doctor said in the emergency room. He looked over me at this nurse, you know, and he said, 'Another Cuban criminal, probably a pimp.' So I opened one eye and I said to him, 'I am an old crusader. You have no idea who I am.' And the doctor looked down at me and said, 'You're right. I don't.' And he kind of smiled and looked right through me. He didn't know anything, and he didn't care, you know."

"Doctors have all their skill in their fingers," Parker quipped. "Don't let it bother you."

"Well, they will find out about us whether they want to or not," said Maraña. "I was thinking that Castro has made his history for everyone and it's covered with sugar. And we have made our history . . ."

". . . and it's covered with shit," cracked Parker.

"And it's covered with shit," Maraña agreed. "We have a shit-covered history."

"Well, you can't change that," said Parker. "What are you going to do, tell everybody that it was Pepe who shot you?"

"No," Maraña replied. "Of course not. And you should forget about that rose," he told Carmen.

"What rose?" she said.

"Good," he said. "I was just thinking about being more visible, that's all. Being even more of a *chivato*, so they will notice me. Maybe I should even get out of the country for a while."

Carmen and Parker exchanged significant looks. "Are you sure they got the bullets out of him?" asked Parker.

"I don't know," said Carmen. "I think maybe you should get a nice quiet job for a while, like maybe selling fireplace equipment in Coral Gables."

"That's good," grinned Parker.

"Or if it has to be dangerous, maybe you should drive a race car," said Carmen. "That way I would at least know when I have to worry and when I don't."

"You are wonderful," Maraña chided. "A man reveals a life crisis to you after getting shot, and you make jokes. Well, forget about it. I've got to figure out some entertainment for Pepe." The idea seemed to excite him.

Half an hour later, Parker pushed his way into the straggling reporters outside Maraña's hospital room. He spoke gravely in place of the wounded man. He said Maraña would live, he thought, but he had not seen the assailant because he was too busy dodging the bullets. Parker did an absurd, gallumphing, bullet-dodging dance for the reporters, who seemed to enjoy it. They said it was just like Maraña to claim he had dodged the bullet. Then, becoming serious again, Parker described how Maraña had made a great effort to whisper that he thought the idea behind the shooting was to shut him up; someone wanted to kill Maraña for all the help he was giving the police on the Taliente murder. This caused a considerable buzz. An hour later, Parker flirted loudly with all the women at the nurses' station while Maraña slipped out by the back stairs.

Maraña drove up and down Eighth Street for two hours before he found Pepe Lopez's car outside Yayo's Restaurant, a stucco structure that was either orange or pink. Whatever color it was, there was a lot of it. Maraña parked and sat still for a moment. Then he ripped the bandage off his neck, pulling out hairs and bits of skin, and he took his package out of the car.

Pepe Lopez had three men and two women with him at his table, all of whom were infected by his good mood. He was telling them stories. His left forefinger lay lightly and elegantly against his temple, revealing a gold cufflink and a embroidered cuff, as he gesticulated gracefully with his other hand. Lopez was telling them about how he had made his father happy the previous Sunday by baking him a boneless whole chicken, Cuban style. He told how he spent the entire morning on the delicate task of deboning the chicken from the inside, and he pantomimed himself in the act of sewing the chicken back together with the butter and spices sealed inside. For the past few months, Pepe Lopez had been a new man. He seldom talked of politics and never of old hatreds or disgraces, or even of Castro. Happiness had settled on him out of nowhere, said his startled friends. Lopez papered the town with his insurance policies, making his customers feel good, encouraging whatever they wanted encouraged, and at night he put on his white shoes. Ever the charmer and the storyteller, he was admired by an endless succession of women, none of whom got closer than a dance. Lopez was still a loner among his tough old comrades from "the life," though now a pleasant one. He encouraged them brightly, just like his customers, but he avoided their nightly shell game of conspiratorial meetings.

Lopez, by spiritual osmosis, felt Maraña enter the restaurant before he saw him. He looked up and said, "Hey, look who's here." His companions fell silent. Lopez's voice sounded like a man talking quietly while falling down a deep well. It trailed off into eeriness. Other tables quieted down, too, in both dining rooms, though almost no one recognized Maraña or Lopez by sight. Yayo's was not that kind of restaurant. It was a family place, full of wicker chairs and kids and red-checked tablecloths, but everyone hushed for Maraña. Something about him stole appetites. He closed the door and stood loudly in the doorway, smiling and looking around but ignoring everything he saw, including the hostess and all the waitresses. They knew without asking not to talk to him. Maraña cradled his package as he stared at Lopez. His look was neither menacing nor friendly. It was mostly concentrated and fixed, blotting out everything else, just flippant enough to be saying, well, isn't this a nice surprise.

Maraña suddenly marched across the dining room, so resolutely that it seemed only pure luck that he didn't run over a table. He stood directly behind Lopez, who was sitting up straight in his chair, a foot taller than his companions. The old humiliating fear had returned to brush his forehead with a sallow clamminess, but he did not flinch when Maraña opened the package. Instead he maintained a sickly leper's smile that many bystanders would try to forget that night in their beds. Now they watched him. Lopez and Maraña stood out in the restaurant like two dark cavities in a clean row of baby teeth.

Maraña took a dozen red roses out of his package and, after clearing a place among the dishes, laid them politely in front of Lopez. Then, with deliberate gravity, he took off his old CIA Rolex wristwatch and placed it among the blooms. He smiled broadly at the people around the table and said, "Congratulations, Pepe." His left hand went lightly onto Lopez's shoulder, which made the woman next to him suck in an anxious breath. Maraña's hand looked well-molded and feminine, like Lopez's, but Maraña inspired a terror in her that the hand might in a flash break Lopez's neck and resume its cultured repose there on the shoulder. She turned away and could not make herself look at the hand again.

Leaning over slowly, Maraña put his lips next to Lopez's ear and whispered, "I am going to let you live, Pepe. You should be grateful. And you should realize that you need me alive to keep the fire in you."

Maraña leaned farther forward to await a response. Lopez turned and found himself staring at the wrinkled, purplish gunshot wound on Maraña's neck. The sight angered him. "That is shit," he whispered. "You are coming after me, and all this is your little show business."

"Take it easy," Maraña whispered in reply. "If I were going to kill you, there wouldn't be roses in that box. There would be a little girl's dress."

Lopez clenched the tablecloth in both fists, turning over a glass of water, which he ignored. Then he opened his fists with some effort. "Please get out of here before I get mad," he whispered.

Standing up to survey the place, Maraña looked at all the people who were pretending not to notice him. He did a much better job of pretending not to notice them, as he pushed his dark glasses back into his hair, into the poolside position. Casually, he leaned over again and stared pleasantly at Lopez, who did not like the look. Maraña was outlooking him in every dimension, more friendly and fearsome and relaxed and alert. "It's so nice to have someone around who understands you," said Maraña quietly. "I know what your true pleasures are, and they are really something. I've seen it before."

"You are an arrogant bastard, Carlos," whispered Lopez.

Maraña patted his shoulder. "See the fire?" he smiled. "See how your tracks are always right behind you? You are very smart, Pepe, very smart. When everything else is gone, you are smart." He smiled around the table and walked briskly out toward his next errand.

Many parents at Yayo's had to tell their children to stop asking questions and eat. But the questions would persist among the adults in Little Havana, and the rumors ran ahead of the questions. Some believed that the Rolex gift meant Maraña was retiring from "the life" in fright, while others were convinced that he was branding Lopez a CIA stooge. Interpretations of the roses—and of the roses in conjunction with the watch—ran from heartbreak to voodoo. Lopez paid them no attention. He went home from Yayo's and fell into a black mood in his room. After two hours of silence, he carefully removed his perfumed shirt and began rhythmically pounding the coffee table with his fists. At first it was mechanical, but slowly an odd look of pleasure replaced the wood in Lopez's face. He took out his knife and went into the bathroom where he savagely slashed all the towels into shreds. Then he went to bed, and the next morning he sold insurance with bubbling good humor.

When Max Parker came home from the hospital, he found a sunburned man sitting under the security light outside his apartment building, eating a banana. The man seemed otherwise absorbed in a thick book devoted to the issue of exactly when Fidel Castro's mind could first be described accurately as a communist one, a label that distinguished Castro from his fellow Latin American *jefes*, reflecting his optimism about the poor and social regiments and above all his hostility toward the United States, which played Goliath to his fame. Parker knew—and was bored by—the book, so he tried to pass unnoticed through the door.

"Are you Max Parker?" asked Howell.

"Yes," hissed Parker, holding on to the doorknob.

Howell rolled himself to his feet. He was wearing jeans, sneakers, a red pullover that accentuated his pink skin, and a classy-looking Panama hat, courtesy of Bobby Ziller. "I'm David Howell," he said. "I'm the one who's been pestering you for an interview."

"I know," said Parker, giving nothing.

"Uh huh," said Howell. He shifted the book from his left hand to his right elbow, pinning it to his ribs, the banana from his right hand to his left hand, and then the book from his right elbow to his left one—all in preparation to shake hands. During the fumbling, Parker edged into the door and a thin paperback volume fell out of Howell's tome on Cuba. "Excuse me," said Howell, stooping down to pick up the book with his right hand.

"Listen, this has been a terrible day for me," said Parker in the harried-exit ploy. "Why don't you call me tomorrow and we'll get together some other time?"

"Suits me," said Howell. "But let me shake hands, if you don't mind, just to celebrate laying eyes on you after three nights. That's why I brought these books, to help with the wait."

"Sorry about that," said Parker, mildly chastened. "It's something we learned in the Company. Never show up for your first appointment with a strange person. Security, you know."

"Uh huh," said Howell. He gave Parker the thin book, and they shook hands.

Parker did a double-take. *"Tales of Suhani,* Volume 28," he beamed. "You read those?"

"Every one of them," Howell affirmed. Suhani, an eighty-year-old sorceress of Inca origin, could grip slick walls with the ridges of her fingertips, and she could decapitate thirty men at once with her long fingernails, which were also good for bending steel or lasers. She could make atoms or hearts sing her tune, and she could, if necessary, drain all the libido blissfully out of male potentates with her ugly old body. Suhani was very bright. She starred in a successful series of pulpy, satirical spy books, in which the satire was much subtler than the pulp.

"I didn't know Number 28 was out yet," said Parker.

"New," Howell nodded. "Just picked it up at the airport."

Parker leaned back against the door. "Okay," he said. "Come on in and tell me what you're up to. I've got a little time."

"Good," said Howell. "I can only stay a few minutes anyway. I want to see the last game of the World Series."

They wound up watching the game together and drinking beer. Howell let Parker talk about the game while he wandered about the apartment, which was much neater than his but similarly cluttered with objects of literature and sports. Unlike the other Cuban houses Howell had visited that month in Miami, the apartment had no Spanish furniture or crucifixes or pastel watercolors of the Madonna. To Howell, it was Cuban only in the lively smells of cologne and espresso coffee, along with the Spanish books.

And it was weird because of all the wires and antennas. One room in particular looked like a radio repair shop after an earthquake.

Howell was thankful to observe that he and Parker shared a number of
traits in addition to their taste for Suhani, including a tolerance for sloth.
Howell's curiosity was benign. He loved being around new people when
they were unfolding themselves to him, and even when they weren't he had
a high capacity for self-amusement. Howell would absorb what was there.
His good nature was remarkably self-sufficient, gave no signs of predatory
feeding, which many people mistook for a lack of ambition. His job was to
notice things, and he believed there were things to notice everywhere. Only
hostility or run-of-the-mill pretension disturbed him. While Washington was
a problem in the latter area, with its cubical rooms and ladderlike minds,
Miami was a vacation in more ways than one. Everything was new, and
Howell could call himself working while being slothful. This was a supreme
goal for an informal reporter—to hang out in the cloakroom, to drink and
run outdoors and make wisecracks, all in the name of research.

In due course, Parker asked him how he had come to Miami. Howell,
because of all the beer, decided to respond to the question in the grander
sense. "Well, I went into the Peace Corps in Africa to get out of North
Carolina," he said. "And I went to Washington to get us out of Vietnam.
And I wrote about Washington to save the world. And now I've come to
Miami to get out of Washington, I guess."

Parker nodded. "Typical *Americano*," he grinned.

Howell nodded back, inwardly relieved that Parker had not pounced on
his declarations with anticommunist slurs. Parker did not conform to his
image of the fiercely reactionary Cuban exile—full of fierce unhappiness
and routine excitement, like a circus roady, with a sad tale and a romantic
plan and a diamond on the pinky. He struck Howell as more like an American. He had no trace of a Spanish accent, or the lilting cadence of speech
or the matador's posture. He hung his muscular body idly over chair legs
and radiated the kind of bemused cynicism with which Howell was familiar.
Howell wondered about the invisible Cuban part of Max Parker, and he
risked asking glibly where it was.

"It comes and goes, but it's in there," said Parker without hesitation.
"There's a lot of American in me, too. My grandfather was born in New
York in 1877, and he was the second youngest member of Teddy Roosevelt's
Rough Riders. You know about them?"

"A little," said Howell.

"Well, the Cubans fought to overthrow the Spaniards on and off for
nearly fifty years," said Parker. "About 60,000 Spanish soldiers died, mostly
of disease, and the Spanish army killed and starved untold thousands of
Cuban rebels. Then, just when the Spaniards were about to give up anyway,
William Randolph Hearst and Teddy Roosevelt went roaring down to Cuba
with the American army to be saviors and heroes. There were only a couple
of battles in a couple of months against the last Spanish stragglers. It was a
joke. The biggest battle was at San Juan Hill, where about seven hundred

Spaniards were surrounded by about six thousand Americans and Cubans, including the Rough Riders. Do you see how crazy it is? I mean it was nothing, but the Americans took colonies all the way to the Philippines. And when the Spaniards left Cuba, they turned the keys over to the American army and the Americans ran Cuba until Castro. The Americans did not like the Cuban rebel armies because they were disorganized and had too many Negroes, so they stripped the Cubans of all their arms and started to 'civilize' them. What do you think of that?"

"I knew a little of it," Howell smiled, "but I didn't realize how ridiculous the war was."

"It's true," said Parker. "You can check it if you want."

"That's all right," said Howell, who looked away and started laughing to himself. "I was just thinking of Teddy Roosevelt leading the United States into the twentieth century by riding a bicycle up San Juan Hill in his khakis. That's about right. Do you think that's what great powers have to do?"

Parker's eyebrows twitched several times but otherwise he gave no warning. "Yes!" he thundered, as he banged his big fist loudly on the coffee table, sending beer bottles flying. "Yes! That's what they do, but it's not funny if you're the ones getting run over! The great powers are blind and nothing is funny to them. They will get theirs one day, too. I believe they will get it, but time is too short."

Parker's voice was suddenly raspy; he was animated and fearsome and ugly in ways that would have seemed impossible seconds earlier. When he said "get theirs," he made the sign of a throat being slit. He said "fonny" instead of "funny" and moved with a quickness that scared Howell. This was a completely different, unpredictable Parker, Howell thought warily. This was the Cuban side.

"I'm sorry," said Howell in a panic. "I'm sorry." His mind scrambled for a neutrally sober thought. "I didn't realize that the army kept a garrison in Cuba after that war," he remarked nonchalantly, as though at a cocktail party.

"Yeah," said Parker, sinking back into his chair, the passion having gone by. "Not much of one because the soldiers got sick all the time, but there was a military governor. General Wood. My grandfather was one of his staff officers. He stayed on and on in Havana because he was treated like a king. He made and lost one fortune dredging harbors, then another one in real estate and another one in imports. Always, he lived well because he was an American. When I was little, he told me glorious battle stories about Roosevelt, which I found out were all bullshit. My grandfather had so much fun that he didn't marry until he was forty. Neither did my father. My father was almost broke when he got married in the Depression, but he was considered good enough to marry one of the richest women in Cuba. Then he ran through her money, and she went to New York to be a schoolteacher. In Cuba I was the *Americano* and here I am the Cuban. No country and a lot of worries. A very sad story, no? I am sorry to be so touchy about ancient personal history, okay?"

"That's all right," said Howell, who realized now that his heart had been racing with fear.

"But you see, David, how so many turning points in American history are tangled up with Cuba, don't you?" smiled Parker. "I mean there's the Monroe Doctrine and the Spanish war and the Bay of Pigs and the missile crisis. And it was the Cubans who broke into the Watergate, of course. All of it with the Cubans. The Cubans and the Americans are destined to dance together in their funny dance, like the lion and the fox. So it's maybe not so crazy for me to be tangled up myself, no?"

"Maybe not," said Howell.

"That's right, you see?" laughed Parker. "Maybe not, you see?"

The phone rang and a left-handed slugger hit a home run on television simultaneously, which caused excitement in the apartment. Parker picked up the phone and was transformed again. His eyes lit up and all his intensities, especially his laughter, seemed to line up on his chin to jump into his face. He spoke in musical volleys of Spanish in the Cuban style, fast and clipped. Howell understood only every tenth word or so, but he could read the florid changes in Parker's face—now laughing, now surprised, now intent, now thinking, now irritated, now laughing. Parker's entire body seemed to come alive in the conversation, and Howell felt comparatively dull as a talker. He felt dull, not only personally, but also nationally, as though Americans were all accountants and administrators.

As he watched Parker, Howell mused to himself about what it must be like to have two cultures and histories so separate and yet so close in one body, and he remembered the things from his own past that he carried with him the way Parker carried the history of the Rough Riders. For him they were more prosaic—things like the sputtering wooden clap of the screen door shutting on his grandmother's porch, or the old coal stoves, or the way the shins of the very old ladies had been burned brown by the coal stoves as the ladies tried to keep warm in the old days. He also remembered the time, just before Kennedy took office, when two stooped black ministers in identical blue suits had presented themselves for admission to a service at the old church outside High Point, how the kids were wide-eyed and the adults fanned themselves busily, how the beloved pale preacher took a long time explaining why he didn't like having to call the sheriff to escort the black preachers away, and how as a sign of good will there was an offering taken up specially for those two black churches just in case there might be hard feelings. He remembered those things and how they seemed to be relics and memories even as they were happening, and he could shake his head and laugh over such disappointments because even their cruelty had a frail and tender side. They whetted Howell's curiosity. He was intrepid, a dare-taker, and he would jump off things or walk into strange places. But Howell had never in his life walked into a fight or a war or any form of violence personally—for him it was always adventure seasoned by a little phoniness and pain—and he found that violence brought out his tentative side, as he liked to call it. If he had lived Max Parker's life, perhaps his own curiosity would have developed a haunted, volatile quality, or perhaps it would no longer exist.

Max Parker hung up the phone with hurry in his face. "I have to go," he said. "What do you want from me, anyway, my friend?"

Howell tore his gaze from the World Series. "Well," he said, "I've got two bosses I'm hiding from down here. One of them wants me to do a story about Miami as the center of the new American decadence, about drugs and the Mafia and the beach hotels and the spies and ex-dictators everywhere. He calls Miami a city of bleached money. The other guy wants more of a news story about those three big Mafia guys who got bumped off down here after they said they knew something about the Kennedy assassination. He wants to know why all these lingering political murder investigations seem to have a Miami angle—even Jimmy Hoffa's—and he wants to know about all the secret agencies down here squabbling over who the bad guys are.

"Anyway, I'm trying to satisfy both bosses and steal a long vacation. I'm not too good on the rough stuff so far. I've never done a murder story before. But there does seem to be a lot of squabbling down here. And a lot of old secrets. Everybody gives me a sly look and says I don't know the *real* story, which is always dirty and underneath. And since I've been interviewing all these cops and these amazing Cubans down here, I've developed my own interest in the Cubans and the exotic secret history of Miami. I guess I'm looking for the underworld."

Parker smiled. "Wow," he said. "If you're looking for the underworld, you should have stayed in Washington."

"Uh huh," nodded Howell. "Maybe so. But that's the white-collar underworld. Or the overworld, maybe. I'm after something else."

"Oh," said Parker.

Howell stared at Parker and put his hands sheepishly into both his front pockets. "You're not telling me you don't know anything, are you?" he drawled. "Everybody says to talk to you. Maybe it's because your English is so good."

Parker was pulling a seersucker sports coat over a red knit shirt. "No, I'm not saying I don't know anything," he grinned. "How's your Spanish?"

Howell looked at the floor and took a deep breath. "Mine Spaniard is no well," he said, in Spanish.

"You're not kidding," laughed Parker. He walked out the door with Howell trailing, waiting. "Well, maybe I'll take you around," Parker called back. "You call me later."

In relaxed Coral Gables, where photography teams are often seen shooting still lifes of a sitting room or a lawn facade, Carlos Maraña's headache was getting worse late at night as he knocked on the door of Edward Noel, the CIA's dyspeptic station chief. He had to knock sharply several times before the door cracked enough to reveal a pipe and a growl. "What do you think you're doing here, Carlos?" demanded the growl. "I thought you got killed today anyway."

"I did," said Maraña. "But that is another story. Listen, I'm sorry to intrude like this, but I don't know where you hide your office anymore. I need to talk to you."

Noel stared irritably through the crack, sucking on his pipe. He was a tall, urbane man with a thin, sleepless face and silver gray hair. His skin was also silver gray, both on his face and on the skinny bowed legs that dropped from his Japanese silk bathrobe to his well-worn slippers. Noel was all one color, and he was hard to impress. His comment upon learning of Stalin's death had been "Oh, really?" At the time, he had been a rising star in the Agency's Soviet Bloc Division, advancing by intelligence and by connections from birth to Harvard. Years later, under President Johnson, Noel made a mistake in his campaign to displace a rival in the executive chain of succession. He and his supporters all through the Agency had argued that the CIA should secure its strongholds in Africa, Latin America, and the Middle East rather than pour its resources into the secret war in Vietnam.

The Noel faction lost badly. When it was announced that Thomas Houseman, not Noel, would become number two man in the Directorate of Plans, Noel said, "Oh, really?" and went on a three-week drinking bout. They offered him his choice of two consolation jobs: chief of the Office of Records or chief of the Miami station. "A librarian? How nice," he said icily of the records job, and he went to Miami a much reduced man. It was a career humiliation, for the station there was a ghost town after the great clandestine wars against Castro. It was a sinecure, and many people felt that Noel should resign rather than to submit to it. Among these was his wife, who left him to marry a hard-boiled columnist in Washington. But Noel stayed, and so did most of his supporters in the Agency, many of whom received $40,000 a year to work crossword puzzles at the office. "My tired old security risks," Noel quipped of them, and he laughed that a lot of them might defect if there were the slightest evidence that spying for the Russians would be more fun than crosswords. Noel himself took lonely refuge in literary bitterness and Chivas Regal.

Maraña extended a fresh bottle of Chivas toward the door. "Here," he said. "This bottle will last long after I leave."

Noel took his pipe out of his mouth and his lips bent into a partial smile, as though pried open with a crowbar. "Shame on you, Carlos," he said. "Attacking my weaknesses, eh, just like always?"

"No," said Maraña. "Just sharing them."

"That's better," said Noel. He let the door swing open for Maraña. "You realize, I presume, that I never allow Cuban agents or former agents in my home?" he asked.

"Of course," said Maraña. "With a few exceptions."

"Very few," said Noel.

"I'm honored," said Maraña.

They walked through a well-appointed house that Noel, like most CIA officers, had furnished with acquisitions from his world travels. There were prints and candlesticks and Balzac bookends from Paris, tapestries from India, rugs from Iran, teak endtables from Malaysia, a patio of hand-painted antique tiles from Spain—everything but the standard blue elephant sculptures from Vietnam. Whenever he could, Noel would tell old hands from the Agency how proud he was not to have those elephants cluttering up his living room, which was his way of reminding them that he had been right on Vietnam, wrongfully shunted aside.

Noel sat in a fanback wicker chair not far from the ice bucket on the patio, his favorite nighttime retreat. "It's been a long time, Carlos," he sighed. "I hope you're not still angry about the Congo."

"Only when I think about it," said Maraña.

"That's good, I suppose," Noel said laconically. "You were always so irreverent, so skeptical of patriotic appeals."

"I know," said Maraña. "And you always lied to me."

"And so literal," Noel added with a smile. "But I still hated to lose you to those idiots in the FBI."

Maraña sat silently through a few of Noel's condescending remarks about FBI agents, whom he referred to generally as "vainglorious bartenders" and "indoor scoutmasters."

"Do you want to know who killed Taliente?" Maraña asked, after a pause.

"So that's it," said Noel, refilling his glass. "Well, now that you mention it, not really. It doesn't matter. Why? Did you do it like everybody says?"

"That's a good question," laughed Maraña. "With my mouth maybe, but not with a gun—just like a good American case officer."

"Precisely," nodded Noel, playing along.

"And it doesn't matter to you that your last Cuban supporters are mad at you for letting Taliente and his grand plan go poof?" asked Maraña.

"No," said Noel. "Taliente was stupid. He wanted to be a hero, and he thought he could start a clandestine movement against Castro with only one-thousandth of the political and military support he needed. He caused everybody a lot of trouble, including me."

"I once wanted to be a hero, too," Maraña said absently.

"I know," said Noel. "But you learned how to wait."

"I learned how to survive," said Maraña.

"This is tiresome," said Noel. "In all candor, Taliente got himself killed just when he was supposed to. He dragged out the hope of getting rid of Fidel for three more years. He entertained everybody, as you call it, and now our remaining Cuban agents don't expect to go after Castro anymore. We have other things to do. More mundane ones, generally."

"You are being too honest for me to understand," said Maraña. "What's the matter?"

"There's no reason to be inventive on that subject anymore," said Noel. "In any case, it's no surprise to you, and I don't think it's what brought you here with those holes in your neck."

"That's true," said Maraña. "I need a job."

Noel put his glass down and gazed momentarily at his fingernails. "Splendid," he pronounced. "I'll write you a glowing letter of reference. Let's see, something like, 'Legendary paramilitary agent with checkered background and gunshot wounds seeks spy employment.' How's that?"

"I'm serious," said Maraña. "I don't want to work here in Miami, and I don't want to work for the Company. I want to work for one of the intelligence services down south, in Nicaragua or Venezuela or Colombia or Panama. You've got Cubans working in every one of them, and I want you to mention me around to get me placed, too. I can still play hide-and-seek with the Russians and all the rest of the games."

"Very interesting," said Noel. "And why would the government, which I still represent, through fair weather and foul, want to have an uncontrollable man like you working for one of our little Latin allies?"

Maraña looked back pleasantly, knowing that Noel was trying to provoke him. "Because I'm going to get the job anyway, and it would be better for you to have helped me. That way I would be more inclined to tell you about things down there and here in Miami also."

"What kinds of things?" queried Noel.

"Like the fact that all hell's going to break loose here over the next six months. Taliente is only the beginning. You used to own Florida from the Keys to Lauderdale, but when the killing is over, I'm not sure you'll even be able to live here anymore."

"I see," said Noel. "How unpleasant. Tell me, where would you like most to work?"

"Panama," said Maraña. "With San Jenis."

"Can you survive this uprising you say is coming if you don't get out of the country?"

"Certainly," said Maraña, a bit huffily. "But it will be harder."

Noel sat back to reflect. His first instinct was to promise Maraña anything and then forget about it. That would be the easiest and least dangerous thing to do. Then it occurred to him that the wiser course might be to get Maraña and as many of his troublesome imitators as possible out of Miami, leaving it a more tranquil city. Then there would be fewer snarled plots and puffed-up conspiracies, which would suit Noel perfectly.

"What about Pat Shea?" asked Noel. "You think he's going to like it if you run off out of town and leave him?"

"I don't care what he thinks, and you don't either, I hope," said Maraña. "If we have to worry about him, we're really in trouble. He doesn't even know who's following him and who's ahead of him. I'll be all right regardless of what he does, which will probably be nothing."

"Well, I see that your confidence is still high despite your unfortunate experience," said Noel, wondering how much Maraña was covering his fear. He laced his fingers in thought. His distaste for the juvenile, sing-song timbre of Maraña's voice was more than offset by Maraña's natural use of the word "regardless." Pat Shea always said "irregardless," which irritated Noel beyond endurance, especially since he could not afford to correct him.

Shea also said "just between you and I," which annoyed Noel even more because he knew Shea thought he was showing off his polished grammar. To have such elementary language out of place in the upper chambers of government demeaned the national security mandate, Noel thought sourly. Shea was an embarrassment to him, more than the gum chewers in customs or even the uneducated, wife-swapping would-be gangsters in the Drug Enforcement Agency. Maraña looked good by contrast, and yet there was something about him that rankled Noel. He decided it was Maraña's lack of respect for hierarchy, which was so unusual in a Cuban. No matter how skilled or mysterious he was, Maraña was still a Cuban—which meant that he was impulsive and a bungler and would talk his head off rather than keep a secret. And therefore Maraña should not say such bad things about a superior like Pat Shea, even if they were perceptive. Humorous insubordination is what it is, Noel decided, and it is the kind of sin that makes it difficult to keep face. He made an effort to conceal the haughtiness that was creeping into his distant eyebrows as he said, "I'll think about it, Carlos. Where can one of my deputies reach you if something turns up for you down south?"

"Have them call Carmen," said Maraña. "She always knows where I am. Here is her number." Noel was still looking at the paper, thinking what a great change it all was from the times when he and his colleagues would stay up all night spending millions and knowing that Cubans and other agents would die happily for them, when Maraña slammed his front door.

By that time, David Howell was giggling incoherently upstairs in Bobby Ziller's blue round room. There were many reasons for the laughter, but the main one was the laughing gas, of which Howell had a lungful or so. Having returned from the Cuban underworld agog as usual with tales of gunrunning and bomb-building and money-toting for straitlaced causes, Howell found that his revelations earned him but a "far out" or a "wow" among the hippies back at Ziller's roadhouse. Howell felt somewhat slighted that his newsy tales of secret political struggles all over the hemisphere were valued only as entertainment—they drew only a laughing, witty comment or a passing nod, like a new piece of furniture or a whiff of perfume. They were not taken *seriously*, he fumed, but then again nothing ordinary was taken seriously there. That seemed to be the whole idea, and in that light it was a high compliment that his stories had drawn a giggle instead of the darting look of boredom.

Of course, no one really had time to laugh very long about any one thing at Ziller's. Too many events crowded in from the outside. Just today, a filmmaker named Sidney had arrived from Hollywood full of script talk and nonsense, both of which were very popular, and two nomadic hippies had sailed in from Barbados on their own sloop. Actually, they were sailing it for someone else, an Englishman who lived on the island of Ibiza and who came from the top of an old industrial family and who was an intimate friend of the filmmaker, it turned out, which everyone thought was neat.

There was also a folksinger who looked like a banker and a rich Miami Beach lawyer who looked like a French sailor, and there was a great deal of excitement over the arrival of an airplane pilot named Arlington Spencer who was blond and winsome and handsome as an actor, and who could still remember the day he quit the prestigious Washington law firm of Covington and Burling. "We were representing ABC," said Spencer, "and one day after a meeting I saw Frank Reynolds and Howard K. Smith walking down Connecticut Avenue. They were stiff as flagpoles, man. They had their chests out and their jaws set, not looking at anybody. They had the weight of the world on them from their head down to the asshole. And I couldn't believe them, man. And then I saw that *everybody* on Connecticut Avenue walked like that and I was learning how to do it too. So I quit the next day." Spencer giggled when he talked, even without the laughing gas. He was rumored to be a genius, having made several fortunes himself in obscure enterprises. To Howell, he was a very attractive, partial man.

Everything at Ziller's was partial somehow. There was money without work and nudity without sex and hilarity without a tragic backdrop. Everything was suspended, which made it easier for Howell to laugh. That way the unreality was not bothersome. At Ziller's there was a kind of familiarity among all strangers. Downstairs, Arlington Spencer was telling everybody about a village in Mexico, outside Oaxaca, where the local priests also drove the ramshackle buses up and down the steep mountain roads. Whenever the parish treasury ran low, said Spencer, the moonlighting priests would step on it, careening around the rims and ledges at even greater speeds than usual, frightening the native passengers out of a chicken or two for the parish. More than one priest had driven his bus into fiery airborne glory on this maneuver, just for the church, said Spencer. He made everybody feel good, though narcotized, with his stories.

Moonbeam crawled into the giant bed next to Howell, shedding her poolside towel. Like everyone else at Ziller's, she came and went on an arbitrary basis, contributing her adventures and a share of her souvenirs to the common good. Nobody seemed to know much about her, which was natural.

"You want some?" she asked, sitting crosslegged on the bed. A joint and a match appeared in her hand from nowhere.

"Sure," said Howell, sitting up and beginning to giggle. Moonbeam seemed so intent about sharing the joint that her determined jaw almost overshadowed the daffy insouciance that was rumored to be the essence of Moonbeam. Howell wondered where she had concealed the joint. He also stared at her breasts, comfortable and not distinctive, except for the veins. What was important, thought Howell, was that Moonbeam herself was at ease with the breasts as she awaited the moment when they would be the center of the world to a young creature. Howell didn't think he would be so at ease, because he thought the breasts were too bouncy and too obvious a reminder of their milky purpose. They were so funny and touching, so ignored by Moonbeam despite their striking claims of color and texture and prominent placement on the body, that the breasts threw Howell's mind back to old conundrum.

"What's the matter with you, too much nitrous?" asked Moonbeam.

"No," laughed Howell. "I was just wondering why men have nipples."

"Huh?" muttered Moonbeam. "You're weird. I thought you only worried about Cubans, anyway."

"I'm serious," insisted Howell, though he did not look serious. "These little things I've got have all the air let out of them, so I can't figure out what purpose they have in nature." He began pinching his left nipple to no apparent effect and at the same time he pulled the entire top sheet of the bed into a ball in his lap to cover his erection.

"Well, you'd look pretty funny without them," said Moonbeam. "Your chest would look like it's erased." She started giggling again, looking Howell over.

"That's just because you're used to them," he replied. Her giggle made him self-conscious of his dual activity there, pinching with one hand and pushing down on the sheet ball with the other to punish and tease the erection. So he pinched and pushed harder. "In evolution," Howell declared, "physical characteristics develop for some biological reason, like survival. So I figure that maybe five million years ago, men had breasts to help out with the nursing, and then we lost them to atrophy when you guys got so good at nursing and we had to go out and spear mammoths. That's one possibility at least. But I don't think men have nipples just to trim out the look of our chests."

Moonbeam's jaw had slackened during Howell's prolonged speculation. "Why not?" she asked.

Howell rocked gently on the bed. "What do you mean, why not?" he asked. "I mean I think evolution had to have some functional purpose for these things, not just decoration or to make them reminiscent of yours. That's not reason enough."

"Man, you're far out," said Moonbeam. "You've got a grim idea of nature. Why couldn't nature be having a little fun? Or why can't there be a little decoration, like the bright feathers on the myna bird?"

Howell stopped his pinching and pushing, and for the first time he was intent upon what Moonbeam would say next.

"Yeah, why not?" she said. "Maybe your nipples are necessary to attract females. Maybe they are part of the mating call and they help keep us from mating with a caribou or something. Maybe they're like a scent or something to attract us." Moonbeam paused, mouth open, to stare at Howell's nipples with a look that went from curiosity to boredom in refutation of her ideas. "If that's so," she shrugged, "I'll admit that yours don't work so good."

Howell's cheeks billowed. He pulled an imaginary arrow out of his chest with a grin and toppled over on the bed like a felled tree. His body shook in a spell of laughter, deeper and more dignified than the previous giggles. Moonbeam seemed pleased with herself for having contributed to such a change. She rolled over on her stomach and assumed the sunbathing position.

When Howell recovered, he began to administer a spontaneous backrub to Moonbeam, starting with her shoulders. They were rounded and narrow, with three or four dark Miami freckles buried in the tan. Howell circled them and crisscrossed them with pleasure, always with his fingers and never with his palms. He was sensitive about his palms. His fingers were nimble and could pick out a loping country song or coax a vibrato from a single guitar string, but his palms were pudgy and small—or so he thought. They belonged to a different hand, and Howell had to adjust by making his fingers even more dexterous. He exercised them and drummed them and whittled with them, with the result that he could become quite self-absorbed whenever his fingers were moving in their complicated patterns of ten. In this spirit, Howell found himself lost in Moonbeam's tan with his fingertips sliding over her skin and then kneading the loose muscles so that the freckles moved in promenades and do-si-dos. Howell played wordlessly up and down her spine, knowing that neither he nor Moonbeam wished to speak, but he could not help laughing when he realized that his recreational finger art had cost him his erection. There was a dent in the sheet ball. His laughter fell out of his chest much more awkwardly than his fingers were moving.

"What's the matter?" Moonbeam called over her shoulder.

"Nothing," said Howell. He tried to recover by moving straight to the soft spot between the dimples atop her buttocks, a place that had always intrigued him. It felt like a subcutaneous hot water bottle. He leaned into Moonbeam's with circular parallel thumb motions, using his eight fingers only for light perimeter caresses. "This area," he pronounced in a whisper, "is the center of the body's liquids, I think. They used to call them the bodily humors—black bile, yellow bile, blood, and so forth. Anyway, they're connected to everything. The bad feelings and tensions tend to collect here, and if you relax you can feel the good juices spreading out from here to every part of your body."

"No shit," Moonbeam moaned. Her response inspired Howell to leap down to the foot area. In Howell's experience, the feet were more complicated than the genitals. The variations in sensation between geographically proximate locations—the heel as opposed to the instep, or the ball of the foot as opposed to the crevices between the toes—were so different in kind and reached out to such different parts of the body that the combinations one could produce with ten skilled fingers were beyond tabulation.

Moonbeam's feet were unusually sensitive to Howell's combinations, and they forced him, after getting several reflex kicks, to abandon the area with regret. He moved up the backs of her legs, concentrating on the calves and the backs of the knees, moving from patches of hard muscle to ones of unfamiliar nakedness for Moonbeam who squirmed. She kept squirming as Howell played lightly over her thighs, but she calmed down somewhat when he started rolling his fingers over the mounds of her ass. For Howell, this slope, the stark soft altitude of the ass as it perched there, was the most exciting feature of a woman lying on her stomach, causing him to plunge in with all the wandering strength of fingers and thumbs. His excitement was partially offset, however, by the gelatinous depth of the area, which, in

116

contrast to the sinews elsewhere in the body, almost cried out for a whole hand massage, palms and all. This made Howell uncomfortable—doubly so because it was such a quirk and it broke the rhythm of his elation—so he gave the ass inexplicably short shrift before circling by degrees to her vagina. Moonbeam moaned, but when the first quiver began to rise in her she yanked herself away.

"Please just touch me," she said through a face filled with pain.

Howell was nonplussed and worried. "I thought that's what I was doing," he said, attempting feebly to laugh.

"I know," she said. "But no more, okay? Just that. It would mean a lot to me. Please?"

"Okay," said Howell. "But I'm surprised at you. I thought you made love to dolphins on a whim." He reddened as soon as this escaped him, because it meant that he took the dolphin story as a sign that Moonbeam was an easy lay. And she would see that.

"That's different," she said. "Besides, I don't know you as well as I know my dolphin."

Howell's eyes bulged as he absorbed this remark. Moonbeam convinced him against all odds that she was in earnest. Her face was soapsuds innocent, wacky, of flickering brightness and passing secrets. Howell believed her, and his guilt vanished. He started laughing. "Wow," he rumbled. "I'm not going to touch that right now. Let's just say that you don't like my nipples. Anyway, I promise not to do anything more than touch you. You have my word."

Moonbeam searched his laugh. "I believe you," she said. "That's exciting."

After a long sweet massage, Moonbeam turned to Howell with red cheeks and a look of suspicion that unnerved him. "That was for you," she accused, "not for me. You *liked* it."

"Huh?" said Howell.

"I thought I could trust you," Moonbeam said coldly. "But you took something from me and you cheated me. You just wanted to get your hands on me, and I let you mess with my head."

"What are you talking about?" asked Howell. "Of course I liked it. I thought that's what you wanted, and I wanted it too. What's wrong with that?"

"*You* know," snarled Moonbeam with such menace that Howell felt a chill. She looked away from him, panting with rage. She seemed much younger, no more than twenty, but the pain had returned to her face many-fold. "You are different from the rest of the men here," she said, in a prosecutor's low rumble, "so I expect you to give me a straight answer. I want to know what you're running from."

Howell stared at her in bewilderment. In panic, he tried to escape through humor by looking around behind him, as though Moonbeam were talking to someone else. "Where did *that* come from?" he grinned.

"I want to know what you're running from," Moonbeam insisted.

"I'm not running from anything," said Howell, giving up the ruse. "What are you talking about?"

"Everybody is running from something," said Moonbeam. "I know that."

"Where did you hear that?" demanded Howell. "What are you running from, then?"

Moonbeam grabbed her ankle with one hand and pulled it up under her, viciously. "I'm running from all the people who say everybody is running," she said. "But *you're* running from something else."

"Maybe so," soothed Howell. "But if I am, I don't know what it is. I think you should take it easy. It's no big deal, and I didn't mean to insult your dolphin." He looked at her apprehensively, but he was still not prepared when she sprang across the bed and wrapped her arms around his neck. Her momentum carried them both off the bed with a thud. Howell grunted and whined at once until he realized that it was not a karate attack but instead a desperate embrace. Moonbeam had flipped again.

"Please hug me," she pleaded. "You *are* different. You are nice. You put up with me."

"Thanks," Howell managed as he tried to loosen one of her arms. "You are choking me," he gasped.

"I'm sorry," said Moonbeam. She let go of his neck and hugged him around the chest. "I'm sorry. It's just that I get scared sometimes. I'm not normal, I guess."

"That's all right," said Howell.

"Just let me stay here a few seconds," she said, squeezing him tighter. "That's all I need. Just until my karma wrings itself out."

"That's all right," laughed Howell. "Wring it out all over me." He was happy that the alien fury had passed.

"There," said Moonbeam after twenty breaths. "It's over."

She jumped back up on the bed and seemed to be somewhat herself again, though subdued. Howell followed carefully, wary of a mistake. He gazed silently at her until it became uncomfortable. She was not going to say anything, he realized, and he didn't know what to say either. So he laughed. "Well, after all that, you've at least got to tell me something about the dolphins," he said. "I can't stand it anymore."

Moonbeam lost her pensive look and smiled. "Okay," she said. "You won't believe it." And she told him about her life down at the research tank with the dolphins, which had a sad ending because her particular dolphin —Antioch, the one she was in love with—had been transferred away from her to San Diego. She had heard that Antioch died thereafter of a broken heart. Or maybe she just felt it across the continent, as one can do with dolphins. The story, though sad, brought Moonbeam back to life. Howell asked her a hundred questions about her courtship of, and communication with, Antioch, and she told how he would swim on his back along the surface with her sitting on his tiny penis, rubbing his skin, which feels like a smooth oiled olive, and reaching around for his dorsal fin in ecstasy.

Moonbeam drifted off amid the flow of Howell's questions, and he watched her sleep. Even in slumber she amazed him by moving into her inchworm position, which he had never seen before. This, of all the strange things he had seen in a typical evening at Ziller's, made Howell conclude that he needed a walk. He put on a pair of shorts and strolled into the outdoor night air, which in Miami is the same as the indoor night air. Walking along past the banyan trees and the eucalyptus trees and the spotlighted, manicured palms around the wealthy homes, he mused about the bizarre urge that kept him shuttling back and forth between Max Parker's old colleagues and Moonbeam. By day it was serious, churchgoing, anticommunist fighters, with a promise of terror and a touch of a joke, and by night it was across the bay and across the universe to the farthest extensions of hippiedom and Dada, where Moonbeam and Arlington Spencer played mental roulette with the promise of a joke and a touch of terror. Howell wanted more of it. He wanted to surprise himself and stretch it as far as he could, but he also thought he might be running from something after all, like she said.

VI

APPROPRIATELY, ONLY part of Henry Woodruff realized that he had a split personality. This same part hovered in the air over the bed as a spectator to Woodruff's experience—the more vivid the experience, the more vigilant the spectator—looking down on the pathetic naked figure there in repose, hands folded and eyes sunk, bent at the waist from the hurt of it. From the air, it appeared to be a dramatic moment, of the kind that will mark a person in the manner of birth and death or war or love, except that it is unexpected and unprepared for by either the species or the person. The man on the bed had obviously received some sort of comeuppance that was special. It was not like a politician coming to grief for a lifetime of lies or a farmer losing his whole crop to locusts or even like a lover losing his heart to another, for all these are known hazards of the games. This looked different. The fellow on the bed was in shock, but he was peaceful, and the look on his face was neither pain nor blank fear.

Woodruff had not felt anything like it since he was a small child, learning to count, lying in the top bunk bed late at night with his eyes open in the dark, measuring off in his mind the time between first-grade summer vacation and second grade summer vacation, which was immense, and then counting—one, two, ten, a hundred, thousand, a billion zillion—all the while growing scared of time. The fear would crawl into him and conquer his little brain and obliterate his body until all he could sense of himself was a minute speck of nothing, and sometimes it would take a drink of water or an extra toothbrushing to get rid of it. Occasionally it would even take two drinks of water. Now that same fear had come back in adult form, and instead of making a visit, of dropping by like a pasty relative or a bad television show, it arrived by physical force and shoved a pipe down his throat. Had he not been paralyzed into calm, he would have gagged when the pipe, as thick as his fist, pushed through his throat and down into his stomach.

Then the switch was thrown and Woodruff's mouth opened involuntarily. The pipe sucked out his insides, starting with his stomach and liver, then rattled up over his vertebrae to suck up his heart and lungs, and finally his tongue. Woodruff's eyes popped out lazily. He couldn't breathe. The terror inflicted its own kind of pain down the middle of him, but it was unfamiliar and not quite real. Woodruff would have welcomed any regular pain in its place; a cut or a stubbed toe would do. But the machine kept sucking silently within him, cleaning out the dry spaces between his ribs. He was a thin paper husk. All he could think was that he was being worked over by the cosmic vacuum cleaner.

The very idea of the cosmic vacuum cleaner brought the trace of a smile to Woodruff's mouth as he realized that this was the first thought he had managed in some time, since the fear had taken possession of him. He seemed to float upward from the bed to get a view of himself, and this time the scene appeared more absurd than dramatic. There he was, surrounded by Casey's paraphernalia, including Excelsior, the stuffed frog, and walls covered with about a hundred new photographs showing only the legs of male tennis players. He did not know why she had put them there, but he suspected it had something to do with his own legs, which lacked the graceful muscle tone and the glistening tan of the pros. It amused Woodruff slightly that he was having an epiphany of sorts in such a setting, amid her doodads, as human creatures will do. He listened to the water running in the bathroom, and it occurred to him that he could take an ordinary shower if he could only shake these crazy thoughts of cancer and think of it as an ordinary divorce. What kind of world was it in which romantic worries would leave a person so ridiculous, afraid to take a shower?

He tried to think of a cancer cell as just like any other little cell, growing and reproducing and making its way in the world, but then the euphemism gave way and so did his mind. He felt the cells crawling all over the crust of his body, causing waves of revulsion that were neither dramatic nor absurd. There was something repugnant about his body or his essence, and it brought him more than just a passing hurt. No, this was his condition. He would have to live with it. His thoughts could not cure it, and in fact the condition subdued his mind easily, being much stronger. In this state, time stopped for Woodruff. As much as he had feared the march of time moments earlier, now the stagnation of it was even worse. The irony of this was a thought that helped rescue him again, though this time it was more difficult. He got outside of himself after a struggle and was even higher above the bed.

Present events took on a profound cover for Woodruff. He decided that the unexpected ferocity of his misery was a demonstration for him that he could not rise above flickering human passions, including his own. Previously he had believed so instinctively. He thought most things in life intrigued his mind only. Wars and corruptions bothered his spirit no more than the rain dents a good slate roof. All the vagabond desires—the conflicts, jealousies, and short-lived ambitions—seemed temporary and petty to him beside the permanent truths of history and science. So he devoted himself to those ideas that applied to *all* people, preferably across the ages, in order to "cancel out" the human factor as much as possible. It would not be easy, he acknowledged grimly, but at least he would concern himself with the edifice of civilization, with the ideas that built upon one another in so formidable a way that people would not quarrel with them like they quarrel with everything else.

In this light, Woodruff's marriage to Casey was an accomplished fact that he regarded with lingering sentiment, but it belonged, nonetheless, to the realm of lesser things that people had been doing for eons and for which they would get little credit on history's scorecard. Woodruff treated his marriage like his college diploma—as a necessary step toward the higher achievements by which he would one day measure himself. Now Casey was obliterating those dreams by showing him how easily and completely he could fall prey to these dastardly frail feelings. Worst of all, he could not understand them. He could feel the cancer, but he had no idea what it was. For all he knew, it could derive from either a fundamental mental failure or from something as silly as the way he walked or the shape of his tennis legs. It was some comfort to Woodruff simply to understand that these arbitrary emotions held dominion over him, for the understanding itself was a sign of hope. It gave him something to think about. On the other hand, he decided he was thinking mostly to shield himself from how desperately he needed Casey. Locked in physical catatonia, Woodruff went back and forth between the pain and his ideas. Propelled by the tension within himself, he went higher and higher off the bed like a rubber band in flight, one end snapping ahead of the other.

Casey had looked back on her first passion with a touch of sadness and a hope of better things. It had been a high point. The moment she had finally discovered did not wear well. At first she blamed Clayfield for spoiling it. They did the right things together, once he decided that it was prudent to be seen with her and she loved the evenings at dinners or embassies or the Kennedy Center. She liked entering the foyers of the embassies on Massachusetts Avenue to be announced grandly by name by a handsome formal crier in a uniform festooned with ribbons, and she liked moving through the receiving lines past the ambassadors and potentates, watching Clayfield play the game and say frostily cordial things or carefully indiscreet things or whatever was correct. And she enjoyed his candid reviews of these characters, which were caustic and even cynical to Casey but never depressing, because Clayfield loved the game so much. He loved it so much, in fact, that he told Casey of his bureaucratic strategies at great length back in her bed, which was where the problem began.

To Casey, the formality and glitter were all right on their own, but their chief value was as preludes of finesse and restraint to the new joys at home, about which Casey was highly enthusiastic. Without such fulfillment, the formalities were just that, formalities, open to the ridicule Henry Woodruff always threw at them. As in many other matters, Casey came to appreciate Woodruff's point of view here even as her chemistry was drifting away from him. After a few months with Clayfield, her joy had atrophied so much that even the sex of it did not much appeal to her, though it was better than with Woodruff. She even suspected that his soft orgasms were not affirmations of love as a whisper in the universe but simply of how little of himself he put into them, or, worse, of how little of him there was.

She had thought about Woodruff a great deal, as always. As their separation became longer and more painful, she admired him more. They were into their sixth or seventh negotiating phase, having tried silence, intensity, counseling, and self-analysis, always fluctuating wildly between optimism and utter despair. No one had yet mentioned divorce seriously, but Woodruff had made jokes about it. Casey laughed at them. She laughed at everything Woodruff intended to be funny, even the words that hurt her, for she appreciated the odd twists of communion between them—how she could express anger with her crackly ankle, how Woodruff deflected his frustration with jokes. Seldom did either of them escape the channels of behavior that had been settled upon between them, usually when Woodruff would get carried away into rapture in a monologue about how complicated their problem was, how great a challenge it posed to mind and spirit, how awesome a small and common event could be when you considered its deepest refractions, always soaring along on the backs of words and paradoxes, such as the notion that marriage itself might be an impediment to an understanding of marriage. On such occasions, Casey might do more than crack her ankles. She would squeeze her fists white wherever she was, on park benches or at lunch tables or in a car, and she would stiffen from formality into a marital glare.

Woodruff would always apologize humbly and there would be silence, followed soon by the end of the session, and Casey would later think of a longer, more eloquent speech than the one she had made. She hated it when he treated her like a concept, but it was impossible for her to sustain her anger when separated from him. Then she was always scissored between her admiration for him and her guilt over what she was doing to him, with the result that Woodruff, who had always encouraged the rebel in her, would turn into a concept of his own.

Once, when her hopes were breaking down, Casey had run into the house and smudged her Album with topsoil as she scribbled a single sentence under that morning's long entry: "Maybe it can happen again." From that moment, she felt a renewed strength that sent her chugging through her days with romantic sunbursts in her head. Whenever she considered reproaching herself for the saccharine quality of such fantasies, she only had to remind herself that they were bought with all the pain she had concealed. So she would not apologize for her hope. Besides, who could deny that it was possible? After all, Casey, at the age of thirty, had broken her own will in half to commit her first cardinal moral transgression, swerving from a lifetime of practiced shoulds, and the result had been the awakening of the very woman in her, with new blood rushing through her body in fulfillment of fantasies she had never known.

Casey wanted another breakthrough. It could be less intense or it could be a surprise. That would be all right. She didn't deliberate over the nature or the likelihood of what she wanted very long, because she knew it wouldn't help and she wanted to preserve the mystical nature of the hope anyway. But the premonition that came to her that evening in the yard was a very powerful one. She thought of other famous breakthroughs—of the Selma march that Howell talked about with so much feeling as a breakthrough in civil rights, of Woodruff describing the Pentagon Papers as a breakthrough in public skepticism about government, of the pill and Tampax and I.Q. tests as breakthroughs for females, of Einstein and Freud and the systematic theology of Tillich. She thought of feminist breakthroughs, closer to home, such as that of her friend Eileen. After a lifetime of reading magazines on how to be demure, Eileen had suffered greatly when her strong-willed environmentalist husband went bonkers over an adolescent guru from the East, becoming his legal and economic adviser, and there was only the tiniest hint of liberation on Eileen's demure cheeks when she walked up behind her husband at the dinner table and dumped twenty-four servings of saffron rice over his head. That, too, was a breakthrough, although Eileen had since gone equally bonkers over the cause of touchy-feely feminist elementary schools. Still, it had been a breakthrough in independence for Eileen, and Casey had gone so far as to urge her toward divorce. She and Eileen both felt an alien thrill, like the bad girls in junior high who used to smoke in the boys' restroom.

Casey's notion of a breakthrough quickly mushroomed into all her hopes and beyond them, as such notions often do. If there were another one, another change of that magnitude, there was no telling what might happen. The great moment would come when Casey would recreate her first breakthrough, but she would do so with Woodruff, her chosen one, and she would show him that she could. She would settle for that alone. Then, having been there, she could have an equal say in the area of subterranean, animal, and therefore highly improper activities of the species, which turned out to be wonderful. In fact, she might have more than an equal say, for Casey was entertaining the heretical thought that Woodruff, for all his worldliness, did not really know all that much about the subterranean side and how easily it could enslave all his imposing qualities—his vast ambitions and childish wisdom, his generous pomposity and lofty tenderness, the determined clarity that made people cling to him and made Casey, at a distance, smile all over. With just one more breakthrough, no less possible than the first one, unbounded romance and harmony and wisdom and independence would come within reach. Casey, in short, tasted the desire to have it all. She appreciated for the first time the way Woodruff and the others must have felt when they came to Washington in the whistling tumult of the marching decade, each one wanting all he could imagine.

Casey behaved very strangely over the next few weeks. She let the house slide. She stacked dirty dishes in the sink and let Excelsior, the stuffed frog, sleep all day on his back amid rumpled covers. She tossed dirty laundry into the closet in the Woodruff manner instead of piling it neatly on the top shelf, and in the bathroom, pantyhose wrappers clogged the trash cans and toilet paper rolls sat handily on the floor. She lost sight of the benefits to be gained from the labor of putting the toilet paper on the tricky roller. She nursed her patience with every sort of artifice she could think of. She took long evening walks through the November coolness of Glover Park. She pulled out her old easel and produced a rough portrait of the big bang's creation of the universe, with lots of cloudy swirls and shiny spots, and she even went to a few passable dinners with people she didn't like, just to pass the time. It was so unlike Woodruff not to have called after so long a separation. Casey suffered nightmarish visions of Woodruff down there in Austin all agog over some millionaire Texas lady with creamy skin and no bra and a mind like Hannah Arendt; she could see them at the beer garden surrounded by literate yahoos as the Texan wowed Woodruff with some recondite Greek palaver in a discussion of something awful like the under-pinnings of totalitarianism. Casey wondered why Woodruff looked up to Hannah Arendt the way barbers look up to Marilyn Monroe, and this very thought drove her back to the easel to slap more color and confusion into the big bang. Casey welcomed the stirrings of jealousy, however, having never felt them before. It was a good sign. Her yearning for a breakthrough had taken hold and was now in the nature of an accepted faith. The remaining question marks were the last-minute details, such as whether certain sexual associations were transferable, and Casey was confident that, now that she knew what she was looking for, the expected chain reaction would occur. All she needed was something to remind her of the perfect mixture of the wholesome and the illicit, and to Casey, this problem was neatly resolved by the backup photographs of the tennis legs, with their downy hair and hard calf muscles.

Finally Casey broke down and called Woodruff at the Senate, where he said he was being ambushed by liberals opposed to his plan to end poverty. He said he had been giving Casey more time, as she had wished, but that he was more interested than ever in saving their marriage, because of realizations that had come to him. He sounded as accommodating as ever, which was bad, but he also sounded serene and almost mystical, which Casey decided was good. Nervously, she came straight to the point and invited him for dinner that night. Woodruff calmly suggested Chez Odette in Georgetown, which was also good. It was a perfect compromise—French for Casey, less snooty than most for Woodruff.

He picked her up in their car at their house, where Casey had been living alone with their furniture and an assortment of Woodruff's belongings packed in boxes upstairs. Woodruff still had a housekey, which he used, but he rang the doorbell simultaneously. Casey opened it almost instantly, pulling Woodruff's key out of the door. Casey was pleased with the way she looked and even more pleased with Woodruff, who was indeed dressed well above his ordinary capacity. He had gone so far as to splash on some shaving lotion from an ancient bottle, which Casey liked, although it smelled like lighter fluid. They stared at each other. Woodruff broke the spell by asking for a tour of the house. To oblige, Casey took him by the elbow and escorted him briskly along, the way a real estate agent hustles a client who is obviously too poor. They paused awkwardly over the boxes of Woodruff's effects, but otherwise Casey kept things moving. In return for the house tour, she asked Woodruff to let her drive the car.

Aside from Casey's jitters, the dinner at Chez Odette was different from longstanding practice in that Casey thumped her watch several times and seemed indifferent to the food, whereas Woodruff lingered over the social amenities and commented on things like the garnishments and the china patterns. Casey nodded through conversation, as though all talk were interesting but nevertheless an obstacle in the path to the heart of things. Woodruff was treasuring the small surprises. It was a complete reversal of their normal behavior together. Woodruff, following Casey to the cashier, stumbled across her old friend Eileen at a corner table, and made inane small talk with her, which was most uncharacteristic. Casey stayed out of sight behind him, and she tugged at his arm until he nearly fell out the door.

As they drove home, congratulating themselves frequently on how much they had learned, how many things seemed different, no alarm registered on Woodruff's face, though Casey had an urgent foot on the gas. Nothing showed when she insisted that he come in for a nightcap or even when she shepherded him and the drinks up the stairs to the bedroom. But when she stepped swiftly out of her shoes and removed her blouse without warning, Woodruff's Zen facade was broken into tiny pieces. His mouth hung open for a time, like a beginner in speech therapy, and he pitched forward on his toes, like a skier. "Is this really you, or am I dreaming?" he managed before he spilled his drink.

"Come on," Casey replied. "We're still legal."

Casey leaped sideways onto the bed and wiggled around while flashing Woodruff her half-grin, which he had never seen before. She grew more excited as she watched terror and lust mix in with the shock on his face while he stripped, but when he crawled toward her she saw that the hunger in his eyes was touched with reverence. Neither could tell whether it came from fear or self-importance or from an awe of the moment; to Casey it didn't matter. The look wasn't one of light celebration, and it cost Casey her grin. "Hurry up," she urged. "You won't believe this, but I don't want the foreplay."

"The foreplay," laughed Woodruff, mocking her expression.

His laughter vanished as he went inside her, and when this happened, strange things happened to Casey. Her senses were extinguished, one by one, first smell and then taste. It became very clear to her that it was judgment day and her merits were being tested, and Woodruff's skin was the parchment on which it would be written. It felt like parchment anyway, though it had always seemed like perfectly good skin to her, and then her

126

sense of touch vanished. She heard air escaping through a tight valve deep inside Woodruff in a continuous sigh, and then she could no longer hear. She opened her eyes and became afraid. Woodruff's eyes were closed and his mouth open in supplication, like a baby bird waiting to be fed. He was diminished, though his features still pretended to authority. She pitied him, as a first step toward repulsion, and then she lost her sight.

All this happened so fast that Casey didn't realize that she couldn't breathe. Had she been able to hear her gasps, she would have thought that Woodruff might take them for a new passionate release, but she couldn't. All she could do was to feel her insides. It was a terrible smothering sensation, grainy and bulging, as though someone had stuffed a huge towel between her lungs, and it brought unspeakable claustrophobia. She began to panic, and as she did, needles of pain began to shoot from her chest down to her groin. Casey arched her back and heaved. Her residual strength made a dash to get out through her mouth.

She had no idea how long it took her to sit up on the side of the bed, moaning. "I hurt," she gasped. "I think I've got cancer. That must be what it is." Wobbling in delirium, she made her way to the bathroom and sat down in the bare tub. The water made a bleak sound as it struck the drain plug. Casey waited, with her head between her knees, for it to rise.

By the time the bath was lapping around her navel, Woodruff appeared, leaning wearily against the door. He was dizzy, having fallen down at last from his mind's flight, and his central system was shorted out from a tangled overload of realizations, among them that there were only two photographs of tennis players' legs in the bedroom instead of the dozens that he had seen earlier. Woodruff hated illusions. "Casey," he said, in a very small voice.

She made no reply. There was none she could think of. Besides, her head would never move from its rest there, in position to stare down through the water's wrinkled light to her dark and unfamiliar crotch, the outlet of the cancer's pain, which was finally abating. The hurt was relocating to her chest, as she numbly told herself that there could be negative breakthroughs, too, as horrible as her fantasies were magic. It is so unfair, she thought, in the refrain of a lost soul.

"Shit," said Woodruff. "We are all lost souls. It's just a question of whether we know it or not."

This stirred Casey. It was just like Woodruff, she thought, to verbalize something from an obscure corner of her privacy and thereby lay claim to it, make it real for her. "You're really an optimist tonight, Henry," she whispered without looking up.

"An optimist?" sighed Woodruff. "Christ, how can you make cracks like that? It wasn't *my* idea to do this. *I'm* not the one who's talking about cancer."

"I know," sighed Casey, not wanting to argue.

"Never mind," Woodruff said apologetically. "I don't think you really have cancer, if that's any help."

"It doesn't matter," said Casey.

Woodruff stared at her. "You know the thing that really gets me is that I thought I had finally gotten over the idea that sex was the great barometer of a marriage. I had myself all convinced that the other things brought peace and closeness, and then the sex would take care of itself, like you have always said. And just as I finally get there, you go the other way. I don't understand it."

"I don't either," said Casey. "Maybe we're both right. Anyway, words don't help."

"I guess not," said Woodruff. He watched her for a long time, but she did not look up. "I don't have any," he said, quietly closing the door, "except that I hope you have a nice bath."

Casey looked up toward the sound of the door. "Be careful on your way home," she said helplessly.

Woodruff rolled down all the windows, turned the radio up, put his left arm out the window, and concentrated on perceiving every ordinary thing he could, the more mundane the better. The unperturbed normalcy of stone walls and streetlights and sappy rock tunes and high school playgrounds and the wind made him feel better, driving at a crawl, so slowly that when he reached Howell's empty apartment the water in Casey's bath was already cool.

VII

DAVID HOWELL could not make himself comfortable on the Coca-Cola crates in the dingy office even before El Navajo pulled out the "boomcake." This object, packed in a plastic trash bag inside a cardboard box at the bottom of a deep drawer, turned out to be an excellent likeness of Fidel Castro sculpted in some sort of white silly putty. Two cherries gave Castro red eyes, and the wavy strands of his beard had been shaped carefully with a serrated knife. He rested there, face up, on a platter made from the lid of a small grease drum.

"Boomcake," declared El Navajo. He grinned savagely, but with an unmistakable pride of authorship.

"Very nice," said Howell, who was both impressed and hungry. He leaned back to wipe away the perspiration that had collected under the brim of the big Panama hat Bobby Ziller had given him for protection against Miami's winter sun. By this hat, Howell had already become known in the cafés of Little Havana. He leaned forward to get a better look at the cake, and when he did the two crates under him pinched his bottom. "Ow!" he shrieked. Then he chuckled, "Castro's crates here don't like your artwork, I guess."

"What you say?" asked El Navajo.

"Nothing," said Howell.

El Navajo appeared to be puzzled and slightly suspicious. He looked back to the cake. "Boomcake," he repeated. Very much agitated, he reached down among the papers on his Gulf Oil desk blotter and pulled out two wires which he jabbed into Castro's skull. "Wires here like so," he said. "Through magic box to phone." Placing what looked to be a small transformer on the blotter, he put on a hurried pantomime of circuitry and waved himself out of the garage. "Go away," he said, now pantomiming a frenzied man dialing a phone. "Call here and BOOOOOM!!" El Navajo lifted his skinny arms to their full wingspan and stood there in his dirty T-shirt, a pack of unfiltered cigarettes protruding from a pocket on his sunken chest. His eyes were mad with delight. "No more Castro," he said. "Everything happy again. I go home to Cuba."

Howell noted the sublime release on El Navajo's face and then turned back to the cake. "Huh?" he said.

"Boomcake," El Navajo explained, pointing a bony left forefinger at his creation. "Kill Castro," he said. He studied Howell's face for approval, and it registered on him that Howell's ignorance remained. El Navajo became impatient with the language barrier. "Say kwatro!" he shouted. "Say kwatro!"

Howell looked blankly at Max Parker, needing help. He knew very little about El Navajo, but he believed instinctively that it was not wise to let him grow frustrated.

"Say kwatro!" shouted El Navajo.

A worried Howell knew that something needed to be done. "Okay," he said weakly. "Kwatro."

"No Kwatro!" shouted El Navajo, now clearly irritated. "*Say* kwatro!"

"I *did* say 'kwatro,' " Howell protested rather politely.

"No, you two, wait a minute," laughed Parker. His jovial mood intruded on the confusion. "David, what he's saying is Spanish for C–4. That's *ce-cuatro*," Parker explained. "That's the name of a plastique explosive we used to use in the Company. It's an odorless, white, petroleum-based compact bomb, just like Fidel in the cake."

"You don't say," mused Howell.

"No say," corrected El Navajo, stamping his foot. "Say kwatro."

Howell rolled his eyes. "*Si, yo comprendo,*" he said. "Say kwatro."

"Say kwatro," agreed El Navajo, now immensely pleased.

Parker had been unable to control his laughter through the exchange. "Boy, you two are really something," he said. "It's funny to talk that way, but C–4 is very serious stuff. A cake like that would blow this garage out into the swamp."

Howell looked at the boomcake with fresh respect. Two light wrinkles creased his forehead, gathering sweat beads and stretching them into lines. Howell stared quietly at Parker, who was still tickled, and then at El Navajo, who was quite sober in his picaresque glory. "Tell me, Max," said Howell. "This particular boomcake here could be made of say kwatro, but actually it is not, right? That's really icing or caulk or something, isn't it?"

Howell's face made Parker cautious. "Don't worry," he said.

"You mean . . . ?" asked Howell.

"Don't worry," said Parker, "but it is the genuine thing."

Howell threw up a long sigh, turning his face from the boomcake for fear that his very breath might set it off. He shook his head. "I just don't understand it," he said.

"Don't worry," said Parker. "Understand what?"

Howell looked at Parker and then at El Navajo. "I don't understand what I'm doing here, for one thing," he replied wanly. "But mainly I don't understand why, if that thing's a bomb, we are in the same room with it. That doesn't make any sense to me."

"Well, that is a point," said Parker. "However, El Navajo is one of the best in the business, so we are perfectly safe. I assure you."

In the midst of all this English talk, El Navajo's face drooped into uncertainty. His faith in Parker was such that he nodded positively along with his words even though he understood almost nothing of what Parker was saying. He did see the fear in Howell and he did understand the word "safe," however, and these combined to bring him an idea. "Safe!" he cried, like an umpire, so loudly that Howell feared the percussion would jar the boomcake toward explosion. "Very safe!" El Navajo added, now rifling through his desk in a hurried search. He pulled out wads of used carbon paper, old insurance calendars, grisly photographs of executions at the *paredón* in Cuba, four or five bottles of after-shave lotion, and his high school diploma before coming across the item he desired. It was a small mayonnaise jar, wrapped in a rag, from which El Navajo retrieved several dozen small pieces of the white clay. They were scraps from the boomcake. Howell took in a sharp breath. El Navajo, with a broad grin of mastery, kneaded the C–4 into a single piece of dough.

"Oh, boy," sighed Howell. And Parker, remembering his old training, shouted, "No!" But it was too late.

El Navajo tossed the C–4 briskly at Howell. As it flew toward him, he froze and suppressed an instinct to bat it away with his hands. There was no time to dodge, so Howell, with the improbable quickness that had once made him a star in dodge ball, went over backward faster than the missile. The crates flew out from under him. To keep farther away from the plastique, he arched his neck and threw his shoulders back, like a limbo dancer. This was fortunate, for Howell's neck was protectively braced when the back of his head struck the metal leg of El Navajo's antique gum machine. All at once, Howell felt the shock and heard shouts and saw that the C–4 was following him relentlessly and let loose a small grunt of surrender. The plastique plopped on his chest before rolling across the dusty concrete floor.

Parker picked it up and handed it to El Navajo with a look of rebuke. "Are you all right?" he asked the victim.

It was some time before Howell could speak. In the interim, all he could do was listen to El Navajo's remarkable laugh, a high-pitched cackle that could peel rust off a ship's hull. El Navajo put one hand over his stomach and flailed the air with the other. There was nothing he enjoyed more than gallows slapstick.

Howell gingerly reseated himself on the crates. "Boy, that was fun," he whispered, rubbing the back of his head. "I'd like to believe that stuff is make-believe, but I'm afraid I know better."

"I hope so," said Parker. "Don't let Eduardo know you doubt his materials, or he'll put on a demonstration for you."

"No, thank you," said Howell. "Not today anyway."

El Navajo, having calmed down, delivered a lengthy speech in Spanish, which Parker translated. "He says you can kick C–4, hit it with a sledge-hammer, even burn it, but it won't go off without the proper electric spark," Parker relayed. "He says that his Company explosives trainer threw a ball of C–4 at *him* on his first day of training, back in 1962. That's what they always do. It's like throwing a kid into the water to swim. You've got to get over your fear of the stuff before you can work with it. Eduardo's seen men faint and pee on the floor and break windows when that stuff comes at them, so don't feel bad about it."

"Thanks," sighed Howell. "So Eudardo was an explosives expert for the Company, is that right?"

"No," said Parker. "He is a firearms man. Explosives are a sideline."

"A what?" asked Howell.

"A sideline," said Parker. "A hobby."

"That's what I thought you said," chuckled Howell.

El Navajo, happy to see Howell so fully recovered, smiled expansively and tossed him the C–4 again. This time he caught it, in spite of the legions of distracting goosepimples that leaped up along his spine. The clay was light, smooth, malleable, and very soft. Softer than Moonbeam's breast, Howell thought, after his fingers suggested the comparison. It unnerved him to think such a gentle substance could in an instant disappear, changing its mind, leaving unsightly destruction. Howell's smile shuddered off his face. He determined to do everything he could not to offend the C–4. To give it space to breathe, he lifted the ball to a perch atop all five fingertips, the way one might hold a thistle. Then he breathed deeply himself until he could formulate a simple question in Spanish. "Where does this stuff come from, Eduardo?" he asked.

Consternation struck El Navajo on the spiny bridge of his nose, between his beady eyes, as he was thrown backward in time to a familiar but piercing discomfort. This was an *American* speaking, demanding information, being far more direct than he had been before. To El Navajo, Howell appeared to be an oaf who cared about "the life" only for his amusement, but you could never be sure. It might be a ruse. In the old days, many Company officers expected a Cuban to tell them every single thing he knew at any time, regardless of security regulations, as though the simple fact that they were American automatically overrode classification. But others—generally the young ones and the security types—would cajole information out of a Cuban agent and then berate him for revealing it. You could never be sure. It was complicated enough back then, and now it was even worse. Americans were now bad, yet here was Max Parker urging El Navajo to speak honestly to one, an outsider, for the first time. El Navajo did not know what to say about the C–4, so he froze helplessly with a friendly but obsequious smile on his face. Then he shrugged and shook his head slightly in the negative, feeling humiliated.

"That's okay," said Howell, who turned to Parker. "Ask him to get back to the story in Africa, Max," he said. "I don't know what made him pull out the boomcake in the first place. Where were we? Let's see. I think El Navajo was on a jeep just behind Michael Hoare about thirty miles outside Stanleyville. Is that right?"

Halfway through Parker's translation, Howell knew he had made a mistake. El Navajo's face clouded up. He frowned, and a small pouch formed at the junction of his eyebrows, turning red as he lit another cigarette. With a vengeance, he crushed the match in his palm. Then, making a supreme effort to control himself, El Navajo put his hands behind him in the parade rest position and tried to recite. He did not get very far. Even before Parker got to translate anything, El Navajo spun around and smacked the wall behind him in a spasm of violence. Then followed a harangue full of hate to Parker, with sidelong glances toward Howell.

Parker soothed him with gestures and words before turning to Howell. "I don't think Africa is a good topic for him to talk about," he confided. "He says there are many things about it that you will never know. And he says none of it matters anyway because Castro is still alive."

Howell said, "That's all right. Just ask him if Stanleyville was his last mission for the Company."

Parker looked at El Navajo, began to form the question, and then turned back to Howell. "By the way, you look ridiculous," he said.

Howell looked blandly at the C–4 doughball next to his ear. "Nice of you to notice," he said. "I feel like a waiter."

Parker almost laughed, but nodded instead toward El Navajo who was upset and who did not understand all the English. "I don't think it's smart to ask him anything about Africa now," he said. "I can tell you myself that Stanleyville was his last mission, if that's any help. When El Navajo gets like this, all he can really see is his red spot for Castro."

"I see," said Howell. "Does it seem strange to you that all of a man's hopes would rest on the death of another man? Boy, that takes a lot of concentration. Do you know if he has always hated Fidel like that? When did it start?"

Parker relayed the questions in Spanish, and El Navajo seemed to relish the change of subject. He spat out a few choppy phrases of obvious invective before drifting into a balmy mood. Howell was startled by the new, enraptured El Navajo with his lilting cadence and his bony left forefinger lightly scratching his temple, sending a sharp elbow almost into the window fan. El Navajo might as well have been speaking of the first time he held hands with a schoolgirl.

Howell thought he caught a key word. "*Béisbol?*" he asked.

"*Sí, béisbol*," bubbled El Navajo, who proceeded to warble along in Spanish.

"Wait a minute," said Parker. He hushed El Navajo. "Now. He did not begin to hate Fidel until a revolutionary tribunal executed one of his girlfriend's relatives on television," Parker summarized. "In his opinion, the head of the revolutionary tribunal was settling a personal grudge. That was the first thing, and others happened after that. For one thing, a 26th of July university student took over the cigar workers' local where Eduardo was a steward. He didn't like that. But he did not always hate Fidel. In fact, he used to play catcher for Fidel when Fidel was a pitcher at the university."

"He did?" asked Howell. "A pitcher?"

"*Sí, peecher*," said El Navajo. He was pounding a fist into the palm of the other hand, ready to take the field.

Howell was astonished, but he was also skeptical. "I didn't know Eduardo went to the university," he said.

"He didn't," Parker replied, hushing El Navajo again. "But he belonged to the same group as Fidel."

"Group?" asked Howell.

"Yes, group," said Parker. "In the old Cuba, almost every organization was called a group. The university was very important in national politics because of the student revolution in 1933, so every group there was a coalition of students, labor unions, and politicians. In Miami, it is the same now —everybody belongs to a group, and the groups are always changing. Anyway, El Navajo and Fidel belonged to the same one, called the MSR."

Howell was glancing back and forth between Parker and the pounding El Navajo, unable to take it all in. "That's weird," he said absently.

"Not really," said Parker. "I don't think so. In America, you have an intellectual, a media adviser, a legendary fundraiser, a connection to Hollywood, and so forth. You call groups 'parties,' or 'administrations,' or 'factions.' It is all the same."

El Navajo could no longer contain himself through such idle English talk. He interrupted it with a long excited tale and with a series of full-fledged pitcher's windups, stepping straight toward Howell. From Howell's point of view, El Navajo's pointed left shoe looked like the tip of a skewer bearing down on him. His pitching stride covered most of the floor space in the office.

Parker rolled his eyes when El Navajo urgently beckoned him to translate the tale. "Uh, Eduardo says that as a pitcher, all Fidel had was a fast ball," said Parker. El Navajo nodded with delight as he threw another make-believe pitch. "He was very fast but very, very wild. He could not change and never learned anything until . . ."

El Navajo, anticipating the punch line, broke out into his theatrical guffaw, watching for Howell's reaction.

". . . he threw his first curve ball by betraying the revolution," Parker concluded with a wince. "That is what Eduardo always says," he added apologetically. "That's his joke. He says that since then Fidel only throws curves."

Howell laughed carefully—just enough to please El Navajo but not enough to disturb the C–4. It was a genuine low-key belly rumble, however, for Howell was amused by the mixture of baseball and explosives, by the sight of El Navajo, and by memories of Henry Woodruff's futile efforts to use the baseball analogy with Casey as a catalyst for discussion of sex. These and other associations kept the merriment going until Howell saw El Navajo spit into his hand, rub the sticky mixture deliberately into his nonexistent glove, and call for the ball. El Navajo had a demonstration in mind.

"I think he wants you to give him the stuff," Parker observed mischievously.

"Please tell him no, Max," pleaded Howell. "I'm not kidding. I'll buy him a real baseball." He stood up from the crates and backed across the office, searching feverishly for a substitute ball. El Navajo, full of holiday cheer, started forward to take the ball and show Howell his harmless change-up.

The tires of an approaching car crunched across the gravel outside and spared Howell. Glancing out the front window to see who it was, Max Parker lost his grin. The muscles on the back of his neck hardened into concrete, and his manner put the room into battle alert even before he spoke.

"Pepe," he spat at El Navajo, trying to sound casual.

"Who's Pepe?" asked Howell.

The two Cubans ignored him as they exchanged anxious trills of Spanish under their breaths. Pepe Lopez was turning off his car engine outside. Howell tried to keep from laughing over impish thoughts about how grown men could go from playing like school kids with a combat explosive to worrying like somber generals over the approach of an ordinary human being. His fear helped Howell keep such thoughts under control.

Having settled upon a plan, the Cubans moved to action. Parker went to the desk and threw the wrappings of the boomcake into the trash. He picked up the boomcake itself and thrust it into the crook of Howell's left arm. Howell was stunned. Parker snatched the ball off his fingertips and put it on Castro's nose so that Howell could support the boomcake box with both arms. Then he pushed Howell toward El Navajo and went out the door to stall Pepe. Not a word was spoken.

El Navajo opened the padlock on the inner back door of the garage office and ushered his guest through with an exaggerated bow, like a Victorian coachman. He ordered quiet by pressing a yardstick of finger to a wagon-wheel of lip, to which Howell was unable to respond. Then he repadlocked the door, leaving Howell alone in the more legitimate of El Navajo's two gun rooms.

After ten minutes at stiff attention, Howell realized that the boomcake was getting heavy and that fear would no longer occupy all his mind. He considered various ways to put the boomcake down, because he knew that he could not think as long as he held it there, with a possible shoot-out building up in the next room. His head was not functioning. There was no way to guarantee silence. So Howell simply squatted down on his haunches, trembling lest his knees crack, and after a series of sweating maneuvers that included holding the boomcake box between his knees while he laid a muffling towel on the floor, he finally laid down his burden. Only then did his ears tune in to the sound of the conversation in the next room.

Most of it was an effusive, sunny monologue by the visitor, Pepe Lopez, who appealed to Howell with his soaring laugh. Parker and El Navajo spoke rarely and always in monosyllabic mumbles, the way shoplifters explain themselves to store detectives. Howell decided that he had nothing to fear from this visitor, Pepe, but he was not sure about the guns. His previous acquaintance with firearms had been entirely cinematic, and this arsenal struck him as more sinister than the ones in movies. Assorted rifles were everywhere, in vertical stacks and horizontal stacks, and on top of the cupboards pistols were shelved like spices. Howell tried to think about how he would present this experience in his article for Marner and Drake back in Washington, but the culture gap was too great. The guns unnerved him, and, much to his own astonishment, he soon concluded that of all things in the gun room he was most comfortable with the boomcake.

El Navajo found Howell sitting on the floor with the boomcake in his lap, playing a game, tilting the box so that the C–4 ball rolled in patterns around Castro's face. On other days, he might have been impressed by Howell's rapid progress, but now he was all business. He had things to worry about, and Parker had places to go. All along the swamp highway back to Miami Parker was preoccupied, oblivious to the wildlife. He gave Howell a brief sketch of Pepe Lopez's background, but otherwise he answered no questions. His brooding bothered Howell, who was only thankful that he didn't know enough to worry about the right things. Parker didn't either, actually. It was vague and yet far too complicated to explain to a novice *gringo*. But there was something about the way Lopez had acted. He was "too happy," as El Navajo had said, even for someone who had turned into the pleasantest man in Miami. All that talk of soccer and television and El Navajo's insurance needs without a single nervous joke about Maraña. No questions, no mention of guns or politics—just passing the time of day without a hint of care in his face. The act was almost supernatural, beyond anything Parker had ever seen. Evil premonitions took hold in his mind.

Howell was relieved to be back at Ziller's. After a hard day among the plots and bombs, the familiar banyan tree became a refuge of normalcy. This sense of homecoming lasted through the early evening's activities, beginning with the sweeping arrival of Donessa, heiress to an Argentine cattle fortune, noted for many things including her affairs with such diverse luminaries as King Hussein of Jordan, Harold Pinter, and Danny the Red. Howell did not question her reputation, for he could sense in her authoritative face the kind of superior aloofness that would drive proud men mad, make them squander their most precious talents trying to move her. Donessa wore purple sandals, a diamond tiara, white sailor's pants, and a halter top that Howell could have worn for a bracelet, he thought. The thinness resulted from her steady diet of fruit juice and amyl nitrates. She got that from a jet-set dropout who was both a macrobiotic guru and the president of the Sierra Club chapter in Goa. Arlington Spencer talked of this man with such offbeat wonder that Howell decided he was making a play for Donessa.

Howell felt utterly uninformed in these areas, having confined himself for so long to readings in public affairs, so he could say nothing. Everything was going too fast, and he had to get by on his feat of striking a match on the seat of his pants. Ziller and Donessa appreciated it heartily, but Spencer did not. His desire for Donessa had already made him competitive, and he wound up searing his thumb trying to duplicate what Howell had done.

In due course Ziller decided that it was time for an excursion to the Boom-Boom Room at the Fontainebleau Hotel, and went upstairs to change his blue bandana for a red one from Guatemala. All of them, including Marvella, piled into Ziller's Mercedes and took off like gypsies, stopping along the way to buy Donessa a jolt of mango juice. In the lobby of the Fontainebleau, the Ziller entourage walked through like the owners, admiring the thousand-piece chandeliers and the imitation Louix XIV stained furniture and the Shriner couples from the Midwest who were on their way to the Boom-Boom Room for the show, along with some zootsuited pickpockets and well-escorted girls in prom dresses. Howell sighed over the very scope of it all, but his remarkable feeling of detached serenity kept coasting along with Ziller, throughout the third-rate bawdy floor show, until a tall blonde woman wearing a pink sheath dress and reddish brown fingernails plopped down in his lap and asked, "C'mon, stranger. How 'bout doing the devil's dance?"

Her accent was a mixture of Zurich and Harlem. Howell gawked at her, flicked his nose with a finger, and replied, "How long will it take?"

She threw her head back to laugh. "That is very good, dahhhling," she bubbled. "It will only take as long as you have."

The light from her eyes bounced back and forth like the hooves of a deer in flight. Howell decided she was actually a transvestite, which to him meant that he would either dance in whirling abandon or not at all. "I'm too tuckered," he drawled.

"Oh pooh!" cried the woman, who turned to Ziller. "How about you, Jiminy Cricket? Would you be so rude as to refuse a princess who wants to do the devil's dance?"

Without hesitation, Ziller grinned, "Whatever's right," as he usually did in situations of stress or ambiguity. He made devil's horns with his fingers and twirled around the floor with the princess, outdoing her. When he returned to the table, Donessa took the hand of the exhausted princess and nudged her back out under the pale blue lights.

Later, in the round bedroom after an escapade of backgammon, Howell decided that he had come full cycle. Now he was looking forward to the morning's breakfast in Little Havana, to the strong smell of Cuban coffee and the routine talk of secrets and betrayals. He had no idea what to expect with the Cubans, but at least he knew what kind of things to expect. Or so he thought. At Ziller's, he often felt like a wayward traveler who had been stranded six months in a carnival tent. He was falling into surprisingly pleasant dreams about circus animals when someone drove a spike of sound through his head.

"There's a big guy downstairs asking for you, Fidel," snapped Bobby Ziller. "I wouldn't argue with him if I were you."

Howell rolled out of bed and into his pants. Ziller's unfriendly tone cleared his head. "Who is it?" he asked apprehensively.

Ziller ignored the question. "Don't bring him up here," he commanded.

"Okay," said Howell.

"And do me a favor," said Ziller. "Don't let any more strangers come to the house."

"Okay. I'm sorry," gushed Howell, so shaken by Ziller's hostility that he got his T-shirt stuck over his head. He didn't know what to make of Ziller, who loved having strangers in the house unless, of course, they were too sincere. "Who is it, anyway?" asked Howell.

"A spic," said Ziller.

Howell flinched. "Oh, right," he said, feigning comprehension. As he went down the stairs, Howell felt Ziller's eyes in the middle of his back, and he decided that there was nothing worse than the inexplicable fury of a dedicated *bon vivant*.

"Max!" he cried, rubbing his eyes. "What are you doing . . ."

"Get your shoes," Parker interrupted. "Hurry!"

"What's gotten into everybody around here?" asked Howell. "Moonbeam, would you please give my friend Max a few blasts of laughing gas so he can relax?" Howell regretted the words before he finished them, and he kicked himself for being sleepy and afraid. It was just possible that loose talk about drugs was what had upset Ziller.

"Some other time," Parker said sternly. "We need to take a ride on the Reading. Now. You will enjoy it. As for the nitrous, I would love to share some with the lady another time." He looked at Moonbeam, who looked ill herself, and forced a bow. Moonbeam returned a curtsy that was tinged with sarcasm.

Howell returned in his tennis shoes. At the door, Parker let out a jolly, "Wake up, my friend," and proceeded to wrap his meaty elbow around Howell's neck. This was a common *machismo* gesture, a mixture of the Latin *abrazo* and the boxer's postfight hug, but there was something wrong about this particular one. Howell hoped that he was just being paranoid, that Parker was just being extra friendly this late at night. But he knew better.

Parker pushed Howell into the passenger's seat, slammed the door, and leaned through the window. He slapped Howell on the back with a heavy thud and shoved his face toward the glove compartment. "Don't look up!" he hissed. "I mean it!"

"Wait a minute," snorted Howell, finally rising to rebellion. "I'm not a goddam accordion, Max! What the hell is . . ."

"Shut up!" said Parker, swiftly pushing Howell back into his jackknife position. "Now stay there until I tell you to move. You don't know what's going on!"

Howell gave up. "That's for damn sure," he whispered, half to himself. When Parker revved up the engine and screeched back out of the driveway, Howell's back was vibrating with a nervous chuckle.

Parker heaved a sigh as he took off, and Howell mistook it for the all clear sigh. His neck crashed into the heel of Parker's hand before it rose two inches. "Ow," said Howell. "Do you know karate?" The speed of the car gave him a false sense of levity and release.

Parker was all business. "Did you know that house was being staked out by two DEA guys in separate cars?" he asked.

"Two what?" cried Howell, his fear quickly sharpened into a cops and robbers motif, with himself as the innocent, and therefore vulnerable, hostage.

"Drug boys," said Parker. "The narcs. In two separate cars. That means they're spending some money on you and your friends."

"On me?" cried Howell. "What do you mean, on me?"

"I thought you were just a roving journalist," Parker teased.

"My God," said Howell, who felt a strong instinct to confess something. "I mean I've seen a few harmless drugs there, but nothing to get the cops excited about. They might as well stake out any house on the bay from what I hear."

"Don't tell me," said Parker. "I believe you. But I'm not sure the DEA guys behind us will believe you."

It suddenly occurred to Howell that perhaps the bear hug escort he had gotten to the car was Parker's way of hiding their faces from the stakeout men. The idea came without specific stimulus, as ideas will do in a panic, and it further disoriented his mind. He felt a burst of admiration for Parker's romantic savvy, checked by sophisticated doubts about his theory. "Huh?" was all he could say out loud.

"The DEA guy behind us," Parker repeated. "One car is following us. That's good."

"I'm glad to hear it," said Howell. "Why is it good?"

"Because if they were going to bust us, both of them would be on our tail," said Parker.

"Oh," said Howell. "That *is* good, I guess." He had second thoughts, as usual. "Can't I sit up now? What are we going to do?"

"No," snapped Parker. "Stay down. I'm going to lose them so we can go on our way, that's all."

"You're going to *lose them?*" asked Howell.

"Yeah," said Parker. "Pretty corny, isn't it?"

"This is too much," Howell said breathlessly. "It's the first time I've ever been followed."

"Pretty neat, isn't it," said Parker. Before Howell could answer, he swerved sharply to the left and commenced a series of rapid but not hair-raising maneuvers to elude the agent. It did not last very long. Once Howell felt the car stop, back up, and ease off in a fresh direction, but the exercise was much more relaxed than he would have imagined. Howell's mind wandered. He found himself looking at his day's activities like a movie reviewer even as they were continuing, and decided that although his experiences were always vivid, they were not always real. So they were disjointed. He was reminded of the vaccination trek through the outer regions of the Tugen territory, where he had come across the heads of some Sudanese unfortunates who had strayed too far onto Tugen lands. The small dried heads were on poles as a warning, and the sight of them after so many miles of clean empty nature had chilled Howell. He tried to take a picture of the skulls, whereupon he was ambushed and taken off to the nearest village to be accused of making a mockery of the holy signs. The chill lasted through all of that, even though Howell never quite connected with the danger. The memory was simply vivid, as was the memory of three village elders poring through their first copy of *Playboy*, smuggled in by a flunky of the Information Minister. They were vivid but not real somehow.

Howell, dodging narcotics officials with Max Parker at the end of a long and difficult day, told himself that it was perfectly natural under those circumstances for him to be thinking about odd things. When Parker finally pulled the car to a stop and told him he could sit up, he creaked his spine into a more or less straight position over the concerted protests of a great many neck muscles. He looked over at Parker who seemed no longer larger than life, and said, "Max, look here. I've got to know what's going on here or I'm just gonna pack up and go home."

"You'll see," said Parker. "It won't hurt."

"No, wait," said Howell. "You've got to understand that I am only a reporter who is trying to get away from home for a while. I came down here because I'm *curious* about the spies and the underworld and all that stuff, but I don't want to be *part* of them myself, you see?"

"Ho ho," rumbled Parker. "You are very fonny. That's just what I said."

"I'm serious . . ."

". . . It's what we all say."

Howell consoled himself with the observation that they had stopped in front of a downtown high rise and not in an obvious shoot-out or body disposal area. "I don't like it when you say 'fonny,' " he said.

"Beautiful," said Parker. "I'm glad you got it off your chest. Now let's go, *chico*."

Maraña had learned to open his door more carefully after the shooting, but Carmen had convinced him that the safest way was not to open it at all. So she appeared to answer Parker's ring herself, carrying a bowl and an eggbeater. "Good morning," she beamed. "Would you like some breakfast?"

"Oh no!" grinned Parker. "That is a terrible idea." He rubbed his stomach with anticipation before adding, "Carmen, this is David Howell, the *gringo* I've been telling you about. David, this is Carmen."

"*Mucho gusto*," Howell said awkwardly.

"How do you do?" Carmen replied. She allowed Parker to plant a kiss on her cheek as she eyed Howell. "I bet you want some early breakfast, too, but I see I'll have to give you the low-calorie toast, like Max."

"Well," a blushing Howell stalled, already smitten by her beauty and by an invisible line of confidence that ran down along her nose to the corners of her mouth. It was pure power, he decided, like a force field, and it played off her soft face like shadows in a painting. "Well, I guess so," he managed.

"Max's stomach is made out of black beans," said Carmen. "But yours is not so bad. It is still hard." She was pointing.

"Thank you," Howell shyly replied, and he reached out to find himself shaking hands with the dull blades of the eggbeater. This snapped him out of his half-trance, and he tried to pass it off as a deliberate joke as he stepped past Carmen into the apartment, thankful that Parker had gone ahead.

Maraña emerged from a bedroom conference with Parker and greeted Howell without looking at him. He nodded curtly, declined to shake Howell's hand, and took a seat on a divan at the head of a coffee table. The furniture was modern, dominated by glass and curved brass.

"So you are the one who has been asking so many questions in Miami, eh?" Maraña asked.

Howell leaned back to allow Carmen to put a plate of eggs before him. "I guess so," he replied. He noticed that both Carmen and Parker had on blank faces and were resolutely ignoring him.

"Uh huh," said Maraña. "If you had a gun and could kill Castro at the sacrifice of your own life, would you do it?"

Howell blinked. "No."

"I wouldn't either, but there are a lot of liars here who say they would. What about if you could kill him and get away cleanly? Would you do that?"

Howell looked around for an escape route. Maraña was boring in on precisely the questions he wanted most to avoid with the Cubans. "No," he replied.

"Well, I would," Maraña said coldly. "I suppose that makes us different, doesn't it?"

"I guess so."

"Would you be happy if I killed him?" asked Maraña.

Howell squirmed. "No," he said.

"Or if he had me killed?"

"No," Howell replied more easily.

"Thank you," said Maraña with a cold smile. "It's tough to make you happy, isn't it my friend?"

"No," said Howell. He resented being grilled this way, but Maraña's authority made him submit. He had not yet been able to look Maraña squarely in the face. All he sensed was a strange mixture of bright, handsome, energetic youth and a kind of bottomless age. "I guess I don't get my kicks that way," Howell added.

"That is very noble of you," Maraña said. "So what is your opinion of Castro then, my friend? You can be honest. No one is listening."

Howell felt tremendous pressure to answer before he could think. Maraña's manner puzzled him. "Well," he said, "I hear he has a very good curve ball."

"Uh huh," said Maraña without a laugh.

Howell felt the neutral silence and discarded the idea of an escape through humor. After squirming some more, he closed his eyes and said, "Well, I respect him immensely for what he has done. He has survived many years against very powerful enemies. I don't think I could live there myself, because he is still a *jefe* and he makes everyone smile about the

141

revolution with those identical permanent smiles, like the born-again Christians. But I don't have to live there, so it doesn't matter. And I am very ashamed for what my own government has done to Cuba since Castro, and before him."

"Uh huh," said Maraña, very far off. Howell was fully prepared to believe that Maraña might rub him out for being too sympathetic to Castro. He had heard of one Cuban whose brother-in-law sliced off his ear after he predicted that Castro would live to be sixty. There had been many crazy but vivid developments from lesser men than Maraña. Howell thought Maraña was making the air heavy around his head. There was a dull hum between his ears.

"But you don't know a tenth of what your government has tried to do to Castro, do you?" asked Maraña, leaning forward.

"I guess not," said Howell. "That's what I'm finding out."

Maraña grinned. "And you don't know a tenth of what your government has done to people like me either, do you?"

Howell shrugged. "Well, I'm a little bit of a liberal, you know." He chuckled.

"That is very interesting. What do you mean by that?"

Howell was relieved to see the first glimmer of curiosity in Maraña. He looked sheepishly to the floor. "Well, I'm always ready to be even more ashamed, I suppose. That's one thing."

"Beautiful," said Maraña. He leaned back and turned the heat off Howell, as though at intermission, and turned to Parker. "I think you're right, Max," he said. "He looks honest to me, but I don't see all the spark you've been talking about."

"I think he's a little nervous," Parker observed.

"Wait a minute," said Howell. "What's going on here? Do you mind if I ask a question?"

"Go right ahead," Maraña said graciously. "You are in your own house." Maraña was a different person from the one he had been seconds before, now full of easy kindness.

"Well, for starters, I'd like to know the reason for all the James Bond stuff you guys do with me, like waking me up in the middle of the night and driving me over here with my head between my knees and talking to me about people following us and everything," said Howell, with gulps of indignation. "And now all this pointless examination and stuff that doesn't make any sense to me. What is it all about?"

"That seems like a fair question to me," Maraña remarked. "What do you think?"

Parker nodded and so did Carmen. Howell saw that she had pulled up a chair and was listening with one ear, unlike the other Cuban women he knew who always withdrew quickly from sight to cast baleful looks now and then toward the male company. Howell thought they disapproved of all the conspiracy talk by the foolish would-be heroes, but he had also overheard a few women berating their men as cowards. In no case did they appear to be in harmony with the whispering and chest-bumping by the men.

"Well, we like to keep you off-balance," Maraña said quietly, "especially if we're not sure what's going on ourselves. We learned that from the Company. They liked to keep us off-balance for years. It's harder for you to make trouble when you're confused and afraid, and it's much harder for you to tell a convincing lie. Don't you think so? When you're shaky, things just pop right out of your mouth. Right, my friend?"

"Maybe so," Howell said. "But I would have told you the truth without all that."

"But then it wouldn't have been as much fun for them, David," said Carmen. "This has become a habit over the years. When they go to the store for cigarettes, they still have to have a plan and a backup plan, and they have several false starts for security before the real thing. That all makes the cigarettes taste better."

Howell smiled appreciatively at Carmen, while a sardonic Maraña said, "Thank you, *querida*" as though he had said so often before. He turned back to Howell. "It has a purpose," he said. "Besides, I hear there really were some DEA people watching your house. Who would expect that if you are just an honest journalist?"

"Believe me, I don't know anything about that," said Howell, shivering slightly. "How could you tell they were narcotics agents?"

Parker smiled enigmatically. Maraña shrugged. "There are so many secrets and hidden things," he said. "Even with your own father and mother or your own country. Always surprises. Now you know a little about how the Company made us feel. All you have to do is to imagine that Max and I are holding back from you the thing you want most in the world."

"And that's getting rid of Castro, I suppose," said Howell, annoyed that Maraña would presume to tell him that his parents held deep secrets from him. It unsettled him to think that Maraña was probably right, that underneath them were hidden people he scarcely knew.

"Oh, it could be anything," said Maraña. "It could be that we want dignity or survival or a week's pay or just a straight answer. It doesn't matter. Whatever you want, it will bother you if somebody else is keeping you off-balance. Those DEA guys put *Max* off-balance while he was supposed to be working on you, so everything gets complicated, right?"

"So what were the drug guys there for, if they were there?" asked Howell. He assumed Ziller was dealing on the side.

Maraña shrugged. "How would I know?" he said. "Drugs are very dangerous, and we political people have to keep ourselves very pure."

"Very pure," smiled Carmen.

"I see," smiled a dubious Howell.

Maraña paused significantly. "But I will give you a few straight answers," he said, "because that's one thing we stupid Cubans have never done. We have gotten too used to the Company's life of lying and keeping quiet about everything. So I have decided to tell you about our life if you want to hear the truth. You have strong ears, don't you?"

"Sure," said Howell. "Can I take notes?"

"You can do anything you want," said Maraña. And he proceeded to tell stories, past two and three and four in the morning. He told of eating crayons in the first grade and of setting off crude gasoline bombs in the twelfth grade under Batista's post offices. He told of his exploits as a young *commandante* in the 26th of July, when he showed each new hair of his fledgling beard to his quick-eyed spitfire of a girlfriend, who wanted to be a dancer at Radio City and who left Cuba when her mother died and Castro closed the casinos in the same year. He told of the Bay of Pigs, having followed the spitfire to Florida, and of early life in the Company, sneaking into Cuba on night missions with death on the tip of his tongue, of twice falling into the water off landing craft and ruining some of the secret writing materials he was supposed to deliver to frightened members of the under-ground. Howell filled up half a notebook with Maraña's stories of dealings with Robert Kennedy and various CIA bigwigs, and he laughed at Maraña's acidic theories about how Arthur Schlesinger, Jr., had labored to stack the anti-Castro leadership with Cubans who had gone to Harvard. He knew Marner would love such stuff back in Washington. Maraña told him amusing tales of "reeel characters" in the Company, and he also told what it was like to kill twenty Africans in thirty seconds—"for me it was nothing then, like turning out all the lights in a big house." He amazed Howell by speaking of himself with detachment, as a fool recounting the echoes of his past, full of irony and winsome disillusionment. He spoke casually of having lost his four children "to a piece of linoleum in New York" and of having been bombed in a rented car "by my best friend, next to Max." Howell was both moved and horrified. He thought Maraña should have had all the juices squeezed out of him long ago, leaving him vacant, like a city stripped of people or like an empty schoolyard. There were signs of that in Maraña's face, but it was also full and inquiring.

"Well, that is enough for a beginning," said Maraña. Parker had been asleep for an hour, and Carmen was painting her toenails with a clear pungent liquid, listening and nodding and being alluring enough to make it hard for Howell to concentrate on his note-taking. Maraña slapped his knee. "What do you think, my friend?" he asked.

"I think it's an amazing story," said Howell. "It's hard to take in all at once. You are much more cynical and hard on yourself than the other Cubans I've talked with." Howell checked himself before telling Maraña that he was also more intelligent.

"No, no," chided Maraña impatiently. "That's not what I mean. I *know* it's an amazing story myself. All I want to know is whether you can make it a bestseller here in America. I want number one bestseller! That's all. Not number two. Number one. That's all I will take. Nothing else, my friend."

"Oh," Howell said uncomfortably. Maraña's agitation woke Parker out of hibernation. Carmen quit painting.

"Well?" said Maraña. "Can you do it? Tell me the truth like you say you do."

Howell fingered his throat to pry away an imaginary noose there, and he coughed a few times before saying, "No, I don't think so."

Maraña dismissed these words with an angry wave. "Why not?" he demanded. "All I want is one book, and I know for a fact that the story is better than the other shit. Why can't you do it?"

Howell looked hopefully to Carmen for support, but she seemed to share the question. "Well, I don't know, Carlos," he said. "I'm not sure. But the thing is that for one thing I'm not a book writer, and for another thing you are a Cuban and this is America. Americans don't really care that much about Cubans, no matter what they've done. Not even about Desi Arnaz or Luis Tiant or any of you. Americans think of all of Latin America as one big mariachi band on a permanent adolescent stage, you know." Howell tried to laugh, but he saw quickly that it wouldn't work.

"I don't believe it," hissed Maraña.

"I'm sorry," shrugged Howell. "But you asked for my honest opinion, and that's what it is. I don't think Americans will pay any attention to you or any other Cuban."

"They will *have* to," Maraña said quietly, with the menace of a lit fuse. "You know why? For all these years we have been the stubby ugly hairs on the legs of your empire, my friend. Nobody has seen us, but we have been there, and we have been doing a lot of the dirty work. And now that the pants of your empire are falling down a little bit, everybody will *have* to see us. We will stand out like black stickers on a porcupine, you know."

Howell waited for the heat to drain out of the silence. "Well, that may be the way it looks from Miami, Carlos," he said, "but I don't think it looks that way from New York. Americans don't even think of themselves as having an empire, for one thing."

"Of course not," hissed Maraña. "That's the only time you can really have one. That's when you can push everybody around, but think you're only being good to them. That's when you can be Caesar and Jesus, too . . ."

". . . Wait a minute," Howell interrupted, seeking time to recover from Maraña's string of images.

". . . We are your mirror, your dirty angel," sputtered Maraña. "Your *something*."

"Maybe so," mused Howell. "You are always ours, something in relation to us and nothing on your own. Except for Fidel, I guess. That's why most Americans don't like him, because he's something on his own in spite of us."

Parker frowned from his chair, his arms folded like a sphinx. "What was that again?" he asked.

"Nothing," Howell retreated. "I was just thinking, Carlos. Another problem is that your story doesn't really have an ending yet."

"You mean I'm still alive?" smiled Maraña.

"Well, that is part of the problem," said Howell with a wink. "But it's more that you and the Cubans haven't really come to anything. You haven't achieved anything, really, and you haven't given up either. You've just changed. You're kind of in mid . . ."

". . . shit," said Maraña. "We are in midshit, you are saying." He stood up abruptly and walked to the bedroom, summoning Parker behind him.

Howell exhaled slowly in relief. He was exhausted and nervous. Without thinking, he sniffed his armpits and caught an odor of stale vegetable soup before he noticed that Carmen was staring at him, smiling. Her black hair was now bunched up under a red baseball cap, and her legs were crossed demurely. "A very long night for you, I guess," she said.

Howell glanced at his armpit again with some embarrassment. "Very long," he sighed.

"You get used to it over the years," she advised. "Don't worry about Carlos. He's anxious about talking to you, because he's never done anything like that before. Just don't lie to him."

"Oh, I won't," said Howell. "Thank you." He tried to think of something personal to say to her, but he lost his nerve in a gurgle of sexual attraction.

"Tell me," said Carmen. "Do politics and the revolution make your heart run faster?"

"What?" cried Howell. "You ask those sudden questions too, just like Carlos?" He grinned with amusement in spite of himself.

"I have my own questions," said Carmen.

"I don't doubt it," said Howell. "Well, actually politics and the revolution make my heart heavier. Climbing stairs makes it run faster."

"That's okay," smiled Carmen. "I'm not sure it's good, but it's okay. And women, do they make your heart run faster, or only stairs? Are you in love?"

Howell stared at Carmen in an adoring stupor, and when he first began to speak he choked on a wave of passion. "Excuse me," he said. "Uh, well, I fall in love every five or ten minutes, I think," he said. "Then I fall out of love or in love with something else. Women make my heart purr for a while, but it's kind of a sporadic purr and I always get in trouble while it's resting. Women get mad at me for no reason at all." Howell looked puzzled by his own words.

"I don't believe you," said Carmen.

"See there?" laughed Howell. "My heart stops purring for five seconds while I think and you get mad."

"I'm not mad at you," chided Carmen. "Boy, you are too sensitive. You're like all these spies and politicians."

Howell misplaced his reply somewhere in the folds of his frontal lobe. Maraña and Parker cut short his suffering by returning from the bedroom with compromise on their faces.

Maraña noticed something amiss when he sat down, and he studied Howell and Carmen alternately to find it. "There, you see," he told Howell. "That's why I think it's bad for Carmen to talk with my business partners. Five minutes with her and their heads are all full of shaving cream and candy, like yours." He leaned over to slap Howell playfully on the shoulder. Carmen threw out a look of pride mixed with disgust.

When Howell offered no rebuttal or riposte, Maraña said, "Well, forget about it. I'll decide about my bestseller later, and for now I'll help educate you about the Cubans. What do you think of the ones you've met so far?"

Howell forced his head into gear and dredged up summary impressions of a few Cubans. The impressions were rather perfunctory, for Howell was weakened by desire for sleep. Tiny grains of sand were falling on the tops of his eyeballs.

"And what about El Navajo, Eduardo, the garageman in the swamps? What did you think of him?" asked Maraña.

"Oh him!" Howell brightened. "He scared me to death, and I thought he was absolutely crazy, some kind of Don Quixote of terrorism. He scared me, though. I think he would walk a mile to save a butterfly's life, but at the same time he'd wipe out a whole town of people without a second thought. Is that fair?"

"What's fair?" shrugged Maraña. "El Navajo had never touched a gun in his life until he came to Miami at the age of thirty years, you know. He is a cripple, in a way."

"A cripple?" asked Howell.

"Yes, part of his mind is crippled," said Maraña. "Have you ever heard of that? It's possible, of course. But never mind about that. I heard you went to see the famous Orlando Mendoza all by yourself. How was that?"

"Unusual," said Howell. "Very unusual. I went to see him at his newspaper office, and he received me in this seedy little room covered with paper and trash. He was sitting in a wicker chair with a big guy in dark glasses standing on either side of him. There was Beethoven on the record player, and he had two very fine brandy snifters in his hand. He gave one of them to me and said, 'Mingle this fruit with the spirit of your quest,' or something like that. He said it was from Gorky, his favorite writer. I thought he was a weird combination of cheap, sinister, and effete, like an intellectual taxi dispatcher."

"That's Mendoza all right," smiled Maraña. "And I suppose he told you about fighting for the communists in the Spanish Civil War?"

"Right off the bat," nodded Howell. "And the next thing I know he's pulling out fingernails for Batista, and he said it was perfectly consistent with something called the Thermidorean illusion. And he was telling me that Bukharin was the last free man in Russia and that by that logic, whatever it is, Batista would ultimately be recognized as a left-wing deviationist. He asked me what I thought, and I told him Batista looked like a thieving conniver to me. And he said, 'Simple minds get simple answers.' Then he bragged about stealing nine million in cash from Trujillo, which he claims he sent to some liberation group in Austria, of all places. Finally, just as I was asking him about the current state of affairs among the Cuban exiles, the phone rang and his two goons marched straight toward me like robots. I had to leave, and I still don't know what to make of him."

"Mendoza is what you call a con man," said Maraña. "He confuses everybody with his bullshit while he is stealing their money."

"Then why does he look so poor?" asked Howell.

"He is several times a millionaire," said Maraña, "but in his con games he plays the thinker and the soldier, and for both roles he must look poor, you see."

"Well, he is amazing," said Howell. "I have another appointment with him at ten o'clock this morning, so maybe I'll understand him better."

"You'd better hurry," Maraña advised.

"What?" asked Howell.

"I said you better hurry. Mendoza will not be around much longer."

"What do you mean by that?" asked Howell, fighting back a wave of fear.

Maraña shrugged. "Just what I said. All our days are numbered, my friend. Just hurry, that's all."

Howell tried to stare at Maraña for clues, but he couldn't. He had a hunch that even Carmen was troubled by the drift. "How about Pepe Lopez?" he asked. "I've heard a lot about him and I almost bumped into him with Max today. What do you . . ."

"He is a killer," spat Maraña.

Howell bolted upright from the kick of Maraña's words, realizing that he'd only seen a fraction of his power before now. His nerves buzzed. "Well, Carlos . . ."

"He is a killer."

Howell's pupils dilated before he could manage a thin, wan smile. "Well, I've heard he's killed people, but it seems everybody down here has done some of that," he tried to joke.

"Be quiet," Maraña commanded. "You are talking like a baby now, because you are out of your element."

"You're telling me," said Howell.

"Killing is usually transportation," Maraña droned from far off, "but for a very few people it is food. Pepe Lopez is a killer. Just now. Very recently. Do not ask any more, okay?"

Maraña rose to shake Howell's sweaty hand before Parker ushered him out the door. When they were gone, Carmen turned to him and said, "You should not have frightened him like that, Carlos."

"I know," said Maraña.

Carmen decided not to press the point. She faced Maraña and put her hands on his shoulders. "What did you and Max talk about in the bedroom, my tired one?" she asked.

Maraña was transformed by the question, smiling at her with affection. "Not a thing," he replied. "We were sharing a quick bit of refreshment."

"That's what I thought," said Carmen playfully. "Some of it is still on your nose." She brushed it off with her finger, which she licked for the taste of cocaine, and then she pressed her ear to Maraña's breastbone for a prolonged, lazy embrace.

A weary Howell arrived on time for his appointment with Mendoza, but he was not awake. As he circled the block toward the office from his parking place, his mind was on Maraña and on what he would tell Ziller about the drug stakeout. His senses were dull. Fatigue screened out the morning sun and the conversations of passing pedestrians, as Howell made his way around to Eighth Street. At first the flashing blue lights did not register on him, nor did the crowd. It was a strangely silent assembly except for the excited small children who were scampering in all directions from the cordon of adults. Howell squinted ahead and thought, car crash—a bad one, he concluded, after noting the number of squad cars and the stunned looks. Then he saw that the windows on both sides of Eighth Street were missing or reduced to webs of cracked glass. A rare Miami breeze blew out the curtains of the boutique next door to Mendoza's newspaper. Howell's first thought was that he was glad he had not eaten breakfast. He walked up behind the mass of colorful short-sleeved shirts and plain dresses. Howell tasted metal as he peered over the crowd—three or four people deep in a horseshoe all across Eighth Street, opening on a side alley—to see the remains of a car, twisted and buckled inward like a knock-kneed squatting hulk, with no trace of a hood or motor at all and with its roof actually open and jagged like the mouth of a volcano. The front tires were gone, but the back ones were miraculously intact. Newspapers that afternoon would say that the bomber or bombers had either miscalculated by a factor of ten or had intended to leave a depraved, unfathomable message.

The papers would also say that pieces of Mendoza were located as far as 250 feet away from the car. All Howell saw, wedged between a wall and a signpost, was a mess that looked as if it might once have held a brandy snifter. He could not blot out the sight no matter where he looked or didn't look. He called up the memory of the mounted heads in Africa to abate the sickness, but it didn't work. He was too much a part of this. Howell began moaning softly and whispered to a nearby woman, "Mendoza?" She nodded gravely with the news, and neither she nor many other bystanders would forget the ashen face of the *Americano* under the Panama hat who ran away. It was all Howell could do after his eyes met the gaze of one of Mendoza's goons across the cordon, and after the goon started tugging at the sleeve of a policeman.

Howell abandoned Ziller's extra car at the airport, where he waited without luggage for the next plane.

VIII

On the living room floor of his apartment, Howell found a pair of wirecutters big enough to snip the suspension cables on the Golden Gate Bridge. Next to them sat a can of green spray paint, and a metal baking dish full of freshly painted metal shavings so thin that they almost cut Howell's fingers. A trail of green metal dust ran from the baking dish over to a spot in front of a window where a sofa had once been, whose space was now devoted to two naked wires that connected a wall socket to a pair of powerful vibrators designed for sexual purposes. The vibrators were wedged tightly, business ends upward, between the back of a dining room chair and one end of a twenty-foot strip of industrial aluminum ductwork. The upper half of the ductwork had been sheared off, no doubt with the wirecutters, leaving a U-shaped trough, and at the midpoint of the long trough there was an assortment of cans—once used for beer, oil, coffee, and chocolate chip cookies, left to right—placed into individually tailored holes in the aluminum. A maze of coathangers crisscrossed among the cans, supporting by strings about thirty shopping-reminder pencils with magnetized tips. Furniture was stacked haphazardly throughout the living room, dining room, and hallway to make room for the long flying bridge of ductwork.

From the high end, with the vibrators and the pile of green metal filings and the chair atop the thickest pile of books, the ductwork spanned five more dining room chairs and two spare ones, sloping gently downward to the dining room table itself where Henry Woodruff was working on a collage of candlesticks, clothesline, and magazine covers. Handily beside him on the table, like a bureaucrat's coffee cups, rested a cordless vibrator and an oak-and-steel knife rack, recently unscrewed from the wall of Howell's kitchen.

"You are just in time," said Woodruff, slowly making his way out of a deep concentration.

Howell shook his head in amazement. "It looks like I'm too late. My God, Henry, what is this thing, anyway? I can't leave you alone for a minute."

"I finally got to you, eh?" Woodruff exulted, coming alive. He got up, wearing a white T-shirt and striped suit pants, and slid in his socks around the creation. Howell and he exchanged a wallowy embrace. "Good to see you," said Woodruff.

"You, too," said Howell, but he was staring at the apparatus.

"Nice hat," said Woodruff. "Panama?"

"Yup," said Howell. "Come on, Henry. What *is* it?

Woodruff executed a majestic, car salesman's wave over the breadth of his handiwork. "You'll never guess, will you?"

Howell rubbed his stomach. "I doubt it," he said glumly. "It may be a David Smith sculpture from the period when he was sniffing paraquat."

"Joke all you want," said Woodruff. "This, ol' buddy, is a *reason*."

Howell rubbed his stomach dubiously. "It may be a reason why we have no place to eat dinner," he said. "It may be a reason for you to move out of here . . ."

"Wait a minute," cried Woodruff. "Don't be so harsh until you see the demonstration. I'm almost ready. Then you'll see why Processa here—that's what I call her—is a reason why I'm going to resign from the Senate tomorrow."

"You are?"

"Yep."

"Are you all right, Henry?" asked Howell. "It's all right with me if you're in another world, but you don't have to build the goddam thing out of my furniture. Have you gone over the big chalk line?"

"Certainly not," Woodruff declared. "Don't be impatient."

Howell shrugged. "This better be good," he said. He went into the bedroom to put on his favorite pale lime boxers and to exchange his Panama for a striped blue railroad brakeman's hat. When he returned, Woodruff was arranging his collage so that each candlestick rested on one of the cans in the middle part of the ductwork. The magazine covers dangled between them. Their titles added up to a splendid exhibition of devotion to the higher levels of policy. There was *Public Policy*, the *Journal of Public Administration*, the *Review of Social Innovation*, the *AMA Journal*, *Health Systems Management*, the *NEA Journal*, the Newsletter of the Association of Association Executives, and the Newsletter of the National Rifle Association. Hanging above them all, from the tallest candlestick, flew a cover of Howell's own *Washington* magazine.

Woodruff was pouring more green filings onto the upper end. "Don't worry," he said. "Your magazine is there only for purposes of representation. For the name, you know."

Howell twisted the top off a root beer. "That's good to hear."

A gleam brightened Woodruff's eye. "Now watch closely," he advised, "and you will see the reason." He seized each vibrator by the throat and turned it on full blast. There was a screech, then a groan, and finally a loud metallic whine. Some of the green shavings jumped up in the air, as though pinched from behind, before sliding nervously down the ductwork. Some of them seem to be revolving on the march.

As the foremost shavings slid under the cover of the *Review of Social Innovation*, a few of them leaped up to cling to the head of the first shopping-reminder pencil, and the shavings that passed by speeded up to encircle the beer can. They actually rushed to make a pile around its base. Howell leaned over to inspect the underside of the ductwork. He found bandages of tape and tongue depressors under all the cans, supporting magnets, he figured, wondering where Woodruff could have found them.

Succeeding waves of shavings embraced the other cans and jumped to the dangling pencil heads. Only a small fraction of the green things made it to the dining room table, where Woodruff greeted them. He walked to the other end and silenced the vibrators with authority. "Well, what do you think?" he asked.

Howell's eyes were lame. "Of the art work?"

"No," snorted Woodruff. "Of the concept. Wait a minute." Busily he brushed filings off of cans and pencil heads with a long brush. "Just wait a minute, and I'll show you the real thing. That was only the static model. Now. What you see here are the magazine covers of some of the groups that have attacked me in the last month for my income redistribution plan. What I did was simple. Some other folks on the Hill and I have tried it before, in fact. We just take all the income transfer programs and all the poverty programs, including Social Security, and we distribute that money in taxes to the poorest quarter of the population. Straight. Just write them a check. That cuts about eighty percent of the administrative cost for the planners and administrators and counselors, and it keeps any of the money from going to people who aren't poor. Poor people would get more than twice as much money as they now get from welfare and so forth. And you know who shot me down, don't you? All the poverty bureaucrats and the planners and the health business people, of course. They reamed me even worse than those National Guard types. Both the Republicans and the Democrats— they slaughtered my memo in the Finance Committee so badly that the boss asked me to sit at another table in the cafeteria last week. Can you imagine that?"

"So?" blinked Howell. "What did you expect? Isn't all that consistent with your theory of geometric overmanagement or the idler gear principle of reorganization? I can't remember them all."

"Yes!" cried Woodruff. "And no! What's different here is that this is *personal* for me, and that's more than a refinement. It's a quantum leap."

"That's wonderful, Henry," sighed Howell. "But why couldn't you just tell me? Why'd you have to build this big sliding board in here like this? Oh, well." Howell's preemptory shrug warned Woodruff that his mind was about to unplug from the intended import of the demonstration.

"Wait a minute," said Woodruff, throwing on the vibrators again. The green pile quaked and came to life. Woodruff had to shout over the noise.

"Now just listen a minute, David! In the past four months, I've made feeble attempts to tackle one of the most urgent problems in the country, if not *the* most urgent! And that's white-collar featherbedding! That's the whole-sale creation of jobs in oil companies, consulting firms, public utilities, and in all kinds of government-type work for people who speak the language of the decision-making process and who can't explain what they do to an intelligent teenager in less than an hour! They are highly paid, they work like beavers, they accomplish little or nothing of value to anybody except other people in the same racket, and they speak their jargon on automatic pilot, like portable computer terminals! You know them as well as I do! Every paycheck they draw is another future claim for justice against gluttony and pretense!"

Woodruff was quite worked up. His normally sallow cheekbones had taken on a luminously amber hue that Howell had never seen before. He stared at the cheeks in worried awe, which Woodruff believed was the only proper attitude for the reception of these ideas. He held up a forefinger across the ductwork toward Howell. "Wait here!" he commanded.

Woodruff ran to the dining table and returned with the portable vibrator and the magnetic knife rack. "Now!" he shouted, going into a crouch, one instrument in each hand. "This green stuff is wealth, of course!"

"Of course!" mocked Howell, as the happy little filings neared the can and pencil maze.

Woodruff ignored him. "And this array here is none other than the De-cision-Making Process! Hence Processa, of course. Now here in the dy-namic model, I'm going to apply national anxiety—this vibrator here—and the forces of ideology and challenge like you and me. That's this knife rack! Now watch!"

He went into a deeper crouch, like a piano player on an invisible bench, and raked his two objects across the underside of the ductwork in all directions. The filings went wild along with Woodruff. They hopped and leap-frogged when the vibrator passed under them—sometimes even jumping from one pencil to another. And the magnetized blade of the knife rack caused mayhem throughout the entire system. The pencils swung madly around, sticking to other pencils, sticking to cans, grabbing some filings out of the air and throwing others through the air to magnetized homes else-where. There was havoc in the rafters and a green mist among the cans. One of the tongue depressor patches fell off the bottom, allowing a handful of small square magnets to crash to the floor. Most of the filings around the demagnetized can became instant refugees. Woodruff's arms were a flailing blur. His eyes radiated the sweet frenzy of the maestro. Howell felt as though he was watching a high-wire artist's first performance without a net.

Woodruff, peaking, threw aside the national anxiety vibrator and the ideology knife rack. "There!" he cried triumphantly.

"Bravo," said Howell, applauding softly. "Even I can see that the Deci-sion-Making Process has become a ridiculous tangled mess, covered with money."

"Precisely!" said Woodruff. He looked down, distracted by the magnets on the floor. "Uh oh. Something's wrong. The entire Planning sector of the economy has fallen apart. All its money seems to have relocated over to the Disputes sector. That could never happen."

Howell shook his head sadly. "I'm sorry, Henry." Woodruff paid no attention. Howell said, "I still don't see what's so personal."

This revived Woodruff. "You don't, eh?" he cracked.

Howell massaged his temples. "Could you please turn off the dildos?"

"Vibrators," Woodruff frowned, but he complied. He was growing steadily more agitated. "What's personal about all this is that the last little pencil in the decision-making process here is *me*," he said. "I have become a good example of white-collar featherbedding myself. It's never really hit me before. The Processa defies the laws of nature. It's more than a tar baby or a master of jujitsu. Even if you're trying to destroy it, it takes your effort and makes it help you *and* the Processa at the same time. You're just contributing your energy, and in return you get covered with money."

"Oh, come on," said Howell.

"I'm serious," said Woodruff. "I make thirty-eight thousand five hundred dollars a year, and I've decided that for all this angst I need a raise soon. That's absurd. It's why I've decided to quit."

Howell whistled. "What are you going to do?"

"I don't know. All I know is that I've spent almost eight years here, and when I look back, it looks like all I've done is talk on the telephone and plan meals. I haven't taken any real risks of any kind, and on the whole I think I'm facing failure on my own terms even though I think I'm an outstanding Senate employee, pretty low on the scale of sloth and self-aggrandizement."

Howell sighed, fearing a long sloppy speech or an emotional leak. "Take it easy," he said. "By the way, how's Casey?"

Woodruff went through a slow motion pause, like a jungle beast thinking about the tranquilizer dart in his neck. "Oh that," he said flatly. "It's finished, I guess. We've already started the grisly part. Last week I went over there to divide up the common property. She told me to take anything I wanted, even her grandma's heirlooms, but I just picked up some kitchen stuff and some knick-knacks. I was very gracious. I told her I had no material desires. I was a willing martyr to marital despair."

"Ugh," Howell grunted, patting his stomach and working around to a smile. "I think that's a fishy area there, Henry. It sounds to me like a small but very important part of you is hoping that Casey will say, 'Oh, his love is pure after all' and change her mind. Your ulterior motive is just behind your lack of any other motive."

"Huh?" asked Woodruff.

"You get what I mean," said Howell.

"Maybe so," said Woodruff. He pondered without enthusiasm and rejected the idea of nitpicking over Howell's meaning. "Yeah, I guess that's possible," he admitted, "although I really didn't want any of that stuff. I just wanted to get out of there."

"Uh huh," said Howell, with a trace of doubt.

Woodruff's bottom lip quivered slightly. Then he sighed. "Well, it's not easy for me to say that I'm what you might call the emotional underdog here. I mean, that's the one who dreams up these gushing reconciliations. The worse things are, the better the dreams. I could probably come up with a gut-wrenching scenario for a reunion twenty years from now. I've been thinking about it, and I've decided I don't believe these people who say their separations are exactly mutual. I just don't believe it. At some level of honesty, there is always an underdog, the romantic fool, and in this case I'm it."

"Oh, Henry . . ."

"Well, the point is Casey will say she doesn't see how she's gonna make it, and I'll sit right there and give her advice. I know she's being honest, but it's weird. It's like she threw me overboard, and now she's asking me to throw *her* a lifeline."

Howell made a sour face. "Ugh," he winced. "That's really bad, Henry. You should stay away from nautical stuff. That line sounds so bad that you must have rehearsed it before on some other poor soul."

Woodruff frowned. "Well, I did say something like that to Casey. It doesn't sound so bad to me. You goddam writers and editors are always ready to ambush an idea."

Woodruff walked around his Processa toward a jumble of furniture in the corner. "Lately, however, it seems that I've fallen prey to more familiar and mundane desires, such as wanting to get laid," he said, plopping on the relocated couch.

"It's hard to do with so much on your mind," needled Howell. "Have you scored?"

"More or less. I mean, maybe five or six times over all this time, but it's been a hell of a lot of work. All of them, except perhaps the owner of those vibrators, are strangers to you. And with every single one of them, I've felt like a stone. Nothing. I haven't even felt human. Oh, I've learned stuff. Like some of them really seemed to get off on me, and that was nice. One made so much noise it made my ears ring. I thought she had a heart attack. But otherwise it has been terrible. I feel like I'm masturbating with a person, only it's worse."

"What do you expect?" asked Howell. "You're a predator out there. You don't care about any of the women except to prove something about Casey. Holy shit. You better stay away from good women with talk like that."

"Oh horseshit," snorted Woodruff. "Even women don't always fuck under ideal conditions. They have selfish reasons and every other kind of reason. I don't dislike the women I've been with. It's just that I feel nothing. Zero. In fact, I have this perverse habit that while we're making it, my mind insists on thinking about chess problems and history lessons and tennis players and . . ."

"Casey?"

"Well, almost."

"Sorry."

"Yeah, actually I do. I can think about her *and* the chess problem. It doesn't matter. I can't get them out of my mind, even though I'm doing something very personal and enjoyable. It's like that Dostoyevsky essay where he defines evil as the desire to punish yourself by wiggling your loose tooth, you know."

"Sounds like masochism to me."

"I'm not a masochist."

"I didn't say you were."

"You implied it."

"Well, Henry, all I'm saying is that you ought not to complain about what you're getting from these women, because you're not putting anything into it. You're expecting too much. You can't go out to get laid and then bitch because you don't feel romantic about it."

"Oh, God," moaned Woodruff. "You sound just like Mantell. Just like her. I'm telling you, David, they've got you well trained."

"Yeah, right. Well?"

"Well what?"

"Well, have you made it with her?"

Woodruff eyed his friend cautiously. "I'm going to answer that question. I certainly am," he stalled, mimicking a senator.

"Good," smiled Howell. "And none of that 'more or less' bullshit either."

"Certainly not," said Woodruff. "And the answer is no. But I have to admit that we've talked about it. We've probably talked it to death, as a matter of fact. That Valerie is a talker. I guess I am, too."

"Uh huh."

"And anyway, among other things, I told her I wouldn't feel right about it until I talked to you, you know, about your own situation, and I didn't think it would be good to do it over the phone with you down there among your palm trees. So I decided to wait. Pretty good, huh?"

"Uh huh."

"So what do you think?"

Howell rummaged through the debris around the wall until he found the bar, or the remains of it, and then he poured some bourbon directly into the thin mouth of the root beer bottle, spilling some. "Shit," he said.

"Bourbon and root beer?" cried Woodruff.

Howell took a long drink and sat down on the floor with one bottle in each hand, like oars. "Yup," he said. "I look at it like this, Henry," he drawled. "I'd be pissed off if you hurt Valerie while you're getting your kicks, but she's old enough and smart enough to take care of that herself, I figure."

"She sure is."

"Uh huh. Otherwise, all I know is that Valerie and I will always be friends, whether we ever sleep together or not. I'll miss it if we don't. I'm not saying I wouldn't. It's not going anywhere. But it's a comfort to us. And I guess you two would be going after bigger game, though I doubt you're in any condition for it."

156

Woodruff had been studying Howell's face for signs of false emotion. "That's what Valerie says," he sighed, rising from the sofa to pace slowly around Howell as though he were a bonfire. "She says a man or woman in the throes of divorce is not fit company for the opposite sex for at least two years. Until then I'll be a menace to womankind, she says. Can you believe that shit?"

"Yes," grinned Howell. "She is a smart lady."

"Oh, come on, David. You know it's not that bad."

"Hey, argue with her, not me. I just came home, and I haven't even gotten over your vibrator trough yet. I'm not trying to barge into anything."

"Ah hah!" said Woodruff. "So you *do* think I'd be barging in on you and Valerie."

"I didn't say that . . ."

"You didn't have to. I *knew* I couldn't trust you two with all that easygoing good friends bullshit! There's got to be more to it. It doesn't make sense. I mean, either both of you have completely lost your romantic hopes, in which case I wouldn't want to be with Valerie, and she would be lying, or you haven't, in which case you can't be so goddammed casual. I mean Christ, if you enjoy making love with somebody who's your friend, what else is there? You can't tell me it's nothing to you and it's all so perfectly balanced between you! Even I know better than that!"

"Take it easy," Howell said urgently. "If the old bat comes up here with her walking stick, it's gonna be your ass, not mine. She'll take one look at my sunburn and know that I'm too mellow to be yelling." He looked up at the circling Woodruff, took off his railroad hat and wiped his forehead with an arm lined with bleached hairs.

Woodruff kicked the floor with a slippery sock and nearly fell in the process. "Fuck her," he groused. Some of his intensity had subsided, but he still looked suspiciously at Howell.

The hat rested again above a new, conciliatory grin. "Now listen, Henry," said Howell. "I'm not going to fuss about how rude it is of you to expect me to explain my relationship with Valerie to somebody like you, obviously crazed by a new desire to make a hundred on life's love exam . . ."

"Okay, okay," Woodruff conceded.

"All I can make out of it is that Valerie and I both think we're good for each other about one or two days a month. Anything more than that and we get on each other's nerves. She thinks I'm a drifter, and I think she's on a power drive with her women. That's all there is to it, I think. Maybe there really is a deeper drama going on, but I think if anybody could find it, it would be Valerie with all her shrink talk."

"She does believe in shrinks," said Woodruff. "You're right about that. She's really been pushing me to go to one myself. I think it's because she looks down on Casey, and she thinks a shrink would help me get over her quick. I, of course, think I could help Valerie get over shrinks, and I tell her horror stories about the Bavarian stress specialist Casey and I went to. She makes me defend Casey. I make her defend shrinks."

"Sounds like a real meeting of the minds."

"Pretty twisted," Woodruff acknowledged. "I don't understand it. All that shrink from Bavaria kept saying was 'Get in touch with your anger. Deal with it. Get mad. Let it out. Get mad.' Getting mad was his solution for everything."

"Well, that's just what coach Rock Buford told all the linemen on my high school football team," Howell mused.

"Yeah, right."

"Don't knock it. We were thirty-two and four my last three years, with a lot of excellent mad linemen."

Woodruff paused somewhere between amusement and exasperation. "Well," he said, "I can see that you're in no frame of mind to bore in on the nature of your own relationship with Valerie so we can get this thing settled."

"You said it."

"Well," sighed Woodruff, "we'll come back to it. There's only one other thing I wanted to tell you, but it's got to be off the record. Okay?"

Howell brightened. "Completely off the record? Not just deep background?"

"No," Woodruff said firmly. "I know the rules. Not just deep background. This is serious, especially if you were to blab to Valerie or Ziggy. Completely off the record, okay?"

Howell pretended to think it over. Then he rolled his eyes and nodded assent.

Woodruff's eyes swept the room for bugs and intruders. "Okay," he whispered. "Sudsy and I slept together, but we didn't do anything."

"Which part is off the record?"

"Very funny. *Both* parts," Woodruff whispered loudly.

"Uh huh. I guess you hesitated because you were worried about what Ziggy might say."

"No, actually that wasn't it, not at all," said Woodruff. He sounded rather pleased to be so sure of himself about a story in the realm of gossip. "Sudsy and Ziggy are finished again. For good this time, I think. Ziggy has a new girlfriend, who is blonder and much poorer than Sudsy. Ziggy took all of his stuff out of her place and gave her credit cards back. He's never done that before. He says he's got to make something of himself, and he says Sudsy always makes him think nothing is worthwhile doing. Sudsy says she's finally realized that Ziggy is a liar—not a little liar but a great big one. She won't tell me what it's about, but it's ugly."

"Oh shit," sighed Howell. "There goes one of the least boring couples I've ever known. Are you sure this isn't just another memorable scrap?"

"I don't think so. But I know what you're thinking, and I'm pretty sure I'm not being used as a pawn here. Maybe that's why we held back, though. Who knows? The main reason *we* think we held back is that it's hard to change from friends to lovers after you've known each other so long. We feel like brother and sister, you know. On our big night, we kept sitting there

158

talking about how much sense it would make for us to sleep together. But nothing happened. We talked about special feelings and magic, and how nice it would be, and how we were just right for each other. But it got too conscious. I'd say, 'Do you feel anything?' And she'd say, 'Nothing too special. Do you?' "

"Oh cut it out, Henry," scoffed Howell.

"It's true," said Woodruff. "It turned into kind of a joke. The moment passed by us if it was ever there, and it felt like we were trying to board a moving subway. Hopeless. So we asked each other the questions in the dining room, then on the sofa, and finally in the bed. But nothing happened, so we just went to sleep."

"I'll be damned," said Howell. "That's good, I think."

"You do?"

"Yeah," said Howell, calling back from the kitchen, where he was opening another root beer. "But now I understand your Processa better. It's obviously the work of a sexually frustrated man who needs to pour his creativity into a large symbolic vessel."

"Maybe so," Woodruff said, "But fuck you, anyway."

Howell ambled back into the living room, casting looks of awe at the contraption. "I'll give you one thing," he said, "You really plunge right in there, Henry. I hate to think what kind of sculpture you'll do about women after you finish with Valerie and Sudsy."

Woodruff swallowed carefully, not sure just how he was being made fun of. "Too gung-ho, you think? I decided today that I need to relax some. I can't solve all this by tomorrow. I'm pretty upset by it all, though. I mean it's hard enough to accept what a divorce means, but why does all the rest have to pile in on top of it?"

"Don't worry," shrugged Howell. "It's nothing unusual from what I've seen. You've got to face one thing, Henry, as Drake would say. And that is that you're past thirty. You've been in the government a few years, and no matter how much of a radical you have been, you are naturally turning into a bureaucrat and a right-winger at the same time. That explains both the sculpture and the women." Howell had ditched his root beer in midsentence, and by the end he was diving headfirst across the floor beneath two chairs supporting the ductwork.

Woodruff was up with a pillow. "You sniveling wordsmith!" he yelled. "That's the lowest scumrotting remark I ever heard!" With that he pitched the orange weapon toward his cackling friend. His aim was poor, however, and he succeeded only in banging up the ductwork. At impact, a cloud of green dust appeared above the can area and settled downward onto Howell's back and shoulders, the heavier parts first. The ductwork itself appeared to swivel its hips slowly from side to side three times before the upper end came untethered and crashed to the floor.

There was a painful silence, after which Howell rolled over wearily to face Woodruff. "Nice going," he coughed through the haze.

Woodruff had been cringing behind his palms. He peeked around them woefully and said, "Oh, shit. It's gonna take me a whole day to rebuild it. I'm sorry, David."

"I'll help you rebuild it. Don't worry," Howell offered with a menacing grin. "We'll rebuild it, all right."

"Well, why wouldn't we?" sniffed Woodruff, taking offense. "It's your fault anyway. You've got a lot of nerve calling me a right-winger after *you're* the one who's been hanging around with all those goddam guacamole gauleiters down in Miami."

Howell winced. "Cubans don't eat much guacamole, Henry," he corrected. "You're thinking of Mexicans. Or Texans."

"Oh," said Woodruff. "Well, whatever. Brown shirts and black beans. I don't care what you call them. They're right-wingers, aren't they?"

"I suppose so," said Howell. "Mostly they're just crazy exiles."

"Uh huh," muttered Woodruff. He was entertaining an idea that promised to divert attention from his misdeeds. "By the way," he said, "how did it go down there? Did you ever get to see the garage mechanic whose arms got stretched by a machine gun?"

"Yep," sighed Howell. "That would be El Navajo. The story is an exaggeration, but so is he. Everything in Miami is a long story for a country boy, I guess. I made it through all right except that somebody put a bomb in a car this morning and blew up one of my sources."

Woodruff started to laugh but checked himself when he sensed Howell's fear. "What?"

"Yeah, made a mess of him," Howell quaked, staring once again at the pulpy dismembered hand. "I had an appointment with him and got there just in time to see the crowd and the cops and parts of my man Mendoza out in the hot street. I'm not kidding. He was literally blown apart. The funeral parlor will have to organize a search party."

"Holy shit."

"And that's not the worst part."

"Uh huh?"

"The worst part is that last night another one of my sources all but told me it was going to happen," said Howell, whose lips were turning blue. "There I was, working up to the nice journalistic conclusion that our political history is all involved with the gangsters, and the next thing I know *I'm* involved."

"Wait a minute," cautioned Woodruff. "Did the guy say, 'Mendoza is gonna get blown up in the morning'? Did he actually say that?"

"No. When I told him I was going to interview Mendoza, he said a couple of times that I'd better hurry. He said Mendoza wouldn't be around much longer. Something like that. It's borderline, I guess."

"Sounds like you're a material witness to me, ol' buddy. Hot dog!"

"Cut it out, Henry," Howell ordered. "This is not funny. I know my coverup lingo. I'm telling you, when I saw that blood on the street and remembered what the guy said last night, I got so scared that I could barely drive the car. I came straight here. I don't have my books or any of my clothes. I didn't say good-bye or anything. I just ran."

160

Woodruff looked around the apartment to verify the empty-handed return. He walked over to the bourbon bottle on the floor and took a warm swallow with some distaste. Things were sinking in around his temples. "Jesus, David," he pronounced reverently. "Why didn't you tell me before?"

In studied disbelief, Howell gazed at Woodruff, at the Processa, at the green grime all over him, and then back at Woodruff. "You're kidding."

"You're right," Woodruff confessed. He disappeared into the bedroom and returned quickly with a small stenographer's notebook. With sober deliberation, he inscribed a few minutes' worth of thoughts in it while Howell looked on.

"I give up," said Howell. "What's that?"

"It's my little Mao book," said Woodruff. "I've been putting my romantic flounderings in here ever since the shit hit the fan with Casey. Things change so fast. And there's a lot of self-criticism in here, too. Like I just wrote about how utterly self-obsessed I've become. That's bad, you know."

"Uh huh." Howell smiled wanly.

"I'm gonna have to do something about it. And I'm sorry about not noticing how fucked up you are. You look awful, come to think of it."

"Thanks."

"No sleep?"

"Just about."

"Well, let's have it. How did you get tangled up with these thugs?"

Howell, still seated and green, was warming up through about five minutes of Ziller-and-Maraña stories when a loud knock sounded at the door.

"Oh, shit," moaned Howell. "The goddam countess on my first night home. This is your fault, Henry."

Woodruff was equally panicked. "This is no time to think about blame," he said. "You should be thinking about what you're going to say."

"What *I'm* going to say?" said Howell. "Why me? It's not my thing. I didn't throw anything, either. I'm not even dressed, for God's sake. I can't answer the door."

"That's ridiculous. When have you ever worried about what you wear?" Woodruff demanded. "Look, don't be a coward. This is your apartment, and I don't even know the woman."

Howell ignored both Woodruff and the persistent knocking. "I'm not *gonna* get dressed, either," he announced. "It's late, and I'm innocent."

Howell sat on the floor with a determined glare and was thus at a disadvantage when the phone rang. The sound was muffled. Howell spun his neck before realizing that he didn't know anymore where his own phone was located, or under what. Woodruff did. "I'll get it," he called eagerly as he sprang toward the messiest pile of newspapers. He extracted the transmitter and crooned a good-natured hello into it, savoring his new, unavailable position in regard to the door-answering problem. He shrugged helplessly with a wink. The knocking became more thunderous.

Howell, checkmated, looked irritably at Woodruff and then eyed the door with the shaky courage of a teenager about to greet his second blind date, the one he'd sworn never to have. Outside the fear region, he was torn between indignation and his exhibitionist tendencies, which were inflamed into hilarity by the prospect of welcoming Madame Delacroix in his boxers.

"Of course, operator, I'll accept the charges," Woodruff said in the background, making sure he would be overheard.

Such casual license prodded Howell into action. He stalked resolutely to the door and flung it open, with his chest out and an eye peeled for the dreaded cherrywood cane.

The woman's small mouth stretched and curled around her teeth in exaggerated forms, like a linguist at diction practice, as she said, "Aaaaaiiiiiiiooooooouuuuu." Her bare feet were about the size of a tall man's kneecaps, and Howell saw that they had a few small nicks and cuts on them. They were runner's feet, outdoor feet, and Howell suppressed as untimely his urge to investigate the cuts. Above them, she wore baggy white knickers and a blue T-shirt stretched over two unfettered breasts that somehow struck Howell as melodious. Her tiny rounded nose took ten years off a face that was playful except for the frightened, dumbfounded eyes. They were hazel, and Howell guessed that in normal times they would be determined ones, matching the tomboy's wiry arms that had made those ferocious knocks seconds before.

"I'm sorry," gulped Howell. "You must have the wrong apartment."

"No!" shrieked the woman. She put her left hand on the door, lest Howell should close it, and she peered at the devastation behind him. "It's urgent," she said, gulping. "Otherwise I wouldn't think of bothering you until you're finished."

"Finished?" blinked Howell. "Finished with what?" He followed the woman's eyes to the scene behind him. The chaos, the wirecutters, and the green stuff, some of which was smeared on Howell, brought home to him the unsettling idea that the woman might be thinking he and Woodruff were in the middle of some dark ritual such as was rumored then to be going on in the capital among diverse cliques. "No," he said vaguely.

The woman dismissed the entire subject with a sharp stab of a tiny hand in the air, fingers splayed. "Are you the one Miss Lily Snow calls the nice young man who always says hello?" she asked, with her eyes narrowed to business.

As soon as Howell said "Oh," with a smile of recognition and relief, the woman pushed by him. "Thank God," she gushed, beginning to cry. "Miss Lily has fallen in her apartment and I can't find anybody in the building to help her. I think she's broken something."

Howell reverted to distress. "Oh, no," he said.

"David! Hey David!" Woodruff shouted from around the corner. "It's somebody named Moonbeam on the phone and she's upset! Is that a code name?" Woodruff was enjoying himself so much that he tacked on an extra, incredulous cry of "Moonbeam!"

Howell ran both hands through his hair in a sign of maximum self-pity. Then he held up both hands to the woman in a plea for patience and yelled over his shoulder, "Moonbeam is from Bobby Ziller's, Henry! Tell her I'll call her later! I've got an emergency now! Somebody's hurt in the building!"

Dashing into the bedroom for clothes, Howell could barely hear Woodruff's next round of messages. "Moonbeam says she understands everything!" came the report. "She says the world is a sparkling blowhole, whatever the fuck that means, and that she knows why you have to run!"

"Get her off the phone, Henry!" Howell retorted impatiently while pulling on his pants.

"She says she's only worried that everybody has started bogarting the orange stuff Marvella got for you! Who's Marvella?"

"Forget it!"

Howell had one tennis shoe on when it resumed. "She says she won't hang up until you tell her what to do with the orange stuff!"

"Tell her to mail it here!" Howell yelled. He bolted back into the living room to find the woman staring and Woodruff entering from the opposite direction in a self-satisfied stroll.

"Boy, she is a lulu," said Woodruff.

Howell was looking at the woman. "It's not what you think," he said, opting for a blanket assurance.

"I hope not," said the woman.

"Uh, this is my friend, Henry Woodruff," Howell introduced. "And this is . . ."

"Haven Pinder," said the woman. "I live downstairs. I saw you here last week dragging a sliding board into the elevator," she told Woodruff.

"The old lady down the hall has fallen," Howell said abruptly. "You want to help us go see about her?"

Woodruff, staring at Howell, gave a careworn sigh. "Not unless it's critical," he said. He glanced nervously at Pinder, who was edging toward the door, and then beckoned Howell to his side. Woodruff managed to look more worried than his two companions. "Make it snappy," he whispered. "We've got a lot to talk about, and there's a poker game at Sudsy's at nine."

Howell drew back and confirmed to his disappointment that Woodruff was serious. He nodded doubtfully. "Don't wait for me," he said, and took off after Pinder, who had left without saying good-bye.

He saw her going down the hall, first in a low crouching silent run on padded feet, like an Indian, and then, as though suddenly overtaken by two hundred years of bourgeois femininity, she switched to a stiff-legged majorette's run with her back as straight as a harpist's.

She arrived just ahead of him at Miss Lily Snow's small, dark apartment, which smelled of oatmeal, urine, and old Bibles. It was a previously rich old lady's apartment, full of nice things long neglected. There were two oil paintings of well-dressed ladies on dirt roads, and several ancient photographs of dead ringers for Sigmund Freud. The living room had half as many working lamps as it needed and twice as many claw-footed Queen Anne chairs. The mahogany cabinet with scalloped glass, the Civil War prayerbook, the embroidered Dutch sewing box, and just about everything else that came to view might well have furnished the back room of an antique store in the Catskills.

In the bedroom, between the bed and the bathroom door, Miss Lily Snow lay on the floor, looking calmly at the ceiling. Her thick walking cane lay next to her. She wore a plain navy blue dress with a white shawl around her neck, and on her feet she had the kind of shoes a ninety-year-old nurse would wear. She seemed half a foot shorter than Haven Pinder, who was no giant herself, and everything about her was frail. The only exception was that her round angelic old lady's face, with the sharp Yankee nose, lit up occasionally under her snow-white hair.

It lit up after Haven Pinder, bending down into a ball with her knees in her armpits, took a hand and said, "It's all right, Miss Lily."

"It's you!" she beamed. "Thank heaven. I'm in a deuce of a fix." There was no more color in her face than before, but the pallor brightened. Her voice was proper, clipped Connecticut, but it sounded small and distant.

Howell looked over her from above. "Well, if it isn't Miss Snow," he said cheerfully. "You look gorgeous tonight as usual."

The old lady's eyes opened farther when she heard the greeting that was familiar to her from her sidewalk strolls. "It's you, too," she said. "Well, well. Isn't that the limit?"

"How come you're lying there on the floor, Miss Snow?" asked Howell with a smile.

The old lady squeezed Haven Pinder's hand, and Pinder passed along a look of concentrated response, a childish oomph of the heart, that squeezed Howell. "Well, that's just the question," said the old lady. "That's just it. I seem to have mismanaged myself somehow, but I don't know how. I was on my way to the lavatory after dinner, and now here I am. My legs are being frightfully rude."

"You must have fallen, Miss Lily," said Pinder.

"Precisely," came the game reply. "So, there you have it."

"Maybe you tripped on a tuft in the rug," quipped Howell, trying to lighten the predicament.

"Hardly, young man," said the old lady. "I danced all the tufts out of this rug before you were born."

"Oh, well, let's see if we can get you up."

Pinder and Howell gripped Miss Lily Snow under her arms, with bracing hands on her rounded shoulders, and hoisted her up to a standing position. Her eyes bulged and her cheeks quivered. She made a funny noise, "Uuuuooee," rhyming with dewy, and listed to Pinder's side.

"Steady," said Pinder.

"That's right, steady," Howell agreed.

Miss Snow's head wobbled toward Pinder and she said, "What's this steady, my dear? I'm not a ship."

Pinder was impressed with this chipper rebuke and nodded so to Howell.

The old lady wobbled around to Howell and repeated, "Just so. I'm not a ship, am I?"

"No, Miss Snow."

"Of course not," the old lady agreed.

"Well, let's take a walk, then, and try out those dancer's legs," said Pinder.

"What a lovely idea," Miss Snow beamed. "I can't think of two friends I'd rather take a walk with. Forgive me, but are the two of you married?" She tugged on each of their arms.

"No, I'm not," Howell said reflexively.

"We just met, Miss Lily," said Pinder, more easily. "We both live here in the building, but we're not married."

"Well, that's all right," chirped Miss Snow. "I'm not either. But that's a long story. Father kept me too busy taking care of him and those horrid insects of his." She pronounced the word "father" with great solemnity, the result of long feeling and practice, the way presidents say nation and America.

"Pardon me?" asked Howell.

"I'll explain later," Pinder said quietly behind the old lady's back. Then she puckered her lips in determination and said, "All right, Miss Lily, let's move out."

"That's just it exactly. Let's move out," agreed Miss Snow, still standing unsteadily.

Howell, charmed by the grit in Pinder's lips, added an extra-playful, "Do your stuff, Miss Snow. Send a message down to those nice legs."

The three of them leaned forward together, and after a delay, the old lady's black left shoe slipped six inches ahead. "Ah," she gasped, looking surprised.

The helpers offered congratulations, but Miss Snow looked doubtful. She seemed to be trying to communicate with her right leg, the one on Howell's side. It was hanging back, leaning behind her at an angle. Suddenly she took a sharp, raspy breath. The helpers saw pain on her face. Her forehead had become milky and translucent at once.

"Are you all right, Miss Lily?" asked Pinder. "Where does it hurt?"

"It doesn't hurt a bit," Miss Snow lied, "except for perhaps a trifle around here." She waved her hand slowly and uncertainly over her entire right side.

"Here?" asked Howell, touching her hip lightly.

"Yes."

"How about here?" he said, touching her leg.

"Yes."

Howell and Pinder shared a nodding diagnosis of worry. He tried to cover it up with good spirits. "What's the matter with that message there, Miss Snow? Is it not getting through to your legs?"

"It's getting through perfectly," chirped the old lady with a weak smile. She always smiled with her lips closed, with a certain delicacy, the way people of her manner were trained to chew food. "That's just it. The message is getting through perfectly, but someone is ignoring it. Isn't that the limit? Maybe I am a ship after all."

Howell watched Pinder go through both a laugh and a heart squeeze at once. "No, you're not," she said.

They retreated, giving up the half step by the left foot. "I guess I'll have to go to New York now," said Miss Snow. "That's where I was going when you came in to see me."

"New York?" asked Howell.

"On the train, of course," she said. "On the parlor car, where I won't have to put up with those sleek ruffians from Philadelphia, you know."

Pinder shooshed Howell's budding questions, leaning behind the old lady's back to whisper, "New York is a lot of things. It's home. It's any trip. And it's also the . . ." Pinder mouthed the word "hospital."

Howell nodded. About a third of the puzzlement went out of his face. After a silent, head-gesture conversation with Pinder, he leaned over and said, "All right, Miss Snow, we're going to go get that hip of yours fixed up, okay?"

The old lady brightened. "In New York? Surely you're not coming on the train with me? I'm not sure I can get you on the parlor car. Father could, of course."

"Uh," said Howell, debating whether to lie. He appealed silently to Pinder, who said, "We're going to stay right with you wherever you go, Miss Lily. Now we've got to get you bundled up. It's cold outside."

Ten minutes later, the trio was making progress through the hall when Miss Snow said, "I've got just the thought." Her face brightened, and the procession stopped to listen. "Those people in New York aren't much to talk to anymore, my dear," she said to Pinder. "They're ninnies as a rule. So I think I'd better take the children."

"The children?" Howell was getting weary of the strange talk, even though he knew that the old woman could not help it, being in shock. He bided his time while Pinder, who seemed to understand, studied Miss Snow's face. To Howell, both of them seemed upset, sharing something private, perhaps something between women. Then Pinder put Howell's hands under both of Miss Snow's arms and ran away.

When she returned, Howell heard her sniffling behind him before she arrived. "Here, Miss Lily," she said, presenting her the pillow. "We'll take the children."

Howell got all bleary-eyed before he had time to think. There were a dozen tiny animals laid out on the pillow, side to side, covered by an embroidered table napkin that served as a blanket. The heads of three or four stuffed mice were visible, along with two dogs, a two-inch elephant, several bears, and one little girl, who looked funny because she was shiny plastic. From the dust on the snouts and heads, the fairy-tale bed seemed to be quite old.

Howell managed to laugh, "That's very cute."

"Some of them are, I quite agree," said Miss Snow.

"They won't fall off, because I've looped the blanket in the back, Miss Lily," said Pinder.

166

Howell stared at Pinder. His tentative recovery laugh turned into a very broad grin and then he began to titter. "Would you please say that again?" he asked.

Pinder figured out Howell's face. Her teary smile turned into indignation as she recognized that he, like others, was intrigued by the way she said things, such as loop and Lily, when happy round sounds seemed to bounce from her tongue to her palate and out. It was girlish, she thought, and even worse it was cute. "No," she snapped at Howell, and when she realized that this word also might have a petulant blip to it, she leaned behind Miss Snow and mouthed an unmistakable "Fuck you."

"Oh," recoiled a chastened Howell.

"What's that?" asked Miss Snow.

"Nothing, Miss Lily," said Pinder. She took an arm with one hand and the pillow with the other.

Woodruff found no trace of Howell three hours later when he returned from the poker game. He spent some time repairing his couch for sleeping, and then he began pacing. Several miscellaneous items got under his feet and he kicked them irritably away. Woodruff was in a bad mood. He had many things to say to Howell, he had developed several new and troubling directions in his divorce ruminations, and he had lost seventeen dollars at poker. All of these he handled gracefully, but the spray paint he stumbled over was such a petty and unnecessary burden, he figured, like traffic jams and burned toast, that he kicked it viciously.

When he calmed down a bit, Woodruff thought about drafting his letter of resignation from the Senate. He didn't get very far. It didn't matter much, although he did think it would be nice to leave behind some telling thoughts on the Senate as a troubled institution. It would be all right to function as an ego playpen, he thought, except that there were too many things at stake. He could not bring himself to think of any, however, and his mind jumped to the stenographer's notebook. He picked it up and stared off into space for about fifteen minutes before writing:

Innocence——The Obsession?
Pubic hair——Acceptable?
Anchor——The heavy burden of romance

Woodruff always wrote in such shorthand in the notebook. He was searching for the key obsession, trying to isolate the force that kept him pinioned to thoughts of Casey long past the time when he knew it was over, even after he knew it had never been all that good. He had a list of possibles three feet long. In the latest round, Woodruff speculated that he might have made Casey into a fetish of innocence that he could not afford to part with after absorbing so much smarmy noninnocence elsewhere. This notion spun round and round but always came out as some play on the old pedestal theory of women in general and Casey in particular, which was thoroughly covered in the notebook.

The idea of pubic hair arose about the same time as the musty smell from his armpits. It fell into the physical category along with a number of Casey's parts that Woodruff previously thought might have been the cause of it all. Her pubic hair was special, he realized, not just as the maddeningly quiet emblem of woman as a shape and siren, but in its own right. It was very black and very, very silky, as he remembered it with a few thumps in his neck, and in that regard it was infinitely preferable to some of the scouring-pad pubic hair he had recently encountered. Definitively preferable, he thought—a clear factor—but could it be unique and powerful enough to be his chief tormentor, the misplaced heart of romance itself? He questioned whether it would be acceptable or reasonable, in the cosmic scheme of things, to have such a hook built for him or anyone else.

The anchor notion arrived just after the lure of pubic hair subsided in his mind. It followed from the actual sturdiness of the pain Woodruff felt, which he calculated was a direct function of the strength of his feeling for Casey. He went on in this vein until he concluded that it was the strongest and most undeniable of the passions he had, stronger than the power lust to create revolutionary theories that would save worlds and earn him the smiles of history—stronger even than his attachment to thought. And then he reasoned that perhaps this very stubbornness was the reason he held on to it so stubbornly. It was one thing to count on, leaving him free to explore everything else. There was so much pressure on romance after other sacred pillars had fallen, thought Woodruff. He was drawn to the idea of Casey as his anchor, and he tried to beat the pain out of his chest with that idea. He thought of every bad thing he could think about it, what it said about him, and so forth, but in the end he gave up, dialed Casey's number, and let the phone ring twenty times.

Casey probably wouldn't want to know his latest ideas anyway, he decided, though some of them might have merit. He sighed before collecting a number of noisy metal items to pile before the apartment door, in case Howell should arrive. After masturbating, he put them back and moved his running thoughts to the sofa for the night.

Ix

Bobby Ziller patted his forehead listlessly with a blue bandana covered with white half moons. He was standing in a hothouse of a phone booth, just off Collins Avenue, on one of those days when the sun touches the ground everywhere in flashbulbs white enough to blind a welder. Ziller was wearing his reflecto sunglasses. Leaning unexpectantly against the hot glass, he dialed a number he had long since memorized.

"*Díme*," said a hollow Spanish voice.

"Uh, *un momento*," Ziller stammered. He was so surprised to get through that he jostled the phone booth's walls with his elbows when he tried to take the phone from under his chin. "Uh, excuse me," he said nervously. "I am the *Americano* with the white beard. Excuse me. I am looking for . . ."

". . . I know who you are looking for," said Maraña. "What are you sitting on this time?"

Ziller forced a thin laugh. "I don't know, but it feels like a blowtorch."

"What a pity."

"Well, um. It depends on where you're sitting, I guess. Uh, listen. I need to have a little private chat with you about your government experience. I'll buy you a milkshake."

Maraña was silent.

"I'm getting tapped pretty hard," Ziller said. "It looks like I'm about to get dealt out of the game."

"You people play a different game than us *Cubanos*. I don't see how I could help you."

"Oh, man, I wouldn't call you for nothing. This is a mayday."

"No meetings," said Maraña. "It's too hot out there. But it's okay, my friend. You can tell me the problem now, if you like. You sound funny, though. Are you alone?"

"Yes," Ziller said faintly. "I just didn't expect to find you, that's all. I've been trying for months."

"That's a long mayday. So what's happening?"

Ziller opened the phone booth for air, then closed it for security. He turned in a tiny circle, twisting the burning phone cord around his neck. "Well, those powder noses I told you about are squeezing me right up into the big time," he said. "They've got me doing a huge business but making a piker's dough. They need a lot of samples for their files, you see."

"Of course," snickered Maraña. "They have to be very thorough."

"And they force me to make a fool of myself by being too eager," said Ziller. "It's just a matter of time before one of my twenty new associates catches on. I figure the boys are just making gravy with me as long as I last."

"I've heard it before. Have you thought about retiring?"

Ziller stared miserably at the broken fan over his head. "And do all that time? I'd take the long nap before I finish. And besides, I think the powder noses would just let word slip about me so they wouldn't have to do any work."

"Probably so," Maraña said thoughtfully. "You have associated yourself with a fine group of gentlemen, it seems. Are any of them Cuban?"

"No. You know them all. They're not Cuban unless you know some who like fettuccine for lunch."

"Well, what can I say? You've got to disappear and stay disappeared, or you've got to get the needle boys off your back. I can tell you one thing. Don't go to any lawyer in town. It's too late for that. Your health would not hold up during the negotiations."

"Yeah. Well, I was hoping you might help me with the off-my-back part. That's how it is. I'm yours, man. Your joker. Play me however you want. I've already told you my life. You know that. Don't you have a few extra favors stored up with the big fuzz somewhere, so you could drop a dime or two on them, let them know that I've paid my debt to society?"

There was a long silence. "That is not possible, you see, because I am in a different situation than you, my friend. That would unbalance me with those people, you know, and they would have to retaliate to keep the balance. The problem is that you have moved into a league above your head, you know. So I suggest you see a travel agent."

Ziller bumped his head disconsolately against the wall. "I'm a good actor. I can still act like a son of a bitch," he said, "but I can't direct myself anymore. I'm beggin' you, man. I can't stand having those guys toy with me anymore."

"This is not a begging world. Listen, you don't want to get involved with me in the first place. You are crazy to trust me. All I can say to you is that when somebody is breaking the law against you, maybe you should consider talking to the authorities . . ."

". . . Ah, come on," Ziller said.

"I'm not kidding. I'm going to hang up the phone now."

Ziller bumped his head softly for nearly a minute, and finally he began whistling a jaunty tune by the Ink Spots, whose music he considered a cultural landmark in the present century. He walked three times around the phone booth whistling louder and louder, feeling the inexplicable happiness of one who has decided upon his next move from the worst conceivable position. He began nodding, agreeing with his own thoughts, telling himself that the move would be easy and casual. Then rubbing his hands together like a kid about to open birthday presents, he stepped back in the booth and thumbed through the phone book. It had not been stolen or mutilated, which Ziller took as a good sign. When the call ended a few minutes later, Ziller emerged from the booth and shook the sweat off his head. He whistled the Ink Spots' "That Cat is High" all the way back to his car. At home, he put the song on the record player in the cathedral room and performed a softshoe routine for Marvella, Moonbeam, a vague skinny lawyer, and two wealthy women in old clothes who made Ziller turn the volume down so that they could tell him that he must be needing money since he always advertised such a need by drawing attention to himself. Ziller chanted, "Tote that hormone! Lift that *kvetch*! Can't take no scolding 'cause ah gots doz happy feets!" Ziller turned up the volume and resumed his dance.

"Oh, Bobby," retorted one of the women, "you don't even know what a hormone is."

"Sho I doos," cried Ziller, rubbing the air in circles. "A hormone is a chemical with a personality."

He kept dancing. The two women looked highly displeased and examined their fingers once or twice in marvelously impressive boredom before stalking brusquely out the door.

Ten days later, Ziller arrived early for his second meeting with Dave Damico. The site was a remote clump of white pines that left a bed of needles eight inches thick, soft, shady, and cool, near a stream of slow, dark water that ran behind an eight-hundred-year-old abbey north of Miami. The abbey had been ripped out of Spain by William Randolph Hearst, who wished to reconstruct it around his pool at San Simeon using the prayer chambers as dressing rooms and the alcoves as a long running bar, but then the stones were lost in Brooklyn during the Depression and not reclaimed until thirty years later, when the Episcopal Church paid the back taxes and turned the old crates into a lovely stone tourist attraction in the holy relic's natural climate.

Ziller felt secure there in the woods, sitting by a prearranged tree. He was wearing a tailored blue suit, a rather flamboyant white silk tie with a small pink flamingo amid a pattern of foliage, a white shirt of some gossamer Indian fabric, and cordovan loafers that had been walked in just enough so that he couldn't see his face reflected in the shiny tops. He was newly barber-shaved and trimmed, looking wealthy and loud, like a recently divorced Wall Street executive or the president of a recording company. Ziller wanted his panache to be noticed, and he knew better than to be subtle with a G-man.

In his unofficial garb, Dave Damico dressed like a college student on the spring beer binge, in a GATORS T-shirt and paint-splattered jeans. Incon-

171

gruously, he also wore his standard double-width FBI brogans, without which any agent would risk ostracism and career disaster. The passion for square shoes had been traced far back into Bureau history, but its origin remained uncertain. Most agents leaned toward the persistent rumor that it had grown out of Director Hoover's notion that narrow shoes were dainty and therefore the telltale sign of a fairy. At any rate, agents lived in fear of being shod in too slim or pointy a fashion, and this fear grew in the exaggerated paranoia of that particular bureaucracy until all agents wore shoes like galoshes and galoshes like wheelbarrows. An agent who for any reason believed his job to be in jeopardy was likely to go out and buy a pair of still wider shoes to dispel suspicions along those lines, and many grateful agents could remember the moment when a kindly older man had advised them how to stuff foam rubber along the sides of shoes to fill up the extra width. All this made for difficult undercover work.

Damico wore his wide shoes dutifully, but otherwise he was a mild iconoclast in the Bureau. He disliked banks, for one thing, and was outspoken enough to say that he resented the Bureau's preoccupation with bankers. He also hated heroin, partly because a Brooklyn cousin of his had died a junkie's death, and he regularly composed fervent memos recommending that the FBI change its "play it safe" tradition of avoiding narcotics investigations. Agents in the Miami office considered him the young Hotspur idealist, always itching to take on the big boys, whom he called "hoods," always dismissing stifling regulations with his impatient, "Yeah, yeah, yeah." He was still something of a storybook cop, of humbler than normal origins for the Bureau. When he reached five years of age, his father had put him to work in the bakery making up dough for bread and pasta, and every morning a sleepy young Damico made mistakes in his simple chores—leaving out the salt, doubling the flour—even after he wrote large reminders in crayon on the walls of his little dough room.

Damico remembered all the smells from that room, along with the banter between his huge father and the bakers and customers up front, and the reassuring honest fatigue of several thousand working days that began before dawn and the proud morning when he was first allowed to work in a sleeveless white undershirt like the men, but he also remembered the helpless rage in the bakery when three well-dressed, ugly men wrapped an assistant baker's leg around a water pipe until pieces of bone stuck out of his shin. Such things happened more than once a year.

Mrs. Damico believed with all her heart that her firstborn son could put a stop to the old ways. She pushed him through college and New York University law school with equally large doses of ambition and rosy hope, so that on the glorious day when he was sworn in as an FBI agent Dave Damico felt truly called to a high mission. The conflicts grappling inside him made the mission more difficult, and therefore higher. He was to be the family's respectability, always placed dead center in photographs of the Christmas throng, but he was also supposed to be the Robin Hood who would square things with the rich thieves.

Damico looked around to make sure there was nobody else within sight. Then he folded his arms, put his back to Ziller's tree, and slid down acrobatically to the ground. "Hiya," he said.

"You're early," said Ziller, who was happy Damico had come at all. "How did it go?"

"So far, so good. Part of your story checks, anyway. I saw them watching your house night before last. They are DEA guys and the bastards are *paisanos*, which makes it personal."

"So what's next?"

"So what's next is you gotta answer some more questions."

"Whatever's right. Like what?"

"Like who is the little brunette with one blue earring that I saw coming out of your driveway?"

"Oh shit." Ziller stood up abruptly and dusted the pine needles off his suit. His jaw muscles had twisted into two little burls, and there was a faint blue spot under one temple. "I knew this would happen," he sighed. "Somebody like you just can't help squeezing a zit, can you? You just can't wait to pull in the bystanders and make them hostages in your shit. Look, I made you a business proposition on very favorable terms to you, because I'm desperate. I admit that. But that doesn't mean I'm gonna rat all over everybody else, too. That woman has nothing to do with this. You don't need leverage out of her . . ."

". . . Sit down," Damico said wearily. He was picking his teeth with a pine needle. "If I wanted to squeeze you, I could. And I'm tempted, because I don't like you. But I'm not after that woman. I'd just like to run a name check on her. The drug boys could have planted her in your house for all I know."

"Yeah, right," said Ziller. He squinted with one eye for a second of doubtful thought before circling the tree to face Damico, calming down. "We need a better understanding here. How are we going to get through the difficult weeks ahead if we keep up this stuff? I don't want to know anything about the people who go to *your* house, so why do you want to lean on the people in mine? Let's devise some evenhanded rules so we can be equally underhanded."

"Don't be a smartass," Damico said easily. "You're a talker, aren't you Bobby?"

Ziller pawed the ground with his shiny right shoe, looking a bit subdued. "Well, I was little when I was a kid and I couldn't run very fast, so I polished my tongue until it got real smooth, you know."

"Yeah, well did your tongue get you in hock with the narcs? You want to tell me about the bust now?"

"No."

"That's all right. You see how reasonable I am? Now why don't you tell me about the brunette? I'm not trying to get a hook into her, believe me. This is for defensive purposes."

"You betcha. Well, as it happens, I don't even know her name. Everybody calls her Moonbeam. She's got an apartment up in Hialeah somewhere. I think she's a part-time photographer. She showed up at my house in a big crowd of acid freaks during the Republican convention and she's been coming around ever since."

"Uh huh. You sweet on her?"

"Yeah, I like her."

"Are you ballin' her?"

Ziller smiled. "No, man. The chick's a trifle unstable. She jumps back and forth between the speed freak jitters and the bourgeois blues, with some weird shit in there that even I've never seen before."

"Forget it," said Damico. "You really are a talker." He was shaking his head in genuine wonder, but inwardly he was hoping that Ziller wouldn't see how happy he was that Ziller didn't seem to know much about Moonbeam. "Look, I'm gonna talk to you about the overall score as I see things. You ready?"

"No."

"Tough shit. Now, you tell me the narcotics boys have got a thirty-year sentence hanging over you if you don't play ball with them. And playing ball means that you keep clueing them in on deals and dealers. But instead of making busts, they just line their pockets and probably their noses. Let's say I believe you that far, okay? And I'll go another step with you that they'll push you until some hood finds out you're a snitch and snuffs you. They couldn't care less, right? That's the feeling I get from you, and it sure as hell wouldn't surprise me about them. Okay? Now. Let me tell you something, Robert. I *like* capital punishment. As a loyal FBI agent I'm not supposed to comment on it, but I don't give a shit. Some guys maim and kill people and do things that make you sick, and I don't want to pay for their prison food, you see. Their lives aren't that important. Fair is fair, but it doesn't mean you can't kill anything, okay? I mean, maybe we should let the veterinarians put them away 'cause they're more humane than the prisons, but let's just hurry those people on out of here and be clean. Okay, Robert. After all that, I still don't think you're in the bunch that should fry, from what I can tell about you."

"Thank you very much," said Ziller, trying to smile. He was still sitting with his back against the tree, staring up at a pair of well-muscled biceps on a light heavyweight's body. Damico's had stood up to pace through the leaves as his lecture heated up, but he had stopped, put his hands on his knees, and leaned over to make his point. Ziller could feel the heat off his face.

"Don't mention it," Damico said loudly as he paced off to the side. "And on top of that, there's something else. Let's say I did want you to fry, okay?"

"Let's not."

"Well, even if I did, I don't think it ought to be done like this, Robert. I mean a judge ought to explain it to you and have it done proper. It shouldn't be done privately and all informal, the way my countrymen over in the good ol' DEA are doing it to you, you see? That's my opinion. They're just using you as bait to troll with through the underworld for sharks and money. That's not right, is it?"

"No." Ziller got halfway through a nervous laugh before a hiccough of self-pity drowned it. Damico turned away from the emotion.

"I'm trying to tell you that I don't like those bastards over there in DEA either, you see? I'd like to nail 'em too. And I'd like to nail all your big pusher friends. Okay?"

"Okay."

"Okay. Now that's the good news." Damico wrung his hands as though something had been accomplished. Then he resumed his pacing. "Now the bad news is that you're still up the creek, Robert. It ain't gonna be easy to get you out, and it sure ain't gonna be free. 'Cause you don't want to testify against the drug cops, do you?"

"Right."

"You hate narcs, but you're more scared of 'em because all they have to do is let it slip that you've been snitching on everybody in town, right?"

"Right."

"Well, you're gonna have to think about that."

"Oh no. I couldn't . . ."

". . . Shut up and listen. We're just working on our understanding here, Robert. Now even if you were willing to testify, we'd have to get evidence. You'd have to wear a wire, man. We'd have to nail 'em cold. And what I'm trying to get you to appreciate is how unpleasant it will be for me to go in to my boss Pat Shea, who is a pansy, and tell him how I'd like to put a wire on one of DEA's informants so he can spy on DEA because the informant says DEA is crooked. That will not be well received, Robert. Can you see that?"

"Yeah," sighed Ziller.

" 'Cause DEA is a government agency and you're a collared pusher and a snitch, you see."

Ziller took a deep breath. "I wish you wouldn't call me a pusher," he protested. "The people who hawk beer and deodorant on TV are pushers, man. I don't advertise. I don't even have a sales pitch. My customers come to me. I'm an importer."

Damico whirled in a rage and snatched Ziller up by the flamingo tie, tearing a ragged patch out of the Indian shirt. The patch floated lazily to the ground like a plate-sized flake of dandruff. Ziller hung limply, so Damico had to use both hands to hold him there while he made growling noises, waiting to find out if his temper would slip its last notch. The moment passed, and Damico looked at Ziller with consummate disgust, frustrated over being caught halfway between reason and fury, holding a dead weight and not knowing quite what to do next. He had to work for every breath.

Ziller closed his eyes and said, "I'm nonviolent, man."

"Shit," said Damico. He opened his hands and Ziller dropped to the ground. After canvassing his body for serious injury, Ziller began massaging the places where the tie had disappeared into the meat of his neck. "I'm not trying to razz you," he said quietly. "I really don't like the rough stuff. That's why I'd like to retire from all this."

"Save it," Damico said wearily, almost in a whisper. "Just don't ever say anything nice about dope around me, okay Robert? I hate the stuff. I hate the people around it. It's all weakness and grime to me."

"Then stay away from it," Ziller advised.

"Shut up before I get pissed off. Now the fact I'm trying to get through your head is that even if we had the goods on the drug boys, and even if you were willing to testify, and even if we rigged it some way so that your 'importer' friends wouldn't come down on you, even with all that I'm saying the odds are heavy against us on whether the Bureau would push for a case against the drug boys or even bring pressure on them. It will be called a pissing contest, and most guys in the Bureau won't want any part of it."

"Great."

"I'm just giving you the facts of life, Robert. You've got to be mighty clean and pretty crazy to push a corruption case against a fellow cop. What's in it for anybody except a lot of grief? So I'm not guaranteeing you anything except that I won't snitch on you myself, okay? All you have is my word that I'd like to nail all those guys on your back just to clear the air around here. And what it boils down to is this, Robert. You've got to take a dive on another rap. Sooner or later. I don't care. But you can't hope to get away with a free ride, and you can't survive any rap tied to dope. Your enemies aren't that dumb."

Ziller looked blank and shrugged. "What about maybe if I arranged to get busted on a small drug charge in another jurisdiction? How's that?"

"Well, you can try it, but it won't work," said Damico. "The feds would just tell the locals that you're a vital part of a very important secret drug investigation. They'd spring you, and then you'd just have another rap over your head."

Ziller stood up and smoothed his tie over the window in his shirt, walking around the tree in a pensive trance. "You guys have to work things around to a confession every time," he said. "I don't like it. Besides, I'm just a regular businessman who's caught up in a web of unfavorable circumstance."

"You don't look like you've worked a day in your life, Robert," Damico said sourly. "And you're not rich enough to live off the sap. I'll bet my Dolphin tickets you've got something back there in your past that will do for us, so out with it. Something small. Something federal. You'll be out in a year, and by then maybe I'll be a hero."

Ziller circled the tree again. "I don't want to go to jail," he said.

"One more crack like that and I'm leaving, Robert," Damico said quietly. "You should have crossed that bridge long ago, before you called me. Now you're wasting my time."

Twice more around the tree and Ziller's forehead took on a weighty curvature at the edges. "Here goes nothing," he said. "You ever heard of the Miami Beach Service Center for the Visually Handicapped on Jefferson Street?"

"No. Keep going."

"Uh, well, most of the people there are not visually handicapped. They're hustlers. Of one sort or another."

Damico shook his head. "It figures I'd get stuck with a guy like you," he sulked. "A petty con. Fleecing the blind folks, eh?"

"Visually handicapped," Ziller corrected. "That's important on your federal grant applications . . ."

". . . Mail fraud . . ."

". . . for things like money and marijuana permits. We say blind on our direct mail solicitations. Tax deductible, you know."

"More mail fraud. Tax fraud. Better."

"You can do a lot with a home for the blind once you get it established," Ziller said, beginning to stroll as he talked. "Last year we had a celebrity benefit at the Eden Roc. It was a smash."

"Congratulations."

"With the proceeds, we sponsored a Latin Holiday for blind people. Blind people from all over got businesses to sponsor them for a raffle fee, and we raffled off six places on the holiday. I was the tour director. We took two real blind people and four entrepreneurs of my acquaintance . . ."

"Jesus."

". . . all over South America to hear the sights. As prizes, we brought back a large number of hand-crafted Peruvian backgammon boards, capes, tapestries, and glasswork. We sold them a few months ago at the charity bazaar. We also brought back two crates of Spanish-language braille equipment. It was hollow."

"Uh huh. Filled with?"

"Ten kilos. You can cut it right there in the back room of the Jefferson Street headquarters. Nobody ever bothers a home for the blind, you know. You get a lot of leeway. I've learned that most people would rather have been seen than see anything, so even our rich board members never drop by . . ."

"All right, all right," Damico cut in. "Do you know what you're doing? Do you *really* know? You're braggin' your goddam head off. That's what. Con men always do that, and I don't like it."

Ziller stopped walking his circle. A certain rosiness had in fact come up in his cheeks, and there was a wistful cast to his clever eyes as his mind drifted back over other scams, including the Dade County Industrial Chemical Company, which had disappeared. "You may have a point there," he smiled. "You mind if I tell you a brief historical note?"

"Probably."

"Well, anyway, my old man sold corporate surety bonds until he went broke in the Depression, and then he hustled booze, fronting for a few speakeasies. All I knew was that he went to work and did okay. But just before he died, he took me out by the pool where I live now and admitted to me all the things he'd done. He looked ashamed, you know. And I said, 'Wow! You really did all that?' I thought that was the greatest thing I ever heard. So the old man actually hugged me he was so happy. Jewish fathers aren't so good at that. It was a big deal. And when he got all loosened up, he told me that he felt more legitimate selling booze than surety bonds. He was excited telling me about a few of his big moves. You could see it in his face. When he was talking about that stuff it was the only time I can remember when he wasn't ugly. Can you understand that? And you see I get the same feeling on a scam. I'm acting, playing parts, humming along. I can snap my fingers at a stranger and tell you what he digs and what he'll fall for. And when everything works, it sparkles like nothing else can."

"Well, you'll have a lot of time to reminisce about those wonderful scams later, Robert. Right now . . ."

"I didn't know you guys really say shit like that," chirped Ziller. The flow of words had brought him a good mood. "But it's all right. I just wanted to say one thing, man, now that I've confessed and all. It's something weird to me. As good as it felt to pull a short con, I always felt a tinge of regret. Not much of one, I'll say, but a little bit, because the people who contributed to my ventures didn't do it with their eyes open, you know. They were mostly greedy assholes who deserved to be relieved of their money, but still, the transactions were not quite straightforward. You may not believe it would bother me, but it did. And the weird thing is that when I shifted some of my assets into the contraband business and started moving merchandise that people really wanted straight up, one-on-one, just the way my old man's customers wanted booze, I felt like a fucking reformer. And here I am in all this goddam trouble for just being good."

"A reformer, eh?" scoffed Damico.

"I just wanted you to know that. No charge, no obligation, and now I'm finished with it."

"A reformer," said Damico.

"Relatively speaking."

"When this is over, I hope somebody knocks the smile off your goddamn cocky mug and puts you in a room with a bunch of kids strung out on heroin, with rust in their veins and blood coming out of their ears. And see how long you feel like a reformer. You little shit."

Ziller stiffened, but his voice became softer. "I've seen people wasted by a lot of things. Some of them they pick, and some of them other people pick for them."

"Oh, fuck you," grunted Damico, waving Ziller away in disgust, almost laughing.

"Whatever's right, man. Truce, okay?"

Damico sighed. "Yeah, truce. I'm gonna carry the torch right alongside of *you*, Robert, God help me. Let's get at it." And he gave Ziller his instructions.

Three hours later, a restless Damico was camped in the easy chair next to Pops Shea's desk while the boss talked on the telephone to his wife, Helen. She was advising him on people to call to bring pressure on the local GSA administrator to fix the air conditioner at the FBI's Flagler Street headquarters. Instead of cooling, the system was dripping water into the evidence room downstairs, and the senior agents were refusing to come to the office because the modern tinted security windows could not be opened. Only the junior ones were there sweating it out with Shea, popping in with useless messages to demonstrate their eagerness. The Bureau was in a bad way. GSA workers no longer volunteered to do night repairs at headquarters, and ordinary citizens had the temerity to give agents the brush-off. The GSA's deputy director, a Cuban, held such a grudge against the FBI for arresting the best Class A helmsman at the Verdadero Yacht Club on bomb charges that he had twice changed the locks on the building without notifying Shea.

It was all symptomatic of a bad year. Since the Taliente murder, there had been seven more major political assassinations, including that of Mendoza, and there had been more than eighty known murders related to drug racketeering. Numerous other people, both Cubans and rich young Americans, had disappeared. Not a single one of the murders had been solved, and there was too much blame to heap it all on the local cops. Some of this was beginning to seep into the papers despite the tourism crisis, which was acknowledged by all the town fathers after even the bare-knuckled Teamsters Union moved its convention from Miami to Las Vegas for fear that wives would be molested by "foreigners" in Miami.

For Shea, things were no better at home. His wife had determined to add a Florida room to their home, prevailing over Shea's opinion that they did not need such a room, being in Florida, and she had ordered, unordered, and reordered her way through several contractors and designers before a perfectly honest-looking builder from Georgia dared to abscond with a large sum of the Florida room money. Shea had been mortified when his wife insisted on excoriating the assembled agents of the Miami field office for not finding the man, pacing there in the conference room under the Hoover portrait as she scolded them smartly and at length, in precisely the manner that was being urged on Shea himself by the "get tough" faction.

The "play it by the book" faction was contending with the corner-cutters, as usual, and the crime specialists tilted with the generalists in disputes garnished with personal feuds and jockeying, but Shea had lost his zest for moderating the fray with neutralism. Sometimes he caught himself fantasizing about chucking it all to take his pale rounded body off to a distant tropical jungle, where he could eat coconuts and flirt with young Irish waitresses. No more Helen. No more agents needling him ceaselessly to do things beyond his limits, as the young fireball Damico was doing now with his crazy scheme to chase drugs and fight the narcs at once—two of the least appealing ideas Patrick Shea could think of.

He hung up the phone and gave Damico the uncomfortable hurried smile of an undertaker about to gloss over his fees. "Excuse me, Damico," he said. "Now what was it you were proposing to do with this fellow Zipper?"

"Uh, Ziller, sir."

"Yes, yes. Well, why don't you put all the ins and outs of your plan in writing for me if you wouldn't mind? I know we have too much paperwork around here, but on something like this I think it's important to reduce all the input to black and white. Don't you agree?"

"Yes, sir, but I'm afraid this is a special case. That's why I asked to see you privately, without Miss Whipple."

"I see," said Shea. "Sensitive, eh? Detrimental to the Bureau? Too sensitive even for the classification system to handle it?" Shea leaned back and made a whistling sound between his polished upper cuspids. Damico and all the other agents knew this presaged a sidestep.

Damico jerked himself out of the chair and gripped its arm as he blurted, "Chief, the reason I've kept this orally confidential is that I have reasons to believe that your daughter might be involved. It's in the high range of probability."

Shea made little clicking noises with his tongue. He looked like a crisp, mild-mannered dentist tempted for the first time to go on a rampage and break up the office furniture. No one had ever seen Shea lose his temper at headquarters. He closed his eyes. "You'd better tell me you're wrong within thirty seconds, David," he sighed, "or you damn well better be right."

"I'm sorry, sir."

"How do you know?"

"I've seen her twice while I've been watching Ziller's house, and I checked out a vehicle that belongs to her," Damico said quietly, seeming humble and efficient, out of character. "I checked it personally on the license, without making a request."

"Thank you."

"Uh, and the information I have is that she has been spending a great deal of time at Ziller's for about two years, but she doesn't use her own name. She's known only as 'Moonbeam,' apparently. Is that possible?"

"Yes, of course it's possible," Shea snapped. The buzzer sounded. He cradled his forehead with one hand while punching the intercom with the other. "No, Miss Whipple!" he boomed. "Whatever it is, no! I am status do not disturb until further notice. That's in capital letters. Please keep all those clowns out of here."

"Why, *sir*," squeaked Miss Whipple through the box. "Certainly, sir." Shea's violent tone threw a scare into her, but later it gave way to indignation. She told her most trusted coworker at headquarters what had happened and how she had not deserved such treatment, and everyone in the building soon knew that the boss and Damico were in the middle of something deep.

Shea folded his hands on the desk and sighed. "Since this case looks like it's going to be personal for me, I'm glad it's you, Dave," he said.

"Thank you, Chief."

"Well never mind about that," Shea recovered. "The point is how we're going to get her out of there. Do you have any ideas on that?"

Damico crossed his legs in the easy chair. "Well, sir, I'm just starting on this, but I guess that the easiest way would be for you to visit her at her apartment or telephone her there and advise her of the potential danger she's in, assuming she doesn't already know. She may know that the house is a drug interchange but not how serious the situation is regarding Ziller."

"Uh huh," Shea nodded, losing strength. "That would be the simplest approach, wouldn't it?"

"Yes, sir."

"I suppose so."

"Yes, sir. And I suppose if there were a real emergency, we could go right into Ziller's house itself, or probably it would be best to send someone in and extract your daughter directly. But that might be dangerous. Ziller's on tenterhooks, sir, about anybody finding out that he has government contacts."

"I understand," Shea whispered faintly, turning to look out the window. "Damn this air conditioning. Oh, boy. You know I can remember when we didn't even have *fans* in the Bureau, much less air conditioners. Isn't that something?"

Yes, sir," said Damico, holding his breath. Shea's suffering had a simplicity to it that helped Damico tolerate the diversions.

"About that approach you suggested, Dave," Shea said. "The only problem with it is that I'm afraid it would backfire on us. That's a strong possibility, I'm afraid, because Helen, my daughter, uh, has a long history of doing exactly the opposite of whatever I tell her to do. She once spent two weeks traveling with that rock 'n' roll band that puts live spiders in their hair, after I explicitly told her to stay away from them." He shuddered quietly at the thought of the spiders.

"I'm not familiar with that group," said Damico.

"That's all right," said Shea. "It doesn't matter. But the point is that a personal appeal from me or her mother would probably be counterproductive, irregardless of the danger or how it is done."

"Uh huh."

"Uh, this fellow Ziller might be on tenterhooks about his contacts, but I'm afraid my daughter is on her own tenterhooks about having the FBI SAC for a father. She hasn't wanted anybody to know that since that business up at Kent State years ago. Maybe before that, really, if you want to know the Lord's truth."

"Yes, sir."

" 'Fraid so. And let's see. If she knew that I knew about her and Ziller, it might even make her more loyal to him, you know. She might even tell him who she is, and that wouldn't be good, would it?"

"No, sir. We don't want that to get around."

"What a mess." Shea pushed his high-backed swivel chair away from the desk, put his elbows on his knees, and stared at the floor. "Maybe I should just call her, though," he opined, half to himself. "Sound her out. Maybe she's grown out of it and is just looking for an excuse to make up with us. You never know with kids, Dave. It might be worth a try."

Damico said nothing. "But it's a real, real long shot," Shea continued, refuting himself, trying to laugh. "The last time I went over there, I took her some new stationery her mother had picked out, hoping she'd write us, since she won't call, and she refused to take it and said her mother had been beating her over the head for twenty years to tell her how great she is, which of course is a little strong. Then she accused me of having her bugged, for God's sake, following her around and stuff. And right there in the door she lit a marijuana cigarette and said she'd learned more about the universe from a fish than she ever had from the Catholic Church. I said *that* was out of school and I told her that to me there is a lot of room for all kinds of fish in the Mother Church's universe. And she just said I was hopeless and showed me out with a little peck on my cheek."

"I'm sorry."

"Yeah, well, not half as sorry as I am. It makes me glad we only had one kid. I don't mean to push the soap opera stuff on you, especially with you being a subordinate official and all, but I'm just trying to show you why I don't think I'd get very far. I think the country's in a hell of a fix when an SAC can't even warn his own daughter about a crime situation, you know. She got those political-type ideas in her head way too early in her life, from the Beatles on. Yeah, but I'm still not proud of the state of affairs now, Dave. I'm really not."

Damico started to say something perfunctory and then simply nodded. He wanted to say that if it were his kid he would storm Ziller's and drag her off under his arm if he had to, but that would conflict with his strategy. Also, he was touched by his boss's open torment.

"Let me think about it," said Shea. "But for right now, let's assume we're gonna work around my daughter. What are the other options? You got anything on them?"

Damico pretended to consider other angles as though he had not already done so. Then he moved to the next phase. "Well, Chief, the way I see it she is only in danger because she's around Ziller, unless there's something we don't know about, and if we can't get her to separate from Ziller we'll have to separate Ziller from her."

"Right."

"And the way I figure, the easiest way by far to do that is for DEA to put a hard bust on the guy and *keep* him busted until the action drifts away from his house. You know? 'Cause that would remove the main source of the problem."

One of Shea's salty eyebrows dive-bombed at an angle toward his nose. "But you don't think they'll do that, right?"

Damico looked grave. "I doubt it," he said. "Unless Ziller's lying from start to finish. He's a good liar, but it doesn't make sense that he would slit his own throat with me just to do it. So I think these guys over there may be milking him for all he's worth. It wouldn't be the first time. And that means they won't bust him unless they have to."

"Those bastards," said Shea. His fingers sounded a few distracted drum rolls on the desk. "Maybe it's on the up-and-up though, Dave. Couldn't they be working toward a big dragnet that's about to come down on Ziller and all the rest of 'em?"

"It's possible. That's what we've got to find out, Chief," Damico earnestly replied. "We don't have any choice but to wrap an ear around DEA's whole Ziller operation. Real careful but thorough. I know it's dangerous . . ."

". . . You're damn right it's dangerous. Can you imagine what we'd do if those guys stuck their noses in one of ours and said we're dirty?"

"I know, I know. We may have to leave Miami if we blow it. If their show is legit, we may just have to sit tight and hope the bust comes soon and smooth. But if those guys really are heavy on the take . . ."

". . . Then we'll knock a few heads together, that's what we'll do," declared Shea, testing his own resolution. It sounded good to him. His anger was rising above that of the standard office crisis. "We'll do more than *that* if we have to."

"Okay." Damico allowed himself a slight anticipatory grin. "And if things work just right, we might even get jurisdiction to roll up Ziller's pusher friends while we're at it."

"Well, if DEA's really not gonna do its job, I guess we'll have to do that, too. But I don't understand those young guys over there, Dave. How could they get sucked so deep into something like this?"

Damico pushed back a cuticle or two while he pondered. "Well, sir, those guys specialize in undercover sales, as you know, and to establish their bona fides in that element they've got to flash around a lot of bait money and a lot of contraband samples. They've got to speak the criminal lingo and hang out a lot at the Anvil Restaurant on the Beach."

"They've got to be more Catholic than the Pope," Shea summarized.

"That's right. It's part of the job. And it's not easy . . ."

". . . Yes, yes," smiled Shea, who was honest in everything outside of golf scores, taxes, fringe benefits, and domestic conversation, too proper and too timid for outright graft, but who nevertheless was reassured to hear the subject of official corruption introduced in the context of operational necessity. "But the people who have the most sensitive responsibilities are the ones who must be above reproach, Dave. In the Bible, they only use angels to punish the wicked, you know. That's always amazed me."

"Uh huh," said Damico, uncomfortable with the piety, worried that it signaled a retreat.

"By the way, do those guys get promoted any faster than us?" asked Shea. "I'm just curious."

"Well, a little bit faster. They're a newer outfit," Damico replied. He could tell he was about to lose Shea. "There's one more angle I see in this, Chief. Maybe we could bust Ziller ourselves on one of our raps. It would have the same effect, 'cause while we've got him under wraps Moonbeam—uh, your daughter, excuse me . . ."

". . . That's all right."

". . . would drift away. That's an alternative for us. I've already picked up one pretty good report that this guy Ziller is a con artist. I'd like to run that down, too, and we can choose later which way to go."

Shea nodded mechanically. "That's good," he said. "It's always better to have options. Look, you're go on that, Dave. You're go on anything you want in this one, as far as I'm concerned. Just be careful around the subjects, please. I don't have to tell you that, do I? Because if any of the subjects find out after some screw-up, the shit's gonna hit the fan around Ziller and Helen could get hurt."

"Yes, sir."

"And that would kill her mother and me. We may not be close to our hippie daughter, Dave, but still, you know."

"I understand completely," said Damico.

"Thanks," said Shea hoarsely.

"I'll be careful," Damico vowed. "Believe me. I want this one bad, Chief. It's gonna work out."

"Thanks for handling it like this too, Dave," said Shea. "It's got to be closely held. If the personal side of this thing came out, it could hurt the Bureau all around, with the DEA and everybody. It could go public."

Damico nodded. He could barely contain his zeal now that his mandate was ordained with the aid of luck, Shea's personal sore spots, and no small measure of Damico's cunning. For the first time in five years of criminal administration, he saw a reasonable chance to be a hero instead of a bureaucrat. His combative instincts rose to the opportunity to make up for a few things by taking one all the way. The phrase in the Bureau was "to the hilt." The thought of it lifted Damico out of the depressions he made in Shea's carpet.

Two weeks later, without consulting his wife about the strategy, Shea went to Washington on a dual mission. More worried than ever after the first trickle of reports from Damico about his daughter, including an especially ominous one that she had twice visited Colombia with Ziller, he wanted to press forward with the arrangements for transfer and possibly early retirement, and accordingly he visited Sandy Morgan, congratulating him immediately on his new position as director of FBI personnel. He greeted a livelier and much more dapper Morgan than he had seen the year before, for Morgan exuded the rare enthusiasm of one whose faithful pursuit of a single goal over thirty years has brought more, not less, satisfaction than expected.

Shea told him almost everything over lunch at the Old Ebbitt Grill, omitting only certain details of Moonbeam's involvement with Ziller. He stressed the negative developments—the rampant murders, the return of his peptic ulcer, the sticky-fingered rascals at DEA, the "wrong crowd" proclivities of Moonbeam, the latest embarrassments in the search for the Florida room swindler. It was high quality material, and Morgan sympathized through it all. Shea wound the subject around to his firm inclination that now was the time for a transfer move, prompting Morgan to wind around through the foibles of the members of the Personnel Review Committee toward the conclusion that it could be done if everything were handled just right. It couldn't be Ohio, he said, because one homeless curmudgeon on the committee always asked specifically if senior officials were being pastured in their home states, which practice he thought detrimental to the Bureau. Shea groaned, but revived again some time later when Morgan figured out that he could have the small office in Huntington, West Virginia, just across the Ohio River. Morgan was smart that way. He even knew of jobs there in security and corporate public relations that would calm Shea's anxiety about his money situation.

In the taxi on the way past Dupont Circle, Shea thought that perhaps his anxiety was nothing more than this—he was going to see a stranger on awkward family business. But it was more than that. Shea was so nervous he could barely light his cigarette. He closed his eyes and blew a lungful of smoke at the Cosmos Club as the taxi cruised by it, with Shea inside trying to hold onto himself.

The Jamaican security man gasped when Shea announced himself as FBI, and from all the stalling and low talking he did with the people upstairs it was apparent that he had thrown the place into confusion. Shea felt better, but in the elevator the anxiety surged again, still more as he knocked on the door. When it opened, he stuck out his hand with a grin and said, "Pat Shea, young man. What branch of the service were you in?"

Howell gulped. He was still tucking in his shirt, and the collar of his suit jacket was twisted in two places. Haven Pinder was tidying him up from behind while he tried to decide whether to be afraid, cool, or stupefied over such a greeting. "Uh, I wasn't in the service at all," he said meekly, rather ashamed of himself for not making this more of a positive statement against Vietnam.

"That's all right," said Shea. "I wasn't either. Didn't get the chance. Too young for the big one and tied up in the Bureau by Korea."

"You're with the FBI?"

"That's right."

"Uh, is it about Madame Delacroix?"

"Who's that?"

"Uh, well . . ." Howell turned to seek guidance from Pinder's face.

"Never mind," said Shea. "May I come in?"

Pinder stepped from behind Howell. "Is this official?" she asked suspiciously. Howell cringed.

"Not exactly," Shea replied, looking apprehensively at Pinder, who was barefoot and blue-jeaned and wearing the kind of look that makes bullies think twice.

"Well," said Howell.

"That's not good enough," said Pinder. "You've got to be careful in these things David, or you'll find out you've granted entry for an official search and our plants might get knocked over and everything. I'm trying to be polite, sir, but is this an official entry or not?"

"Uh, no, ma'am, if you ask it that way," said Shea. "This is more personal. I'm not from this office anyway. I'm from Miami."

Howell cringed again, almost drooping with guilt. "I knew it," he sighed, stepping back from the door. "All these months I've been telling myself different, but I knew it would work out this way. I should have talked to you people a long time ago."

"Pardon me?" asked a puzzled Shea.

"Let him ask the questions, David," said Pinder.

"I know, but . . ."

"Would you like some cheese and crackers?" Pinder offered.

"Love some, if it's not too much trouble," said Shea, stepping inside. "Nice place you got here."

X

HOWELL WOULD tell Haven Pinder on occasion that the Shea visit was a "personal snapping point" for him, not just because it broke his heart—for it broke hers even more—but because he realized how many leaden weights he was carrying inside in addition to the Mendoza death and his guilt over not having reported his conversation with Maraña. The burden had accumulated during what Howell called a "gear-shifting period" among his friends, whose lives had a way of switching themes harmoniously every year or two, a pattern due in part to the homogeneity of activity in the capital. There had been several "fire drill" periods, for example, brought on by war or scandal or election, during which everyone worked furiously until midnight, giving orders like martinets, containing various crises, flopping into bed every month or so with a complete stranger. There had also been periods of escape and money worry and ideological transition, but no previous phase had been nearly so unsettling. People changed so drastically as to startle their best friends. Whole sections of personalities melted away to be replaced by others, changing the resonance of combinations such that old friends would question whether they had really known each other.

It had all started when Ziggy Rosen had suddenly quit the FCC to buy a small radio station just outside Baltimore, a city in Maryland full of such ordinary people that most Washingtonians had never heard of it. The station was dirt cheap, but it could beam a weak signal all the way to Clyde's in Georgetown. This was precisely Rosen's intention once he assumed command of WIZY radio, and in April he had moved to Maryland after a small farewell ceremony at the Tidal Basin. Susan Hartman cried briefly there when Rosen handed her a satchel of junk from their previous lives.

In the late transition period, the inhabitants of David Howell's apartment often swerved into a commemorative descant on the subject of Ziggy Rosen, which, for everyone except Haven Pinder, was a relief from the complicated lives in Washington. It was not that she didn't like Rosen. The two of them had shared a subterranean channel of affection ever since she had once interrupted one of his political discourses to tell him he was "squishy," which pleased him immensely and prompted a dance without music. That was fine, but Rosen had long been an irritant to Pinder's boss and as such his name called up the job anxiety that Pinder was enduring along with the Howell anxiety.

The boss, during his formative years, had made a name for himself by leading marches against oppression, lecturing widely on conspiracies and socialist theory, and coining a phrase or two. He kept in his office at the Alternative Political Coalition a striking photograph of himself in a Guevara beard and a bullet-studded bandolero, leading a student protest in the old days against racist and imperialist vegetable purchases by the university. Although feminist protest against the strident sexism of the pose had long since forced the boss to take the photo off his wall, out of sight, he still cherished that manly gaze more than anyone suspected except Haven Pinder, who not only knew about the secret drawer where it was hidden, but also had felt the brunt of his commanding instincts for two years.

Pinder had just about had enough of it. In fact, she would have quit already without the sustenance she got from her secret, nonpolitical pursuits. She was proud of her work, considered herself a craftswoman who could take a pamphlet from an idea to the post office—writing, editing, layout, printing, illustrating, the works—and her ambition did not look past such complete tasks, certainly not enough to overcome her disdain for self-promotion by office politics. Pinder simply desired to pull a reasonable load for a pure cause, as she had done all her adult life. It was not the shortage of causes that brought on her disenchantment; it was a perception that the boss was a "creep." One night, after the participants in an office conclave left behind a million words on militarism and two hundred cigarette butts on the floor, Pinder had told him so.

Martin, the boss, pretended not to hear, and then he laughed. His response was an official one, as usual, in the form of hints over the next few months that Pinder's commitment was floundering. In his world, commitment was measured not just by how late one stayed at the office, though that was important, but by a steady imperviousness to personal developments as contrasted with general ones. Personal discussions were useful only for empirical data that might help one refine a consistent general political outlook, and in that vein the boss reminded Pinder that her father had "bad politics."

Pinder was sensitive about her father, a rather eccentric gentleman who had dropped out of the family law firm in New York to become a seed merchant. He packaged seeds for flowers, vegetables, and fruits, caring infinitely more about the seeds themselves than he did about their issue. In his leisure time he puttered around in the yard in a three-piece suit from one barely begun chore to another, leaving a rake in the leaves or a saw stuck in a half-severed limb, always yanked away from practical matters by some rhapsodic thought on a particular kind of seed. The elder Pinder knew everything about seeds. They made him bubble and smile, and he would forsake any worldly emergency just to sit around the table and talk to his family of seeds and what miracles they could accomplish with only some water and dirt. One of his truly bizarre habits was that he never drank wine without ceremoniously dropping a few seeds into his glass, preferably heavy ones, after which he would watch them sink toward the stem as he rendered a touching, often funny, pronouncement on the merits of the particular species. Haven Pinder loved her father for his grace in all this, and throughout her youth it made no real impression on her that his personal beliefs went no further than a serene faith, a conviction that there was a "perfect picnic spot" worth searching for on every outing, a wish for a healthy spring germination period, and perhaps a toast or two for old school chums out there "roughing it up" in politics, such as John F. Kennedy.

This had changed for young Pinder on the weekend of the huge antiwar march in Washington, the same one at which David Howell had first run into Casey Woodruff, when the atmosphere was ionized with excitement. Pinder experienced the mass religion of several hundred thousand minds and bodies touching in both power and transcendent goodness and Pinder, having never felt anything like it, went immediately home to tell her parents again of humanity's political bonds and of the evil in people who did not understand them, and of course her father did not understand because for him such quaint meetings had little or nothing to do with a healthy spring germination period. The daughter tried to draw an analogy between her people and his seeds, but it was to no avail, and thereafter daughter and father were sadly mismatched. She thought him an irresponsible hippie in his political views, while he thought similarly of her patched jeans and floppy breasts. She thought him far too serious about his seeds and pleasantries, while he urged her to lighten up about the normal sour course of world events. They were quite similar in material but opposites in construction, like mirror images, and years later the boss could still inflame Pinder by calling up the bad politics in her background.

For Pinder, it had been rough, but no rougher than back at Howell's apartment, where Henry Woodruff was equally derisive of her association with the boss. Woodruff soared off on long diatribes against the ungrounded nature of life in the alternative political conclaves, as in all the decision-making process, he said, where people speak of "raising" money instead of earning it, preserving thereby an aura of selfless purpose about their pursuits. He also ridiculed the boss's difficulties in transforming himself from an "organizer" to a "radical statesman," making oblique arguments on the follies of those who proudly refer to themselves as "organizers" as though the term conferred a distinctive and virtuous outlook when, he said, a penchant for organization was the commonest trademark of the age, hailed alike by old Nazis rebuilding their apparatus and by business executives assembling a conglomerate and by oil ministers creating a cartel, and by Haven Pinder organizing a rent strike.

"Fuck you, you creep," said Pinder as she tasted the cold leek soup she and Howell had concocted merrily that afternoon.

Pinder said this casually and in good nature, as a frog might leap off a hot flat rock into the pond, and it was likely this very peskiness that obviously pained Woodruff, who looked at her in disbelief and shock as he wondered how anyone could so shabbily dismiss his ideas just when their heated inertia was producing an up-draft in his mind.

Howell frequently urged Pinder to go easy on Woodruff in those days, Woodruff's transition being the starkest of all. When called upon to speak at his divorce trial, Woodruff had risen wearily and stated that he was neither for nor against the divorce, that he would take no responsibility for it nor stand in its way, that he was necessarily more tentative in his beliefs about his own marriage than he was about the larger issues of which marriage is a part, which in itself was quite tentative. Woodruff went on in a shaky, disembodied voice at a rhetorical level he later compared with Sir Thomas More's scaffold speech, causing extra grunts and wavings of toothpicks among the pickpockets and vagrants there in the Superior Court, and he was just getting around to the *apologia* when the judge cut him off with the gavel. At which point, Casey Pendleton formerly Woodruff *nee* Charlotte Pendleton became quite upset and was escorted out by her courtly lawyer, Langdon Howard, who was still trying to figure out why Pendleton, having rebuffed his advances on the doorstep after fourteen consecutive dinners, had grabbed him one night behind the neck and pulled his evening clothes off right there on her living room floor. Pendleton explained this enigmatic attack of passion to him and to Woodruff as an act of self-disgust brought on by frustration over her continued sexual attraction to Richard Clayfield, which had outlived her respect for him. In the hallway outside the courtroom, Woodruff mumbled his good wishes to both Pendleton and Howard without knowing what he meant, and they parted, flushed with consolation.

Woodruff cashed in his Senate retirement policy and figured that it, plus his savings, would carry him through the two years it would take to write his book of essays on American history, entitled *The Curve of Liberty*, which would incorporate a number of his theories as well as some historical minutiae and disjointed predictions, all of which plans combined—or didn't combine—to make the project worth a paltry advance from Lester Hershey's New York publisher. Woodruff didn't care. It was his dream. He planned to do some revision to the benefit of President John Adams and to the detriment of the priggish Woodrow Wilson, to project the legislative decline of the Senate, and to discuss the psychohistorical impact of the way people think of time and its path—in circles as opposed to straight lines or upward spirals or ellipses or other geometric forms, among other theories—and all this drove him whistling every morning to the Archives or the Library of Congress, whose beauty restored him.

He was divided in his mind as to whether his personal troubles enriched or impeded his research. On some days it would seem that his affairs with lawyers, heiresses, stewardesses, and legislative aides would infuse the dry lines of his thought with flesh and blood, but at other times his perceptions of them led nowhere. Woodruff always remembered at least one salient detail about every woman and also, surprisingly, about the atmosphere she created around them, whether it was like a casbah or a hunting lodge or a rainstorm, but each affair felt isolated and frail to him, like a cut flower suspended alone a hundred feet in the air. He suspected this was related to his feeling like a stone and so advised Valerie Mantell, who abandoned her designs on him.

He also told Susan Hartman, who was grieving in a rather whoopee fashion over Rosen's final departure, Woodruff thought, and Sudsy's response, characteristically, was to mock him with a long judge's face and a circular death-row trudge before she giggled and said, "My goodness, aren't we serious today, Henry?" She rattled her bracelets and loosed such a full-hearted laugh that Woodruff could only smile, too.

Sudsy's father owned a huge strip of forest land bordering on the Rappahannock River, whose waters run between half a dozen Civil War battlefields and over millions of stones in all shapes and sizes, carrying the muted, lively sounds of nature and history. Hartman often teased Woodruff there about his angst proclivities, calling him "Stony" or "Mr. Stone," especially when he was, in fact, under the influence of drugs, which was for him not unusual during the transition. The Hartman land served as a weekend retreat from the campaigns in the city, a place where she and her friends could run naked as ponies through the river and innocently sit on rocks to forget about midlife crisis and the president's chances. This was Hartman's element, a place where she was not at war with her family since the gentry loves open land as much as hippies or anarchists do. Dancing around the river banks, many people had their glimpses of the famous Rosen heavy timber, much in evidence along with the other furrows and dangles on holiday there in such numbers and such splendor that it was truly remarkable how everyone refrained from coupling on the riverbanks. There was something reserved about the spirit of the place. An abstinent streak of some years was running one day when Woodruff and Hartman, lying face down on a towel, ran out of things to talk about.

This was mostly Hartman's fault. She did not want to hear Woodruff's reflections on romance, and she certainly did not want to hear about his book. She had heard most of it secondhand from Mantell, anyway, and it was more fun for her to make Woodruff banter on unfamiliar subjects. This day he fell silent. Hartman pulled a leaf apart under the sun, dropping small bits in the sand, as she told him of her latest boyfriend, a spindly trout fisherman from Wyoming who had come to Washington to lobby for the wilderness and proved to be something of a genius, wearing a tattered hat covered with homemade trout flies into congressional offices where he spoke with a persuasive air of democratic trust, learning the quirks of Congress and growing more and more absorbed in the nuances to be read there in the faces of the aides and the wording of messages and so forth, for these affected votes on the wilderness.

Within six months, said Hartman, her new man had grown obsessed with events in the Congress and would come home late at night with long earnest tales of breaks and betrayals, but he did not recognize his own seduction even after a weekend on the Rappahannock when he lacked the will and concentration to tie his trout flies. Potomac fever, Hartman sighed. The story delighted Woodruff. He interpreted it as another example of brilliant fishing by the Decision-Making Processa, casting across a continent and a million realities to catch the homespun fisherman, and he belabored the analogy until Hartman said it gave her a headache. Woodruff admitted it gave him one, too.

As they sorted leaves from pebbles, a moment they had long postponed swallowed them up. Nerves went into gear. Each of them was instinctively aware that the other was thinking the same thing, which was that although they had been naked and alone before without consequence, they had never felt the question the way they did then, and now even avoidance would change things, perhaps ruin their friendship. Unspoken urges and hesitations swirled back and forth between them.

Finally Woodruff looked at her and said very sincerely, "I don't know, Sudsy."

And Hartman looked back at him, fought off a smile and replied, "Aw, come on, Henry."

On this note, their affair had begun. It built slowly through the last of the hot days, with the emotional effects lagging considerably behind the practical ones on the apartment situation. By this time, Woodruff had been living in Howell's building well over a year and the new Pinder romance had created confusion over who would sleep where. Howell and Pinder kept their apartments and arranged their evenings as a prolonged home-and-home series between the fifth and fourth floors—or at least it evolved into such—and it did not always work out with Woodruff there on the sofa bed he bought for the living room. Woodruff developed a taste for reading alone late at night in Pinder's apartment, but he had to respect her desire not to spend all her evenings at Howell's, so there was a lot of adjustment. If Pinder wanted to be alone for a night at the same time that Woodruff received an unexpected female companion, there would be shuttling back and forth, which grew tiresome. Howell, more than once, slept at Lester Hershey's, and Pinder and Woodruff shared the Howell apartment often while Howell typed away all night down at Pinder's on articles for Marner and Drake. In the rush of daily life, this made for messy entanglements, worsened by lost keys, telephone messages, and diaphragms that were always in the wrong location.

Hartman joked that she came complete with her own apartment, which was more than she could say for Woodruff, but the extra apartment simplified nothing. In practice, they spent most of their nights together in the

Howell-Pinder building because Woodruff could not stand Hartman's neighborhood or her cats, nor they him. As a result, the two couples maintained a state of logistical flux that they knew was odd for Washingtonians in their thirties, as household refugees and privileged transients. They got by on a surfeit of humor and old friendship.

All the pairings among them worked well except possibly for Woodruff and Pinder, the newcomer, who thought Woodruff rather callous at times, especially when he did not show any interest in Miss Lily Snow. In return, Woodruff considered Pinder "too emotional" at times, such as any time she took up for Casey Pendleton during his rambling oral treatises on marriage. These discussions would become quite contorted, for Woodruff himself would usually be reciting lessons he had learned, angling toward some proposition of Pendleton's with fresh arguments to her advantage, but he always did so in a controlled and closely reasoned manner that made the lesson more acceptable to him, whereas Pinder tended to shake her head and say, "I sure don't see any fun in that for Casey." This greatly annoyed Woodruff, for he preferred to see the question as one of justice more than fun, and to the extent that fun intruded he thought it should do so fairly. He accused Pinder of arbitrarily siding with Pendleton on the basis of common sex. Howell was happy to see the Pendleton topic fade away with the arrival of Hartman.

The new couple cohosted a celebratory poker game for themselves. Hartman blew her bangs constantly and made lusty comments in Woodruff's direction, while Woodruff was wry and delighted. Howell congratulated them for completing yet another circuit on the great Washington penis-vagina network. This pairing seemed to make sense. They were toasted optimistically by mutual friends as a brainy, lanky, irreverent twosome, as sterling types who had been slightly damaged—he by marriage and she by family money—but were now preparing to right themselves together. They were serious but unconventional. She lightened her frontal assaults with catlike twists and puffs of intent; his cerebral orbits brought comedy through such acts as pouring coffee into the sugar bowl or rolling a glass of whiskey instead of a cup of dice onto the backgammon board.

Shortly before Halloween—that is, a few weeks before Pat Shea's surprise visit to the Savannah—Woodruff and Hartman lay holding hands on Pinder's bed at midnight, absorbing rare waves of peace. Woodruff, always alert to the dangers in his own deepest sentiments, thought long and hard about the shaky progress of his affection for Hartman before he allowed himself to smile. "Uh, Sudsy," he began tenderly in a tone neither of them had ever heard before, packed with sincerity and childish tremor.

"Uh, yeeees," sang Hartman in reply, laughing at Woodruff's labor but squeezing his hand.

"You're okay, Sudsy." Woodruff announced. "In fact, everything seems okay. This is very good stuff. Where did you get it?"

"From my refrigerator. I've had a stash of MDA in there for seven years, and now I'm beginning to run low. I don't take it more than twice a year, just to keep up the special potency. You see why we call it the love drug 'cause of the amazing lift it gives you in the heart area? Do you feel it?"

"Yeah, I think so," replied Woodruff, trying to be scientific. "I think you could tell me I'm a bankrupt human being from every standpoint and it would be all right. I mean I think I'd appreciate your being able to say that to me and I'd still feel benevolent about everything."

"That's the idea."

"I see, I guess," said Woodruff, who thought for a second or two and then made the whole bed vibrate.

Hartman gave him a protective hug. "Are you cold, baby?" she asked.

"No, I'm okay. I was just giving a cosmic shudder for all of our friends trying to get through this."

"Through what?"

"Through whatever we're getting through."

"Oh, that's what I thought."

Woodruff sat up in the bed. "Sudsy, would you say 'what' again for me, please?"

"Huh?"

"It's an experiment. I'll tell you in a second. Just say 'what.' "

"What."

Woodruff looked intently at the air between them, and then his face turned slightly as though he had been lightly slapped. "Amazing," he said.

"What?" asked a puzzled Hartman.

After a pause, Woodruff appeared to get slapped slightly harder. "Even more amazing," he said.

"What is it?"

"I don't really know how to say it," he replied. "Let's see. You know how slowly a ball bearing sinks through thick motor oil, or a pearl sinks through thick shampoo on one of those TV ads?"

Hartman gave Woodruff a worried look. "Uh huh," she said. "What's that got to do with 'what'?"

"Well, that's the way your words come at me. It's like slow motion, and each word is on this wave. And when the wave hits me, I literally *feel* the word. And not only that, I feel whatever feeling you put behind it. Does that make any sense?"

Hartman shook her head in friendly disbelief. "What?"

"There!" cried Woodruff. "It happened again. I felt that 'what' and it was different from the other ones. 'Cause that time you were trying to give me an affectionate warning like maybe I'm too stoned, right?"

"Well, that's possible."

"But the thing that gets me is that I'm getting waves off every word, even the 'the's.' That's really something. I mean, now that I think about it, I should expect to get an emotional contact with loaded words, full of hate or boredom or affection, like the way you say 'baby,' but to also get it off the more neutral words, supposedly neutral. And of course it's not just the word

194

itself that matters now. It's you, who you are, you know. And the way you say it. Oh, boy. It's like every conversation is an incredibly complex emotional bombardment through our own personal channels."

Hartman put her other hand behind her head. "It's very interesting, Henry," she said noncommittally.

Woodruff, in a semilotus position, nearly lifted himself off the bed. "Goddam, Susan, this is wonderful stuff," he exulted. "You may have to open up your refrigerator and let me eat another fistful or two."

"Not a chance. Any more and it would leech your insides like a limestone pit, you fool." Hartman was giggling slowly, softly caressing his back.

"Fool?" recoiled a wounded Woodruff. He looked thoughtful, his head cocked to one side, as he peeled the layers of emotion off the word at his leisure, pondering Hartman's use of endearing insults. Somehow the drug seemed to put a floor under the disparaging or depressing meanings of the word, and a smile passed across Woodruff's face as he contemplated the good things about fools—the lovable fools of history, the lessons they have taught that could be taught in no other way. He turned back to Hartman and said, "That's very sweet."

"I know," she said, as though she had followed his imagination.

Woodruff slowly reclined on the bed. "Ah," he sighed. "Listen to this, Sudsy."

"Yes?"

"I feel tender enough to make love a thousand times, but I don't have the energy or the buzz or whatever it takes to make a hard-on. I'm sorry, but it's so pleasant that I'm not really sorry. From here it seems like you've got to have almost some aggressiveness and some aloofness to make love, like a lion or something. I know I'm not making any sense . . ."

". . . Take it easy, baby," Hartman cooed. "Don't hurry so much or you'll always wind up in the same place." She rubbed his chest several times to calm him. "Now you just forget that you ever made love before and follow me, and I'm gonna follow the tenderness."

"I don't see how this is possible," whispered Woodruff.

"Don't worry."

The final success was a cooperative maneuver, with Woodruff sitting up straight on his knees and Hartman doing the guiding, after which the laughter subsided as he lay quietly on her breasts. After five minutes of repose, Hartman said she thought that was the way love ought to be made. Woodruff agreed. It took another lazy half hour before there was enough genital blood for any friction, and even then they rubbed aimlessly, as though keeping time to a dream of landscapes.

Woodruff, losing all sense of proportion, sank through her skin into a liquid expanse covered by a red sky. It was not dark or claustrophobic, as he had expected it to be, but rather like a giant open hothouse in the autumn. He came across colossal objects of a cushiony pink construction, which he took to be Hartman's internal organs. They were as tall as skyscrapers and purring contentedly. A sign appeared, saying "Library" in one direction and

"Furnace" in the other, and Woodruff was just accepting the bodily journey fantasy—determining to search out a smooth blood corpuscle the size of a subway car and ride it to explore the Library, which he took to be the brain —when a wave of appreciation for whimsy, which reminded him of Howell, washed over him with the familiar gentle force of the drug and swept him like a fleck of silt through a very long absence of gravity, which was all right. A gigantic soft curtain was closing around an equally gigantic smiling pink mushroom, which Woodruff took to be the head of his own penis. He was just beginning to bounce upward off the spongy curtain when the entire red-skied universe began to rustle with a single whisper, "Henry, you old codger, this isn't a trick, is it?"

Woodruff, having severed familiar connections to time and space, whooshed around in whirlpools of both before replacing himself there in the bed, in an abnormally large body, retaining from the earlier instant the appreciation of whimsy and the sight of the mushroom, which he now tried to wiggle. As he did, it struck him how an entire universe of inanimate and animate things can have its own essential character, such as the universe that had just whispered to him in a timbre of feisty apprehension.

"Is that you, Sudsy?" he whispered groggily.

She rubbed his hair. "Don't even try to tell me where you've been," she smiled.

"I won't," said Woodruff. "What do you mean a trick?"

"Well, I mean you're not doing all this with me when you're still in love with Casey, are you?"

"Casey?"

"Your former wife," she prompted.

"I know," he said. He looked up to take sightings on the familiar objects there in Pinder's bedroom, papered heavily with photographs of Indians, and having taken these bearings he waited a few seconds for the arrival of the cosmic vacuum cleaner. He did not expect a full-fledged attack, or anything like one, but when he scanned across tumbling images of Pendleton and received not so much as a tiny stab or rattle under the lungs, he felt a strange, light awe. Something had been amputated, but he was whole, or so it seemed, and he could not imagine what part of his interior it had been attached to. "I guess not," he said.

"You sound surprised."

"I am."

"Oh."

Woodruff saw her disappointment. "No, Sudsy," he pleaded. "It's good. It's very good. It's unbelievably good."

She satisfied herself of his face but forced a doubtful smile. "You're peaking," she said. Her voice had a clinical edge.

"Hey, please," said Woodruff, fearing that she was trying to reduce the uniqueness of the moment. "I thought you were going to follow the tenderness."

"Mmmmm," she said. "I forgot." She undulated slowly and saw Woodruff close his eyes. As he did, it seemed to her that the skin of his neck and face drained to a translucent jelly, penetrable down to the bones, giving Woodruff a skeletal appearance. He looked a generation or two older, at least, but the eerie smear of his face corresponded to no specific age. To Hartman this was a familiar apparition. She saw it in herself in the mirror, and she saw it in the gaunt faces of exiles with whom she worked late at night in church basements to produce passionate literature against various dictatorships around the world. They all had flashes of age. Hartman had accustomed herself to the vision. It was a sign of maturity, she thought, to think nothing of it, to look at Woodruff and see that age was part of him, too, although she chuckled to herself that he did look better with the cover on his skin.

His face returned to normal, and Hartman, still undulating slowly, thought of all the different people with whom she had already been in bed by the age of thirty-two, of her early virgin fantasies and her coy phase and the long era of the sensuous rebel. All these were still there in part, and now there was a new, mortifying element that she could only identify as the childless woman syndrome. It was creeping up on her in spite of all she believed, causing her to think of mastodons and saber-toothed tigers and the great tradition of reproduction, even though she did not give much of a hoot for tradition. There was even a small room inside Hartman that was closed except in the presence of men, when the lights would go on for a brainless hospitality toward all of them. She could bear to contemplate this impulse only on the benevolent cushion of MDA, and she wondered what Valerie Mantell would think of it. She indulged in the impulse only for a few seconds, during which she clutched and almost chewed Woodruff's penis with her soft walls. It was a celebration, but it was also a primitive appetite that was satisfying, not because it tasted good, which had been the joyful appeal of sex in the early pill years when she pretended to get seduced, but because she was hungry.

XI

FRESH, UNCERTAIN couples would become a trend of private life in the capital, and, as often happened, there would be a parallel trend in the larger scope of public and world affairs. It had been a time of transition, with slippery coalitions and forgettable ideas. Political columnists complained that no recent president had been able to invent a label for his era. There was no New Deal or Great Society, and the floor of the White House pressroom was littered with failed slogans. In the thematic vacuum, even surprising news died quickly for lack of context. Reporters tried desperately to stretch an isolated event into a framework for the next month's news.

So said Marner in his essays for *Washington* magazine. He flourished in bad times, when political observers were thrown back on their own resources. With his elegant panache, reminiscent of Sydney Greenstreet, he seemed to rise to fullest life in moments of honeyed derision, of disgust enlivened by amusement. His voice—a thick Valentino bass with a slight reedy edge—was well suited to this tone. Marner called himself an idealistic cynic, whose idealism was grounded in the belief that there would always be an abundance of stylish scoundrels to elicit his chosen pleasure.

Continuous inspiration kept Marner writing late many nights until the occasion of his semiannual dinner with "the kids," as he called them, when he alone caught sight of Valerie Mantell stepping demurely out of her pantyhose in the kitchen to cool herself informally before bringing in the dessert. No one noticed the sudden epiphany, which Marner himself would have denounced as ludicrous and alien. Its only discernible effect that evening was to thicken the sarcasm of Marner's remarks about Mantell's feminist vocation. He always twitted her skillfully. No matter how abstruse the topic of discussion, something undefined in his manner always raised inside Mantell a primordial insecurity about such things as carburetors and skyscrapers and steel mills. He made her feel guilty about enjoying the fruits of mechanical engineering, a male preserve, even though she knew that Marner was as ignorant of the rough practicalities as she. He projected a claim on them, and he also projected a profound skepticism about Mantell's qualifications for existence.

This much was normal, but over the next few weeks the heat of it rose markedly. He called Mantell to volunteer new criticisms. He sent her books, presuming to educate her, and he went so far as to plant the idea among her friends that Mantell needed lessons about the nature of money. Mantell was thus prepared, in an odd way, for the letter in which Marner starkly announced his intention to woo her. At first she assumed it was another barb, a parody of courtship at her expense. But then Marner repeated his declaration to others. He said he had no idea how to go about his quest, but would never rest with failure. He loved to analyze his prospects and catch up on the romantic conversation he had missed for twenty years—oblivious to the embarrassment of his listeners—and Mantell finally admitted she had a problem. She said she was being ambushed by the nineteenth century.

The new Marner was inexplicably transformed. Even Howell worried that he was only one slip away from becoming one of the deranged hobos who wander the streets of Washington shouting speeches about farm parity or psychosurgery. Marner shed his old habits so completely that he ignored his work for two months, during which time he startled childhood friends in distant cities by reading them poems over the telephone. He changed his bank account several times, forgot his dart board, and shut his door to all routine business. Then, much to the relief of Mantell, a spectacular episode in the *Post–Times* rivalry returned the stinging delight to his typing fingers.

The essential facts had been reported later in a *Time* magazine cover story, "Four Days of Crisis." On Day One, General Byron Wade, the president's national security advisor, was flying from Frankfurt to Cairo when he suffered another attack of "imperial epilepsy," as the reporters privately called it. Hurling packets of nondairy creamer at his aides, the general insulted every political leader in Europe as he stalked the aisles of his air force jet. He was especially harsh toward the French president, who, he shouted, "would not know a fine wine from a bottle of Polish piss!" Finally the general calmed himself and told the accompanying reporters that what they had just heard was off the record, as usual, and he charmed them with some tidbits from the hidden mosaic of his plans. On Day Two, the press dutifully reported on the prospects of the Wade mission, but the mood of high diplomacy was destroyed the next morning when the *Post* reported every seedy detail of the general's airborne fit.

It was a quick, clean scandal. The president held an emergency morning press conference less than four hours after the story appeared. All three networks flashed dramatic news briefs throughout the day, and by evening Wade was gone.

The press angle excited Marner. He knew that Hershey had been after General Wade for more than a year, working as only Hershey could work

—late into the night on the phone, threatening, intimidating, lying about what he already knew, making deals, asking four or five staccato questions in a row, all of which made up his famous interrogatory technique, known as "woodpeckering." Hershey had thus extracted several stories on the subject of Wade's vulgarity and instability, but the *Times* editors rejected them for want of substantive dignity. Months later, Hershey offered stories on Wade's double-dealing, his betrayal of various allies, and his ruthless bureaucratic campaign against his rivals, such as Secretary of State Carlyle, but the editors rejected these on grounds of patriotism, saying the international situation was then too precarious to attack someone in Wade's position. This enraged Hershey, who became obsessed enough to write an entire book on the general. The manuscript was completed just in time to become useless after Paul Sternman and the *Post* "nailed" Wade with one story.

Sternman, for his part, did not want to write the first story of the Wade scandal. In fact, he resisted it and wound up writing a memo disclaiming responsibility for the decision. But he had no choice. The story reached him cleanly, untainted by breach of the agreement Wade reached with the reporters on the plane. Sternman's lead came from a friend at the Pentagon. He did not know that the Pentagon man had received it from Richard Clayfield, who in turn had received it from a pockmarked wire service reporter named Sneed, who had been on the plane. So Sternman thought nothing amiss when Clayfield himself called directly to say that columnist Jack Anderson was about to break a sensational story on General Wade. Sternman felt numb. He made twenty calls to verify what he had heard. Then he and his editor went to their superiors to play a rather complex philosophical game—since the editors had already heard the story as a matter of prime gossip but not as news—and it was decided that all obligations could best be kept by going public.

At four-thirty on the morning of Day Four, when the four-star edition of the *Post* came off the presses with the last of the hundred changes resulting from all the arguments and diatribes over the fateful stories, Sternman had put a copy under his arm and staggered to his car. He could smell the burnt adrenaline about him, which he loved and always would, but he felt disturbed nevertheless by the night air. Somehow he had lost the afterkick of a big story. He had experienced this before on the police beat—a special mixture of satiation and regret, such as occurs after a sumptuous feast of mediocre food. Sternman knew the feeling would pass, but he did not want to be alone in the interim. So he drove across the Fourteenth Street bridge into Virginia, down to Alexandria, up past the huge Masonic Temple to a neighborhood of gingerbread houses, and parked. He walked stealthily around to the back door, used his special keys, tiptoed up the back stairs to the bedroom and turned on the light. "I'm sorry, LaLane," he said. "I just had to be with you."

Two stretching arms appeared from a lump under the thick satin spread, followed shortly by a head and a crumple of white nightgown. Rayburn rubbed her eyes. "It's all right, honey," she said huskily. "I was having bad dreams anyway."

Sternman kicked off his shoes and started pacing intently on the carpet. "Your hair looks nice," he said. "Really nice. It's the first nice thing I've seen in two days."

"Oh hush. It's a mess." Her hair, confused by a succession of trial arrangements, fell about her shoulders in an assortment of spirals that touched Sternman as a wanton release from the severe beehive.

He had already forgotten her hair, however, and was staring off through her suburban wallpaper toward an earlier scene at the *Post* when he and ascending layers of editors had debated General Wade's fate. They huddled in various spots, covered by smoke and noise, watched closely by other reporters who maintained a respectful distance, and argued in the usual pattern. As a rule, the higher editors spoke less and used a greater proportion of expletives, so that on crucial stories the game often turned on the relative strengths of the cusswords applied to the parties. When the salty Yank of a top editor issued his sententious decree, "Okay, fuck it! Stick it to him!" it ought to have conferred an air of nobility on their course, for the decision to publish went against the top editor's prevailing ire. But for some reason there had been no rush of delight. And perhaps, Sternman shuddered at the memory, he spoiled whatever rush there was with his flat response, "Oh, shit." In that instant, newspaper veterans would have sensed a general doubt as to Sternman's future in the hierarchy. He was too laconic and formal, and far too unnatural a cusser. Indeed, he swore in a trance of hollow mechanics, the way a coal miner punches the time clock.

"Are you all right, honey? You're not in trouble, are you?"

"No. I mean yes, I'm all right." Sternman's voice, in the ionized quiet of predawn, had a grating loudness to it.

"Shhhhhh. You'll wake up the kids."

"Sorry," he said, lowering the pitch but not the volume, rattling loose change on the bedside table.

Rayburn lifted the covers. "Come on," she invited. "If you need a hug, it's got to be here, 'cause I'm too sleepy to get up."

Sternman stripped to his shorts. He liked clear signs and thin mysteries, and this was his call for warmth, not sex. She knew this, and she also knew by his groan in bed that his humors were bottled up. As he slid in on his stomach, she rolled partway over him and spread the loose folds of her nightgown over him before dropping the covers. "Oooooh, you're cooold," she shivered. "But not for long."

Sternman breathed in snorts and jerks.

"It's about General Wade, isn't it?" she whispered. "Is he gone?"

Sternman nodded.

She rubbed her hand lightly along the back of his neck and let out a gurgle of relief. "I thought so. Now you listen here, Paul. I can't stand to see you worry yourself to death over somebody like 'Beau' Wade."

"I know," said Sternman.

"He's not worth one less breath in your life, much less any blood pressure. He's the only soldier I ever knew who had calling cards printed up with his new rank before the promotion lists came out."

"I know," said Sternman.

She moved closer to his ear. "Okay," she whispered. "I won't talk about him. You don't want me to, do you?"

"No," he said, and the sound of it shook the whole bed.

"Shhhhhh," she whispered. "Can't you whisper?"

He turned his tight neck to her and mouthed a negative. Trying again, the word "no" blared forth like a horn.

"Huh?" she giggled in a breathy night laugh. "*Everybody* can whisper."

"I never could," said Sternman.

She cut short her laughter and rubbed his neck with greater sympathy. "Well, don't talk then," she whispered, "and let me tell you about my bad dream. I was dressed up in a strange yellow uniform made out of rubber with little green sequins down the side. Kind of cute, but I'd never seen anything like it. And I was floating like greased lightning through the sky over these black mountains, you know. Nothing like Texas. I could walk right there in the air over this way and that way, but I still kept moving. And there must have been some more funny little yellow pilots behind me, 'cause I kept wavin' 'em on to go faster. But I never could see anybody. So I just kept going and exploring things as best I could. And I was having a pretty good time. But then all of a sudden I just whooshed into this huge cathedral of a room with a shiny floor. There wasn't a soul there. So I gulped and said 'my gosh' and stuff and wandered around. And then this great big sliding door opened up from a hallway. Scared me to death. And this cute little thing with no face walked up to me and asked in a real friendly voice, 'Well, what is your report?' it said. 'Is everything going to be all right?' And I was so glad I didn't know what to do. I cudda hugged that little shmoo. I almost jumped up in the air to say 'Yes!' but when I started to explain I realized that I couldn't hear myself. And then I couldn't *see* myself either. All I saw was the shmoo standing there by itself in that huge room, and I wasn't anywhere. I tried to talk and raise my hand and everything I could think of, but I just wasn't there anymore. Anywhere. So I couldn't give my report and I couldn't fly anymore and I thought that was the worst thing that ever happened to me. I was getting all shook up about it when you woke me up."

"I don't like dreams," said Sternman. "Probably 'cause I don't ever remember any."

"Shhh. That's all right."

"But I like the way you rub my neck. And I'll tell you something else, LaLane. I feel good about coming here. And I like hearing you tell me stuff that I don't really understand. And I wish it could be different between us, because it's more to me than just coming here, you know. I can't say it right, just like I can't whisper. But even if we are so different, we don't *seem* so different to me." Sternman sighed in midthought. Such intimate expression exhausted him.

"Go on," prompted Rayburn with a purr and a squeeze.

"Well, I don't know. You are only nine years and three months older than me. That's something, but it's not all that much. We count in the same generation."

"Thank you." Her soft laughter had already begun over Sternman's attention to the minute facts, for which he was famous.

"Well, that's something. And besides. Well, it's just consistent with that."

"Are you trying to tell me that I don't always feel like your mother?" she whispered.

"Something like that," he admitted. "Thank God you're not like my real mother."

"I'm sorry you didn't like her."

"Well, that's beside the point. The point is that I don't even feel like a reporter around you most of the time. I don't talk to you all the time about the paper. We're just us, that's all. I don't want to talk about it anymore."

"Hey, that's okay," she said freely. "I just want to know how come you always say your sweet things when I'm sleepy."

The commotion around the Rayburn breakfast table a few hours later reached a high pitch, as the three children—the eldest was away at the University of Texas—fussed over the taciturn man with the tired, square face who appeared in the company of Mom. Noise broke out just after the introduction when, with no one knowing quite what to say, the older girl realized that Paul Sternman was the same one whose name had been in the *Post* for years and was that very morning written under the banner headlines about General Wade. This daughter still modeled herself after her martyred father, having been his favorite. She questioned Sternman about the Wade article, touching with uncanny accuracy all his sorest spots—why would the *Post* stoop to such a thing, what could motivate such an intrusion into the private life of yet another military man the liberals wanted to "get," and so forth—and she chewed both his unresponsive grunts and her spartan bran with a carefully practiced distaste. In all this she was in striking contrast to her eager little sister, who was thirteen and in pigtails and precocious. She spilled things, and she wanted to know everything, particularly about the famous former girlfriends of Sternman whom she had read about in the *Post's* own gossip pages. These questions brought coughs to everyone except her brother, who laughed. Pigtails herself went on to say, "I just wanted to know how intense is your relationship with Mom?"

"What kind of dumb question is that?" scolded the son. "He spent the night with her, didn't he?"

"Really, Bobby," huffed the older daughter.

"Well, he did," said Bobby.

"That doesn't mean a thing and you know it," said the younger daughter, standing her ground.

The older daughter dropped her spoon in disgust. "Please!"

"Oh, shut up," said the son. "You just don't like men from the news media."

"I do," said the younger sister. "But I just don't think Mom's ready to get flipped out over anybody yet. That's all."

"She's not flipped out," said the older daughter confidently. "Besides, she can decide for herself, Karen."

"Not necessarily," said Karen. "Especially not with a younger man like Paul who's been around a lot. Younger men are harder."

"Oh, hush!" shouted LaLane. "All of you! And get out of here before you're all late for school!"

The kids were all up and bustling, with Rayburn checking necks and pockets and shoes in the morning ritual. "Now just a second before you go," she cried to quiet the throng.

"Uh oh," said Karen, recognizing the tone that comes just ahead of an emotional jolt for kids.

Rayburn nervously clutched two hands before her breast. "Um, look here y'all," she drawled. "Um, Paul and I are friends. And we wanted you all to know that. But we don't want anybody else to know, y'hear? We don't want it to get around all over the place. So do us a favor and don't tell anybody, okay?"

Karen was worried. "Can't I just tell Sarah?" she begged. "Please? I can swear her. Really."

"No," said Rayburn. "Not anybody, Karen. This is a family secret just for us, okay? Sarah might talk to somebody who knows somebody else, and pretty soon it might be in the papers. We can't let that happen. It would make everybody unhappy."

"The papers?" gushed Karen, bugeyed. The thought of so important a secret instantly erased her crestfallen look.

"Right," said Rayburn.

Karen surrendered the point. "Okay," she said. "It's just like not talking to all those reporters who kept calling when Daddy was gone, isn't it?"

Rayburn drew back slightly. "Yeah, something like that, honey," she said.

"Just a second here," said Bobby with some suspicion. He shifted uneasily and could not bring himself to look directly at Sternman. "Um, I can see why Mom might want to protect her privacy," he said, "but you're in the papers all the time. Even Karen's read about you. I don't understand why we should keep a secret for you, you know."

Harriet, startled to hear her rebellious brother say something she agreed with, sidled over next to him to wait for an answer. They did not appear to be from the same family—she with her long clean lines and he slouched over beneath his mop hair, wearing a brown leather jacket covered with homemade decals of skull-and-bones poison labels pasted over photographs of bacon and sugar and white wine and X-ray machines and so forth.

As Sternman drew a breath to reply, Rayburn interrupted him. "Well, I hope you would do it for me, Bobby," she said. "Because I asked you to. I'm sharing something with you that I wouldn't be comfortable sharing with the whole world."

Bobby looked troubled. The gnarls of the problem made fresh dents on his youth. "I understand that," he said. "And that's okay by me. But I don't understand about you, Mr. Sternman. How come you want to hide things?"

"Yeah," said Karen, not in tune with the gravity.

"Hush, Karen," scolded Harriet.

"It's not the papers I'm really worried about, Bobby," said Sternman. "It's just that I'm a private person. And so is your mother."

Bobby was not quite satisfied. "Something's weird," he said. "No offense please, but you wouldn't do anything like *exploit* our Mom, would you?"

"I hope not," laughed Sternman. And then he said no more firmly.

"And I'd give him an Alamo haircut if he tried!" said Rayburn jovially. "Now you kids get out of here before you put both of us on the couch." She kissed them one by one as they clamored out the door.

Rayburn collapsed into a chair. "Whew!" she sighed. "It's hard to have an affair when you have teenagers."

"That was rough, all right," said Sternman. He was staring vacantly at the WADE FLAP GRIPS EUROPE headline.

"I know," she said, reaching over to touch his hand. "But now that they're gone, would you like to go upstairs and exploit each other?"

"You're damn right I would," said Sternman. "But I can't. I've got to get to the office."

"Oh," said Rayburn, biting her lip.

"That old bastard Wade is gonna give us a fit all day, I know. So I may not make it for dinner tonight. But I'll make it up as soon as this dies down. Okay?"

"Okay."

"And your kids are amazing. They love you a lot. I'm just not used to it, that's all."

"I know, Paul. It's all right. I just want you to know how much I love you for coming down here in front of the kids. It meant a lot to me."

Sternman looked away from her. "Um, we can't do dinner tomorrow night," he said. "I'm sorry. I forgot that I've got to go over to Mrs. Graham's. Maybe I'll come over later again, if that's all right." Sternman drew himself up to full height, as he always did when threatened or touched.

"It really did mean a lot," said Rayburn, with tears appearing.

Sternman twitched before jumping over to give her a furtive but powerful hug. "To me, too," he moaned. Then he snatched up his paper and left.

"Hey, that was almost a whisper!" Rayburn called after him. When he was gone, she hugged herself and bit her lip laughing.

Sternman drove away in conflict. He was thinking poorly of Woodruff. Sternman had no doubt that Henry Woodruff would never allow himself to be seen with LaLane Rayburn in the presence of any children, let alone her own, and he sensed that Woodruff had caused one of her deepest wounds by avoiding all contact with her for more than a year. He had shunned her, really, out of guilt or haughtiness or embarrassment over their wildly different appointments. It galled Sternman that Woodruff could do all this and still be considered less aloof, less quarrylike, then Sternman, and Sternman could only guess how Woodruff had mastered the forms of intimacy. With indiscretion. That's how he did it. Indiscretion and sloppy, gossipy facts and some intellectual pretense. Sternman admired Rayburn for many things and high among them were her discretion and honor. She would not even tell him—and he was skilled in extracting information—whether she had ever gone to bed with Woodruff, but he felt so from the way she spoke of him. The same discretion now protected Sternman, and he was grateful for it. Their affair was clandestine, incubated far away from the cold eyes at the *Post*. They went to dinner in Virginia, to the Eastern Shore of Maryland for the weekend, but Rayburn never made the acquaintance of Sternman's professional colleagues. It would ruin him at the paper if they even got a look at her bio sheet, he figured. Within a week, he would be "Tex" or "Mr. MIA." Reporters had to be careful about acknowledged lovers, and Rayburn was out of the question for a man of Sternman's ambition. Her discretion protected him, but it also helped him commit the same sin as Woodruff and that was galling. But at least he was not as bad as Woodruff. He went to her, and he showed himself to her kids. And he liked it. Part of it. Sternman made a mental tab of points in his favor against Woodruff, and his mind turned easily from there to the dangerous General Wade.

Rayburn hurried to her morning appointment on Q Street. Her own career was still in flux, and had been since she abandoned motherhood and MIA activism. After the Conference Board rejected her for fear of controversy, she worked for a short time as a volunteer at the Center for the Promotion of Local Self-Reliance. Discouraged, she decided to forsake politics for work in hard commerce. Four months later she obtained a license to buy and sell real estate.

Two bureaucrats, a husband from the Veterans Administration and a wife from the Civil Rights Commission, spent most of the late morning with Rayburn on a tour of a dilapidated Victorian brownstone. The prospects were statistical-minded veterans of three previous renovations. They were all business as they honed their calculations on how much it would cost to pitch out the old rusty beds and refrigerator carcasses and waterlogged junk, how much to open the fireplaces and cover the walls, and how many years before enough blacks would be moved out to ensure a profitable resale. Rayburn gave them her answer, a trifle too honest for the game, that it would be about two years before a surge in value on that block. Too long, the prospects tentatively decided. They moved on after brainstorming with Rayburn about properties nearer the roving edge of prosperity. The rookie salesman carried a cloudy mind down Q Street, past an old church to her car.

She did not quite fit in anywhere, in love or in politics. And in real estate she had trouble finding the intermediate territory between the prime turf, dominated by agents with French and British accents, and the slums where speculators played rough. Everywhere there was money. A high tide of it washed over properties in the capital, raising values five and tenfold in a few years, dazzling people, making ordinary folk feel like Rockefellers. Real estate talk displaced war, elections, and scandals as the premier topic of dinner conversation. For many, it was a first taste of capitalism, and there was a giddy, larcenous elation that came from knowing one could double or triple a healthy salary in a year simply by buying ahead of the wave. Naturally this sort of bonanza had paradoxical effects on the personal beliefs of the citizenry.

Rayburn despaired of making sense out of it. She had already seen one Republican couple make a killing and then bicker themselves to divorce trying to decide whether to take the money and run to the country (wife) or plow it back through another renovation (husband). And she knew of four anticapitalist communalists who bought a house together for a "community of sharing" but soon ran afoul of the bonanza. When they tried to split up after two babies within two years had made their arrangement impractical, they found their house had increased its worth by nearly two hundred thousand dollars. No one could afford to buy anyone else's share because no one would take less than market value, though in principle they did not believe in windfall profits.

Rayburn herself sat in on a few of the gut-wrenching sessions when the communalists swung from esoteric points in Marxist idealism to a banker's crystal-eyed calculations of risk. The hard realities of the real estate boom tested their most cherished beliefs in racial brotherhood and socialism, grinding them up in bitter arguments that went on to grind up their communalism, too. On her last visit to their house, Rayburn found them trying to divide up the furniture and household items amid petty squabbling that would have reflected well on no doctrine at all. There were crude plywood walls splitting many of the rooms. Worst of all for Rayburn, the communalists in their desperation sometimes lapsed into personal animus against her—the southerner, real estate agent, and ex-military wife—as being somehow implicated in their vexation.

Rayburn fell prey to an entire collection of such bad feelings from her recent memory. They mingled with memories of tender discovery that had also come to the surface, leaving her a pulpy mass of sentiment as she piloted her station wagon west on P Street toward her next appointment. Her mascara ran slightly when she let go over this or that, and Rayburn found herself calling on the old Longhorn discipline to keep from falling apart.

She pulled up next to the Dupont Plaza Hotel and an unorthodox button of a woman stepped up to the car window. "Miz Rayburn?" she inquired.

"Yes," she sniffled. "Miz Pinder? Please get in."

The two women eyed each other curiously, although neither appeared to be in a sociable mood. Rayburn sniffled again and said, "Pardon me, but you don't look like the kind of person who would want to buy a two million dollar building."

Pinder frowned.

"Don't get me wrong, please," said Rayburn. "I like it. And frankly I don't like most of the people who do buy those buildings, anyway." She eyed Pinder, who was dressed in a turtleneck, white old-fashioned knickers tied at midcalf over striped athletic socks, and running shoes. She looked like Bobby Jones's prettiest caddy.

"It's not for me," said Pinder. "I'm just looking at buildings for the people I work for. And I'm not too happy doing it."

"Well then, I'm sure we'll make quite a pair, 'cause I've never really had any commercial sales. I don't really know what I'm doing."

"Good," said Pinder.

Rayburn laughed and wiped her eyes. "Okay, now that we're settled on all that, let's do the best we can for as long as we can stand it, okay?"

"Okay."

"Now. This first building is already under contract to be sold, but it's contingent on the buyers being able to clear the building of the tenants living there now."

"Oh great," sighed Pinder.

"Well, I know what you're saying. But anyway you might want to put a backup contract on it, in case the other deal falls through. It's supposed to be a grand old building full of old people. I've never seen it."

They both fell into frosty moods as Rayburn drove down 21st Street toward the Corcoran Gallery. "Hey, I live near here," murmured Pinder.

"Lucky you," said Rayburn. She eased up on the side of the street and dropped her jaw. "Well, I'll be," she said, reaching to double-check the address on her clipboard. "I played poker here one time."

"Where?" asked Pinder sitting up abruptly. "Not that one. That's where I live."

"That's it!" cried Rayburn. "I can't believe it."

"I *don't* believe it," said Pinder. "Nobody's told us anything about any sale."

"I'm sorry, honey," said Rayburn. "But here it is. Sold to Crown Realty Associates, Inc., on October 31. That was Halloween. They just haven't told you yet."

"Oh, my God," sighed Pinder, staring at the clipboard. "Oh, my God," she repeated with lilting wonder. Then she leaned over to clutch herself. "I have a stomachache," she said.

"Aw, honey, I'm sorry," said Rayburn. "I didn't really want to sell you this building anyway."

"I know you didn't," groaned Pinder.

Rayburn looked surprised. "How did you know?"

"I could tell from your face," said Pinder. "Faces are the only complicated things I can read anymore. Yours says you've had a hard day."

Rayburn studied her profile. "I'll say I have. You're pretty sharp. I just came from trying to sell a house at 14th and Q, and when I went to my car these two young boys in secondhand suits tried to pick me up as a prostitute."

Pinder uncurled. "Really?"

208

"Yes!" wailed Rayburn. "I started to turn up my nose and tell them I am a *real estate agent*, not a *prostitute*, but that didn't sound right so I just ran off crying."

"I'm sorry," said Pinder. But when she and Rayburn looked at each other in sympathetic stupefaction, the corners of Pinder's mouth turned slightly upward in spite of all her efforts to hold them down. She quivered, and one tiny squeak of a laugh escaped. "I'm sorry," she said.

"That's all right," said Rayburn. She sniffled again, then looked undecided. "It's okay if you laugh 'cause I know in a way it's funny. Maybe I am a prostitute. That's how I *feel* sometimes." She convulsed into a sob and pulled out of it into laughter.

"No, you're not."

"Hooooooooooo," sighed Rayburn. "And then I come over here and try to sell you your own building on a contingency in case the other buyer can't throw you out."

Pinder joined a new round of laughter with slightly diminished enthusiasm. When it calmed she said, "I've lived there seven years. What am I gonna do? What are all those old people gonna do?"

Rayburn drew away from her frustration. "Well, sometimes it's just one thing after another," she said. "I already feel all washed out and it's not even noon."

"So do I," said Pinder. "Listen, I don't think I want to look at any more buildings today, if you don't mind. I'm in shock."

"I understand. Do you want me to drop you off somewhere?"

"Yeah, drop me off the Key Bridge, please."

"I'm sorry honey, but it's not that bad."

"I know. But I don't know what to do. The last thing I want is to face the people at the Coalition. I guess the only thing I can do is to go to lunch."

"Go to lunch?"

"Yes. That's what my father does in New York whenever the kids come home. When he gets tired of arguing about unions and unmarried couples and the draft and stuff, he just throws up his hands and says, 'Well, let's have lunch.' And he can make everybody forget the arguments while we're eating because he's always in a picnic mood."

"Sounds like a wonderful father."

"He has terrible politics, but he's wonderful, you're right," said Pinder.

"Well, that's better than the other way around, believe me."

"Thank you."

"You don't think I'm some kind of prostitute for selling buildings, do you?"

"Huh?"

"Well, you know how you can look at things in different ways. You know, your father probably looks at prostitutes differently than you do, and I know I probably look like an old sow to you 'cause I'm a military wife and an old beauty contest girl—I entered a lot of them, but never won anything higher than third runner-up to Miss Soybean—on top of my real estate and all."

Pinder recoiled ever so slightly, for these features were indeed heavy blows against her idea of a desirable person. But when she saw an instant pulse of hurt in Rayburn's face, she gave out an involuntary, sympathetic groan. "Ooooh, I don't think you're anything like a prostitute," she said. "And even if you were, I'd still like to have lunch with you. How about it?"

"You would?"

"Sure. We're unhappy about a lot of the same things," grinned Pinder.

Rayburn agreed, and in due course the two of them discovered their common acquaintance with Woodruff and Howell. "That was before my time," Pinder said of the poker game, and soon they were reminiscing like old friends while the stationwagon's engine still purred.

It was Pinder's idea for Rayburn to order two lunches at the corner café. Pinder herself went into her building and found Miss Lily Snow sitting in the lobby watching people come and go. They hugged and made their way down the sidewalk together, as they often did, with Snow taking tiny brush steps of six inches or less. Her bodily strength, having retreated from the extremities, was concentrated more than ever in her eyes and face. These were set off nicely by her white hair, which was thinner after her stay in the hospital. Age muffled her voice, a spritely soprano divided by thick husks. She sounded like a flute in a box of feathers.

"Isn't this a lovely surprise?" beamed Snow as she inched her way around the table where Rayburn was sitting. "Two young ladies to have lunch with. Must be my lucky day."

"Miss Lily, this is LaLane Rayburn," said Pinder.

"Very nice to meet you, Miss Snow," said Rayburn. "Haven's already told me a lot about you and the other tenants at the Savannah. She says you're the liveliest one there."

"Oh she does, does she?" said Snow. "Well, she is the sweetest thing in the world to me, but I dare say she can exaggerate things a bit. Yes she can."

"Oh," said Rayburn.

"Of course, Father always exaggerated, I'm afraid," said Snow. She was just now easing into her chair, with Pinder's help. "I remember once he predicted that some of those wicked roaches of his would take over the world by the end of the century."

"Maybe they will," said Pinder. "I don't think they're wicked, Miss Lily."

"Nasty, then," said Snow. "Well, I don't think they stand a chance. I'm more worried about the rats. But that prediction of Father's got him in a frightful ruckus with his colleagues around the world. Some of them attacked him in scholarly papers, and I remember Father telling me he couldn't bear to be with them at their conventions, which were usually in Europe. The Europeans are very good on bugs, you see. I think Father's severest critics were the Hungarians—maybe the Austrians. At any rate, I know he lost his appetite for almost two years."

"He did?" asked Rayburn, full of wonder.

"Dr. Snow was the chief entomologist at the Smithsonian for years," Pinder explained.

"Oh," said Rayburn.

"There you have it," said Snow. She turned to the young waitress who was delivering the dry toast and tuna fish that the café owner sent out automatically on sight of her arrival.

"Uh, what was your father's favorite insect?" ventured Rayburn.

"Favorite?" replied a puzzled Snow. "Why he didn't have one. That's just it, you see. Father was trying to get rid of them. He had these big blown-up photographs of the most horrid-looking creatures you ever saw, and he was always naming one of them the newest public enemy. That's what he called them, 'my little public enemies.' "

"Oh," said Pinder. "Well, he must have liked them a little bit if he spent his whole life around them."

"That's just what my mother and I always said, to be quite candid," said Snow. "We thought it was strange. But insects were a man's business back then, and we never questioned Father's judgment. Never." She spoke with a bright pride and defiance, like the captain of a clipper ship.

Rayburn had been nodding slowly. "And you've lived pretty much in this neighborhood all your life? That's what Haven says."

"Since then, yes," said Snow. "We lived in a gorgeous house around on Florida Avenue for a time, and before that we lived a few blocks away on Hillyer Place. Georgetown wasn't nearly so stylish back in those days, I assure you. And then I moved into the Savannah right after Father died."

"When was that?" asked Rayburn.

"Oh, good heavens, a long time ago," sighed Snow. "I don't quite remember. Let's see. Just after the war, I should say. That's it."

"Which war?" asked Pinder.

"Which war?" Snow said vacantly. "Goodness knows. Let me see. I tried not to pay any attention to any of them, you see." Snow's hand shook as she took a bite of toast. Her face withered a bit, and the light went out of it for the first time in the conversation. "I can't think," she said faintly. "Isn't that the limit? Let me see. I think it was the war that was on the radio."

"World War II," said Pinder. "That's what I thought. She's been there about thirty years."

"The one on the radio," smiled Rayburn. "That's pretty good. It's a long time. So I guess you're the senior tenant in the Savannah, right, Miss Snow?"

"Nonsense," she chirped. "Not a bit of it. Miss Hope and her mother had been there for years when I moved in, and they're still there. So is Admiral Jefferson's wife and that awful woman with the poodle who used to run around practically naked. There are a lot of them. I guess Mr. Davis is the senior tenant. The old coot."

"Old coot?" said Rayburn.

"Precisely," said Snow with delight. "I hate to say it, but that's exactly what he is."

"Well, maybe this Mr. Davis is a coot," laughed Rayburn. "But most of your friends and companions are in the Savannah, aren't they? They must be after all these years."

"No they aren't," said Snow. "That's just it, you see. Most of us don't have that much to say to each other. Some people think any two old people will have a lot to say to each other just because they're old, but it's not true. Most of them are not very interesting, you see, any more than they were when they were younger."

"I see," said Rayburn.

"I do run across interesting people every now and then. Like some of the hippies and street people, though most of them are quite disagreeable in appearance. And I even like the Chicken Man."

"The Chicken Man?"

"He's one of the local winos," Pinder explained.

"Oh," said Rayburn.

"The most dreadful manners of anyone I've ever met," Snow proclaimed, "but he always has something provocative to say. I'm afraid I usually bore him. It's a terrible thing to feel you're boring the Chicken Man, I can assure you."

"He cock-a-doodle-doos," said Pinder.

"Oh," said Rayburn. "Do you have any family, Miss Snow?" she asked, continuing her inquiry as to Snow's sources of refuge in case of disaster at the Savannah.

"Yes," she replied. "I've got one sister left in New York. We had another one, Sarah, but she died. She was the only one who married. Married a Catholic, too. Too bad."

"You keep forgetting that I'm a lapsed Catholic, Miss Lily," chided Pinder.

"Oh dear me, that's right. I'm sorry," said Snow, in a manner that left Pinder in doubt as to what she was sorry for.

"How is your sister?" asked Rayburn.

"My sister Maggie is a will-o'-the-wisp," said Snow. "We communicate very seldom, for some reason. I'm not quite sure what it is, though I've got a fair idea of it. Maggie is tall and beautiful and was a far better dancer than I was."

"I didn't know you were a dancer," said Pinder with glee.

"Certainly." said Snow. "Maggie and I both danced in New York ballet before the Great War. It was quite a daring thing for two sisters to do back then. Maggie even smoked cigarettes and got quite a bad name for a time. At any rate, she was a better dancer and I was better at taking care of Father. We were both devoted in our own ways, but she was more aggressive and I was purer. That's what some people said to tease me about my name and so forth, you see. So Maggie stayed in New York with the ballet and later with Broadway and other places with dancers—any kind of dancers, she was quite versatile, you see—and I brought Father to Washington. There was no dancing here to speak of back then, so I dabbled in the theater."

212

"You did?" said Pinder. "Miss Lily, why didn't you tell me this before? I didn't know you were a ballerina and an actress!"

"I wasn't much," sighed Snow. "But I was very good at swooning and we had a lot of swooning scenes in those days. Father didn't approve. He didn't approve of theater or dancing, for that matter. He said Maggie and I were just making displays of ourselves and it wasn't proper."

"Aw, pish," said Rayburn.

"Well, he was right in a way," said Snow. "Father was never completely wrong, and he was frequently completely right as far as I could tell. But he came to tolerate the little companies I played with, and we got along famously. I took care of him and went away with him constantly, and that's when Maggie first came to disapprove of me."

"She did?" asked Pinder, dismayed.

"Why?" asked Rayburn, who reflected on her manners and added, "May I ask?"

The old lady looked wistfully out the window and said, "Well, it was mostly over Gigi, I'm afraid. We were sisters before that—the dancer and the actress, you know, though I really did it for fun—but after that we've never quite gotten along. Maggie thoroughly disapproved."

"Gigi?"

"Luigi Mariani," said the old lady. "I called him Gigi. He was the best lover I ever took. The *only* one, really."

Pinder drew a sharp breath. "Miss Lily!" she smiled. "You never told me about a lover."

"Well, I'm sorry, my dear," said a slightly wounded Snow. "You'll just have to live with it, I suppose. I think I'm old enough now to say I've taken a lover in Rome. I told the vicar years ago, and I think he's gotten over it by now."

"I hope so," said Pinder. "Please, you don't understand . . ."

"Well, there you have it. I've said it," said Snow, pursing her lips. Mingled with the spirited shame, there was some tenderness around the pink edges of her eyes, presumably for Gigi.

". . . I think it's neat," said Pinder.

"Neat?" asked Snow. "It was hardly neat, I assure you."

"I mean good," said Pinder. "I think it's wonderful, as long as it was good for you."

"Well, thank you, Haven. You're always kind," said Snow. "but I'm afraid your friend doesn't agree."

"No, wait, please," blurted Rayburn, who was moved well toward tears by the frail carriage that had preserved such an isolated passion over so many decades. Age had robbed her of much, but what remained had a purity untainted by circumstance or calculation, a simple heat in contrast to the complicated wrinkles in Snow's neck and in Rayburn's life. "Excuse me," said Rayburn, touching a napkin to her eyes. "I don't mean anything at all, Miss Snow. I just think it's a nice story, that's all."

"Well it was quite a story," said Snow. "We walked all over Rome while

Father was in session with his insect colleagues, and I used to amuse myself by stitching Gigi's name in hotel towels."

"Then what happened?" asked Pinder.

"Well, that's just it. I don't really know. One night he said something very dashing about having to run off to Brazil or some place in South America on business, and I never heard from him again."

Pinder nearly purred in sympathy, and Rayburn went back to her napkin. "I'm so sorry," she said.

"Those Italians are quite the impetuous ones," smiled Snow with a glint of appreciation. "You can't count on them for much, but they can be splendid at times. Are you Italian, Mrs. Rayburn?"

"No, I don't think so," sniffled Rayburn. "I mean I don't really know anything about my extraction. My family's just Texan, I guess."

"Sounds perfectly exotic to me," said Snow.

"Maybe you are," said Pinder, studying her face. "But I think you look too reliable."

"A trifle so, yes," Snow agreed.

The unusual lunch lasted long past the food and the three cups of coffee until Snow, tiring badly, began to misplace fragments of her thoughts in unreachable portions of her brain. Then there was a ceremonial departure that included two kisses from the café owner, and Snow inched her way back to the Savannah with a companion on either side. Afterward Pinder and Rayburn made a compact to protect the old woman's last bit of life by keeping her free from eviction and stress, even if doing so meant giving up a sale or moving the Progressive University somewhere else, and they parted comrades by chance and partners in nobility.

Within days, events had twisted their bargain into a matter of intrigue. Rayburn found out that she had already violated her real estate firm's strict admonition against disclosure of the tenant removal contingency in the Crown Realty Associates contract. She had to call Pinder and urge secrecy on her, lest she be fired for endangering a sale. This was a humiliating experience for Rayburn, who regretted the indiscretion and positively loathed the sneakiness that followed. She was a woman who made almost a fetish of being straightforward, a trait she derived most likely from her schoolteacher mother whose children and pupils had been reared to believe in James Madison and honest debates and fair fights. On many occasions Rayburn had embarrassed her husband by asking his few CIA buddies from Southeast Asia why they made such a big deal of "sneaking around under the covers." "Under *cover*, dear," Colonel Rayburn would correct her, trying desperately to make light of her naiveté. There would be some clucking among the men. But Rayburn, undeterred, would quote Benjamin Franklin about how difficult democracy is to keep even when it is practiced by a few citizens in a town meeting, and she would say "Goodness gracious, how can we hope to keep it when it is huge and under the covers?" Some of her first prickly moments with her husband had occurred in such discussions, and now her peace was besieged by the lie in her throat and she was as irritable as she had ever been in the old days. She kept at it for a detestable jumble of motives: to help Lily Snow, to cover up her indiscretion, to keep food on her children's table.

For Haven Pinder things were no better. She gave the news to her boss before Rayburn called, which was bad enough. Worse, to her surprise, the boss was inflamed by a desire to possess the Savannah despite all the unfavorable circumstances adduced by Pinder, such as her living there. His mind was seized by the greater possibilities—to establish the university of the left *and* save the old people! He tested the idea on key financial backers in New York, and, with their approval, became feverish with excitement. He would use the first two floors of the Savannah for the university and the top three as low-cost condominiums for the tenants. It would be a housing program and a learning program under one roof, a creation, an innovation, a tonic for the forces of practical idealism.

His enthusiasm swept up even Haven Pinder, whose instinct had been to fight all developers and keep the Savannah a place for renters. She was attracted to his picture of "peoples' ownership" in victory over the luxury developers, to a campaign battle over bricks and mortgages and other hard-nosed realities, but also with surpassing symbolic importance. This combination touched a deep longing in Pinder, for it would fuse the tangible and the important, mingling the immediate goodness of her father's seeds with the evangelism of an ideological act. Pinder was one of millions struggling to escape the dullness of real things like furniture or manufacturing or accounting without getting seduced by the vagueness of the exciting things like a peace framework or a new religion, and she would fall for anything that offered hope. Washington promised the exquisite blend and kept promising it, although, for Pinder, it had always been one mirage giving way to another, in a city where everyone wanted to make defense policy but no one wanted to face a gun, to make health policy for the whole world without being exposed to diseased flesh.

On the second Thursday in November—a little more than two weeks before the Shea visit—Crown Realty Associates pitched the Savannah into chaos by delivering eviction notices to each tenant in a letter introducing that company as the building's new owner. Mrs. Beecher simulated a continuous heart attack in the lobby. Even Howell's bits of shocking nonsense could not bring her out of it. Mr. Davis celebrated his ninetieth birthday giving tenants his thorough analysis of the sales package, calculating that a condominium in the Savannah would require a monthly payment eight times the current rents. Two elderly homosexual "cousins" on the second floor moved out of the building almost immediately for reasons no one could understand. The demented old lady with the poodle on the fifth floor, who had indeed knocked on Savannah doors often, wearing slip and bra and carrying enough Scotch to get her once again through the tale of her mother's near-suicide and subsequent shock treatment in 1937, became hysterical. Poverty had already reduced her to a diet of embassy buffets to which she gained entrance nearly every night on the strength of her pedigree and her nerve and her moth-eaten furs, giving ingenious grande dame performances in the receiving lines. No one doubted her resolution to die rather than move from the embassy neighborhood. "I simply *must* stay here, darling!" she would swear, in a voice like molten brass crackling over cellophane. "I've got to stay on the list!" This woman led a diverse group of complainers so ferocious and/or pathetic that no one from Crown Realty wanted to face them.

Haven Pinder pretended to be surprised by the eviction notices, which made her feel bad, and within a few days she had to pretend not to be surprised by the boss's scheme. Her suspicions were so ugly that she remained calm by patrician instinct, gathering evidence and squirming inside. The boss's political mind had raced ahead of the game. Craftily, he told Pinder that she must not let on to any of the tenants that they might be rescued by the Alternative Political Coalition or the Progressive University. He did not wish to raise false hopes or expose his plans prematurely, he said, but he was so insistent that Pinder grew afraid. She had to watch her fellow tenants agonize over what to do—to obey meekly and leave their home of many years or to stay and make an unseemly fuss—without offering any solace at all, making her feel like a collaborator in their misery. A stream of tenants announced plans to give in and move to Baltimore or old folks' homes, and as their number grew the boss became more excited. He stepped up his secret meetings with bankers and contractors and the New York "movement millionaires," and it occurred to Pinder, who was not blind, that he was waiting for enough tenants to vacate to make room for Progressive University. By holding back, the necessary evictions could be charged to Crown Realty and not to the boss or his colleagues. The boss kept a list of evacuees, marking them with big black X's on a secret chart in his office, cheering inwardly as their number approached two floors' worth.

Pinder could not stand it. She broke security and told a number of wavering tenants on the sly that help was coming. Not to despair. Thus Pinder compounded her inner turmoil by entering another clandestine effort at cross-purposes with the first one. Only Rayburn, who was similarly engaged against her own firm, understood the inner tension of it. She urged Pinder to drink more milk in order to protect her stomach from its acids.

Henry Woodruff burned off several coatings of milk with his midnight discourses on the crisis, aiming always toward a higher palliative understanding. Pinder, listening to his lengthy analysis, felt like a snail crawling over sandpaper. She said she understood all too well already—too well, perhaps, to permit a remedy of action. As it was, her anger was divided and stalemated, and so were her loyalties and principles. Woodruff replied quite sincerely that she would profit from a more general perspective on the situation—one that would explain her behavior and her boss's, along with Crown Realty and just about anybody else she cared to include. They were all, he said, subject to the overwhelming power of the Scissors Theory.

"The Scissors Theory?" said Pinder.

"Precisely," said Woodruff. He ignored three worried faces and went off to fetch a portion of his manuscript from Pinder's apartment downstairs. Returning, he waved off all objections and derision. It was important, he said, a rare fit of theory and complex reality. He read excerpts in a sonorous, half-humorous voice. According to the Scissors Theory, all political empires undergo a prolonged midlife crisis, during which the Scissors Phenomenon appears most vividly in the empire's epicenter.

"Las Vegas?" asked Howell.

Woodruff replied with a look of strained tolerance. "Better known as the capital," he continued. He held up a pair of shears. "The phenomenon works like this," he said. "Over time, the scissors open wider and wider, and of course this means the ends of the two blades get farther and farther apart, you see . . ."

". . . That's very good, Henry," interrupted Susan Hartman, "but I'm sure Singer Sewing Machine has already thought of it."

"Sudsy, this is serious," he sighed. Taking first the lower, downward-pointing blade, he discussed it as an index of declining political sensibility and vitality, arguing by historical example that a widespread condition occurs whereby action and thought are grossly mismatched, and one thought parodies the next one. People will say the world is falling apart and then discuss this as to how it might affect the labor secretary's standing in the cabinet this week. Or they will say everything's all right and then go on to propose a moral and political and economic transvaluation. In Washington, he said, the best evidence of the downward blade is the nearly universal diagnosis of political malaise that exists along with a curious devotion to trivia. Only farmers and movie stars debate major issues any longer. Insiders carp at one another and say little of substance, but at the same time they use increasingly expansive words—"clearly," "totally," "ultimately," "absolutely." Everyone gets more serious as the level of nonsense rises. Outside Washington, the downward blade is evidenced by the growing number of people who tell pollsters that they neither agreed nor disagreed with the president's speech but, instead, laughed at it.

This made Howell laugh.

"Just like that," said Woodruff, pointing at his friend. "The president will be up there struggling with something deadly serious, and an alarming number of people will be laughing at him."

"Oh, come on, Henry," protested Howell. "You laugh yourself."

"I know," said Woodruff.

"Just last week you laughed at the Human Rights in Turkey speech," Howell accused.

"That has nothing to do with it," Woodruff said drily. "The point is that large numbers of people are doing it, and it's evidence of the downward blade. Okay? I don't care whether you call it the difference between the Salk vaccine and the swine flu vaccine or what, but it's real. It's a fundamental failure in public discourse, and it's because a lot of our words like 'rights' and 'markets' have been swallowed up by the decision-making process and don't mean anything anymore. I've got a little poem in here somewhere on that. Kind of trite, I guess. Let's see, it winds up, 'Farewell Freedom, Farewell Skill/Hail Processa, Work Your Will.' "

Hartman's face was buried in her hands. "No more of the poems, Henry," she said. "Please."

"What the hell is the Processa?" asked Pinder.

"That's very complicated," said Woodruff.

"Excuse me," said Howell. "You remember that contraption up here the night Miss Snow fell, the thing with the air-conditioning duct and the green shit all over the place?"

"Sure," said Pinder.

"Well, that's the Processa," said Howell.

"Oh," said Pinder.

"Never mind," said Woodruff. "The important thing is the consensus about the down-the-tubes trend. That's this blade here. And the other one is the rising index of snippish materialism. It runs up at the same angle the other one runs down. And it means the flowers in the parks get prettier and prettier. More sleek office buildings go up. More houses get renovated. Continental restaurants spring up all over the place. People drink wine like water. And the radicals who once sweated blood all summer cutting cane down in Cuba now lie on the beaches near Havana and toast the revolution. Everybody goes up gradually. It all goes on invisibly, and nobody feels privileged because everybody is too anxious about that downward blade underneath, you see . . ."

". . . Well, that's just great, Henry," sighed Pinder, "but . . ."

". . . What makes the scissors open, according to the Theory?" asked Howell with dry amusement.

"My hand," deadpanned Woodruff.

Hartman led the others in laughter. It was the first sign of life she had given, having previously learned that Woodruff's cerebrations put a capsule of stale air between them.

Woodruff, encouraged by Hartman's laughter, became serious again. "No, really," he said. "The opening force is a matter of great debate. In fact, it's what a lot of the silly finger-pointing in Washington is about. I mean it's silly because nobody really makes any sense and nobody in Washington admits benefiting personally from the force. Some say it's bigotry or corporate power or government regulation or whatever, and everybody says it would be all right if their point of view would prevail. Which is bullshit, I think. And everybody fights with everybody else over this in our own special Washington way, which is subpoenas and studies and meetings and publicity campaigns and so forth, and the Processa picks up the tab for all of it. I think it's human nature, mostly, you know, that appetites will find a way to win out over integrity after a time, on average. But I haven't really pinpointed the force yet. That's the next chapter."

"The next chapter, eh? Great," Pinder said sourly. "I suppose then you'll spell out what all this bullshit has to do with our getting thrown out of the Savannah."

"It has a lot to do with it, Haven," said Woodruff. "We're getting thrown out because the upward blade here means that this little apartment is worth about a hundred acres of prime Iowa farmland. It's crazy, but most people in Washington say that's good. Clean. Upgrading. But down on the other blade is all the nonsense about why it's happening and all the trivia. And your boss man Martin is trying to make a profit and a revolutionary act out of it at the same time. It's perfect."

Pinder and Woodruff, equally prone to social withdrawal, differed in that Pinder would become quiet and cloudy whereas Woodruff would blabber endlessly on his own isolated plane of discussion. Pinder, therefore, offered a far smaller target for Howell's therapeutic humor—fewer words, fewer bland meanings to twist playfully. Howell had to improvise, as he was doing in the shower with Pinder on a Saturday afternoon in November. He was lumbering around under the suds, humming a Beatles song called "In My Life," a tender though melancholy reprise of things past, changing the lyrics to wildly incongruous real estate lingo items, ending "in myyyyaiahh coming-up-fast area, I'll love you more." He had been overperforming since Pinder came home in an especially foul mood with the news that her boss wanted three floors for the university, not two. Economic pressures would force him to sell off the top floor apartments as luxury residences, leaving only the fourth floor for "hardship cases" among the surviving Savannah tenants.

Howell sallied forth again. "It's all right, baby," he said. "We can move downstairs with Miss Lily. And the Guccis, on their way up to their posh condos, can throw loose change out into the poverty demonstration area."

Pinder, back turned, rinsed vigorously in silence.

"And with Martin's socialist realism art classes downstairs, we'll have a fully integrated experience here," Howell pressed. "We can call it Progressive Condoversity."

Pinder turned off the shower and stepped out of the bathtub in one motion. "Hey!" cried a well-lathered Howell. "What are you doing? I'm sorry. We'll call it anything you want!" Whining to himself, he managed an emergency rinse and followed Pinder to the bedroom.

She lay on the bed, not moving when Howell slithered up behind her. They were like two spoons on edge, closely lying in parallel curves. Howell nuzzled under her hair and whispered. "Please don't put me in the doghouse, Haven."

She said nothing. He could tell without his eyes that she was comatose. Her breathing made no sound. With the fingertips of his left hand he began to massage the top of her scalp, parting the hair back and forth, kneading a light comfort into the blood vessels nearest her brain. "I'm sorry, baby," he moaned. "I just didn't know what to say, that's all . . ."

Pinder responded to the massage only with a slightly more audible breath, though her head was purring. Finally she murmured, "Please don't make a joke."

"I won't," Howell promised urgently, but then he giggled slightly in spite of himself. "I'm sorry," he whispered. "I don't know why, but that was just funny somehow."

Pinder curled more tightly into her spoon. "I just can't take it any more, David," she sighed, close to tears. "Martin spends all his time making people feel small. He tells people they're not working hard enough. He tells people what to think. He pretends to listen when I tell him how crazy this building plan is, but then he just tells me I don't understand what's important. Or he ignores me. He keeps talking about what the correct position is and stuff like that, and I can't stand it any more . . ."

". . . Well, Haven," said Howell, continuing to rub her head, "you've always known a lot about Martin and how he . . ."

". . . No, please, don't talk about him," Pinder interrupted. "I know what you're going to say, and I just want to say he makes people feel small, that's all. And so does Henry. He's crazy, you know."

"I know," whispered Howell.

"And that's all right. But my God, he just uses people as examples all the time, and he makes me think that's all I am."

"That's just his way, baby," said Howell. "Henry's troubles come in through his cock and go out through his head, that's all."

Pinder stirred all along the line of contact between her back and his front. Then she gave a mildly irritated kick with one foot. "You're making a joke," she accused, in a way that made Howell believe she would have pursued his comment were it not for her adverse mood.

"No, I'm not," whispered Howell.

"Well, it's like everything in politics and everything else is all going on inside Henry's skinny head, and the rest of us are just illustrations," sighed Pinder. "And that makes me feel small. And so do you sometimes, with your jokes."

Howell stopped rubbing. "Why?" he asked.

"Because you hit all my soft spots," she said quietly to no one. "You make fun of Henry and me and even yourself. We're all jokes. You just deflect everything. Ha Ha Howell."

Howell rolled over away from her and pounded the mattress thunderously with his fist. Pinder lay inertly, without flinching. "I'm trying to hang onto something," she continued in her hushed monotone, "and you make me feel small for it with your jokes."

"Well, what the fuck *else* do you want me to do?" Howell said bitterly, his nose buried in a blanket. "You want me to say I think Martin is a great man? Well, bullshit! I'd much rather have a laugh or two than anything he can offer the world. He's turning into a hack, baby, let's face it. Politics is the opiate of the bourgeoisie."

"We're all bourgeois," said Pinder softly. "That doesn't mean anything."

"I know," sighed Howell. "I just thought I'd try something intellectual, I guess."

"No jokes."

"Why not?" Howell asked. "I've got to hang onto something too, you know. And why shouldn't I? Everybody I know with half a conscience is all strung out over something these days. Everybody I care about. My poor old insides are already churned up over them, so why shouldn't I try to laugh about the gurus and pretensions they hang onto? At least it's friendly." He waited for Pinder to say something. Then he said, "Well, maybe it's not always friendly, but it's alive. I guess. Fuck, I don't know. You've got me talking to myself."

Howell's roar was a revelation to both of them. It conveyed the jolting primitive anguish of a woman's scream, the voice from a separate region, but it also had the breadth of a tenor. "Noooo!" he cried, over and over. He jumped up to crack a flat fist against the bedroom door. The loud report and his stinging knuckles were both drowned out by the anger in his feet as they stomped around the bed. "No, no, you can't do it, Haven!" he shrieked. "You can't hurt me and be hurting and be wonderful all at the same time, goddammit! You can't! I can't stand it!" By the end of this, he was kneeling at the corner of the bed next to her head, and he snatched up her wrist in his left hand. She had not moved. He shouted "No!" once more, with diminished force, in the direction of saying please.

Pinder finally moved to look at him with the eye of a salmon in a bear's paw, a certain blankness on top of terror on top of something unknown. "You're crying," she announced as though this, and not his berserk fit, were the news of the last twenty seconds.

Howell dropped her wrist. "A little bit," he admitted, but his collapsing anger made it a little more. "What's wrong with that?"

"Nothing," she said, looking through her own tears for the first time at his wounded eyes. She gave out her clear groan and averted her face. "Nothing," she said again. Still hiding her face, she flung her arms in the air at a rakish angle, elbows rigid and fingers splayed.

Howell fell back on the floor with a thud of the ass. "I don't believe it," he sobbed. "Now you want to hug." He saw Pinder nod her head in the affirmative, which made him shake his in wonder. He sniffled, grinned, and said, "Oh, boy," as he jumped over the baseboard.

They squeezed and rolled, oblivious to the intervening towels. "Why did we *do* that?" moaned Howell. "Why? Just when we need each other most, we go off into bullshit like that."

Pinder squeezed him silently and then asked, "Is that as mad as you get?"

"What?" said Howell. "Oh that. Yes. Jesus. That's as bad as I've ever done."

"I can handle it then," said Pinder.

"That's as bad as I can get," said Howell, with no inkling that the next year would prove him wrong. "Ow, God!" he whimpered, holding his right hand gingerly above them. "I mashed my knuckles into castanets on that fucking door."

"I can handle it," Pinder repeated, with pride and satisfaction. "I love this hand," she said, kissing it. "You poor wounded warrior."

Howell withdrew his hand. "You're making fun of my melodramatic tendencies again."

"No, just your weakness," she laughed, and with that she grabbed him about the chest and rolled him over her. It was quite an achievement, especially since her short arms reached only part way around the barrel. Howell grunted, laughed, and rolled her over him. They went back and forth like wrestlers, mimicking each other's noises.

As lovers, Howell and Pinder were talkers. Conversations broke out intermittently by voice and by eye. They liked to stare at each other, noses touching, during the long stroke in and again during the long stroke out, measuring the excitement by the tiniest increments through wide and glassy eyes. When it became too much to bear—when an eye would flutter or a smile would burst forth or a shiver would rattle a spine—they would laugh joyously and rock from side to side. Sometimes Pinder would make her enthusiastic purring noise.

"Uuuunnnhhh!" she breathed, when a rush of pleasure put her mouth into a twitching grin.

Howell was just behind her. "I don't see how we can be so wounded and confused and still get so much pleasure from each other," he smiled. "It feels too good for an honest man."

"I think we're doing all right."

"You do?" asked Howell.

"Yep."

They reestablished nose contact and watched each other through the undulating stillness of four identical hazel eyes. Tiny yellow splashes danced around their pupils. Even an outsider would have noticed changes in their faces. Soft ripples chased smoothness across cheeks and foreheads, and colors appeared here and there like splotches of autumn, mostly orange and red. They both kept smiling, but after a time Howell dropped two tears on Pinder.

"What's the matter?" she asked.

"Not a thing," said Howell. "I just can't get over your face when you make love. There's so much going on. Oh, boy. You are very beautiful."

"Thank you," said Pinder. "But what's so sad about that?"

"Nothing," said Howell. "It just touched me, that's all."

"But you do look a little sad."

"Well, yeah, but . . ."

". . . That's all right . . ."

". . . I guess I was actually thinking of Henry and Casey there for a flash," sighed Howell. "You know, they've both gotten to the point where they can admit she never came close to an orgasm in eight years as lovers, and it hit me that her face never got to bathe itself in love like yours does and that Henry never got to see it or anything like it. That's what it sounds like, anyway. And it just hit me as very sad for a second. What people miss. What it must do to them over years."

"I know, David," said Pinder. "But they're doing all right now, I hope. I saw Casey last week. I think she is."

"Such a loss, though," said Howell. He pressed her to him, and his body quivered.

"I know," sighed Pinder. "But it all goes into the mix."

"What mix?"

"Of sad and happy. You can't always tell. Like sometimes you think I'm sad if I cry when we're making love, but I'm not. It's just full, that's all. And rich."

"Maybe so," sighed Howell. "A rich mix."

"Uh huh."

Howell abruptly raised his head like a turtle. "This is ridiculous," he said with a determined grin. "I was watching your face, but now I've talked myself into a funk."

They stirred on toward a desperate headlong yelp and a prolonged Pinder noise, after which they lay still a while before congratulating each other. "Very good," said Pinder.

"Came all the way from New York," moaned Howell.

"And cleaned my windshield," said Pinder.

After two long hugs, Howell girded on his towel and strolled out of the bedroom.

A few minutes later, Pinder appeared naked in the living room doorway. He did not see her. "Can you hear it?" she asked.

"Oh," started Howell. "You scared me."

Pinder nodded toward the television screen. "You can't really hear it," she said. "Don't you want to turn it up?"

Howell blanched, realizing his mistake in keeping the sound low. He had been too clever by half. "Not really," he said.

"How much time left in the quarter?"

"Uh, it's college basketball," said Howell, shuffling miserably in his towel. "They don't have quarters. Um, there's a lot of time left."

Pinder leaned against the framing, her arms crossed. "David, have they had the intermission yet?" she asked.

Her words landed heavily on Howell's conscience, shriveling him in advance. "Halftime," he corrected. "Uh, yes."

"How long ago?" Her voice was thick with stern disappointment. "Just now?"

Howell cast a glance at the torrid action on the court. He licked his lips. Looking furtively back at Pinder, he groaned miserably over the disjunction of realities. "Haven, it's the Tar Heels," he pleaded. "I'm from North Carolina."

"How long?" she persisted.

"This is a misunderstanding," he sighed. "Um, the second half started five minutes ago."

Pinder's lips were slightly blue. Hugging herself to keep warm, she stepped back into the kitchen and peered warily around the door. "So all this was during the halftime?" she asked. "You came in to take a shower with me and make love to me, and it was all during the halftime?"

"Now wait a minute!" cried Howell, stamping a foot in frustration. "This doesn't change anything! I'd forgotten all about the game, but then I got scared by what I felt between us! I swear!"

"So you thought some football would make you feel better?"

Howell buried his face in his hands. "Basketball," he said.

"Basketball, then. Basketball would make you feel better."

"I didn't say that! I just meant that the *game* is basketball, not football," said Howell, sweeping his arm toward the screen. He was distracted by a spectacular play, and a bandit's grin hit his face. "Look at it this way," he shrugged. "We had a lot more time with basketball. If it was baseball, we'd only have between innings."

"Good," said Pinder. She was gone before Howell could work up a puny laugh to hide his error. "Wait a minute!" he cried after her. "This is ridiculous!"

She was meditating on the side of the bed when Howell arrived. "Please, baby," he said. "I'm sorry about the baseball joke. Let's not let a stupid thing like sports come between us, okay? It's nothing. I was just a little overloaded from being with you, and I was watching the game for a second to get my mind off things. That's all. Look, sports is an escape for men."

Pinder did not look at him. "It's not that you went back to the game," she said quietly. "It's that you came in here during the halftime. I can't quite handle it yet. I feel like a pom pom or something, one of the halftime's highlights."

"Ha ha!" twittered Howell, in a laugh that tripped over his chin. "That's very good. I didn't know you knew about halftime highlights." He sat down next to her and tried to seem cozy.

"No judgments, no demands," she said vacantly. "I'm not one who wants to keep you away from your sports to be kissyface and earnest all the time. It is a big jump though. I need something just like your sports, I guess. I need to be alone for a little bit."

Howell stood up to seize the opening. "Hey, that's fine," he said. "That's all right with me. But please don't turn into a robot on me. Let's not lose it."

"So," she prompted.

"So?"

"So get out of here," she said firmly.

"Huh? Can't I just go in the other room?"

"No," she growled. "All the way out of here. Now."

Howell turned in a small circle. "I'm not dressed," he said. "I live here, too."

"I don't care!" cried Pinder. "Just go. You can go down to my apartment if you want."

"Come on, Haven," said Howell. "Can't we just make up now, before I go. It's not good to let things fester."

Pinder did not reply. "Oh, boy," sighed Howell. He snatched up his keys and padded barefoot out the door.

Ten minutes later, Pinder listened to a chagrined man through a crack. "Look, we're gonna have to figure out some other way to be apart," he said.

"Henry and Sudsy are having some kind of fight down there. I don't think they're getting along too well. Anyway, they don't want me around even more than you don't want me around. And besides that, Madame Delacroix saw me in the hallway wearing my towel. She gave me her praying mantis glare. I thought she was gonna use the fire extinguisher on me."

"Tough shit," grinned Pinder.

"That's better," said Howell, pushing his way in.

"The tar feet are winning," said Pinder.

"Tar *heels*," said Howell. They tried a hug, but it was unsatisfactory, less than a complete atonement. They could not know why, or speak of it, and they spent the next half hour swimming uneasily through each other's silence. The fateful call from Felix, the Jamaican desk man on the house phone, had found them in such a state.

Pat Shea further unnerved Howell, who ate most of the crackers and cheese. Everything about Shea touched a fiber of panic—FBI, Miami, military credentials, smooth teeth, even the aquamarine necktie. Howell was transfixed by him, especially by the droning irrelevant talk of the sun in Miami and the president's new reorganization plan and the positive trend in unemployment being offset by a negative one in manufacturers' durables. To Howell, who prided himself on a feel for the human amusements in any personality, it became obsessive that he could find no discernible body temperature in Shea. It was as though he came from a wind-up species, and Howell knew enough to fear his own hostile detachment.

"I can't believe you're Miss Lily's nephew," said Pinder.

Howell took another bite of cracker. "He is?"

Pinder looked bewildered, then annoyed. "That's what he just said, David."

"Oh," said Howell. "Sorry."

"She's quite a lady, yes, she is," said Shea. "Not quite as spry as she used to be, though. I guess she's going on eighty-five now. That's getting up there."

"Yes," said Pinder.

"Sure is," said Shea. "Yes, sir. And she thinks the world of you two. Yes, she does. Both of you. And that's why I thought I should stop by here to see you like this. Very good cheese here, if I do say so myself. I really hate to see Aunt Lily getting on like she is. I really do. But I don't guess we have much choice about it, do we? No. She's gotten pretty feeble in the few years since I've last seen her, you know. Don't get up here as much as I'd like to anymore. It's a myth, really, about the Bureau paying us to travel a lot to catch criminals all over the place and have a good time. Wish we did. I watch those television shows and I find myself saying, boy, I'd really like to join that outfit. I sure would. But in real life you can't just go TDYing around without a lot of good reasons in triplicate, even if you're a SAC. That's what I am, by the way. Or an inspector. So anyway I try to stop in to see Aunt Lily whenever I get the chance. There aren't many Snows left in our family.

I'm a Shea, of course, but my mother was a Snow. And we're getting a little concerned about the possibility that Aunt Lily might need better medical attention than she's getting here on her own."

"Uh huh," nodded Howell.

Shea went on until Pinder interrupted him. "You don't want to put her in a nursing home, do you?" she asked.

"Not necessarily," said Shea. "Not necessarily at all. Now we're just exploring the options. Out-patient and in-patient, full-time and part-time. You know, talking to the medical personnel and friends like yourself and other individuals. And Aunt Lily herself, of course."

"What does she say?" asked Howell.

"Well, now that you mention it, just about all she does is criticize the manners of her doctor," said Shea. "That's what she does."

"That's her all right," said Pinder.

"It's a question of timing, like everything else," said Shea. "It really is. I mean you do something now or later, and sometimes you move too soon or too late. And there are so many factors to evaluate, without airing the family's laundry right here in front of you, I mean there are some practical considerations, too, such as finances and distances and supervision and so forth. She refuses to move to Florida. Yes, she does. Quite a mind of her own."

"Mr. Shea, it would be terrible to put Miss Lily in an old folks' home," said Pinder. "She loves it here. It's her whole life. She walks to breakfast and lunch every day, and she sits in the lobby in the afternoon. I'm pretty sure she'd want to stay here no matter what."

Both Howell and Shea shifted uncomfortably in their seats. "Very good cheese," said Shea.

"Thank you," said Pinder.

Shea crossed his legs. "It's not pleasant to think about, is it?" he sighed. "I know it's not. I mean, we all do, of course. But you'll understand that I have to be concerned about the medical attention. The building's management told me she had a fall some months back . . ."

". . . But she's all right now," said Pinder.

"We know about that fall," said Howell. "That's how Haven and I met. Down at Miss Lily's, helping her to the hospital."

"I see," said Shea, studying Howell's cordial smile. "How unusual. That's nice. Well, I know how much the two of you care for my aunt, and I want to tell you again how much we in the family appreciate it. This is a hard thing for all of us to go through. And it doesn't look like it's going to get any easier, I'm afraid. I see the notices downstairs that the building's been sold for condominiums. It looks like we'll have to move her, no matter what."

"Not necessarily," said Pinder. "The Savannah has a tenants' association, and we're trying to block the conversion. Or at least to make the developers keep Miss Lily and some of the others on as renters. You know, the ones who have been here thirty and forty years. It's not right to kick them out."

226

"Well," said Shea, clearing his throat. "That might put her through a lot of stress, I'm afraid."

"So would moving," said Pinder.

"What do you think?" Shea asked Howell. "I'm trying to do what's best, you know, and I appreciate your advice."

"Uh huh," said Howell. "I don't know. It's hard to know what's right." He had something else to say, but it was paralyzed in his throat.

"Yes, it is," said Shea. "And it's kind of sticky. Being in my position in the Bureau and all, it's kind of hard for me to go along with seeing my aunt in some sort of sit-in or anything. Anything disruptive. I'm kidding, of course."

"I think it would kill her to be all cooped up in a home," said Pinder. "She wouldn't have anything to do."

"Well, maybe," said Howell. "I know she doesn't want to go anywhere, Mr. Shea. She always talks about how long she's been around this neighborhood, even back with her dad."

"Yes, yes, I know," said Shea. "Well, I don't mind telling you, it's not easy. That's the one sure thing."

"Sure is," said Howell.

"Sure is," said Pinder. She tried to ape Shea just enough for Howell to catch on. He gave her a warning look.

When Shea finally left, Pinder started to shriek. "Why didn't you *say* something?" she demanded. "He's an asshole. He doesn't care about her at all. You should have told him!"

Howell put his hands over his ears. "Please," he said. "Please, baby. I'm sorry I couldn't talk too much, but I'm telling you that guy made me think of the Cuban with the hand blown off. Talk about a small world! FBI. Miami. Miss Lily's nephew. It's weird. Everybody in the whole world is only one and a half acquaintances away from everybody else. It's amazing, like when I ran into the only white person on the Sudanese border in 1967, in a hut in the middle of nowhere, and six years later I found out that it was Paul Sternman's first wife."

"I know, David," said Pinder. "But you still should have told him."

"I can't believe he's really with the FBI," said Howell.

"God help us," said Pinder. "I thought they'd be a lot less boring and a lot more sinister."

"I just couldn't bring myself to be tough on the wimp," Howell apologized. "We're not family. Basically, we're helpless. I don't know what good it would do."

"I know, but it would make me feel better."

They tried to make up, but something was fractured between them. They debated what it was for a month. Both major incidents—the halftime letdown and the Shea visit—were so bizarre as to render analysis unsound. Pinder said Howell could do anything he wanted. She said sports and intimacy were not incompatible, but that wasn't quite what she meant. She reproached herself for wanting to put tails on sweet moments. Howell kept excusing his stricken timidity in the face of a wimp like Shea as a sensible choice against *machismo* nonsense. But he didn't quite mean it either. Valerie Mantell consoled Pinder with the observation that only a confident woman could pitch Howell out of his own apartment. This provoked considerable debate. Woodruff consoled Howell with the idea that both incidents were too trivial to interfere with a romance of any substance. Somehow, the Howell-Pinder romance went on. They had many laughs, and they stirred the mixture on many nights and not a few afternoons. Underneath, however, they were conscious of a flaw, something missing, something in keeping with the unsettled times.

Four days before Christmas, a mortified Pat Shea knocked on their door again and begged for help. They were taking his aunt, he said, but she was suffering from fiendish delusions. The three of them rushed downstairs.

An attendant standing by the wheelchair made no attempt to calm Lily Snow, whose eyes were as large as eggs and rimmed with pink. "Help!" she squealed. "Help! Help!" When she screamed, her entire body convulsed as though racked by terminal hiccoughs.

"Oh, my God!" cried Pinder, rushing up beside her. "Miss Lily!"

"Help! Help! Help!" squealed Snow.

"We're here," said Pinder. "It's all right."

"Help!" shouted Snow. "Is that you?" She stared blindly between Pinder and Howell, who were kneeling no more than two feet from her face. The room was alive with the smell of sour turpentine, of acidic body odor and urine and fear.

"What's the matter, Miss Lily?" asked Howell, attempting feebly to be jolly.

"It is you! Thank heaven!" cried Snow. "Please help me. I don't quite know what's wrong. That's just it, you see. But I know there are these horrid creatures on the train trying to do away with me."

Shea shook his head sadly. "I haven't really told her anything," he said. "She just got these ideas in her head all of a sudden. I think the attendant set her off."

"We've got your hands, Miss Lily," said Howell. "You just squeeze if you want anything."

"And mighty fine hands you have, indeed," said Snow. A hint of vision was settling back into her eyes. "Please do what you can to stop this train. I've never seen such wretched dark country!"

Shea twirled his finger next to his ear in a fatalistic loony sign. "It's all right, Aunt Lily," he said. "The doctor will take a look at you soon and fix you up."

"Doctor? What doctor? I didn't send for any doctor. My goodness! I need a conductor, not a doctor."

The attendant leaned over and whispered in a soothing professional manner, "Let's go, Missy. We'll be all right."

"Help!" squealed Snow, instantly blind again. "Help! Help!" It was louder than ever, a scratchy yell trying to tear its way out of her body.

"Oh, my God," cried Pinder. Howell gripped her shoulder, and Pinder said, "It's okay, Miss Lily. We're right here with you."

"Help!" cried Snow, less loudly. She did seem to hear. Leaning over toward Pinder's hand, she said, "Please, dear, get me off this train. I'll be so grateful! Hide me in a pile of leaves or something!"

The attendant started gently forward. Howell and Pinder looked desperately at each other and went beside her, soothing her once again toward the hospital, which turned out to be the Georgetown Nursing Home. Shea, all the more upset from Pinder's caustic looks, excused himself just after the administrator admitted the old lady to her room.

Howell and Pinder developed the art of sulking. Pinder sagged further at work, where the boss was feverishly estimating the stalwarts and slackers among the tenants, readying himself for a move against the Savannah. Without Snow, the venture had no purpose for Pinder. She became lethargic, a condition that contradicted the sparkling bantam look of her. She no longer hummed to herself in the morning, and she lost interest altogether in Howell's problems at *Washington* magazine.

At the Savannah, Howell said to Pinder, "Something has definitely been lost in the transition." She agreed after the usual survey of their friends. They felt blocked, mute about it. Only when they visited a rapidly failing Lily Snow at the Georgetown Nursing Home did their blood move, as Snow gamely complained of the "lunatics" and "nitwits" and "lionfeeders" there, holding hands and demanding kisses on the head.

Near the end of February, Howell was tempted by an offer to escape to Miami. Bobby Ziller called with the announcement of a spectacular two-day bash in honor of Donessa and Arlington Spencer who had purchased a yacht together. They had rented a castle, he said, and the guests would be awarded at random airplane tickets to distant places in the world. Howell was tempted as an observer. The champagne passed under his nose. There was mystery in it.

The mystery became irresistible when a distraught Marvella called two days before the party to say that Ziller had disappeared. Gone for a week. She begged Howell not to say anything about it, a request that baffled him, along with her manner and all the facts. Howell could not sleep for two nights before deciding to go to Miami for investigation on all fronts, from Ziller to Shea.

Haven Pinder hugged him at the door, then squeezed him as they caught part of the old mixture and savored it. "Be careful," she said.

XII

F<small>OR ALMOST</small> two weeks, in Miami, the palm trees had been dancing all night, which is what they say about the endless prelude of conspiracy when tires screech and tight conclaves explode or drag on to postponement, with traitors and communists and the law always somewhere in the shadows, dancing. The tension reached out into the Everglades, where business was brisk for El Navajo. Stale rumors nourished him between customers; he took the hot news with him to bed. El Navajo was so excited when the battered, cream-colored van pulled into his station that he could not speak with the two occupants. He gave them the *abrazo* and then pointed sadly to his mouth. He was operationally mum. They laughed and hit him on the arm several times apiece, hard enough to hurt but soft enough to be playful. They understood him. One stayed at the van while the other, at El Navajo's joyful insistence, went to inspect the new luxuries. El Navajo had gone first class. His shooting range was now a hundred feet wide, a great swath through the swamp, featuring specially made new paper targets of famous faces, including Marilyn Monroe and the Red Baron. There was a brand new green carpet in the office, slightly stained with oil, and on it sat six brand new pinball machines. Not just anybody got to use them. El Navajo beamed through all this and then sprang to his tasks. He filled the van with gas and changed its license plate. As the van lurched off he could only wave, but he found his voice later and cried, "Kick one for me!"

The two Cubans kept their guns ready all the way into Miami, seeing ambushes at every intersection and ghosts in the swamp canals. Their purpose was to stay alive and to earn a huge quick profit for themselves and their associates by delivering the shipment to Carlos Maraña, the middle man of the deal. This straightforward criminal motive made the two escorts unique among those who would touch the conspiracy that night, for this transaction would be a contorted one even by the standards of Miami.

Tonight there would be cops trying to arrest cops, cops trying to keep crooks out of jail, crooks trying to get into jail, among other unorthodox moves. The participant who could keep straight all the twists and reverses would be the winner. This was almost always Maraña, whose moves made sense only to himself.

Max Parker was grumbling about them, in fact, when he saw the van pull up outside Maraña's condominium, about a hundred yards away from Parker's lookout post. Parker watched one of the escort Cubans enter the building. Then he ducked around the corner of a dress shop and dropped money into a pay phone.

"Yeah," said a voice from a phone booth in a coffee shop near the heart of Miami.

"It's going down right now," said Parker, scared. "Just like I told you."

"Don't be fucking with me," growled Damico. "This is too important to me."

"Lay off!" spat Parker. "This is it, I tell you!"

"Awright, I'm a little tight. What's the gig?"

"Two drops, heavy and light. The oilies don't like it, but that's the way it is. Hard, fast, and now. The crate is a plain tan van, man."

"Where do I get my shot?"

Parker bit his lip. "Drop one," he said. "Vizcaya."

"Where?" Damico was incredulous. "Goddammit, Max! None of your bullshit. Don't tell me the hoods have time for a party."

"Hey, I don't have time for you, man! That's it. Drop one is light, half and half. My car's already there. He goes on from there. I fly with the heavy down payment."

"He working with hostages?"

"Yeah, and trust. He trusts his friends."

"Shut up. How much time do I have?"

"I figure fifteen minutes, at least. If I'm standing outside the tan van, everything's okay. And don't tail us, okay? He's better on that than any of us, and it'll queer things."

"Save it," said Damico. "Where is this joint, anyway? I've never been there."

"Gotta go, man," spat Parker. "I'm good for names, not addresses." He hung up.

Maraña, wearing a tan suit without a tie and dark glasses, sprang out of the building like a jaguar. He jumped into the van as the second escort jumped out. Maraña nodded tersely, but as he drove off alone he took both hands from the wheel and shrugged comically.

Maraña slowed down to allow Parker to jump in on the run. "Smooth," said Parker, dusting himself off.

"I hope so," said Maraña. "Did you snitch on me to our friend Damico?"

"Of course," sighed Parker. "But he is not stupid, Carlos. He must have figured out by now that we're running this thing together."

"It doesn't matter. The only thing that matters is that we've got an FBI agent sticking his nose in a drug case where he doesn't have jurisdiction. Why do you think he's doing it?"

"I don't know," Parker replied. "All I know is that he didn't seem too interested in this deal until I told him about the idiot wops who are making the buy tonight. That really turned him on for some reason. Maybe he's after those guys."

"I don't think so. I think these wops are dirty with the DEA, and my guess is that Damico is trying to make a case against his brother feds, the narcs. I'd bet on it."

"Maybe so," said Parker. "But he's still got to make a living. And there's gonna be too much confusion out here tonight to fight corruption . . ."

". . . Yeah, but Damico doesn't know that."

"Big deal. I'm not worried about him, Carlos. I'm worried about us. With all these cops all over the place."

"They all got the word?"

"I might as well have put an ad in the paper," sulked Parker. "I don't like any of this."

"Good."

"Good," mimicked Parker. "You say good. But I could get all shot up or get a bloody nose or something—all for nothing. That doesn't make sense." Parker's sing-song manner made it impossible to tell how serious he was.

"You're getting old, my friend," said Maraña.

"Hah!" snorted Parker. "I am young and strong. I should be looking for a woman instead of trouble."

"You're crazy," said Maraña. "Nothing could be more trouble than the armadillo you're going out with now. When she talks, it's like someone is pouring tomato soup in my ear."

"But she adores me," said Parker.

Maraña flipped his dark glasses up on his forehead and turned to Parker with a hard, sardonic dare in his face. "What's the matter, Max? You're not having fun?"

"Oh, sure," nodded Parker. "Tons of it." He shook his head and started to giggle.

Maraña coaxed the new mood. "You feel the old buzz going, *chico?*" he laughed. "You feel the shit move inside you like ice?"

"Okay, Chief," grinned Parker, rocking forward in fear. "I'm ready."

"That's better. Here. I think you should test some of the stuff before we get there."

Half an hour later, before dusk, hobbling old gentlemen in white coats were lighting evening torches along the rock paths that wound in a maze through a thick forest of ficus trees and strangler figs. There were parking lots in many lacunae of the forest, and at the remote end of one of them Max Parker leaned back against the snub nose of the van and whistled to himself. He carried in a sagging coat pocket his ancient CIA "freedom pistol," a gift to him from a grizzled OSS veteran who had dropped the pistols to the Resistance in the Second Great War. Parker had saved the veteran from drowning in a freak accident off the Caribbean island of Vieques, and while the pistol carried a sentiment approaching the gratitude the veteran felt—he cried with nostalgia whenever he dusted it off—it was made of cast iron and was functionally imperfect in that the gun tended to blow up in the user's hand. Still, it would make a great deal of noise in case of trouble, which is what Parker would want to do, and the pistol's history would make quite a story for the authorities. So Parker was outwardly relaxed, cleaning his fingernails, heart thumping, when Damico sneaked through the dense underbrush at the back of the van.

"Hey!" he whispered. "Let's get going."

Parker did not look around or up. "It's not locked," he replied. Damico skittered along the van commando style and hopped in on the passenger's side.

Parker listened to the silence for almost a minute before ambling back to the door. He also pulled out a walkie-talkie. "*Chico*," he said over the static, "any sign of them yet?"

The sight of the walkie-talkie made Damico queasy. He checked himself before yelling and bared his teeth to mouth the words, "What the fuck are you doing?"

Parker looked blandly at Damico while listening to the receiver. "No," crackled Maraña's voice. "And don't call me anymore! Over and out."

"Same to you," shrugged Parker. He took out a stick of gum. Damico was gesticulating furiously at the walkie-talkie.

"It's okay, Dave," said Parker. "I turned it off. Just trying to see how much time you have. You're wasting it, by the way."

Damico looked suspiciously toward the instrument. He beckoned for it, verified that it was off, and tossed it on the dashboard. "Where'd you get that thing?" he asked.

"I made it," Parker replied.

"That's really dumb, Max," he said. "Somebody could hear that transmission and be down on our ass. If they come, I'm gonna break you in two."

"Take it easy," said Parker. "Here I am risking my life for you and you say you're going to break me in two. How am I supposed to feel about that, Dave? I betray Carlos for you—and Carlos would kill me if he found out I betrayed him—and now you are so nervous and ungrateful. How am I supposed to *feel?*"

"Cut the horseshit," Damico commanded. "Look, just because I work for the FBI doesn't mean I'm automatically dumb, okay? *I* know you've been doubling back on me with Carlos, okay? That's natural, okay? And I don't mind spending the money, okay, 'cause I need you for something big that's about to go down the drain if I don't move fast. I'm about to lose these guys. They've gotten rid of my snitch." Damico was perspiring heavily. He pulled a lever to open the heater vent on the floor of the van. After inserting a small magnetic recorder in its mouth, he flicked the lever back to defrost.

Parker stared out the window. "You got a court order for that?" he inquired.

"Shut up," said Damico. "You know better than that. I can't go just after dope. I'm after something bigger."

"And it's not Carlos?"

"Not now," grinned Damico. "And after this, probably not ever. Look, I already *told* you that. So don't worry. I don't know why in the hell Carlos would want to do business with these bozos, but that's his problem. As long as he doesn't try to corrupt anybody tonight, I won't bust him for the dope. I couldn't, anyway."

"He wouldn't dream of corrupting anybody," said Parker.

Damico unscrewed a brush handle from what seemed to be a dark brown glue bottle. Then he lifted army blankets off the bales of marijuana stacked high in the back of the van, and slapped liquid from the bottle here and there. There was a whine of hurry under his grunts and groans. "There," he said. "D.D. I like the personal touch. This is a lot of boodle."

"It's nothing," said Parker. "I didn't know you Bureau guys knew how to put the firefly on a load."

"We don't," said Damico, still scrawling his initials. "Or I don't. But I've got a buddy in customs." He folded the last of the blankets back into place and jumped forward.

"Aren't you going to light up the dessert?"

"Huh?"

"The dessert," said Parker. "Under your seat in the flight bag. That stuff back there is just hay. I wouldn't touch it myself."

Damico retrieved the bag. "Holy mother of the devil!" he sputtered, as he ripped into the cellophane shroud. "Jesus! How much is this?"

"Enough to turn on every sparklehead between here and Palm Beach," said Parker.

"Oh, boy," sighed Damico. He scribbled in a frenzy and made little moaning noises, the bag resting on his knee.

"Put it on the tape," Parker suggested. "The cellophane's not porous enough to hold it."

Damico jerked the zipper shut. "Thanks," he said. He sniffed the sweet odor of the coating. "Fan the door a little, will you?" He replaced the bag, pulled a small object from his coat pocket, and slid out the door under the van. "Wait here."

Parker whispered after him, "Tracer?" Hearing only grunts and dim clanking sounds, he said "What else?"

Damico, breathing heavily, stuck his head back into the van. "Bon voyage," he grinned. "I hope Carlos talks a lot to whoever rides with him, and I hope he talks a lot to me on Monday. And I hope you all stay healthy. There. Don't ever say the Bureau never gave you a kind thought."

"Thanks," said Parker. "I think you're a straight guy, Dave. That's why I worry about you."

"Glad somebody does," said Damico. He crawled back into the underbrush, and Parker got out with his freedom pistol to resume the watch.

234

The parking lot sat on the landed end of a huge hammock that reached out into Biscayne Bay across the grounds of the magnificent Vizcaya, a priceless Italian villa whose stonework alone required the passion of a thousand artisans. It was now a city-owned museum, rented occasionally for private parties. On the sea side of the hammock, near the mangroves that flanked the formal gardens, Maraña strolled around a pagan altar the size of an elephant, from early Rome, of white stone carved with delicate wreaths and laughing faces and muscular torsos. He paused briefly, then headed back toward the villa. Two men hurried down a nearby foot bridge and fell in step behind him. Each carried a large briefcase.

"Good evening, gentlemen," Maraña said without stopping. "Let's just walk for a while."

They obliged. The first man was lean and tall, with black hair and a springy walk and mischievous blue eyes, dressed in an expensive blue Cardin suit. The second was an older and less springy replication of the first.

Maraña let them get closer. "This is a very international place, my friends," he said. "You see here on our left the exquisite Jasmin *Simplisefolium* hedge perfected in Italy by the spaghettis, like yourselves." The two men bristled. Maraña waved his arm like a tour guide toward the serpentine maze of hedges near the path. He was exercising his memory over the names of the foliages, which was one of his affectations, but he was also casting a wary eye across the gardens for intruders. "And here you see the bright green Bermuda grass in its winter growing lull," he continued. "And over there, like billy clubs, are the Japanese yew, or *Podocarpus*. Behind us in the distance are the lovely Australian pines, and between us and those statues of gods and goddesses over there you will see the amazing Virginian oak. See how in that long row of trees there the leaves have all grown together and they are trimmed flat and square like a giant bar of green gold. It is very beautiful, no? The Americans have made something good, no?"

Maraña lifted his dark glasses and turned to his companions as he walked. The older one was gazing around on his turret of a neck, impressed by the sights and descriptions. His colleague stared intently at Maraña, on the other hand, ignoring everything but Maraña's face. This may have been a mistake, for the sight seemed to have the effect of removing the sting from the best taunt he could think of. "Nature boy," he snickered.

Maraña lowered his glasses with a measured smile. Abruptly, he turned right through a high arching door in a giant wall of coral rock. It appeared to be a fortress, though it was nothing more than a minor architectural bauble in the gardens. The high inner walls were frescoed at the top with gnarled swirls of stone foliage. Beneath them, more delicately, swans lofted streams of water made of stone that trickled down the walls to pools made of water. Maraña walked through several grottoes within the compound and took a seat on the back of a peacock.

"Where are we?" groused the younger shadow.

"In the secret gardens," replied Maraña. "It seemed like the place to go. I just wanted to take a peek in your briefcases. A formality, you understand."

"Out here?" gasped the older man.

"Sure," said Maraña. "Don't be so nervous, my friend. There is nothing illegal about a lot of money. Now which one is the big share?"

"Mine," said the younger.

Maraña snapped his fingers and patted his lap. "Here," he commanded. He opened the briefcase and contemplated the inevitable stacks of money for barely an instant, then repeated the process over the lesser amount in the second. "There," he said. "No problems. No mess. We are building a working relationship, you see. Now this little one goes with me. And the big one goes with you. And I go with you. All together now." After snapping the briefcase shut, he walked briskly out of the sunken grotto, up the steps through the arching door and toward the villa's south wall, the blue-suited pair in tow.

"Hey!" growled the younger one under his breath. "Let's go around the building, not through it."

"I need some champagne," Maraña said glibly. "Wait here and I'll bring you some, if you like."

The pair, lockjawed with displeasure, followed Maraña toward accordion music and tinkling glasses and the conversational buzz of three hundred voices. They crashed a large private party by entering one of the castle's three huge stained-glass doors, twenty feet high, separated by stone columns and crowned with three arches of more stained glass depicting a sailing frigate between two seahorses. Maraña stood in the middle of a Neapolitan mosaic on the marble floor in the center of the tea room, the gardens behind him through the stained glass and the party ahead of him in the villa's courtyard. They were on the fringes of a crowd that was considerably enriched by the palatial setting, a crowd of more leisure than formality, silver hair but no gloves, more jewels and sandals than neckties.

A tray of champagne floated by. Maraña took two and wafted the bearer toward his new companions. As he did so, he caught sight of a lone figure leaning against a column at the far end of the glass doors, staring rather forlornly at the last glow of sunset. Amber and rose shadows were sprinkled on him through the glass pattern. Maraña drained one glass of champagne before sliding over next to the man. "*Americano,*" he said. "How come you never come to see me any more?"

Howell gulped from one dream to another. "Carlos?" he asked. "You are Carlos?"

"Max told me you would be here, but I didn't believe it," said Maraña. "I had decided you are a myth, David. I see your fonny stories now and then, but nobody ever sees you. You are becoming a shadowy character."

"Carlos," mumbled Howell, still in a stupor. "I can't believe it. Don't tell me anything strange, please. You probably own this palace. It's unbelievable. I feel like one of the pope's chimneysweeps."

"You do look a little below caliber," said Maraña. "What are you doing here?"

"I don't know." Howell blankly replied, looking down at himself. He was wearing a white dinner jacket over an orange Orioles T-shirt, blue jeans, and striped tennis shoes. "Oh, this?" he said. "Well, I went to an Orioles game today at spring training. It saved me. It really did. If you've been gutter-blind for a long time, then baseball can be a great antidote with all that sunshine and the kids and the hot dogs and stuff. I know that doesn't make much sense."

"Sure it does. Remember, Cubans love baseball," said Maraña. He put both champagne glasses on the floor, twitched, and glanced backward at the two men immediately behind. They were on the verge of a tantrum. The younger one jerked his head in the exit signal. Maraña took a quick breath. "Come see me soon, David," he said. "I still want to talk to you about my proposition, and you can explain why you are so upset by a nice party like this one. Okay?"

"Wait," blurted Howell. His head had cleared to its new prevailing mixture of secrets and fear, and he instinctively reached out to Maraña. "Just one thing!" he cried, glancing apprehensively at the two men behind Maraña's shoulder. "I may not see you! You always disappear!"

"Later, David," said Maraña. He whirled and walked off with the briefcase, followed closely by two unhappy companions.

Howell looked desperately after them, on his tiptoes. He pulled a scrap of paper from his coat pocket, and when urgency overwhelmed his reticence, he scrambled after Maraña, bolting around the two men, waving his paper in the air. "I can't stand it, Carlos," he pleaded, running alongside Maraña's business walk. "This weird note came today about my friend on the beach where I stay," he panted. "Does it mean anything to you?" He held it before Maraña's face on the run. "Seven years" was all it said, in pasted magazine letters.

Without stopping, Maraña jerked his head backward, his dark glasses jumping deftly to his forehead, and then he gave a look so frightening to Howell that he dropped the paper onto the blue mosaic. The Maraña party trampled it. One of the blue suits turned to retrieve the scrap for his own purposes, but Howell was there before him. He picked it up and started to run after Maraña again. Before he advanced the second step, the heel of a meaty palm struck him squarely in the chest. A sharp thud echoed through the tea room. Howell gasped. He thought he had swallowed his tongue, but then he realized that the noise had terrified him most. It was thunderous and unexpected. Heads turned in the room. The elder blue suit stood his ground but said nothing.

"Easy," Maraña said quietly. He was smiling contentedly, like a hobo in his long-lost ventilated shoes, but the volcanic tension was rising from his shoulders. He was just beneath the flash point. The blue suits felt it in their mouths and backed off. It further slackened Howell's jaw. "Why don't we get together soon?" smiled Maraña with a sense of theater. The gawkers around the tea room returned at least one eye to their business. Maraña put down his briefcase and shook Howell's hand warmly. "So we will see you tomorrow?" he smiled. He reached into his own pocket for pen and paper and began scribbling on his knee. The party returned to normal, except

237

for the blue suits. They had become progressively undone by this new Cuban and his holiday meanderings on the job. Edging as close as they dared to Maraña's elbows, they hung over him, vultures with glistening wax heads.

"There," said Maraña. "Thirteen twenty-one Thirteenth Street, my friend." He turned to the frowning blue suits. "No secrets," he assured them, waving the address for all to inspect. To Howell he turned quite pointedly and delivered a hypnotist's command: "Ten o'clock in the morning exactly, David. American time. Not late. And ask for me. It's a big place. *Ask*, my friend, and do not be afraid, okay?"

Howell nodded, still panting and spent but much better. He waved good-bye to the trio.

"Some stunt," muttered the younger blue suit as he pursued Maraña past a marble statue of Bacchus and down the grand stairs toward the path of torches. "No wonder you guys couldn't touch Castro."

"Who is that bird, anyway?" asked the leader.

"A friend of mine," chirped Maraña. "My Washington connection. He acts like a clown. That's his cover."

"You guys have different ways," said the younger.

"Yes, we do," said Maraña without interest. He stopped in the path and pulled out his walkie-talkie. "Now don't get jumpy," he said patronizingly to the pair. "I'm just calling home to make sure everything is all right."

Two very tense trigger hands warmed inside coats as Maraña said, "*Chico*, I'm coming home now. Is dinner ready?"

There was a brief crackling pause before Parker replied in his best imitation of *Casablanca* pidgin, "Oh, Carlos! Ze night she eez so dangerous, and I feel safe wiz you onlee."

Parker had his gun out by the time they passed through the last pair of torches. Nearing the van, Maraña motioned to the one without the brief-case. "In there," he said. "You've got thirty seconds to check it out." One man jumped into the van.

"I still don't like it," said Parker. "Why don't we just make the whole trade right here and go home?"

"Not a chance," said the blue suit. "If your *Latino* buddies want to jump this load, they'll find pieces of Carlos here."

A head soon poked out of the van. "Looks good so far," it said. "I'd guess eighty on the snow."

"Finest quality," said Maraña.

Not another word was spoken. Maraña jerked his head toward Parker, who received the suitcase from blue suit, who in turn nodded Maraña toward the driver's side of the van. Parker and the young one trotted off through the gravel toward their respective cars, while Maraña eased the van out into the road, the tester beside him, comforted with his gun. The van went ahead of the two cars up over the gridwork of elevated highways that traverse downtown Miami. Parker veered off back toward Carmen, who would be free as soon as Parker delivered the money to the two Cuban escorts. Damico, at a discreet distance, followed the van and its tail northward on the interstate.

"Turn right toward the beach," growled the tester. He was facing Maraña, wedged between the door and the back of his seat.

"Be happy to," said Maraña. "How far do I go with you?"

"Far enough."

As they swerved down the arc of the feeder lane that would put them eastbound over the Julia Tuttle Causeway, the back of Maraña's neck bristled. "Ah, my friend, this is a fonny business," he smiled. "You think I'm dealing you a hand, but of course I'm only shuffling the cards. Somebody else is dealing, I think."

"Shut up."

"Okay, but I'm very nervous. Cubans like to talk when they're nervous, you see. I guess it's all that strong coffee."

"I said shut up."

The van pulled out into the traffic, three cars ahead of its escort. Suddenly, two black sedans pulled from the shoulder of the highway across the mouth of the feeder lane. The leader lurched backward, as if to turn around, and bashed into its twin. They wound up in a minor tangle all across the lane. One man got out and held up a finger of apology to the cars behind. He had a word with the other driver. A woman from the car immediately behind the absurd mishap got out and tried to shoo the miscreants to the side. A screaming blue suit sat on his horn, trapped behind the blockade.

When Maraña crested the second of three small hills on the causeway, he cried, *"Mierda!"* and slammed on the brakes. The van skidded in a half arc down the acclivity as its terrified passenger whirled to see the blockade across the highway. Pulsing flashes from police lights bathed the night in red, turning a blue suit purple and a yellow neck sickly green. "Back!" screamed the tester. "Before they get too close!" He jammed his gun into Maraña's ribs.

Maraña grunted from the pain in his side and screamed a hoarse, "No problem!" But as he jerked the van around to retreat against the traffic, another flashing car leaped out of a crease in the divider and cut them off, forcing the van down a gentle grass slope toward the bay. It came to a precarious rest, penned in by two blockading sedans. Armed men rushed pell-mell toward the victims.

"Hold it!" screamed the tester through the open window. "I've got Maraña here, and if you birds let me go you can have him and the load! If you don't, I waste him!" With his left hand, he twisted Maraña's collar viciously.

"We're federal officers!" cried the leader. "DEA. You're under arrest, but if you want to shoot somebody, suit yourself!"

The tester listened to the scramble of feet outside as he whined in desperation. "Drive the crate into the bay!" he commanded, twisting Maraña's shirt even tighter.

"I can't swim," gasped Maraña.

A knock of metal sounded on the window behind the blue suit. He turned to face a gun, just as someone flung open the van's back doors. "Okay, okay, take it easy," he surrendered. "Sorry about that hostage play, pal," he said quickly to Maraña. "I thought it might've been some of your buddies. It was worth a shot."

"No problem," said Maraña.

There was not the slightest post-bust letdown for anyone, no backwater of wasted adrenaline. If anything the pace picked up, much to the surprise of the suspects. They were thrown briefly against the sides of the van and frisked. Doors were already slamming, tires screeching. Blue suit was yanked into another car, and Maraña found himself in the passenger's seat of the van. "I'm Mike," said the driver.

The van lurched back on the highway. Maraña braced himself. "Isn't this an unusual procedure?" he asked. The agent ignored him. Maraña rubbed both hands distractedly through his hair and then began to tremble. "What are you going to do to me?" he wailed. "I know I'm on your side. I know it. Please let me go!"

"Big tough Carlos Maraña," sneered Mike.

"Where are we going?"

The DEA agent leaned back against the driver's seat with exaggerated nonchalance. "Well, that's up to you, ol' buddy," he advised. "I'm either gonna slap the cuffs on you in a minute and put you away for about twenty years if I'm lucky, or I'm gonna give you some money and let you convoy this load right up Miami Beach just like nothing ever happened. How does that sound?"

"It sounds like you're trying to get me killed. Please don't do this. I'm begging you, man. I don't even know where to take the stuff, anyway. That other guy knew where to go."

"Hold it a second." Mike pulled out his walkie-talkie as he drove and carried on a muttered conversation. "Uh huh," he concluded. "Well, your Italian pal squealed, Carlos, so we know where the rendezvous is."

Maraña made small fearful noises. "Oh no," he said. "I don't believe that guy talked. Not this quick. You guys must have an in with these characters already. What do you need me for? Why don't you just let me go? I'll give you all the money, man. Money's no problem."

"You better shut up, Carlos," said Mike. "I'm disappointed in you. I heard you were a classy Cuban, and now you're gettin' all emotional when I'm tryin' to offer you a hell of a deal."

Maraña meekly succumbed and took the wheel of the van. Mike directed him north on Alton Road, up the west side of Miami Beach, and was spitting out orders on what Maraña should say about the arrested Italian and about the one who had been detained behind the highway roadblock. Maraña gulped along uneasily. Mike planned to hop out of the van shortly. He was telling Maraña what terrible things would happen to him if he reneged on the deal when the van crossed a small hump of a bridge over one of the canals that bring pleasure craft from Biscayne Bay to the interior of Miami Beach, not far from the Ziller home. Maraña interrupted the briefing as he drove on. "Excuse me," he said. "We've picked up a cop or two, I think."

There was a bolt of silence in the van. Mike studied Maraña, who appeared to be staring straight ahead, casually. Too casually. It took a few seconds for the DEA agent to realize that the eyes behind the dark glasses on the composed face were darting about from one rear view mirror to another. Mike leaned out his window to catch sight of the Dade County police squad car following clumsily behind. "Take it easy," he said. "That bonehead's probably not after us. If he is, he's an idiot in a fuckin' big pile of trouble. You just keep drivin' and drop me off anywhere as soon as we're out of sight of him." He sounded husky, like a lover.

"No problem," said Maraña.

As the road approached a larger canal, an elevated bridge rose from its center and twisted into a banked left turn before descending gradually on the other side. Maraña stayed in the right lane as long as he could, heading toward the flatter span that curved to the right, and then he eased into the steep narrow one on the left. The squad car did the same. Sight of its lazy pursuit twisted the silence in the van another turn.

The elevated lane bent most sharply at its zenith, some forty feet above the roadbed on either side of the canal. Passing this point, the occupants of the van obtained something of an aerial view—Miami across the bay in the distance, a grid of city blocks ahead and below with their gold streetlights playing on low white buildings. They also saw squad cars converging at high velocity on the mouth of their ramp. Flashers began to blaze.

"Shit! Shit! Shit!" roared Mike, his head jerking vehemently like the kick of artillery. "You had somethin' to do with this, you goddam black beaner!"

Maraña said nothing. He was peering stonily from side to side, as though estimating the pain of a jumping escape to the water on the left or pavement on the right.

The agent pulled a gun from his shoulder holster. "No tricks out of you, asshole," he growled. "I'd just as soon shoot you now for tryin' to escape."

Maraña stopped the van and raised his hands like an outlaw. Doors were opening on police cars a hundred feet away, front and rear. Mike gave Maraña one last look of rage. Then he nearly kicked his own door off its hinges and jumped out to scream at the top of his fury: "HOLD IT YOU FLATFOOTED BIRDFUCKERS! C'MERE, GODDAMMIT!" He stomped his foot as he waved his captors forward.

Crouched next to the front tire of his squad car, one of the uniformed policemen became rattled by the conduct of this drug suspect, armed and raving as he was, and so he promptly fired two warning shots over Mike's head. At first Mike did not believe it had happened. He soon changed his mind, however, for several other uniformed cops and even some of the undercover drug detectives let fire at the van. Mike, cursing plaintively, dived back in, as Maraña crawled in the back to lie flat on a bale of marijuana. As incoming slugs cracked the windshield, Mike fired a couple of rounds through the back window of the van to keep the officers in the trail car at bay. The gunfire almost deafened the two men in the van, who were squirming and making strange noises they were not aware of. Maraña summoned the presence of mind to wave his handkerchief out the window.

Mike threw his gun around the window post. It went skittering down the street toward the downhill cluster of the posse and was instrumental in restoring the peace, along with the bullhorn of a tall beer-gutted tubular man in a loud yellow sports jacket. He was the chief investigator from the state attorney's office, more or less running things along with the lieutenant in charge of the narcotics squad and the chief of the tactical antiterrorist unit.

Ten seconds had passed since Mike first left the van. In the precious silence that followed the cessation of hostilities, some participants were thankful to hear familiar sounds again—passing cars, police radios, distant airplanes, the canal breeze—and more than a few lifted silent prayers. The chief investigator kept telling everybody it was over.

Exiting the van with the utmost caution, the suspects faced an approaching posse whose mood was now as surly as it had been shaky before, burning off residual fear. The chief investigator lit a very long cigarette as he moved in behind his men and his bullhorn. Suddenly, his voice rose high above the police chatter. "Well, looka here, boys!" he cried. "We got two big ones here! Real big! We got mister international master spy and bomb man himself, and on top of that we've got us a fed, it looks like. Howdy, Mike! It sure is a surprise to see you!" His joy grew as the dimensions of his catch registered on him, so that by the end his face was shining with the demonic pleasure that comes rarely to those so well versed in the wormy aspects of human nature. There was champagne in his voice. All that remained of his emphysema was a tiny crackle of popping hot grease.

The DEA agent dropped his hands, finally recognized. "Very funny," he sneered. "You guys really know how to fuck up an operation, all right. All you need is a tent and you'd be a goddam circus! Now gimme my gun and get the fuck outa here! This is a federal case. No yokels!"

Merrily, the chief investigator held up his palms. "Now hold it, hold it, hold it," he said. "This guy's your collar? Is that what you're sayin'? He doesn't *look* busted to me. You didn't notify *us* that anything was going down tonight, now did you?"

"You know better than that," growled Mike. "You didn't notify us either. I had me a nice little convoy here heading toward the big guys, and you guys blew it for me. Nice work!"

"You always ride *with* your convoys?" chortled the investigator. "Just to help out and make sure things go smooth, eh?"

"None of your business," said Mike.

Maraña was bouncing primly on the balls of his feet. "I do my best, Mike," he said in a heavy Spanish accent. "We almost make it."

Mike stared sideways in shock. "Shut up, spic!" he exploded, and caught Maraña on the jaw with a whirling backhanded roundhouse. Several of the onlooking officers blinked. Maraña fell back against the van, his mouth bleeding profusely from tooth wounds.

The chief investigator tucked his bullhorn under his arm and looked at the pavement in sour disappointment. "For God's sake, Mike, you can't say that kind of shit around here," he said. "Maybe in Washington, but not here. We have some minority language officers right here on the narcotics squad."

"Yeah, " said one officer in the background, who went on to make a spic joke or two at the expense of officers Diaz and Medrano, who responded with jokes of their own. Everyone was nervous. There was no feeling of resolution to this bust, owing to the peculiar circumstances. The DEA man said nothing. He did not even acknowledge the words of the chief investigator and instead looked directly at Maraña. The hatred in his face was tinged with puzzlement, as ideas and suspicions tried to crowd their way in among the heaving passions. An intense, transparent struggle appeared there and threw attention on Maraña, who was daubing his mouth with the surrender handkerchief. Maraña did not look right to anybody. There was an air of achievement and even serenity about his carriage as he leaned against the van, and his cheeks, fully visible now that the blow had knocked off his dark glasses, seemed to be growing more youthful and full even as his eyes lazily surveyed the scene.

"Something smells here," Mike declared quietly. "Something really smells."

"For you, my friend, that is quite an observation," said Maraña with an unmistakable gleam. "You are a real—how do you say?—piece of work."

The chief investigator, who was also troubled by Maraña's projected well-being, exchanged nods with the narcotics lieutenant, communicating thereby a conviction that the dialogue was unpromising. The lieutenant snapped his fingers. "Let's get the cuffs on Maraña there," he said to no one in particular. "Uh, as long as Mike here will promise not to slap him anymore. So let's get on with it."

Mike, amid the police bustle, tapped the side of his nose while thoughtfully sniffing for clues. "You weren't like this, all chipper and all, when I got hold of you," he mused of Maraña to no one. Turning to the chief investigator, he snapped out of it. "I'm gonna need to know your snitch," he announced. "You might as well get used to the idea, 'cause this case is too important. You don't realize how big it is. It goes all over the country and into several foreign countries, too."

The chief investigator was amused. He sidled over and replied in a whisper, "You give me your snitch first, and then we'll talk."

"Boy, you better snap out of it. I'm not out here with cobras like him just for kicks. Now I'm telling you and the cops that you're all in a lot of trouble if you don't cooperate with me. You've already fucked up a U.S. case right in the middle. You've fired on a federal officer. You've failed to exercise control over the men under your supervision. You've fired the first shot without sufficient provocation. You fired without announcing yourselves or your purpose. You've broken every rule in the book, and now you want to stand around and keep secrets. I'm gonna have your fat rich ass canned, and then you'll have to go to work for one of those wiretap companies you love so much."

The chief investigator took umbrage at these remarks, and reared up to the full advantage of his superior height. "*I'm* in trouble, eh?" he snickered. "Let me tell you something, Mike. For all I know you're a rogue narc, see? They're all around. You could be in on this. You know, riding shotgun for Carlos Maraña doesn't look too good to me."

"It was a very sophisticated operation," said Mike.

"Uh huh," came the reply, "And how many other buys did you bust tonight besides Maraña? And where are they?"

This question the DEA man pondered with care. "I'm not authorized to tell you," he replied.

"Oh yeah? Don't give me that shit."

"Yeah. Have another helping."

The argument continued in this vein, without material advancement, as technicians dusted the van for fingerprints and tagged the evidence. They estimated the briefcase cash at four hundred thousand. Backup men from the DEA arrived to support Mike's side of the dispute and to insist on double-tagging the evidence with their green and black stickers. The entire scene took on a devilish glow from the carnival of whirling red lights, still in full force when Dave Damico trudged up from behind.

"You guys sure do have traffic backed up," he said by way of greeting to the chief inspector. "What's going on?"

"No hook in it for you, Damico," said Mike.

"Hey, that's okay. I've got plenty of business. Mind if I take a look at the booty?"

"Help yourself." Several shoulders in the executive group around the yellow sports jacket turned toward Damico. They snubbed him together and shared a flicker of unity, having in common a dislike for the Bureau.

Damico left them to their work and inspected the van like a car salesman. All he knew since getting delayed behind the two-car roadblock on the highway was that something fishy had happened. Now he saw that there was no blue-suited Italian there with Maraña, whom he greeted with feigned surprise. He managed to retrieve his recorder from the heater duct without detection. Then he sauntered back over to the cabal, trying not to look depressed. "You guys working this case together?" he asked.

"Kind of," replied the chief investigator. "What's it to you?"

"Oh, nothing. I just wondered whose tracer that is under the van there. Right there. It's a handy little thing to have on a tail."

This question caused much consternation, as Mike and the chief investigator eyed each other warily, figuring the angles. Not to claim the tracer might be to forfeit a stake in the bust, which would be bad. On the other hand, anyone who claimed the tracer might have to explain it, which would be tough for them, given their ignorance of how it got there. Which was troublesome to both, especially to Mike. He had a more delicate operation to worry about, and if there were tracers there could be other things. And of course, Damico could be lying just to make a fool of the man who would come forward to claim a nonexistent tracer.

244

After fumbling as long as possible, Mike said, "I told you you could look around, Damico. I didn't say to inspect the crime scene." He pushed his way to the van without committing himself, ahead of the perplexed investigator. On his hands and knees, Mike yanked the tracer off the drive shaft. "See?" he grinned. "Didn't even need it."

"I don't like this at all," said the chief investigator.

"You guys don't seem too sure of yourselves tonight," said Damico, trying to grind as much uncertainty into Mike as he could. "You sure you're okay?"

"Yeah, big daddy," Mike replied. "We're okay. You can shove off now."

Damico left with a lingering frown, anxious to hear his tape but fearful that the crunch had come too soon to make a corruption case. His delicate trap had been trampled upon during its construction, and Damico felt the direst of premonitions—that he would never get another chance.

At the jail Maraña walked between the yellow sports jacket and the DEA man into the glare of television lights. Both officers handled the media reception awkwardly, doubtless because of the troublesome questions that might arise from the two separate arrests and the dual custody. Mike was gaining the upper hand, but no one could tell it from his demeanor outside the jail. He all but ducked his head. Maraña, on the other hand, smiled expansively and raised his manacled fists in the air. He detoured slightly into the gaggle of reporters who were shouting questions and his name.

"Hey, Carlos! Did you shoot anybody tonight?"

"How did it happen?"

"Were you going to bomb Castro with grass?"

"How does it feel to have somebody snitch on you for a change?"

"Have you switched from politics to drugs?"

"Hey, Carlos! We heard it was a mixed load of cocaine and grass and a lot of money. How much money? Isn't that a wacky kind of smuggling?"

Maraña hushed the crowd a bit by responding to the last question as the chief investigator dragged him through the crowd. "What's crazy about it?" he grinned. "Anti-Castro Cubans *always* have half a million in cash on them when they go smuggling, my friend. And we *always* have a good man from the DEA riding with us all the way. What's so fonny about that?"

"What?"

"Who rode with you?"

"What are you talking about?"

"Are you saying it was a set-up?"

"Shut up," said Mike, pushing his way through.

"Did Castro have anything to do with this?"

"How about the CIA?"

"Are you saying those weren't your drugs on the van?"

"No," said Maraña over his shoulder. "They weren't mine, and I wouldn't sell them, anyhow. If they *were* mine, they were for my own personal use!"

There was a wave of laughter under the shouting. "Three *tons* of marijuana for your own use!?"

"That's enough!" shouted Mike. "You'll find it all out in court."

"How much can he get for this?"

"Life," said the chief investigator.

"You bet your life," Maraña called out, making a victory sign high above his head as he went through the cellblock door.

The following morning, as the hour of ten approached, David Howell walked back and forth on the pavement in front of a cavernous white building situated in a cluster of such buildings on the shoulder portion of Miami, by the map. Howell's look was aimless. Staring one last time at a scrap of paper in his hand, he shrugged off toward the mastodon called Public Safety.

"Excuse me, I'm looking for a man named Carlos Maraña," he told a mutton-chopped attendant at the information desk. "Do you know if he works here?"

The attendant peered over the silver spectacles that relieved his sallow complexion. "I believe you're serious," he said. "Mister Maraña seems to be the most popular man in the whole building this morning. It's very exciting. I'm not supposed to say that, but it is. Earl, one of the night guards, says Maraña broke a window upstairs just by looking at it. Earl swears it. I don't believe that sort of stuff, but it never hurts to listen. No, to me it doesn't hurt."

"What's exciting?"

"The whole thing. They call him Third Cat, because he's already used up his nine lives twice. He's mixed up with the Russians, if you ask me. They're mixed up in this somehow."

"Mixed up in what?" queried Howell.

The attendant looked about in a conspiratorial manner. "In this," he said, pointing toward a tiny article that had been rushed into his morning *Herald*: STRANGE TRAP NETS MYSTERY SPY—MARAÑA NABBED IN SHOOT-OUT. The article described how a "combined strike force of federal and local officers" captured Maraña the previous evening in a blazing gun battle. It summarized the public knowledge of the suspect's career as an explosives expert with rumored ties to Castro, the CIA, and several foreign governments, who had survived at least five attempts on his life by bomb and pistol. Howell grew wobbly as he read on through hints that the arrest might not be what it seemed—allusions to strange unprofessional conduct by Maraña, smuggling a smorgasbord of drugs and money through the heart of Miami Beach in the early evening, and references to conflicting statements by unnamed officers.

"Beats everything, doesn't it?"

"Sure does," sighed Howell, who was pale.

"You know him?"

"Kind of."

The attendant gave a clandestine wink of understanding. "You must be CIA," he said. "One thing they missed though."

"What's that?"

246

"The voodoo."

"The voodoo?"

"Yes sir. You better believe it. The Cubans around here are thick in the voodoo. Not like the Haitians, of course, but I'm telling you that Little Havana is full of witches and dolls and chicken necks and stuff. Sure is. And I'm telling you. You put the Russians together with the voodoo and what do you think you get?"

Howell was still staring at the newspaper. "Russian voodoo?" he guessed vaguely.

"That's right," said the attendant with undue satisfaction. "You get Mister Maraña there and a lot of trouble for Uncle Sam. That's why he's got them buffaloed. All the lawyers in hell couldn't figure it out, if you ask me."

"Uh huh. Tell me, what's the address here?"

The attendant told him.

"That's what I thought. How would I go about calling on a prisoner?"

"Go back outside and walk around to the big side door. You can't miss it."

"Thanks," said Howell, moving away.

"Don't mention it," said the attendant. "And one more thing, since you're, you know, *working* on Maraña. I know the score. Well, you don't have to believe in it, but I recommend that you put a little dab or two of aloe on the tip of your nose at midnight after every time you see him. For protection."

"Thanks again," said Howell.

The attendant nodded brightly and went back to his horoscope.

Howell, fortifying himself on the march, resolved to concentrate on the mysteries close to his own life and to ignore the others. He wanted to know about Ziller. On this thought, he walked into a large basement chamber filled with echoes and sobs. Shocked relatives of car thieves and pugilists clung to each other as they endured the room's cold humiliation, waiting to see freshly nabbed young ones. Lawyers and bondsmen and more veteran relatives passed the time of day in chairs around the perimeter of the room, oblivious to the sobbers. Relatives and skinny young arrivals in handcuffs were escorted occasionally through a heavy metal door on the far side of the room. Next to the metal door was a small window, behind which sat a sergeant who had dulled himself to the proceedings over the space of three years.

"Uh huh?" he droned at Howell, as he picked slowly at the loose skin on the back of one elbow.

"Um, I'd like to see a new prisoner named Carlos Maraña. I believe he was arrested last night."

"You do, huh? Got a badge?"

"No."

"You a relative?"

"No."

The sergeant ran his tongue over both rows of teeth and twitched his nose slightly, like a cow clearing gnats from a runny nostril. "Reporter?"

"Um, well. More of a personal friend."

As much as anything could be said to strike the sergeant, this struck him as unlikely. He looked sideways toward a jail passage out of Howell's view. "One friend a week," he muttered. "Regulations. Official visitors have priority. Then relatives. There's nine ahead of you, all official. Try again in March, maybe."

"March? Listen. He *asked* me to come see him. Can't you check somehow?"

"Uh huh," grunted the sergeant, so bored that he might just as well have called Howell a liar.

"Really," urged Howell.

"When?"

"Um, I got a message last night."

"Uh huh." The sergeant tried a drop-dead look on Howell, who dared not retreat, and then he took his face out of gear to reach lazily for a phone. Howell fidgeted for five minutes. On two occasions he saw the sergeant's jaw move slightly. Finally, he hung up the phone and slid a pink card under the window. "Fill this out," he said.

"You mean I get to see him?"

"And have a seat over there."

Howell did as he was told. The room seemed quieter to him, and he felt the pressure of many eyes. Several men in conservative suits eyed him carefully as they tapped new shoes on the concrete floor. When a young body-builder of an officer banged through the metal door to call, Howell jumped out of his seat. He walked shakily out of sight, feeling cold everywhere except for a hot spot in the back of his neck. The officer heaved the door shut.

"This way," said the officer, heading down the only corridor there was. He turned right, climbed a few stairs, and led the way past a row of small doors that reminded Howell of squash courts. There was a smell of hot sweat and tobacco. The officer opened one of the doors and Howell went into a small compartment with two chairs and a thick metal grating that divided him from Maraña.

Howell collapsed faintly into a chair. "Good God, Carlos. Why didn't you tell me you'd be here? Are you all right?"

"I am alive," said Maraña. "No man in jail is all right." His smile was drawn, and a tautness about the eyes and forehead evidenced a hard night.

Howell studied Maraña and then ran his eye over the compartment, imagining what lies and sad pleadings had passed through the partition between them. "This is just like in the movies," he said, and then, shaking away his thoughts, said, "Please be gentle with me, Carlos. I can't understand your world and I don't think I want to. Besides that, my stomach doesn't feel so good, to tell you the truth. I've lost my grip a little bit. Now I know you've got worries of your own right now and everything, but I'd really appreciate anything you could tell me about Bobby Ziller."

"I knew him slightly," said Maraña. "A very entertaining fellow."

248

"I thought you did, from what you said at Vizcaya . . ."

". . . Beautiful palace, isn't it?" Maraña interrupted. "How did you like the party, my friend?"

"It's a fairyland," sighed Howell. "The party really threw me for a loop. This guy I met at Ziller's named Arlington Spencer rented the place to impress his new girlfriend. I went there expecting to see all the hippies and radicals and bohemian rich brats having a big time—you know, like the ones I knew in New York and Washington, only older now . . ."

". . . And they weren't there?"

"Yes, they were there. But so were a lot of Cubans, you know. People I'd interviewed. People I couldn't imagine in the same room were there. My night world and my day world came together. Pepe Lopez was there, even."

Maraña's face hardened. "He was? Are you sure?"

"Yes. He asked me to say hello to you if I saw you, but I didn't think I would."

Maraña looked off and then seemed to relax. "Oh well, we are safe in jail," he smiled. "Don't worry."

"I wasn't worried. It just threw me off. The right wing and the left wing were there together and they turned out to be not as opposite as I thought."

"It takes two wings to fly," grinned Maraña.

"Pepe was very nice, I thought. He said he was out of the conspiracy business. He didn't seem like a killer to me."

"You are a baby, my friend."

Howell cleared his throat. "Anyway, I wanted to find out something about my friend Ziller, so I've been playing private eye all weekend. And nothing makes sense. Nobody from Ziller's family wants to report him missing, and nobody really wants to talk about where he's gone. So that was bad enough, but then that note arrived yesterday . . ."

". . . The one with the address on it?"

Howell did a double-take. "No," he said. "The one that said seven years. Come on, Carlos. Don't do this to me. *You* gave me the one with the address on it."

"I'm sure it was the other way around," Maraña declared. He looked very somber.

Howell stared at him in disbelief. His weak laugh gave way to fear and he rubbed his eyes. "That's not funny, Carlos," he said. "I know you gave me the one with the address on it. *This* address! That's how I got here!"

Maraña pretended to mull this over. "Mmmmm, that is very interesting, my friend. I will have to tell my attorneys, you know, because if you are so sure that I told you I would be in jail *before* I was arrested, somebody might think I knew all about it in advance, you know. Like the whole thing was an undercover operation that went, you know, haywire."

Howell rubbed his eyes further as his tongue swam in a rush of saliva. "You can see that I'm still very slow in these things," he said. "Please don't get me into this, Carlos."

"Beautiful," said Maraña. "I sure am glad I insisted that you come see me."

"This is not a joke, Carlos. I'm trying to get out of one thing, and I step right into another one."

"Just like your country, eh?"

"Oh, come on."

"I'm sorry, David. I don't want to offend your patriotism. I know how patriotic you are. But for my own selfish reasons, I'm happy you remember that way about the note. And I know you'll see it as your patriotic duty to keep the note and tell the truth about it if my lawyers call you to the court."

Howell lowered his eyes from Maraña's easy gaze. "You're just toying with me," he accused. "You're using me to get yourself out of something, and you don't really give a damn if it gets me in trouble, do you?"

"But you are learning a lot, no?"

"No. I'm not, really. You haven't told me anything about the seven years note . . ."

". . . It's all right, my friend," Maraña interrupted. "I want to be fair with you, believe me. Fairer than you deserve. Believe me. We will not need you in the court, I don't think. So you can forget about that. I was just thinking about what a good time we could have if you told everybody about it. And if you described the two nervous spaghettis who were with me. You don't realize how much trouble you could cause."

"That's just great," sighed Howell.

"And about the note," sighed Maraña. He folded his hands before him in a pose of menacing tension. "You are not going to like it, my friend. It is very sad, and very very stupid. The note means that the baghettis are going to punish your friend's family for seven years."

Howell squirmed in his chair. "What? What baghettis? What does that mean?"

"Well, you know what is a bagel? Okay? And you know what is a spaghetti? So the baghettis are the alliance of those two, and they have been very important in this country for many years. But now the Cubans are pushing the baghettis out of the drug trade. That's what I hear, anyway."

"Uh huh."

"Of course. And the baghettis have many stupid customs. One of them is that when they discover a betrayer, they dispose of him in a way that will punish and disgrace his family. It's personal then, not just business. That's what they say. So I'm afraid your friend's body will never be discovered. That means he cannot be declared dead for seven years, so his estate and his will are frozen. His insurance will not be good until then, and his family will suffer because they will not even know for sure he is dead." Maraña made an impish sign of the cross.

Howell's numb mind contemplated a vision of LaLane Rayburn and Bobby Ziller at a crowded press conference at the Mayflower Hotel, discussing MIAs of different worlds. "Why?" he mumbled.

Maraña paused. "What's the matter, my friend? You don't seem as upset as I thought you'd be. I thought this man was a good friend of yours."

Howell stared, face flushed, at a blur of the jail grating. "Well, I don't even know he's dead, for sure," he said softly. "Not that I don't trust your opinion. And besides, I don't know what kind of friend he really was. He was a really spirited *character*, I know that. But I only saw him a few times, so I don't think he's a friend, or was a friend, especially now if he's a memory and I realize that maybe all I got and all I have is a salty glimpse of him. Oh, why?" He licked his lips in distraction. "You know, Carlos, I'm not sure what this means, but I'm not really reacting much. It scares me."

"Rumors are very scary."

"Why? Why would anybody kill him?"

"Well, from what I hear, your friend was a small-time, subshit drug dealer who got caught, and the authorities turned him into an informant under pressure, you see, for their own purposes. That much I'm pretty sure of. And my impression is that the baghettis found out. So poof! They kill him and throw him in the bay like one of those new diapers, what do you call them?"

"Pampers?"

"Yes, and it's stupid," Maraña declared, squeezing one hand with the other. He was getting angry. "Stupid, I tell you. And you know why? Because if *I* were the baghettis and *I* found out that he had been informing against me all this time, and that the federal authorities were playing footsie with him like they always do, you know what I'd do?"

"No," murmured Howell, shrinking from the wrath.

"I'll tell you!" spat Maraña. "I'd call him in and say, 'My friend, you are my number one man!' And he would be my eyes and my ears with the authorities. Within a month, I would know every weakness and every personality, if I didn't know it already! And I would *have* them! My advantages would grow because they are weak and dirty and because I feel no *guilt*, you see?"

"I think so," quavered Howell.

"But not the baghettis! It's all because of their *heads*, you know. They think they are the bad guys in a cowboy movie, so they act like the bad guys! When one of their guys gets in trouble, they have to kill him, you see. It's pathetic, really. They have these silly little rituals, like college boys. I don't even think that seven years business is a law anymore, but they still write those notes for the fun of it. They are a backward people, you know."

"Uh huh," came the lame assent. Howell, looking downward, spoke under his breath, "Just tell me, Carlos, that you didn't have anything to do with getting Bobby killed. Just for me."

Sitting back in his chair, Maraña beamed with pleasure. "For you, David, I will give the denial," he laughed. "I don't know why, but I will. Maybe it's your pale face or the harmless way you try to catch on. I will say this to you, David. My belief is that your friend and I were involved with some of the same people, for different reasons. And I think maybe they were trying to

251

jump from him to me without a clear idea of what they were doing. Without any idea, really. And without a brain, how can they have any principles? So maybe they were finishing with him to get to me. But I did not wish him dead. I had no reason. That would be unkind, don't you think?"

"I don't know," Howell replied. "It just seemed to me that if you knew he was a snitch, you could have hurt him if you wanted to. I don't have any idea how this is done, but I hear from important Americans that you Cubans can't keep from talking about what you know."

This seemed to add to Maraña's cheerfulness. "I've heard that one myself, David," he said. "Many times. It has always amused me, because it shows how blind you Americans can be. You think you are infiltrating us, and we are really infiltrating you. You think Cubans don't know when to talk and when not to. It is very strange, you know. I remember in your Watergate business, the Cubans accepted sentences of forty years and didn't say a word, while very important Americans all the way up in the White House broke down in tears completely and conspired against their friends to keep out of jail for six months. I have seen stupid Cubans take life sentences in quiet while the greatest of the American silent spies are gabbing all night with their newspaper friends, but still you hear that the Cubans can't keep their mouths shut. And it's fonny . . ."

". . . Well, I agree on that . . ."

". . . because listen, my friend. There has been a long time when all you Americans had to know about anybody around the world was whether they are communist or anticommunist. That's it. Nothing about the heart, nothing about the language or dreams. Even the CIA. That's it. But not anymore. Because you are just some of the happy foreigners doing complicated things. Like me, you see." Maraña spread his arms from one side of the jail booth to the other and took a bow.

Howell slowly raised his eyes. "You know, Carlos, I don't know how you got in this jail or what you're gonna do about it," he said, "but I get the feeling you *like* it a little bit."

Maraña changed form. "No!" he thundered, slamming a fist onto the desk in the booth and turning around in the same motion, so that when Howell's pulse returned and the ringing in his ears became bearable he saw only a heaving back above the tan trousers with a jagged sweat line under the belt, like a mountain range in the distance. And he saw one of Maraña's clenched fists pull out a bloody handkerchief as he whirled back toward the grating. "No, I do not like jail!" hissed Maraña. "Nobody likes it! I can be fonny about where I am, my friend, but *you* can't. Do you know there are people in this jail right now who are sworn to kill me! Do you know that I have asked to be put in solitary confinement for my own protection! Do you know that three Cuban groups have condemned me to death this morning in the newspaper! Do you understand anything! I try to be hospitable to you while I am doing the things I *have* to do, David, but that doesn't mean I like jail. Understand?"

Howell had put his head between his hands in shock and, without realizing it, was half breathing and half whistling a pop tune whose lyrics run, "Chains! My baby's got me locked up in chains." He ceased when Maraña's silence demanded it. "What happened to your mouth?" he asked quietly, observing the blood in one corner.

Maraña's whole body jerked from side to side, as though picking a spot in the wall to storm through. "From one of the idiot spaghetti authorities I met last night!" he exclaimed, calming to a tight, mocking anger. "One of the shits, David. That's what I deal with all the time—the shits and the subshits. What do you think of that?" He wiped his mouth carelessly.

"Not much," Howell replied. He bounced slowly up and down as his curiosity chased his fear. "I'm sorry you got hurt, Carlos," he said, "but there's something I don't understand. I don't understand why you *do* all this. You're smart and you're too cynical for the causes. Why don't you just retire and live a quiet prosperous life somewhere with your war stories? Why don't you just get out of all this shit?"

"Aha!" Maraña exulted, seizing the metal grating with two bloodless hands. "Now you are talking about something, my friend. You are talking about motivation!" He squeezed the grating as he settled into an intense whisper, "And I will say, David, that I became fascinated. Yes, fascinated. Fascinated." He seemed to glory in the word, emphasizing its penultimate syllable. "You see, I tried to know everything about the world and the other worlds, and maybe I tried to know too much. And I became fascinated. Fascinated, David. Sometimes you can feel it on your skin. I became fascinated with the target, like a fighter pilot. Do you understand what I mean, David?"

Howell, wide-eyed and transfixed, nodded dumbly.

"Well, you know we had the T–28 fighters in the Congo with Cuban pilots, . . ." said Maraña.

". . . Yes, I talked with some of them . . ."

". . . and the best of them and the first to die was my friend Arturo," said Maraña, excitement rising. "And we used to talk at night about the perils of being a fighter pilot, you know, because Arturo knew he had it. He was the most alive of any of us, the only one who learned any tribal language. He was always climbing trees like Tarzan and giving the kids rides on his shoulders, and he even took some of the Africans up in the plane with him, against orders. He had a very happy disposition. But, my friend, he was also fascinated. And one day, way in the sky, Arturo *stayed* fascinated with the target. He hit the ground at over 300 miles an hour. Poof, you see? Fascinated!"

Howell shuddered.

"There!" cried Maraña. "You feel it on your skin?"

"Um, nothing wrong with the plane?"

"Not a thing."

"Was he a kamikaze or something, some kind of suicide?"

"Of course not. There were only Africans there. Nothing to hate, for a Cuban. It was the pure fascination, David."

"Uh huh."

"In 1964. Yes, and I saw the wreck. I saw the telegram President Mobutu sent to Arturo's family, very secret. And I saw my boss put the cash in Mobutu's hands once or twice, always on Friday. Very secret. And I saw the wreck. It was fascinating then. Now it is nothing."

Howell was still collecting his will. "Um, and what's the target now?" he asked.

"Ah, the target!" grinned Maraña. "That is a different subject. I don't think you know enough for that. We are only talking about motivation."

Howell's slow thoughts gave way to a loud knock on the door behind Maraña. "Time's up," growled a bored, laconic voice, whose owner stuck a face that matched in the room as the metal on his hip hit the door.

Maraña turned to face him. "Just a minute, please, Officer," he said graciously. "We are just planning my escape."

Howell swallowed awkwardly. The officer's wooden face walked around the booth by inches before cracking into a mischievous leer. "All right," he drawled. "I'll get your gun. One minute."

"Two minutes," Maraña called after him. He turned back to Howell. "Nice guy," he said.

"Uh huh," Howell sighed. "You are one tough enchilada, Carlos. I'm just saying I wish you could move up to a cattle ranch near Pensacola or something, and be fascinated up there. That's all."

Maraña, still holding the grating, his head resting on an arm, looked suddenly bored. "Ah, you are a dreamer, David," he said testily. "Listen. I have been in one conspiracy or another for fifteen years, since I was twenty-one. My life has been sneaking in and out of countries, moving weapons, shooting people, trading rumors, staying up late at night, and always a lot of waiting. I have always done the same thing. Once I was a noble part of your government, and now they hunt me. But I do the same. You think I should go back to college or something, David? The time is gone, and inside me I have lost the formation for the happy normal life. To me, I am normal. So enough of that. *You* go to Pensacola and farm the cows!"

Howell leaned back briefly to study the face that had closed abruptly, wiped clean of everything except square edges and corners, a cubist face with dark boxes for eyes, its roundness leeched out of it. Howell chuckled in spite of himself. "You know, it's fonny," he said, mimicking Maraña, "I'm not sure I'd do any better with the cows than you, Carlos. I ran around all through my twenties, too. My sit-ins and my sympathies and my words have been going all over the world. I'd have trouble with the cows. Fascinating."

Maraña showed no sighs of fascination. Instead, he let go of the grating and lowered himself to his chair slowly, as though the air were seeping from his legs. The anger was gone. He seemed quite weary. "I had a rough night playing with the police, David," he said. Then he looked slowly at Howell, liquid pools forming inside the arid borders of his face. "My life is ruined, you know. That is what I've been trying to tell you. That's what I want you to write for me. I am a very unhappy man, David."

Howell said nothing, waiting for the next word. In the silence, he heard bursts of mournful Spanish in the corridors, along with clanging doors and confined echoes and other jail sounds fitting for Maraña's confessional metamorphosis. Howell fidgeted for his intrusion, as no further words came from Maraña, who appeared lost elsewhere. "I thought you were fascinated," Howell said gently.

Maraña ignored him. "It is not the honor," he opined, mostly to himself. "*Latinos* care a lot about honor, you know, but I've learned that honor can come later. You don't have to feel it at the time. I mean, David, you can rob and steal now, and if you're good at it the honor will take care of itself, like with Rockefeller and Franco and Cortez and the viceroys of India. And Joseph Kennedy." A sardonic smile flickered and died. "I could be a good gangster and maybe make my son ambassador to Spain or something. But I don't have the purpose and the belief, David. Do you see that?"

Howell said nothing.

"I have no purpose. The more clearly I see, the blacker is the hole I look in. Can you *see* that, David?" he pleaded.

Howell cleared his throat. "But you don't *want* it to be that way," he said. "That's something. Right?"

"Sometimes. Sometimes I don't care about it. But the thing is, David, I used to have a purpose. I used to trust and believe, and I would sacrifice myself. And then your people crushed it over the years. Very important people. I could give you the names and dates and places of where it happened. *That's* what I want to do. Those crimes and lies are the great corruption, and I want your people to know about them. Power is blind and never accepts blame, you know. But you Americans stole my purpose and left me unhappy deeper than I ever was afraid of. And I am pretty mad about that."

Maraña stared like a blind man. Howell felt no anger from his words, but he did feel the booth trembling slightly and it occurred to him that all Maraña's rage had been compressed into a solid atom of control somewhere in his body. Howell felt the waves of it, the hints of the possible explosion, as he tumbled forward instinctively. "You know what I think, Carlos?" he asked politely. "I think you have to make your own purpose and not blame the Americans or anyone else for deceiving you. That's what you should do. You shouldn't be blaming anybody for what you are. I know it's late, but you are still strong enough to do that."

Maraña's eyes rolled slightly as he considered this quiet outburst during a fearful moment for Howell. "Tell me something," he said enigmatically. "Would you have said that without this screen here between us?"

"No," said Howell.

"That's what I thought," laughed Maraña.

"Not a chance." Howell tittered off into his own relief.

Footsteps approached. Maraña was laughing high in his range as he stood up. "You know something, David," he said. "I snitched on myself to everybody in town to get myself arrested. What do you think of that?"

"You what? What are you talking about?"

"I can't tell you all my secrets," Maraña replied.

The door opened, clearing the laughing dream from Howell's mind. "Wait a minute," he said, feeling his answers dragged back toward the cellblock. Howell had forgotten he was in jail. "Wait a minute," he repeated. "Carlos, is there anything I can do? How long are you, I mean, what are you planning? What can I write? I don't know what to say."

"Let's go," said the officer.

"Write me a letter," smiled Maraña. "You have the address. And tell Carmen to bring me a *Time* magazine. Okay? *Ciao.*"

Howell watched him leave and then made his own way uncertainly back through the corridor. A guard opened the big metal door for him, and as he stepped through, two flashbulbs went off in his face. Howell blinked and ducked toward a corner of the waiting room to sit down. He saw the representatives of various government agencies stirring around the perimeter. Reporters, mostly Cubans, had been trying to interview them, and now they fired questions at Howell.

"The only thing he really said about this case was that he had informed on himself all over town to get himself arrested," Howell shrugged.

"Yeah, right," said one reporter. Howell chatted with them for twenty minutes, answering probing questions about his own background and introduction to Maraña. None of it satisfied anyone, including Howell, who glanced frequently across the room to the solitary figure of Carmen Vilar, wearing a light blue satin pants suit and looking decidedly more garish than Howell remembered her. She barely acknowledged him, but one intense look of recognition told him she did not wish to speak.

Back at the Ziller household, Marvella's febrile efforts to nurse the assorted victims of the Vizcaya party out of their stupors without waking them to full paranoia as to the whereabouts of Ziller were, most abruptly, ruined by the arrival of two gentlemen from the FBI in full regalia, including the obsolete felt hats. Crisply and doggedly, they insisted upon an audience with a woman they would identify only as "Miss Moonbeam." Arlington Spencer roused himself to challenge their entry to the house, while Marvella did some shrieking and a large number of naked rumps were collected from around the pool like so many canteloupes.

Some of the professionals within the group—one pediatrician, three lawyers, a "laughing gas dentist," a stockbroker, and an English banker residing in Colombia—reared up to their full dignity, which was no mean accomplishment given their states of mind, to face the law and to stem the panic among their own party. Some hasty organization followed. One anguished soul wound up holding a lobster pot over the sea wall, poised to drop a cache of drugs into the brine. A less resolute man of the Buddhist persuasion hummed "We Shall Overcome" softly to himself, and a few people closer to the edge of American productivity moved bravely toward the front ranks. The FBI agents saw none of these results, however, for when Arlington Spencer had stalled as long as he could, he agreed to produce Moonbeam at the door if the agents would not arrest her or enter the house. Soon thereafter, the object of the commotion appeared, heartily encouraged from behind. There was no consternation on her blank face, but she did walk delicately, expecting the floor to cave in at any moment. After a few private words with the agents, she announced her intention to go with them. She satisfied about half of her stunned defenders that it was voluntary, and waving kisses, departed without a further word of good-bye.

Howell arrived in the immediate trail of this event. His best guess as to its connection with Ziller's fate—or at least with Maraña's version of it—was that Moonbeam had probably been busted on a drug run along with Ziller and was therefore subject to similar retribution from the Mafia, from which the FBI might be attempting to protect her. Several hard-liners scoffed at this because it tended to cast the Bureau in a favorable light. Some hinted darkly that Moonbeam might be the cause of it all. Some doubted everything. A few sage heads resigned themselves to "whatever comes down," and others gave way to the inner pandemonium. One woman called her son at a Connecticut prep school and told him to stay on the campus until further notice. Howell's own mind went on similar skeins of flight. He managed no repose in peace or laughter and could not stop his gizzard from spinning, suffering as he was from both cultural claustrophobia and dispersal. He could not keep from talking, though he made no sense, and his hands trembled so badly that he had trouble slicing the aloe leaf in the yard in order to apply the milky salve to his nose, just in case. Jittery beyond his experience, Howell watched anxiously for a police tail on his airport taxi. He sat on his suitcase until the midnight economy flight left for Atlanta, where he waited again for the flight home.

From the Greensboro-High Point airport, Howell drove a cheap rented car through the dawn and between the pine trees all the way to Thomasville, a mill town erected when the furniture industry moved south after the Great War. Little about it had changed. The Southern Railroad still ran through the heart of it, and the world's largest chair still stood three stories high at the corner of Main and Salem, testament to the sturdy vocation of the inhabitants. Just two months earlier, Howell knew, the fire department's only engine had helped boost Santa Claus into the huge concrete seat of the chair, from which he would wave and toss Hershey's kisses to the children crowded below, among whom for many years had been Howells. Such memories crowded in on him. He remembered the hot dog battles in the school cafeteria, which reminded him of the comically flatulent dietician, barely contained in her white uniform, and of other notable sights that lined up in a long row of daguerreotypes from the seasoned time in the back of his head—items of strong, deep lines, but old—jarring what little continuity remained in the flashier registry of the questful journalist just in from Miami.

Down one of the business side streets past the Howell Cabinet Company and its surrounding grounds and warehouses to the place next door, which, owing to the peculiar construction of the city, was a residence. Many of the old furniture men had pulled right in next to the railroad and thrown up a one-story brick home next to the shop, among them the hard-nosed James Orson Howell, who was currently at odds with a host of external forces—chiefly the business school graduates who had run the craftsmen out of furniture and who were equally at home selling motorboats or stereos, but not excluding the soft woods and the prefab construction and the Japanese, for whose television sets the Howell Cabinet Company slapped together ersatz mahogany cabinets, and certainly not excluding the bespectacled men and women from the federal government who were always ordering the raising or lowering of the water fountain by minute degrees, as the elder Howell told it. Only a few grizzled old foremen still knew how to taper the legs of a cherrywood table, he complained, though he himself also knew. In fact, working with the routers and lathes and saws and glues in his little garage workshop was one of only two pastimes that would, without fail, bring contentment to the elder Howell and melt the hard pose of his deprecations. He made tables and chairs and music boxes there of the finest wood, for friends or for nothing, stealing as many moments as he could before and after going to the office to contend with the external forces. He was there when his son walked in, shivering.

"Hello, Pop," said Howell.

The old man, struggling to remove a round tabletop from a circle of wood clamps, began to frown as he always did when someone intervened in his workshop. But within an instant he recognized the voice as belonging to one of his descendants, his second and greater pastime, and immediately there was a brightening across a band of his face that encompassed his cheekbones and eyes and a portion of his forehead. It was as though he took a narrow mask off a rather leathery countenance, wizened by a few folds of age at the neck, to reveal a strikingly boyish layer of himself, with prankster's blue eyes and bouncing eyebrows that drew attention to a full head of straight black hair now fallen, as after all his exertions, into a line of bangs. The stern, ruddy woodmaster lit up with the puckish gleam that he had transmitted to his progeny.

"What have we got here?" sang out the old man, whirling to hold out his arms. Surprise goosed his joy a notch higher.

"Hello, Pop," grinned Howell, rushing to embrace him. Their chests clapped together and they went through a few rounds of their own special greeting, alternately lifting each other off the ground as they twirled in a mutual bear hug, laughing. The old man had the advantage of the bottom grip and of the stronger hands, his being disproportionately large and well-worked in contrast to Howell's twiddly paws, but Howell had the advantage of swinging the lesser weight. His father was of a smaller frame and had accumulated a less expansive paunch from the cheese and peanut butter crackers in his own vending machines than Howell had derived from the daily guzzling of white wine in the capital.

Happily exhausted, they beheld each other from within arm's length. "Good to see you, Son. What's the occasion?"

258

"Uh, nothing. Just a surprise visit."

"Your mother know you're here?"

"Not yet."

"Uh huh. Lost your coat up in Sodom?"

"Nope. I just came in from Miami."

"Oh. Down there again? It's cold here in the winter, you know."

"Yeah, I know."

"How's your lady, Haven?"

"Just fine."

"Feeling anything special?"

"She's pretty special."

"Any special news?"

"Not that I know of."

"Uh huh. How's Henry?"

"Fine, I guess. I haven't seen him in a few days."

"Uh huh. And Soapsuds?"

"Sudsy. She's fine. Sparklin' like always."

"Uh huh. And everybody else?"

"Okay, I guess."

"Good. Magazine still afloat? Marner and Drake behavin' themselves?"

"Barely. Same as always."

"Uh huh. I saw your article about the war with Venezuela, bombing and losing and stuff."

"It was a satire."

"Uh huh. I didn't understand it."

"It's nothing. I'm sorry."

"That's all right. They still paying you?"

"Barely."

"You need some cab fare? I know you need a lot of cab fare in a big city. You need a few hundred dollars?"

"Not just yet, Pop. I'm okay."

"You sure? I've always got some tucked away here and there in drawers and boxes, you know. It won't hurt me."

"No, it's all right."

"Don't tell your mother, though."

"Okay."

"You just passing through? Just sayin' hello?"

"Well, not exactly."

"Uh huh. I figured you had some business. You look kind of like you swallowed some turpentine. What is it?"

"Well, I don't know."

"Uh huh."

"It's complicated. So many things have happened right in a row."

"You're not in some kind of trouble, are you?"

"Not exactly. I don't think so."

"You sure?"

"Pretty sure. It's more personal, I think. It's hard, Pop. You know, all these things . . ."

". . . It's all right."

"Thanks. Um, you know, what I'd really like to do is to work with you a little bit right now and talk later."

"Uh huh."

"I mean I can help you move stuff, at least."

"Well, I don't want you to hurt your fingers or anything."

"Aw, Pop."

"Sure, Son. Love to have you."

"What are you making?"

"Breakfast table."

"Looks nice."

"Here. Feel this."

"Wow. Like glass. And I can't even see the seams. Still got the touch, eh? What's next?"

"Gotta make some dowels and some groove fittings for the underside and then lathe there around the claws on the stand."

"Uh huh. How's Sam?"

"Fine. Old and hardly working."

"Mom okay?"

"Yep. As long as there's hope for the United Nations, there's hope for me."

"Aw, Pop."

"You know, if it hadn't been for you and the Peace Corps, she never would have gotten hooked on that stuff. I haven't forgotten that."

"Uh huh. Sorry. How's business?"

"Hanging in there. Working more and more for those sorry Nips."

"Easy, Pop. No wonder Mom's dragging you to the UN."

"Never would have dreamed it back on Okinawa. You know what particle board is?"

"Kind of. I'm not sure."

"Sawdust mashed together with glue."

"Uh huh."

"Well, that's what they've got us making their TV cabinets out of. We put a veneer on it painted with a Chippendale design."

"Uh huh."

"They're smart, though. I'll give them that. And they work their tails off."

"I know."

"How do you know?"

"Well, that's what I read."

"Uh huh. Well, they do. They're through here every few weeks, and your mother always has some of them to supper."

"She does?"

"Yep. You think that's funny, don't you?"

"Sorry. Didn't mean to laugh, but I could imagine some funny things."

260

"Uh huh."

"Do you use chopsticks?"

"No. Here. Help me lift this top out of the clamps. I gotta go to work. You look a little better."

"Thanks. Ugh, I bet particle board is a lot lighter than this."

They worked on for half an hour at a steady rhythm. Howell's lack of skill forced him to stand around a lot, and he used up the time by caressing the wood. His mind was still at a tilt from what it was carrying and from the alien hot comfort of home, with the awkward slippage that sets in after the first primal squeezes.

The old man could not help noticing the occasional quiver on his son's lips. He watched them as he sanded and carved, and he also watched them as he stood back to study an incorrect fit before making another run at it. There was music in his work, even in the long delicious pauses, as the old man had a basic pulse about the shoulders and arms. He always perspired. Despite the chill of February morning, his labor soon produced abundant beads of it, including the characteristic drop that always clung precariously to the tip of his nose, which was slightly crooked as a result of two school-yard punches from Sterling "Snuff" Waters, who had been lucky in both the match and the rematch, as the old man told it.

Howell stared at the drop a long time, waiting for it to fall. The old man looked up at him as he tried to work the teeth of a brace into the gums of a beam. "You know, I've always worried about you and all those people up there trying to straighten out the State Department, son," he said. "Trying to figure out all the bad things in the world and putting in all the good ones. You've gotta be suckin' wind. I couldn't do it."

"Well, I don't care that much about the State Department," said Howell.

"Well, all the departments, I mean," said the old man. "They're all a puzzle of air with a million pieces—foreign and domestic and what have you. Economic. Hard to get hold of, and nothing works. That's why I stick to the sports pages pretty much, and my nature books."

"I understand," Howell said quietly.

"You do?" asked the old man. He held up the smooth pine brace. "You know, son, sometimes I get my neck bowed right after I get up in the morning. About some stupid thing somebody says on the radio about what's going on in Syria or some place. Think of it. Six-thirty in the morning and I'm already bent out of shape."

"Uh huh," said Howell, still watching the drop of sweat, fearing that his father's solemnity and his unusually long string of words presaged a pitch for the old-time religion.

"And the thing is, I don't get any satisfaction out of yelling at the radio to set it straight," pronounced the old man. "And it wouldn't even do any good if I was *on* the radio telling Syria what to do, especially since your mother always says just the opposite of what I do. I don't get any satisfaction out of it."

"Uh huh."

"But if I take this piece of bracing here and it's three-sixteenths of an inch too long, I can cut three-sixteenths of an inch off of it and it will be all right. Perfect. Or two inches or six inches or what have you. And if it's too short, I can make another one. And when I'm finished, I have something that will last, and I can tell that I've made it. I can tell my work. I don't mind if people see it. And that gives me some satisfaction."

"I know."

"I just wanted you to know that . . ."

". . . it's good . . ."

". . . in case you wonder what I do here while you run off searching for something else."

"Oh, Pop."

"I don't know why I said that."

"I do."

"Beats me. Maybe you can take a little of that satisfaction with you. Or maybe you can get some when you come home. It's not much. Your mother and I always wanted you to find something better." The old man stopped, looked quizzically at the brace, and shrugged.

"Oh, Pop."

"We just worry about you, Son. It's natural. Good to have you."

Howell pressed both hands over his face and shook gently.

The old man looked all about him, at a loss. "Let's go see your mother," he said, putting an arm around Howell. "I guess this trouble can't be too bad."

That night the three of them had dinner, at the conclusion of which Laura Lee Howell went out of the kitchen and returned peering over her half-focals, the kind with the chain attached behind the ears, carrying a large pile of books and magazines and yellowed newspaper articles from the *Christian Science Monitor*. She was quite deliberate about it. Howell, still chewing, watched her with pregnant curiosity as long as he could and then asked, "What are you doing, Mom?"

"I think your mother has something to say to you," observed the old man.

Laura Lee Howell suffered this remark without comment.

"She's got out her theology books," the old man continued. "Her Eric Hoffer and Bonhoeffer and *hasenpfeffer*."

"Hush, Daddy," she scolded.

"Who's Hasenpfeffer?" asked Howell.

"Rabbit stew," she replied with distaste. "Daddy can't even step on a bug, and here he is talking about stewing those cute rabbits."

"Oh," said Howell.

The old man's ears reddened near the top. "Sorry, Mommy," he said. Then to Howell, "This is important, Son. She's been working on it a long time, and I agree with her."

Howell gulped and then his face flared into a Chaplinesque parody of dread that he had learned from Haven Pinder. He erased it. Having never heard his father give such an advance endorsement to his mother's views, most especially those views nurtured by her reading matter, he felt the full weight of the moment's expectation.

As she nervously shuffled her papers, she gave her husband a kindly look of gratitude for his support. She had the heart-shaped face of a race that had swept only briefly through the British Isles, and in combination with her other features, such as the delicate hands she contributed to her children, it produced a lasting impression of near saintliness on everyone she met. She endeavored constantly to live up to this impression, which was no less a burden to her than her husband's opposite image was to him. His flinty elements struck fear in strangers. The two of them were anode and cathode, circuited powerfully through their offspring. Her present fluster was a tribute to this flow. She moved one set of notes ahead of another, and, clearing her throat, she placed the Bonhoeffer volume and a tract from the Unitarian center in Greensboro on the blond maple lazy Susan her husband had made for them, moving aside the Heinz 57 meat sauce she tolerated for him.

"You may have to help me here a little bit, David," she said. "Do you remember the first time Daddy and I came up to Chapel Hill to pick you up for Christmas? The very first time, when you were a freshman?"

"Huh?" asked Howell. "Boy, you're really sneaking up on me, Mom. I guess I remember."

"Well, I do," she said. "And so does your father."

"No, no. I'm sure you do," said Howell. "I mean I know you picked me up a lot that first year, and I remember being all upset. That was in '63, right after the Kennedy assassination."

"That's right."

"Uh huh."

"And in the car, you were telling us about some of your teachers and your courses," she continued. "And you told us all about how you had decided there is no such thing as a selfless act. You said you thought there was a selfish motive behind every human word and deed . . ."

". . . I did?"

". . . Yes, that's what you were saying. You'd thought about it a lot, and you couldn't defend any other reason why people in general would do things. You talked about people going into wars and things and sacrificing themselves, and you said that even in those cases the people would get some kind of pleasure out of the sacrifice. You said otherwise why would they do it? You can see here. I wrote down as much of what you said as I could remember. You talked about hidden motives and self-deception, and there's something here about a utility curve."

"There is?"

"I couldn't find out anything about that."

"You're lucky," Howell tried to laugh, but he was furrowed up in his past. "I might have said something like that back then, Mom, but I don't remember it."

"I do."

"I was an Econ major then, Mom. They'll say anything for a buck."

"You didn't say it like an Econ major," she countered. "You said it like my son who had just quit going to church."

"Uh huh," sighed Howell.

She looked down at her hands. "And I don't mind about the church part of it," she said. "Excuse me, Daddy, but the churches around here are terrible. Maybe they are everywhere. But I don't agree with you about the selfishness. And neither does Daddy. So I've been studying up on it."

"My God," Howell whispered in awe. "All this time?"

"Yes, it's very important to us. Let's start with Martin Buber," she said. "Now he says that love is the absence of self-awareness and the height of self-awareness at the same time, so it is a paradox . . ."

". . . Wait a minute," said Howell. "I've upset you about this all this time, is that really true?"

"Well, we've loved our children more than anything else," she said, looking at him through a blur.

"Aw, Mom."

"But we want to do right about it and not hold on to you, and we want to be proud of everything you learn, so we wanted to make sure we knew what we were talking about," she said, glancing at the old man. "Didn't we, Daddy?"

Howell turned to his father, who was busily trying to touch his puckered lips to his nose, making quite a show of it, the better to divert attention from his glimmering eyes and from the battle on his chin, where pride was losing ground. "Uh oh," quivered Howell.

"Yes," said his mother, as she reached for the Bonhoeffer. "And I know you don't like theologians, but I think some of these arguments are sound. This fellow says . . ."

". . . Wait a minute!" Howell said, pushing himself back from the table. "I can't stand it. Oh, Mama, please forgive me for hurting you."

"That's all right . . . you didn't . . . I mean I enjoyed reading on all this . . ."

"I know, Mama, but I don't care about defending anything to those guys. Not one of them is worth a good hug from your Mom."

Howell picked his mother up from her accumulated notes and squeezed her and sniffled with her. When they leaned back to look at each other squarely, they were in the same wet nest of adoration. The old man joined them in kind, and they gave in to it. Before long, they were laughing.

"What a slobbering mess," said Howell.

"I guess it's all right to cry together every fifteen years or so," said Laura Lee Howell, a bit later.

"A family needs a little soldering every now and then, I guess," said the old man.

"What *was* it that you used to say about theologians?" she inquired.

"Oh that," sniffled Howell. "I said a theologian is a philosopher with an excuse."

"Yeah, that's right," said the old man, feigning offense.

"Boy, you two really hit me with both barrels today," said Howell. "What got into you?"

"I'm sorry, Son," said the old man. "Maybe we just had this instinct you've been unsatisfied. Parents get feelings, you know."

"No, I'm glad you did," said Howell. "Believe me."

"But are you going to read all the passages I've been collecting on selfishness?"

Howell looked warily toward the stack. "I don't know, Mom," he laughed. "Some of them."

Just then a large group of Howell's siblings pushed through the door to greet their brother. They arrived with spouses and children and with the news that Howell had that day been elected to the Thomasville High School Glee Club's Hall of Fame, which caused much merriment. The musical achievement officially cited by the alumni committee in its induction notice was Howell's solo performance of "I Wonder as I Wander" at a countywide Christmas assembly attended by two candidates for governor, but everyone including Howell's parents knew that his first big hit was Roy Orbison's soulful "Runnin' Scared," which he let loose in locker rooms and pep rallies. After that, people said the boy could really sing, and a number of elders thought he should have gone to Nashville instead of the Peace Corps.

Howell collapsed of fatigue soon after everyone left. He said tender good nights and retired long before Carlos Maraña went to sleep on his creaky jail bunk in Miami. It had been a busy two days—two visits from Carmen, filled with warnings, two sessions with his lawyers, and nineteen unhappy official visitors, most of them trying to plug up the holes in the story of the Vizcaya night bust. Dave Damico was disconsolate enough to say outright that the tapes, while tantalizing, were not good enough for the SAC, Mr. Shea, who declined to push after the drug cops. Maraña cheered Damico with a full sworn statement on how he watched Rolando Carvajal murder Taliente two years earlier. He remembered that Carvajal had been wearing a green shirt. He remembered the license number of the rented car. He remembered everything. Carvajal was now in the same jail. Maraña had sent him a note saying, "Be silent and don't pee, okay?" There were two more death sentences pronounced in the papers against Maraña. He was wide awake, thinking. He knew most of what was about to happen. The next day his attorneys would secure his release on the faulty drug charge and he would disappoint both Carmen and Dave Damico by flying straight to Panama without notifying either of them, and there he would take up his new job in the Panamanian intelligence service. Carvajal would go free for lack of a witness against him, becoming a figure to reckon with on account of his new status as slayer of Taliente. The newspapers would print speculations that Maraña was in Havana, in any of eight South American countries, in Israel, in a barrel at the bottom of the Caribbean, or elsewhere. Some would place him in the midst of brilliant plots headed by Castro or Sadat or even by the hefty American photographed coming out of the jail, but no one would guess that Maraña might be running from his fear of one man. He lay awake wondering if Pepe Lopez knew.

Howell could not sleep either. At one o'clock he called a sleepy Pinder in Washington. She mumbled, "Hello, baby. Where are you?"

"Hello, you're wonderful," he replied. "I'm in Thomasville. Stopped to recuperate a day after Miami. It was rough. Too many surprises."

"Like what?"

"I'll tell you tomorrow. Just wanted to make sure Henry hasn't built any contraptions in the living room. I couldn't take it in my condition."

"Nope. Just me alone in one long Savannah tenants' meeting. Henry's had an accident You won't believe what happened to him."

XIII

HENRY WOODRUFF stalked past the Gutenberg Bible on the first floor of the Library of Congress. "Now I'm cooking," he whispered to himself, blowing nervously on his hands although it was quite warm. "Now I'm cooking," he repeated. He jumped up in the air with a skip step and turned sideways to dipsy doodle out into the huge vestibule, staring up past three tiers of balcony to the Renaissance mosaics that cover a ceiling of billowing arches. If he were the president or even a senior adviser to the president, Woodruff thought, he would have a reception in that magnificent room. It was the only good reason for a party he could think of.

He stopped, falling into a soft-shoe stance of puzzlement—legs crossed, one toe on the floor, finger to the point of his chin. Woodruff was leaner than he had been in a decade, and there was a leathery grace to his spryness. Some heads in a flock of tourists turned toward the strange sight of a self-absorbed cricket who paid them no notice. His body controlled itself while his mind hesitated several times in the direction of the door to the main reading room. Not yet, he decided. He tried to crack his knuckles, but they made no sound. Woodruff had no reliable nervous habits, such as nail-biting or foot-tapping or cigarette-smoking, no steady and unobtrusive drains on his anxiety. This he regretted at times. His choice in normal fare was to think or walk and in charged moments, which occurred at least once a year, both these functions would get the better of him. His gait became twitches and jigs. Strange cerebral forces vaulted over six or eight synapses to slap him in the face. At such times Woodruff felt like a stranded pedestrian on the highway of his own energy.

"Hurry up," Woodruff said unconsciously, and then, waking up with a start, he nodded politely to a passing scholar who took umbrage at his command. Woodruff jumped into a trot, elbows churning, down the stairs to the basement, sliding partway on the brass rail, on through the photographic exhibit headed as always by snapshots of the president, whom Woodruff saluted in passing, and into the depths of the library. Bouncing through the snack bar and its odd mixture of solitary students and chatter-box cardplayers, he addressed a vending machine. Money was exchanged for an apple, but Woodruff could not bring himself to bite it. Instead, he examined the fruit carefully as his thoughts returned to the implications of the DNA molecule. Appetites grappled with one another, and Woodruff weighed the time. Is it there yet, he wondered. He would have liked to eat half the apple and then check the reading room again, but he decided not to risk any chance of being ejected from the library and from his treasure for possessing half-eaten food. He considered eating half the apple and throwing the rest away. This idea he rejected after realizing that he was not hungry and, morever, that his true purpose in acquiring the apple was not eating anyway, but passing time, which he could do just as well by walking. So he sighed and tucked the apple into a pocket in his parka before retracing his steps to the floor above. He talked to himself on the way, and his chest moved oddly forward and backward in transit, like an egret hurrying along the ground.

Loud expressions of delight are not common in the main reading room. Upon hearing the sharp handclap and the shrill whoop of joy that went on to echo all around the cavernous dome of learning, an attendant at the central desk instantly concluded that someone was listening to the finale of a sports broadcast on the radio. His glower located Woodruff, who was rubbing his hands gleefully over a stack of large books, the size of atlases, that had been delivered to his appointed seat. The attendant, failing to reach Woodruff with a visual reproach, sauntered over to a colleague behind the circular desk and muttered, "Hey, keep an eye on that dude over there with the medical books. Could be some kind of philiac or something."

For the first five minutes they watched him closely. To them, Woodruff was teetering between enthrallment and perversion. He turned the large folio pages in a frenzy and ran his right index finger up and down the charts, mouth moving slightly and his left hand caressing the opposite page. Abruptly, Woodruff slapped both hands over his eyes and turned his head upward like a sun worshipper. His torso wobbled a bit in the chair. When his hands fell, he kept his eyes closed and appeared to be searching his eyelids for a glimpse of the epochal star. With both hands on his inner thighs at the crotch, he pushed his full weight down on stiff, rocking arms. After whipping through several more folios, Woodruff's hands went from face to crotch again as he beseeched a distant oracle. The attendants looked askance at one another. It could be epilepsy. It could be a primitive sect, a speaker in tongues. Or, with the medical books, it could more likely be the satisfaction of a longing in some rare manner unsuited to a quiet, populated area. Whatever, Woodruff could be one of those who periodically require a uniformed escort from the library.

He surprised them, however. The inner commotion left his face, and he meditated in utter stillness for fifteen minutes, during which time the attendants lost interest. He was breathing deeply but calmly, refreshed by what he had gleaned from the book. When Woodruff opened his eyes, he scribbled some notes in a small spiral book and fondly inspected the folio in front of him. Then he rose. As he returned the books, the hurry seeped back into him. He looked as though he had just navigated a treacherous passage and had important news to tell.

Just outside the door, he ran into a man in a dark pin-striped suit. "Henry!" the man greeted cheerfully, detaining Woodruff as he swept by. "What are you doing up here?"

"Hello, Jerry," Woodruff replied. "Not doing much. Just some reading, you know." He began backing away slowly, moved by urgency.

"Good to see you," said Jerry, also backing away. "I gotta hand it to you, Henry," he called. "You were right to get out of here when you did. There's not much going on except the campaign. It's gonna be bloody."

"Yeah," said Woodruff. "Well, my money says that the man on the white horse will win this time over the man who won't do any harm."

"Maybe so," said Jerry, who stopped retreating and broke out in a conspiratorial look. "Say, Henry," he said. "I think your old boss has got a good chance at being number two."

"He's too fat," said Woodruff. "Got to lose some weight."

"No, really," said Jerry, moving toward Woodruff. "He's already put Edie and two other staff people on the campaign task forces. They're better than the people over there, and I'm telling you Henry you could *run* some of the foreign policy shops if you came to the meetings. Most of those guys don't know analysis. They don't know structure. They don't know budget. All they do is look at the polls, you know—like sixty-one percent of the voters think we pay too much attention to Africa, stuff like that."

Woodruff was still retreating. "Well, believe it or not, I might just have one more campaign in me," he replied. "I can't do it now though, Jerry. But as soon as I finish this work I've been doing on my own, I'm gonna be back in shape."

"That's good, Henry. You can't stay out of the game too long or you lose your touch. What are you working on?"

Woodruff stopped. "Well, today I was working on the structure of the DNA molecule," he beamed.

"Huh?" said Jerry, stopping.

"Hidden properties. Unbelievable stuff," said Woodruff, starting forward.

Jerry caught a glint of insight. "Genetic warfare," he guessed. "Some national security angle? You think it's coming?"

"Maybe," came the coy reply. "I'm working on just the opposite, though."

Jerry's face went stale. "Sounds interesting," he lied, beginning to retreat again. "I know there's a connection in there somewhere. You and your oddball projects, Henry. That's what we need now. Ideas and stuff."

"Save me a place on the Executive Committee of the Future," Woodruff smiled. "Right now I've got to take a piss."

"Sure," waved Jerry. "Let's have lunch sometime."

"Right," called Woodruff. He resumed his trot and whispered the word "toady" to himself.

Woodruff rushed downstairs to the bathroom, swelled and bursting as much from the epiphany in the reading room as from kidney pressure. He felt a strong beacon of pleasure at the top of his bladder and another one in his immediate memory, where the flavor of Jerry brought a new, condensed perception of the unctuous ambition that grows in the Senate, sometimes slowly and against all intention, but more often like wild bright-colored weeds in infinite variety, a catalogue of the personalities clustered around the desire to lay down an uncontradicted opinion.

Simultaneously, Woodruff was purring over the possibilities of DNA, and to him there was a special zest to any moment that could so vibrantly engage that discovery and Jerry and the thrill of urination all at once. He tingled and effervesced. The light itself seemed to pulse at the corner of his eyes with whatever property serves to convert a dull pattern into a rhythm, calling out the primal response. His mind skimmed like sled runners over the territory of Alexander the Great, picturing a large dirty tent somewhere in Asia where the Hellenist emperor, sated with the affections of his generals and with the godhead achieved by conquest, might casually imagine a dispersal of his global estate such that new climates and biological hardships might, in a few thousand years, produce the slightest modification in the genetic codes of Alexander's descendants.

Woodruff's brain frolicked in a zone joining the biological inheritance with imagination. The very notion of imagination enraptured him as he thought of imagination's role in all things, including ordinary sight, where it helps bring life to the cold molecules ahead. Such a wonderful enhancer and creator, Woodruff thought, that it seemed too sweet to recognize any commerce between it and the biological tour of genes through time, so magnificent in its own right. Yet certainly the embrace of sperm and egg, twined at many trillion points, could transmit a capacity for imagination that had worked its way to the core of the human legacy somehow, necessary for stark survival and holy comfort and spitfire entertainment. And surely one axis could change the other with but a blink of the universe, as, for instance, Einstein's whiff of intuition may yet bring dark or light shades when the nuclear dew he secreted works its way down the long resonant bowstring.

Playfully, Woodruff sent causality in both directions—genes to imagination, imagination to genes—and then he arranged them without causality at all, as dancers or mirrors or fishes and sea. The fanciful zest of his ruminations engaged him more than any accuracy they could spawn, for Woodruff was in the first glow of intuition. It was a paradoxical mixture of pure sensation and pure thought—the flaps of the brain down into mechanical concentration, yet a leap of mindless pleasure. He conceived of himself as situated on a thin wispy neck between two great tangled empires, thought and emotion, touching the physical world, and while riding this nexus Woodruff thought the sensation was indeed too sweet—something like the

270

hypersensation immediately after orgasm when he could not bear to touch the white jelly at the tip of himself because of the delightful, shuddering, sexual chill.

Which reminded Woodruff that he was, in fact, in the basement of the Library of Congress, eyes closed at the urinal. A piss to remember, he thought. As no other excretory event stood out in his memory, he recognized this one as some sort of lifetime milestone. Woodruff smiled to himself and squeezed himself, fluttering as he raised to consciousness yet another point of elation. He swayed in the stall. Sex and imagination and genes went soaring through evolution in striking combinations, each appearing as the essence of the other two at times, on past amoebas and Alexander and scenes both lofty and humble. Woodruff experienced a great crescendo of inspiration. At the end, he kicked the flush handle like a frenzied maestro, but then his practiced hands made a crucial error almost as rare as the slip of mutation.

Woodruff gave out a rasping, hissing scream caused by a sharp intake of breath over a constriction of shock in his throat. There was no sound of voice, but there was a terrible clashing of air such as one would make while being choked or thrown into a pool of ice. Reflexively, he started to double over toward the urinal and his hands shot out to the walls for bracing. Then Woodruff was bright yellow all across his mind from a second streak of pain. He undoubled back to a slight crouch, still sucking air. For an instant, Woodruff thought he was reliving a dream of succumbing to ether for a tonsillectomy at the age of six—he saw a garish clown riding a miniature bicycle around the inner rim of an upright clock, faster and faster amid smoke and flying sparks, a gong sounding loudly at the top of each revolution. It was a dream and then a joke, but the stinging pain came out of the clouds to bite even harder. He accepted a slight portion of the cruel reality before moving by impulse to flee. Rising up to move, he was stabbed by another streak of pain in his crotch. All motion of any kind made the unbearable pain even worse. Woodruff tried not to pant. It was then that he realized that he could scarcely hear anything above the deep pounding of his own heart in his ears.

"Are you all right, buddy?" asked a voice from behind that Woodruff thought he might have heard before. It was very far off. He turned slowly at the neck, having learned quickly that the agony commanded stillness, and as he did so the extra blade arrived with a vengeance that made his jaw drop.

There was a capital policeman just behind him, trying to look bored. "You got a problem or something?"

Woodruff's mouth was stretched into a flat grimace, which he labored to make look like a smile. The result was an absurd row of teeth and cheesecake thin lips, a close-up of the class outcast trying to cut up in the third-grade photo. Woodruff groaned. He tried to shoo the policeman with a look of indignation, but the officer was staring at Woodruff's feet. He's embarrassed, thought Woodruff, withered by shame. Or maybe he's relieved that there's nobody else in here.

"I'm all right," grimaced Woodruff.

"Yeah," said the officer, so flatly as to conceal his meaning.

"Thank you," said Woodruff, nodding every so slightly in dismissal.

The officer did not move. Woodruff leaned forward to flush the toilet a second time. Groaning freely behind a camouflage of noise, he prayed earnestly for the officer's departure, and, when the roar settled down to its high-pitched aquatic sigh, he had reason to give thanks. Alone, he contemplated his misery for the first time. The head of his penis barely protruded from his jeans, shrunken to the size of a thumbnail and pitched unnaturally to one side the way a hangman's victim lolls about above the broken neck. Partially escaped, the organ thus obstructed Woodruff's view of the trouble on the underside, so he placed one fingertip very, very gently below and traced the path of the zipper. Its steel teeth ran in separate rows beneath the accident, Woodruff's mind numbly recorded. Malfunction. Then the rows came together. He followed their united track upward to a streak of extra pain. He retreated for ten seconds before feeling along even more gingerly. This time he estimated that there was approximately an inch and a half of united zipper under the first point of distress. He decided to rest again and to whimper slightly, and while doing so he noticed blood on the tip of his finger. "Oh, my," he whispered to himself. "Oh, my." It had been his maternal grandmother's favorite phrase, uttered hundreds of times a day. Woodruff longed to reduce this disaster to a burned cookie sheet or a missed crochet loop or another of the crises he had heard his frail grandma declaim.

He tried simply standing there in the stall and waiting for something better to happen. Nothing did. He stalled by flushing the toilet a third time. Then he tried to peer around the top of his organ to examine the area of the wound. Pain prevented it. He was pinioned. No motion was possible without a severe price. He could not even stand upright, because doing so pulled the penis against the zipper. The pain was stable only at the original semi-crouching zip-up position. He was frozen into the exact attitude of impact. At the slightest crouch, the pants tended to ride up with excruciating results.

Desperately, Woodruff took the fly between the thumb and forefinger of his right hand. One yank, he thought. It had to end. Nothing could be worse. With hot forehead and dry mouth, he experimented a micrometer downward to unzip. It was useless. Woodruff felt lightheaded and saw tiny clear dots swimming in his vision. He felt so insignificant in the face of the hurt that even the idea of challenging it frightened him. The pain had needles in it—the slightest touch to the talon pushed pins in everywhere from the ankles to the back of the ears—but at the same time it was foggy and nonspecific. A vaporous genie effused from his trousers to lord over him. Woodruff forced himself to reexamine the problem. Beneath the talon he saw small bits of loose flesh protruding slightly outside the zipper teeth. Squeezing a fist around a ball of raw hamburger would make something similar ooze out between the fingers. Woodruff moaned. "Not much blood," he whispered to himself by way of encouragement. It occurred to him that he might try to zip on past the biting point, which he located an inch or so behind the glans of the penis on the underside, and then perhaps he could pull apart the rows of zipper teeth from behind, liberating the half inch of plowed flesh. An experiment along this line failed instantly.

Panic arrived. Woodruff surrendered to an overwhelming desire to do something. He moved whatever part of himself he could move without penalty, which was not much. His face indulged in epileptic excursions. One hand rummaged roughly around his scalp. When the energy spilled over. Woodruff pitched himself into the task of unbuckling his jeans. That was the solution! He would take his pants off and untangle himself from the inside without hindrance or claustrophobia. He fumbled excitedly, sucking in air as though he might inhale all the distress, and he actually started to divest himself in three or four different ways before he realized the impossibility of the venture. He could barely touch his pants, let alone take them off, and the predicament of being sewn inside his jeans drove home an appreciation of the functional oneness between clothes and the body. He thought of that. He felt more kindly disposed to the idea of underwear than he had dreamed possible. He cursed himself for his previous, casual opinion that underpants were a stupid, dirt-fearing nuisance. He cursed himself for giving in to the bare impulse—all the better, he sneered to himself, to daydream of sexual escapades while contemplating the genetic history of the emotions and other subjects there in the Library of Congress. The incongruity of it all made him laugh. The laughter was ambushed by pain. He was glad when it subsided enough for him to notice the first signs of throbbing. A whimpering desire to cry out for help clashed with a stronger one to hide, to reveal this to no one. He might remain helpless there in the stall for days having no idea what to do. His ordeal was obliterating even the practical functions of his mind, separating him from the memory of the great speculative joys he had found ten minutes earlier in the reading room. His body had kidnapped him in cahoots with stupidity, and he resented the endless stretch of captivity ahead. "Fuck!" he hissed. "Shit!" He forgot grandma.

Footsteps sounded on the bathroom tile. Woodruff flushed the toilet again, almost reflexively by now, and in the commotion he began to take off his parka. It was a slow process, for even the minor torso twists required to slip out of the sleeves caused terrible repercussions below. Finally, Woodruff pivoted to leave the stall, clutching the parka to his chest to conceal the affliction. He discovered quickly the wisdom of small steps, one at a time, so as to prevent his own legs from pushing the jeans' legs apart. Every motion of his gait proved hazardous, for the slightest shift in penis or jeans brought consequences beyond endurance. Woodruff inched along, slightly bent over, prematurely aged. He put one hand in the small of his back to present the spectacle of himself as some kind of spinal ailment.

He was sure the basement guard would remember him, mark him as a smuggler of rare quartos, and search under the parka, but he slipped by with his fears and went on to a surprising scrape in the revolving door. As he was

273

resting halfway through the exit, an eager scholar entered with enough brisk force to expel Woodruff, throwing him forward and off-balance into the cold, howling. One foot caught most of his weight; the other stumbled behind. Woodruff clapped a hand over his mouth and very slowly brought his feet back together just outside the revolving door. Scholars passed him. One elderly gentleman advised Woodruff to put on his coat.

For reasons peculiar to Washington, the Library of Congress is a cruel spot for anyone who hopes to catch a taxi. Woodruff knew this. He watched them pass by, full and empty, yellow and black and white, drivers unmoved by his emergency gestures. In the despair and the dirty cold, he gave way to macabre visions of a small newspaper item in keeping with the era, "Ex-Hill Aide Zippers Self/Suicide Probed," that would perk up even the battered formica souls at the *Post*. Fifteen minutes later, teeth chattering, he made two decisions. Choosing to expose himself to humiliation rather than the elements, he put on the parka. This left him with only the small spiral notebook for crotch protection. It was a bitter option, stoutly resisted. The notebook was a poor sentry that could not cover all the angles. Woodruff felt ridiculous pressing it to himself, and he did not fully accept the change until the cold air dulled the pain around the wound. Then he decided to walk, with no destination in mind or the speed to get there. Just for the activity, which he deemed worth the danger of movement. He was making his slow way along the curb toward the Supreme Court when a horn blasted behind him.

"Henry! Need a ride?"

Woodruff jumped, grimaced, began to turn around.

"Where're you going?"

"Anywhere!" cried Woodruff, just as he recognized Paul Sternman in the back of the cab. "Paul!" he smiled. "Oh, please. If you share that warm taxi with me, I swear I'll bad-mouth the *Star* for a year. Don't mind if I do. Thank you, yessiree."

Sternman was all business. "Let's go."

Woodruff couldn't move fast enough. "You're the best-looking Saint Bernard of the winter," he quipped, stalling for time. "You on deadline?"

"Yep," said Sternman.

Woodruff, reaching the open door, confronted the task of entry. It would not be easy, he realized, since he could not lean over very far, or lift his legs, or fall backward onto the seat without torn tissues and pandemonium in the agony lobe. He felt Sternman's displeasure. Improvising in fear, he began humming a tune full of spirited, erratic leaps—Tchaikowsky's "Capricio Italien"—so that when he closed his eyes and bent backward into the seat he could mask his grunts as attempts to reach the next octave. His song, if raspy and discolored, was recognizable until Woodruff's ass hit the seat. Then it stopped abruptly as he groaned unmelodiously, slapped his left hand on the floorboard and arched himself, feet still in the street. His right hand still held the notebook in place, but Woodruff used it furtively and desperately to tug his pantlegs upward. He had to take the pressure off. He needed slack to sit down.

274

"Are you all right?" asked Sternman.

"Yes," gasped Woodruff. His back to Sternman, he reached with his right arm under his legs and lifted with all his might, falling against the back of the seat, into the cab, left hand still braced on the floorboard. He managed to close the door, but he couldn't put all his weight down or turn toward Sternman. He faced out his window, a bit toward the front. "Sorry," he said.

The taxi eased away. "What's the matter with you?" asked Sternman.

Panting, not turning around, Woodruff fought exhaustion. "Back problem," he grunted. "Books too heavy, I guess. Library accident. Sharp pain through the quick of me. Sorry. Rough day."

"I guess so," Sternman said, with a truculent, puzzled frown. "Where are you going?"

"Oh," groaned Woodruff, pausing at length to further advertise how much conversation taxed him. "I don't really know," he said. "Drop you at the *Post* and I'll take it from there."

Sternman looked at the back of Woodruff's neck. "Not telling, eh? Something confidential?"

"Yeah," Woodruff replied, without interest.

"What's her name?"

"Zippy."

"Who?"

"Nothing. It's not a woman."

"Oh. Who is it, then?"

"Don't know, really. I think I'll go see a doctor about my back."

"That's interesting," said Sternman with a trace of sarcasm. "Sorry about the nose. It's the job."

"I know."

"It's gotten a lot tougher lately," said Sternman, casting subtle doubt on Woodruff's claim to know about reporting. "On the big stories, especially. You gotta stick your nose in hard."

Woodruff said nothing. He felt poorly, not only from the pain and the expectations of embarrassment and the paranoia about his genital future but also from the atmosphere there in the taxi. He was putting falsity into the air, and he reproached himself for it. He was sending out shame and evasion at a most inopportune moment, and Sternman was responding with coldness. Sternman could be hard. Woodruff was disappointed.

"Carlyle's yanking the ambassador to Turkey tomorrow," Sternman announced. "They're gonna be pissed. Probably gonna invite the Russians in for talks within a week."

Woodruff waited a long time and then said, "Yeah."

"Carlyle's been tough since Wade left," said Sternman. "No pansy any more."

"Uh huh."

Sternman looked away, out his own window. "Boy, I hope Meyer likes it better than you do," he said. "I was hoping to lead the paper tomorrow."

"Sorry," moaned Woodruff. "You on foreign now?"

"No," brightened Sternman. "I'm doing some national security stuff sometimes, but this one is mostly intramurals. There's a big fight over this in the cabinet. Treasury's pissed because this is going to send the market all to shit."

"Uh huh."

"But Carlyle's winning anyway."

The taxi driver turned up the volume on his radio, but the jaunty reggae failed to dispel the brooding hostility in the back seat.

"How can he miss," sighed Woodruff, "with Clayfield at his ear?"

"You don't like Clayfield, do you?"

"No."

"I don't either."

"Nobody does. That's how he stays ahead. He your source?"

"You know better than to ask that," Sternman bristled. He tried to smile in Woodruff's direction in order to put some jovial spin on his remark, but of course he saw only the back of a parka, which reminded him of the way Woodruff had turned his back on LaLane Rayburn. Sternman thought he should not be talking so much about a story. He was jumpy and combative, in contrast to his trained habit. Usually, Sternman pushed doggedly but privately ahead on his work, relying on it to earn a respect he could not gain by charm, and he made a point of remaining aloof, glacierlike, from the witty needling that passes for friendly conversation among colleagues. He was annoyed with Woodruff for being able to annoy him.

Woodruff said nothing. "I don't talk to Clayfield much," Sternman added testily. "We had a big argument years ago about oil import quotas. He thought foreign oil was going to stay cheaper than domestic. Now he won't admit he ever said that."

Woodruff rocked forward slightly to relieve zipper tug. His head was clearing as he adjusted to the numb pain. Still, the very thought of movement, pressure, torn flesh, terrified him. He savored a position of stillness. "Ah," he sighed, "that's just a political disagreement. It means you can't be friends, but he can still be a source. Right?"

"Yeah, right," said Sternman. It was all he could think of. His chest heaved a couple of times as he strained to think of something that would make Woodruff turn around. "How come you care so much about Clayfield?" he asked, surprising himself.

"I don't, really."

Sternman tried to laugh. "I know," he said. "You don't really care about stories, but you like to find out about the sources."

Woodruff said, "Yeah, right.'

"When it's Clayfield, especially."

Woodruff nursed himself briefly, speculating on what was making Sternman fester. "Say, are you having a bad day, by any chance?" he asked.

"No."

"A bad night? A Guild meeting or something?"

"No," said Sternman, tight and accusing, still remembering his parting words with Rayburn the previous evening, how it was too complicated with the kids and the *Post*, how understanding she was, how he had worked all night in a fit of misery. "It's gonna be a damn good story, Henry," he said coldly.

Woodruff nodded vigorously in agreement but declined to comment on the proposed story because he knew he could not do so sincerely enough to mollify Sternman. He decided to try a placating move with a tidbit in the guise of raw surrender. "Maybe I am too curious about Clayfield," he said. "You know he was my exwife's source for a year or so. Source, as in lover. Helped split us up."

"I haven't really kept up with your private life since the poker games stopped," said Sternman. "But I heard that. Does it bother you now?"

"No."

"Come on," scoffed Sternman. "What is it then?"

"What do you mean, what is it?"

"Why do you talk about him? Why do you care?"

"Well, shit," sighed Woodruff. "Goddam. First I was plain hurt and then I was wounded by Casey's bad taste, I guess. And then about a year later I decided it was just part of the overall sadness, you know. And now I guess it's just interesting."

"Interesting?"

"Yeah, *interesting*," said Woodruff, bristling himself now but still speaking in a breathy groan. "Goddam, Paul. A hundred years ago I might have had to kill the bastard. Now we're just part of each other's growth process. That's a big transition, and Clayfield and I are related in it, like it or not. That's *interesting*."

Sternman banged a well-tailored knee with an unpracticed fist. "Fuck, no!" he said. "It's not interesting worth a damn!" Sternman spoke in a conversational monotone but with an arctic fury and a profane relish that would have shocked all his fellow reporters and one of his former wives.

Woodruff cringed. "Wait a minute," he said, raising up on his floorboard arm, trying to twist around to see Sternman's face. "Is this a joke? What did I do?"

"Interesting, bullshit," glared Sternman. "Fucking selfish, stealing, fucking stay out of the way and don't get hurt, that's what interesting is. Superior, dodging horseshit and stuff, Henry, and you know it."

"Know what?" gasped Woodruff. "What are you talking about?

"It's gonna be a damn good story."

"What?"

"Interesting," mused Sternman, in a controlled snarl. He had several hot beams going at once. "That means you just let it go by, Henry. The government, women, everything. Shake the fucking dust off and go on, you know. Make comments and nice fucking-sounding criticisms and stuff, but you're not responsible for anything, are you?"

"Huh?" cried Woodruff, almost bucking upward off the seat. He tried to shake off the chills from his head, not believing this was taciturn old Sternman, but the words also made a new hot pain seep outward from his groin. "Are you loony?" he asked.

"Yeah," came the smug reply.

Woodruff could see him now from his craned neck, and what he saw was the familiar stolid face with a touch of madness, but madness of a hard coinage, Republican madness, he would say, like a tested general in battle. Woodruff gulped. "Wait a minute," he said. "Let me try here. You mean I'm a shirker emotionally or something? It's all right, but I mean, *you're* saying that? That's really something. I mean you don't exactly play in the rush hour traffic, emotionally, yourself. Now that you've brought it up." Woodruff tried a high-pitched, fearful laugh, hoping to coax one out of Sternman.

"You're an interesting assistant, I think" said Sternman. "Assistant president, assistant senator, assistant editoi, assistant boyfriend, assistant person. And you find ways to make things interesting by looking down on me and my stories."

"That's not fair," Woodruff protested. "I don't look down on your stories. I think it's very valuable to have someone like you trying to sort the bullies from the patriots."

"Just like that," pounced Sternman. "That's not what I do. I just write stories. You fuck around to be interesting. I find out and I fuck up and I record stuff. I don't care if the country goes down the tubes—somebody's gonna want to know how it looked when it went down . . ."

". . . That sounds very nice, but . . ."

". . . And you try to make a burlesque out of everything I do. So does Howell, but at least he's attracted to the dance."

"That's pretty fancy language, Paul," Woodruff deflected. "If you don't watch out for that, they'll stick you over in the 'Style' section."

"Bullshit," said Sternman. "I'm not fluff, and I'm not a splinter running around looking for fingernails to burrow under, you know. I just write stories. And if I can get important writing stories, so much the better, 'cause that's what the town's about. And I hurt for it. I hurt for it right out in the open. I like the whole town. I like watching everybody squirm and butt heads. I even like watching people like you sniff the pile, you know. But I don't like it when you turn up your nose at me, goddammit. 'Cause I know what I'm doing and I don't think you do. So stay away from me, okay?"

"Hey, I don't need this," cried Woodruff, struggling in anger to sit upright. "What's going on here? What happened to you?"

"This is my cab," Sternman declared. "And you've had this coming for a long time. I've been thinking about it up there in my little cubicle. I work a lot, but even a robot like me has things to say, and just this once I'm doing it. You're just like all the rest of us, Henry. Except you're harder and more of a liar. And it's gonna be a good story."

"*What* story?"

"My story tomorrow about the ambassador . . ."

". . . What are you *doing* calling me a liar, Sternman? Jesus Christ! You're bonkers. You're not making any sense . . ."

". . . Bullshit . . ."

". . . Are you on the sauce or something? You don't look so good, Paul. Maybe smelling too much of that printer's fluid. This is crazy. Have I *done* something to you?"

". . . Okay, fact number one! You're here just like everybody else and you want to run things and be important. But you won't. 'Cause you're scared. You want to be pure. And you're gonna get run over! That's a fact, Henry! One day you're gonna realize this place has run over you. You won't even think you've been part of it, but you'll know it's run over you. And you'll be nothing. And you'll make excuses . . ."

". . . Hey, cut it out! Who asked you for your crystal ball? I'm the same . . ."

". . . You'll make excuses and blame everybody else, but it'll hit you hard. You think it can't touch you. Well, let me tell you something . . ."

". . . Lemme tell *you* something . . ."

". . . Listen to this . . ."

". . . I don't believe you, you know . . ."

". . . Listen to this. What you *do* think can touch you is your women and stuff, you know, with all your talk about how you're feeling and how things have changed with this woman or that woman and all that sensitive shit you lay out, your stuff, you know, pure Henry Woodruff reflective romance stuff. Yeah, you know that stuff, yeah?"

"Yeah?"

"Yeah, well that stuff doesn't touch you at all, Henry. That's the kicker. You're all backward. You just go flying by on that stuff and you hurt people you know and all you get out of it is you decide a little later that some of it was *interesting*. Not all of it. Just some of it. The way so-and-so yelled at you all the time was interesting because it showed how she thought you didn't hear her. What's that? Even I understand it, and it's nothing to you. But with me . . ."

". . . Hold it a second, goddammit. That's pretty personal stuff, Paul. Who've you been talking to? Sudsy didn't tell you any of this, I know. Are you just making all this up? You don't know any of the women . . ."

". . . with me, it's different. With me the bad things hit very hard. I don't think I recover, to tell you the truth. You don't have to believe it if you don't want to."

Woodruff felt a change. An alarm galloped by in a different direction. He studied Sternman's face, which was composed though tight and almost metallic, miraculously stable for all the fury that had passed through, and he saw that the expression had not changed at all except for a slight downward pursing of the lips. Yet Woodruff, still stupefied by the hostility, sensed that Sternman was about to fall apart. He was afraid, having never been in the presence of anything like this. There was a fine moisture in the taxi, as though Sternman's entire personality were about to be wrung from a sponge. "Paul," said Woodruff. "What happened? Where is all this coming from?"

"Hard," said Sternman, far off, trying to be gritty. "And I hurt for it. Hard. You asshole."

"Uh huh," said Woodruff. "So I'm the asshole and you're the hard-livin', hard-lovin' guy."

Sternman jerked his head.

"Hey," cried Woodruff, shrinking back, holding up his hands.

Sternman blanched suddenly. "You're bleeding!" he exclaimed.

Woodruff saw the blood, which was bright red but not copious. "I know I'm bleeding," he replied.

For a reporter, Sternman was not good on blood. As a rookie, driving to crash and crime scenes, he always fortified himself for the worst with his imagination and his discipline, and even then he often lost his composure. "My God!" he cried. "Driver, stop the cab! Call the police! Who did this, Henry?" He was looking toward the bloodstains on the jeans, which Woodruff could not hide completely with his hands.

"I did," Woodruff confessed.

"*You* did?" asked Sternman, slipping from mortification to disgust.

Woodruff looked to the ceiling of the cab. "Yeah, I zipped myself up by accident back in the Library of Congress and I don't know what to do."

"I never heard of anything like that."

"Well, neither have I!" shrieked Woodruff, who, forgetting his bondage, moved too much in the effort. He winced and groaned.

"Ugh," gagged Sternman. "I thought you hurt your back."

Woodruff sighed. Then the taxi's position registered on him. "Driver, I don't want to stop!" he ordered. "I want to go to a doctor. Let's go."

"Where to, sahr?" asked the frightened driver. His radio was off.

"I don't know. I don't have a doctor."

"You should go to the hospital," said Sternman. "Take us to George Washington emergency."

"I don't want to go to a hospital," said Woodruff. "I hate hospitals. It'll be a circus."

Sternman was pallid, wiggling on the seat from discomfort at the sight of such a wound. "Why don't you have a doctor then?" he begged.

It's a long story. Who's yours?"

"Dr. Isaacs."

"Where?"

"Watergate."

"Oh, shit. I don't want to go there."

"Why not? There's nothing wrong with a doctor in the Watergate. He's all right."

"Oh, boy," sighed Woodruff. Needles were stinging his cheeks. He rubbed his eyes with a bloody hand.

"Don't do that," said a squeamish Sternman.

"Do what?"

Horns sounded from a line of cars blocked behind the taxi on 15th Street. "Where to, sarh?" asked the driver.

"Never mind," said Sternman.

"Okay," said Woodruff. "Driver, drop Mr. Sternman here at the *Post* and then take me to the Watergate, please."

"You don't need me to go with you?" asked Sternman.

Woodruff, looking at him, shook his head as if to clear it. "No, thanks," he said.

Sternman did not impose himself. "Okay," he said. "Maybe I'll call ahead for you."

"No," said Woodruff. "I'd really rather you didn't say anything, to anybody really. I think I can do it. Dr. Isaacs, right?"

"Yeah."

"But I don't really expect you to keep quiet for me, I guess, after . . ."

". . . Well, I didn't know . . ."

". . . I know . . ."

The taxi was idling outside the *Post*. Sternman opened his door and swallowed. "Well, I don't know what to say now."

"I don't either."

"Well, good luck," said Sternman. He swallowed again, trying to suppress the residue of all the conflict he had disgorged. Then he got out, straightened himself up to a professional stiffness, and strode toward another day of news as though nothing unusual had happened. He mentioned the incident to no one, not even to LaLane Rayburn, whom he would call that night to propose the idea of reconciliation.

Woodruff was alone with his blushes and the driver, who seemed to speak with a Jamaican lilt. "Kind of weird, isn't it?" Woodruff tried to laugh. "Sorry about the commotion. We're old friends. We never argue."

"That's all right, sahr," said the driver. "I seen it ohll. I have Lyndon Johnson in here. And General Westmoreland. I have two stabbings—one stab me, one stab somebody else. Many, many robberies and one baby born back there. Yes, sahr. Baby come out in sack. Cop have to bite it open. Everybody screaming all over the place. I seen it ohll."

"I guess so," said Woodruff.

Reggae music resumed loudly on the offbeat, and Woodruff eased back to the cramped position his wound preferred. He found himself wishing that his affliction and his quarrel held a higher rank in the driver's collection of notable occurrences. And as he puzzled over the trail of Sternman's accusations against him, he wondered why he had immediately thought of Susan Hartman when Sternman called him hard and untouched by women. Interesting, thought Woodruff, musing savagely back on himself. Interesting that his reaction then and now would be to find it interesting, just as Sternman said. And telling. Woodruff felt a desperate sad tug from all Hartman's spirit and beauty, longing to be so swallowed up by her that he would find nothing interesting at all.

Nearly an hour later, after a painfully drawn-out encounter with Dr. Isaac's receptionist over whether he had an appointment and other matters —including the necessity of filling out forms in the waiting room and the receptionist's shrewd and motherly explanation of how he could and should have kept his Senate medical insurance even after leaving the Senate, which led to Woodruff's explanation of why he had chosen not to do so even though he had known the bureaucratic moves required, which the receptionist made clear she doubted—Woodruff found himself on a different floor of the Watergate building in the offices of a urologist to whom he had been referred by Dr. Isaacs. He stood in one of the dressing rooms between the waiting room and the *sanctum sanctorum*, surrounded by a stout nurse in pants, a thin pretty one in a uniform, and a doctor in a lab coat. The doctor was just what Woodruff wanted—professional, with perfect fingernails and indoor skin and very dry teeth, without a single stub of a renegade hair protruding from neck, nostril, or ear canal. His face, clean and expressionless, set off by a reassuring pair of dark-rimmed glasses, appeared to have been molded by a dozen articles on clinical technique. To Woodruff, all this was welcome as a barrier against a host of human-interest embarrassments.

Woodruff was sweating. He groaned impressively at each light touch on the zipper by the doctor, who had squatted a bit for access after carefully hitching up his lab coat and trousers. He stood up. "I see," he said.

"See what?" asked Woodruff.

"Superficial lacerations. Nothing to worry about."

"What do we do now?"

The doctor pondered as he touched thumb and forefinger delicately to the rim of his glasses, as with a camera. "Nothing to it, really," he said. "Minor surgical procedure. It's really more of an engineering problem than a medical one."

"Oh," said Woodruff. "Now? Here?"

"Yes," said the doctor. He bowed slightly. "Make yourself as comfortable as possible, Mr. Woodruff. I'll be with you in a moment or two. Miss Rogers, you know what to do."

The doctor left. Woodruff suspected that Miss Rogers did not, in fact, know what to do. She fussed briefly with a jar of tongue depressors and followed the doctor.

"Oh boy," sighed Woodruff. "This is going to be fun." He glanced at the stout nurse, who was pretending she was alone. "Betcha never had a case like this," he said.

"Superficial lacerations?" she replied.

"Well, I mean this kind, you know," stammered Woodruff.

"Not exactly," said the nurse.

"Oh," said Woodruff, looking around vainly for help. He was reconsidering his desire for professional service. The people administering to his emergency let on nothing beyond a tight membrane of discomfort. Otherwise they had the personalities of cotton swabs—or *appeared* to have them, which is what bothered Woodruff because he could see hints of jolly beer-drinking times on the stout nurse's face and he could imagine the doctor with his feet up on his desk right now, cackling merrily to his med school buddies on the phone. Woodruff decided it might be better to break on through to one good guffaw and a poke in the ribs. The professional treatment, he mused, would have been better for the gonorrhea episode, which flooded back to him. Everything was backward. If he could only do it over again, he would take his penicillin shot here with the cotton swab doctor, and he would take his zipper over to the public health clinic. Might as well have a big time. He'd tell those dudes he'd had a fight with his girlfriend—tell 'em that's how he won a thousand dollars in a bizarre game of chicken in the back room of an exclusive Georgetown bar, something like that. Pop their eyes out.

Woodruff laughed out loud to himself. The stout nurse looked askance at him and became visibly uncomfortable. Now she was worried. Woodruff struggled to sober himself.

Miss Rogers returned with two pairs of shears, which the nurses used to hack away at Woodruff's jeans. Up the legs on both sides from cuff to waist, around the pockets and through the groin—cutting, pulling, trimming until all that was left were two strands of zipper knit together at the wound. Woodruff was naked except for a copper-and-blue, Western-style bow tie hanging below the neck of his penis. In the appropriate place, there was a swelling the size of a golf ball.

"This way, please," said Miss Rogers, picking up a tray she had prepared. A surgical napkin covered the contents.

"What's that?" asked Woodruff.

"Just some ointment and equipment," she shrugged.

"Let me see," Woodruff demanded.

The stout nurse obeyed, against her better instincts. Her patient sagged on the table.

"Wait a minute," trembled Woodruff, transfixed by the sight of a large hypodermic needle in the center of the tray, garnished with a mixture of gauzes and tweezers.

"It's not going to hurt much," said the nurse.

"It already hurts," he whined, quite afraid. "I need to make a phone call. One quick phone call. I'm entitled to that."

On the way to the treatment room, clad in a gown, Woodruff dialed the Environmental Protection Agency's Chemical and Nuclear Waste Management Procedures (CANWAMP) Task Force, where Susan Hartman traveled as a part-time photographer gathering shots of barren industrial moonscapes and piles of crud.

"I'm sorry, Miss Hartman is in a meeting and cannot be disturbed," sang the secretary, trained to prim sadism.

Woodruff sighed. "Listen," he said quietly. "I want you to break in and tell her that Mr. Woodruff from the White House is about to have emergency reproductive surgery after an accident. He said he *must* speak with Miss Hartman before the anesthesia. Okay?"

The veteran secretary was not fazed. "May I have the number at the White House where Miss Hartman can return the call from Mr. Woodruff?" she countered.

Woodruff knew better than to falter or explode before this crucial response. "Four-five-six-seven-oh-nine-four," he said, making up a number off the White House exchange. "But Mr. Woodruff is not at the White House. He's at Doctor McIntyre's office in the Watergate, about to leave for George Washington hospital, and I know Miss Hartman would be upset . . ."

". . . I'll see if I can reach Miss Hartman if you'll hold please," said the secretary in a tone of unappreciated sacrifice.

"Thank you," said Woodruff, shaking his head in relief.

"Henry!" cried Hartman. "What's the matter? Where are you?"

Woodruff groaned. "I'm at a doctor's office in the Watergate," he said woefully. "It's a long story, baby, but I sliced up my you-know-what in my zipper at the library . . ."

"Eeeeww!" Hartman recoiled. Woodruff could hear her body jerking.

". . . and the doctor's gonna operate now," said Woodruff.

After a pause, Hartman said in a cautious low voice, "This isn't a joke, is it? Is Howell there?"

"No," Woodruff whispered.

"Sorry, baby. What can I do for you?"

"Could you get me a pair of trousers? They had to cut mine off."

"Sure thing," said Hartman. "I'll be there."

"Thanks," moaned Woodruff.

Two hours, one injection, and four disappearing stitches later, the doctor exhaled at length and said, "There!" He smiled broadly in miraculous transformation and reached out to shake Woodruff's hand. Woodruff was speechless beyond muttering thanks. He shook hands. The doctor vanished with his aides. And shortly thereafter, heading toward recuperation at the Savannah, Woodruff was thankful to be able to walk at a full gait.

XIV

HOWELL ARRIVED home on Monday night with a dufflebag and a sunburned nose, waving loose sheets of paper, smiling and full of tales. He found Haven Pinder at the dining room table. Her white knickers and gray socks curled under her in the chair as she studied a peculiar white paper canvas the size of a wall poster. Howell's eyes were all on the knickers. "Ah, boy!" he grinned, rushing up from behind. He reached over the chair, grabbed both her ankles, and scooped the bundle of her up into the air, at some risk to both of them.

"David!" cried Pinder. She wiggled free to eye him mischievously. She put the backs of her hands to her hips and patted her foot. "I thought you were all strung out from bad things in Miami," she said. "What happened?"

"I was," said Howell. "Still am, I guess. I don't know. You'll have to ask somebody else."

"Huh? What do you mean by that?"

"Nothing," shrugged Howell.

"Then why are you so happy?" asked Pinder, smiling but with a residue of purpose in her face. Howell had interrupted a business mood.

Howell absorbed this with mock indignation, then astonishment. Finally, he laughed. " 'Cause I missed you when I was off with the wolves," he said. "And now I get to see you." Howell was amused. An idea was formulating somewhere out of the range of expression—that his pleasant anticipation of coming home to Pinder had been goosed into a higher zone by actual sight of her in such characteristic attire and position, especially the position, for when Pinder curled her legs there was no hint of posed protection at all, only a light air that she was cozy with herself, and this in combination with the offbeat knickers and the shape of her gave Howell quick whiffs of presence far better than any anticipation, leading to superabundant delight. "Yeah," he said. "I get to see you."

Pinder leaned back to study him. "Wow," she said. "What happened down there? Must have been something."

"Well, the news from Miami is bad," sighed Howell. "First of all, Carlos Maraña is in jail."

"He *is?*"

"Yep. That's where I saw him."

"You did?"

"Yep. And that's the least of it. While I was there, two FBI agents showed up at Bobby Ziller's house and carried off this woman named Moonbeam."

"Moonbeam? Who's that?"

"Well, she's a pretty regular part of the menagerie down there," Howell sheepishly replied. "Young, pretty, flaky, high shock value, insightful, weird —the works."

"Yeah, I'll bet," said Pinder with playful suspicion. "What did they want with her?"

"I don't really know," said Howell. "That's the damn thing about it. I can't really tell about anything. That whole scene is an Edgar Allan Poe mystery written by an undercover magician. Moonbeam may be an FBI informant on drug smuggling, or they may have been trying to make her *look* like one. I don't know. And Carlos. God knows what he's doing. As best I can tell, he got *himself* arrested on some petty marijuana charge. Why, I don't know. Maybe it was to be safe in jail or to do something in jail, or maybe it was just to make the cops look silly in some plot. I don't know."

There was a glaze above Pinder's smile. "Sounds confusing, all right," she mused.

Howell sighed. "I know," he said. "But all this is not fun and games. The real bad news is about Bobby Ziller. He's still gone. I'm pretty sure he got himself tangled up with Mafia heavies, and I think he's been killed."

"Oh," whispered Pinder.

"Uh huh. Like in the movies."

"I'm sorry," she said, putting her ear softly to his chest.

"I wish you could have met him," sighed Howell. "He was such a whoopee sort of person that something like this is hard to imagine."

"Oh, David," squeezed Pinder. "I'm sorry. And you're not even sure about that?"

"Whew," sang Howell. "You got it. That's one reason I had to stop off to see the folks." He shook his head to clear it. "How about a favor?" he smiled. "How about if we forget all this for a while?"

"Okay."

"And you tell me about Henry. What happened?"

"No."

"No? Why not?"

"Because I'm tired of talking about it already," she replied. "I've listened to Henry's story about six times, and I know all the symbolic meanings he's dreamed up. And I've seen the stitches. He shows everybody the stitches." Pinder was about to smile in spite of herself. She looked soberly at the floor to conceal it.

"What stitches?"

"Just the stitches," she replied evasively. "Never mind for now, okay? You've got enough to worry about. Besides, I've got an emergency of my own."

"You do?"

"Right over there," said Pinder, pointing to the dining room table.

Stroking his chin, Howell ambled over to investigate. It did not take him long. "This is a map," he declared.

Pinder made a face. "Brilliant," she said.

Howell defended his dignity with a glance. "I'll bet you're gonna rob a bank," he remarked. "Or liberate some documents or something, aren't you?"

"Close," said Pinder.

"Uh huh. Is this where Henry received his mysterious wound?" Howell guessed wryly.

"No." Pinder was curt, and Howell, slightly taken aback, returned to the paper. He scrutinized the shape of the crude drawing—the indications of hallways and doors and staircases, along with a few words. "Fourth floor," he said to himself. And suddenly his head dropped a foot closer to the map. "LS," he said. "Is this the Georgetown Nursing Home?"

"Yep," said Pinder.

Howell slowly sat down. "Is Miss Lily all right?"

"Noooo," groaned Pinder. "She's shriveling up. She's not eating, and she hates the whole place. Says she's in the trash."

Howell put his face in his hands. "Sounds just like her," he rumbled. "Now I see, Haven . . ."

". . . I can't stand it anymore!" she cried. "You're not gonna believe how much worse she's gotten just over the weekend . . ."

". . . I know, baby," moaned Howell, "but you can't go kidnap her out of a nursing home, for God's sake!"

"Why not?" asked Pinder. "Just tell me why not."

Howell was shaking his head. "Why not?" he brooded. "Just tell me why not. All right." Then the nodding came to a halt and he began to study Pinder's face. "You're serious," he decided. "You're not putting me on."

"Well?" challenged Pinder.

"You *are* serious," sputtered Howell. "You realize, of course, that it's crazy? You realize that, don't you?"

"Well?"

"I don't mean zany whacko wonderful crazy, Haven. I mean criminal deranged no-no crazy. It's kidnapping, for openers. You can get life in jail for that. Her nephew runs the FBI in Miami, and he'll be all over our ass. Besides that, it's February. You can't take a ninety-year-old woman out in the snow in her nightgown. She'll freeze. She'll fall and break her hip. And even if she didn't, we don't have any place to put her and nobody to take care of her. Other than that, it's a great idea." Howell stood up and grinned with an exaggerated shrug. He twirled around in place several times as though to dispel the lunacy, but then, seeing Pinder unmoved, fell back into the chair. He sagged with remorse. "I'm sorry," he said. "I know what you go through when you visit her. Believe me. I just don't think it's a good idea, that's all. I'm sorry."

Howell moved toward her for a hug, but Pinder remained still in a curious daze. Her lips formed a small circle and her skin was waxen, smooth and filled with liquid. She took one step away from Howell.

Howell winced out loud at the sight of her. "Oh, shit," he moaned.

Pinder cocked her head slightly to one side. "I've thought of all those things," she said quietly.

"All what things?"

"All those things you said about why it's crazy."

"Oh."

Pinder tilted her head to the other side and wobbled around in a rubbery, snooty, taunting look, acquired in her high school days. "You're not sorry," she announced. "Because you're gonna do it."

Howell's head bounced on his neck as he watched her. "Just like that, eh?" he quipped, snapping his fingers. "You're right. Let's quit wasting time! This is Washington, but forget policy! Forget Latin intrigue! Let's heist an old lady!" He spun around toward the kitchen, then reversed himself and went back toward his dufflebag. Pinder watched. Howell was suddenly jittery. He scratched his head viciously. "Mind if I take a second to think this over?" he asked, fumbling through the dufflebag. "Goddamm it . . ."

". . . They're right here," said Pinder, turning around to a bookshelf behind her.

Howell, bending over, looked up from the dufflebag. He rose into a look of awe. "Well, I'll be damned," he chuckled. "How did you know?"

Without a word, Pinder tossed him the pale lime boxer shorts. She also threw him the striped railman's hat.

"Good ol' crisis drawers," beamed Howell. "I couldn't believe I really left these things here. Sure could have used them in Miami."

A few minutes later Howell returned from the bathroom via the kitchen, wearing the hat and the lime shorts and a faded T-shirt commemorating the New York World's Fair. "I'm ready," he declared, clutching tonic and Mount Gay rum.

"Are you sure?" asked Pinder. She spoke with a slight tremble.

Howell nodded. "Brief me," he said.

"Okay," said Pinder, warming up. "Now the first thing I found out is that Pat Shea doesn't have legal authority over Miss Snow. He just put her in there by fiat. That's what happens with almost all of them there. Some relative just shows up and sticks them in."

"Uh huh. How did you find that out?"

"From Doris," said Pinder. "She's one of the nurses I made friends with."

"Does Doris like Miss Snow?"

"Every now and then she squeezes her hand as she walks by," said Pinder.

"They prop Miss Snow up in the hall about three hours a day in a wheel-chair, strapped in, and the nurses come by with food trays and medicine. Slap them down on the run."

"Oh, boy," sighed Howell.

"You know what it's like."

"Yeah. So what does keep Miss Snow in there if she wants to leave?"

"Inertia, mostly."

"I can't believe that," said Howell. "That place has got to have more protection than that. It sounds like the nursing home could be charged with kidnapping."

"Well, they got her to sign a release for all claims that might result from their treatment," said Pinder. "The relatives have to sign it, too. Pat Shea signed it. That's an agreement to have her there, in a way, and it protects the home from what it really worries about—malpractice suits by the relatives after the patient dies. But the release doesn't give the home the right to keep Miss Snow there against her will. In order to do that, Pat Shea would have to get her declared incompetent by a judge and get a court order to keep her there."

"Uh huh," said Howell. "Why didn't he do that?"

" 'Cause it costs money and is a lot of trouble and is a waste," Pinder replied. "Who needs it? Miss Snow has no effective will. She can't leave, and she wouldn't have any place to go anyway."

"All right, what's your plan? How would you get her out?"

Pinder lit up. "You mean you'll do it?"

Howell rocked backward and rotated his neck under the pressure. "Not necessarily," he drawled. "I've got to know the plan first."

"Oh. Well, let's assume for a minute that the plan will work and we can get her out," Pinder ventured. "Then would you do it?"

"What do you mean, 'work'?"

"Well, I mean we don't go to jail or anything like that and Miss Snow is safe. How 'bout it?"

Howell rubbed his neck.

"Your neck sore?" grinned Pinder.

"Yeah," groaned Howell. "Look, I don't want to dump on this idea, but I mean there are a lot of things to think about with something this serious. Like where would Miss Snow live and who would pay for it and who would take care of her? Stuff like that."

"Well, I think she should live here, in the bedroom. You and I can have the fold-out couch. It's bigger than the bed anyway. And we can use my place some. Henry and Sudsy might have to move back to Sudsy's. And I can spend a lot of time with Miss Snow because I quit my job at the Coalition."

"You what?"

"I quit. In fact, I went to unemployment this morning. Martin's still trying to buy the building, but I don't think he's got a chance. Neither do we, probably. Half the tenants have moved out already."

"That's great," said Howell. "We'll have no job and no place to live and the FBI after us for an old lady."

"David," chided Pinder.

"I can't believe you quit. What are you gonna do?"

"I don't know. But I didn't quit just because of this plan, if that's what you're thinking. I wanted to quit anyway." Pinder stood up and began to pace behind Howell, who exercised his neck trying to watch her. "You've missed a few things. The day after you left—Friday, I guess—Miss Hope called me up and told me somebody was in Miss Snow's apartment, so I went down and found Shea there. He had a mover and was going through all her stuff telling him what to ship to Florida and what to junk and stuff. He wasn't too happy to see me. I walked in and asked him if Miss Snow had died . . ."

". . . Oh, Jesus, you can't . . ."

". . . Well, it was like he was dividing up the estate before she even dies, and I just didn't like it. I wasn't obnoxious, really. But I told him I didn't think Miss Snow was doing too well in the home and said you and I would be anxious to take care of her if we could get just a little part-time help, you know . . ."

". . . Thanks for telling me about it . . ."

". . . Well, I thought you'd go along, you know, and I had to say it then. There's not much *time*, David. She's gonna die. There really isn't. I tried to convince Shea of that, but he just said he thought it would be better to have her near a lot of medical care. He was very nervous. He went back to Miami this morning. Didn't even go see her."

"The son of a bitch," muttered Howell.

"He's not really so bad," said Pinder. "He's just busy with arrangements, mostly. Kind of removed and harassed or something. I think he's pretty much of a sympathetic asshole, like everybody else."

"Well, that's just it," said Howell. "I wouldn't want to do this out of bravado or anything. And there's no duty involved or anything like that. No family. No financial necessity. No larger issues at stake. And if I don't hate Shea enough or love Miss Snow enough . . ."

". . . What's enough?" asked Pinder.

"I don't know," said Howell with a trace of irritation. "That's the question, I guess. But we should really know, because we could really fuck up here. I mean bad. You and I could split up over it. Miss Snow could die . . ."

". . . Well, I think she's gonna die within a month anyway . . ."

". . . That's what you think, but we don't really know. She might die here, too, and we'd be haunted by it, if we thought we were responsible. Or she might live ten more years. Are you ready for that? Some sort of miraculous recovery? It could happen. I know you. You might just turn her on and have her kicking up her heels . . ."

". . . She loves you, too, David . . ."

". . . Well, she thinks I'm funny." Finally he took a deep breath and looked at the floor. "Would you do this by yourself?" he asked quietly.

Pinder looked out the window. "I don't know," she replied. "I don't want to bargain about it too much. There are some things you just *do*, that's all."

Howell appeared to sink into a trance. "Uh huh," he said, staring off. He swallowed. "You know, sometimes I can't tell whether things just happen through some sort of destiny or lucky sequence or whether I kind of arrange for it to happen, but looking back so many times there's this bizarre poignance to things."

"So we'll get her then?"

"How do I know?" groaned Howell. "How do I know whether I would jump out of an airplane or bet everything on one solid instinct at the track? I won't know until I'm right there. And I'll be scared one way or the other."

"I will, too," smiled Pinder. "You're wonderful."

"Uh huh, that's great," said Howell. "I think I feel the old buzz saw heading this way. How would you feel if this thing backfires?"

"If we try, I think I would be sad but proud," sniffled Pinder.

"Sad but proud," mocked Howell. "That's perfect. You're sounding more like a southerner all the time."

"Fuck you," said Pinder.

"Well, I learned one thing," said Howell. "Next time I go to Miami I'm taking you with me."

"You got a deal," beamed Pinder.

In furtherance of their agreement, Howell rented a bright red luxury automobile the following afternoon. The car sported an all-white interior of tufted leather, dual armrests, a shiny instrument panel, a smell of fresh polyurethaned paper, and seats adjustable along three axes by an electric motor.

At precisely half past four he pulled up outside the Savannah to find Pinder waiting there with the equipment: two blankets, a jar of honey, two large shopping bags, a pair of wool athletic socks, a Bible, an Episcopal hymnal, a roll of paper towels, a pair of dark glasses, a scarf, two pillows, and a wool hat. Pinder piled it all in the back seat before diving into the shotgun position. She was wearing a print dress from the thirties, with shoulder pads and a full skirt over boots. Howell was in his only suit and his heavy-traction climbing boots, looking like a bulldozer driver after a visit to his congressman.

Moving west on M Street, Howell stopped at the second alley east of Wisconsin Avenue. Engine running, brake on, he leaned over to give Pinder a desperate bear hug. They stared at each other and mutually rolled their eyes in dizzy apprehension. "I don't believe this," said Howell with amused adoration. "Go do your stuff, Scout." Pinder did not look back as she ran up the alley through the dirty snow.

Howell turned right on Wisconsin Avenue and inched his way up the hill lined with ice cream parlors and French cafés and theaters and boutiques, an area that had never appealed much to him. The Georgetown Nursing

Home had no lights, nor much of a sign at all. Howell almost missed it, though he had been there several times before. He was jumpy, beating back panic, when he saw a column of darkness falling onto the street. He stopped the car in traffic and jumped out for the signal, but only after squinting up toward the huge recessed building could he see Haven Pinder on the front porch, holding up her thumb.

Howell drove around the block and up the alley over Pinder's footprints. After turning around at an intersecting alley, he made his way in reverse gear until he backed up to the nose of the blue hearse. He took the shopping bags and the honey with him, locked the car, and gazed about over the cold smoke of his breath. The alley dead-ended into a *cul-de-sac* at the rear of the nursing home, large enough for six or eight cars. There was a curved brick wall of about six feet in height on the side opposite the alley, above which could be seen only the scraggly naked branches of a middle-aged elm tree. The curved wall ran away from the rear corner of the nursing home like a rib and butted into the side of a three-story, windowless brick building that faced north. On the south border, opposite the curved wall, ran a straight brick wall at a slightly oblique angle so that the wall jutted into the space squarely behind the home. It appeared to surround the yard of the building next to the home. On the far side of this wall loomed red shoulders of another brick hulk. Howell thus surveyed an enclosure of mongrel shape, a rhomboid with a round belly, so shut off from light that the late afternoon sun left no shadows at the damp terminal of the alley. A dark green trash dumpster stood next to the hearse. Behind them a concrete loading ramp sloped gently up to a set of oversized industrial doors, flanked by handrails and covered by a metal awning. On the right side of the large doors was a smaller entrance topped by a small, inhospitable painted sign reading "Visitors." It opened as Howell approached at a fated trudge.

"You all right?" whispered Pinder.

"Yeah," whispered Howell. "How's Miss Snow?"

"Don't know. Haven't been up there yet."

"Why are we whispering?"

Pinder looked cautiously back over her shoulder. "Beats me," she said.

Howell walked by her. "Now look," he said out loud, "we can't spook ourselves, okay?"

"Check," said Pinder. She followed Howell's eyes to the large room on the left of the corridor, glass along the corridor wall waist-high, valentines strung in loops along the glass. Inside, one uniformed lady was pounding out "Rock of Ages" on a sour piano and another was leading a classroom of wheelchairs in song. Hers was the only distinguishable voice except for two or three of the spryer patients, seated in regular chairs around the perimeter. Among the wheelchair congregation, some voices scratched vaguely along the tune while others made miscellaneous sounds sporadically, on their own antiquated rhythms.

Howell pushed the elevator button. "No," said Pinder. "That thing takes forever. Let's walk." They made their way eighty feet down the hall past the administrative offices and the kitchen to the front door and the muffled sound of traffic on Wisconsin Avenue. A staircase ascended on the left.

"What if she's already asleep?" asked Howell, following upward.

"I don't know," Pinder replied. She stopped briefly on the second floor landing to peer down its hall, which was oppressively dim. Faint glows of orange spilled from what few doors were open. They might have come from candles. Only a nurses' station at the midpoint was well illuminated. Beyond it, two or three silent figures slumped next to the walls like urns in a small-town hotel.

"Jesus," shuddered Howell. "Are you sure this place is legal?"

"The floors get lighter as you go up," said Pinder. "I don't know why. My guess is that you start on the fourth floor and move down the longer you're here."

The fourth floor was indeed clean, gleaming, and cacophonous by contrast with the others, with bright fluorescent lights, a bustle of nurses, and patients lined up thickly along the walls—food gone, medicines down, trays still up for the preslumber sitting. Howell breathed deeply, thankful to be back on familiar ground. He took the lead toward Miss Snow's room.

"Hello, Doris," said Pinder, as they approached a stout nurse leaning over a tiny white-haired man who looked dapper in a red-checked shirt. He had a beatific smile on his face and a small stuffed giraffe in his arms, the only such toy to be seen on the corridor. Doris was combing the old man's hair. "Well looka here!" beamed Doris. "Miss Snow's gonna have a big time. Hello, Haven."

Pinder towed Howell to Doris's side. "Is she still awake?" she asked.

"Well, honey, she's still sittin' up," said Doris, "but we already cut her engine for the night."

"Oh," said Pinder. Howell inched up from behind. He thought he detected by some wise glint that Doris was winking about the scheme, but he couldn't decide whether this was good or bad.

"Let's go," said Pinder, touching his elbow. Howell jumped before smiling at her, and they followed Doris down the hall.

Doris swung her arms freely while walking, a habit she had embellished years earlier as a carhop for a drive-in restaurant. One arm sidled out casually to tweak the nose of a skinny old man in a stupor, with metallic blue hair and dark blue shadows in his sunken cheeks and a row of ferocious lines on his forehead. "Goddammit!" barked the old man. He kept staring straight ahead.

"Hush, Sidney," laughed Doris. "I done tol' you about that kind of talk." She never stopped, calling out other names down the row. Sidney scowled so actively that his head teetered about on a weak spring of a neck. "Goddammit!" he squeaked.

Lily Snow was in the third wheelchair from the back end of the corridor. Her sparse white hair, neatly combed and tied in a small bun, was the most visible part of her, as her face slumped over and her head hung like a cap on a peg. She was strapped in around the chest. "Wake up, Lily," said Doris. "Company's here." She curtsied off back up the hall.

Miss Snow did not move. "Uunnnhh," moaned Pinder in her sympathetic noise. It was involuntary, and as soon as she recognized her own sound she pulled out of it into a cheerful, "Hi, Miss Lily."

Howell stood back, making sure it was indeed Miss Snow. There was always some doubt, because the speed of her decomposition and the blur of frail wheelchair occupants obscured Howell's memory of the lively old spinster from the Savannah. This time it was her skin that struck him as unfamiliar. There was less of it hanging on her bones, but to Howell what seemed alien and unfair about it was the color. It was a clear jelly flecked with gray, as though the large raised veins were casting dirty shadows all through her protoplasm. Her arms looked like fillets of a dark-meat fish, caked here and there with a flourlike paste. Howell hoped it was baby powder as he squatted down on the linoleum along with Pinder to look up into Miss Snow's face.

"Hi, Miss Snow," he said.

"Who are you?" rasped Miss Snow over a blank look.

"Haven and David, Miss Snow," said Howell, giving Pinder a look that he might be better off elsewhere.

"From the Savannah," added Pinder. "Here. Give me your hand."

"Well, there you are!" cried Miss Snow with a smile. "How nice of you two to come see me. I think you're both perfectly lovely. Don't you?"

Pinder felt better, although she noticed that the top half of Miss Snow's face remained numb. "Thank you," she said, rubbing her hand. "Sometimes we're nice, I guess."

"Of course you are," said Snow. "You're as nice as you can be."

"Thank you," said Howell. "How have you been, Miss Snow? Have you found any new friends up here?"

"Of course not," Snow replied. "I haven't even talked to anyone, to be quite candid. They all act like babies. They think they're ancient."

"Oh," said Pinder. She and Howell eyed each other awkwardly. "How about somebody to hold hands with? I know you like to do that."

"That's just it," said Snow. "I haven't found anybody worth holding hands with."

"Oh, Miss Snow, you're just joshing," said Howell.

The old lady cracked a smile. "It's in my nature," she said. "But I do love holding hands with you and your wife, it's true. Both at once whenever I can manage it."

"That's easy," said Howell, taking her other hand in both of his. "How's this?"

"That's just right," she pronounced.

"Good," said Howell. "Don't go away. I just want to take my parka off." He released her hand and began to strip off the parka.

"Help yourself," said Snow. "You can take off all your clothes if you like."

Pinder shook her head to clear her ears. "Excuse me?" she said.

"I said he can take off everything as far as I'm concerned," Miss Snow repeatedly soberly.

"Miss Snow!" sputtered a gleeful Pinder, who had not heard an attack of Miss Snow's ribaldry since the Italian lover story. Howell was laughing out loud. "Did you hear that?" he asked Pinder.

Miss Snow also laughed, lifting up her tiny oval face. Howell and Pinder each knew that the other was noticing how the life had swelled back into the top of the old woman's cheeks, all around her bright blue eyes that were strangled at the edges by patches of doughy tissue.

". . . There you have it. Yes I am. I'm not as old as these old fossils who can't do anything but complain and answer questions and make nuisances of themselves, but I do think I'm old enough to tell your husband that, don't you?"

". . . Well, yes . . ."

". . . Good . . ."

". . . But . . ."

"And it stands to reason that I'm old enough to tell you two that I love both of you, even though I scarcely know you . . ."

". . . Oh, Miss Snow," smiled Howell.

". . . But I do. There's nothing you can do about it, I'm afraid. Is there?" She looked imploringly at them.

"Don't *need* to do anything," said Howell. "We both love you too."

"Yep," said Pinder.

"How lucky that it's all working out," said Snow.

"In fact," said Howell, "we wanted to ask you something. Do you remember when they brought you here with your nephew, Mr. Shea, and you didn't want to come and you asked us to hide you in a pile of leaves?"

"From New York?" asked Snow

"No, from Washington," replied Howell.

"I haven't been to Washington for weeks," Snow declared.

Pinder and Howell gave each other apprehensive looks. "We're in Washington now," Howell said gently. "In Georgetown."

"Oh, Georgetown!" said Snow. "Yes, I like it quite a bit."

"You were leaving the Savannah," said Pinder.

"And then I went to New York?"

"Well, on your way here," said Pinder. It made her uncomfortable to see Snow suddenly grope with time and travel.

"Anyway, do you remember asking us to hide you in a pile of leaves?" asked Howell.

Snow struggled with the question for some time, looking off, losing strength, forming parts of words with her lips. "Leaves?" she asked. "I believe so. I believe I do. Where would we be without them?"

"That's a point," said Howell. "But what I meant was . . . about the leaves, Miss Snow. The leaves aren't important . . ."

". . . Aren't they now?" asked Snow, the emptiness returning to her face.

"Well, sometimes," struggled Howell. "Sometimes they are. But what I

295

meant was that you wanted to escape from here. You wanted to hide in the leaves."

"That sounds lovely," said Snow.

"Uh huh. But we'd like to know if you'd still like to leave."

"Leaves?"

"Well, leave any way we can. There aren't any leaves now. There's snow everywhere."

"How dreadful," said Snow. "It must be cold as the dickens."

Howell sighed. "Yes, it is," he said. "Have you heard from Mr. Shea, your nephew in Florida?"

"Him?" said Snow. "Pat? Not that I know of. He's a lawyer, you know."

Howell sighed again. "How about your sister Maggie?"

"Oh, yes!" Snow declared. "Father talked with me about Maggie just this morning. I'm afraid she's on the rampage again."

"On the rampage?" choked Pinder, whose spirit was retreating through the confusion.

"Quite right," said Snow. "Father went over there for a visit and he said, 'Maggie, I wish you'd tell those girls living upstairs to behave themselves.' And Maggie said, 'Father, there's not a thing I can do about it.' 'Well,' said Father, 'perhaps I should have a talk with them.' And it was not very satisfactory as I recall, so then Maggie said, 'Father, I think they'll quiet down if I go with you to the Catskills for a time.' And Father decided that was just what to do. I said, 'Exactly right,' and Maggie said, 'Let me get just a few snips together.' But she didn't visit for some reason. Changed her mind. Maggie and Father both are always changing their minds. Inconvenient, probably. So Father and I rode the train up together. He arrived again just yesterday looking fit and proper as ever and said, 'Let's take a trip.' I said, 'Fine. Where's Maggie?' And I was just getting ready to go . . ."

Snow's mouth dropped open silently and her breath caught on a ratchet somewhere inside her. She appeared stricken, although there was no sign of pain in her face. Pinder, who had been awestruck through Snow's monologue, dropped a tear on her cheek when she made her involuntary noise. She watched Snow's entire torso contract as though a bubble of air were passing through her. Even Howell's small hands would fit around Snow's wispy chest, which was troubled by passing storms and changing colors. Frightened, Pinder grabbed Howell's knee with her free hand. She thought Snow was having a seizure, some kind of freezing up of her internal workings, but she also thought it was possible that Snow was in the grip of a bowel movement. Then she hoped it was something much less, some breakdown in slow motion between the family realities in Snow's gut and her mouth, which ordinarily ground them down into words. Pinder realized that she was no less paralyzed than Snow.

"Are you all right, Miss Lily?" Pinder groaned.

Snow swallowed. "Yes, thank you, dear," she smiled.

Howell leaned forward next to Snow's ear. "Miss Snow, will you excuse us for a minute?" he asked. "We need to get some water, okay? Don't you run off."

They rose from the floor and looked surreptitiously about before stalking around the corner to the water fountain.

Howell blasted out some stale, angry air. "Holy shit!" he whispered into Pinder's ear. "I thought she was gonna croak."

"I don't know if I can do this," said Pinder.

"I don't either," said Howell. "We've got a catch-22, I think. When she's bad and helpless, I think we're not qualified to take care of her and she's about finished anyway. When she's good, I figure she doesn't need us and this place isn't so bad after all. Either way I wonder how the hell I got here. Except I know how I got here."

Pinder pursed her lips together in a white line. "Oooh," she sighed. "I feel so tight."

"Me too."

"I kick myself for babying her sometimes—always talking about her old friends and the Savannah and stuff—'cause every once in a while she jumps right past us with something pretty sophisticated and I think she must resent us for treating her like an idiot. God, they're so many people inside her I can't stand it. What should we do when she starts talking about her father like that? Should we tell her he's been dead forty years?"

"I don't know. How about all that traveling she does? She sounds like a train schedule."

"She's a train person," said Pinder. "Doris says she doesn't say a word to anybody for as much as a week when we don't visit. She says some of them go for months. I guess the live part of them has to go somewhere. It's so weird."

"Well, I don't know. She sounds like she's having a pretty good time on some of those trips."

"This is ridiculous," whispered Pinder. "What are we gonna do?"

"I don't know," said Howell. "But I tell you one thing. I don't want to keep coming back here feeling like this. Let's either do it or forget it."

"Gulp," said Pinder.

"So why did you cut me off when I was asking her whether she wants to leave?" asked Howell. "I figure we at least ought to make the effort."

"Well, I was chickening out," winced Pinder.

"Oh," said Howell.

"I'm sorry," said Pinder.

"Wait a minute," said Howell. "Listen, Haven, I *know* you love Miss Snow whether we kidnap her or not, okay?"

Pinder looked down to smile. "That sounds funny," she said.

"I mean it," said Howell, flicking the side of his nose. "You don't have to prove anything to me or Miss Snow or anybody else."

Pinder smiled warmly. "You always flick your nose when you're tender," she said.

"Fuck you," said Howell, looking hurt.

Pinder hugged him and made her noise again. Howell hugged her back. "Enough of this," said Pinder, breaking it off. "I refuse to filibuster ourselves into a nondecision. The patients down at the songfest will be coming up soon and we'll lose our chance to take her down." She stamped her foot for resolution and, craning her neck stealthily around the corner, peered at the row of wheelchairs. "On the other hand," she sighed.

"What?" asked Howell.

"Well, I have always identified with deers," said Pinder. "Because of their tentativeness."

"You? Tentative?"

"On the important stuff," she said, bowing her head. "Tell you what, David. Let's take her downstairs and decide then."

Howell stared at her silently until she looked up for a brief and friendly, but indecisive, conversation by eye. "Here," said Howell, handing her the shopping bags. "You get her stuff together okay? I want to talk to her just a second."

"What for?"

"Well, I want to try to talk to her straight," replied Howell. "If she can really speak her mind on something like this, I don't want her to miss the chance just because I'm too squeamish to lay it out for her."

Pinder smiled. "I'm glad we agree on so much," she said, but she grabbed the bags and skirted the corner before Howell could say anything.

Howell squatted low and took Miss Snow's hand in his. She was staring at a nearby piece of air. He rubbed vigorously. "Miss Snow, come in please," he called softly, mimicking a pilot. "Come in, Miss Snow. Mayday."

The old woman squeezed his hand. "Oh, there you are!" she cried. "You are a perfect dear with your warm hands."

"Thank you," said Howell. He leaned forward close to her face and marshaled all the intensity he could. "I need to talk to you and I don't have much time," he whispered. "Please, Miss Snow. Concentrate on what I'm asking you and tell me just exactly what you think. It's very important."

Snow seemed to brighten slightly. "My, my," she said. "That's good. Father says I'm much more competent on important matters than on trivial ones."

"Good," said Howell, who wasn't sure her cheerfulness was a positive sign. "Now this is serious, maybe even criminal for us. Haven and I are thinking of taking you out of here. Not for a visit. Not for a ride or anything. But permanently. For good. We're thinking of taking you out of here for good. Understand?"

"Sounds lovely," said Snow.

"No," whispered Howell. He squeezed her hand five or six times, firmly enough to make her wince. "It may not be lovely at all. Listen to me, please. The people here in this hospital won't like it, Miss Snow. You're not supposed to leave. And your family probably won't like it either. Your nephew won't like it. And Haven and I aren't your family. We're taking a risk. We think people are going to try and take you back and bring you here again, Miss Snow. It might be very unpleasant for you. We don't want that, if you don't. Understand? We really don't. Basically what we have in mind is to sneak you out of here and take you back to the Savannah to live with us."

298

"That *is* important," said Snow. "Yes, of course it is. I love the Savannah. Always have. I'm going back there to live just as soon as things are ready for me. Next week, probably. I was there last week and the whole place was still quite irregular."

Wearily, Howell sat back on his heels. He ground his teeth, eyes closed. "No, Miss Snow," he groaned. "That's not right. This is a nursing home in Washington, and you're not supposed to leave here. Please try to tell me what you want us to do, but you should understand that nobody else is ever going to take you back to the Savannah. They want you to stay here. That's the whole point. They think it's best for you to stay right here and not go back to the Savannah, Miss Snow. That's it. I'm sorry, but it is."

Howell searched Snow's crinkly face for signs of comprehension or apprehension or despair. He felt cruel, waiting what seemed like minutes as he watched light whip blankly in and out of her eyes.

Snow nodded her head at the end of her deliberation. "Well," she said, "I don't see why they shouldn't."

"Shouldn't what?" asked Howell.

"Shouldn't take me to the Savannah," said Snow. "Isn't that what you asked?"

"Yes," said Howell, blinking.

"Well, there you have it," said Snow. "I know where I am and where I'm going, so I can't for the life of me imagine why anyone wouldn't take me to the Savannah."

"Well, that's a point," said Howell, shaking gently as his insides commenced a laugh. "But we're thinking of taking you ourselves because we really don't think anybody's gonna help. How's that?"

"Splendid," beamed Snow. "Father loves the Savannah, too."

At this, Howell paused, swallowed, and sighed. "Miss Snow, you're really something, you know," he said. "That's what Mr. Davis says about you, come to think of it. He always says, 'I can't figure that woman out. She whipsaws me with her tongue.'"

"Oh he does, does he?" said Snow. "He's amusing in his own gruff way, but romantically he's as cold as a plate of salad."

"Miss Snow!" winced Howell.

"Well, it's the truth and I can't do anything about it," said Snow.

Pinder emerged from the room with a look of accomplishment. "Well, look at you two," she said, noting Howell's wet cheek and Snow's open mouth. Snow always laughed in mime.

"She's about to call Mr. Davis a coot again," Howell explained. "And I think the plan is okay with her."

"What plan?" asked Snow.

"It is?" gulped Pinder.

"Yep," shrugged Howell.

"What plan?" asked Snow.

"Okay," sighed Pinder.

"*The* plan," said Howell to Snow. "And the plan right now is for us to go downstairs for a little bit of singing with the Salvation Army group. How's that sound?"

Snow looked puzzled. "Well, if you ask me, it's not much of a plan at all. I can't abide the singing, frankly. These creatures in here can't sing worth a nickel."

"That may be," said Pinder, "But it doesn't matter. It's part of the plan."

"I beg your pardon?" said Snow.

Howell gave the hallway a conspirator's scan. "It's just a trick," he whispered to Snow. They eased the wheelchair down the hall past the demanding stares and incoherent sounds of Snow's neighbors to the interminably slow elevator and down to the first floor. Twice Pinder puffed her cheeks to the bursting point to let off pressure. Howell rubbed his stomach, finger-cleaned his ear, and sniffled energetically as though he had a cold.

The songfest was entering its final ten minutes when the Snow party pulled up in the middle of a hymn. A number of the singers continued through the Amen and would no doubt keep going through the remaining ones, Howell guessed. He watched the singers and felt them watching him with a peculiar intensity—accusing, hoping, scolding, begging. No one watched Snow at all except Pinder, who leaned over to examine a blank face whose alertness had fled.

Pinder stood up and whispered to Howell, "She's conking out."

Howell kept looking at the crowd, marking the location of the single nurse in attendance. "That's probably good," he replied. Then he bent down to place his ear in front of Snow's mouth, near enough to feel a light breath and to smell the combined odor of shampoo and urea and a mealy, breadlike substance that was mysterious but not unpleasant. Howell nodded his agreement as he stood up. "She wants to ride in the hall for a minute," he announced to Pinder, who nodded in response. They backed out into the hall and made one pass up and down.

"We forgot the hymnal," whispered Pinder.

"I know," said Howell.

"I don't think we're very good actors anyway."

"I know."

"I think it's time."

"Yep."

"Oh. Are you all right?"

"I don't know."

"Okay," said Pinder. She took off through the door without warning or good-bye, leaving Howell feeling abandoned with his charge. He tried singing along with the group inside, but he could manage only a vowely tenor chant, like a crude imitation Japanese.

When Pinder shouldered her way back in through the door, she brought with her the sound of a running engine. For an instant she gazed around, wide-eyed and spine-gripped from cold fright, and then she dropped her bundle on the floor. "It's too cold!" she whispered.

"It's too everything," said Howell. He shared with Pinder a look of extreme suffering from impatience. "Okay," he said, reaching under Snow's knees and behind her shoulders. "Easy, Miss Snow," he whispered. "I'm only gonna pick you up for a second." Stiffening his back like a weightlifter, Howell miscalculated the effort required. He nearly threw the old woman into the air. "Jesus!" he whispered. "She's light! Hurry!"

Pinder, moaning softly, spread both blankets in the wheelchair and at the same time watched furtively for company. Howell lowered Snow back into the wheelchair and the two of them fumbled to wrap the blankets around her.

"I can do this," shivered Howell. "Let's get out of here. Is the car warm?"

"Getting there."

"Where are the dark glasses?"

"She doesn't need them. It's already dark out there. Not much glare off the snow."

"Oh. Can I see?"

"Yeah."

"Sure you want to do this?"

Pinder grabbed him about the waist from behind and cupped her body to his. "Yes," she gasped. "But let's do spoons for about a week. Promise?"

Howell tried to quiet his chest. "Jesus!" he whispered. "I can't stop breathing like this. I'm a failure in this line of work . . ."

". . . You are not . . ."

". . . My knees are weak. It's all true. All the cliches are true . . ."

". . . You're all right. You remember the signal?"

"The what?"

"The signal."

"Oh, yes. Don't talk about it."

"Knock on wood. See you in a second, Miss Snow." Pinder decided not to kiss the white face with the half-closed eyes. She made a face and squeezed Howell instead. Then she ran out.

Howell dropped to his knees and fumbled with the socks, pulling them over old feet that seemed glazed and poreless, like high quality sculptures. He bundled the socks inside the old blue blankets. Hurry, he thought. The scarf went six times around her neck. Howell let her head fall back against the chair after wrapping it. "Fuck," he said. Snow did not seem to notice. The pullover wool hat was the last and easiest move. It engulfed her small head. Howell stood up. "This is no time to hesitate," he whispered to himself. "It's gonna be all right, Miss Snow. It's gonna be all right. You be sweet, okay? He scooped her up.

"Help!" cried Snow in a small voice, buried in the wool. "Help! Help!"

Howell was stricken white and paralyzed. "Shhhhhh," he whispered to the ceiling. Snow's disembodied wail touched the deepest spot of his fear.

"Help! Help!"

"Shhhhhh." Howell spun in a circle. Desperately, he rocked his bundle like a baby and nuzzled the scarf. "Don't do this to me," he begged. "I'm skidding. It's gonna be all right."

"Help!"

Howell was in another miserable spin when he heard an automobile horn sound lightly in the distance. He froze. The horn sounded again.

"Ohhhh," whimpered Howell."

"Help!"

Fury seized him. "Shhhhh!" he hissed. "Goddammit! Somebody's coming!"

He heard the soft crunch of feet in the snow. "Help," he moaned. He put Snow back in the wheelchair as the door opened.

"Help!"

Howell dropped to his knees and yanked off the wool hat. He heard two deep-voiced men pass behind him, arguing about the rival quarterbacks for the Washington professional football team.

"Help!" cried Snow.

Howell blindly dropped his face on hers. He rubbed cheeks, partly to comfort himself. He felt very weak. His mind refused to make any suggestions on what to say to the authorities. The voices faded.

"I should have known they wouldn't pay any attention to you, Miss Snow," Howell whispered. The breathlessness was returning. He looked around at the fluorescent glow and down to the hat in his hand. "Does this hat bother you?" he whispered.

Snow's face acknowledged the words but she made no further reply. Howell, with a big sigh, slipped the hat back on."

"Help!" cried Snow.

"Uh huh," grinned Howell, scanning the hall. "Well, Miss Snow, you've got to trust me for a minute. I am the help this time, I think."

"Help!" cried Snow.

Howell scooped her up again, took three steps to the door, and banged it open with his ass. Down the ramp and through the snow he went, feeling exhilarated and settled at once.

Pinder threw open the passenger door and piled two pillows next to her right shoulder. Howell laid Snow on the seat, back to the pillows, blankets stretched toward the door.

"Are you all right?" squeaked Pinder. She was just entering her fear, having been alone with the suspense.

"Of course," swaggered Howell. "And so is she. Nothing to it."

Pinder looked highly distressed. "Those guys came over to talk to me!" she whispered. "I didn't know what to do. Did you hear the horn in time?"

"Yeah," said Howell. "It's all right. Here. Put your arm around backward to keep her from falling forward."

Howell jumped in. "Go," he said.

"We did it!" said Pinder on the road, but she could scarcely talk. She was gulping, too full of raw triumph, awe, and fear. "Nobody ever checked out of that place like you did, Miss Snow," she managed.

All the way home they darted about like a pair of spring dragonflies in the air. The words lagged far behind their conversation. Every detail of the

302

evening struck them both as unbearably hilarious. With pride and relief pushing hard from behind, a glance or almost any detached word could trigger the giggles. And then, at the same time and with no warning, both of them would be pierced by a terror that Lily Snow would die there in the car. Always it was mutual, and this helped pull them out of it off in another direction. The timing never failed. It was still going after they had put Snow to rest in their own bed at the Savannah and listened twenty times apiece to her shallow breath, and after they had showered and folded out the big sofa bed in their new living room quarters. Then there occurred a simultaneous outburst of frisky energy. They scooted around the bed in each other's arms, hugging like lovers, flipping like wrestlers, laughing like children, shushing each other lest they wake up Snow.

"I feel this tingly excitement like I did when I was sixteen," said Pinder between bursts of scooting.

"You what?" giggled Howell.

"No, listen," she said. "I used to go to the movies with my first real boyfriend and I'd be so excited that when he put his arm around me and touched my bra strap I felt naked all over and I couldn't sit still. I'd be squirming around, and the very *idea* of his stomach or his underpants or anything was just more than I could stand."

Howell tried to look wounded. "I thought I made you feel that way all the time," he whined.

"Well, not exactly," blushed Pinder. "Not that kind of kid's naked. You do something else."

"Aw, shit," grumped Howell.

"Come on, David."

Howell grinned. "I know," he said. "I feel exactly the same way."

"You do not," doubted Pinder.

"Yes, I do," he insisted.

Pinder gave him a frumpy, thinking woman's smile and then she initiated another round of rolling and scooting, three times up and twice across the bed. In time, the energy subsided into the romantic zone and they pulled strings through each other's hearts.

Howell toppled over in a stupor. "I have severe aftertingle," he sighed.

Pinder cooed quietly and took a deep breath. "That's all I ever want," she said.

"You're kidding," said Howell.

"No, I mean it," said Pinder, speaking in the soft, dumbfounded tone of epiphany.

"No, I know you mean it," said Howell. "It's that I was thinking the same thing again. If this comes again, that's wonderful. But if it doesn't, it's enough. Like that?"

"Well, it's a lot," smiled Pinder. "Yeah."

They talked on for hours about Snow and Pinder's career gamble and Miami and their friends and the FBI, always in balance like a juggler's two hands, until, at ten o'clock, they decided after a sequence of thoughts that

Howell should make a phone call. Pinder watched him collect himself. After the pleasantries, she heard Howell say, "Um, listen. One reason I called is kind of funny. You remember talking about cutting off the boards when they're not the right size, Pop? . . . Uh huh. . . . Yeah, Mom. He said if it's so much too long he cuts it off so much and stuff. I liked that. . . . Yeah. . . . Well, what I mean is that I think Haven and I have cut off a pretty nice board today ourselves. We think so, anyway. Cut at least three or four inches off one. . . . Naaaw, Pop. It's not medical. . . . Don't make me laugh. It's symbolic, you know. . . . No, it's not marriage either. . . . No. Well, I don't want to say right now. It's hard to explain . . . Uh huh. Well, I'll tell you later. It's just that we're pretty happy about it. . . . Yeah. A little scared but happy. And we wanted you to know. That's all. . . ."

SPRING BROUGHT social disturbance to Pinder and Howell. No one invited them to dinner. A few of the old regulars tried when the news was hot, but the first mention of Snow made people squirm. No one knew exactly why. The subject slapped at friends and guests alike as it hung there, looming, a conversational goiter. Howell and Pinder did not know what to say either. They tried simple description, jokes, steadfast silence, and many other ploys, but Lily Snow was a demanding live ghost whose story was at once too personal and too significant for ordinary Washington discourse. It carried the force of a taboo, independent of meaning, and what meaning there was refused to fit in the normal packages of gossip or political abstraction. People who relished a marital scandal among their own friends—and who could blithely analyze genocide or incest or billions of dollars—fell into bilious muteness around the kidnappers or liberators or thrillseekers or desperate family mutants, as they were variously styled out of earshot.

LaLane Rayburn was the only regular visitor. Having no need to reach a conclusion about every development around her, she proceeded simply on her desire to be around Lily Snow because she enjoyed it. She showed up every week or so once the threat of immediate jail passed, which was soon. At first she allowed Pinder and Snow a full hour to walk the two short blocks to the corner café for lunch. The old woman's walk had been further enfeebled by inactivity at the home, and it took her nearly a month to work back up to her full six-inch step. At the café, the three of them became regulars. The waitresses welcomed Snow back as a minor celebrity. The Chicken Man stopped by occasionally to make strange pronouncements, always fishing edibles from his various pockets as he spoke. It made no difference to him that Snow did not seem to know quite what was going on. This attitude spread to Pinder and Rayburn, who came to value both her lucid moments and her dim ones. Usually, at the end of lunch, Snow would lay down the

305

last crust of bread and summon a bill from the café's mistress. Then, ceremoniously, the old woman would scratch out a few numbers and a flat signature on one of her bank deposit slips. "It's my treat today for you youngsters," she would say proudly as she handed the worthless slip to the owner, who always returned gracious thanks.

By April, holdouts occupied only nine of fifty apartments in the building, and Crown Realty stepped up the siege. The company boldly ordered demolition begun on the vacant apartments, demonstrating confidence that the tenants' weakened union would lose its various appeals. Jackhammers roared and plaster dust flew. Crown Realty then sent word that anyone who vacated a holdout apartment by June 1 would receive five thousand dollars; anyone waiting beyond then would receive nothing but the full weight of eviction orders that were slogging through the courts.

These harsh terms were delivered with a heavy sigh by agent LaLane Rayburn, who had worked her way into a clandestine position of delicacy. On the one hand, she stood to gain one half of her firm's commission on the sale of the Savannah, which funds were in escrow pending final solution of the tenant claims. On the other hand, she was dedicated to the cause of Lily Snow and the other aged tenants. Howell and Pinder trusted her fully through many tests, including the grand madam's rumor campaign that the three of them were in cahoots with Crown Realty and for a specified sum had agreed to sabotage all settlements until the tenants moved out by attrition, in psychological collapse. The grand madam called Crown Realty at one hour of extremity and offered to move out for twenty thousand, giving as a sign of good faith the information that LaLane Rayburn had been conspiring with the holdouts instead of bulldozing them in the manner of a conscientious real estate executive. Rayburn acutely sensed a new mood of suspicion at Crown Realty, and after a series of emergency calls to Pinder, arranged for a vice-president of Crown Realty to "see for himself" that she was only reasoning with the tenants. The man walked into the only tenants' meeting Lily Snow ever attended. He faced a carefully arranged semicircle of people eighty and upward, flanked by Pinder and Howell, and he was unable to function in their presence. He stared at them in great discomfort and could not answer questions ranging from the leaky faucet in apartment 307 to the reason for his bad manners in not having made himself available to people much his senior for consultations about their homes. Miss Snow said he was a nice young man. The vice-president retired hastily, and Rayburn's liaison role was never again challenged.

All parties to the real estate dispute, including Crown Realty, found themselves miserably short of cash by spring. Tempers grew short. The tenants' union economized with some group spaghetti dinners during the demolition phase, and at one of them it was decided by hand vote to approach three of the known rich people in the building for a loan to carry on the union fight. The mother and daughter Hope declined to contribute, but Mr. Davis astonished Pinder by writing out a check for a thousand dollars without hesitation. He said no one had ever asked him for money before—too scared, probably—and that he would help out because he was going to die soon anyway from all the excitement in the building. Everyone was profoundly shocked, but not as shocked as they would be when they found out that the financial affairs of two old ladies were in the hands of none other than Milton, the Jamaican man at the reception desk, who had, over the years, worked his way into their hearts, wills, and checkbooks with his sympathetic ear at all hours. The ladies had bequeathed Milton a number of fine antiques and a pile of money, and he planned to use some of the latter to purchase one of the small luxury condominiums at the Savannah. He would stay on the reception desk because he liked it. But the management of Crown Realty rejected his application on grounds of the bad impression it would make to have an uneducated man—a glorified janitor—roving the halls with the privileges of ownership. Milton secretly threw in with the tenants' union after that. No management phone call went safely through his switchboard.

Having quit her job in February, Pinder lost her unemployment benefits in March as the result of a squabble so unattractive that Pinder swore Howell not to tell her family. It had to do with Martin. At first their relations improved when Martin abandoned his scheme to make the Savannah into the Progressive Condoversity, accepting instead an appointment as the token radical on the President's Task Force on Youth Mobilization. He planned to resign in protest after a few months' vacation from the Coalition —or so he told Pinder. She showed little interest one way or the other, and it was perhaps this very indifference that caused him to refer unkindly to Snow as "your eviction-proof hostage." This enraged Pinder. She made some remarks over the telephone about how badly he was aging as a brilliant political hustler. Martin replied testily that this was petty, and he shifted their hostile dialogue to the more suitable plane of a political issue—namely, whether the medical delivery system in Thailand was progressive or regressive. A kind of sour truce prevailed for a week. It fell apart when Pinder received official notice of Martin's letter to the government declaring her unqualified for unemployment assistance. Martin laid claim to the highest of motivations—honesty in government. Pinder ridiculed the claim, but when she lost the unemployment benefits she consoled herself with the idea that it was better to be on her own. She herself began hustling. She brought her light table and her scissors and her glue pots and blue editing pencils back to the Savannah, and within weeks she was making pamphlets and articles ready for the printer, cutting and snipping piles of analytical words that meant little to her, enduring the freelance work by humming to Lily Snow.

Howell also suffered financially during the shock period that followed the creation of his odd family. Some of the trouble was not of his own making. It derived instead from a new national mood—or at least a new mood in Washington—of pervasive bitterness and scorn to the point of self-derision, so that the previously clear bombast of the great commentators gave way to snide comments on small matters. The fever arrived slowly and promised to last for some time. Finger-pointing and blame-dodging continued as always, but with the crucial difference that no one seemed willing to assert much of anything beyond a complaint. As a result, politicians high and low sounded like trapped animals gnawing their own legs, and they came to trust statements of vague belligerence as the best means of gaining attention. It was a time of pessimism without disaster even at *Washington* magazine, where two of Howell's best articles were denied cover billing on grounds of excessive warmth.

Something had changed at the magazine when Howell could least afford it. He found himself no longer able to harmonize the conflicting eccentricities of Marner and Drake, and, without his old gift for wiggling, laughing, and puffing through doctrinal clashes that no logic could resolve, Howell fell under the failed magician's curse. Those with the fondest memories became the most disappointed in him, and his long trail of good humor at the magazine evaporated now that he could no longer take a bitter dispute and make a peace with his prose. Howell hoped the decline was temporary. Marner and Drake thought he had "lost it" after the Lily Snow episode and his Miami broodings. Drake complained specifically about Howell's refusal to write an article on the nation's cruelty to its old people, an article extolling Drake's plan for a volunteer clearinghouse of old and young citizens. Baby care would be traded for companionship, accumulated wisdom for fresh spirit, and so forth, with unimagined benefits from the startling reaches of Drake's brain—all showcased around Howell's experience with Lily Snow, which would provide what was known in magazine parlance as "the flesh and blood angle." Drake called it "the grabber." He could not understand why Howell would not use his own personal knowledge to help generate goodness on a larger scale. To him, Howell had become churlish and narrow. He and Marner worried about it.

On the morning of the first Saturday in June, Woodruff left Hartman's apartment after breakfast and walked in a partial daze toward the Savannah. He felt nothing but the familiar sense of suspension, stranded between some forebodings too small to bother with and others too large to define. In such a state, he decided to visit his besieged friends. He knew Milton well enough to get passed upstairs unannounced. "What's the matter?" he asked Pinder, just after she had cracked the door to reveal a face full of tense displeasure.

"Hi, Henry. What's the matter with you?"

Woodruff thought an instant and realized he was smacking his lips unpleasantly, like a traveler with his first mouthful of sulfurous water. "Oh," he said. "I guess I got cement dust on my tongue downstairs where they're working. Tastes bitter. Is Miss Snow okay? I just stopped by . . ."

". . . Come on in," Pinder said hurriedly. "She's okay. It's just that David's on the phone with the FBI guy in Miami."

"Oh, great," muttered Woodruff as he entered to behold the back of Lily Snow's head. She was seated in an armchair facing out through the living room window, a strip of sheet tied loosely around her waist. The late morning sun made incandescent filaments of her hair.

"Say hello to her," said Pinder, running off. "I gotta go hold David's hand."

Woodruff tried to do as he was told, but he found Snow's eyes closed. He leaned over very near to check her breathing, which was soft but steady. Woodruff decided it was a sun-induced nap.

"Excuse me?" Howell said into the phone. "I don't understand what you mean by prejudicing your other options." He gave Pinder a harassed look as Woodruff walked into the living room.

"A lawsuit?" sagged Howell. "Oh boy, here we go. Would you please explain that to me, Mr. Shea? I'm not fond of lawsuits. . . . Uh huh, but you think that would most likely be against me, though, don't you? I mean the parties who are responsible. By that you mean . . . Well, yes, sir, she lives here. Since she was forced to give up her apartment because she couldn't afford it . . . No, we're not, but I don't think that makes any difference. I know it doesn't make any difference to your aunt . . . Yes, sir, I know it's a responsibility. In fact, it's a very important responsibility to us. We spend a lot of our time with her, Mr. Shea. To us, it's hard but it's more than a responsibility. It's a privilege. Haven and I have both learned a . . . Pardon me? Who should think about what? . . . Uh huh . . . Uh huh . . . Well, I think we should try to keep the two separate, Mr. Shea. Really. It's not for us, you understand. We would be perfectly happy if you sent some support directly to a nurse or to the doctor. Or even if you just sent the papers up so we can get the Medicaid help. We're happy to pay for the room and board. That's not much. But we've had to pay the doctors more than five hundred bucks just in these few months . . . That's right . . . Well, we did think of that. It's just that we did it, anyway . . . No . . . Yes, I know you do. I mean I'm sure you do, and I would like those people to be satisfied, too. I just wish they could all come here . . ."

Howell's cheeks had turned white. He lowered himself into a hardback chair, and as he listened he beckoned Pinder to him. She rubbed his shoulders from behind. Howell touched her hand gratefully. He looked very weak when he smiled a greeting to Woodruff, and afterward, while Shea's side of the conversation dragged on, he acted out a brief comic pantomime indicating that the person on the telephone was loony but was also putting Howell through quite an ordeal.

"Believe me, I know that's a burden," said Howell, sounding desperately sincere, "and we're not trying to avoid the inevitable. And if there's anything we can do to help ease things with your relatives, please let us know . . . *You* do? We *all* do? I don't understand that, Mr. Shea . . . Uh huh . . ."

There was alarm in Howell's voice. He stood up and covered his face with both hands, cradling the receiver. Without moving his feet, he twisted his body back and forth several times, almost writhing. Woodruff sat down. Pinder's mouth dropped open and she walked around Howell to see his face. His voice, when he finally spoke, was surprisingly soft and seemed to be held down by a self-control that was invisible and volatile, like the downdraft that makes a kite dip wildly in the air. "I think so," said Howell. "But could you go through that again, please? Her sister and she . . . Uh huh . . ." Howell clenched his fists. "I do, *too*, Mr. Shea, and so does Haven. We all do, but Haven and I know that place isn't the way to do it . . . Yes, yes, yes, we've met most of them . . . I know, but I wish you could come up here and see her now and I wish you had seen her over there . . . *Competence?* There's more to it than competence . . . No, sir. I'm not trying to tell you about training. Let's forget that if we can. We can all agree that it's Miss Snow's money and we want every penny of it to be spent for her benefit and health, right? And I can't tell you how sorry I am that it's come to this . . . Yes, sir, I believe you're sorry, too . . . Please do, especially about the Medicaid papers. Okay . . . Yes. Right. I'm clear on that. You don't forfeit anything by talking to me . . . Excuse me? . . . Well, no I don't really mind . . . Well, you don't really need a witness to establish that she's here, I assure you. We've told everybody that from the first day. We're not trying to hide anything . . . Okay, I hope she does . . . Good-bye."

Howell hung up the phone and slumped over it. There seemed to be some doubt as to whether he would explode in anger or deflate, but he soon resolved it by going limp. "That twerpy son of a bitch," he moaned softly.

"Sounded like a lot of fun," quipped Woodruff.

Pinder resumed the massage. "What did he say, David?" she whispered in his ear. "Was it that bad?"

"Pretty bad," said Howell without looking up. "Pretty bad. He said first of all it's all in the hands of his wife, who's pretty angry. He says he's on our side. But his wife has talked to a lawyer and she plans to start legal proceedings to take formal control over Miss Snow's affairs if the welfare agencies up here don't take her away for them."

"Uh huh," said Pinder.

"That's not so bad," said Woodruff.

"And the kicker is that he said she told him to notify us that we were instructed to return Miss Snow to the home, just like their letter said, and that if we didn't and she dies in our custody, they would bring a wrongful death action against us. Big bucks."

Pinder stopped massaging. "No," she cried. "What's he talking about? We don't have any money."

"Great," sighed Woodruff.

"He knows that, I think," said Howell. "It's just pressure. I'm gonna have to talk to Drake about how he keeps the magazine's creditors off his back. He says it's easier if you're really poor."

"It's not funny, David," chided Pinder.

"I know," smiled Howell.

"Nice try," said Woodruff.

"But get this," said Howell, in warm sarcasm. "This is what really got me there. He says we all have a financial interest in putting her back in the home. He said it like I was one of the boys and he was punching me in the ribs in a bar or something. He was *trying* to be one of the boys, anyway. He said, 'I'm gonna confide in you because I want you to know that my financial interests and my humanitarian interests are completely in line.' "

310

"Uh oh," sighed Pinder. "Here it comes."

"Apparently, Miss Snow's father left about two hundred thousand in trust for Miss Snow and her sister Maggie in New York. I don't know where he got it. They're not allowed to touch the principal, and the old man set up the trust so that the inheritance flows through the estate of the sister who lives longest. In other words, if Miss Snow outlives her sister then all the money goes through Miss Snow's estate. And Shea just told me he knows he's the sole beneficiary of Miss Snow's will, but he thinks he's not at all in his Aunt Maggie's. He says Aunt Maggie is the black sheep of the family."

"So why didn't you just promise to keep Miss Snow alive for a long time?" queried Woodruff.

"That's the whole point," said Howell, who suddenly lost his temper. He banged a fist loudly on the telephone table and looked angrily about for another inanimate object to hit. "The point is that the asshole believes the way to keep Miss Snow alive is to surround her with as many doctors and nurses as possible! He really believes that! What can I say to a guy like that? Huh? He kept talking about all the specialists and the emergency equipment at the home, like all these experts are gonna plug Miss Snow into some machine and keep her goin'! And he's so sure of himself. He kept saying that he'd had the training in the FBI to know when he doesn't have the proper training for a job, and that's why he wants her back in that rathole over there—for her sake and his."

Howell sat down again. Pinder looked off in the next room at the bowed head of Lily Snow and made her noise of primal sympathy, but halfway through it turned into a near growl.

"And you guys think she'll live longer on love than medicine?" asked Woodruff.

"Fuck you, Henry," muttered Pinder.

"Easy, Henry," said Howell.

"Okay, okay," soothed Woodruff.

"And I know it's very convenient to Shea that he doesn't believe he has the training," said Howell. "So he doesn't have to do anything himself. I'm sure it didn't occur to him to put her in a home down there in Miami so he could visit her. And I doubt if it would occur to him to spend a dime of his own money on her . . ."

". . . You think he's putting all this pressure on us just for the money?" asked Pinder. "I mean just because he thinks that nursing home's the best way to keep her alive?"

Howell's gushing speech stopped short. He gave Pinder a look of gratitude for the warning, and sighed. "Well, I don't think that's completely fair," he admitted. "I'd like to. But he got me in an uncomfortable position when he was talking about how he has a responsibility to the rest of the family to make sure Miss Snow's taken care of, and how can he do that when these two young strangers have run off with her? Stuff like that. And what can he tell them, and who are we? Hard to answer."

311

"I thought he didn't have any family, except Maggie in New York," said Pinder.

"Well, I don't think he does, really," said Howell. "Except his wife and a daughter. Talked a lot about them."

Pinder looked suspicious. "Oh," she said. "Well, what was that at the end about hiding stuff?"

"Oh, that!" said Howell, stimulated by the memory. "That was cop stuff. He had a secretary listening in on the phone. That's what he told me. Said he wanted a witness establishing that we have possession of Miss Snow. Can you believe that?"

"Amazing," said Woodruff. "Hard to get a secretary in the office on Saturday morning."

Pinder ignored this. "Boy," she sighed. "We probably never should have called him."

"Wait a minute," said Woodruff. "You called *him?*"

"Yep."

"Why?"

" 'Cause he's got control of Miss Snow's papers she needs for Medicaid," Pinder explained. "And we hadn't heard any fussing from them in so long that we hoped maybe they'd given in. Fat chance, I guess."

"He's got all her stuff," said Howell. "Furniture and everything. And he went to the post office and got all her mail forwarded to him, including her checks."

"How can he do that?" asked Woodruff.

"Easy. He just did it."

"Oh."

"Son of a bitch," muttered Howell. "He's getting her Social Security checks and her dividend checks off the trust. Giving them to his wife for safekeeping, he says. I'll bet she's cashing them. I'll bet two-to-one. God, this is an outrage. I thought I had lost my outrage. Did you hear me warn him about the money, Haven? When I said every penny ought to go for Miss Snow? Do you think I was tough enough?"

"Sure," Pinder said generously. "That was good."

"Well, I couldn't be too tough," sighed Howell. "Our position is too weak."

"Uh huh," sighed Pinder.

A gloomy silence ensued. Then Woodruff leaned back in his chair. "Well," he said, "have you guys considered bumping off the sister in New York? How about that?" He twinkled with self-satisfaction as he examined the glum faces before him. "Think of it. Then the old bastard down there would have his inheritance assured. Okay? So then the tables would be turned and he wouldn't want Miss Snow to live anymore, right? In fact, the sooner the better as far as getting his hands on the dough. So in that situation, he wouldn't *want* her to go back to the home anymore and you could keep her without any more hassle. How's that?"

Howell and Pinder had buried their faces in their hands, paying no attention. Woodruff studied them nervously, insecure in the role of mood levitator. He cleared his throat. "I'm just thinking out loud, you understand," he offered. Still receiving no response, he said, "Not that I have anything against your nontraditional approach to starting a family, of course. Nothing at all. I actually like Miss Snow. Do you think she'd like to have a cigar with me?"

"She doesn't want a cigar," Pinder said numbly.

"She doesn't want a cigar," said Howell.

Woodruff broke into a genuine, nontheatrical smile after a few seconds of intense study. "You guys are really out of it," he laughed. "Smoke a cigar. Wow."

"He's making fun of us, David," sighed Pinder.

"I guess so," chuckled Howell, waking from his trance.

Woodruff stood up abruptly. He stretched his arms toward the ceiling and sniffed valiantly for fresh air. "Sudsy was right," he teased. "You two need a break. My mission is to lure you for an afternoon on the Rappahannock River, featuring nature and possibly some extremely dangerous drugs."

"Unnnnh," moaned Howell, feigning a stab wound. "That hurts. We can't. We have to stay here and mope."

"How come?" asked Pinder.

"Well, *one* of us has to stay with Miss Snow," Howell replied.

"Huh?" said Woodruff. "Let's get a babysitter, for Christ's sake!"

"A ladysitter," Pinder corrected.

"Whatever!" said Woodruff. "You can't stay here all the time! We can come up with the money. I don't care whether the old bastard ever sends you any. Spend it now. You'll probably be in jail later, anyway."

Pinder and Howell gave Woodruff parallel looks of weary disgust. "Henry, we've gone through this many times before," said Howell. "Do you realize how hard it is to get a ladysitter for a ninety-year-old woman? Do you know any parents who will let their teenagers sit with an old lady?"

"Well, no," groused Woodruff. "Goddam." He gave the distant Snow a resentful glance.

"The only person we've had much success with is your old friend LaLane Rayburn," said Pinder. "But she has to be with her kids on the weekend."

"I see," squirmed Woodruff. "How is she?"

"Fine," said Pinder.

"Okay, forget it," said Woodruff. "Do you want to hear the latest news about Valerie and Marner?"

"No thanks," said Pinder.

"Oh," said Woodruff, disappointed. "Not even the headlines?" he pressed. "You've got it all—the hundred and seven consecutive days of roses? Crying at the office? Valerie worried about . . ."

". . . We know all that," laughed Howell.

"Boy, you're a lot of fun today," snorted Woodruff.

"Where's Sudsy?" asked Pinder.

Woodruff leaned back to give his scalp a languid fingertip massage. "Back at the apartment," he sighed.

"Is she all right?" asked Howell.

"I suppose so," Woodruff replied lamely.

"Why didn't she come with you?" asked Pinder.

"You two doing okay?" asked Howell.

"Hey," said Woodruff. "What is this, 'Issues and Answers'?"

"Henry, you look depressed," said Howell. "You can't be depressed. *We're* depressed."

"Oh, you're just temporarily depressed," scoffed Woodruff.

"Is it Sudsy?"

"Sort of."

"Is is something sexual and extremely personal, or is it something we can't talk about?" Howell pried.

Woodruff looked uncertainly at Pinder. "I can leave," she said. "I'd be happy to talk to Miss Snow." She took a deep, prideful breath.

"No," said Woodruff.

Pinder rose to leave. "I know you're gonna use all those big words anyway, so I might as well . . ."

". . . Cut it out, Haven," sniffed Woodruff. "It's not that, really. It's just that Susan and I haven't had as much fun together since my, um. My accident." Woodruff seemed quite sheepish about the subject.

Howell became sympathetically tickled. "Your accident?" he guffawed. "Well, I can't imagine why not. I mean just because you cut yourself to pieces . . ."

". . . David," scolded Pinder, although she was laughing herself.

"Maybe fun is the wrong word. I just mean I've felt very remote from her since then. From everybody, really."

Howell and Pinder looked apprehensively at each other.

Woodruff crossed his legs and let out a confessional sigh. "And I think the reason is that I've been withdrawn even more than usual because of a new obsession of mine, and Sudsy's not particularly interested in it," he said. "But I can't let go of it. And I think it's the reason I had the accident in the library in the first place. In fact, I know it is. I was thinking about it and my mind lost track of my fingers. So whatever it is, it's already wrecked my penis and kept me apart from Sudsy. I get very excited by it and very depressed by it at the same time . . ."

". . . You sound like you're in love," said Pinder. "Is it another woman?"

"Hardly," Woodruff declared.

Howell leaned forward, looking as though he had just knit together some clues. "Is it related to the Scissors Theory?" he asked.

Woodruff closed his eyes to think. "Tangentially," he said. "It's a minor derivative, I suppose, but this one's much broader and sweeter."

"Oh, Henry, I *wish* you were gonna talk about Sudsy," said Pinder, gushing with disappointment. "You already sound more intimate about this whatever it is than you did about her."

Woodruff pursed his lips and exhaled through his nose. He was annoyed with Pinder for destroying the verbal momentum he had felt—for constraining him at a moment of excitement and revelation. Such was the penalty for bringing up a difficult subject in her presence, he figured. Pinder was unsure of herself at certain levels of articulation, and therefore she maneuvered the conversation to suit herself. This was all true, he thought vehemently. On the other hand, there was not much he could do about it now, because he did not wish to take her on at all, especially with Howell there. Besides, Pinder's heartfelt objections touched him in a familiar place near the one Susan Hartman touched at difficult moments, and this sensation was what it was all about to Woodruff. It was a sharp sense of remoteness simultaneous with a heightened yearning, plus an excitement at the mixture itself. Woodruff wanted to keep the sensation alive. It provoked a raging sense of inquiry, diluted by a consistent alien quality, which was subtle and not beyond logical explanation but nevertheless disturbing and intriguing in a primordial way, like a blind man's wink. Woodruff's heart gave a thump as he realized that this sensation was, of course, at the core of the new obsession he had been about to describe. The excitement returned. He thought he might even become Pinder's friend if he could communicate this to her.

Turning to Pinder, he looked tenderly sheepish, and he swallowed. "I'm sorry, too, Haven," he said. "But different people open up different ways, just as hearts break in different ways. And mine is a weird one." His laugh covered his flank.

"Oh," said Pinder.

Neither one of them could put anything into words. Howell waded into the emotional mist between them. "Excuse me," he said. "What was the name of that new thing of yours, Henry? The broad and sweet one I mean?"

"Oh, that," smiled Woodruff. He paid no attention to Howell's teasing. "Well, it's called the Template Theory."

"Uh huh," said Pinder, who was beginning to wish they had settled for the previous small moment and postponed the actual theory until some distant month.

Howell mimicked the hard-boiled reporter. "Template, eh? Template, template," he said. "Have to remember that one. Feels good in your mouth, the word does."

"Thanks," said Woodruff.

"What is it about?" asked Howell.

"Well, it's symbolically derived from the DNA molecule and chromosome theory," Woodruff replied grandly. He reached into his hip pocket to extract the folded papers he had brought from Hartman's.

"You don't know anything about chromosomes or chemistry, Henry," grumbled Howell.

"That's not important," said Woodruff.

"Oh," said Howell.

"Now look," said Woodruff, as he spread several large photocopies on the dining room table. "Here are some of those standard models of a DNA molecule. You've seen those, right?"

Pinder and Howell nodded. "Yep," she said, "Tinker toys on a spiral staircase. I studied that in high school."

"Double helix," Howell agreed, peering at the reproduction.

"Right," said Woodruff. "Now the thing you've got to envision here is the length of this molecule. The proportions are truly amazing. Even in the miniworld of molecules and atoms, the DNA double helix is incredibly skinny. If you were to blow it up several billion times so that it was as wide as that pencil there, the double helix would be several miles long. Like a pencil from here to Arlington Cemetery. And if you take the molecule at its actual diameter, which is, well, I don't know what the fuck these measurements are. . ."

". . . Which is *real* skinny," Howell suggested.

"Yeah," said Woodruff. "And if you were to take one and put another one and another one end to end for 93 million miles, all the way to the sun— okay, got that? And if you did that *sixty times*, sixty strands to the sun, you'd have a total weight of about an ounce. That's really something."

Pinder was nodding mechanically. "Uh huh," she said. "Let's stipulate, David. They're skinny."

"Right," said Howell. "Goddam, Henry, I can't imagine where you're going with this. So far, it's just one of those sci-fi numbers games like the space people and the brain freaks pull."

"Be patient," said Woodruff. He picked up the pencil and pointed it out the window. "Now. Suppose I'm holding this blown-up DNA molecule like this—just one molecule, see—and I'm pointing it toward Arlington Cemetery. Okay? Now each time this molecule reproduces, the two helices have to unravel from one another all along the incredible length of this thing, okay?" Woodruff peered down the length of the pencil and off into the distance. "So you have two unbelievably long skinny spirals, and each of them takes half the sugars and phosphates and stuff that had linked them together . . ."

". . . The stairs of the spiral staircase," chimed Pinder.

"Right," said Woodruff. "You know what a Contac cold capsule looks like, don't you?"

Howell frowned, "Of course."

"Well, all those tiny little colored balls in there would be carbon and hydrogen and nitrogen and oxygen and phosphorus atoms and so forth— millions of them—piled along the two spirals here all the way across the Potomac over there. Okay?"

"Here, let me help you," Pinder offered, taking the pencil. She made a big show of pointing it out the window toward the Virginia heights on the opposite side of the Potomac. "Boy, this is heavy," she smiled.

"Not really," said Woodruff, holding his own imaginary half. "Now look. Each of these is a template. It's a half a DNA, a mold or a model. And each of them has the capacity to reach out into the cell around it and reassemble its other half from all the Contac balls swimming around out there, which is basically our food broken down into its smallest elements. Okay? So all

316

along the miles and miles of this tiny peashooter millions upon millions of sugars and phosphates are attracted and lined up exactly in mirror to the template. So then we have *two* DNA molecules."

"And then they screw each other," quipped Howell.

"Noooo," groaned Woodruff.

"Just kidding," said Howell. "Look, Henry, I know this DNA stuff is fascinating and everything, but it's not your field and . . ."

". . . Wait a minute," said Woodruff. "I'm getting there. I just wanted to give you a rough idea of these incredible molecules, which is pretty much what I have. And what a template is and stuff. To me, it's amazing just that something with those mindboggling proportions—you know, so unlike any living thing we know—can come unraveled all along its length into two perfect template halves. It's the longest, tiniest, and most perfect zipper imaginable."

"Aha!" cried Pinder. "There's the connection."

". . . Come on, Haven" pleaded Woodruff. "That's not it. Hold on. On second thought, maybe it is in a way."

"Sounds fishy to me," said Howell.

Woodruff flicked the air impatiently. "No, wait," he said. "This thing's complicated enough without you guys throwing in stuff like that." Woodruff cleared his throat. "Now this is what I'm driving at. Let's take this DNA template as the model for all living reproduction, okay? Not only for cells dividing, but for the genetic stuff, too, where a male template gets together with a female template, makes certain genetic adjustments, and then starts reproducing. Something like that. It's good enough for me, symbolically anyway. And this chromosome, with DNA as the active ingredient, as the aspirin people would say, carries aboard the incredibly long split peashooter all the information necessary to produce both the species and the individual. In other words, it says whether you're an anteater or an oyster or a person, and it also makes you unique, okay? It determines your cheekbones and how long your tongue will be and everything. That's the awesome beauty of the physical template. And so . . ." Woodruff hesitated and his eyes began to waver uncharacteristically from the faces of Howell and Pinder. In normal times his direct look was harmlessly imperious. Now it was intense but shaky.

Woodruff was able to plunge ahead. "So what I'm proposing here is a psychological equivalent of the genetic template. A psychological template, sort of. I don't know exactly how it will turn out yet, but the idea is to look at this template here stretched all the way over to Arlington as a model of psychology. So we have a template instead of an id, or what have you. And this psychological template does all the things the genetic template does. In fact, I guess they're related somehow. In other words, *this* template produces the unique individual just like the genes do. That's the personality, of course. And at the next level up, it produces psychological clusters just the way genes make races and families look alike. That's culture, of course, if you look at culture as a group personality. So there is family culture and

Chinese culture and hippie culture and military culture and so forth. Okay? Now here's the kicker. At the most general level—the same level at which genes make things look like people instead of manatees or wildebeests— there is a basic psychological template. And I think that template is all about attitudes toward death. Pardon me, but that's what I think. Psychologically, I think death is the bottom line. It distinguishes people from animals and people from people and so forth and it also links them together." Pausing to swallow, Woodruff glanced apprehensively at his audience.

Howell appeared to have sunk into the mood of a solitary fisherman in an empty boat at the end of a long day. Beneath the placid torpor on his face there were some signs of curiosity, mostly slight frowns and roving eyes, as though he were troubled from time to time by the imaginary sound of fish swimming nearby. This curiosity, plus the silence at the break in Woodruff's speech, brought his back off the chair. He sat up and flicked his nose. "Now I see why you've got your template peashooter pointing toward Arlington Cemetery," he drawled.

Woodruff did not expect a reply from this vicinity of thought. "That was inadvertent," he said, looking out the window.

Howell looked at Pinder, who was reclining with her hands folded and no apparent inclination to speak. Then he looked back at Woodruff through the tension and his belly rumbled slightly. "Death is the bottom line," he chuckled. "Jesus, Henry. A number of people have made that point, you know. Like Moses and John Maynard Keynes."

"I know," Woodruff frowned irritably. "You think I'm crazy, don't you?"

"What difference does that make?" said Howell.

Woodruff heaved a put-upon sigh. "Look," he said, "I'm not trying to cram this down everyone's throat. It's not something I go around talking about. I mean I don't want to be like my friend Sidney Lloyd, who was a very funny be-bop piano player and all-around goof-off until he became a Buddhist in college. And after that he joined various evangelical movements and I lost track of him until one day in New York when I saw him on the subway. He was very sharp and very witty, but he had an intense look to him and he used to accost strangers on the subway with things like, 'Why won't you look into anybody's eyes?' and 'I can help you with whatever it is you're avoiding.' "

"Nice guy," said Howell.

"Yeah, well he was very smart, and he had good instincts about people and what they use to protect themselves. He took Nietzsche's plunge, which is a nice thing to do but not to dwell on, and of course he became one of your more intelligent, high-class lunatics at Bellevue."

Howell eased back into the chair again. "That's great, Henry," he said.

"I'm sorry," said Woodruff. "But the point is I'm not accosting people on subways." He smiled softly. "Not yet, anyway. I'm just talking to you two. And I'm embarrassed by it, and I care what you think, you know. And what I hope, and what I guess I want you to tell me, is that there's some value to this. I'm not trying to stare at death all day, and I'm not trying to cure it or

anything. Though of course if I could cure death I'd be a famous man . . ."
Woodruff trailed off into a shy fantasy and looked up for a response. Howell
and Pinder were smiling routinely. Woodruff cleared his throat. "It's just
that it seems almost obvious in a way that death is the fundamental psychological factor in life, as it were, and I think it ought to be recognized for that
at least. I think it makes things clearer. And it's closer to the truth. And it's
not necessarily harmful . . ."

". . . Boy, Henry, if you weren't so strong you'd be crazy," smiled Howell.
"But now that we're at it, let me get something straight. You say death is the
key to life as far as the psyche is concerned, right?"

"Uh huh."

"It underlies culture and the differences between the species and all personality, right?"

"Uh huh."

"Okay, but a month-old infant can have a lot of personality. My little
brother did, I remember. And Hershey's kid did. He was hyper and outraged
at two weeks. And that's years before an infant has any awareness of death.
And they seem free of death worries to me . . ."

"Well, all I can say is that most babies get all kinds of emotion poured into
them from the day of birth. Hugs and goo-goos and songs and stuff like that
from parents and nurses and so forth. And suppose they take on some of
them somehow. Some of them take. Well, what the baby gets is raw emotion
from people, especially the parents. And emotion is what personality is
made of. I mean, emotions in an infinite variety of combinations are what
I see laid out along that psychological template Haven's got. And since I
think everything along that template is a reflection of or expression of the
awareness of death, you know, it follows that I think all the emotions conceivable are related to death. In other words, they wouldn't have any meaning without it. Hugs and smiles and songs are all emotional conduits, and
they transmit something to the infant about death. It's like an emotional
transfusion. It's not conscious, of course, and the good thing is that the
emotions still *feel* despite their source. So if you're dancing, you just feel the
dancing without worrying too much about where the good feeling came
from . . ."

". . . Well, maybe if you kept reminding yourself that you were only dancing because of the grim reaper, you wouldn't have so much fun," said Howell.

Woodruff hesitated, wondering whether to take this personally. "That
would be morbid," he smiled. "But it's pretty much what a lot of churches
have done when they try to wipe out dancing."

"How about a giraffe, Henry?" Howell asked with some mischief. "Put me
a giraffe on the template there and tell me what you come up with."

Woodruff paused again. "I should have known," he sighed. "I should have
known." He gave Howell the semidespondent grin of a burnt-out prospec-
tor. Then he glanced at Pinder, who was lightly massaging her closed eyelids, as though oblivious to the proceedings. "Look," he told the ceiling.

"This stuff gives me a headache, too. I don't have it all figured out by any means, and I'm just telling you because it all relates to Sudsy, believe it or not."

"Bullshit," said Pinder, without opening her eyes.

Woodruff gaped at her in surprise, waiting for himself to recover and for Pinder to open her eyes. She didn't. Woodruff started to say several things but only shrugged quizzically at Howell. "Giraffes," he said. "Okay, now a giraffe has a personality. They're shy and docile and so forth, and I'm sure individual giraffes have their quirks. To people, a lot of the giraffe's personality derives from the way they look with their long, funny necks and their geeky faces and their strange, awkward but graceful walk and stuff. And their looks derive from genetics, which is the physical side of the template. Okay? And of course we Darwinians believe that the genetics come from survival and the struggle against death, so that most of an animal's personality is a function of looks and survival behavior, which are related to death by evolution. There's personality all right, but precious little of it is independent of evolution. Maybe none. Maybe it's that way with people, too, but it sure looks like the physical and psychological templates are separate in humans. In other words, a complete history of giraffes would pretty much coincide with their evolution and how it produced them and the latest threats to them, like people and zoos and so forth, but we think of human history as something pretty separate. It's what has happened *since* the last evolutionary change, in the time since people who looked almost exactly like us started piling rocks together and making wars and stuff."

"Aren't you just saying people have relatively big brains?" queried Howell.

Woodruff stared at Howell in a heated daze. Suddenly he grinned. "Yes," he replied. "In a word. Have it your way."

"Jesus Christ, Henry!" fussed Howell. "You put us through all that to talk about a brain! I get nervous when you talk about evolution."

"Wait a minute," said Woodruff. "Bear with me a minute. I'm near the end. Look, I was kidding about the brain."

"You're kidding."

"Anyway, forget the brain," said Woodruff. "I think people have hyped the brain to glorify themselves. Think of it as a computer for logic or whatever. But the engine behind it comes out of the emotions, which means off this template over here." He motioned toward Pinder's pencil, only to discover that she had discarded it in her lap. "This one," he said, retrieving it to point out the window. "Okay. You know, like the brain is the place where the emotions rub against each other or something. Anyway, human history as we know it comes off this template here. This one is what makes empires and Woody Allens and makes folks worry all the time and go to church. Because, whereas the psyche of animals seems pretty well balanced with the requirements of survival, people seem to have a few extra sections on their psychological template here beyond what they need. If you take a blank human template, with all these infinite trillions of ways to reflect or perceive mortality, any personality or culture is gonna be only so successful in handling them. What's left over is psychic energy, worry, ambition, or whatever. That makes the good things in history, but it also makes the bad ones. It's the most naked part of the human preoccupation with mortality. Okay? Now. You may ask what good is all this?"

"Go ahead," said Howell, after he blew his nose into his handerchief with a clear, soprano honk.

"Okay, I will," said Woodruff. "Well, I think there have been only two effective bandages, or containers, or channels, or whatever you want to call them, for the spillover part of that anxiety in history. One is religion, which is the oldest and most universal . . ."

". . . And the other is baseball," suggested Howell. "With God on the mound and Big Adam Apple at the plate . . ."

"Come on, David," pleaded Woodruff, stamping out his own wry smile. "Baseball is not big enough yet. The other one is less than four hundred years old. It's the whole idea of progress. You know—science, efficiency, a better future, secular heaven, all that stuff. The whole modern *schmeer*, life as an escalator instead of a merry-go-round. That runs pretty deep with all of us. It's in revolutionaries and businessmen and schoolteachers and parents and even baseball players. Everybody but hobos, maybe. It's still seeping all over the world, making people restless. Americans have been the most restless, which meant the best. The restless win all the time. But now —my God. The escalator is stopping. It may not even be real. People are freaking out about it because their psychological attachment runs deep. And the scary thing about it all is that we're on the downward curve of both religion and the belief in progress, although both of them are still really strong. I think individual people may be able to adjust to losing them, but I don't think societies can. Without cataclysm. Like in the Dark Ages before the idea of progress. In the big picture, it's impossible to imagine a third bandage on the scale of religion or progress. And that leaves nonbelievers with the challenge of trying to make do without their crutches while everything is falling apart, or falling on them. What do you think?"

Pinder opened her eyes to look at Howell with disappointment. Howell flicked his nose again. "Of the big picture?" he said. "Well, I guess it's time for baseball to make a move. I don't know. What do you want me to say, Henry? I was never that big on progress, and there have always been cataclysms. I believe in foibles, proportion, sentiment, and harmless diversions."

"Uh huh," Woodruff nodded skeptically.

"And besides, this sound a lot like your Death of Progress Theory from seven years ago," Howell chided.

"It is," said Woodruff. "But that was at the level of economics and world history. Then when Casey and I split up it kind of stunned me into thinking I'd left out the whole psychological and emotional side, you know. It was all too rational. So that's where the template stuff came in, after some painful exploration."

"Oh," said Howell.

Woodruff looked to the floor. "Look," he shrugged. "It doesn't matter. It's just another chapter in the manuscript. You haven't said anything, Haven. You're making me feel foolish."

Pinder rose slowly. "Well, I was just waiting for you to talk about Sudsy and your accident," she said.

"I did," said Woodruff.

Pinder squinched her nose. "Huh?"

"Yeah," said Woodruff. "I did. That's what I was talking about, you see. The point is that I zipped myself up because I was in a reverie one day over this goddam template. Okay? And since then I've been all involved with it, and I haven't gotten along very well with Sudsy."

"I can see why," Pinder said softly. "Some of it's interesting, Henry, but it's a lot of weight on your head."

Woodruff signed. "Listen, I wish you wouldn't reject it like that without debating the merits. That's part of it with Sudsy, too. I keep telling her that this template thing has a personal side, too. All the time. Like I told her how I realized from the template that all my life I had never really appreciated the way women die."

"Excuse me?"

Woodruff flushed. He twisted his fingers around each other and became very uncomfortable. "Yeah," he said huskily. "I know it sounds weird, but it's easy. At a certain level, I thought of men as struggling and fighting and getting ulcers all the time. Going against the grain. More preoccupied by death and more prone to horrible ones. Okay. And on the other hand I thought of women as floating along somehow, like petals on the river or something. Somehow insulated from the grim realities. Which meant at bottom that I didn't think women face death the same way men do. I *know* it's stupid. But if you think that, it's hard to respect a woman or anybody else. *Any* woman. Except Hannah Arendt, of course. So I realized how important an instinctive shared belief about death is to the whole notion of respect. That's a little thing, I guess."

Pinder frowned painfully. "You thought all that?"

"Look, I'm admitting it, aren't I?" Woodruff defended. "Gimme a break, will you?"

"I'm trying," said Pinder.

"No, you're not," said Woodruff.

Pinder groaned and stood up. "I'm gonna let you two thrash it out. But you can't solve it. You gotta live it." Howell tried to interrupt but she walked out past Lily Snow into the bedroom.

"Oh boy," signed Woodruff. "Now I've done it."

Howell shrugged. He said nothing, but he followed Pinder and left Woodruff with a look that he should understand.

Pinder was sitting on the side of the bed. "Why are you so patient with him?" she asked softly.

Howell slid around her to lie face down on the bed. He was rubbing her back and thinking of a reply when Woodruff appeared at the door. "I'm sorry," he said. He sat on the floor next to Pinder. "Listen, Haven," he said, "I know you're tired of the soap opera, but let me just say I know I'm awkward about the way I reveal myself. I mean, I thought that's what I was doing and you sure didn't want to hug me, did you? I talk at my fears. I fight 'em."

"Sudsy hugs you," said Pinder. "I know she does. She loves you."

"I know she does," said Woodruff. "But, well, there's something lacking. The tougher I am on myself, the more I realize that for me the examined life lacks charm. It's stripped. I don't have any special gifts or answers. I don't guess anybody does."

"I do," chirped Howell, his head buried in the pillow.

"Uh oh," cautioned Pinder.

"What?" said Woodruff.

Howell rolled over to put two hands on his belly. "Well, the way I see it, I'll get through the second half of eternity just about the same way I got through the first half."

Woodruff thought about this a second and then chuckled. "Oh, David," he scoffed. "That's an old trick."

"Yeah, Henry," said Pinder. "These are just the halftime highlights."

Woodruff's jaw dropped. He stared at Pinder with fresh respect and then amusement. "Halftime highlights?" he cried. "Where did *that* come from? You don't know anything about sports!"

"Yes I do!" Pinder retorted, "I know a lot."

Howell hugged Pinder from behind. "I once got in a lot of trouble over this," he chuckled.

"Huh?" said Woodruff. His mouth was open when the phone rang.

Howell sat up in a panic. "Oh, shit!" he cried.

"Don't worry," soothed Woodruff. "We haven't been making any noise this time. Besides, the old bat can't fuss with all the construction noise in the building."

"I'm not worried about Madame Delacroix," said Howell after the phone rang again. "It's that FBI guy calling back. Oh, God, the jig is up."

"Wait a minute," said Woodruff, rising to battle. "I'll handle this. You guys need a rest."

"That's right," said Pinder. "Stall him. Tell him to call back tomorrow."

"Feed him some of your template stuff," Howell suggested. "That'll hold him."

"Right," said a fortified Woodruff. He grabbed the phone. "Hello? *Who?* Casey! Well I'll be damned! You were? Well, yeah, I know where to find myself, I think. That's what we were just talking about, actually . . . Never mind. What's up? . . . Sure. When? . . . Uh huh. How long will it take? . . . Uh huh . . . Uh huh . . . Hold on a second, okay?" Woodruff put his hand over the receiver. "Casey says she has something important to tell me," he announced. "She says it won't take but a few minutes. I got an idea. How 'bout if I try to lure her over here to spend the day with Miss Snow while we hit the country with Sudsy? She might like it. Would she be all right with the old lady? . . ."

It was arranged within a minute. Everything became kinetic. After a flurry of phone calls and preparations, Woodruff took a walk around the neighborhood with Casey Pendleton. Then he walked over to pick up Hartman and his long white cruiser while Pendleton received a briefing on Lily Snow. She arrived upstairs at the Savannah looking immensely relieved, wearing her weekend garb of crisp jeans, a polo shirt, a ponytail, and jogging shoes, carrying a Gothic novel, a volume of the tax code, and an apple (being on a diet). Sitting on the sofa in front of Snow, Pendleton listened attentively to glowing introductions from Howell, and she was drawn aside by Pinder for a lengthy list of things not to worry about. Paleness, funny nasal noises, twitching—these symptoms and many others had sent Snow to the hospital in the early days of panic, when Howell and Pinder were rookies. Pendleton enjoyed the tales. She asked the right questions. She also beamed with such spillover warmth in the presence of Lily Snow, who was herself in a good mood, that Pinder wished she were closer than a peripheral friend. Upon taking her leave, Pinder reached past the handshake to impose a hug and a kiss on the cheek. The ladysitter reciprocated with pleasure, but Pinder would remember that she hugged with a stiff back.

Woodruff maneuvered wordlessly through the city traffic, across the Key Bridge, and up the George Washington Parkway. The congestion plus a radio broadcast of the usual fractured news subdued the passengers under the cares of the city until they eased up to the crest of a commanding piedmont and caught a whiff of plowed ground on the big highway through Virginia. The old country rush hit them all simultaneously. "Kick it, Henry!" Howell cried from the back seat, but Woodruff was already doing so. Pinder rolled down her window to put her head outside with a luxuriant grin, skiing through the warm air at sixty. Hartman fiddled with the radio. When she found a high-spirited shuffling blues tune by a singer named Leon Redbone, who could imitate the sound of a Dixieland trombone with his vibrating lips, she juiced the volume and the quartet escaped on a high wave.

Pinder ducked back inside. "All right," she hollered, "who wants a bologna and potato chip sandwich?"

"A *what?*" shouted Hartman, above Redbone.

"A bologna and potato chip sandwich!" Pinder replied.

This concerned Hartman enough to turn down the radio. "What are you talking about?" she asked, craning her neck to the back seat where Pinder was invading her goodie bag.

"You'll see," said Pinder.

"It's her special junk food reward for times of acute stress," offered Howell.

Hartman made a face and then flipped around backward to watch Pinder, who had slices of bologna laid out on her lap. Potato chips and a jar of grainy mustard were handy nearby. "I don't believe this," said Hartman. "What goes on the inside, the bologna or the potato chips?"

Pinder looked surprised. "The potato chips, of course," she said. "If you put them on the outside, they'd crumble all over the place when you bear down on the sandwich."

"Oh," said Hartman. "Excuse me."

"Here, see for yourself."

"Sure," smiled Hartman, who then fought off an attack of uncertainty as she examined the package. "My God," she said reverently. She took a deep breath and went for the big bite.

"It's an experience, isn't it?" quipped Howell.

Hartman swallowed. "I think it needs a higher potato chip ratio," she said.

"That's what they all say at first," Pinder replied sententiously. Smiling, she was increasing production. "Want one, Henry?"

Woodruff took a long time to answer, demonstrating quickly that he was not part of the excitement over the sandwich experiment. "No, thanks," he said, eyes on the road.

Hartman sighed. She looked at Woodruff like a first-grade teacher until she broke into a mischievous grin. "All right, out with it!" she commanded. "What did Casey say?"

Woodruff paused thoughtfully over a long stretch of highway. "You won't believe it," he said, shaking his head.

The other three shared an inquisitive look. Pinder staked each of them to another sandwich. "She wants you back," she guessed, trying to make light of it.

"Nope," said Woodruff. He turned his head to his fellow travelers. "She's gonna have a baby," he declared.

The listeners skidded to an alert stillness, as though sensing a hidden trap. Woodruff had been known to lure friends by means of his sobriety down long roads of fanciful gossip. "Say that again, Henry?" asked Hartman, poised to weight authenticity in word and tone.

Woodruff watched the road. "She's gonna have a baby," he repeated. "At least that's what she says. And you guys, by the way, are sworn to secrecy. No kidding. This is serious. Because she's still trying to decide who the father's gonna be and she doesn't want anybody in her law firm to hear anything until long after it's done."

"What!" squeaked Pinder. "She doesn't know who the father is?"

"It's not done, yet," said Woodruff. "She has just made the decision. That's all. She said she's been thinking about it for a long time, and she's decided to pick somebody carefully and do it by sneak attack, kind of. And she will take complete responsibility for the kid. That's all she wants. Natural artificial insemination."

"Wow," sighed Pinder.

"That's the way I'd do it," Hartman muttered in soft awe.

"Are you and I candidates for the golden spermshake?" asked Howell, still suspicious of a ruse.

"Nope," replied Woodruff. "We're out. She wants a stranger. A chosen stranger. That's what she said. I'm telling you she announced all this in her duchess voice. Cold resolve. I doubt anything will stop her."

"I don't believe it," said Hartman.

Pinder blew out a stunned breath. "Boy, you'd never guess she'd do something like that in a million years," she said. "My God."

"Is she gonna try to stay in the law firm?" asked Howell. "In Washington? You think she can?"

Woodruff nodded affirmatively. "That's what she says. She says they won't like it, but in the end they'll have to accept it. I don't know. Anyway, she's convinced she can have the kid and stay on the job. She won't leave Washington. And she's developing a fanatical attachment to the law as the source of her independence. That's what she said. She said, 'I've decided men are easier to give up than law.' "

Howell flicked his nose. "That's the most depressing thing I've heard all day," he said.

"Maybe she'll find a lover later," Pinder suggested hopefully. "Maybe she'll even fall for the guy she picks to, um, to do her."

"To *do* her?" laughed Howell.

"To help her conceive," coughed Pinder.

"Well, she knows it will be a lot harder to find a lover or a mate or whatever once she's got the baggage of a kid," said Woodruff. "But that's a conscious choice she's making. She's thirty-three now, and her most recent suitors have been disappointments to her. She's decided she's looking for a good mate and father instead of fireworks, anyway, so she might as well be up front about it. Literally. Have the kid first. Weed out the slackers."

"You sound like you approve of it, Henry," said Hartman.

Woodruff looked at her and shrugged. "Well, shit," he said. "What am I to say? I think it's a sad situation. But at least she's not deluding herself about it, I don't think. And she knows it's gonna be a ton of troubles in the future, and she wants to do it anyway. She might pull it off. Who knows?"

"Did she ask for your blessing?" asked Howell.

"Nope," said Woodruff, after thinking. "I don't think so. Not explicitly, anyway, and I don't think at all."

"Then why'd she tell you in advance like this?" asked Howell.

"You got me. Old times' sake, maybe. Something. Maybe she just wanted to tell somebody semiofficial."

"Oh," said Howell, dropping the subject.

"Do you think she'll tell you who the father is, Henry?" asked Pinder.

"I doubt it," said Woodruff. "I wouldn't if I were her. It would just mess things up, probably. I guess that'll just be another unsolved mystery."

"Big deal," smiled Howell. "Most mysteries stay unsolved these days. Like who killed Jimmy Hoffa, and who killed all those Cubans down in Miami, like Mendoza."

"And whatever happened to your friend Bobby Ziller down in Miami," Woodruff added.

"Yeah," sighed Howell uneasily, surprised by the comment and by how forcefully a distant memory could rush upon him. "And for that matter, I don't believe the mystery of your gonorrhea episode has been cleared up to this day, has it?" he crooned.

326

Woodruff cleared his throat. "That's true," he acknowledged. "The established facts do not square with medical knowledge."

"How's that?" asked Hartman. "I forgot."

Woodruff shot a vengeful snicker back to Howell. "Nice of you to bring this up," he said.

"Sorry," said Howell, trying to sober himself, with mixed success.

"Well," said Woodruff, "the medical authorities swear that I had it, but each of my two possible female communicants swears that her medical authorities say she didn't. So there is a discrepancy. Which is not important to anybody anymore. Except it nags me a little to think that I may not have had it at all."

"Oh," said Hartman.

The weighty silence returned. After a pause, Hartman and Pinder launched a conversation about Casey Pendleton's plan—about the social ramifications, about who else would and would not do such a thing, and why. The subject touched a number of sparks, but there was a current of melancholy running beneath it that was accentuated by Woodruff's billowing silence. His mood dragged their dialogue down to a perfunctory exchange, and finally to a halt. Hartman turned the volume back up on the radio. She watched Woodruff quietly down ten miles of highway, finally turning to put her feet up on the seat, elbows on her knees. Eyeing Woodruff, she shook her head just to feel her long hair undulate on her shoulders.

Howell spoke up from the back seat. "Excuse me," he said. Hartman and Woodruff turned expectantly toward him. Howell coughed. "I was just wondering whether either of you has ingested a dangerous drug in preparation for our river walk," he said.

Woodruff frowned momentarily before giving way to a look of sly escape. He pulled a cellophane bag of orange powder from his shirt pocket and dangled it before the crowd.

"My psilocybin?" gasped Howell.

Woodruff nodded.

"My God, Henry. That stuff is old," said Howell. "It's probably moldy by now. I doubt if it's any good."

"Probably not," Woodruff agreed. "I didn't take enough to get stoned anyhow. Just a pinch to get some surf up in my head, maybe. I was waiting to offer it to you guys on the river."

"I'll bet you were," kidded Pinder.

"I was," Woodruff insisted. "Here, you want some now?"

After a brief debate, Howell and Pinder declined. "Somebody's got to stay straight to take care of you guys," she said, as the long white car approached the highway bypass around Warrenton, Virginia. Ahead, perpendicular to their path, stretched the majestic Blue Ridge mountain chain, the eastern edge of the Shenandoah Valley. Around them lay rolling pastures of horse and farm country. But on the bypass itself suddenly appeared a slender, isolated apotheosis of asphalt civilization. In the bare space of one half mile before the pastureland abruptly resumed on the far side, appeared a stark museum, magnificent in its own way, like an Inca ruin or an aerial photo-

327

graph of New York. Representatives of all the great national chains stood side by side, noses up to the highway telephone wires—McDonald's, Howard Johnson's, Holiday Inn, Kentucky Fried Chicken, Burger Chef, Burger King, Arbee's, Arthur Treacher's Fish & Chips, Gino's, they were all there, along with chains of a more local vintage, two large shopping centers, a bowling alley, a gas station for each of the major oil companies, and a last local hangout called the Frost Diner. At the midpoint of "the strip," as it was known, sat the Seven-Eleven Store, specializing in less nutritious food products, for people in an extra hurry.

"Hey Henry, let's make a pit stop at Seven-Eleven," cried Hartman, who always got excited on the strip because it marked the near end of the journey. The river was quite near. "Haven's out of supplies."

"I could use some orange juice," said Howell.

"Okay," Woodruff conceded.

He pulled into the parking lot and the others tumbled out ahead of him into the compressed market, where shelves of foods, novelties, and household items were packed tightly around a square checkout counter tended by two bored women in peppermint frocks. Woodruff followed, wandering over to the corner devoted to racks of magazines and paperback books. He studied the magazine rack from a medium distance. The strip was visible in the background, above the rack and through the floor-to-ceiling window. All the organs of national communion were there, hundreds of them, the few literary ones and the solid news journals and the vast hordes of celebrity sheets. There were sober *dicta* on national affairs along with screaming headlines like the one about the woman in Idaho who claimed to have been impregnated by the ghost of a pop star named Elvis Presley, and to Woodruff's blurry mind it all melded together into one piece, a garish assault of bright colors and red opinions and expressions of frozen extravagance, fishhooks for dreams and comportments. Woodruff became mesmerized, feeling quite still before the shrine.

After a bustle of talk and cash at the counter, the sporting trio looked around a moment later to find that Woodruff was nowhere in sight. "Where's Henry?" asked Howell. The shrugged at each other and waited. When time produced nothing, they fanned out in the store but came up empty. "Where *is* he?" asked Hartman, shaking her head. "That man has been a pisser all day." She went outside, ducked around the corner, and returned with another shrug. "We've only been here a second," she said. "He couldn't have vanished. Could he?" Worry grew in fits. After consultations, they fanned out to search the store again, for lack of anything better to do. Pinder, on a hunch, went out to check the car. She thought Woodruff might have been stretched out on the back seat. She returned without success, however, and the search resumed.

On his route, Howell felt rather silly, looking under shelves and under packing boxes in a store designed explicitly so that not even the smallest item could hide. In the rear corner, he absentmindedly opened a metal door the size of a large porthole on a large refrigerated bin. Howell shut the door and jumped back three feet. He looked furtively around, down the aisles and out the window, before returning to the door. It was waist-high. He opened it, and then he winced so extremely that his face almost made a noise.

"Henry!" he whispered. "What the fuck are you doing in there?"

"I'll be out in a minute," smiled Woodruff. He was crouched inside with his arm resting on a pile of ice bags.

Howell's eyes bulged. "Goddammit, Henry!" he gasped. He jerked his head from side to side. "Somebody's gonna see up! You can't do this!"

Woodruff leaned toward the door from the inside. Howell backed off an inch or two. "I'm all right," said Woodruff. "I'll be out in a second. Shut the door!"

Howell shut the door softly and walked away in circles until he found Pinder, whom he grabbed sharply by the arm. "Come with me!" he commanded through his teeth with conspiratorial urgency, saying not a word until he had found Hartman and drawn the pair aside. "Guess what!" he whispered. They were frightened, saying nothing. "Henry's over there in the ice machine!"

The three of them fluttered around in fear and mirth, in epithets on mental instability and in disbelief. They craned their necks around to observe the scene, where the huge silver container was adorned with one word, ICE. No one came by there.

"We gotta get him out of there!" whispered Howell.

"I don't believe it!" challenged Hartman.

"Then why are you whispering!" whispered Howell. "Go see for yourself! And get the psilocybin away from him just in case the cops come!"

Hartman blew smoke out of her ears and then she laughed. As she did, she had a premonition about a redoubtable woman who was entering the Seven-Eleven wearing orange stretch pants beneath a torso shaped like three doughnuts on a spindle. The woman walked away from them.

"Uh oh," wailed Hartman. "Uh oh."

"What?" whispered Pinder.

Hartman pointed to the woman, who reached the far end of the store and turned toward the rear corner, where the icebox stood.

"Oh, my God!" whispered Hartman. She placed her slender fingers in front of her face.

Howell and Pinder craned their shoulders around the shelf to bring the icebox into view. Hartman turned away to grab Howell around the neck. She didn't see the woman open the icebox door. Nor did she see her take the bag of ice that was offered to her from within by a pair of familiar hands. But she did hear the loud gasps from her two friends, and she pulled out of her cringe in time to see the woman arrive at the checkout counter and plunk down her ice. There was nothing in her pale routine face beyond porkchop shadow and steady dissatisfaction.

Howell clamped his small nimble paw over Pinder's mouth, and the three of them otherwise clutched desperately at one another until the woman was safely out the door. Howell doubled over. "I have never seen anything like that," he whispered. The small of his back shook at the ceiling.

"I don't believe it," sputtered Pinder. "I just don't believe it. I've gotta go outside to laugh. I can't stand it!" She had tears in her eyes.

"What *happened?*" croaked Hartman, who was weak from laughter and stupefaction herself. "What did she *do?*" Howell and Pinder tried to describe it for her, but the words were too tangled in mirth and awe. This went on for some time, during which they forgot the man in the container.

Thus was earned the nickname Icebox Woodruff, which would have been christened with an immediate celebration had it not been for Carlos Maraña. Howell was still bent over when he saw him—or his clone—emerge from a powder blue Dodge with unofficial plates, which had pulled up to the Seven-Eleven. The driver stayed put. Three men got out of the back. One of them appeared to be an athletic businessman in dark glasses, but he stretched his arms above his head and twisted his hips with an abandon that didn't fit. Maraña stood on the other side of the car. He had been seated in the middle. He wore silver-tinted sunglasses and a kelly green suit with an open shirt. If he stretched his cramped muscles at all, he did it so subtly that he did not disturb a single thread of his suit. He just stood there, hands folded in front of him.

Howell yanked in a sharp breath and stumbled toward the front door to make sure. He had just risen to full height when he paused, partly out of shock and partly to let the third man pass by him. Seven-Eleven's newest customer was a tall, dignified American with silver hair, whom Howell had no way of recognizing as Edward Noel. Howell watched him stroll to the counter and ask for a pack of cigarettes. Then, as Howell put a hand on the door to exit, something about Maraña made him freeze. He could not move. There was too much contrast between the inner commotion he felt from the carnival terrors and the stillness of Maraña, who was standing in the bright June sun. Only two parts of Maraña moved. His head swung very slowly, almost imperceptibly, from side to side, which Howell took as a negative against the greeting he had in mind. And Maraña's hands were trembling slightly. The very idea of Carlos Maraña afraid made Howell afraid. Fears in Maraña carried such a deadly reality that they obliterated Howell's fears from icebox escapades and romantic impasses and template speculations, which suddenly became the stuff of consciences too long at large.

Stiff-legged, Howell hurried back to the two women. The sight of his face splashed them with panic that lacked an underside of humor. "What's the matter, baby?" asked Pinder with alarm.

"I'm gonna pee," gasped Howell. "That's Carlos Maraña out there."

"*Who?*" frowned Hartman, alarmed and testy, about to be provoked by one twist too many.

"*Where?*" hissed Pinder. "are you sure?"

"Right there," Howell whispered through his teeth. "The one looking right at us. With the glasses. And the face like an abyss. Don't move too quick!"

Pinder stole a look. Howell leaned over to Hartman's ear. "He's the Cuban spy I talk about all the time," he told her. "The one I saw in jail. Last supposed to be either dead or in Panama's secret police."

Pinder leaned into the huddle. "But why are you so upset, baby?" she asked. "You don't think he's after us, do you?"

"No," Howell winced in frustration. "I don't *know* why I'm upset. Except he makes me upset. And he looks afraid. And he motioned me not to speak to him. I think. I think he's under arrest or something. And I want to know why he's here of all places. It's creepy."

Hartman looked back and forth. "*I'll* tell you why he's here," she whispered. "He's here for the same reason Henry's in that icebox over there! To ruin my Saturday in the country." Her breath sounded like a furnace.

Howell blinked twice before assimilating this comment. Then he smiled quickly, although still afraid. He kissed Hartman on the cheek. "You're all right, Sudsy," he said. "Give me your car keys."

"What are you talking about?" gasped Hartman.

"Hurry! They're leaving! I just want to follow them a little bit and see where they're going! C'mon, Haven!"

Both women's eyes darted between the icebox and the blue Dodge. "No," said Pinder. "I'm gonna stay here and help Sudsy with Henry. I have to. And I don't want you to go."

"I'm going," Howell said. "I'll be all right, and so will Henry. Hey, they're leaving! Hurry!" He peremptorily flung open his hand for the keys.

"David, you don't know a thing about spying," grumbled Pinder, as Hartman pulled the keys from her pocket.

Howell was backing away. "I won't be long," he said. "Check in at the bowling alley. I'll call there if there's a message."

"Be careful," called Pinder, but Howell was gone. She and Hartman exchanged stunned looks.

"Is it these men?" mused Hartman. "Or is it us?"

"It's them," said Pinder.

XVI

HOWELL WAVED good-bye to their confusion as he screeched off down the highway. The Dodge had gone west, toward the Blue Ridge, which was a surprise. He had thought they'd be heading for Washington. Howell turned on the windshield wipers by mistake. He told himself to calm down, but he worried that perhaps Woodruff was seriously undone. Impossible, he consoled himself. Woodruff had performed stunts like that before. He laughed to himself, and then he cleared his throat to focus on the danger ahead. It was best to stay about a quarter of a mile behind, he decided. Howell tried to think like a detective. The circumstances pointed to the CIA, he figured, because Warrenton, Virginia, was CIA country. He could see the mountain-top antennas of the Agency's world communications headquarters, and he knew from his reporters' bull sessions that a training center and the CIA archives and storage warehouses and countless retirement homes for Agency people were scattered about the countryside. Indeed, the CIA was rumored to be the county's largest employer, with secret roots scattered widely. Preston Hartman's plumber was thought to work there, and so was his gardener. Howell could accept the idea of a CIA rendezvous nearby, but not with Maraña. Maraña hated the CIA. He had left it years before for other agencies and was last rumored to be a freelance narcotics informant. Howell decided it didn't make sense. He shrugged and sang along with the song on the radio.

The Dodge turned off the main highway about three miles outside Warrenton, into farm country of narrow hilly roads. After five miles and one turn, Howell reached the summit of a hill and saw no Dodge. He pulled over to think. A dirt road went off to the right, dividing forest land behind from a farm ahead that was surrounded by a white picket fence. The fence came to a corner at the dirt road. Perimeter trees concealed much of the fields behind it, but they seemed to be extensive. No house was visible.

Howell spotted a few horses grazing in the distance. On the left side of the road, wooded land fell off to a stream that wound off into a clearing. Several hundred yards ahead, a paved road went off to the left toward the clearing, and there was a second side road farther ahead.

Howell jumped on the accelerator to speed to this last road, hoping to find a dirt surface with dust still settling. He found dirt but no dust. Howell decided he couldn't be too precise in his conclusions since he didn't know how fast dust settles. It was a disturbing piece of practical ignorance. He sighed and determined to go on what little he had. If the Dodge were a CIA car, he reasoned, the horse farm with the white picket fence would be an unlikely destination because a working farm was too elaborate as cover for a safehouse, even for the CIA. He eliminated that and the two dirt roads, leaving the road he had passed on the left. It was a standard gentry driveway, with a blank mailbox, a name (Out to Pasture), and a no trespassing sign. That's it, he concluded. It was a hunch confirmed only by the unorthodox, amusing farm name. Howell chuckled to himself when he realized that after all this sleuth work he lacked the nerve to venture past the no trespassing sign toward an unknown reception.

He turned left onto the second dirt road, stopped, and turned off the engine. A knee-high fence of stacked stone indicated that he was at the corner of the Out to Pasture estate, which Howell figured must be a large one since stacked stone fences date back to slave labor. The fence ran parallel to the dirt road as far as he could see. There were trees and clearings inside it, but the land was even less open than the horse farm. After protracted debate, he decided to drive along the dirt road in hope of sighting the house and perhaps the Dodge.

Unfortunately, the road sloped downward and to the right after about half a mile, so that the stone fence was veering away from him at the top of an embankment. Again, Howell stopped. This time he turned on the windshield wiper deliberately and toyed with the knob as he listened to the rasp of rubber on dry glass. Somehow it seemed appropriate to the moment. He sighed, mentally previewing scenes of himself returning to the Seven-Eleven with his tale of failure. It was a silly idea anyhow, he thought. He wished Pinder were there. She would point out some magic in the landscape that would make the journey seem worthwhile with or without the Dodge. She would want to climb the embankment just to see what was there. Howell glowered at the dirt. Then, in a burst of energy, he hurtled his way over road and ditch to scamper up the steep incline. A visual blur awaited him at the summit. He made his way through prickly underbrush, past the mottled bark of sycamore trees into a thick stand of poplars, until he found the stone fence about a hundred yards from the road. It was crumbling here and there, but it still made a fine perch. Crouching on it, he peered through the forest to a narrow clearing that ran parallel to the fence. On the other side of the clearing, a double row of red oaks lined a driveway leading up to a white farmhouse with two porches and three chimneys. "Oh, boy," Howell shivered to himself as he sat down on the fence. He saw not one but three blue Dodges lined up in the driveway, and a thrill of triumph swept over him. The vision shone as the spy's reward for having persisted through a reversible world of wispy clues and forget-me-not disappointments. Even though he had no idea what it meant for Carlos Maraña to be Out to Pasture in a blue Dodge, Howell savored the thrill, independent of substance.

He was still savoring it, sitting on the fence, when he heard a wooden door slap shut. He jumped, and when he landed his bladder hummed for attention. Howell cursed his chemicals. Leaning forward, squinting, he saw a lone man standing in the backyard just outside the house. There was something in his hand. Howell thought it was Maraña, but he didn't trust his judgment in such a state as his, at such a long distance. Impatiently, he tried to make the man move with his eyes, but nothing happened except the man kept staring off toward the Blue Ridge skyline and Howell's bladder kept swelling. He stood up to pee, watching the man but not breathing. When he was about halfway through, the target began to stroll away from the house across the lawn. From the gait—a fluid glide from the waist down, but pitched slightly ahead, with the shoulders slightly thrust forward—Howell was certain it was Maraña. "Oh, boy, oh, boy," he moaned to himself, savagely boosting the flow. The distant chills brought him the unusual sensation of feeling less relieved empty than full as he cast one last look around at the peaceful trees and, receiving no countermanding orders, lurched off through the woods parallel to Maraña.

He quickly gave up hope of finding a quiet way to hurry through the woods, surrendering himself to the mercy of the man he imagined in the house sighting down on him through a telescopic lens. But nothing happened. Howell was thankful for summer, when the underbursh crunched instead of crackled. Keeping an eye out for stickers and a watch downward for stepping spots of bare ground, he tried to keep track of Maraña and plot strategy at once, but this was too much. Unpredictable panic kept inviting in irrelevant concerns like forest smells and poison ivy dread. It was all he could do to press ahead and hope Maraña's walk carried him far away from the house. Which it was doing. Howell started angling toward the huge clearing. Maraña was about a furlong ahead of him gazing silently at the surrounding vistas. Howell could not help musing on the incongruity between the present setting and the Latin spy, who looked for the moment like a charter member of the Sierra Club. But he longed to catch up. The house was far behind. The trees thinned out as he edged near the long promenade of grass, and Howell began dashing from one to another. It was liberating for him to run swiftly on the soft grass, hearing no sound but his heartbeat and the wind in his ears. He reached another tree and was thinking about giving a call when Maraña slowly turned around. His silver glasses gleamed. He held a drink in his left hand, and with his right one he reached casually into the outside pocket of his jacket to pull out a revolver.

Howell sank to his knees behind the tree, instantly breathless. "Carlos?" he gasped. "It's me. David Howell."

Very slowly—cruelly, Howell thought—Maraña put the gun back in the pocket, keeping his hand there. He began walking toward Howell's tree. His face betrayed no hint of thought or purpose. Maraña appeared to be preprogrammed, a few degrees more pleasant than a robot. Howell glanced instinctively back toward the house, Maraña's gun having transformed the snipers into trusted authorities. He wondered if the Dodge drivers could hear a gunshot from there.

Maraña stopped about fifteen feet from Howell's tree. "How are you, my friend?" he smiled. "I thought it was you, but you can never be sure with these tricky CIA people, you know?"

"Huh?" gushed Howell, breathing gratefully. He realized that he was hugging the tree, which was embarrassing, so he raised himself to his feet. Good ol' Carlos, he thought, but he was wary.

"You should stay behind the tree," Maraña pleasantly warned.

"Okay," Howell said eagerly. Then he frowned at the bark in front of his nose.

"Not from me," said Maraña. "But you should keep out of sight in case the gentlemen from the Company are watching from the house."

"Oh," said Howell, edging his way toward the back side of the tree. "Why? Is it dangerous?"

Maraña looked blank for an instant, and then he smiled hesitantly, as though he had forgotten with whom he was dealing. "No," he laughed. "It is just these security people. Everything is security for them. So if they see me talking with someone out here, they'll probably decide to sell this beautiful safehouse for security reasons and I'd have to find another place next time. That would be too bad. Security people are the same everywhere. The shits and the subshits again. I have them, too."

"You do?" said Howell. "You've been in Panama, right? That's what I heard."

"I have been all over the world, my friend," smiled Maraña. "I'm hot right now. My name is privately on the lips of presidents on three continents. Most of them are sneering, of course."

"Oh," said Howell.

Maraña raised his right hand from the gun pocket to remove his silver glasses, an act that pleased Howell on two counts. Maraña's eyes were a thin mask of paleness in the middle of his tan. "But you're right, David," he said. "I've been mostly in Panama, chasing you Yankees around our canal. How do you like that?"

"That's what I heard," chuckled Howell, bursting with camaraderie now that Maraña seemed somewhat human and disposed not to shoot him. "Still tweaking the Americans, eh Carlos? I thought you were getting over that. It's good to see you."

"Not tweaking them enough, my friend," grinned Maraña.

"Oh, come on," said Howell, resting a shoulder against the tree.

"Believe me, it's true," said Maraña. "And it's sad, you know. Because I won't be tweaking and peeking much more, my friend. I am about to retire from my international career, David. It's true."

"You are?"

"Yes, I am," Maraña replied. "You don't have to believe me. It doesn't matter what you believe, as usual for a *gringo*."

"I believe you," said Howell, though he was not sure he did. "But why?"

"You're asking that of *me*?" said Maraña. "After what you told me that day in the jail about how I should take care of myself and not blame anybody? Remember, I don't forget things. You were lucky, David. People get mad when somebody steals what they love to blame, and I have a terrible temper. It was only because you were so nice to visit me. You were the only one who wasn't a shit or a subshit that day. I don't forget it."

"Thanks," said Howell, making an effort not to sound too sincere. "Yeah, sure," he added.

"The truth is all I know," Maraña grinned. "I'm going on my own for good."

Howell coughed into his armpit. "You've *always* been on your own, Carlos," he said. "I just meant that you should start with yourself to make your happiness. That's all."

"Happiness? What's happiness?" Maraña said icily. "Remember where you are."

Howell looked about at the landscape and trees.

"This is Company property," said Maraña.

"Oh," said Howell.

"You are a secret guest," said Maraña with a hint of menace. "Don't forget that."

"Never mind," said Howell, shaking his head, breathing deeply. "So you're quitting. I see. Is this your last big operation?"

"If *you* say so," Maraña replied. "I'm only sightseeing."

"Oh, come on," prodded Howell, kicking the tree with his sneakers. "You've gotta tell me something. Look, I almost fell over when I saw you back there at the Seven-Eleven. You can't do something like that to me without telling me a little bit about what you're doing. It's not fair after I did all this good following work and tore my pants in the bushes."

Maraña eyed Howell up and down, twinkling with a smug appreciation that the latter found most unsettling. Then he turned around wordlessly to look at the mountains, hands clasped behind him. "And what are you doing out here in this beautiful Company land today, David?" he asked pleasantly, as though he had just happened upon an old friend at a horse show. "Were those your friends giggling in the store?"

Howell sighed. "Yeah, they were," he said. "We were just on our way out to spend the day in the country. My friend Susan's father has a farm out here on the Rappahannock River."

"I see," said Maraña, in the neutered tone of the interrogator.

"Really," said Howell. "We just wanted to sit in the river and get away from Washington."

"I believe you," said Maraña. "And how is Susan?"

"Not so good, if you really want to know," sighed Howell. "She's having boyfriend troubles with my friend Henry."

"What's the matter?"

Howell stared at Maraña's back, at the Blue Ridge in the distance, and then he looked anxiously from side to side, puzzled, fearing that Maraña might be anesthetizing him with such talk for an ambush. He saw nothing unusual, however. He looked up in the tree directly above him and still saw nothing. "Well, I don't know," he said. "Susan's wonderful. She's a little haunted, but she's wonderful. And Henry's too busy trying not to be disillusioned to love her right, I'm afraid. But who knows? They don't know themselves. They don't fight, but sometimes they just come unplugged."

"Too bad," Maraña said flatly. "I didn't know Americans could be like that."

Howell bit one lip. "Carlos, you don't really care about . . ."

". . . and how is *your* girlfriend, David?" Maraña interrupted. "That was her dressed like a farmer?"

Howell chuckled in spite of himself. "Yes," he replied. "That's Haven. She's terrific. We're doing all right, but we're being ground down pretty hard lately because we've put ourselves in a strange mess. The guy who's on our backs is from Miami. You may know him, come to think of it. Pat Shea, head of the FBI office?"

Maraña shook his head slowly. "I've heard of him," he said. "What did he do to you?"

"That's very complicated," Howell sighed. "Basically, his aunt is an old lady who's lived in our building a long time, and Shea stuck her in a rotten old folks' home and took all her stuff, for some reason. Something to do with money, maybe, but basically he doesn't like being around her. So Haven and I brought the old lady home to live with us and now Shea's climbing all over us with threats and stuff. We don't know what to do. We're at the end of our rope."

"That's terrible," Maraña said wryly. "You are a very fonny man, David."

"Okay, okay," said Howell. "I realize you don't want to talk about why you're up here from Panama. I give up. How about something else? Can you at least tell me what was going on when you got busted down in Miami? I never have figured that out."

Maraña rose up on his toes, and back down. "I already told you," he said cheerfully. "I informed on myself all over town to get myself arrested. Some friends helped me. I'm surprised there weren't more agencies involved, really. Some of them were loafing."

"But *why?*" pressed Howell. "It doesn't make sense. You could have gotten killed! You almost did get shot, for God's sake! Why take the risk?"

"Many demented persons have tried to kill me," said Maraña. "And many others are sworn to do so. I take precautions, but I take a risk when I walk out the door. Getting arrested is not so dangerous, my friend."

"But I don't understand *why*," said Howell, who was getting worked up. "Why the risk? What for? It seems like much ado about nothing."

"Aha!" Maraña laughed with pleasure. "That's what it is, David. Any honest man in the spy business will tell you that's what it is for everyone but the suckers."

"Come on."

"You are really something, David," laughed Maraña. "Now let's suppose there are some times when it's good to be in jail. Can you understand that?"

"Uh huh," Howell said vaguely.

"And let's suppose there are some things you can do and say in jail that you can't do on the outside," Maraña added with a mysterious lilt. "Okay? And let's suppose that there are times when it's good to leave a country under a cloud instead of just walking to the airport, okay? And let's suppose that sometimes a little mystery is good for its own sake. To put demons in the heads of your enemies, okay? And on top of all that, let's suppose that there are certain things you can accomplish with the police by getting arrested, okay?"

"Wait a minute," protested Howell. "Okay. I'll be the mouse and you be the cat, but run that last one by me again."

"It will make me happy," beamed Maraña, enjoying himself. "You are so much like a child, my friend . . ."

". . . Well, I don't know . . ."

". . . Believe me, it's good. Okay? Now you know I told you about the security shits and the subshits, okay? You should picture them as the food tasters around the King of Spain. Something like that. Their job is to make sure nothing bad happens to the king. So naturally they don't want the king to eat any food at all, right, because he might get poisoned? And naturally they don't want to eat the food either. So they are in a false position. And if they are your enemies and you *know* them, then you are lucky because of that. You can starve them. You can send them fattening food. You can play with them . . ."

". . . But what has that got to do with a drug bust, Carlos?"

"That's easy," replied a jovial Maraña. "That's what I'm telling you, David. But you don't listen. Maybe you are more interested in the beautiful mountains there. The Company owns them, I hear."

"Oh, come on, Carlos," snickered Howell.

"I'm not sure about that," Maraña admitted wryly. "But the king's guards, I am sure about them. And on top of everything else they are the *king's* guards, you see, and for that reason they cannot afford to be embarrassed for anything. They depend on the king's favor, and the king will not be embarrassed. And there are a lot of them, fighting among themselves. And if those guards are your enemies, David, you must understand that they want to have a good time and they don't want to be embarrassed. So what do I do? I show them a good time, and I convince them that if they interfere with me they will be embarrassed. You see? It's simple. And I can guarantee you those people from the DEA will never make any more problems for me, David. They have already been embarrassed a little bit, and next time it will be much worse."

338

Howell was concentrating intently on the back of Maraña's neck. He shook his head slowly as he checked the grounds once again for intruders. "I think I have it," he asserted, mimicking a student with a fresh insight. "So you are up here now tying knots in another group of the king's guards, right?"

"Of course not, David," protested Maraña. "I am serving the public interest. I am bending over backward to protect the rights even of the hypocrites."

"I give up," sighed Howell. "I've never heard you speak in so many parables and shit, Carlos . . ."

". . . And I've never heard you ask so many questions . . ."

". . . You were a lot more straightforward in the Dade County Jail."

"You are very kind."

"I'm kidding. By the way, did you really know you were gonna be there when you wrote out that address for me at Vizcaya?"

"Certainly."

"So where will you be tomorrow?"

After a long pause, Maraña responded only by rotating deliberately to face the white farmhouse, so that Howell was visible in the left corner of his eye. This motion made Howell realize how still he had been.

"Tell me, my friend, do you know any officials in the State Department?" asked Maraña, absorbed in a distant plan of his own.

"Huh?" puzzled Howell, who shrugged and smiled, "Sure. Do you want a job?"

The joke bounced lamely off Maraña's mood. "Somebody you can get in to see on a few hours' notice? Doesn't have to be too high, but I want the secretary of state to have heard of him. Do you know somebody like that, David?"

Howell suddenly felt quite uneasy, not being sure whether he was just outside of a conspiracy, or in one. "Sure," he replied unsteadily, thinking of several acquaintances, including Richard Clayfield.

Maraña pondered this for some time. "I might be able to help you with your FBI problem," he said nonchalantly.

"What FBI problem?" burst Howell.

"Didn't you say you were having some kind of personal problem with Pat Shea in the Miami FBI office?"

"Yeah, but that's personal, not FBI business."

"I might be able to help you then."

Howell was becoming exasperated. "Come on, Carlos!" he pleaded. "I need help, but you can't be so goddam cryptic, okay? What's it got to do with the State Department?"

Maraña did not waver from whatever was in his head. "What is your telephone number?" he asked.

Howell stared blankly, and then started fumbling through his pockets. "I'll write it down," he said.

"Just tell me," said Maraña.

Howell told him.

"Good," said Maraña. "And one more thing. Can you think of a place in downtown Washington where we can meet outdoors at seven o'clock on Monday morning? Some place pretty and quiet?"

"Seven o'clock?" gasped Howell. "There's no good place to meet that early."

"Sometimes it is necessary to make up for all your nights of fun," Maraña said drily.

Howell, under duress, thought a moment and said, "I know one nice place that I've always thought would be perfect for spies to meet there and pass the microfilm and stuff. It's in the embassy district though. Is that all right?"

"Sure," said Maraña. "Tell me."

Howell gave directions. Maraña began to ease away down the lawn even as he was repeating them. "Wait a minute," called Howell. "This is crazy. Are you sure you're gonna be there?"

Maraña did not turn around. "Call Max if I'm not," he said. "He might know something. Good-bye, David. I've got to entertain the subshits now. And one more thing, my friend. Wait here a minute while I leave and then try not to make so much noise going back, please." Maraña tossed a quick chilly grin back at Howell and glided out of whisper-shouting range.

"I thought I was pretty quiet going through there," said Howell, though Maraña could not hear him. He sagged back against the tree and tried to figure out whether or not to classify this encounter as a success. He shook his head and shared a quiet laugh with the Blue Ridge before making his way back through the forest to the white cruiser, and from there to Warrenton Lanes, where he found his friends around a pinball machine in somber moods. He told them of his adventures as the four paddled around in the Rappahannock River next to a pile of clothes, and he laughed upon hearing Woodruff's point of view on the lady in the orange stretch pants—how she looked from within the ice machine, why handing her the bag of ice had been "nothing more than the instinctive crisis mode of a former devoted public servant," and so forth. But the day was abbreviated and the somber mood lingered through it. Haven Pinder rubbed Hartman's neck most of the way back to Washington. Howell worried about Lily Snow. He knew there was something wildly funny about the very idea of entrusting her protection to someone like Carlos Maraña, but his whimsy failed him. Nothing wafted up. And Henry Woodruff, when not exercising a manic new curiosity about Cuban affairs, kept murmuring, "Boy, what a day."

At the appointed hour on Monday morning, Howell made footprints in the dew past the embassy of Israel to the chosen spot. He found a reception committee of two, neither of whom was Maraña. The Chicken Man was there, fishing miscellaneous items from his tattered coat, washing his face without water and otherwise preparing himself for the day, all the while trying to seize the attention of Miss Hope, who was also there with her two shopping bags of peanuts and stale bread. Howell sensed that he was intruding on some dawn ritual, although both these elders remained oblivious to him.

Miss Hope, moreover, remained oblivious to the Chicken Man. She was beaming down at her mass assembly of squirrels, cats, and pigeons, moving her lips in private endearments. Howell had never seen her in the element for which she was famous in the neighborhood. He watched from a respectful distance. Every so often, Miss Hope would reach in her bag for another brightly colored bowl and place it down without hesitation, in moves so familiar to the setting and the animals that Howell decided she must have a discrete spot for each bowl—one next to the lamppost, four along the curb, two under the park bench, others scattered along the sidewalk and under certain bushes—and an aggregate order perfectly understood by the animals, especially the cats, who gathered in twos and threes around the bowls while the other animals generally scattered in the munching area. When all the bowls were set out, Miss Hope nodded here and there toward what Howell imagined as various checkpoints of her domain, and then she sat down on the bench with a slight residue of busy care on her beatific face.

As she sat down, Miss Hope naturally turned toward the Chicken Man, who had been going through his own motions in the street some fifteen feet away, and the Chicken Man did not let this opportunity pass by wasted. Instantly, he slapped the backs of his hands to his armpits and began flapping his elbows up and down with all his might, his head thrown back and his face inflamed in a joyous crowing motion that would have done any rooster proud except that there was no sound. This silence occasionally got the Chicken Man in trouble, for some magistrates had taken it as a sign of a rational and therefore responsible strain somewhere deep in the parabolic recesses of his mind, and things go hard with flaky drifters caught pulling fast ones. On the other hand, the Chicken Man got into less trouble because he no longer woke up influential residents with his namesake cry.

Howell watched mesmerized from a southern corner of 22nd Street and Decatur Place, charmed into titters and awe by the odd dignity of the performances and by the notion that they took place there within a rooster's call of a thousand ordinary Washingtonians who were dreaming their way through grand strategies for arms sales, conquests of secretaries, throatholds on public opinion, and other serious schemes to grasp a bit of tribute at a bargain. He had both hands over his mouth when he saw Maraña walking up Decatur Place, moving fast.

Howell quickly scanned the site for a place to talk without displacing the feeders or the flappers. Miss Hope's area was uphill ahead of him in the cusp of a dead end in 22nd Street, bordered on the left by a thin strip of woods and on the right by a walled mansion. On the far side of the area stood a sculptured stone water bath, behind which a broad bordered row of curved steps rose through a shaded, cool space to another dead-end cusp of road above. An awkward overhang in 22nd Street was thus mended by a tree-covered grotto of stone, but there was no convenient spot secluded from

Miss Hope. Howell nodded a greeting to Maraña and went ahead of him up the steps. He took a seat at the top.

Maraña sat lower, giving Howell his back. He did not seem to notice the theater ahead of him, even when the Chicken Man gave one last elbow flurry and toddled off toward the morning street scenes. Maraña radiated alertness. "No questions," he commanded, with the soft intensity of a bank robber's private orders to the teller.

Howell tried to be pleasant. "Okay," he said.

"I want you to go to your best contact in the State Department," said Maraña, sounding far away. "Today. And you tell him that I have come up here from the government of Panama to help you, and the Company is bottling me up for its own reasons. Tell them a plan is well under way to assassinate Secretary Carlyle when he visits Caracas at the time of the OPEC conference."

"Oh, great," sighed Howell.

"Tell them the assassin will be your old friend Pepe Lopez," said Maraña.

Howell sighed again but said nothing.

"Tell them Pepe has become very accomplished," said Maraña. "They can confirm that with the FBI, if they want to let the FBI in on this, but only those who have seen Pepe work lately know truly how dedicated he is. I told you he is a killer, David."

"Yeah," Howell said weakly.

"Believe me. You have a problem. Pepe is already in Caracas. The sub-shits in Venezuela will never find him, and they can't protect Secretary Carlyle unless they hide him under the bed all the time. But I can find him. Maybe I can talk him out of it. Who can say? But I will not go to Caracas without some backing from the United States. The subshits down there are not gentlemen, my friend, and some of them don't like me. So the officials in the State Department should find out quickly and do what they want to do. It doesn't matter to me either way."

Maraña shifted one foot down a step, and Howell cried, "Wait!" in a whisper. He thought Maraña was leaving. "Oh, boy," sighed Howell, "And you want me to . . ."

". . . Yes," said Maraña.

"But I don't understand why the CIA won't tell the State Department themselves."

"That's not part of your message," Maraña said sharply. He paused and then relented somewhat in tone, "But who knows, my friend? Maybe they will. Right now the Company people are acting fonny. Some of them think I'm a Castro agent trying to make Secretary Carlyle back out of his trip, you know, and look bad. Some of them think I'm too close to the Israelis and I'm conspiring to keep Carlyle away from the Arabs. Some of them are worried because Pepe and I are both old Company boys and this might embarrass them with the president, I guess. The Company people really want Carlyle to go to Caracas because he will make the Arabs talk a lot among themselves about the United States and then the Company will hear things through its people, you know. It is all very complicated, David. Some of the Company guys just don't like me because I have been working for the FBI, you see?"

"Not really," said Howell.

"Well, it all means that to be a good spy in these times you've got to be a good bureaucrat," said Maraña. It was a close brush with levity, though he was still wound very tightly.

"Oh," said Howell.

"That's why I'm retiring," cracked Maraña, with leaden sarcasm.

"Right," said Howell. "I forgot."

"One other very little thing, my friend, said Maraña. "Some people in the drug agency have told the Company that I brought a suitcase full of cocaine with me from Panama. They say I had it with me in Miami when the Company man met me at customs there. That is a nasty rumor. The Company people are very upset about it because it would make them look bad, you know, so they are spending valuable time trying to check that out when the life of the secretary is at stake."

"Jesus Christ, Carlos," reeled Howell. "What a rat's nest. Is it true?"

"I want you to tell them I said that," said Maraña. "Tell them I have nothing to hide, and this rumor may be getting in the way of important business. The drug people are neutralized, you know, and it makes them feel better to try to ruin my reputation."

"I guess so," Howell said lamely. "But is it true?"

"Of course not," Maraña replied. "I am the representative of my government on important matters. I only follow orders, my friend."

"Yeah, right," said Howell. He became puzzled suddenly and stared at the back of Maraña's head for some time. "You know, it's amazing," he said quietly. "I don't have the slightest instinct whether you're telling the truth about the cocaine or not. I've never drawn a blank like that before with you or anybody else. I'm getting zero. Nothing. I don't like it. And I had such a good sense of you in the jail . . ."

". . . We were just talking then, David," Maraña chided. "This is business. Don't make it hard for yourself. You don't have to know what's true. Just deliver the message. It's your duty now."

"Great," said Howell. "Just great. I don't believe this. I've never arrived at a murder before it happened."

"That's not true, my friend," Maraña countered. "I told you in advance that Mendoza was not long for this world, didn't I?"

Howell rubbed his head with both hands. "That didn't register that way," he said numbly. "It didn't hit me until later. This is hitting me now."

"Don't feel bad about it," Maraña advised. "Forget about it. Besides, I have some good news to make you feel better."

"Great," sighed Howell.

"I am in a hurry," snapped Maraña. "It's about your problem with Shea. I'll help you for friendship only, David. How's that? There's nothing for me but risk, and that's not wise. Okay?"

"Okay," mumbled Howell.

Maraña turned his neck to face him. He spoke like a seer, with clear diction and authority animated by a foreign presence. "When you need to, David," he said, "you give word to Pat Shea that on the morning of Taliente's murder, more than two years ago, there was a mosquito in his French toast at the Concord Cafeteria. And the mosquito heard him give orders not to warn Taliente. And the mosquito can still talk, okay? You tell him to think about that, and he'll leave you alone."

"A mosquito?" Howell echoed. "I don't understand."

"You don't *need* to," Maraña replied kindly. "It's probably better if you don't. Just tell him you heard that, and the rest will take care of itself, okay?"

Howell replied with a weak, troubled nod.

"Okay," smiled Maraña. "And one more thing. Maybe you better tell Shea to ask Dave Damico what a mosquito is. The FBI has them, but Shea is a buffoon and he may forget."

"I don't blame him."

Abruptly, Maraña stood up and smiled briefly. "Well, good-bye my friend," he said warmly. "Good luck with the State Department and with your old lady. And wish me good luck in Caracas." Twisting his body, he reached down to shake hands.

"Good luck," Howell said, and he shook his head slowly with bewilderment in tempo with the handshake.

"And don't follow me today, okay?" grinned Maraña, moving away.

"I won't," said Howell. He watched Maraña skip briskly down the stairs and through the middle of Miss Hope's feeding area. A mass of pigeons made a great whooshing hum as they took to the air. Maraña did not notice Miss Hope's look of reproach. Howell tried to apologize for him, but Miss Hope was too preoccupied with her private animal matters to take solace from his words.

By four-thirty that afternoon, the meeting in Richard Clayfield's conference room at the State Department had attracted a number of extra participants, including two pleasant security officers who looked rumplish despite their elegant clothes. They introduced themselves, whereas the two more aristocratic arrivals from the State Intelligence Office, INR, did not. They only nodded and asked questions, looking pointedly skeptical about the propriety of having so many free words exchanged in such a mixed group. One of them listened to Howell for a few minutes, whispered briefly with one of Clayfield's assistants who was taking notes, and quietly disappeared. He had just stepped back into the room when Clayfield seemed to run out of questions.

"Very interesting, very interesting," muttered Clayfield, sitting on the corner of a sturdy antique desk. He had his pipe going and his thin necktie slightly askew, a common sign of ambition and of willingness to take policy risks. Clayfield's career was at a turning point. He and most inside observers believed that if he stayed at Policy Planning another year he would lose the impetus of his rapid rise as a junior whiz and acquire the image of a shooting star on the fade, destined for nothing better than the high-level backup jobs. Clayfield needed to move soon. The right ambassadorship or some visible position at the National Security Council would do wonders toward advancing him the last step to the plateau of permanent diplomatic success. He had to act shrewdly, but it was no longer important for him to look smart, which may have explained why the thick dark-rimmed glasses of his early career had given way to a pair of classy thin silver rims that would make a good impression at hearings on Capitol Hill. He pushed the glasses delicately up the bridge of his nose and smiled, very much relaxed and in command of the room. "Very interesting," he mused. "It's a damn good story, David, even if it doesn't check out."

"I think it will," said Howell, who was on the small sofa next to Woodruff.

"I'm sure you do," said Clayfield. He shook his head and chuckled softly to himself. "And it was very considerate of you to bring this matter to me."

"I'm sorry," said Howell. "It wasn't my idea for Carlos to tell me this stuff. I sure didn't pry it out of him. He dumped it on me this morning."

"And you just ran into him over the weekend out in Virginia, eh?" asked Clayfield.

"Yep," said Howell.

"And did you see him, too, Henry?"

"Henry's never met him," said Howell. "He was kind of on ice this weekend, so I saw Carlos alone."

"Oh," said Clayfield.

Woodruff gave Howell a sidelong warning look as he cleared his throat. "It was my idea to bring this to you, Richard," he said. "Because you are the highest guy either one of us knows here. Sorry about that."

"That's okay," smiled Clayfield. "Where would I be without a crisis?"

One of the security men leaned forward toward Howell and asked, "Do you remember what the address was of the house in Virginia where you met Maraña, Mr. Howell?"

Howell frowned. "Those big houses out there don't really have street addresses," he replied.

"Oh," said the security man, who dodged a condescending look from his colleagues.

"Pardon me, gentlemen," called out the INR man who had just returned. His words asked for pardon, but his tone would have kicked in a door. "I might have something for you, Mr. Clayfield," he announced, striding over to give Clayfield a piece of paper and the confidential look of a shared secret.

"Excuse me," said Clayfield. No one spoke as he scanned the one-page memo. He raised his eyebrows significantly at the INR man. "Did you get this through channels?" he asked.

"I obtained it through *a* channel, yes," the INR man smiled enigmatically.

Clayfield looked dissatisfied, but he let it go. "Well," he said, "it looks like at least some of your story is true, David. The names you're throwing around are definitely not children."

Howell took a long breath. "I know," he said. "Is that about Maraña and Lopez?"

"Yes," said Clayfield. "It's sketchy, but it fits."

Howell's face brightened with curiosity. "Does it say anything on there about Maraña's mission to the Congo in 1964 for Lyndon Johnson?"

Before Clayfield could answer, the INR man cleared his throat in disapproval, drawing Clayfield's eye. "It's all right," Clayfield told him. "They've brought us something, and I wouldn't give them anything new or any sources." He turned back to Howell. "You're not gonna write anything about what we say here, anyway, right? That's the agreement, straight up."

"Yeah," Howell conceded. "But I can write about Maraña, and I do think it's interesting that *he* didn't put anything off the record." Nerves choked his laugh.

"Maraña doesn't have the interests of a government to protect," said Clayfield.

"Oh, come on," smiled Howell. "He's got his own life to protect, and he's not operating out of a big office on the seventh floor."

This did not please Clayfield. "Well, as to your question, yes it does say he was in the Congo in '64," said Clayfield, looking down at the memo. "It says 'reconnaissance and security patrol activities, including direct security assistance to foreign nationals during period of instability.' And then it gives the dates," said Clayfield, looking at the INR man to make sure his discretion had been noted.

"I know the dates," said Howell. "May through August, and hot and bloody."

"But it's an accurate description?" Clayfield prodded.

"Well, more or less," Howell squirmed. "If what Maraña told me is true, and I think it is, that description wouldn't quite capture the flavor of what he did. It would be like calling the conquistadors a mobile anthropology transformation unit or something."

"That's true," said Clayfield. He handed the memo back to the INR man and experienced a visibly restless pause. "Well," he said to Howell and Woodruff. "I thank you guys a lot. You've been very helpful, but I guess we'll have to take it from here. I'll keep you both posted. Maybe you'll get a good story out of this yet, David. Although right now there doesn't seem to be much humor in it."

"Nope," said Howell.

Woodruff's voice broke through the usual rustle of a meeting's end. "Excuse me, Richard," he called loudly. "But I'd like to have a quick word with you about the policy implications of this before we go, if you don't mind."

Motion in the room stopped, and Clayfield gave the subtlest of glances at his watch as he paused. "Sure, Henry," he smiled. "I might have known you weren't going to sit here all this time without getting in your say. But you've got to make it quick, okay? This is not a long-range policy study you guys have tossed at us."

"Sure," said Woodruff. He looked briefly about to communicate his desire to be alone.

"All right," said Clayfield. "I'll talk with Henry and David for a second, and we'll meet back here in exactly thirty minutes. Can you guys find out if the Venezuelans have Pepe Lopez's name on their watch list for the secretary's Caracas trip?"

The lead security man puffed his cheeks. He was having a rough meeting. "Well, we don't have the list," he said. "The Secret Service has got it."

"Well, do you think you could find out about it without letting them know we're interested in Lopez yet?"

"We can try."

"Good." Clayfield turned to the INR man. "Do you think you could use your channel to find out more about Lopez and Maraña?" he asked. "Could they be pulling a scam or something? I'd hate to get the secretary agitated and then find out that it's only some coke dealers doing a number on us."

The INR man looked noncommittal. Clayfield drifted into an afterthought without seeming to notice. "We should probably go over this one more time before we go to the secretary," he said. "Your shop's probably going to handle it when the secretary finds out, but I'll be willing to deliver it with you because it landed here."

"Right," nodded the INR man, calculations in his face. He knew Clayfield would maneuver cleverly regardless of the fact that the Maraña story hardly belonged to Policy Planning, but he was reassured to hear Clayfield speak so flexibly on jurisdiction. This probably meant that Clayfield had no better idea than he whether there was credit or blame ahead.

Clayfield admonished his colleagues to keep the Maraña story out of liaison channels with other agencies for the time being. When the room cleared he said, "Okay, Henry. What's on your mind?"

"Do you mind if I stand up?" asked Woodruff.

"Of course not. Go ahead."

"Thanks," said Woodruff, rising. He smoothed the trousers of his favorite old Senate suit and strolled around the coffee table. "It's Cuba, Richard, as you've probably guessed," he smiled. "I've been thinking about it ever since David got himself mixed up with the exiles down in Miami a couple of years ago, and he and I have been talking about it more or less continuously for the last forty-eight hours."

"I see," said Clayfield. "What did you come up with?"

"Insanity," Woodruff answered, beginning slowly to pace. "I guess the best word is insanity."

"Good," smiled Clayfield. "That's my specialty around here."

"Think of it a second," said Woodruff. "Here we have a Cuban down in Venezuela who worked for the U.S. government for years but is now so twisted that he may kill the secretary of state. Why? Because the secretary has been quoted lately as favoring some sort of vague dialogue with Castro. That's probably it. The papers in Miami say the Cubans are all pissed off. And you and I both know that the secretary's not talking anything serious with Castro. It's just the biennial statement of good intentions, right?"

"Don't quote me," nodded Clayfield.

"So it's an empty gesture, but still he might get killed for it, okay?" said Woodruff, pacing a bit faster. "And we have this former ally who can intrude on the American secretary of state, and the whole thing has to be handled through back channels because of the intelligence implications. Secret histories and stuff. Okay, that's just the first Cuban. Then we have this other character, Maraña, who seems to be able to make the entire U.S. government into his own little plaything because of all he knows and all he's done. He seems to play all the intelligence agencies off against one another to give himself pretty much carte blanche. Nobody knows who he really works for, except himself. Nobody knows much of anything about him except that the U.S. government has got to pay attention to everything he says. That's for sure. And he won't go to jail for any of his crimes. That's a pretty safe bet. And you've got to try to deal with him privately, because he'll slaughter the government if there's ever a fight in public. Okay? Now then there's the third Cuban."

"That would be Fidel," mused Clayfield, smoking his pipe over folded arms.

"Right," said Woodruff, "He's where the absurdity starts. We've pretended his government hasn't existed for twenty years, while at the same time it's been an obsession in American politics. Cuba's this tiny little country with a great tropical spirit, but every time Castro twitches his nose we go crazy. I mean he's the mouse in our fucking kitchen who's had us up on a chair screaming for two decades, doing all kinds of hysterical things. Every dealing we've had with his government has been secret, by and large, whether we're trying to talk to him or overthrow him. And it's all been ruinous. He was first to make it popular around the world to call us sneaky bullies and liars, and he pulled it off because he was right. We're so screwed up and touchy about Castro that I'll lay you odds we'll do something stupid about Cuba right at the beginning of the next war. And the point of all this, Richard, is that I think the three Cubans are all part of the same problem. Lopez, Maraña, and Castro. You take our original, sneaky, lying betrayal and the corruption keeps eating from there."

"Like a cancer," Clayfield mildly suggested. "I've heard that line of thought before on other matters."

Clayfield's wry smile, on his attentive face in the cloud of pipe smoke, brought out a few extra splotches on Woodruff's neck. His ire was rising sufficiently for him to employ his favorite ceremonial gesture—scooping up two handfuls of air in front of him and tossing them sharply into the air, like a lungful of nonsense. "I didn't use the cancer image, because it's tacky," he grimaced. "But I might as well have. I believe it."

Clayfield thoughtfully removed his pipe. "Well, that might be something we could kick around some time, Henry," he said. "But it's pretty abstract, you know. Especially now that we've got an immediate crisis on our hands,

348

courtesy of you two. Do you have any ideas about what we should do on that?"

"Yeah, I do," said Woodruff, making a turn, tossing up a single handful of air. "I think we should recognize the present Cuban government tomorrow. That's number one. Number two, I think we should say that we are no longer gonna hide from the fact that we've acted badly toward Cuba in the past. Number three, I think we should announce that any political group who plans to murder people or blow things up to prevent recognition should forget it, because it's already done. Take it from there, okay? Tell all the hawks Castro won't be able to rally support against the American ogre as easily. Tell 'em we'll get Castro with sugar. I don't care."

"And you think maybe Pepe Lopez would read in the paper that we'd recognized Fidel and that would make him decide not to shoot the secretary?" Clayfield asked.

"I doubt it," said Woodruff. "He's probably a long-gone killer. But who knows? Maybe it would. Maybe if he saw the American government was gonna quit being crazy, *he'd* quit being crazy. I don't know. But I know you'd be striking at the root of what makes people like Pepe Lopez."

"Well, I don't presume to know what makes people like him," said Clayfield. "But I do know you've been around this town long enough to know that Cuban policy is more complicated than ordinary etiquette, Henry. You know as well as I do that we've got nearly a million bullet-voting Cuban exiles in Florida, New York, and New Jersey. We've got a president who doesn't give a damn about Cuba one way or the other. But he does give a damn about the Russians, and to him and everybody else around here Castro means the Russians. And that means heavyweight big power politics. So you don't give something to Castro without getting something from the Russians, basically. Like it or not, you've got to look at it within the context of that larger game. I'm not aware of anybody in the government who's even thinking about recognizing Castro, to be honest with you. It's about as far along as recognizing Peking was in 1960. It would be seen as a major policy failure and loss of influence not only in the hemisphere but everywhere we rub noses with the Russians. That's the way it is, Henry, and you know it as well as I do. So I don't know why we're talking about this, actually.

"You're taking this rather personally, aren't you?" he went on to ask. "Cuba has never been your speciality, has it?"

"Wait a minute," said Woodruff. "I don't want any misunderstandings on that, Richard. Please believe me that my feelings on this have absolutely nothing to do with any personal connections with you. At all. I'm not pretending that you and I have ever been great allies in politics or anything else, but we've come of age together in Washington, and I think you know me well enough to know that I wouldn't make all this up just to fuss at you over old scores with Casey. Which is true, okay?"

Clayfield nodded impassively, saying nothing one way or the other.

Woodruff resumed a slow pace. "I think it's you folks in the government who take Castro too personally. After all, Kennedy tried to overthrow him

349

with a secret army, and then they sent the Mafia down there to kill him. They wanted to get him bad. There was a lot of hatred in it. The whole world knows that, Richard. Everybody. And from that standpoint, it's *already* been a major policy failure. We couldn't kill him. We've already lost a lot of influence. We've looked stupid and immoral and inept. We tried to wreck their economy and sabotage them and all kinds of horrible stuff that hasn't come out yet. But the world knows we've been a failure by any standard. The only question is whether we'll change and whether we'll admit it. And from what I can see, the answer is that we still take Castro so personally that we've refused to apologize to the Cuban government for repeatedly trying to assassinate its head of state. Won't hear of it, by God! And it seems to me that if a country twenty times bigger than we are tried to do to us what we've done to Castro on the sly, we'd think that government had a severe psychological problem."

"Maybe so, Henry," said Clayfield, unperturbed. "Maybe all governments have psychological problems. They're all run by power freaks, you know. Look, I agree with what you say. A lot of it, anyway. But we're dealing with the real world here, as you know. And there are a lot of silly problems. You can't apologize to a government you don't recognize, for example."

"You can if you want to," grinned Woodruff. "Don't make it sound like a machinery problem, Richard. It's a gizzard problem."

"You've learned a lot about anatomy since you left the Senate," smiled Clayfield. "And you've also developed a new phobia against covert operations, if you don't mind my saying so."

"I always had it," mumbled Woodruff.

"Well, I have, too," said Clayfield. "Believe me, we don't particularly like those guys over there at the Agency. You know that. They're always causing stinks. They act like they have a lot of hair on their chests, but they won't show it to you. So I don't like it either. But you've got to have them, Henry. You know that. Every modern state has an intelligence service to do a lot of stuff that's not kosher. That's what they tell us anyhow."

Woodruff speeded up his pacing, six steps in either direction. "Watch out, Richard," he said, trying to control his voice. "Watch out, now. You're gonna get me worked up. I've been good so far, believe it or not. But this Cuba thing has pushed me into a lot of reading about the Agency, and I've decided we've been getting a crock of shit on its value. They say you've got to have a mean-ass intelligence service to have a strong country. Well, my reading of history says that's bullshit. Peacetime spy organizations usually develop their reputations when an empire's going downhill. That's what happened with the British. They built up this whole legend of the great MI–6 and James Bond and all that stuff during the decline of their power, as kind of a mythological salve for their sense of importance in the world. And they passed that tradition on to the OSS, which really didn't do much in the war. Let's face it. Basically, OSS was a lot of prominent types who got to have a lot of romance and a little war without having to wear a uniform.

"And now that we're getting screwed up, the CIA's getting important just like the British spies did. They've put genies and astrology back into politics because they are whatever you want to believe they are. They are the devils or the saviors, and who really knows? They are royalty, because if you really believe in the CIA you don't want to know what they do. You just support them the way we used to support the king. And if you believe that the strength of a foreign policy in a democracy depends upon the depth of public support for it, then you could argue that relying on the CIA makes us weaker, not stronger, because nobody knows much about what we're doing.

"And what I'm saying, Richard, or trying to say, anyway, is that the clues as to why things seem to be falling apart are all there in Cuba. The unrecognized, unapologized-to government that we deal with only under the table in a manner that would shame Thomas Jefferson on his least honorable day, and we've created monsters like Lopez and Maraña who've come back to haunt us because we're so caught up in the afterlife of our own secrecy that we're helpless. They corrupt us in so many ways we're not conscious of. It's like slavery, really. That whole secrecy bit will seep back to the clergy and the courts inevitably, and pretty soon it becomes a whole way of life that makes a lot of sense in a way, but still has that obvious blister of phoniness rubbing away until it breaks. That's why I think a good first step in dealing with the Lopez crisis would be to recognize the government of Cuba."

"Hear, hear!" cheered Howell. "Bravo, Henry. Amen! Preach to me!"

Woodruff fell quickly out of his oratorical haze to wince significantly at Howell.

Clayfield stood up. "Some of that was very good, Henry," he observed. "Did you practice it?"

"A little bit," Woodruff admitted. "I wanted to make sure you got a good dose, just to make me feel better."

"Well, all we have to do then is recognize Castro and abolish the CIA, isn't it?" twinkled Clayfield.

"Right," said Woodruff, flushed with postspeech letdown. "Listen, Richard, I may be naive, but I'm not stupid. I know how quixotic it is to talk about going after something that well entrenched. You couldn't cut a bureaucracy as big as the Agency if its only mission was changing the water in horse troughs in front of public buildings. I know that. I just wanted to get it off my chest, I guess. And sometimes I have these nightmares that we'll look back amazed at how docile we've been."

"Okay, okay," said Clayfield. "Consider it off your chest. Can I get back to work if I promise to put in a good word for recognizing Castro? How about it?"

"That's not good enough, Richard," Woodruff drawled. "I didn't come sliding into town yesterday. I'm starting a campaign on this Cuba thing. Howell's been telling me I've been too withdrawn from the world, and I've decided he's right. Cuba is a good reentry vehicle for me, and I know you can do better than a good word. We don't have to talk about it now. I know you've got yourself a crisis. But we can talk later, after I get churning."

Clayfield paused on the way to shake Woodruff's hand. It was the first time thought interfered with his smoothness. "Let me ask you something," he frowned. "You say a campaign. Could that have anything to do with the fact that your old boss is a favorite son candidate for president? You wouldn't mean that kind of campaign, would you?"

"Not really," said Woodruff. "He cleared that favorite son thing with the president, you know. It's honorary."

"Yeah, well, that was the kind of clearance where the president didn't have much choice, I hear," smiled Clayfield.

"Well, the senator's not planning to do a number on the president about Cuba, if that's what you're asking."

"No, that's not what I mean," said Clayfield. "What I mean is, do you think you could get the senator to take a flyer or two in public about Cuban policy? Understand me now, okay? I could get in trouble for this. But I think it might make a difference if you could get someone like the senator to speak out on Cuba in an election year. I doubt if you can do it, frankly."

"I don't know," Woodruff said. "Maybe I could. And I'm gonna take some flyers myself, now that I've practiced my speech."

"Well, I'd sure like to see how it flies," said Clayfield. "If you can get a vice-presidential contender to speak out in favor of recognizing Cuba, that's news. I guarantee you that the people here would see all the arguments for the wisdom of what he's doing. I might even work out some way for you to see the internal paper. And I also guarantee you that any press you get on the issue will go straight to the secretary's desk. And I'll show you my cover memos. How's that for openers? Better?"

"Yes, that's a lot better," smiled Woodruff. "Thanks, Richard."

Clayfield shook Howell's hand after Woodruff's. "And thank you for the information, David," he said laconically. "You're a real help. I'll see to it that you get a tax audit and a wiretap this afternoon."

"That would be kind," smiled Howell. "And if it'll make you feel any better, you're lucky you got Henry today when he's still rusty. He'll be hell in a week or two."

"I can imagine," laughed Clayfield, ushering Woodruff out the door. "I'm sure he'll be bivouacked in the woods outside Camp David, with a big cigar and fatigues."

Clayfield emitted a controlled friendly laugh as he opened the door to reveal a contingent of the security officials standing outside. Howell and Woodruff passed through their expressions of grave concern.

"Goddam, Henry," laughed Howell. "You didn't tell me you were gonna pull a Patrick Henry in there! You just said you wanted to come along because of your new Cuba kick. What happened?"

"Well, I don't know," Woodruff said sheepishly. "It just happened, that's all. It just came over me.

Howell shook his head in amazement. "A blister of phoniness," he muttered with delight. "Where did you come up with shit like that, Henry?"

"What's wrong with it?" Woodruff frowned, "Look, you're the one who's been telling me not to be so aloof from the world. So if you don't like the lines, you've got to help me find better ones, okay?"

"Take it easy," said Howell. "It's all right. But I've been trying to get you more involved with *Sudsy*, not Cuba, as a matter of fact."

"Oh," grinned Woodruff. "Well, you've got to be more specific."

"It's all right," said Howell. "You've got to promise me one thing, okay?"

"Uh oh," Woodruff said warily. "Go ahead. I'm ready."

"This is serious," said Howell. "Really. I don't care what you say about Cuba or Maraña, but I don't want you saying anything about that weird mosquito threat with Pat Shea. That's my business, okay? It involves Miss Snow, and it's probably blackmail. And it's ugly. And that's for me and Haven to decide, not you. Okay? Promise me."

"Okay," said Woodruff, somewhat startled by the unusual intensity in Howell. "I swear on Lester Hershey's temper."

"That's good enough, I guess," said Howell. "Now, let's forget this stuff a while."

Woodruff agreed, but they talked Cuba back at Howell's apartment nevertheless. Miss Snow had been to Havana, and the Latin spirit of the memory reminded her of her lover, Gigi Mariani, whose memory inspired a reverie on places to walk and the color of the ocean on certain days, which became vague as Snow faded toward sleep. Woodruff became impatient and remained so through Pinder's effort to reconcile her long-standing political crush on Fidel Castro with his weaknesses on civil liberties and women's issues. Woodruff talked straight through the dinner hour and did not straggle back to Hartman's until nearly nine that evening.

There he found a note on his study board. It said, "Dear Henry. I can't take it any more. So I'm leaving. I think I may be able to see for the first time that it can hurt as much to leave as to be left. Maybe I'll think this was all fun some day, but not now. Your template can't land on my runway, for some reason. I don't want to talk about it. I love you, but I love me more. You can have the apartment. I may come back for the furniture. Love and good luck. Susan. P.S. This is real."

Woodruff moved the study board and sat down to read the note several more times. He did not say a word, nor hear any of the street noises. He decided it could be true, but then again he decided that it probably wasn't final. Hartman always signed her notes, "Suds." This wasn't her. Woodruff shook his head and rubbed his dry eyes. It was a crisis, all right, but not decisive yet, he thought. It was a good thing his blood was up after the meeting with Clayfield. Now perhaps he could face the fact that things couldn't go on the way they had been going. He would do something with Hartman, but he wasn't sure what it was. Funny how Clayfield was always around in one way or another at his woman emergencies, he mused. It occurred to Woodruff that Clayfield was probably his best and most complete self as a human being within the confines of that State Department office and the world it enclosed. He wondered if something similar were not true for himself, and then he read the note again. After imagining Hartman coming through the door, upset, he found himself eager to get on with it. He wished she were there, even though he didn't know what he would say. His mind rebelled from the task of rehearsal. He tried to force himself to think about Cuba strategy, but nothing came. Woodruff got up and walked into the bedroom. Empty drawers were open, clothes and suitcases gone, signs of exit. Hartman's favorite books and photographs were also missing. He tried to call Howell, but there was no answer. Probably sneaking out for a sandwich, he figured. Or hiding out for some early evening sex. Woodruff breathed deeply and began pacing the living room very slowly, with more waiting in his mind than thought.

Hartman arrived at Valerie Mantell's apartment with two suitcases bearing her father's monogram. Mantell opened the door with her hair piled on her head and her fanciest dress pin at her throat. "Susan!" she said. "I thought you were Marner. Are you all right?"

"No," said Hartman. "Can I come in for a second?"

"What are you talking about?" cried Mantell, reaching for a suitcase. "Get in here! What's the matter?"

"Oh, nothing much," sighed Hartman, inside the door. But when her eyes met Mantell's, she dropped her suitcase and threw her arms around Mantell's neck. She squeezed as hard as she could and her entire back shook spasmodically.

Mantell made loud noises of affection as she squeezed up and down Hartman's back for a full thirty seconds, her face buried at Hartman's neck. Then she drew back slightly to look at her. "My God, Susan," she said, "What happened to you? What made you cry like this?"

Hartman took one step backward and took a couple of determined breaths. "I'm not crying," she declared, and then she sniffled with a vengeance that was convincing.

Mantell put her hands on her hips and smiled in mock irritation. "All right, you're brave, Susan," she said. "Now let's have it."

"Well, I just walked out on Henry," sighed Hartman. "For good. *Finis. Etcetera.*"

Mantell kept her hands on her hips and took a deep breath herself. "Well, that's bad, Sudsy," she sighed, "but it's not exactly a big shocker. I told you he was a difficult man."

"Oh, don't be so sincere, Valerie," Hartman mildly scolded. "You tried for him yourself, and you know it."

"That's true," Mantell conceded. "Maybe we have the same taste for dangerous men." She tried to laugh.

Hartman looked down at the table. "You don't understand, Valerie," she said quietly. "I'm not just leaving Henry. I'm leaving. Period. I'm leaving town."

Mantell closed her eyes briefly and then opened them in stillness to examine Hartman's face. "You're not kidding, are you?" she whispered quietly.

"Look, Sudsy, I think you're upset. Maybe you should go off to get over this . . ."

". . . That's not it, Val," said Hartman. "I think I'm leaving town more than I'm leaving Henry, actually. That's what I really came to tell you. I'm gonna catch the ten o'clock train out of here."

"To go where?" asked Mantell.

"I don't know. That's the whole point."

"What do you mean you don't know, Susan? You've got to go somewhere. You can't just run off into the night. Where the hell is your ticket for?"

"New York," said Hartman. "But I may get off sooner if it feels right."

"I thought you were gonna stay here with me," Mantell said numbly.

"No."

Mantell looked softly at Hartman and was tearing up when a stab of irritation passed through her. "Goddammit, Susan!" she cried. "This is ridiculous! You can't just leave town! What about all your friends? Your whole life is here. You don't know what you're doing and you've got *me* crying, which is stupid. Now you *can't* leave tonight, I'm telling you. That fucking Woodruff has got you addled temporarily, but you'll get over it and . . ."

". . . Wait a second!" shouted Hartman. The two of them stared at each other in a wide-eyed freeze. At the end of a long pause, Hartman exhaled every bit of air and tension inside her. "Look, Valerie, this is why I told you I'm not crying now," she murmured. "Because this is hard. But I don't have any choice. I've already cashed in most of my stocks. I've got a small fortune in traveler's checks with me, and I'm going. You're the only one I'm even telling besides Henry, and I didn't really tell him. I just left him a note. And you don't have to tell me how hard it is to leave friends here. That's all we've got, really. When all the politics and romance washes out, we've got friends. Most of us left our families to come here. I didn't, but I never really had a family. You know that. My old man is just what I seemed to find all the time in Washington. He's somebody so obsessed with fixing the whole world that he doesn't understand what an asshole he is inside. Maybe he does. Anyway, it doesn't matter. For me this city is sick. Maybe I'm cursed inside. I don't know. But I think only people like you have a chance to keep yourself healthy here. And that's because of you, or what you have with Marner or your job. It's something I don't have. Your steady good feeling. And you're rare, Valerie. You know how rare you are even to have a chance." Hartman bit her lip and swallowed again. "I don't think I've got one. Either the city is getting sicker or I am. So I've got to try to find something else, and I'm sad I didn't find out until I'm thirty-four. And if I do find something else, I promise I'll bring some of it back to you. Do you understand me?"

Mantell's great heaving sadness made it clear that she did. "I'm cold," she said, hugging herself.

"Listen, Valerie," Hartman said softly. "I just want you to know that I'm planning on coming back sometime, but I'm not sure. I'm not just going away for the weekend, okay. And whether I ever come back or not, I want you to know that you've been the best friend I've ever had. In poker and politics and the river and every other goddam thing I can think of. And I'm sorry I can't be here with you to help you make it. I hope you and Marner have a kid, okay. If there was one thing I could change in the world, it would be to change me so that I could stay here. But I can't."

"Okay." smiled Mantell. "Sudsy, you are one unbelievable woman."

Hartman called Mantell twice over the next three days, from undisclosed places. She also called Woodruff, Pinder, Howell, Hershey, and a number of other friends with various tales of mystery. But she was gone before Cuban thickets brushed the fates of Lily Snow and the secretary of state, among others, and those behind accepted the fact that she had wandered off in her own way, like a jazz melody, leaving a constant hum of memory in her trail.

XVII

THE TELEPHONE'S harsh ring annoyed Max Parker, who was kneeling on the cluttered floor of his home laboratory, face down, as in homage to Mecca. Groaning, he pulled his head and his needle-nosed pliers from the maze of wires on the circuit board before him. He dropped the pliers into his shirt pocket, secured a few copper connectors at one corner of his mouth, like diaper pins, and crawled to the phone stand just outside the door. "Talk to me, friend," he sighed, as pleasantly as possible.

"You know who I am?" asked a throaty whisper.

"Huh?"

"You know who I am?" the voice repeated. It was conspiratorial, soaked in sweat and frustration, and it conveyed as much pain as a man freshly slugged in the ribs.

"How can I forget?" cracked Parker.

"Don't say it."

"Okay, okay," Parker said wearily. "What is it? I'm busy."

The man seemed to clear his throat, but he was actually cranking up the first husky word. "There is a meeting tonight at eleven," he said. "We have proof about the Americans, but the *Accion* will do nothing. They are playboys! Do you hear me? They are dirty, focking playboys."

Parker moved the receiver an inch away from his ear. "I hear you," he said. "And for once I agree."

"Good," rasped the man. "We have split away from them. Tonight we denounce them and make our declaration of principles. And we hear evidence on the American traitors in war council. I will be military chief, Max, and I want you to be with us."

Parker sagged back against the door frame. "Well, forget about that, Manolo," he scoffed.

"Don't use my name!" Blue Shirt commanded, in a gruff hiss. "We are not fooling around, like in the Company. The council will impose death for security violations."

"Oh, leave me alone with that shit," winced Parker, removing the connectors from his mouth. "They all say that. The *Accion* people already called me tonight, and that's what they say."

"Be careful, my friend."

"I will," said Parker. "But I want you to tell me one thing. Why is it that you always sound like one of those filthy obscene phone calls? Why is that?"

"Shut up, Max. Shut up and listen to me," said Manolo. "Maybe it's because I have not lost my dedication and I care about security. I hope you realize the risk I am taking just to propose having someone like you in the group? Do you realize that? You are part *gringo*, my friend. And you are the friend of Marãna, who is either an agent of Castro or of the CIA or of the devil, whoever is the worst. I am taking the risk of my life just to give you another chance."

"Thank you very much," sniffed Parker. "And I also think you are full of shit. So why are you inviting me, eh? Are you trying to be tricky?"

Manolo let loose a coarse, impatient growl. "I warn you, Max," he menaced. "You have a destiny, my friend. You will be an example, one way or the other. I am giving you the chance because I think you are *simpático*, despite everything else. And you have skills. And you are very good at manipulating the Americans. And most of all, I know Maraña has mistreated you as his puppet. Now he has run off and left you. He doesn't care. And I think you see him for what he is."

"I do," said Parker. "Who will be at the meeting?"

"You will see."

"Where?"

"Don't be stupid, and don't think we're stupid. I will pick you up. At ten-thirty."

"No, you won't," sighed Parker. "I don't need to know what you're doing. I don't care. Good-bye, Manolo. So nice of you to think of me." He hung up the phone but kept his hand on the receiver, waiting with a wry smile. It rang within thirty seconds. "Yes, yes, I know I'm a *maricón*, dear," sang Parker.

"You will be sorry."

"But I won't have to go to so many of those long meetings," quipped Parker. "Tell me, Manolo. What is the name of your new group, The Beatles?"

This time Manolo hung up on Parker, who chuckled to himself and then frowned. By reaching above him to a light switch, he turned on a complex of electrical systems in his *"cuarto de boudoir,"* as he called it—soft colored lamps, an overhead hotel fan, a sophisticated sound system, and a special shaded light in the aquarium. A jaunty calypso tune soothed Parker as he crawled back to the workroom. As soon as he reclaimed his mind so that it was master of the tangled wires, lost in them by concentration, the doorbell rang.

"*Mierda!*" grunted Parker. He kicked the wall, looked apologetically at the wires, and slithered across the floor to the doorway. "Go away!" he shouted. "I don't want any!"

He leaned outside, hoping to hear the sound of nothing. Instead, he was jolted by a distant but familiar, sassy contralto. "Yes you *do* want some, Max!" cried Carmen Vilar. "Open the door!"

Parker reached the door in an instant. Vilar blew by him wordlessly, in black pants and a yellow shirt and a smile. Parker stood there grinning in the cloud of perfume that followed her, and before he could say anything she was swirling across his floor in a calypso dance, throwing one shoulder and then the other at Parker, moving quickly enough so that her long black hair always had to catch up. It wrapped around her face with a late hug and then flew behind her with abandon when she moved the other way. She stopped before the song ended.

"To what do I owe this privilege?" Parker asked brightly.

"I'm bored," said Vilar.

"Oh," said Parker, less brightly.

"And besides, Carlos just called me, and I'm extra bored," she said.

Parker lifted his eyebrows. "He did? From where?" he asked.

"Caracas," Vilar replied with distaste. "He is in Caracas during the OPEC conference, trying to find an oil well, I guess. He says Pepe Lopez is there."

"That's what I hear," sighed Parker. "He is crazy. He's got every basement soldier in town itching to kill an American. He's just crazy enough to do it, and everybody wants to beat him to it. Some people say he's crazy, and some people say he's got the wrong American. But everybody is turning green. They think Pepe might just get away with it. Then he would be as big as Castro, almost."

"Everybody?" teased Vilar.

"Well, three or four people who count," said Parker.

"That's better," said Vilar.

"I don't like it,' grinned Parker. "It makes me afraid for my father's American blood in me."

"You've always been afraid for your father's blood, Max," chided Vilar.

"Hey!" winced Parker. "Take it easy. I'm talking about getting shot and you're making ethnic slurs on me again."

Vilar said nothing, although her face flickered with jokes and a trace of affection. She appeared lost for an instant, and then she shook her head to wave it all away. "Let's dance, Max," she beamed urgently. "That's another cha-cha-cha. Can you move your magnificent body for a cha-cha-cha with me?"

Parker's face stumbled behind her moods, but he wound up full of pleasure, twirling with his arms in the air. One hand still held the needle-nosed pliers. "Are you kidding?" he cried. "You are looking at Ferdinand the Astaire, lady. The calypso is second nature to me, you know." Parker spun his way through some demonstration steps of syncopated rhythm, touching alternate hands to the breast in rapid moves that resembled a football player transferring the ball from one elbow to the other. There was more aplomb than grace.

"Bravo!" laughed Vilar. "Wait for me."

"First I need a beer for the true dancing," said Parker, dashing to the kitchen.

"Me, too," called Vilar.

Parker returned via his calypso step with two cans of beer. Each of them held one like a belly dancer's fan as they swayed separately into the rubber-spined weave of back and forth. "Can you tell me what is especially magnificent about my body?" Parker asked gleefully in midswirl. "Or is it obvious?"

"I'd rather dance," said Vilar.

"Oh," he said. "I'm sorry I asked."

"I told you I wanted to dance," teased Vilar.

"I know," Parker shrugged in motion. He took a long pull of cold beer and smiled at the blur of black and yellow. "You are the true margarita, Carmen," he said. "The liquor is sweet, but the salt will wrinkle your tongue." Parker revolved away from her in the flow of the dance, but as he did he saw a patronizing glint at the edge of her distracted smile. Vilar's eyes were turned aside as far as she could turn them while still following the dance. Parker started to take offense. Then he thought better of it. He decided maybe it was all part of the calypso. As dancing was a foreign world to him, it was easy to convince himself that nothing there was quite real, that it was a painted theater of bright shadows from which the wiser man takes nothing so real as a clue. And Parker, having already started moving, which was the first and hardest step for him, kept on moving. The smirk left his face when he went into the thick of the rhythm, without reservation, rolling his shoulders so loosely that he might have appreciated the genius of the ball and socket joint had he not been so far away. Parker stepped beyond his proven capabilities to take Vilar's hands and go with her, touching, into the lateral calypso. Hand to hand they went, and it came off quite nimbly, he thought, much to his surprise. It seemed to please Vilar as well. Her eyes were closed and her smile was not so distant. It was a musing smile, far short of vibrant, but it was a vast improvement over the barbed sugar of before.

Parker was just beginning to enjoy himself when he felt something very hard from Vilar's face. Fearfully, he studied her for the cause of the jolt, without success. Aside from the faintest twitch on the side of one cheek, nothing would explain for the effect on Parker, which was nonetheless forceful. He felt the dizzy clang of concussion in his head, and at the same moment it struck him that Vilar might be smiling *because* she could close her eyes to shut out the cathartic energy of the dance in favor of some demanding demon behind her eyes. With a flick of the brain, Parker conjured up a hundred possible demons, mostly having to do with Maraña. He dropped Vilar's hands, whereupon her smile dimmed and her eyes barely opened. Parker stared glumly at her and received no reply. He danced more stiffly now that all his daring footwork had earned him nothing better than a frosty, intimate exile from her, a banishment that made him loathe all his excuses in her behalf. Her compliments now stung. Parker sank so far into moldy self-pity that he nearly tripped himself. I had no designs and no aims, he thought, as a brilliant prosecutor excoriated her before the court of his inner workings. I desired nothing but to help her and to observe her special habits that are like no other woman's, but now I see she has denied me a wish that I was not even aware of—the wish not to be treated as nothing. So far as Parker could tell, none of his heated resentment was transmitting even the three feet to its target, who appeared to be securely possessed by something unpleasant.

They stopped when the music did, but Vilar did not further open her eyes.

"What's the matter, Carmen?" burst Parker.

She looked at him the way a heavy sleeper frowns at a screaming alarm clock, and then she studied her beer. "I told you I'm bored," she said.

"You're bored, eh?" nodded a laconic Parker. "That's too bad. So what can the doctor do for you now? I think you need two jokes, three dances, and another beer. How's that? Just tell me what you need and I'll get it for you," he said, snapping his fingers, trying to smile.

"Oh, Max," sighed Vilar.

"I will," Parker repeated.

Vilar looked him up and down. "What were you doing before I got here?" she asked.

Parker could not reply for some seconds. A simple request for information caught his mind off balance. He had to switch chambers, away from the smooth, silver bitterness. "Well, I was making a sign for Felipe's new night club," said Parker, with a pinch of defiance. "It says AQUI SE BAILA DISCO, and I will make the words light up individually in crazy patterns. It will be something. A little moonlighting project for me. And I wasn't bored, Carmen, if that's what you mean. I like that work."

"I didn't say you were," Vilar said.

"I know you didn't," said Parker. He lifted his chin and stroked it, as though debating whether to shave again.

"I don't see how you can design a disco beat while you have calypso music on your tape," Vilar drily remarked.

"Because I am an electrical genius, of course," said Parker.

"Of course," smiled Vilar.

It was almost enough to pull them out of it. "And before that, I was on the phone with that idiot Manolo," Parker added. "He called me with a new conspiracy and a new group and a new target. He says it's an American, but I think it could be Carlos. He wants me as a feeler for Carlos, I think."

"Manolo is too afraid of Carlos to do anything," said Vilar. "Don't worry."

"Maybe so," said Parker. "But still it's no fun to talk to him. His voice has gotten worse in the years since the dog bit him on the last day of Taliente. It's so ugly. He sounds like a condemned man on his way to the execution with a hard-on, if you can believe that."

"Forget about him," said Vilar. "He's part of what's so boring, Max. It's not the work. How can I say your electricity is boring when I have taken a job myself?"

"You have?" Parker jumped.

"Yes," said Vilar. "Every day I count other people's money, and I stretch my forty-five minutes for lunch."

"Uh huh," smiled Parker. "And I'll bet you still take deposits from your favorite drug dealers and spread the cash among all the tellers' drawers, don't you?"

"A tiny, tiny bit," Vilar admitted, tickling the air with the fingers of one hand. She looked to the floor and pursed her lips with sheepish delight that made Parker want to forgive her. "But things have changed at the bank, Max. There is too much money for the tellers to handle it. I only do a few small favors for old friends."

"Oh," nodded Parker. "When did you go back to work?"

"Yesterday," she replied.

"And you like it?"

"I just told you that, *chico*."

"I know you did," Parker retorted with a grin. "But you haven't told me yet what it is that is bothering you so much. And something really is bothering you. Enough to ruin a magnificent performance just now by the Ferdinand."

"It didn't ruin it," countered Vilar, trying to make light of it. "I liked Ferdinand's dancing. It was very good. Maybe I can get him to dance some more."

Parker involuntarily clenced his fist. "Ruined it for *me*, Carmen," he said harshly. Then he sighed. "Now tell me what it is that's so boring you. What did Carlos say?"

Vilar took her beer to a sofa. "You are very touchy tonight," she said.

"I wasn't until you arrived," said Parker, following her.

"Don't be childish, Max," said Vilar. "Now your talk is boring, on top of everything else."

Parker ground his teeth. "What did he say?"

"Nothing but the usual," said Vilar. "You know it as well as I do. He said it is very dangerous and very complicated. He said he likes the Arabs better than the Venezuelans. He said he will come to Miami soon, but he doesn't know exactly when. He said there is treachery everywhere. He said he likes to hear my voice, but it frustrates him to talk on the telephone. He said I have a nice body. He said I understand. He laughed about El Navajo in the swamps. He asked if you had put him in your will. He made noises with his nose to tell me the *cocaina* is good. He asked me to tell him the rumors about him, so I did. And he said he had to go. He was very busy and it's dangerous." Vilar lit a cigarette and let the smoke curl out of her nostrils.

"That sounds about right," said Parker, unsatisfied.

"You don't have to talk to him to know what he said," she added. "You know that."

"So what?" asked Parker. "That's what's boring? It's happened a million times. Why now? I don't understand you tonight. A lot of what Carlos said is true, as usual."

"Of course," said Vilar. She looked away, sucked smoke between her hollowed cheeks, and said, "I don't like it when he's around Pepe Lopez."

Parker cocked an eyebrow. "Ah hah!" came his singsong response. "So you are afraid Pepe's finally going to kill him. Is that it?"

"No," she said, so sadly that Parker took it as a rebuke.

"I don't see why you should worry about that," he smiled. "Just because Pepe shot him twice and has sworn to kill him as an enemy of the fight against Fidel. I don't see what there is to worry about." It was all he could do to finish the sentence. Vilar's expression stilled his laugh, and Parker wound up with his eyes and mouth in three small circles of curiosity.

"Shut up, Max," she said quietly. "I quit worrying about that years ago. You know that."

"Well, that was very intelligent of you. So then what are you worried about? Are you afraid Pepe and Carlos will become lovers, or partners? Are you afraid they will stay in Venezuela forever?"

"No."

Parker's mouth opened to let out further sardonic protest, but he checked himself. He buried his forehead in the palm of one hand and began to chuckle softly. "I give up," he said. "You are one difficult woman, Carmen. Maybe I should go to South America myself."

"Maybe so," Vilar said. "I just don't like the idea of Carlos being around Pepe, Max. I think that's what it is. I can't explain it. Whether he kills Carlos or Carlos kills him or neither one is not the point, you see. It's the time, I guess. For me the whole contest, the whole involvement with such a man holds no interest. It's like being corked in a bottle or something."

"It's boring," Parker suggested.

"I guess so," sighed Vilar. "But it's worse than boring."

Parker watched Vilar stare vacantly off through the window at the dark night. He nodded his head significantly and put his empty beer can on a magazine. Then he clapped his hands lightly. "At least we're getting somewhere," he said brightly. "Now I know vaguely why you are so upset. One more beer should do it, if I'm lucky. Do you want one?"

Vilar shook her head slowly, still looking away. "No, thanks," she said. "I'll stick with my cigarettes."

"I'll never understand women," he called to her from the kitchen as he popped open another can. He returned with that one and a spare. "Okay," he said. "I know you don't like . . ."

". . . Shut up, Max," she interrupted, just before she eyed him up and down, and purred softly, and shook her head with a good ol' Max look. As she watched him bristle, she tried to imitate a commander's fond and savvy reaction to the shortcomings of a brave soldier.

"Carmen, you've never talked to me like this," Parker whispered.

"I know," said Vilar, as though it were nothing. "Listen, my heart was with you in the fight against Fidel, and it still would be. I'm already too old to change. And I was with Carlos when he turned against the Company, because the Company had betrayed him. I never liked those people anyway. You understand?"

"Of course," said Parker.

"And I liked the international stuff and the spy business and all the rebellion," she said. "It was interesting to me, and I think I helped Carlos keep his head a few times. I have been his partner, too, Max."

"Uh huh," Parker nodded warily. Vilar's pupils were constricting with zeal.

"I was his partner," she radiated. "He could go away for three years like Ulysses and come back with hardly a word, and I would still be his partner because I understood why he was doing what he did. And I understood you, too, Max. All of you. And if Carlos had to play out the rest of the game from here until he got killed, and all he had with him were you and me, I would understand that, too. And I wouldn't mind that any more than I would mind getting killed myself. Because certain things are necessary. And the three of us share a very special and exciting spot on the losers' side of the world. I could do that, Max, I tell you. I could do it and not complain. I could do my part and keep knocking over a few men with my tongue and my high nose and my breasts, Max, and I wouldn't give ground to anybody because I am special, too. I see things in front of me just like you and Carlos, and I know what to do when there is no easy way out. Do you believe that?"

"Sure I do," Parker swallowed, with his mouth slightly open. Vilar's eye had captured his, like a hypnotist's watch.

"I know you do," nodded Vilar. "I know you do, Max." She suddenly smiled at him appreciatively, which caused Parker to stumble from his trance. "I know how good you are at making the hard way look easy," she said. "Don't forget that. It's good. But what's not good is Pepe Lopez."

"Uh huh," said Parker.

"Not uh huh!" blazed Vilar. "That's not it, Max. I'm saying Pepe is not worth a second of Carlos's time! Or yours or mine! Not a second!" she hissed viciously. "There is no tragic destiny in it. There is no reason to be involved with him one way or the other. I say kill him or leave him alone, whichever is quicker. There's no one else in the world I would say that about. To me, Pepe is the only worm in the world. I like Castro's word only for him. Pepe is a *gusano*. Carlos has finally found the subshit he is always talking about, and there is no pride in chasing him to Venezuala, or thinking about him at all, Max. I see nothing in it except a little sadness and a lot of boredom. Do you understand? I cannot care about what happens with Carlos and Pepe, except that it disgusts me for Carlos."

Parker leaned away from her, absorbing all this, and he took a long hit on the beer. As he fought off a satisfied belch, he said, "I don't think you like this guy Pepe Lopez, Carmen. You make it sound like he's Carlos's new preoccupation in life. You sound almost jealous of him."

"*Mierda*," Vilar said through her teeth.

"Hey, take it easy," Parker retreated. He raised himself from the sofa, as though it were hot, and then reseated himself gingerly. "I'm only trying to say that maybe Carlos is not as involved with Pepe as you think," he smiled. "Maybe it's all a ruse. It wouldn't be the first time, that's for sure. Listen. I certainly don't know what he's doing down there with Pepe. I have no idea. He hasn't called me in a month. So maybe you don't have a good idea either. Maybe he's gonna buy Pepe some more roses. Maybe he's gonna set Pepe up for the Venezuelan goons. Who knows? I certainly think Carlos has a right to spend some time worrying about Pepe, because Pepe is a dangerous man who has already tried to kill him. Don't you agree?"

"No," seethed Vilar. "I don't agree, because I know Carlos. And I know he's not afraid of Pepe the way other men would be. Carlos is smart, Max. He knows it's no disgrace to be killed by your inferior. It happens all the time. There's nothing you can do but be careful. But it is bad to be preoccupied by your inferiors while you are living. Carlos has never done that before, but now he's allowed himself to get fascinated by Pepe somehow. That's what's going on, Max. I know it. There is a betrayal about to happen. I feel it."

Parker waited until he thought it was safe to comment. "Maybe so, but I think you should wait to see him before you decide anything. He's been gone like this a hundred times, and Pepe's not the first character you haven't liked. I don't like Pepe either, believe me . . ."

". . . Why should I?" challenged Vilar. "You don't believe me, do you?"

"I just said I don't know," frowned Parker.

"Let me ask you something, Max," said Vilar, after lighting another cigarette. "Do you see any plan in Carlos's mind over the last few years or so? Since Taliente, and especially since that stupid thing with Damico and the Italians? You hated that as much as I did, you know."

"I know," said Parker. He thought while he opened the reserve can of beer. "Well, I agree those things are strange," he replied. "I've been worried a little myself. But I don't think Carlos has ever planned anything beyond the next operation."

"Maybe not."

"He's very good at that."

"I know," said Vilar. "Maybe there's not a plan, but there's a logic to it. And to me the logic points straight to the *cocaina*, Max."

This gave him a pause. "That's not all, is it?" he asked suspiciously. "Tell me what's new about the *cocaina*, Carmen. Without it, how would we have financed the revolution and our kids' educations and our Saturday nights?"

Vilar snuffed out her cigarette with a vengeance. "In the real *cocaina* there is no room for friends, Max," she said softly. "That's what I see. And that's why I feel a betrayal coming, somehow. All I feel of it so far is Pepe."

"You've always laughed at the conspiracies, Carmen," said Parker, trying to smile brightly. He failed. His smile took on a more sober cast, as though a painting had captured his eye and then his interest. "Now you've got one of your own. Who knows? You may be right."

Vilar grimaced. She rested her chin on a hand, elbow on a knee, to stare silently at Parker, who was trying to hold his pose of moderate humor. Vilar watched him, took his measure, and in due course a smile of understanding began to grow visible between her fingers. "You bastard!" she muttered, with equal parts of anger and satisfaction. "You have been thinking the same thing all along, but you've sat there playing fucking Sancho Panza, like always, so you can make me feel like a stupid woman out of her element. Maximilian, you are a lying bastard, and you are a conspirator yourself. I should have known."

Parker did not change expression, but his eyes were deep into her face. Then he leaned back to relax, with a noncommittal smile. "Those are very dangerous thoughts, Carmen," he said quietly. "All of them. There's no such thing as the last conspiracy, you know. There's always one more until there's one too many."

"How profound. Look, Max, you don't have to be so careful, okay? I'm not gonna tell Carlos you're worried about him. Why don't you just tell me the truth about what you've been thinking?"

"This kind of thought can poison your mind," said Parker evasively. "Maybe it already has."

"And stop avoiding me with your bullshit!"

Parker's back stiffened. "Hey, what is this?" he cried. "You come knocking on my door all sad and you want to dance and everything, and the next thing I know you're calling me a liar! Why don't you just try to forget about all this until Carlos gets back, okay? I'm telling you I've seen people crack under stuff like this before, when it wasn't even real."

"Because *you're* not forgetting it, that's why," Vilar said coldly. "I can see your little mind turning over from here. You can play your friendly, loyal, technical, funny Max all you want, but I know it is nothing more than your last bit of camouflage. You have survived a long time in a nasty business, Max, and it has not been done just as Sancho Panza. That would make the fool of both you and Carlos, and I know he values your cunning. Well, now is the time to use it. Why don't you quit playing with your wires and *do* something?"

Parker looked at the floor for some time, flexing the muscles in his jaw. then, with skips and kicks and stutters, he broke slowly into a wicked private laugh that tittered along in fits while he eyed Vilar. When he inhaled, Parker gave out a soft, high-pitched yodel, and he punctuated his laugh with labored cries of "Carmen, you are really something."

Vilar's embarrassment did not take long to smolder. "You are a real bastard," she muttered.

"Look at me!" beamed Parker, throwing his arms open like a performer welcoming applause. "I am already doing something, my lady, and I will show it to you," he exulted. With a flourish, he touched the tips of both index fingers to his temples, clenched his eyelids tightly, and flew off into a mocking, high-pitched squeal: "Worry, worry, worry, worry, worry!" he shrieked. After peeking quickly at a disgusted Vilar, he repeated, "Worry, worry, worry, worry, worry! There! You see? I am worrying very, very hard,

Carmen. I worry very, very hard because Carlos may send Pepe Lopez to spank me when he comes home, and I don't like Pepe Lopez, you see. So I worry, worry, worry, worry, worry. All the time. How's that? Okay?" Parker opened his eyes to shrug, and the wild energy drained quickly from him. He leaned back with a can of beer and became instantly sullen.

Vilar said nothing while Parker's squeals echoed in the silence between songs on the tape. She snuffed another freshly lit cigarette. "Well, at least you admit you feel something wrong about Pepe," she remarked stonily. "That something, I suppose. Otherwise you are a boring clown, Max. I've learned that, too."

She heaved a peremptory sigh and reached to the floor for her purse, but was intercepted by Parker. His hand seemed to glide invisibly through the air like that of his fantasy idol, Suhani, and he clasped Vilar's wrist firmly. "Wait," he said, with ominous pleasantry. He let go of her wrist and tried to smile, but the duplicity was too much for the moment and a bolt of anger traveled around the arc of his body from one hand to the other. With successive spasms of strength, Parker crushed his beer can so that it disappeared inside his palm.

Vilar did not flinch. Instead, she leaned tauntingly toward him and smiled. "Oooooooh, Max," she oozed with sardonic awe. "You are so very, very strong. I'm impressed."

Parker put his nose near Vilar's. "Bitch!" he whispered. "I am happy to entertain you as the clown or the strong man, because it is my duty and I know how awful it is for a fine women like yourself to be bored. It is a terrible thing, especially for a pretty bitch like you. But you should never forget one thing, Carmen, on pain of your life or your pretty nose or whatever you care about. If you really want to play the conspiracy game with a shrewd bastard like you say I am, you better forget about playing it like a woman. You can put on that icy look of yours and talk hard, really hard, about the betrayals you see everywhere, but then you better not turn around with your pretty lips and beg me to tell you the true feelings inside me. You understand?"

Vilar retreated an inch or two from Parker's livid face. "That is a true feeling," she tried to smile.

Parker nodded with a menacing smile and then he leaned forward even more. "That is for you to decide," he hissed. "But as far as I am concerned, you are Carlos's woman. I am Carlos's friend. Beneath that, it's survival, and all of us are doing things to get through the day. I play with cops and wires. I play Max day and night, but it is none of your fucking business, you hear? I don't trust you a bit in the business because all I get from you is lies, Carmen. You come pouting in here all sad and you say you're bored and want to dance. Poor Carmen. And in the end you say what's boring you is Pepe Lopez. Which is the worst lie. It is a complete, bitchy, murdering lie, because the last thing in the world Pepe and Carlos are to you is boring. You hear me? They are all you want to talk about. You have been talking shit to me, Carmen, and then you have the nerve to berate me for not showing you more of my heart." Parker made clucking noises as he waved a finger back and forth in front of her face. "No, no, no," he teased savagely. "I may not even have one."

The first and only wave of pain crossed Vilar's face. She looked straight at Parker. "That is not a lie, Max," she choked. "It *is* boring to me. I swear it."

Parker held a sick smile near her face, but he studied her at length, from the long lashes above her fierce brown eyes to the ball of white knuckles in her lap. "That is for me to decide," he whispered coldly. "There. You see how easy it is? I decide, and you decide. You go to your corner and decide. See?" His forced smile was short-lived. "And for you, Carmen, it is very easy, because if you are not lying and it has all become boring to you—Pepe and everything—you can just throw up your hands and walk away to your father or your pile of *cocaina* money or whatever pleases you. With me it is not so easy to walk away, even from the peeking fools in the FBI. You can go, Carmen. Whenever you want. I know how proud you have always been of telling Carlos that there are no ties and that you can blow away like the breeze the second you feel bored. You have been so proud of your freedom and your position. Well, if you are bored, Carmenita, then do it! For God's sake, go! And don't bring me any more of your boring lies."

Vilar said nothing, nor did she move. Her mouth was set, nostrils slightly flared, and rising blood turned the dark skin of her neck the color of a peach.

Parker's face cracked from the stress. "That was quite a speech for a clown," he blushed. "Wasn't it?"

Vilar rose like a robot. "All right," said a distant voice. "I'm going." And with that, she went at him. Her right hand whipped back and around her like a discus thrower and then her entire body shot forward. Parker did not move. He remained frozen in his angry blush, watching in slow motion. Shock and a small residue of atavistic chivalry kept his cheek on a pedestal so that Vilar hit it squarely with the full thrust of her weight and all the whiplash in her arm. There was a loud crack of woodblock sound, but Parker heard only the beginning of it. He did not blink away the slap like Gary Cooper. The next thing he knew his head was wedged tightly between two pillows that seemed to have wrenched his neck viciously to the side and then yanked him bodily across the sofa. He thought he felt his legs tumbling behind. Popping noises behind his windpipe made him curious about the sensations of a broken neck, but soon he was not curious about anything. Somebody crammed a blaring dog whistle into his left ear. It complemented a searing BOINNNG of reverberating pain, caused by the way his skull was bouncing off the skin of his cheek out of phase with the fluid that was sloshing around inside his skull. Parker winced on one side of his face. The other wasn't working. Nausea following the BOINNNG.

Parker thought he felt Vilar pulling her knees out of his ribs, and a bit later he heard her heavy breathing above the CONELRAD hum in his ear. But seconds passed before he could do anything but groan. Then he took a wavy bearing on the sound of her labored breath and whirled blindly upward with a wounded man's cry of primal anger. His sudden revival would have been a drunken one even if his head had not popped so unevenly from the crack in the pillows. Vilar had time to turn aside so that Parker's hand landed with poor radar but a lot of fury at the back of her neck. Her scream was cut short as the heel of his right palm cuffed her across and over the coffee table toward the television.

"Bitch!" gasped Parker. He staggered toward her, tripped over the overturned coffee table, and fell on his face. Quickly, he managed a lunging crawl to Vilar.

She was already on her back, moaning, with one hand clutching her neck and the other holding the place where the table struck her shin. She was in pain, not shock, and she overcame it the instant Parker touched her. His right hand pinioned her left one to the floor, but before he could grab the one at her shin, she gouged him in the stomach and made a serious effort to tear away a large chunk of his breast. When he howled and went for her hand, she went for his face. But he caught her and pushed both wrists to the floor. Vilar bared her teeth in fury and commenced to kick and buck with strength out of proportion to her body. One hand and then the other reared up. Parker pushed them down like bicycle pedals on a steep upward grade. When he rose up to gain more leverage, she ambushed him with a warm spray of white spittle. Parker shook his head to sling it off him, and as he did he was struck conscious of the humiliation. Vilar sensed an ebbing in his strength. She immediately flailed upward on a maniac's adrenaline, born of hope. Hanging on, Parker weakened further. "Wait," he said. "I've never hit a woman before. I really haven't."

"Let me go!" screamed Vilar.

"Okay, okay," rasped Parker. He lost more strength and sagged to the side. Vilar twisted out of his grasp and rolled all the way across the living room to safety. She sprang to her feet and breathed wildly, staring down at him in triumphant fury. "Hah!" she said, more to herself than to him.

Parker was still on the floor. He was rubbery, eyes closed, trying desperately to hone in on an intuition that had just whispered by him in all the chaos—of himself pounding the floor of the racetrack in Cuba just after the death of Sloppy Kisses. A dumb grin worked its way into Parker's face.

Vilar's anger was already worn out when she saw him. She fought back an impulse to smile herself, out of relief. "So," she said, slapping her hands together as though to shake off the dust. Then she did smile slightly, but Parker was too lost to see it. "You are such a clown that maybe Carlos will let you live, Max," she said. "I don't know."

Parker slowly rolled over to face her, disinterested. "Maybe so," he said. "Anyway, thanks for dropping by." He began to shake from a gentle, weak laugh that was interrupted by pangs of headache.

Vilar picked up her purse on the way to the door. "Don't mention it," she called. "I'll do anything when I'm bored. Anything."

"*Mierda*," sighed Parker. From the floor, he tossed an empty beer can in her general direction. It caromed loudly off the wall and skittered along the floor. She shrugged as she exited with a grin that Parker thought was strange for the occasion. He thought about it for some time after she was gone.

Not surprisingly, this episode grew into a stubborn barrier to amicable relations between Parker and Vilar. They did not see or speak to each other for nearly a month, in fact, and when they finally did it was only after being individually subjected to the blandishments and the temper of Carlos Maraña, who insisted that they join him at the Renegade Club for dinner on the weekend of July 4. Parker had reasons of his own for attending, but he still had to be pressured. In the end, Vilar's presence was bought with many promises and shepherding by Maraña. Tired of seeing them separately, he was determined to patch up the silly feud that had grown up while he was "down south," as he said, although he did seem to enjoy both accounts of the Sancho Panza fisticuffs.

XVIII

DINNER WAS scheduled for nine o'clock on Sunday evening. Parker arrived half an hour late and was the first one there. He screeched to a halt in the curved loading area of the Renegade Club, tossed his keys and a joke to the parking attendant, who responded with a laugh and a fraternal punch on the arm, and then he entered the club's opulent foyer of glass, tall enough for indoor palms and bright red appointments and fountains and grottoes featuring tropical vegetation of every description. Two well-muscled Cubans in white suits and bow ties nodded politely and directed Parker a few feet off to the side to the communications desk, which was a curved console of dark wood encasing enough equipment for the cockpit of a jetliner. One of two striking women in formal black dresses and red smiles, known as the Dragonladies, registered Parker's name and membership number from his card of gold plastic, on which was embossed the image of a ferocious, besworded, one-eyed pirate. Parker nodded animated greetings around the room while she worked. He checked the guest list, took his card, winked, and made his way past the bar and the downstairs showroom, where a tiresome blonde and a piano were putting out tunes from World War II, up the winding stairs up to the east dining room. He handed the *maitre d'* a twenty-dollar bill and a Chinese fortune cookie, his latest affectation, as he sailed by to Maraña's usual table. There were twelve places set. Parker took his seat, two to the left of the head, and summoned a waiter by name. He ordered four bottles of white wine, a round of Bloody Marys, an assortment of appetizers, and he gave instructions that a dozen of the largest lobsters were to be thrown into the pot upon first sight of Maraña, to whose account he charged it all. Then Parker sat back to wait. He was not very good at it. He twirled a finger in two of the Bloody Marys and waved occasionally at fellow diners.

A party of four women and two men, all Cubans, arrived shortly in the elegant trail of the *maitre d'*. Parker welcomed them with restrained enthusiasm. Two of the women were old friends of Carmen Vilar. They were beautiful, of high social standing, and naturally haughty. They sniffed briefly at Parker. They clearly had no use for the other two women, either. These were younger and more given to rapid speech to calm their nerves, though they made a great effort to appear at ease. Maraña, in his fondness for categories, referred to them as "Noses," meaning that they would look pretty, converse sparingly with unexpected visitors, keep seats warm, and rise to other decorative contingencies so long as their noses remained near a glamorous scene and were filled with the euphorious *cocaina*.

The two pairs of women, who seated themselves at opposite ends of the table, had little in common beyond disregard for their companion in the three-piece suit, who sat at the foot of the table and turned his chair sideways, looking off in silence. He was a man of hulking frame and timid mustache and a face of dutiful perplexity, such as one might see pausing at length to fathom an ordinary street sign. Parker knew what kind of gun he was carrying. Although he would be of doubtful value in any serious altercation, he was something of a deterrent, and Maraña deemed him preferable to the renowned bodyguards whose pride always required them to intrude upon the evening, take sides, and so forth. This gentleman displayed no resentment toward anyone, not even toward the gregarious one whose name was Jorge but who was called Sunshine because of his disposition and his trade. The latter embraced a sitting Parker from behind and walked around the table to take a chair opposite him. Sunshine was a dandy of slender proportions and classic Latin features, whose photograph might easily appear in a *New Yorker* advertisement for Bacardi rum. Beneath his tailored suit, he wore a white silk shirt adorned with small impressions of *jai alai* players in action. He wore three silver bracelets on one wrist, and on the other a watch that cost more than a round trip ticket to Paris. Aside from this hardware, Sunshine perpetually wore the look of a jackpot night in Las Vegas.

"How are you, Sunshine?" asked Parker, toasting vaguely around the table with a Bloody Mary.

"Beautiful," smiled Sunshine. "Just beautiful."

"And how's business on the holiday weekend?"

"Really beautiful," Sunshine replied.

The conversation continued in this vein only briefly before the *maitre d'* reappeared in escort of three more guests, who were wide-eyed and underdressed in blue jeans and old sports jackets and fledgling cases of sunburn.

Parker rose with a smile and an outstretched hand. "How are you, David?" he asked, in English.

"Fine, I guess," said Howell, who remained nonplussed even though he was quite relieved to see Parker. "Hi, Max. What *is* this place?"

"It's Carlos's little playpen," smiled Parker, who clasped Howell's wrist like a Roman and pulled him into a one-armed *abrazo*. "Do you like it?"

"It's amazing," said Howell. "Watch out for my hat."

"Oh," said Parker, backing off, looking down between them to see the

372

battered straw hat. "I should have remembered that hat of yours, David," he laughed. "I'm really sorry."

"That's all right," Howell said sheepishly. "You can't hurt old faithful here. The Miami hat. Listen, I'm sorry we're late, Max. We got lost. I thought this place was in Little Havana, and I had no idea it would be this fancy."

"Forget about it," Parker said graciously. He turned to the Cubans seated around the table and said in Spanish, "This is Carlos's friend, the *Americano* who used to walk up and down Eighth Street in that ridiculous hat." The Cubans responded to this with cheesy smiles, as no claim of friendship from Maraña could overcome their foretaste of a stilted night with English-speaking *gringos*. Parker shrugged. The Americans understood nothing but the discomfort and resumed their glassy-eyed examination of the premises.

"I hope we're not intruding on your evening, Max," said Howell. "I really was just calling to say hello."

"You are welcome, David," Parker said graciously. "You know that. Carlos insisted."

"Thanks," said Howell, "And you're sure you've got room for three of us? Haven and I had to come down on some emergency personal business that Carlos knows about, and Henry here has a speech tomorrow, so we decided to come together for a weekend."

"It's all right, David, Carlos needs a lot of help to spend his money."

"Well, we're good at that," said Howell, who then noticed the agitation of his companions. "Excuse me, Max. I want you to meet my friends, Haven Pinder and Henry Woodruff. Max Parker," he introduced.

"*Mucho gusto*," grinned Parker. He bowed slightly as he shook Pinder's hand. Greeting Woodruff, he said, "And you must be the one who made the big speech at the State Department, right?"

Woodruff started to smile but then checked himself and looked to Howell for help, fearing that he might violate some confidence with his first word.

"It's all right, Henry," said Howell. "Max knows everything."

"Oh," said Woodruff. "Well, I did give a little speech at the State Department, yes, but I don't know whether it did Carlos any good."

"I'm sure it did," Parker said vaguely. Then he looked startled. "Here, please! Take a seat and forgive me," he beckoned. "And would the señorita do me the honor of sitting next to me?"

Pinder agreed and seated herself between Howell and Parker. Woodruff aired his independent proclivities by walking around the bodyguard to a place next to one of the Noses, who in turn was next to a rather subdued, nearly eclipsed, Sunshine.

Parker introduced each of his fellow exiles by name and repeated the names of the Americans. Both sides nodded woodenly. Parker leaned over to Pinder. "Haven is a most unusual name, is it not?" he asked.

"I guess it is," replied Pinder, reaching under the arm of her chair in search of support from Howell's hand. She had been in high form, riding her bedazzlement, throughout her first weekend in Miami, at the Ziller household and Castle Vizcaya and the Fontainebleau and other points of interest, but now she was slightly self-conscious, which annoyed her. She sensed that she should be careful, but she did not know exactly how or why, and she was loath to admit feeling some discomfort about her attire—fresh denim overalls, a Lily Tomlin T-shirt, boots, and, mercifully, a ragged lavender suit jacket from the thirties, with shoulder pads, which provided under these extreme circumstances a welcome daub of anonymity. "I guess so," she repeated.

"Well, Haven is a nice name," Parker effused. "An unusual name for an unusual woman, if half of what David has told me is true. You have been his woman for some time now, am I right?"

"His woman?" bristled Pinder. After scrunching up her small red nose unhappily in Parker's direction, she refrained from saying anything. Instead, she squeezed Howell's hand and appealed to him with her comic expression of one at panic in a noose.

Howell cleared his throat. "Um, Max," he drawled. "Not 'my woman,' okay? The Cuban *machismo* talk around Haven will take you straight to the *casa de perros.*"

The other Cubans at the table, who were otherwise ignoring this triplay, took brief notice with their eyes of this awkward Spanish phrase from Howell's mouth.

Parker looked quickly at Howell and then back at Pinder. Then he broke into a full rumbling laugh. "The doghouse?" he laughed. "You will put me in the doghouse?"

Pinder, encouraged by his humor, nodded in the affirmative.

"That's right, Max," said Howell.

"If you only knew, señorita," laughed Parker. "I am *already* in the doghouse, you see."

"You are?" said Pinder, who could not resist a smile.

"Oh, yes," roared Parker. "Just ask those two women there."

Pinder and Howell looked toward the end of the table.

"Those are friends of Carmen Vilar," Parker said merrily. "You've met Carmen, haven't you, David? You know her?"

"Sure," said Howell.

"Well, those two women there have put me deep into the *casa de perros* for offending Carmen," said Parker. "I am *under* it, I'm afraid. I will never get out!"

"What did you do?" asked Pinder.

"Oh, that is too long a story," said Parker. "But look at them," he chuckled, pointing at the two women, sitting next to the oblivious bodyguard. They had interrupted their private conversation to glare at him. "Look at them!" cried Parker.

"It looks pretty bad," said Pinder. She felt much better. "Max, do you mind if I ask you something?"

"Of course not."

"Well," said Pinder. "What kind of dinner are we having here? Are you

374

all friends? I can't help noticing that you are all facing in different directions."

"You have?" Parker said thoughtfully. He casually scanned the table. "That's true, Haven," he concluded with mild admiration. "You are very observant."

"Thank you," said Pinder.

"Well, I guess you could say we are all friends in a way," said Parker. "But we are related to each other mainly as part of Carlos's group, you know. How do you say? His entourage. His hang-oners, really."

"Hangers-on," Howell corrected.

"Right," said Parker.

"Oh," said Pinder.

"And I have been with Carlos the longest by far," said Parker. "So I am either the highest hanger-on or the lowest one to hang on to. It all depends on how you look at it."

"Oh," said Howell.

"And Roberto down there is the newest," said Parker, nodding toward the bodyguard. "He probably won't say anything all night, because he is brand new and very shy. And besides that, he speaks no English."

"I see," Pinder said sympathetically.

"In fact, if you'll excuse me, señorita," Parker confided, "about the only English word he understands is 'fuck.' "

At this instant, Roberto's head jerked a bit, as though a posse of gnats had flown up his ear. The other Cubans looked at Parker also, with disapproval or curiosity. Howell and Pinder chuckled softly.

So did Woodruff, who by this time had abandoned his effort to elicit information from the Nose beside him on the fine points of collective political sentiment among the Cuban exiles. "Excuse me, Max," he ventured across the table. "Could you tell us where we are and what this is, please? This is a private club, right?"

"Sure," said Parker. "That is correct. This is the Renegade Club. That is Biscayne Bay out the window there, looking east."

Woodruff nodded.

"Then where's Miami Beach?" asked Howell. "I don't understand."

"It's over there, David," Parker replied. "You can just see the southern tip of it, not the big hotels. We are very south here, you see, in the rich new condominium district of laundered money."

"Please don't mention condominiums," said Howell. "We left Washington to get away from them. Haven and I are about to get thrown our of our apartment."

"I think Carlos told me something about that," frowned Parker. "But I didn't really understand it."

"It's too long a story," smiled Pinder.

"So what kind of a club is it?" asked Woodruff.

"It's just a social club," shrugged Parker. "What can I say? It's a club full of renegades, I guess."

"And all the renegades must be wealthy," said Howell. "This is a very lavish place."

"You are looking at the humblest member," smiled Parker. "The club is nice because we don't spend any money on golf courses and expensive things like that, such as the Americans do. We are proud of the building, though. It's only four years old this Christmas. The dining floor, where we are, takes the form of a huge clover on this platform, with three separate leaves facing every direction except north, you see. The other two dining rooms have music. We prefer this quiet one. Back there to the north, the building sits directly on one of the few natural hills in this area, and there are the meeting rooms and card rooms and about a hundred suites for overnight guests."

"No tennis courts or anything?" asked Woodruff.

"Nothing for athletes," said Parker. "You can't sweat here unless you are losing money or getting arrested."

"Getting arrested?" said Howell.

"I am joking, David," said Parker.

"Good," said Howell.

Parker nodded. He summoned the waiter to open the wine and ordered another round of drinks. Then he looked more soberly at Howell. "Now that you have raised a serious subject like getting arrested, David . . ."

". . . You raised that, Max," Pinder interjected. "That was you . . ."

". . . That's all right, baby," said Howell.

"You are right, Haven," Parker conceded. "But no matter. I just wanted to say one thing to you before Carlos gets here."

"What's that?" frowned Howell.

"Well, you should take this for what it's worth," said Parker, examining his fingernails, "but I don't think you should spend a lot of time around Carlos right now. Things are very sensitive in Miami these last few months. The atmosphere is fonny because of things like that episode you went to the State Department about, you know. There are a lot of crazy people running around, and I don't think you should spend a lot of time poking around among the action people asking a lot of questions. People have heard of you, David, or they have seen your picture in the newspaper coming out of the jail when you visited Carlos. I've heard people talking about how you were spotted on the day of the Mendoza bombing. And a lot of people don't like Carlos right now, for some crazy reason."

Parker tried briefly to chuckle. The three Americans were paying close attention. Pinder and Howell were nodding along in utter sincerity, mouths slightly open. "You really think it's dangerous now, eh?" said Howell, trying to sound nonchalant.

"Not really," said Parker. "And Carlos would think I'm crazy for mentioning it at all, because he never thinks it's dangerous. But that's Carlos."

"That's Carlos," Howell agreed.

"Well, what do you think we should do, Max," Pinder asked nervously. "David, I mean. What should he do?"

"Nothing in particular," sighed Parker. "I'm afraid I have worried you unnecessarily, Haven. For that I am sorry."

"That's all right," Howell said quickly. "I'm glad you told us, Max. This isn't a working trip, though. I'm not working on a story or anything."

"That's probably good," said Parker.

"It's still a little scary, though," said Howell.

"Not really. Forget about it," smiled Parker, looking solicitously at Pinder. "I just mentioned it because I know how curious David is, and I know Carlos. For all I know he might impetuously invite you on some exciting conspiracy tonight or tomorrow or Friday just to show off, you know. He might like nothing better. And I think you should think twice about going, that's all. This is a shaky time right now for the Cubans and the Americans, especially Americans around Carlos."

"Well, we're leaving tomorrow night," said Pinder.

"No problem then," smiled Parker.

"What exactly is going on, Max?" asked Howell. "I don't like this."

"You see how curious he is?" asked Parker. "You see? I will have to say that is too long a story for now, David. So I owe you one, I guess. But I have my ears to the ground, and I hear a lot of wild threats and so forth, along the lines of the matter in Caracas. That's all."

"Uh huh," frowned Howell. "But have you heard anybody mention me or us specifically? Come on, Max. I don't like the vague fear, you know."

"No, no, no," said Parker. "Nothing like that. To be frank with you, I haven't heard any names but Carlos's lately, and he knows all about that. So don't worry. I'm afraid I have made a mistake."

"Oh," said Howell, who did not appear satisfied.

Parker waved a sauce-dipped shrimp in the air to evoke the carnival whirl of events, and said, "Things are always volatile with the Cubans and the Americans, David. Who should know better than me, eh? I am both."

"I guess so," said Howell, with a reluctant smile.

"What about Henry's speech, Max?" asked Pinder. "Do you think it's a problem?"

"Oh, that," shrugged Parker, after an instant's thought. "Nobody here knows about that. Nobody knows anything about Washington, you know. That's no problem."

"Not the State Department speech," said Pinder. "The one he's giving down here."

"Oh," said Parker. "What's that?"

"Well," said Woodruff. Having the floor, he took a large swallow of Bloody Mary while his mind warmed up for description. "It's early tomorrow night, before we leave," he said, "over at the auditorium . . ."

". . . Excuse me," Parker interrupted. "Here's Carlos."

"Oh," blinked Woodruff.

It was true. The Cubans at the table had already bestirred themselves over the sight of Maraña and Vilar, who were weaving through the dining room, Vilar in the lead. She wore a bright red dress that swept around her body like a tight *sari*, and small red sandals and no make-up at all, and she carried her purse on her thigh in the grip of her palm, with her arm hanging straight and the purse-strap dangling just below. The effect was a bit more sultry than usual, whereas Maraña was as effervescent as ever. He wore a dark pin-striped suit without a tie, sunglasses perched atop his head, and he stopped briefly at two or three tables to whisper in someone's ear, like a politician at a fund-raiser.

"How's everybody?" beamed Maraña, as he seated Vilar on his right, next to Sunshine. "And how are you, Sunshine?"

"Okay, I guess," said Sunshine.

"That's all? Just okay?" teased Maraña, with eyebrows raised. He seated himself amid great bustle, as two waiters were bringing a table and a long-corded telephone to his side. "That's not like you, Sunshine," said Maraña. "Hasn't Max been taking good care of you?"

"Sure," said Sunshine.

Maraña nodded briskly to the Nose on his left as he turned to Parker. "Hello, Max," he said garrulously, and then he focused on Howell. "And David!" he smiled. "You made it after all, I see. I hope you will entertain us with your jokes."

"Well, I don't know," blushed Howell.

"The Señor Sombrero has a big plantation in Virginia," Maraña announced to the table.

"That's not really true, Carlos," said Howell.

"So what?" grinned Maraña. "I saw you sneaking around on one, didn't I?"

"Uh huh," admitted Howell.

"Okay then," said Maraña, looking over the table. "David speaks Spanish like a very small *niño*," he announced grandly in Spanish. "So I'm afraid we'll have a dinner in English." This brought listless nods from all the Cubans save Parker and Vilar.

"And you must be Haven Pinder," said Maraña, offering his hand. "Pleased to meet you."

"Thank you," said Pinder, marveling despite Howell's briefings at Maraña's energy and zest, and at the powerful combination they made with the edge on his pleasant voice.

"Any friend of David's is a friend of mine," he pronounced as he shook hands. "And any girlfriend of David's is a girlfriend of mine," he added with a grin. "Just teasing, Haven. Tell me, what is the date of your birth?"

"Excuse me?" gulped Pinder.

"Your birthday," said Maraña. "Just tell me. I like to know them. I won't forget."

Flustered, Pinder had to think for a second, but she told him.

"And this is my friend, Henry Woodruff, I told you about," said Howell, pointing to Woodruff.

"How are you, Henry?" smiled Maraña.

"Fine," said Woodruff. He waved a greeting, being too far away to shake hands, and as he did so he gained the impression that Maraña was taking an x-ray of him.

Maraña greeted his way around the others. "Okay," he concluded, rubbing his hands. "Is everybody happy?" He turned to a rather taciturn Vilar and then looked mischievously at Parker. "Do you two remember each other?" he teased. "Sancho Panza, I present to you the Slugger."

Maraña and the Noses thought this was uproariously funny. Sunshine and the Americans were not sure. Vilar's two friends knew for a fact that it was nothing of the kind. Roberto didn't understand and therefore didn't think anything.

Vilar outstalled Parker on the response. Some time after the laughter died down, he said, "How are you, Slugger?" with a wry grin.

"In better shape than you," Vilar smiled.

"That's better," said Maraña. "Much better." Satisfied with the truce at the head of the table, he looked abruptly back at Woodruff. "I wish to thank you, Henry, for your speech at the State Department last month," he said. "David says it was a big help."

"Well, I don't know about that," Woodruff blushed. "It wasn't even planned. It just happened."

"Those are the best speeches," said Maraña.

"Sometimes," said Woodruff, unable to resist the qualification. "Thank you, though," he added. Then he leaned casually back in his chair and asked, "How did it go down there, anyway?"

"I thought you'd never ask," teased Maraña.

"No, really," coughed Woodruff. "Did you have much trouble?" He glanced anxiously at Howell, and the two of them engaged in a quick, furtive eye battle. Howell cradled his face delicately in one hand and rolled his eyes at Woodruff, communicating his amusement at Woodruff's headlong professorial plunge into the Venezuelan assassination business. Woodruff's eyes flicked subtly, trying to shoo Howell's away.

"Well, Henry, the secretary of state is still alive, isn't he?" beamed Maraña. "So I must have done a pretty good job down there, I guess. Because there is no question he was going to get shot."

"Really?" said Woodruff. "Are you sure?"

"No doubt about it," said Maraña. "Pepe Lopez is a very dangerous man, as I have said many times. And he would have done it if I hadn't talked him out of it, I assure you."

Woodruff stared blankly at Maraña and then he took a deep breath. "Whew," he said, shaking his head to dispel a rush of paranoia. He was nowhere near certain that he believed Maraña, but the physical reality of a human being who glibly claimed to operate on such a plane was itself unsettling. Especially someone of Maraña's presence. Woodruff had previously discounted Maraña's tales to allow for Howell's tendency to exaggerate. Now he was feeling the impact of the error, and since he blamed Howell for part of his present discomfort, he shot him a frown of unexplained reproach. "I see," he said to Maraña.

Howell saw that Woodruff was temporarily indisposed. "Couldn't Pepe be prosecuted for conspiracy anyway, even if he didn't go through with it?" he asked Maraña.

"Of course," said Maraña. "At least that is what they tell me, David. And you bet the FBI would love to obtain the indictment. They don't like Pepe, and they don't like me anymore. But there are always complications, you see."

"Oh," said Howell. "Like what?"

Maraña shrugged and threw up his hands, to suggest there was a great number to choose from. "Well, the Company would fight it, as usual," he said, "And the State Department is not sure because they don't know what the Venezuelans would think, and so forth, David. And there are many other things in addition to the fact that there are no witnesses."

"Oh," said Howell. "What about you?"

"Me?" exclaimed Maraña, touching all ten fingertips to the lapels of his coat. "Why me, David? How many more enemies do you think I need?"

"Well, I don't know," Howell retreated. "A few more wouldn't hurt, maybe. You say yourself he is a dangerous man."

"Very fonny," said Maraña. "I have done enough, my friend. I went through all that trouble up in Washington over this, some of which you know and other parts are better to forget. That was first. And then I went down to Caracas, and the Venezuelans lied to me about the assurances I needed. They didn't help me at all. Instead of that, they followed me along with some Americans, I think, but I know the Venezuelans followed me all over the place, and they made a lot of trouble for me because I had to give my word to Pepe that I would see him alone, you see. And I had to overcome that with Pepe because to him that made me a liar, you see, and he was in a very precarious position down there, as you can understand.

"And after that, I had to use all my powers of persuasion to keep Pepe from going ahead—even after I told him that the Americans had found out about his plan through their spies—because he was ready to go ahead no matter what. He had given over his mind and he had given over his body, you see, so that all that was left was his instinct, and his instinct was to kill no matter what. I'm telling you that is the truth. If we had had Pepe in the old days, there would be no Castro. I told him that. And so it was quite difficult for me to dissuade him, and when it was all over what thanks do you think I get, my friend? I'm telling you it is really something. From the Americans, I mean. Not from the secretary of state. He is a high official and I expect nothing from him. But the others. Well, they gave me a lot of problems about who was going to pay for my ticket, you know. One group would say that another group would reimburse me, and so forth. Same old shit. And nobody wanted to see me, in the embassy or anywhere else.

"Then after I go through all that trouble for nothing, I come home and what happens? Some of the agencies here are not satisfied with my work and they say they won't be unless I make a fool of myself and testify publicly against Pepe in some conspiracy trial. Other agencies don't want me to pay any attention to those agencies, and those agencies don't want me to pay any attention to the others, you see. So it's a big mess. And the agencies that do want me to testify are really something. They don't seem to mind that even more people would want to kill me after something stupid like that. And why not? Pepe will have to say that I am crazy and I cooked up the whole plot just to discredit the freedom-loving Cubans in Miami because I am a Castro agent, you see. And everybody would believe him because they think I'm a Castro agent anyway and Pepe is a very nice insurance salesman. You can go over there to his office tomorrow and I'm sure that's what he will say. Tell him you heard this rumor about what Maraña says. Maybe I will take you myself. Is Pepe in town, Max?"

Parker had been listening from the lower reaches of his Bloody Mary glass. "I think he is," he coughed. "That's what I hear."

"Too bad," mourned Howell. "We're all busy tomorrow and it's our last day. Maybe next trip, Carlos."

Maraña gave Howell a needling smile. "Next trip, then," he agreed. "Right. But it has to be in the daytime, David, because I am too scared to go see Pepe at night."

"Well, hold it a second," said Howell, turning to Pinder. "Is it okay with you to go in the daytime, baby, or would you rather go at night?" he asked, about half deadpan.

Pinder was still looking at Maraña, with the sound of a thunderous waterfall in her ears. She gulped and gave an ambivalent signal by nodding her head up and down.

"Daytime," Howell interpreted.

"Okay," said Maraña. "You will see."

Howell could no longer sustain the pose of humor with which he had warded off the thud of Maraña's words and most particularly of his words and his face when he described Pepe Lopez in a killing mood. Both Howell's cheeks filled with air and his eyes closed, seeking strength. Then he exhaled wearily, making a funny flapping noise with his lips, like a child imitating a tired horse. "Shit, Carlos," he sighed in surrender. "We'll let you handle Pepe, okay? We're tourists. We went to the Fontainebleau last night."

"That's all right, David," Maraña said gently. "But let me know if you change your mind, okay?"

"Sure," said Howell.

"The papers said Carlyle left Caracas two days early," said Woodruff, by now revived. "Do you know why that was?"

Maraña listened, but he was still studying Howell for clues as to his mood and his attitude toward the mystery of Pepe Lopez. He turned slowly to Woodruff. "Well, I can say this, Henry. I know the secretary left Caracas the very day after the Venezuelans betrayed me and lied to me and followed me to the place where I was supposed to meet Pepe," Maraña recalled. "That is the truth. Now, in my mind, I have to think the secretary left pretty soon after it was confirmed this way that Pepe was in Caracas. But who knows? They say he left early to underscore his displeasure with the oil proceedings. For sure he was displeased, but I don't know if it was the oil or Pepe or maybe even something else."

"Boy," sighed Woodruff. "I always thought Caracas would be a nice place to go."

"It is the pits," said Maraña.

"I guess so," hedged Woodruff.

Suddenly, Maraña shook his head to clear it. "But no more of that nasty business," he pronounced grandly, raising his arms to welcome the two waiters and their rolling trays stacked with lobsters. "We are spared for at least one more fine meal." There followed a wave of appreciation and much bustle and many premeal comments as the waiters did their work, and after Maraña had presided over all of this and dispatched the waiters to bring more wine and four extra lobsters, he leaned ostentatiously to his right, putting his elbow under the table on Vilar's knee. "Sunshine, I have a favor to ask of you," he said humbly, pretending to be conspiratorial.

"What can I do for you, Carlos?" said Sunshine, as the Americans looked expectantly at one another, wondering what joke Maraña had in mind and why he would speak so secretively in English to Sunshine, who preferred Spanish. Pinder sensed all around the table that there were bubbles of anticipation, and the new mood made her ears pop.

"Well," said Maraña, "I have this ferocious appetite because it is so late to be eating, you see, and I always get fat by eating too much at a time like this. I also get drowsy, which is dangerous. Do know any way for me to curb my appetite and keep my wits?"

"I'm afraid that is impossible without surgery, Carlos," Sunshine declared. "Or perhaps you need the shock treatment." He shook his head woefully, but there were subtle movements under the table.

"I hope not," smiled Maraña, raising himself. "It would be terrible." With that, he tried to keep himself from laughing. As he did, he cupped his right hand over his mouth and nose. Giggles broke out among the Noses and Sunshine and even Roberto, but it was not until Maraña had breathed deeply many times from the oxygen mask of his hand, scattering white powder all over his face and the tablecloth and even on the curtain behind him and on the lobster on his plate, that the Americans realized what he was doing. Their jaws dropped open in unison. Pinder cupped an empty hand over her own mouth. She exchanged looks full of wonder with Woodruff and Howell and then with the surrounding Cubans, who seemed to take pleasure in her reaction. Without a word, relations improved instantly. The Nose next to Woodruff gave him a friendly pat on the shoulder. He shared with her a look of amazement. The Americans had learned a thing or two about cocaine, and even Woodruff knew that Maraña had just inhaled about one hundred dollars' worth of dietary inhibition while wasting a like amount in wanton disregard of its value, its illegality, and the fact that he was doing so on display in a crowded restaurant.

Maraña sighed contentedly through his mouth. "That's better," he said, after wiping his face with his napkin, which he shook out vigorously to the side of his chair. "*Salud,*" he toasted. There was a fresh nasal twang to his voice.

He companions returned the toast heartily and fell to their lobster.

"Jesus Christ, Carlos," breathed Howell. "I hope you don't get us all locked up for life. That's not on our schedule, you know."

"Don't worry about it," said Maraña. "You are in good hands, my friend."

Howell nodded weakly. "That was an awful lot," he said. "An awful lot. You realize that, don't you? I just want to make sure. I mean that was an awful, awful lot."

Maraña smiled as he attacked his lobster. "You mean I seem greedy when there are so many drug-starved Negroes in the northern cities?" he asked.

"That's terrible, Carlos," Pinder scolded sternly.

He jerked his head toward her in surprise and then relaxed. "I apologize," he said. Pinder held her frown.

"Well," said Howell, "it's just that to someone like me it's shocking to see something like that. It's like burning money or something."

"Don't worry about it," said Maraña, dipping a clean white forearm of lobster meat into a bowl of hot butter. "Don't worry about it, David. It's not excessive at all, if you know the facts."

"It's not?" Howell nodded dubiously.

"No," said Maraña, turning to him. "It's not at all if you consider that I brought five million dollars' worth into the country on Thursday night without a mishap. Then it's not, is it?"

"Oh, come on, Carlos," scoffed Howell.

"That's nothing," said Maraña. "I'm still new. But you believe what you want, David."

"Don't play with me, Carlos," said Howell.

"I would never mislead a reporter like you on a matter of so much money," teased Maraña. "Would I, Sunshine?"

Howell looked hopefully to Sunshine, who was enjoying a dainty smile.

"Oh, boy," sighed Howell, looking to Pinder. He tried to give her a supportive squeeze under the table, but he succeeded only in getting some butter on her overalls.

Maraña's smile toward Sunshine erupted in a volley of high-speed Spanish. Howell picked up no more than two words of it, but the Americans perceived that it must have been a joke because all the Cubans at the table immediately burst into animated laughter. Sunshine laughed very enthusiastically, with his happy face very near his lobster. He responded with a quick rope of Spanish back to Maraña, which caused more laughter. Then Parker tossed in a rope of his own, and so did Vilar and even one of her friends in quick succession, as the pace of the meal picked up considerably. To the Americans, left behind, it seemed that all the Cubans, and most especially the men, had to eat ever more rapidly to keep up with their talking and also to laugh ever more rapidly in order to give themselves time to eat. With all the talking and laughing and rattling of dishes, the level of merriment ran very high and so did the noise. The Americans ate along as well as they could. It was some time before the Nose next to Woodruff took such compassion on him that she dropped out of the Spanish rope exchange. "You are the one who works for the senator?" she asked in English.

"Yes, in a way," Woodruff replied. "I used to be his aide in the Senate, and now I'm back with him as a consultant in his campaign."

"That is exciting, isn't it?"

"Sometimes."

"Well," said the Nose, "I am glad someone so important as yourself would agree to come down here and have dinner with Carlos and his friends. He is a very impressive man, is he not?"

"Yes, he is. Thank you. You are very kind," said Woodruff.

"Thank you."

A frown crossed Woodruff's face. "But I should tell you," he added, "that the senator I work for is a very liberal one, of course."

"Oh," said the Nose, who reentered the Spanish celebration after a parting blank nod.

Woodruff stared off at the gold conquistador light fixtures on the ceiling, wondering what had compelled him to tell her that his senator was a liberal, which, even if it were true, had no readily discernible meaning that would help either Woodruff or the Nose share the proceedings there at the Renegade Club. Woodruff was thankful Howell had not overheard his remark. Perhaps he had been trying to reassure her that his senator, being a liberal, would be more understanding of the assassination business or of the cocaine, or perhaps he was trying to tell her that even though he was taking part in their world, ogling it, in fact, he and his senator were still liberals and did not share the Cuban exile view of Castro. It did not make sense, Woodruff sighed to himself, as he drifted off to a conversation held just that previous Friday over lunch at the Tabard Inn, in which a well-regarded analyst had pointed out to him that if you take the bilateral and multilateral international credit policies of the United States and turn them on their heads, as it were—or actually not quite on their heads, since certain of the minor policies were to remain in their present mode, such that the inversion Woodruff was asked to imagine for heuristic purposes would have the policies on their heads but at a slight angle removed from the perpendicular—then it would become abundantly clear from the adverse hardware/software mix of the new countries receiving incremental credit under the hypothetical inversion why the existing policies, as a practical matter, would be so difficult to change. Woodruff had entered into a give-and-take with the analyst on a few aspects of this idea in order to show respect and friendliness and to establish qualifications before shifting the subject to the U.S. nonrecognition policy toward Cuba, which Woodruff not only proposed to change but managed to do so by inventing a paradigm of policy modification that was structurally similar to the inversion proposed earlier in the lunch by the analyst, who in the end endorsed Woodruff's notions with certain reservations. Woodruff smiled wanly at the game, and as he thought of this he looked up to find a disturbance in the Renegade Club.

All noise had ceased at the Maraña table. The Americans followed the eyes of the others across the dining room to the area of the *maitre d'*, where in the distance some shouting and shoving appeared to be going on. Then, quickly, six young Cuban men emerged from the cluster to march in single file through the dining room. There was no doubt where they were heading. They would have drawn stares even without the commotion or their grim expressions of resolve, being too rough-looking for the place. An observer with an eye for status might have put them at the level of Roberto, the bodyguard, to whom the lead marcher reported without ceremony. He whispered in Roberto's ear while his comrades stood in the aisle with emergency running up and down them. Roberto then hurried to whisper simultaneously to Parker and Maraña, who sank back into his chair with a look of disgust. Before his back touched the cushion, Parker had beckoned Sunshine with a finger. These two and Roberto promptly led the group of six back through the dining room and out the door with Parker at the head. His face had caught the grimness. Not a word was spoken among them after the messages to the ears.

Maraña ruefully lifted the telephone and punched out a number. He was soon in a soft, well-modulated conversation, as though placing reservations on a Spanish airline.

After a minute of unproductive eye contact among the Americans, Woodruff asked, "What the hell is going on?" to anyone who would answer.

"Damned if I know," replied Howell. He scanned the Cuban women at the table, whose looks told him they would rather not be asked. After wiping his hands on his napkin, Howell shrugged to Woodruff and reached to Pinder for some mutual squeezing.

Maraña finally hung up the telephone, but before he could say anything a buzzer sounded and a small white light started blinking. This time, after a brief conversation, Maraña stood up and left. "Excuse me," he requested.

"Sure," said Howell, in the quiet of his wake.

Not long after, Woodruff stood up and walked around the table to a spot between Howell and Pinder. He felt, or imagined he felt, the weight of numerous eyes around the dining room, and was not sure whether to worry that the onlookers might regard him as a participant in whatever was going on, or, alternatively, that they might be wondering why he was left behind with, and ignored by, the women. Still in doubt and self-conscious, he hitched his shoulders about meaningfully inside his coat and leaned over to whisper in the ears of his friends. "Jesus, Howell, what have you got us into now?"

"Take it easy," soothed Howell. "Look, Henry, you wanted to come, and all I promised you was that it wouldn't be boring."

"He's quite a specimen, all right," whispered Woodruff.

Howell grabbed Woodruff's sleeve for emphasis. "I think we've got to stick together here," he advised. "We don't know what Carlos ran off about. I don't know any better than you do. My instinct is that it doesn't have anything to do with us and isn't dangerous for us or anything, but I don't really like the feel of what Max told us."

"I could tell," said Pinder.

"I don't think Max gives warnings lightly," said Howell. "So I think we should sit tight through dinner and excuse ourselves as soon as it's polite. Something doesn't feel right."

"You're not scared, are you?" asked Woodruff.

"A little," whispered Howell. "But don't worry too much. A little apprehension is the price you pay for Carlos's entertainment."

"I don't really want to go outside," said Woodruff. "This table is probably the safest place around to pick up clues about your man Maraña."

"I don't think we should whisper like this," whispered Pinder.

"I have an overwhelming need to, Haven," whispered Woodruff. "Look here, David, I thought you said Maraña was a spy type. You didn't tell me he was the godfather, for Christ's sake!"

"It's news to me, too," whispered Howell. "He's changed, I guess."

"What do you mean, he's changed?" hissed Woodruff, his neck turning red. He glanced apprehensively around. A filmy smile was his shabby pretense of calm. "What do you mean, changed?" he repeated. "You mean just like that?"

"Henry!" said Pinder.

"I don't know, Henry. Take it easy," whispered Howell. "Maybe he's not the godfather. We don't know what he does."

"Well, he sure acts like one," Woodruff persisted. "What do you think that string of goons was, a chorus line?"

"Come on, Henry," smiled Howell. "They looked pretty young to me— more like gangs from *West Side Story* than hit men. Can you believe what he did with the coke?"

"Boy," sniffed Woodruff.

"You think he'll offer us some?" asked Pinder.

Howell shrugged, and Pinder looked wistfully away.

"What about the five million dollars, David?" whispered Woodruff. "That's a lot of stuff. Do you believe that?"

"I don't know," sighed Howell. "Could be. The cops say they run a lot bigger loads than that, but I didn't know Carlos did it."

"I can't believe he talks so openly about it. That and Caracas and everything. He's not what you call your clandestine mum type."

"Yeah, but you never know how much of it is true," replied Howell. "He could deny it, or say it was a joke. Anything. You can't tell."

"Well, that Pepe Lopez stuff felt pretty true," shivered Woodruff.

"Pretty weird, eh?" whispered Howell. "The whole thing."

Pinder soon dropped out of this review, considering it impolite. She turned to Vilar, who seemed perfectly at peace making her way through a lobster. "Carmen, does this kind of thing happen all the time," she asked. "Do you mind if I ask?"

"No," said Vilar.

"It's just so new to me, and I don't know what's going on."

"I know," smiled Vilar. "I don't think it's anything, really. Usually for something big there is a lot of build-up, you know?"

"No," said Pinder. "Not really."

"Well, a lot of crowing and planning and psychological preparation. It's not important. You haven't missed anything."

Pinder nodded. "Well, what is it like for you to be around this all the time?" she asked. "Do the women ever get up and stalk out? Does it scare you?"

"That is a good question," said Vilar. "Sometimes I like it. And I have to admit to myself that what comes from all this conspiracy is this table," she said, pointing to the lobster feast. "It is a separate life. I could live easily, but not like this."

"Uh huh."

"And to answer your other question, the women never walk out. Usually they are not there in the first place, you see. I have been more than most. Now, less. There is less purpose. And when I am there, I usually don't mind the danger, but I never like the foolishness."

"Oh," said Pinder, her sympathies running into difficulty with the last statement. "I'm afraid I would be just the opposite."

"No, you wouldn't," countered Vilar. "I can tell."

"Well, I'm not sure whether to thank you for that or not," laughed Pinder. "But thank you anyway."

"Most danger is crazy anyway," said Vilar. "So you can't really worry about it. It doesn't do any good."

"Uh huh," said Pinder. She cleared her throat, puckered her lips, and looked at Vilar in a mild torment.

"What is it?" prompted Vilar. "It can't be that bad."

"Well, Max told us he was in your doghouse and made a big deal of it," said Pinder, with a shy tattler's smile. "And I couldn't help wondering how he got there."

"He hit me," flared Vilar, shaking her head for emphasis.

"What?" cried Pinder.

"He hit me," said Vilar.

"That creep," said Pinder.

"Don't worry about it. I got him back," said Vilar, with fond pride at the memory.

"Good," said Pinder.

"Wait a minute, Haven," Howell protested. "I don't think you should jump in there and take sides."

"I'm talking to Carmen," Pinder said curtly.

"Oh," said Howell, whose further reply was broken off by the return of the four men.

"Now where were we?" asked Maraña, lifting a glass of wine. "Has the dessert come yet?"

"Wait a minute," said Howell. "What happened out there? You can't pretend all that was nothing, Carlos. It's not fair."

"I don't have to pretend," Maraña replied. "It was nothing, wasn't it, Max?"

"Worse than nothing," said Parker.

"Well, if it was nothing, you can tell us anyway," Howell persisted.

"Okay, okay," said Maraña. "Just because I'm a happy guy, I will tell you. But it's embarrassing, I should warn you."

"I don't care," said Howell.

"Well, you asked for it," said Maraña. "What happened as best I can tell is that some guy that I never heard of got mad at his girlfriend and told her to get lost because he was in love with another woman, even though he wasn't. And so the girlfriend gets mad and goes over to his house, where he has a beautiful Cadillac convertible, which is the pride of his life, you see. And she has a big knife, and right away that night she goes to his car and she cuts the whole top off his beloved Cadillac convertible. All of it, my friend. Saws it to pieces and then she sets fire to the top in his front yard. She is a very spirited woman, they tell me, but I don't know. So naturally, as you might expect, now he is mad. And he finds out that she already has a new boyfriend who is a member of this club, unfortunately, and he and a bunch of his friends get in the Cadillac without a top to come over here and do harm to the girlfriend and her new boyfriend—after making threats and that sort of thing, so that the boyfriend has a bunch of his friends here, too, downstairs. So they start arguing and shoving each other downstairs and all the way up here to the dining room, and finally I had to go down there as you saw, and now the girlfriend is back in the convertible and everybody is happy except our club member, who is sitting over there in the blue coat and the white shoes looking sad. That's all there is to it, you see."

The Americans, who had made all kinds of snickers and musings and expressions of disbelief and delight to each other over the course of this tale, remained mute for some time afterward. As a rule, their mouths were open in hesitation, for they wished to be entertained by the troubadour without losing their wits to his wild imagination. Howell finally turned around in his chair. "Where?" he asked. "Which one is he?"

"Right there," said Maraña. "The one by himself at the table for two."

"Oh," said Howell. "Come on, Carlos. This is ridiculous. I can't believe that yarn."

"Well, it is not worth arguing about, that's for sure," laughed Maraña. "But I told the truth like always. Didn't I, Max?"

"I'm afraid so," sighed Parker.

Howell looked around to find that further challenge was pointless, and then to Woodruff. "See there, Henry?" he said. "Let's hold tight. You never know."

"Know what?" asked Maraña.

"Never mind," said Howell.

"Good idea," smiled Maraña. "Don't be upset, David. There is much petty stuff going on in low places and in high places. Even in the White House, I'm sure."

"Especially in the White House," Pinder agreed.

"So there," said Maraña. "Now let's get on with it. Sunshine did you order any dessert?"

"Sure," grinned Sunshine.

"Well, we can start before they clear the table, I guess."

"Beautiful," grinned Sunshine. "That's beautiful."

"You are so eloquent," teased Maraña, putting his elbow back on Vilar's knee.

For some reason, Maraña's splattering of the cocaine was even more of a jolt to the Americans the second time. They watched each step, fully cognizant of the drama. And when Maraña inhaled, each of them stiffened in the back and became jittery and high, having received an empathetic transfusion of the drug. They emitted nervous clutters and other unintelligible sounds until a few seconds later when they saw the act repeated by Carmen Vilar. Then they fell silent. Eyes passed to Sunshine.

Pinder coughed her way through the tension and turned to Parker. "I have heard a terrible thing about you, Max," she playfully accused. "But I can't believe it because you seem like such a nice person. Did you hit Carmen?"

"What?" cried Parker. "Who told you such a lie?"

"Carmen," said Pinder. "Is that how you got in the doghouse?"

"Oh," said Parker, "Well, yes. I guess it is."

"I'm ashamed of you," said Pinder, who bumped his arm with the back of one hand.

"Hey!" he protested. "She hit me first."

"That's true, Haven," said Vilar. "First *and* last, both times with good reason."

"Oh," said Pinder.

"I told you not to charge in there," said Howell.

"Well, I feel better anyway," said Pinder.

By this time attention had passed to Woodruff, who was watching the Nose at his side. She was spraying just as much white powder around her area as anyone else, and sniffing just as heartily—having lost all the deference and delicacy that had marked her previously to the spell of the cocaine, which is in certain respects a powerful equalizer of character. She handed to Woodruff what turned out to be an ordinary spice jar, about two-thirds filled with the powder.

Woodruff stared at the jar in his lap. There was a pecan-sized ball of silicon dioxide, a drying agent, tightly wrapped in cheesecloth, lying there partially exposed like a boulder in the sand. Both the jar and the assembly of the ball were in the province of Sunshine. "Wow," said Woodruff. "I've never seen so much." With a lingering sigh of remorse, he passed the jar on to Roberto, who, being on duty, stolidly passed it on to Vilar's two friends. In their eagerness to consume, they had already lost their stuffy looks for the first time in the evening.

"What's the matter, Henry?" asked Maraña. "You don't like it? Don't worry about it. That's all right."

"No," coughed Woodruff. "Actually I do like it occasionally. I don't know what it is. I think it's a little dangerous maybe."

"Dangerous?" smiled Maraña. "Don't worry about that. The *cocaina* only makes you risk death and insanity. Freedom will do that, my friend."

"I've heard that," said Woodruff, with a touch of sarcasm. "I was thinking more of the danger of jail, Carlos. I have to give a speech tomorrow night, and I'd hate to ruin it here."

"Oh," said Maraña. "Well, don't worry about that either, Henry. You are safe here. You are my guest. What is your speech about? Do you want to practice it now?"

"Well," said Woodruff, with a nervous coughing chuckle, "I don't know." Rising to the task, he took a deep breath and then, after a second thought, which was a metathought, he glanced to Howell for assistance.

Howell had just poured about a tablespoon of the powder into his right hand and passed the jar to Pinder. "Well, here goes, I guess," he said loudly, looking around for attention, rescuing Woodruff with the diversion.

"Excuse me a minute, David," Maraña abruptly cautioned, raising his hand sharply to freeze Howell. Then Maraña smiled to the man who had just walked up behind the two friends of Vilar. "Well, here is my friend from the FBI," he said graciously. "How are you this evening, David?"

"Fine," said Damico, who in his office garments stood out like a bill collector in a women's spa. "How are you, Carmen?" he nodded. "What was all the excitement about, Carlos?" he asked.

"Nothing," shrugged Maraña. "The usual domestic quarrel. They brought it to me, I guess, only because I am on the board here at the club."

"I know," said Damico. "Congratulations."

"Thank you," said Maraña. "Even an old patriot spy must assume responsibilities sometime." He winked at Damico.

"I've been telling you that for years, Carlos," said Damico. "You'll find out how tough it is to keep law and order. You'll be cracking heads around here with these hoods before you know it."

"I guess so," sighed Maraña. "I should have listened to you before."

"I told you," grinned Damico, who loved to run a tease off the undercurrent of a sermon.

"You're all right, Dave," said Maraña. "Let me tell you something serious. And I mean it with all my heart."

"Go ahead," said Damico.

"If anybody ever takes me down, I want it to be you."

Damico stared at Maraña's cold face. "Why thank you, Carlos," he replied. "I think you mean that. There's nothing I'd rather do, believe me. But a lot of guys have already gotten there ahead of me, haven't they?"

"I'm not talking about all those play times," said Maraña. "I'm talking about putting me away, which will never happen, of course."

"Of course," said Damico. "Well, I'd like to do that, too, Carlos. We could be together night and day. But I'm afraid I'll have to pass. I'm about to ship out to Philly. I'm going up there to the organized crime squad. My folks are up there. So I'm gonna fight my fellow dagos to please my Mom. You guys down here are too tough anyway."

"I'll miss you," said Maraña. "There is no such thing as the Mafia, you know, Dave. That's what somebody from the Bureau told me right after the Bay of Pigs, during my training."

"I'm too young to remember all that," smiled Damico, above a look of ice. "But I know there's a mob in Philly."

"Well, good luck then," said Maraña.

"You going back down to Panama soon?" Damico inquired.

"From time to time," said Maraña easily. "But I'll tell you this, Dave, since you are leaving. My duties are drawing to a close down there. I'm finished with those people. I'm just gonna come home to my responsibilities. Make some money. Enjoy life. Protect myself. I don't have any more dragons to go after, Dave, so I'm gonna be here on the defensive."

"That's nice," said Damico.

"Sure," said Maraña. "Oh, forgive me Dave. Do you know everybody?"

Damico nodded around the Cubans.

"These are my friends from Washington," said Maraña. "David Howell and Haven Pinder and Henry Woodruff. Dave Damico. The only honest G-man in Miami."

Howell had been suffering acute lockjaw since Damico's untimely appearance, and his mouth was dry but on fire with new tastes of anxiety, as though he had chewed up a bushel of cloves. Awkwardly, he reached over the back of his chair to shake hands with Damico, lefthanded. His right fist still gripped a sweat-soaked lump of cocaine.

Damico nodded at the Americans and then frowned back to Howell. "Don't I know you?" he asked.

"Not that I know of," gulped Howell. "I don't believe we've ever met."

Damico closed one eye to think. "David Howell?" he mused. "Could I have seen a mug shot on you? Have you ever been arrested?"

"No!" cried Howell, taking genuine offense. "Arrested? God no! Well, actually I was kind of arrested once in a civil rights demonstration in South Carolina. But that was fifteen years ago and they didn't take my picture. The mayor of that scummy town, who was also the druggist, had to let me go. All we were doing was registering voters."

"I see," puzzled Damico. He sighed and then brightened toward Maraña. "Well, I'll be off," he said. "What's the next stop, Carlos?" he grinned. "Are we going dancing tonight?"

"Who knows?" smiled Maraña. "Maybe. Enjoy yourself, Dave."

Damico left and Howell sagged toward the tablecloth. "My God, Carlos," he moaned. "What's he doing here?"

"Take it easy," said Maraña.

"How did he get in the club?" asked Howell.

"The FBI office has a permanent guest membership," said Maraña.

"What for?" asked Howell.

"Because it is smart," said Maraña. "It was the first motion I made when I joined the board of directors."

"Oh," said Howell. He sighed and then pretended to sneeze. He took his napkin to blow his nose, and under this cover, proceeded to cram some of the cocaine up his nose.

"Very sneaky, David," complimented Maraña. "But you shouldn't let it get wet like that."

"I know," sighed Howell, obliged to use his water glass to dissolve cakes of it out of his mustache. "But I had to get it out of my hand, and I didn't want to waste it."

"Of course not," chuckled Parker. "And it's safer in your nose, too."

"What did he mean about the next stop?" asked Woodruff.

"Well, some nights a bunch of them will just follow you around from place to place," Maraña replied. "Tonight looks like one of them. They just watch and say hello. It's all right."

Pinder, who had just sneaked a noseful of cocaine, gave Maraña a look of uncertainty.

"It's true, Haven," said Maraña. "Don't worry."

"Is it also true that you're coming back to Miami to make money?" asked Howell, after winking at Woodruff.

"Of course it is," said Maraña. "You never lie to the FBI, David."

"Yeah," said Howell. "Right. So you're gonna retire?"

"Sort of," hedged Maraña. "Yes and no. I'm just gonna stay home more."

"How's that for you, Carmen?" Howell asked ingenuously. "Does it make you feel better that the travel days might end soon?"

Vilar gave Howell a look of unexpected distress. "Not really," she sighed. "It will be different but pretty much the same. Worse, maybe. Now Carlos can worry about being in it and also about not being in it. What can you say?"

"Oh," shrank Howell.

"Carlos needs his worlds to conquer," said Vilar.

"Hey, what is this?" cracked Maraña, looking askance at Vilar. "Is this 'What's My Line' or something? For psychiatrists? What is this shit?"

"I'm sorry," said Vilar.

"That's better," said Maraña. "Don't be so cynical." He snatched the spice jar from the satisfied Nose on his left. "Here, Carmen. Have some more."

"Thank you," smiled Vilar, lighting up quite a bit.

Maraña took a big breath. "Now, Henry," he addressed Woodruff. "What is this big speech of yours?"

"Oh that," said Woodruff. "It's nothing, really." He strained to swallow a rising column of air.

"Is it a secret?" teased Maraña.

"No," said Woodruff.

"We're just advocating U.S. recognition of Castro," suggested Howell. "It's not a big deal."

"That's what your speech is about?" asked Maraña.

"Generally, yes," said Woodruff. "A group of us in Washington have sort of taken up the issue, and we're testing it out a little, in newspapers and speeches and stuff. I realize the idea is not real big in Miami, but I thought I should see for myself. Do you think everybody here thinks recognizing Castro would be the end of the world or something?"

Maraña looked at Woodruff, chuckled devilishly, and shook his head. "Henry, my friend, you are really something," he said.

"Thank you," squirmed Woodruff, trying to rest his chin on his Adam's apple. "Carlos, I think I would feel better if you would get mad and call me a communist or something, and then I could give you a few of my reasons and stuff."

"Why should I get mad?" shrugged Maraña. "If there's one thing I'm sure of, Henry, it's that you are not a communist. Let me tell you."

"Oh," said Woodruff.

"Foiled again, Henry," teased Howell.

"Well, I just assumed you'd be against it, Carlos," said Woodruff, ignoring Howell. "And I wanted to see if we could discuss it or something. I guess I've already learned something."

"Why should I be against it?" asked Maraña. "Listen, you are talking diplomacy and I'm talking survival, my friend. I don't really care what the U.S. government thinks of Fidel. Is the government going to kill Castro or help kill Castro? No. One way or the other? No. Forget about it. It is all the same. To me, the effect would only be that it might make it easier for some of us to get into Cuba to make trouble. There would be more spying. And Castro would have to be real mean for a while to prove the Americans have not seduced him."

"I see," said Woodruff.

"Now that's just me," said Maraña. "But this is a big city, Henry, and there are people who think just about anything you want to hear and some other things, too. Now the big leaders in public will all say it's a terrible idea and another betrayal and so forth. But that's just because they have to speak for the fools, and we exiles are always supposed to be unhappy, you see? Fidel stays in power? We are unhappy. Fidel had his picture taken smiling in Cairo? We are unhappy. Crops fail in Cuba? Well, not bad, but we are still unhappy. Hurricane destroys Cuba? Well, beautiful, but we are still unhappy. Now you are beginning to understand the mind of the exile, Henry?"

"Not completely," coughed Woodruff. "But it's a start. I think we might have to talk this over some other time."

"I have plenty of time," said Maraña. "Where is your speech? Maybe I will listen?"

"At the Dinner Key Auditorium," said Woodruff. "Before the group that's going down to go deepsea fishing with the group of Castro Cubans. I think Fidel is going with them again this year."

"Sure!" cried Maraña, with a smile. "Everybody knows about that, Henry! It's famous. We call it the *fiesta de los pescadores maricones*. The festival of the queer fishermen."

"Watch out, Carlos," cautioned Parker, motioning to Pinder's frown.

"It's a joke, Haven," said Maraña. "But it is true that all Cubans—in Miami or Havana—hate homosexuals and love Ernest Hemingway. That's why that fishing trip has been so successful."

"What if Hemingway were gay?" asked Pinder.

"That would be a paradox," said Maraña.

Woodruff started to say something, but he noticed that there was a tear in Carmen Vilar's eye. She looked so unhappy that Woodruff became flustered.

Maraña had noticed. He shifted his eyes quickly between Vilar and Parker. Then he closed them briefly. It was the first time Woodruff was conscious of seeing his eyelids. "Just a minute, Henry," said Maraña.

"Sure," said Woodruff.

Maraña turned sharply to Parker and asked him in a rope of Spanish, "What did you do to Carmen while I was gone, my friend? How hard did you hit her?"

The table was very quiet. Parker's smile was unhealthy, and it twitched. "What are you talking about, Carlos?" he replied steadily, in Spanish. "That has nothing to do with it. I don't know what's wrong any more than you do."

"Oh you don't? You're telling me you don't?" said Maraña. "Look at her. Have you ever seen Carmen cry before, my friend?"

Parker's eyes moved slowly to Vilar, who was indeed crying softly. Without a word, he shook his head no.

Maraña looked Parker up and down so calmly, so serenely, that Pinder reached under the table to seize Howell's hand in fright. Then Maraña shrugged in slow motion and turned deliberately to Vilar. "Tell me what this is all about, Carmenita," he whispered. "And please don't be sentimental unless you have to be."

When Vilar did not manage to say anything for a number of seconds, Woodruff was moved to speak up from the other end of the table. "I'm very sorry, Carmen," he said.

Maraña was stunned by the intrusion. He looked at Woodruff as if he were a slug. It did not occur to him that Woodruff, not understanding any of the Spanish, thought Vilar was upset because his Cuba speech had pierced her deepest convictions. "Shut up, Henry," said a dumbfounded Maraña. "Have you no manners?"

Woodruff felt lower than ever. But he knew from the moment's terror that he would never again say he wanted to see Maraña angry.

Maraña turned back to Vilar. "What is this fighting with Max really all about?" he asked with a pursed smile. "You can tell me. Have you and Max been fooling around while I was gone?" His smile became impish.

Vilar had a short sniffling laugh. "No," she said. "No, I haven't."

Maraña smiled expansively. "Good, good," he said. "Now we are getting somewhere." He glanced around the table, and all the Cubans responded with anemic chuckles. "I feel better," said Maraña. "So it's not Max, then. What is it?"

"It is, in a way," said Vilar. She wiped her eyes with her napkin, and then she looked steadily at Maraña. "I am planning to be his lover, if I can," she said.

"Oh," said Maraña.

This time Parker was the only one to chuckle, and he did it out of shock and disbelief, so weakly that it didn't last through the instant required for Maraña to turn to him. "Is this true, Max?" he asked casually.

Parker looked all around and swallowed. "I don't believe this is happening," he said. "How do I know, Carlos? How do I know what she plans? This is the first I've heard of it."

"That means nothing," Maraña said quietly.

Parker buried his face in his hands. "This is crazy," he whispered.

Maraña turned to Vilar, whose eyes had dried and who was sitting erect in her chair. "We should go somewhere else," she said.

"What for?" asked Maraña. "These people are nothing, and the *gringos* don't understand, anyway. The *cocaina* feels good. I'd like to finish our little discussion, and then maybe we'll go dancing."

"All right," sighed Vilar, and she looked straight at him. "Carlos, you are no good for a woman anymore," she said. "I respect you enough to tell you so even before I tell Max of my feelings, but it is true. To me, you are now almost like Pepe Lopez."

Maraña looked at her and then reached gracefully for his wine. "For saying something like that, Pepe would kill you with pleasure," he said, drinking.

"And you, maybe without pleasure," said Vilar. "That is the only difference, and I am not sure of that anymore."

Maraña nodded as though this were interesting evening news. "I see," he said. "It is terrible to hear a thing like that after being the same for so many years."

"You're not the same," said Vilar.

"No," said Maraña, holding up a hand in peace. "I do not wish to argue, Carmen. That is our arrangement. I merely wish to know what is going on. If I wanted to argue I would tell you your plan is unfair to poor Max. You would chew him to pieces."

Vilar looked at Parker with her warrior look. "I don't think so," she said. "Who knows?"

"What about this, Sancho Panza?" asked Maraña, turning with a sporty panache. "What are we talking about here, something real or just a game?" Maraña slowly drained the humor from his face until he was looking directly at Parker with two midnight lagoons for eyes. Parker was nearly panting. His worn face had the look of a man whose insides had just explored a hundred miles of new territory at a sprint. The Nose between Maraña and Parker leaned back from the line between them. She would have leaned back to Louisiana if she could.

"What about it, Max?" prompted Maraña.

"It is not a game, Carlos," said Parker.

"Fair enough," said Maraña. "From there, only one thing is more. And that, my friend, is that if you can look at me, your old friend, and also at the strong possibility of being killed, and if at the same time you can feel passion for that woman, you should tell me now."

Parker looked to Vilar and back to Maraña. There was nothing else in his universe. "Funny thing, Carlos," he said huskily. "It seems that I do. It really does."

"That is what I thought," said Maraña. He looked away, but for some reason the pressure from him continued to compress the air around all the faces at the table. Maraña began to fold his napkin very neatly on his plate. "I should tell you two something," he said pleasantly. "There are no hard feelings, of course. I would never hurt either of you for pleasure. You should not worry about that. But at the same time you should understand that I am in a very dangerous business. A reputation is often a man's life. So if you two do something to hurt my position, I may have to protect myself, as I said before." He stood up, snapped his fingers, and pointed quickly to all the Cubans except Vilar and Parker. To them he bowed. "That's it, I guess," he shrugged, and he walked out. As he passed behind Howell, Maraña said in English, "Excuse me, David. And excuse me to your girlfriend." The Cubans, even Vilar's friends, followed him out the door. Shortly thereafter, so did Damico.

Woodruff was the first to move. He rose quietly, stayed bent over, tiptoed to the empty seat next to Vilar, and sat down very slowly, worried about noise—all like a man changing pews during the service. By his looks, Woodruff had not exhaled in some time.

"What do we do now?" asked Pinder.

"That's a good question," Vilar said in English, looking at Parker.

"I think it's time for us to leave," said Howell, noting that the two Cubans had not budged from each other's gaze.

"Not right now," said Parker, who was on the verge of tears himself. "Not just now, if you don't mind. It may sound fonny to you, but I wouldn't mind some company for a few minutes. It must be fonny to you if you didn't understand any of it."

"I understood enough to be scared shitless," sighed Howell. "I felt weak. And I didn't want any of us to get hit in a crossfire."

"I feel weak, too," said Vilar, as Pinder and Howell embraced across the arms of adjacent chairs.

"You might have given me a little warning, Carmen," smiled Parker, shaking his head in a daze.

"I didn't want to," said Vilar. "It seemed right to do it this way. Besides, I thought you had figured it out."

"I think I did, a little bit," trembled Parker. "My God." Looking away from her for the first time, he dropped his head into one hand and began to shake. Pinder soon reached over to pat him on the back, without saying anything.

"I hate to bring this up, Max, but do you have a gun?" asked Vilar.

"No," said Parker.

"A gun?" echoed Woodruff. "I thought it was over."

"It is, basically," Vilar assured him. "But I think Carlos is going to stay very mad at us, you see."

"Oh," said Woodruff. "I'm sorry. He seems like a very dangerous man."

"Well," said Vilar, in a way that meant nothing.

Parker looked up. "This is crazy," he said. "How do you know that I am good for a woman either? How do I know? How do I know about you, even?"

"We don't," laughed Vilar, adding a daredevil shrug.

"That's what I thought," sighed Parker. "I suppose you realize that we can't stay in Miami, don't you?"

"Yes," said Vilar. "I know how to travel."

"I'm not gonna carry a gun around all the time," said Parker.

"That's the idea," Vilar agreed. She started to reach down for her purse, and as she did she put the spice jar on the table.

"Excuse me, Carmen," said Woodruff, on the way to a proposition. "I might need to try some of that, if you don't mind. I could use a lift."

"Help yourself," said Vilar. Woodruff slipped the jar into his jacket pocket and began to look around for the door to the men's room.

Outside the club's entrance, car doors slammed, tires squealed, shoes tapped pavement, and a great many clipped, angry words bounced off hardened ears. It was cacophany compared with what was going on around on the far side, in a dark place on the hill near the east dining room, where a solitary and malignant anger had reduced the waiting man to a sorry state of whimpering. He beat his gloved hands against the bricks and cursed himself for volunteering to go alone. Time had played its part. Every furtive look around the corner into the bright lights had poured a little acid on his nerves. Each sight of the white faces inside tensed every muscle in his body.

The sight of Maraña, whom he loathed and dreaded as his patron demon, had made him whine to himself. Sometimes he looked up to the sky and mashed himself against the wall at the same time, feeling as though he weighed a thousand pounds. And whenever he saw movement at the table —a man getting up, or even looking like he might get up—he did all these things at once because it had to be the time. And he would kick the newspaper from the emergency exit and hold the door and wait. But not a single one of them came down the hall. He thought of running away each time he replaced the newspaper. But he went back to the wall with less nerve and more clamminess. He smelled his redolent self and knew that whatever happened he must burn these clothes. For some reason, this reminded him that he had something to say, and he kept repeating what he was supposed to say, over and over. He was repeating it and repeating it when he decided again that it had to be now, and still when he kicked away the newspaper and heard the steps in the corridor. Then he realized to his horror that he was making a noise already that he could not stop, somewhere between a moan and a growl at the bottom of his throat. So he forgot his battle cry, and all he did was to make this same noise a lot louder when he stepped through the door across the narrow corridor leading to the men's room and fired three hissing bullets into Woodruff's back.

Woodruff sensed the hatred before the first shot. It rushed over him and was oozy yellow and fiendish and vile beyond anything he had ever imagined, such that it paralyzed him. He felt nothing at all in his back. Only a blank period until he was sensible again and saw shapes zooming off at all angles. He had no thought at all, but he was aware somehow that proportion in space was gone. This was confirmed when he decided to feel his chest and realized to his amazement that his arm was many feet away and was not even his, and yet somehow the hand seemed to traverse the immense distance to lie on a chest that turned out not to be his, either. His hand felt it, but his chest felt nothing, and what his hand felt was not really a chest but a warm, pulpy thing, like a mess of hamburger, really, and it was striking how vivid it was. It was then that Woodruff realized he had probably been shot. Which was senseless, too. Still he had no thought, but he did sense an elongated white form before him, a thousand feet high but vaguely human, and so he told the screaming dishwasher, whom he could not hear, "All I was doing was coming in here." Still he didn't think anything, but before he blacked out he did feel an indescribable liquid loneliness and a yearning for the simplest human touch.

Three and a half hours later, the same homicide detective who had earlier excused himself briefly to a small isolated office where he threw aside his clipboard in disgust and cursed his luck for sticking him with a case that already involved not only Carlos Maraña and the vice-mayor's daughter and Dave Damico and some guy named Parker, who claimed to be an informant for both the FBI and the Immigration Department and who was saying all kinds of terrible things he had heard, and also the goddam secretary of state and a mutilated Cadillac and a victim from the Senate who was supposed to have given a speech the next night to a Castro group, of all things, not only were these names and others he'd forgotten in the case but it was also an obvious terrorist murder that smelled from one end to the other like it would never get solved because of the politics and the craziness, which would also guarantee a life of constant grief for the man in charge of it, as any fool could see—this same detective offered a ride to the swollen-faced couple in front of him, for he was naturally kind in spite of his profession.

Howell and Pinder accepted. They had no choice, really, since Parker and Vilar had left them alone following Howell's third sobbing outburst at Parker, in which he screamed hysterically and demanded that Parker tell him of the plot that killed his friend. That fit was the worst one. It earned Howell an armful of sedatives from a nurse who came over from the next building in the Dade County complex, where the jail and the hospital and the morgue and the clinics and courts and police offices were convenient to one another. Except for these wild fits of anger, Howell and Pinder were most grateful to Parker and Vilar for coming with them. The two Cubans

398

were not in very good shape themselves, in shock and stoic fear, although Parker had summoned the presence of mind during the first howling screams to remove the spice jar from Woodruff's coat without being detected.

At the station, they sat across from Howell and Pinder most of the time, saying what things of comfort they could think of. Howell and Pinder would spill without warning from numb, staring silence to quiet talk about the smallest of details about the dinner or Woodruff, or into breakdowns, most of which were just the opposite of the three angry fits. Howell would start shaking and say, "no, no, no, no, no" over and over again, and Pinder would say nothing. She only hugged her own stomach and moaned painfully as she cried.

The detective dropped them off at their car at the Renegade Club and then followed them for a time, with his usual misgivings about their faculties. He swerved off for home when he saw they hadn't run into anything. Inside the car, they spoke of strange things, such as how surprised they were to find the night sky still there after all that time in the buildings and how they did not recognize a single feature at the Renegade Club. They spoke repetitiously past one another, like the choral themes of a long dirge, with Howell saying he should have seen the evil and asking why it was Woodruff, and Pinder telling Howell it was not his fault.

"Where are we going, David?" asked Pinder some time later.

"I don't know," said Howell. "Does it matter?"

"No," said Pinder. "Except I want to get out of the Cuban section. I hate this place."

"All right," said Howell. But before he did, he pulled into a parking lot and stopped the car. "Just a second," he said and was gone.

"What?" said Pinder, who had no fear until she saw Howell pull his nose from a big restaurant window and yank open its door like a madman.

"SON OF A BITCH! SNEAKY MURDERING LYING BASTARD!" Howell shrieked with rage as he hurtled through the late night crowd at the Versailles. He knocked over a waiter and a customer or two, and just before he exploded into the back room he grabbed a sugar container off a table and hurled it ahead of him with all his strength. It barely missed Maraña's head and shattered the mirror just behind with a terrific noise, augmented by the screams of customers. Countless shards of glass sprayed around the room from what had been one of the stately mirrors with the delicate *fleur-de-lis* etching, framed in trellises of etched vines.

Howell seized Maraña from behind an overturned table and lifted him by the jacket, and Maraña was quiet as Howell shook him violently and screamed, "Who killed Henry? Goddammit! Who killed Henry?" Howell did not hear Dave Damico shouting, "Hold it, FBI!" from the side, but he did hear Haven Pinder wailing "A gun! A gun! A gun!" And he felt it when Maraña slugged him in the jaw.

Howell was getting up dizzy but still crazed with fury when Pinder crashed into him and hugged him with a great sob of relief as she put herself between

Howell and Maraña. Then Howell heard Damico's shouts, but what extinguished his seizure like a master switch was the sight of Pepe Lopez standing there with the gun Pinder had spoken of and with a broad smile of complete romantic joy, such as a florist might hope to get rich from.

"My God!" Howell whispered softly.

"That's better," said Damico, coming forward under control. "Put that away, Pepe," he ordered. "Don't spoil it now."

Lopez complied slowly. Maraña was dusting the glass off him with a napkin. Pinder was still hugging, and Howell was holding his jaw. He nodded when Damico asked if he were all right. "Let's all go outside a minute," said Damico. "It's all over. You too, Pepe."

On the way back outside, amid the stares and whispers of the customers, Maraña stopped at the cashier's desk and motioned to a very unhappy-looking man, who appeared to be the owner. "My apologies," said Maraña. He peeled five or six one hundred dollar bills from the wad in his pocket and handed them over. The owner nodded. "Politics," shrugged Maraña. "My apologies."

They all went outside, where Damico asked many questions of them one after another and made many radio calls before he was satisfied as to the facts, or at least that there was nothing for him to do. Pinder and Howell walked arm in arm in small circles in the parking lot, enduring the thick time. Howell's jaw swelled even more than his eyes. At one point, he accused Lopez of the murder and quietly told Damico many bad things about him, but he only shrugged when Damico returned with the news of Lopez's tight alibi. After more circles, he and Pinder walked up to Damico and Maraña.

"I don't know everything, my friend," said Maraña. "What can I tell you except I'm sorry? I knew nothing about it. But I will try to find out for you."

"Shut up, Carlos," said Howell. "You and Pepe deserve each other."

Maraña flinched.

"Take it easy," said Damico.

"That's all right," Maraña smiled easily, pointing at Howell's face. "You should just remember, my friend, that you are not the first one to suffer by losing a friend in a crazy war that's not yours. Understand? Or to feel truly helpless about it because somebody else knows everything and controls everything. Or to be eaten by riddles. Understand? And you won't be the first one to feel fonny about seeking help from your friends in the FBI, will you? How's that?"

"Come on, David," pulled Pinder.

"Say hello to Carmen for me," nodded Maraña. "And I really will try to find out for you, I promise."

After many more little circles, they were free to leave. "I'm driving this time," Pinder declared, and nothing more was said until she got well out of Little Havana.

"I'm too tired and battered to get upset any more," Howell said. Nevertheless, he did get upset after feeling compelled to mention small details that came back to him, such as the lab coats and the blood and how limp Woodruff's body had been when the stretcher men turned it over.

"Shut up, David!" cried Pinder. "I can't take any more of that. If you can't help yourself out of it, help me."

Howell blinked. "I'm sorry," he said. "You're right. There's got to be something good to keep going on with, but I can't come up with it offhand." He put his head back on the seat, and, tearfully, began to laugh for the first time in many hours. It bubbled very slowly. "Listen, Haven," he said. "I know this is even harder on you because you didn't always get along with Henry. He was so removed and so weird sometimes—God, was he far-off there sometimes—that it wasn't human. But it was."

"I know it was," Pinder said gently.

"But he never gave up and he always tried to be harder on himself than he was on anybody else. And goddammit, Woodruff is the only guy I've ever known who could get himself killed trying to make his first speech about Cuba," said Howell, giving way to both laughing and crying.

Pinder made her sympathetic noise and did the same thing, saying, "Oh, my beloved Howell," and as she reached over for him, she allowed the rented car to jump a curb somewhere in Miami where dawn would soon find them.

Epilogue

PAUL STERNMAN worked most of the day on the story, and with minor lobbying he placed it on page one of the metropolitan section of Tuesday's *Post*, headlined "Ex-Hill Aide Slain."

> Henry L. Woodruff, 34, former Vietnam War activist and aide to Senator Nelson Harris (D-Mo.), was shot to death by an unknown assailant late Sunday night in Miami.

Sternman reported the circumstances and the early police speculations, Senator Harris's statement calling for an FBI investigation of the tragedy, and he included several paragraphs on the conflicting statements by Cuban exiles in Miami. Two anti-Castro groups had issued communiques to newspapers and radio stations taking credit for the assassination, calling it a warning to any American who might extend a friendly hand to Castro. On the other hand, prominent Cuban leaders were quoted to the effect that Castro himself was probably behind the murder with his usual intent of dividing the exiles and poisoning relations with their American allies. Sternman went on to describe Woodruff's character and career, including his work of the last two years "on a nonfiction political book which friends and publishing sources describe as a wide-ranging collection of essays on the decision-making process." He closed with the survivors and other obituary material.

By the time the story appeared, Pinder and Howell were tending to Lily Snow back at the Savannah. They had already made their first instinctive decision in the shock of the event, which was to cancel their showdown appointment with Pat Shea on Monday and to expel from their minds all thought of using Maraña's information. They decided to ignore Shea, placing all their trust in his lack of resolution and in the slowness of the courts, which turned out to be wise. Unfortunately, the same slowness kept all their legal actions against the developers ensnared in procedural matters until only five stalwarts were left against the siege. The developers happily agreed to rent a small apartment to Miss Hope and her mother, cheaply and for their lifetimes, and to pay a handsome sum to Snow and to Pinder and Howell, if all legal challenges to their condominium profits were dropped and if the latter three moved out of the Savannah by the first of September. At last, the tenants were forced to capitulate. Miss Hope said that she had known all along she would never have to move, and in the end Snow did not leave the Savannah either. One morning she fell and broke her hip on the way to the café with Pinder, and within four days she died of pneumonia and exhaustion, talking of trains and of Father.

In New York, Maggie Snow died soon after learning that she had outlived her sister, and when the lawyers had finished, a tidy sum remained for a struggling female dance company. The spiteful Helen Shea suspected lesbianism behind this family betrayal, and some of her sentiments worked themselves into the speeches of her husband. After resettling across the river from Cincinnati, on the way to retirement and a second career in security public relations, Pat Shea often held forth in motel conference rooms on his personal experience with the hedonism and loss of discipline that was destroying American youth, giving sad personal testimony about how one wastrel young man had not only corrupted his daughter toward hippiedom but had also, incredibly, snatched the last bit of health from his aged aunt. Helen "Moonbeam" Shea married an outdoor sign painter in California.

None of this touched Howell, who would never learn of the family tie between Moonbeam and Shea. He was quite raw, however, from the two funerals within a span of six weeks, and he was in grave doubt as to whether he and Pinder could absorb these and the Savannah loss and still have enough reserve for him to quit *Washington* magazine, which he had wanted to do for some time. The desire was strong, but so were the inertia and the attachments and the financial practicalities. Then one bright day in October, when walking through a rough part of town on his way to a solitary lunch at the Florida Avenue Grill, he was accosted by a very small black boy of about eight years. Addressing Howell as "mister," the boy asked his assistance in repairing the handlebars of his small girl's bicycle. Howell bent over to examine the screw, whose threads had long since worn off, and after tinkering for some time he said the only hope might be to steal a screw from another place on the bike, such as the seat. But it turned out that there was no screw for the seat. The situation was so bad that Howell was moved to tinker another ten minutes before giving up, figuring the rusty bike was ten years past natural extinction. He told the boy it was too dangerous to ride and that he might hope for a new one at Christmas, whereupon the boy nodded his thanks and picked up the handlebar from the ground. He slipped it loosely in place over the nose of the bike, held the connection with one hand and an end of the handlebar with the other, hopped on the bike at a run and roared off at top speed. Howell was left wincing, holding both arms over his head in anticipation of a wreck, and then laughing at himself.

Two weeks later, after a farewell party, Howell and Pinder climbed into Moby, one of two things allotted to them from Woodruff's estate (the other being the unfinished manuscript of *The Curve of Liberty*), and they pulled a trailer full of belongings parallel to the railroad from Washington through Harper's Ferry and on to the small house they had rented for approximately one-tenth what it would bring in Washington. They were more or less settled there by the time of the November elections. The vice-president had resigned, as expected, but Senator Harris was not selected to replace him on the ticket. The job went instead to an Illinois senator of eloquent voice who had once suggested bilingual education as the best weapon against terrorism. He and the president both visited Miami during the campaign and pledged to end harassment of Cuban freedom fighters by federal authorities. Their opponents did likewise, to great applause, and won the election. Among the realignments this portended in the capital was that of Richard Clayfield, who would lose his title and the office with his own personal government photocopying machine, at least temporarily, during a stint of foreign-policy-in-waiting.

Pinder's birthday was five days after the election. A letter forwarded from the Savannah arrived about a week later. It contained a birthday card, a newspaper clipping, and a photograph of Carlos Maraña seated in an enormous wingback wicker chair. The clipping related the gangland murder of Manuel "Manolo" Valdez, Blue Shirt, a Bay of Pigs veteran whose body was found in the parking lot of a woman's clothing store. "Dear Haven," said a note on the card. "You and David may have reason to be interested in the news here. I have survived many adventures, but as I know of your distaste for ethnic remarks, there is little I can relate to you about them. Most things are not my decision. You and David are always welcome. Perhaps for a meal in the daytime? Yours, Carlos M."

Howell reported this information to the Miami homicide detective, who kept saying, "It all fits. It all fits." Howell asked what fit with what, and the detective explained how the word in Little Havana was that Valdez was responsible for both the Taliente and Woodruff homicides, and that Valdez had been executed by Pepe Lopez on orders from Maraña, his new patron. Howell would not believe in the partnership of Maraña and Lopez until Max Parker confirmed the news from Mexico, where he was "trying to hang on to Carmen," as he told Howell. Parker and Vilar were using a stake of *cocaina* money to breed race horses for the cheap Mexican tracks, and during their long stormy affair the only constant would be that no one ever accused Parker of the slightest dishonesty, medical or otherwise, around the horses. This was considered a holy phenomenon in those parts.

During the phone call, Parker also advised Howell of the whereabouts of El Navajo Romero, whose prosperity was driving him to Costa Rica. El Navajo kept widening his shooting range, not only past any conceivable practical requirements, but also past the boundary of his property, and when certain environmentalists pointed this out to the authorities, El Navajo found himself in a lengthy controversy. As his smuggling wealth rose in rough balance with the tribulations of the fight, El Navajo spent more time in refuge at his customary whorehouse in Costa Rica, whose attractions grew and grew on him, especially after Max Parker fled the country and Maraña retired from active politics. Finally, El Navajo determined to purchase the Costa Rican establishment with all its goods, and he lived there more or less full-time. Whenever one of the tiptoeing African nightmares struck him down, El Navajo would seek comfort from one of his own employees.

Before the next spring, Howell decided that he was stable enough in an uncertain world to speak with Pinder's father. On a weekend visit to Long Island, he waited as long as he could for a suitable moment of privacy, which never quite arrived, and only in desperation, a few minutes before the train was to leave did Howell trudge out into the snow, where Mr. Pinder was standing on a small stepladder in his suit and an overcoat and an apron, clipping branches off a dead tree. "Excuse me, Mr. Pinder," called Howell. "I'd like to have a word with you about your daughter."

Pinder looked thoughtfully at the blade of his tree clipper. "Should I come down?" he asked, as though inquiring whether he should dress for the evening.

"I think so," said Howell, and when he saw the feet hit the ground he looked up and said, "I know this is old-fashioned, but Haven and I would like to ask your blessing. I would like to ask for her hand."

"Well, David, I take it you are asking my blessing as distinct from my permission?"

"I was hoping you wouldn't ask that," smiled Howell.

"Then I won't press the question, of course," said Pinder, and it was only then that Howell began to enjoy the interview, as he realized that the twinkling gentleman was exercising his love of formality. "I am presuming you love my daughter," said Pinder.

"Very much," said Howell.

"Well, I must say I have wondered about her safety in your company sometimes, David. And I am presuming that in light of your mutual weakness for impulsive adventures you have reexamined your own attraction for dangerous and unsavory characters, after the tragedy last year."

"Well, sir, I hope Haven and I will always have adventures," Howell replied. "But I do not feel driven toward the unsavory kind exclusively, if that's what you mean. There's no guarantee . . ."

". . . I'm sorry for that wording," Pinder said gently. "What I meant to express was merely my hope that you and Haven both have a healthy regard for the *terra firma*."

"Oh, we do," said Howell. "We're getting better and better on that."

"Good," said Pinder. "Of course, I am prejudiced in favor of the earth."

"I know," said Howell.

"And I presume the two of you think you can make a go of it financially?"

"Well, we think so," gulped Howell.

"It's merely that of the endeavors I've heard you mention lately after your career transposition—the handy work on houses and the work driving the rescue vehicle and things of that nature—I suppose I should say that I prefer to think of your present occupation as a musician."

"Well, that's all right with me," laughed Howell, "But that's only been singing every other weekend at one of the local steakhouses."

"Still," said Pinder, looking upward.

"I'm making more money writing, even part-time," said Howell.

"I know, but writers drink too much, as a rule," smiled Pinder. "So that until you settle on something permanently, I will stay with musician for the time being."

"All right," said Howell.

"Very well," said Pinder. "All I ask of worldly things is that you make a good effort to keep Haven and your children comfortable and cared for enough to exercise a flexible taste for the finer things in life. Just try not to forget the wine or the picnics, or their equivalent, please."

"We won't," said Howell.

"Good," said Pinder. "And I hope you'll understand that I have not prolonged this talk to take advantage of whatever nervousness you must feel. I have been in your position myself . . ."

". . . No, no, I didn't think that at all," said Howell.

"For you certainly have my blessings and Ann's blessings as well," Pinder said warmly. "I should admit to you that we've both hoped things would come to this between you and Haven. The reason I have gone on so long, I suppose, is that as I get older I realize how few opportunities there are to talk when you are really saying something. So I wanted to make the best of this one."

"I am very glad you did," said Howell. "I'm sorry I didn't say more myself, but I think I was too nervous. You were right."

Pinder glanced toward the house and then said with a suave but slightly mischievous smile, "I think we ought to be going in now, though, and I'll save this tree for tomorrow. No harm in that, of course. Some people inside may be worrying about us out here, getting cold." And they went in to celebrate.

Shortly before the May wedding, Casey Pendleton gave birth to a son, whom she named Samuel. Howell and Pinder rode the train in to Washington to visit her, finding a proud and tender mother. They thanked her for beginning to make up for the losses of the previous year. Pendleton said she could not imagine any difficulty she and Samuel could not conquer, that on the contrary she felt like a pioneer. Having told her own mother of her pregnancy not long after Woodruff's funeral in Chattanooga, she would always believe nothing about her family could hurt her after that. Through the next few years, she would never say who Samuel's father was, though many rumors would arise from her habit of spending Saturdays at a fine antique store on Capitol Hill, sitting across from its owner.

The wedding occurred outdoors at the Pinder home on a magic day, as evidenced by the clear sky and the splash of flowers and the many dances pairing Mr. Pinder and LaLane Rayburn, who would not have missed it even though she was leaving soon to go home to Texas. Ziggy Rosen flew in all the way from California, where he had moved after narrowly escaping indictment in some Maryland tax fraud dispute involving the legislature and a scheme to subsidize outdoor historical museums at old drive-in theaters. He danced mostly with Laura Lee Howell, who was radiant among the broods of Howells, and he talked a streak with Lester Hershey, who was woodpeckering his students at American University with a thoroughness and idealism that astonished those acquainted with the cynical old scandal king, and who was in a rush of optimism over his fourteen-year-old son's prospects as a professional baseball player. Hershey danced mostly with his wife, but he also danced some with Marvella, who came up from Bobby Ziller's old home in Miami Beach. She had married a stone crab fisherman from the Everglades who consistently mortified the neighbors on Miami Beach by parking his frumpy yellow trawler right behind their million-dollar homes, and it turned out that the fisherman was something of a Wall Street redneck who had in fact known Marner at Harvard, which was a surprise to all sides, and he teased Marner with some of the things he remembered that Marner would have preferred not to have written in the *Crimson*, such as his attack on having scholarship students, of which the fisherman had been one. But no teasing could have disturbed Marner on the day of the wedding, which was the first social event he could remember enjoying. He was still too silly over his own bride, such that he was for the first time, as he put it, "holding myself up to public scorn and ridicule, along with the charlatans who really deserve it."

Only Drake began the day in a somber mood, complaining that he had lost not only Howell at the magazine but also his wife, who had left him. It was a trauma that called up inside him all the buried memories of his runaway mother and the Sir Francis Drake swindle. In time, it would produce a rash of articles in his magazine on how to solve the personal costs attendant to a life of public service and also a series of rain dances beseeching his own wife to come back to him, which she would. He did not know this on the day of the wedding, but still he got swept up in the magic of it. The pollination was such that the friendships among the Washingtonians seemed more lasting than the coincidence of their views and more serene than their compulsion to generate melodrama, for a day at least. They already had something of a history together, and when they thought about it on the right occasion they could transmit their good will as easily as the heat in their fingertips, not only to friends but to friends of friends. Which was what happened then. Howell and Pinder glowed at each other all day, of course. He offered a toast to the memory of Woodruff and to the health of Susan Hartman, wherever she was, being funny and poignant about her letters from various exotic spots, promising to be there. Haven Pinder's toast was in honor of all those like Howell and herself who were getting around to things about a decade later in their lives than was traditional. She said it was well worth the delay.

Howell and Pinder went back to their small house outside Washington, and in time they felt grounded enough to hard value in the flow of goods and ideas and feelings that both of them began to lob political notions back over the walls of the capital without fear of being captured by the larger imperfections of the world. Shortly after that, they knit together both their families and the memory of one who had so helped them touch, in the form of a daughter they named Lily Pinder Howell, who from the first day was much more than anything that brought her to being.

It was only after her birth that Howell saw clearly how his ideas could advance his feelings without having to hold them up, and that he could admit to himself how much of a weight to him Woodruff had been at times while he was alive, or how much lighter and more human some of him felt as a memory. He wondered if it might have happened anyway.

He and Pinder still shared a voracious appetite for public events, though sometimes they pretended not to. They devoured the newspaper and they shared some of the deeper and juicier details omitted from the pages with their friend Paul Sternman, who rose to executive positions at the *Post* without ever learning to curse like a newspaperman and who said of any disaster, "You can read about it in the morning for a quarter." Occasionally, Howell and Pinder would recall some of the forecasts in Woodruff's manuscript. Serious disintegrations began much sooner than predicted, but he proved correct in saying that those of the "abstract classes" would claim it was because they did not have sufficient control over things. The members of the Howell family did what they could. They remained confident that no matter what came to sigh for or chuckle over it would not be so bad, that they could keep the mix, and that a great many of their tears would be happy ones.

> *National secrets. Baby shoes.*
> *The shape of tomorrow.*
> *What will I choose?*
> *I'll never know 'til I*
> *Shake those empire blues.*
> —from a song
> by David Howell.